"I didn't come here to fight. I've been watching ever since the calf wrestling, and I think you're helping Sammy," Morgan admitted.

Jolie blinked. Had she heard him right?

"I came to tell you that I'll do whatever I need to do to help you help him," Morgan continued. His amazing blue eyes softened—he was actually conceding.

"G-good," Jolie stammered. As she looked at him, she thought about trying to apologize again, telling him that she hadn't meant to hurt him. But she knew he would only deny that she'd hurt him in the first place. "That's the way it should be. Our past, what happened between us—"

"Is the past," he said, firmly.

"Yes. We should still be able to help these boys even though we once had feelings for each other and it didn't work out."

What else could she say? She'd just come up against one wall after the other with him; he'd made it clear there was no sense in rehashing old history that he had no desire to revisit. So she stopped trying.

For now.

Books by Debra Clopton

Love Inspired

DEBRA CLOPTON

First published in 2005, Debra Clopton is an award-winning multipublished novelist who has won a Booksellers Best Award, an Inspirational Readers' Choice Award, a Golden Quill, a *Cataromance* Reviewers' Choice Award, *RT Book Reviews* Book of the Year and Harlequin.com's Readers' Choice Award. She was also a 2004 finalist in the prestigious RWA Golden Heart, a triple finalist in the American Christian Fiction Writers Carol Award and most recently a finalist in the 2011 Gayle Wilson Award for Excellence.

Married for twenty-two blessed years to her high school sweetheart, Debra was widowed in 2003. Happily, in 2008, a couple of friends played matchmaker and set her up on a blind date. Instantly hitting it off, they were married in 2010. They live in the country with her husband's two high-school-age sons. Debra has two adult sons, a lovely daughter-in-law and a beautiful granddaughter—life is good! Her greatest awards are her family and spending time with them. You can reach Debra at P.O. Box 1125, Madisonville, TX 77864 or at debraclopton.com.

Her Unforgettable Cowboy

Debra Clopton

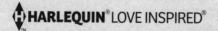

Recycling programs
for this product may
not exist in your area.

 ™ LOVE INSPIRED BOOKS

ISBN-13: 978-0-373-81690-3

HER UNFORGETTABLE COWBOY

www.LoveInspiredBooks.com

Printed in U.S.A.

I will not leave you as orphans—I will come for you.
—*John* 14:18

In memory of Ms. Jo,
Grandma Edith and Grandma Sylvia.
Thinking of each of you makes me smile.

Special thanks goes to Carolyn and Joyce for the
research trip to The Purple Cow—what a fun day we
had. I think you'll see the research paid off well.

Also a big thank-you to my editor, Melissa Endlich—
your insights and encouragement
in this new venture were spot on.

Chapter One

Sunrise Ranch, Dew Drop, Texas

"Calm down, son."

Morgan McDermott's father, Randolph, cut Morgan off at the pass with a rasp of exasperation—which in no way, shape or form even began to match the anger-fueled exasperation Morgan was struggling to contain.

An imposing figure at fifty-two, Randolph had hair as black as the Texas oil pumping from the herd of wells across the ten-thousand-acre McDermott family ranch. The only differences between the two men—who shared chiseled high cheekbones and square-jawed features—was the whisper of white at Randolph's temples and twenty years. Randolph was as physically fit and hard-headed as any of his three sons.

"Calm down?" Morgan gave a harsh laugh. "Are you kidding me? You go behind my back

and hire my *ex*-fiancée, and you expect me to calm down? For starters, Dad, we're partners. I'm supposed to make decisions like this *with* you. Second..."

Morgan was so shaken up by what he'd just been told that he lost his train of thought.

Jolie Sheridan, here.

Randolph pushed back from his desk and rose, meeting Morgan eye to eye. "You know as well as I do that we needed a teacher and we needed one quick. Jolie has graciously agreed to fill the position for one semester—"

"I don't care if *she's* paying *you* to let her teach the boys here at the ranch—I don't want her here." Morgan would never use this tone with his father under normal circumstances. But being blindsided by the knowledge that his dad had gone behind his back and hired the woman who had broken his heart was not normal circumstances. "We're supposed to discuss this kind of thing, Dad."

"I understand your feelings, but there was no time. Besides, Jolie is familiar with the school and will fit right in."

Logically it made sense, but that didn't ease the betrayal. Morgan remained silent, trying to grasp the reality of his situation.

"Your past is something I'd hoped you'd overcome by now. I hated that you got hurt when she left. We all did. That said, I've made a decision and it stands."

Morgan rammed a hand through his hair. "How do you expect me to—" He halted at the stern look his dad shot him.

"I expect you to act like a man, not a broken-hearted teenager nursing a grudge."

His dad's words stung. "I got over her a long time ago and you know it," he growled, not remembering the last time—if ever—that he'd been this angry with his father.

"Did you?" Randolph studied him, unflinching, from across the wide oak desk.

"You know I did. That doesn't mean I want to be around her for the next four months."

"You're strong. You'll make it. Maybe God worked the details out so you can come to some kind of peace with the situation. You may have gotten over Jolie, but you haven't forgiven her. You can't have peace until you do that."

This was a no-win situation. Yanking a noose tight around his emotions Morgan snatched his hat from the hat rack. "I'm late," he said, turning to leave. He pushed open the door of the Sunrise Ranch offices, his father's words trailing him.

"Mind your manners, Morgan McDermott. And remember, those boys out there are watching every move you make and learning from you."

"Some partnership," Morgan growled as the

blazing Texas heat hit him full force. It didn't begin to compare to the sizzling heat of his fury.

His life had just turned into a train wreck.

Ramming his hat onto his head, Morgan battled to get a grip on his anger. Stalking across fifty yards of white-rock gravel separating the barns from the office and chow hall, he fought to rein in his emotions. He had a herd of boys enjoying a very special moment in the barn and he intended to be a part of it come baseball-size hail or high water. And he knew—without his dad reminding him—that they didn't need to see him furious.

Sunrise Ranch was a working cattle ranch and foster home for boys who needed stability in their lives. Morgan took his job as their protector and role model extremely seriously. If he didn't, he wouldn't still be on the ranch in the first place.

Despite the heat or Morgan's mood, excitement rang in the early-morning air hanging over the ranch compound. Quickening his stride, Morgan approached the sun-faded red stable, the birthplace of hundreds of foals over the years. The sturdy, low-slung building had been on the property since Morgan's great-great-grandfather built it back in the early 1900s. Through the years there had been new barns and buildings added, but this lovingly maintained stable and the other historic buildings that dotted the property carried the memories of those who'd been here before him.

This was their legacy to him and his two brothers, Rowdy and Tucker. His family took to heart the responsibility of passing it on to future generations.

Morgan hauled in a deep breath the moment he stepped through the stable's double doors. Instantly the scent of grassy, sundried hay and feed mingled with the smell of leather and horses, filled his lungs. And his spirit.

The stables held lots of memories from years gone by, but it was the hushed whispers of the boys at the end of the building that filled his soul and gave his life purpose.

Before his mother's death when he was eleven years old, Lydia McDermott had had a vision to share the beauty and blessing of their West Texas ranch with less fortunate boys who had no place to call home. She'd died before she could make her dream a reality, but Morgan's dad and grandmother worked tirelessly over the next two years, getting the ranch approved as a foster home.

For the last eighteen years, sixteen boys at a time had made Sunrise Ranch their home. And Morgan, who had become a full partner six months ago, intended to help carry the torch forward—no matter who his dad brought on as the boys' teacher.

Moving down the concrete alley, the clink of his spurs and scuff of his boots bounced off the stalls. The chatter halted from the huddle at the end where a new colt had just been born, and the boys who were new to the ranch turned, awe on their faces. There was nothing like watching the miracle of life.

Yup, that was the only reminder Morgan needed that the boys came first.

Striding to stand behind them, Morgan patted one of the newcomers on the back and looked at the foal.

"It's about time you dragged yourself out here to take a look at the new little filly," Walter Pepper, his horse foreman, teased from inside the stall where he'd been assisting the mother. One of the best horsemen around, Pepper—as he'd been tagged in his early years—had worked at the ranch since he was a teenager, hired on by Morgan's granddad forty-five years ago. A stocky cowboy with a white head of hair, a gruff voice and a heart of gold, he loved to tease.

Taking in the coal-black filly curled up in the soft hay beside his momma, Morgan gave a crooked smile. "Looks like y'all've got it under control."

"She's as black as *your* hair, Morgan," nine-year-old Caleb declared, his green eyes shining. A blond-headed creative thinker and doer, Caleb was a regular fixer-upper, always coming up with ideas and taking tools and machines apart in the shop to figure out how they worked. But right now, he was wide-eyed like the rest of them, watching the mother horse tend to her newborn baby.

"Yeah," B.J. said, a grin lifting the seven-year-old's plump cheeks. "She ain't got no streak a white in her black hair like Beauty or Mr. Randolph gots." He puffed out his chest, proud that he was the first to make the comparison between the jet-black horse with the white lightning bolt crossing her face, and Randolph and his white temples.

"You're right about that, son," Morgan agreed, tousling B.J.'s brown hair as he studied Beauty. She was the first of twenty-five mares on the ranch who were due to foal in the next two months and she was kicking off the season like a pro. When the baby unbuckled her long legs and tried to stand, Beauty began nudging her gently on the rump, encouraging her as she struggled to gain her wobbly legs.

"Look, fellas, she's helping her baby get up," Joseph observed, extending a lean, muscular arm from where he hung halfway over the rail. The oldest boy on the ranch at eighteen, Joseph was long, lanky and a good-natured encourager of the younger boys. He had his heart set on being a large-animal vet and Morgan knew he would make a great one someday.

"It's 'cause she *loves* her," ten-year-old Sammy

whispered reverently, a whole host of wistfulness in his words that cut into Morgan's heart. Sammy had been at the ranch for only two weeks and was struggling. The kid's parents had given him up recently and before he could blink twice he found himself at Sunrise Ranch. The foster care worker had known the ranch had one opening and wasted no time getting Randolph and Morgan to accept Sammy into the mix. But Morgan could tell the poor kid was still grieving and in denial about what had happened to him.

Pepper's compassionate old eyes met Morgan's. These boys knew what it was to have a mother and a father who didn't care. Over the years Morgan had had many boys come to talk to him about how seeing a horse taking such tender care of her baby stabbed at their hearts on a raw level.

The first group of boys came to live at the ranch when Morgan was thirteen. They'd lost their parents, and because Morgan had just lost his mom to cancer two years earlier, he thought he understood what they were going through. It wasn't until he was a high school senior that he finally realized he didn't know where these boys were coming from at all. His mother had loved him with all of her heart. Death had forced her to leave her children—she never would have neglected or abandoned them.

It wasn't until six years ago when his fiancée

gave back her engagement ring and chose a life without him that he felt some semblance of what these guys felt. It was a hard lick to know you weren't wanted.

For a moment, he went back to that day, standing in the drive, his heart in the dirt at his feet, watching Jolie Sheridan drive off into the wide blue yonder. He was over it—had been for some time now—but it had been a long, hard crawl out of the pit he'd fallen into. He'd made some mistakes on the way and fueled plenty of gossip in Dew Drop. But he'd lived.

He'd moved on.

He'd always known his life and dreams were here on the ranch, and even though things hadn't turned out exactly like he'd envisioned them, he'd managed to take hold of what God had entrusted to him and he was content.

Even happy most of the time.

At last the filly got her legs beneath her and managed to take her first wobbly steps, bringing Morgan back to the stable.

"She did it!" Jeb yelled. His nine-year-old enthusiasm startled the filly—she jumped and fell flat on her face.

Horrified, Jeb clamped his hand to the top of his head as the boys around him scowled. In the sudden silence the filly gathered herself up and this time rose more easily, with just a single nudge from her momma. Jeb gave a big silent grin. The excitement the boys were containing over the filly's accomplishment could very easily have blown the roof off the building.

There was a lot to be learned from what they'd just witnessed. Getting up from a fall was a life lesson well worth paying attention to.

"Okay, boys," Pepper said, coming out of the stall, "let's give mother and baby some alone time. You fellas can come back this evening after you get your chores done. You just have to promise to be quiet."

"Will do," agreed Wes, a stocky seventeen-year-old with curly blond hair and a cocky attitude. The boys looked up to Wes and Joseph, and the two teens took their leadership roles seriously. Morgan liked that about them.

By the time they were leaving the stable, rowdy laughter and joking had ensued. Morgan followed the group, somewhat calmer than he'd been on entering but still not pleased. His dad had deliberately made the decision about Jolie without him because he knew there was no way Morgan would have agreed to it. But Morgan's anger wasn't just based on personal grounds—in his estimation the last thing the fellas needed was another teacher who wouldn't stick around. And Jolie was *exactly* that.

As fate would have it, Morgan and the boys

walked into the sunlight as Jolie herself whipped her cranberry-colored Jeep into the ranch yard, sliding to a halt across the driveway from them in a plume of dust. The doors and top were off the Jeep, giving them a clear view of her, with wind-tossed cinnamon hair.

Morgan's gut twisted in a knot and he came up short as if he'd slammed face-first into a flag pole. He had a clear shot of her. Rocks lodged in his throat. She was beautiful.

She had the boys' attention instantly, looking vibrant and full of life, every inch the world-class competitive kayaker that she was, long legs and tanned skin in well-worn jeans and a sleeveless orange tank top. She jumped from the vehicle with a big Julia Roberts smile on her face—and a hundred watts of pure joy slammed into the group.

It felt more like a sucker punch to Morgan.

"*Who* is *that?*" Joseph whistled as long strides brought her closer. There was no mistaking his admiration of Jolie. The kid was seventeen after all.

Wes elbowed Joseph out of the way. "Hubba, hubba, come to papa," he said. Morgan bopped him on the back of the head.

"Watch your manners, hotshot," he warned. "Both of you," he added as Joseph glanced at him, too.

"I didn't mean any harm," Wes said, his blue eyes dreamy. "I'm just in *lovvve.*"

Joseph put his hand on his heart and patted it, then gave his full attention back to Jolie.

"She sure is pretty," Caleb gushed as she came nearer.

True on all counts—Morgan could not deny it. Jolie still had the ability to take his breath away.

"What's up, fellas? How's it going?" She greeted the guys like she'd just seen them yesterday and knew them by name. Looking like a bright beam of sunlight, she seemed to sparkle. She hadn't looked at Morgan yet, focusing all her attention on the sixteen totally engrossed fellas whose lower lips were now sitting firmly on their boot tips.

"You fellas must be my new class. I'm Jolie Sheridan, your teacher."

"You *are?*" Sammy cooed. The rest of them had suddenly become speechless.

"You bet I am." Jolie chuckled. "I'm excited to start school." Those luminescent green eyes met Morgan's for the first time and he was fairly certain he looked as grim as he felt because her smile faltered.

"We don't have to start today, do we?" Sammy blurted. Jolie gave them another sucker-punch grin as she put her focus back on the boys.

"Don't worry, little dude, school's not till Monday. You have freedom today and tomorrow…and then you're *all mine, all mine,*" she sang the last words and ended with a wink. "I'm just getting the classroom fixed up today."

The woman had skills when it came to winning over a crowd. Of course she'd had this fickle group at her first hello.

"I'd be glad to help you," Joseph offered, finally finding his voice.

Wes Grinned. "Count me in." His chest was so puffed out Morgan feared the teen would throw his back out of whack.

Their eagerness had Morgan rethinking some things…like maybe it was time to offer Joseph and Wes some guidance on relationships, and what was acceptable around a girl. Not that the boys were around girls very much because they went to school on the ranch. Still, there were local girls at church and around town. Morgan made a mental note.

Jolie's eyes widened at their offer. "I would *love* some help if you fellas want to. Only if Morgan doesn't have plans for you, though."

Every eye turned toward him.

"You don't, do you?" Joseph vocalized their question.

He wanted to say that yes, in fact, he sure did.

He wanted nothing more than to tell the kids they had other things that required their attention besides Miss Jolie Sheridan. But any cowboy worth his salt knew when he was caught.

The right thing to do—the *courteous* thing to do—was help out the new teacher and offer assistance.

Him included.

If it had been any other person, he wouldn't have even hesitated.

"Nope," he heard himself saying. "No plans that can't wait. Helping Miss Sheridan get settled would be the gentlemanly thing to do, so we'll do that first and then we'll go build the fence."

"I don't want to disrupt any plans you've already made," she insisted.

The guys erupted like squawking geese, assuring her it was *no* problem. No problem at all.

Morgan suddenly wanted to take the boys and get as far away from Jolie as possible. But instead, he said, "Like the guys are telling you, it's not a problem. We can build the fence Monday after school if we don't get it done this afternoon."

She smiled at him and it hit him in the gut like a two-by-four. He was in for a beating while she was around, whether he wanted to admit it or not.

"Well, okay. Thanks."

"You're welcome," he said, his breath jamming in his throat.

She hesitated, her eyes locking on his for a second before turning back to the boys. Only then could Morgan breathe.

"If that's the case then follow me, good men that you are," she directed with a laugh. "Let's go see what adventures await us."

Waving to the fellas to follow her, she headed for the three-room schoolhouse. The boys trotted behind her looking like a litter of puppies with their tongues hanging out.

Morgan watched them go. "Just call me Jolie," he heard her telling them, her voice drifting to him over the distance, like a long-forgotten song.

"I heard she was back." Pepper came out of the stable to stand beside him. "Your grandmother told me she stopped by the kitchen yesterday and said hello. She said they had a real nice visit. Said she was worried about you, though. Me, too. I figure from that scowl on your face you just found out this morning."

So even his grandmother knew.

"How many others knew about this?" he asked, not even trying to hide his anger.

"Don't get me to lying. I just happened to see her coming out of your dad's office yesterday when you and the boys were off working cattle with Rowdy. I asked your grandmother about it."

Morgan shook his head, watching Jolie in the

distance. His stomach rolled like he'd just been thrown from a rough bronc. What had he been thinking when he'd offered to help?

Staring from beneath bushy eyebrows with concern, Pepper clapped Morgan on the back. "You hold your ground, Morg. Dig your boots into that gravel and don't budge. I helped scrape your heart up off the sidewalk once, and I ain't lookin' forward to doing it again in this lifetime."

Morgan shot him a firm look. "You don't have to worry about me. I learned my lesson a long time ago. I'm just looking out for the boys today."

"Good. I haven't ever disagreed with your dad about much, but this time I have to admit that I did. He should have never let that girl come back. It just ain't right, accident or no accident."

Morgan knew about the accident. His grandmother had told him how Jolie had nearly drowned in competition on a river. It hit him hard then and still did now, even if he had gotten over his feelings for her the day she'd given him back his ring.

Tugging his hat down low, he gave Pepper a nod and headed off toward the school. Might as well get this over with.

Despite the anger that still lived inside him, his pulse picked up speed as he started after Jolie. And his boots followed suit, not dragging anywhere near as much as he thought they should, considering he was going to help the woman who'd left him high and dry with his heart—and his engagement ring—in his hand.

Chapter Two

Did I make the right choice coming home to the ranch?

Jolie's emotions had been tumbling around inside her like clothes in a dryer since the moment she'd spotted Morgan standing beside the stables. The cowboy had always turned her world upside down with his midnight-black hair and deep blue eyes. Six feet of lean Texas cowboy with an extra inch added on for good measure—like the guy needed any extra help.

He'd been thirteen when she moved to the ranch with her parents. Immediately she'd thought he hung the moon. He'd probably thought she was a ten-year-old pest but was too kind to let her know it, unlike his brother Rowdy. Instead he'd endured her childish adoration with a patience that she'd tested on a regular basis.

How could she not have fallen in love with the guy?

"Where should this go?" Joseph asked, looking at her desk.

"I think I'd like it over there by that wall." Jolie pointed to the opposite side of the room from where the heavy oak desk was sitting now. She smiled, determined not to let the rush of the past and the uncertainty of the present distract her from getting her classroom set up.

She was impressed with the way the boys were willing to help. And startled and a bit shaken by the fact that Morgan had offered his help, too. Especially because he'd not hidden the fact that he was unhappy about her being here—his eyes had told the tale. She'd hoped time had healed old wounds, but even if it hadn't, she'd had to come home to the ranch.

Needed to come home.

Needed desperately to find the person she'd been, the person she'd lost somewhere in the depths of West Virginia's Gauley River.

She had loved Sunrise Ranch from the moment she'd moved here when her folks had been hired as house parents for one of the two foster homes on the ranch. It had been a wonderful place to grow up. And she was praying it would now be a place where she could heal and find the funny, take-the-world-by-the-horns girl she'd lost beneath the dark water of the Gauley.

The girl she was faking right now for these boys.

Coming up out of that water, her world shaken to its very core, the one thing she'd known upon gasping that first lifesaving breath was it was time to face her past....

Time to apologize to Morgan McDermott.

As if God was in agreement, this opportunity dropped in her lap and here she was.

"Is this where you want it...Jolie?" Joseph asked.

She'd told them right off to call her Jolie. She was just too laid back for anything else, even if she was their teacher. Besides, the ranch was home to the boys. Informality made it all the more true.

"Perfect," she said to the earnest young man.

"You got it, then." Joseph grabbed the edge of the monstrous desk and she was pretty sure he was about to try and move it himself. Not to be outdone, Wes was eyeing the floor-to-ceiling bookcases with determination.

"Hold off over there, Wes," Morgan demanded, coming in the front door and taking charge. Jolie's insides jangled as his presence filled the large room.

So much hung between them. She'd hoped to talk to him yesterday when she'd arrived, but he'd been working cattle at the far edge of the ranch. And so here they were in a room full of bright-eyed students, unable to talk about the fact that today had been their first meeting since she'd given him back his engagement ring.

"We'll get the desk moved first and then the bookshelves, Wes," Morgan said as he grabbed the other side of her desk.

"Thanks." Joseph grinned at Morgan. "We're putting it over there." He nodded his brown head toward the windows.

With Morgan's strength, the two were able to move the mammoth desk with ease. Once that was done they attacked the ten-foot-tall bookshelves. It ended up taking Morgan and most of the boys to move them.

Everyone's eagerness touched Jolie's heart.

She was smiling so much that she was almost able to ignore the fact that being around Morgan was causing her some heavy-duty stress—she could suddenly feel his presence like a weight.

"Where's our desks gonna sit, Jolie?"

Jolie looked down into the big, brown eyes of a wisp of a boy. "Sammy, right?" she asked, and he nodded. Sammy seemed like a nervous little fella. Uncertain of himself.

"We'll need to turn them all to face my desk. That way the light from the windows will stream across your desks. I *love* light and want y'all to enjoy it while you work."

"Can my desk be this one?" His words were as timid as the light touch he laid on the desk closest to hers, almost as if he were certain she would say no.

"Sure. It's got Sammy written all over it. Matter of fact, everyone can pick their desk."

Unsmiling, Sammy nodded and slipped into the wooden seat. "Only till my dad comes and gets me," he added in a quiet voice barely audible over the noise of the chaos breaking out behind him as the other boys began slamming into desks two at a time.

Jolie hardly even glanced at what was happening around her as her heart latched on to Sammy, who was so clearly suffering. "Sure," she assured him. "You can have that desk as long as you're here."

She wasn't sure what else to say. There were times when kids were on the ranch short-term. But most boys were here for the long haul—Sunrise Ranch had always been geared toward boys who had been totally abandoned by their families. The ranch became their home; the people, their family.

The poor kid got a wistful look on his face, then patted the desk next to him. "You can have this desk, Joseph," he called to Joseph—obviously Sammy's hero—as Joseph watched the rodeo going on over who got which desk.

"I'm too big to sit on the front row." Joseph brushed his brown bangs out of his eyes. "One of the shorter kids can sit there, and I'll sit in the back so I can make sure all you goofballs behave. Hey, goofballs!" he yelled, drawing all eyes in his direction. "One of you to a desk."

"Yeah," Wes barked loudly, crossing his arms and stepping up beside Joseph. "What kind of *animals* are y'all anyway?"

It looked as if Wes and Joseph had decided they were going to make certain the boys behaved for her. Jolie hid a grin—and then her gaze met Morgan's. Morgan's eyebrow hitched upward, his dark denim eyes cool.

He has no confidence in me, she suddenly thought. Jolie was fairly certain Morgan would think she needed help in that department—if, that is, he even remembered how she'd let her class get out of control on her first day of student teaching. It had been a long time ago, and he might have easily forgotten the laugh they'd shared over the little boys letting the mice out of their cage and the hysterics that had ensued. Meeting his sardonic gaze, she hiked a brow of her own. "It'll be okay, guys. They're just excited. We're going to be fine," she said to Wes and Joseph, assuring all of them, as well as herself.

"Can you ride a horse?" Sammy asked, drawing her attention. She was grateful for the change of subject.

"Yes, I can. Can you?" she asked.

He shook his head. "Never been on one."

"He helped us work cattle yesterday, though." Morgan stepped up beside the boy, giving him a smile that sent an arrow straight to Jolie's heart. Morgan McDermott had a soft spot for these boys.

He placed a hand on Sammy's shoulder. "You did good, Sammy."

"It was scary. I almost got trampled, too." Sammy's eyes were huge.

"Aw, come on, kid, it wasn't that bad," Joseph called from the back of the room where he was trying out his new desk. "If you stick with us, you'll learn not to be scared."

Sammy didn't look too sure about that.

"I ride," yelped Tony, a skinny kid around fifteen or so who looked like a young Elvis Presley with his swath of black hair, blue eyes and a crooked smile that made his eyes twinkle. He skidded to a halt in front of Jolie.

This led each boy to reveal he could ride. Jolie caught the flicker of fear in Sammy's expression as he realized he was the only one who couldn't ride. She glanced at Morgan to find his guarded eyes staring back at her.

"We're gonna learn to mug steers tomorrow after church," Caleb said, his freckles crinkling with his smile. "You can come, too, Jolie."

Sammy slipped his hand into hers and looked up. "Would you come?"

Jolie melted right there in the middle of the room. Turned right into a pool of liquid. "Sure I will," she said. She was pretty sure she would have jumped from an airplane if he'd asked her. "I love to calf wrestle, and scramble, too. But muggin' is my favorite! I used to be one of the best here on the ranch, you know."

"Seriously?" Joseph jerked to his feet, gaping at her from across the room. He and Wes exchanged disbelieving looks. "*You* can take down a steer?"

Jolie nearly shook her head. *Males.*

"Hey, y'all look like you don't think I can do it!" she teased.

"We just aren't used to girls—I mean, *women*— wantin' to do something like that," Wes drawled, glancing at Joseph and Tony.

Jolie smiled at the cocky, young cowboys, with their worn jeans tucked into their rugged boots and their T-shirts with the arms cut out of them. It was obvious that they'd been working that morning, most likely hauling hay, an ongoing job she remembered quite well growing up on the ranch. A picture of Morgan in that same getup at that age raced through her head and she glanced his way. He looked about as happy as a grizzly bear that had been awakened in the middle of a really good nap.

"I'm a little insulted here! Girls do this sort of thing all the time." She laughed when they all swallowed and looked a bit meek. "You'll find for the most part that I look at life with a bring-it-on attitude." She looked directly at Morgan before shifting back to the boys. "I haven't done it in a long time, but it sounds too fun to pass up. I'll be there." She looked at Mr. Grizzly Bear again. "May I speak to you outside?"

"Sure," he growled, swiveling toward the back door. "You boys don't tear anything up while we're gone."

Jolie thought Morgan was teasing even though he seemed far from a teasing mood. Surely he wasn't thinking the boys were going to destroy all the work they'd just put in. But then again, there *was* the incident with the desks.

Looking back over her shoulder, she was struck by the group. The picture they made reminded her of an old John Wayne movie, *The Cowboys,* about a bunch of ragtag boys who'd needed a gruff old cowboy to teach them life lessons. Although Morgan was far from an old cowboy, it was plain to see that these boys respected and admired him. And needed him.

Smiling at them, she winked. "If y'all want to finish turning the desks and lining them up, that would be great."

They all chorused, "Yes, ma'am."

Smiling at their politeness, she followed Mr. Grizzly outside and then passed him, leading him out of earshot of the class. There was a large, gnarled oak tree still bent over as it had been all those years ago. She didn't stop until she reached it, turning his way only after they were beneath the wide expanse of limbs.

Morgan crossed his arms and studied the tree. "I remember having to climb up this tree and talk you down after you scrambled up to the top and froze."

She hadn't expected him to bring up old memories—it caught her off guard. "I remember how mad you were at having to rescue the silly little new girl." Mad? Actually, furious was more accurate.

A hint of a smile teased his lips, fraying Jolie's nerves at the edges. It had been a long, long time since she'd seen that smile.

"I got used to it, though," he said, his voice warming.

She laughed, encouraged by his teasing. "You had no other choice! I guess if you hadn't rescued me I'd never have made it to my teen years." But she was grateful to Morgan for more than that. She'd grown into a teenager who could handle almost any situation, a girl confident in her own skin. She hadn't been afraid to try anything because she'd been so crazy adventurous—and free to learn from her mistakes, thanks to Morgan and his brothers, Rowdy and Tucker, who had always been there to help her through. She'd idolized them, but at the same time, wanted them to stop babying her.

Morgan especially.

Of course it was Morgan who'd made her the angriest, and Morgan whom she'd fallen for. Their relationship had never been an easy one. The push and pull of attraction had started when she'd demanded independence, and then changed when she'd found herself desperate for his approval. But it became something incredibly complicated when she'd realized she wanted his love.

And then the pull of competitive kayaking entered the equation when Morgan introduced her to it on a lazy summer afternoon and things grew more complicated. She'd been fifteen, and her instant infatuation with the sport had been too much to ignore. For a young woman who craved the adventure world-class competition offered, Sunrise Ranch suddenly seemed…small. When Morgan made it clear that he had no desire to leave the ranch, Jolie decided she had no choice but to walk away.

Looking at him now, she was overcome by the memory of the internal war she'd lived through when she'd made the decision to leave.

It had been six years, but it felt like twenty.

They were standing beneath the shade of the old oak tree, electricity humming between them.

When the smile left Morgan's eyes, Jolie sucked in a wobbly breath, forcing herself to focus on the job she'd been hired to do. "I'm curious about Sammy. Has he been here long?"

"Just a couple of weeks. He's our newest rancher. He's still having trouble emotionally, after his abandonment. It's a tough situation."

"He seems fearful."

"He is, poor kid. He knows his dad has been gone from the picture for a long time. But his mother gave him up to the state and now he thinks his dad will find out and come for him. He'll stretch the truth from here to Alaska, so you might want to tread lightly with everything he says until you give it a reality check."

"He lies?" she asked, a little more frankly than she'd intended. But she needed to know the truth if she was going to help him.

Morgan grimaced. "Kinda. More like the boy who cried wolf."

"The stories don't ever seem to change, do they, Morgan? I just can't imagine how these boys handle their families not wanting them. Or not caring enough to make loving homes for them."

She'd been around kids like Sammy all the time growing up. Some handled the situation with anger, some with denial, but it was all about fear. She understood that on a personal level—three times this week she'd awakened in the middle of the night because of nightmares. She pushed the thoughts away, praying she was up for this job.

"Sammy's a good example of how bad these kids have been hurt. They need people around them who will care for them and stick with them." The hardness of Morgan's tone matched the accusation in his eyes. "What are you doing here, Jolie? Why aren't you taming rapids in some far-off place?"

"I...I'm—" She stumbled over her words, tongue-tied by his question. "I'm taking a leave from competition for a little while. I had a bad run in Virginia and I— It was bad." She couldn't bring herself to say that she'd almost died, that she was lucky to be standing there. "Anyway, your dad was kind enough to offer me this opportunity."

"I heard about the accident and I'm real sorry about that, Jolie. I really am. I wish you a speedy recovery so you can get back out there doing what you love. But why come here after all this time? We dropped off your radar a long time ago."

"This is my *home*. It has never been off my radar." Jolie saw anger in Morgan's eyes. Well, he had a right to it, and more than a right to point it straight at her. She'd just thought she was prepared for it.

She was wrong.

"Morgan," Jolie said, almost as a whisper. "I'd

hoped we could forget the past and move forward."

Heart pounding, she reached across the space between them and placed her hand on his arm. It was just a touch, but the feeling of connecting with Morgan McDermott again after so much time rocked her straight to the core and suddenly she wasn't so sure coming home had been the right thing to do, after all.

A jolt from a live wire couldn't have burned Morgan more than the touch of Jolie's hand. Shock waves coursed through him with a vengeance, his mouth went dry. There had been a time when he'd have done anything for her touch. He gulped hard and hardened his heart against a walk down memory lane.

He wasn't some kid anymore, holding his heart in his hands. He was a thirty-two-year-old adult male with a good brain between his ears. Or at least he'd thought he had a good brain.

"I did forget the past. A long time ago," he assured her, his skin burning where her hand still lay. He wondered if she felt the way his pulse had started galloping at her touch. They stared at each other as seconds slipped by.

"Yes, of course you would have," Jolie said at last, her hand squeezing his arm slightly before it slipped away. "But I was hoping there would be no hard feelings."

His jaw jerked in reflex.

"I didn't mean to hurt you," she said. "It really wasn't personal."

"You broke our engagement, then headed off in search of *better* things. I think I had a right to take that personal."

"That is not fair."

Morgan was suddenly not at all comfortable with where this was heading.

"I wasn't searching for *better*," she said. "I couldn't stay. You know I would have regretted it for the rest of my life."

"Well," he drawled icily, "that makes me feel a whole heap better."

"I'm sorry," she said, her eyes shadowing. "Morgan, I'm so sorry for the way it ended that day. I'm sorry for letting us go so far. I never meant to hurt you. I never should have accepted the ring in the first place knowing my heart was torn."

"On that we agree." At least she hadn't waited until the night before they were to walk down the aisle like Celia, the next woman he'd been fool enough to ask to marry him. Two in a row had made Morgan hang up any thoughts of ever popping the question again. Not that he ever should have started dating Celia in the first place.

"Look, Jolie, that was a long time ago. It doesn't matter anymore. Right now my concern is for those boys. They got hung out to dry by their parents and then their teacher left them for something better at the last minute. They don't need another person leaving. They need someone they can count on to be here for them."

Slapping a hand on her hip, fire flashed in her eyes. "I intend to honor my contract for the semester, and I'm going to do my best to help each of the boys any way that I can."

Morgan met her gaze with fire of his own. "I don't like your being here, but it doesn't matter—you are. I'll just have to hope and pray it all turns out okay."

Turning away he strode back toward the schoolhouse, leaving Jolie standing beneath the old oak. He used the walk to rein in his temper so he could finish setting up the classroom. The last thing he needed was for the boys to pick up on the bad vibes between him and Jolie—and if he wasn't careful, they would, before he even made it in the door.

How, he wanted to know as the schoolhouse got closer and his temper just got worse, was he ever going to make this work?

Infuriating man, Jolie thought, stalking after Morgan. "Stop right where you are, bucko," she demanded, sounding as if she was calling him out to a gunfight at the O.K. Corral. He swung around at the entrance to the schoolhouse, clearly startled. She marched straight up to him.

"You might not have any faith in me." *And my faith in myself might be shaken to the core.* "But while I'm here, I'll give these kids everything I have to give. No holding back."

For the first time since the accident Jolie felt a familiar strength ease through her, and she liked it. She'd had moments since nearly drowning when she'd felt as weak as a newborn, but she still counted herself a strong woman. She prayed that throwing herself into helping the boys of Sunrise Ranch would be a win-win situation for all of them.

"Key words, Jolie—*while you are here.*"

"It doesn't matter to you if I can do a good job, does it, Morgan? This is personal on your part."

"You bet it's personal. These boys are my *personal* responsibility."

Stung by his words and breathless with fury, she glared up at him, trying to ignore the fact that the man smelled of pine and leather. His scent played havoc with her senses. Her eyes, traitors that they were, slid down to rest on his lips. She inhaled, but all the air in the world seemed to have gone missing.

Focus, Jolie. Focus.

"Think the worst of me, Morgan McDermott. However," she said, her conviction ringing true in her own ears, "I will give these boys everything I have to give them."

He stepped so close they were almost touching, and she had to tilt her head back to look him in the eye. "That's exactly what I expect," he said. "They deserve it." His gaze fell to her lips and lingered for only a brief instant before meeting hers. Jolie's heart skipped a beat, and Morgan's eyes were nearly black with dark emotion—yearning? Fury? Jolie was rendered speechless by his scowl. What was going on in that mind of his?

He left her then, continuing toward the school.

As she followed him toward the back door, she was sure of one thing and one thing only: for the first time in weeks she was filled with a great sense of purpose. What God had in store for her and Morgan, she didn't have a clue. But God had plans for her at the Sunrise Ranch school and she was determined to prove herself to Him.

It was probably going to be a lot easier than proving herself to Morgan.

Chapter Three

When Jolie reached the main classroom a few seconds after Morgan, she saw Joseph holding the front door open for Morgan's grandmother, Ruby Ann "Nana" McDermott. Nana was the backbone of the ranch, a former barrel racer who ran the chow hall like a well-greased wagon wheel. Her vision had been essential in making Lydia McDermott's dream come true, and her heart had been essential in making the place what it was today.

Jolie knew that since Lydia's death, Nana had been just as much a mother to Morgan as she had been to the countless young ranchers who'd needed her love. Jolie had loved and adored Nana and the feeling had been mutual. In her sixties, Nana had deep blue, wide-set eyes, high cheekbones and a square jaw, and there was no denying that her son Randolph and her three grandsons,

Morgan, Rowdy and Tucker, were from her gene pool. Before her thick ponytail had turned the color of pale steel, it had been jet-black like Morgan's and Randolph's—a long-ago gift of the Cherokee blood of Nana's ancestors.

Yesterday Jolie had been welcomed by Nana with open arms—there was never any lack of hugs where Nana was concerned. Today Nana hustled into the room like a woman on a mission, her ponytail swinging as she brought cookies to her boys—and checked up on Morgan and "her girl," as she always called Jolie.

She set the large tray down on a worktable beside the computer as the tantalizing scent of chocolate and cinnamon filled the room. Nana's smile was just as warm and sweet as the cookies nestled on the tray.

"Y'all have sure been workin' hard today, so I whipped up some of your favorite cookies." The instant she stepped back, it was like a free-for-all—the boys dived for the chocolate chip cookies, attacking them as if they hadn't eaten all morning.

"Glad you came on out today, Jolie," she said as Jolie gave her a hug.

"I thought it would be best to come and, you know—" she faltered as she looked at Morgan, who frowned at her "—get acquainted, with the boys, I mean, and get prepared."

Morgan looked as if he'd just witnessed her robbing a bank or something, his eyes narrowing in distrust. Jolie gulped and looked back at Nana.

"Thank you for the snacks. These boys deserve it—as you said, they've been working hard."

Nana waved off the comment. "These bottomless pits always need cookies." She planted her fists on her hips, giving Jolie and Morgan the once-over. "When I was coming out of the chow hall I saw you two heading around the back of the building."

Nana looked at Morgan, and Jolie thought she saw worry in her eyes.

"Um, we had things to discuss," Jolie explained. What else could she say?

"Morgan, how's your day going?" Nana asked when it was obvious the boys were too engrossed in cookie devouring to eavesdrop on their conversation.

Exasperation flashed in Morgan's eyes. "How do you think, Nana? Started out with a real bang in Dad's office this morning."

Nana blushed—surprising Jolie, since she wasn't the blushing kind—and she leaned in close to Morgan. "If it makes you feel any better, I told Randolph he needed to warn you."

"And what about you?" he asked.

"I— Well," she said, patting his arm. "We'll talk about this later."

Jolie wasn't sure what was going on, but it sounded as if Morgan hadn't known she was coming. Was that possible? The thought practically made her gasp. If that was the case, then no wonder he was so hostile. His dad had not only made the decision to hire her on his own, but had also kept it a secret—until today.

"You didn't know?" she whispered.

His lips pressed into a tight line and his left eyebrow lifted ever so slightly.

Jolie gasped, looking from Morgan to Nana. It was true—Randolph hadn't told him!

Nana turned to where the boys were scarfing down the cookies as if there was no tomorrow. "Did you fellas know Jolie is a world-class champion kayaker? She gets paid by sponsors to travel all over the world and compete using their gear. Isn't that right, Jolie?"

"Get outta here. For real?" Wes said, stepping away from the cookie fray.

Jolie nodded and her stomach dropped to her feet as a sick feeling washed over her in a wave. *Please don't go there. I can't handle that right now on top of everything else.*

She'd known it was ridiculous to hope no one would mention her kayaking, yet she'd hoped exactly that. She gave a weak smile. "I've won a few competitions."

"Ha!" Nana hooted. "She's top ten in the country."

Morgan crossed his arms, his expression stormy.

"Top in the country!" Wes gushed, suddenly looking a lot younger than seventeen.

"Really?" Tony joined in, his eyes lit with expectations.

Alarms clanged inside of Jolie.

"What's kayaking?" Caleb asked as he and the other smaller fellas looked up from their cookies.

"It's like a plastic canoe that holds one person, and they compete on riding the rapids and stuff." Joseph had come closer, as intent as Wes and Tony. "We have some rapids on the river at this place. Do you know that?"

She knew what was coming next. She knew it and she wasn't even sure she could speak. But she nodded and fought for words as acid churned in her stomach.

"I—I started on those rapids when I was a kid. Morgan showed them to me."

That was all the encouragement the boys needed. They instantly erupted in excitement.

"Cool! Can you teach us?" Joseph said over the others' exclamations. Jolie silently prayed for God to help her.

"I've always wanted to learn," Wes gushed again, grinning like he'd just won the lottery. "Can you teach us?" he echoed as the others chimed in.

Jolie's vision blurred—where had all the air

gone? She suddenly felt unbearably hot as every eye in the room stared at her. Her pulse pounded in her head like the roar of the white river rapids she now feared. Black spots began to spatter her vision like paint drops. She swayed, woozy, and her gaze swung to Morgan—for what? To ask for help?

I can't teach these boys to kayak!

Breathe, she commanded herself, even as her knees turned to jelly....

"Jolie!"

Morgan's voice rumbled down a long tunnel as Jolie sank like a rock.

One minute she was standing and the next she was swooped up into strong arms. *His* strong arms. Morgan McDermott's arms.

The arms she'd longed for since she'd walked away from Sunrise Ranch...six long years ago....

Voices floated to Jolie through a dark fog.

"She fainted," Caleb gasped.

"Passed smooth out," Sammy said in a hushed voice.

"I ain't never in my whole long life seen nobody pass out," B.J. whispered.

Though lost in the fog, it registered loud and clear to Jolie that her head was resting against Morgan's chest. His heart beat against her temple so hard it was no wonder she'd come to so quickly.

"Good thang you gone and caught her, Morgan," B.J. continued. Jolie was surprised how easily she could already identify the boys just by the sound of their voices.

"Yeah, or she might have died," Sammy said solemnly.

"Caleb and Sammy, how about y'all get me a glass of water and a cold rag?" Nana urged gently.

"Sure! I'll get the rag," Caleb volunteered.

"I'll get the water," Sammy said. Their voices were followed immediately by the trample of feet.

"Jolie, can you hear me?" Morgan asked gently.

Jolie lifted her eyes and forced herself to pull her head away from Morgan's heart. Embarrassment warmed her face. "Faint of heart" was not a description of the gal who'd looked down the throat of The Gorilla—the burliest rapids in the toughest of all the extreme kayaking competitions in the world—and felt only an adrenaline rush and excitement. She was not a wimp. Fainting was *not* in her vocabulary...or at least it hadn't been until she'd almost drowned.

"Give her some air, boys," Nana said. Moving in, she fanned Jolie furiously with a booklet she must have snatched from the bookshelf. "Honey, you're whiter than Walter Pepper's hair!"

Jolie would have smiled at that if she could have.

"How are you doing?" Morgan asked, his voice gruff in a way that made her heart beat faster.

"I'm okay," Jolie assured them, looking at Morgan. His eyes were full of concern—and questions. She was thankful they were surrounded by the boys—boys who were silent and looked a little scared. She needed to stand up and show them she was fine.

Even if she was fast becoming a wimp, she certainly didn't have to broadcast it.

"Are you sure?" Morgan set her on her feet, keeping his arms around her. "Maybe you should sit down."

Maybe I need to stay in your arms—
Maybe I need to get a grip!

"No, I can stand," she said firmly, and forced herself to step away from Morgan.

The concern in his eyes almost undid her.

This was the man she'd fallen for when she was sixteen years old. This was a gentler man, not the hard man she'd been dealing with for the last couple of hours. Sadly, she knew she was partly to blame for some of the hard crust encasing Morgan.

Praying her witless knees wouldn't buckle, she was pleased when she stood firm. All she had to do now was come up with an answer as to why she wasn't going to teach the boys how to kayak.

Sammy and Caleb came bounding from the back of the building, Caleb waving a washcloth and Sammy sloshing water from the glass as he ran, the hand clamped tightly over the glass not keeping the water from escaping. His big eyes were huge with fear. She hated that she'd worried him when he already had so many things bothering him.

"Sit," Morgan demanded, pushing her into the nearest seat. B.J. immediately came to stand beside her.

"You're whiter than a marshmallow," Caleb declared, pushing the washcloth into her hands.

"I'm fine," she assured him and the others as they all began talking about how pale she was.

"You scared fifteen years off my life," Sammy said, sounding like an adult.

Jolie had to chuckle at his tone.

"Sammy, you don't have fifteen years to scare off," Joseph teased. "You're only ten."

Sammy frowned. "She scared it off me, though."

Caleb blinked hard. "You scared me, too."

Jolie's heart warmed at their worry. "I'll be honest with you, fellas. It freaked me out a little, too. I mean, really, I blacked out and woke up in Mr. Morgan's arms—*that's* a scary thing!"

She won a round of laughter from all the boys, and keeping the momentum going, she drove the topic away from her. The last thing she wanted was for one of them to ask about kayaking again.

She caught Morgan watching her and her insides did a swan dive straight to her toes. Forcing her chin upward, she gave him a smile and kept her balance as she stood.

Joseph frowned, his lean face looking a little strange without the smile that was usually plastered across it. "You're as wobbly as the filly we just saw born."

"I'm okay." She forced any shakiness from her voice. "Now, let's talk about this calf wrestling I'll be winning tomorrow."

"Winning?" Joseph grinned dubiously, looking more like himself. "I don't think so. I'm wrestling, too."

"Me, too," Wes spoke up, challenge in his eyes. "Which means y'all are lookin' at the winner right here." He pulled his thumbs toward his chest and grinned.

Jolie laughed, feeling some semblance of herself returning. "You boys need to remember to never underestimate your opponent." She let her gaze slide to Morgan. He crossed his arms and cocked his head to the side, his eyes holding steady, assessing her.

She knew she wasn't fooling him. She also knew it wouldn't be long before he asked her exactly what the fainting was all about.

She wondered if he would ask purely out of concern, as any decent person would do, or if he would ask because somewhere behind that shield he wore, he still cared for her. She was just going to have to wait and see.

But in the meantime, she should probably figure out what to do about the fact that she desperately wanted it to be the latter.

Chapter Four

A little unhinged by her afternoon, Jolie headed straight for the Spotted Cow Café to see her longtime friend Ms. Jo. The café was in its mid-afternoon lull when she walked through the lemon pie–yellow door. She was immediately greeted by the moo of the four-foot toy cow just inside the entrance. The cow's hide had bare spots on it from years of kids petting it, but it mooed like a newborn bawling after its mama.

Jolie had good memories in this diner.

The soft buttery walls were covered with all manner of spotted-cow gifts from customers: knickknacks, cattle horns and mooing cow clocks were everywhere. It was a unique place, to say the least. Even the buffed-concrete floor was painted with large, irregularly shaped brown spots. They were supposed to represent the hide of a spotted cow but had come out looking more like cow patties, which was why Chili Crump and Drewbaker Macintosh, a couple of the old-time locals, nicknamed the diner the Cow Patty Café. Needless to say, that made Ms. Jo furious.

Jolie headed for the old-fashioned soda fountain at the back and her mouth began to water the instant the glass case of frothy pies came into view. Her stomach growled, reminding her that she hadn't eaten all day.

Pie sounded like the perfect meal after the day she'd had.

"That'll make you fat," Edwina, the longtime waitress, warned, hustling out of the back carrying plates of hamburgers and fries. She paused to give Jolie a lopsided grin. "But it's worth every calorie and more. You can tell by my hips that I partake of a bite every chance I can get."

Jolie chuckled. Edwina was a character who'd worked for Ms. Jo for years. Skin as tough as boot leather and a personality to match, Edwina loved to tell tall tales. Rough as she was, she was part of the atmosphere and as dependable as all the cow clocks put together.

"You here to see Ms. Jo?" she asked. "She's armpit-high in pie crust—okay, so her armpits aren't involved, but she *is* in the pie dough, if you want to find her."

Jolie grinned. "Thanks, Ed. You keeping the cowboys straight today?"

Edwina huffed and headed toward the two cowboys sitting at the window. "Crazy men, I done told them they weren't welcomed in here but they keep comin'. I know it's not the food or my winning personality, so it's got to be my beauty. It's a curse."

Chuckling, Jolie headed through the swinging doors. She'd made Ms. Jo mad when she'd first arrived in town and only taken time to get checked in at the Dew Drop Inn before heading out to see Randolph. She'd known Harvey, the front-desk clerk, would have it all over town that she was back. By the time Jolie had come in yesterday afternoon, Ms. Jo had been told and was not happy that Jolie hadn't come by to see her. She was probably still a little peeved about it today.

Walking through the curtain into the large, spotless kitchen, Jolie waved at T-Bone, their cook, as she passed the grill and went back to the baking area. Ms. Jo, a compact little gal with short brown hair curled around her ears, worked the dough with a pie roller. Her alert hazel eyes locked onto Jolie as she entered the room.

"I know that look," she quipped, rolling pin wagging at Jolie. "You met up with Morgan, didn't you?"

Jolie gave a weary nod as it all settled down on her again. Keeping her energy up for the kids had been tough, and she was emotionally drained.

"By the looks of you, it didn't go so well." Pointing the rolling pin at the stool by the workstation, she demanded, "Sit down and talk to me." Heading to the sink, she rinsed her hands under the faucet. "How did Morgan react to seeing you?"

Jolie made circles in a small pile of white flour that was on the counter. "He isn't happy. At all."

"What did you expect? Flowers? You *did* hand him back his ring before hitting the trail for parts unknown."

"Gee, thanks for the support."

"You know I love you, but I'm worryin' you're fixin' to get yourself in some hot water."

"I apologized and he didn't take it well." She didn't go into the fainting episode. The last thing she wanted to talk about was the reaction she'd had to being in his arms.

Shrewd eyes held Jolie's. "You hurt Morgan when you left. And then, on the rebound, that boy went and almost married Celia Simpson. And she left him right after the rehearsal." Ms. Jo clucked her tongue. "I'd hate to see you lead Morgan down the wrong road again."

"I would never do that. Besides, he can barely stand to look at me."

"You know he's one of my favorites, Jolie. Kind of reminds me a little of my Clovis. He's got feelings that run real deep and it'll take more than words to prove you're sorry. But maybe working with those boys he loves so much will help."

Jolie was glad Ms. Jo didn't tell her it would be easy—they both knew it wouldn't be. Ms. Jo pulled a pie out of the glass icebox. "How about you and me take a break and have us a piece of this lemon pie with some coffee?"

Jolie sat up at attention. "Do you even have to ask?" She wondered if pie would help erase the feel of Morgan's arms around her. Her heart went erratic just thinking about how she'd felt snuggled against his heart....

"I think this situation is gonna need a bunch of prayers, too. For those boys' sakes, we need you two on speaking terms. Y'all don't have to make up and kiss or anything—goodness knows that would only lead things in the wrong direction. Just bury the hatchet and get it over with."

"Easier said than done, I think."

"In all honesty, this could be the best thing for Morgan." Ms. Jo brightened. "Maybe it'll help him move forward, find someone who'll actually go through with marrying him. Seems such a waste for a cowboy of his caliber not to have someone to call his own."

Jolie put a huge bite of lemon pie on her fork, breathed in the tangy scent and stuffed it in her mouth so she wouldn't have to say anything.

Because even after all this time, the thought of

Morgan and someone else made Jolie want to eat an entire case of pies.

"How you doing, Morg, my man?" Rowdy asked Sunday afternoon.

Rowdy, Morgan's younger brother, ran the ranch's cattle operation and they were sorting the steers for the mugging together. "My boots almost had blowouts when Dad told me what he'd done."

"You think *you* had a blowout," Morgan growled.

Rowdy, who always looked as if he was ready for a good time, with lips that turned up at the edges and eyes shot with mischief, looked as concerned as Morgan had ever seen him. "So how did it go? The boys about talked my ear off at lunch. They're impressed, just in case you didn't know that."

"Thanks, I picked up on that all by myself when their jaws started dragging in the dirt. And Wes and Joseph started showing off their muscles."

Rowdy's lips twitched. "Should make for a good show tonight. But how are you?"

Morgan rested a boot on the bottom rung of the arena and studied the steers closely. "How do you think? I don't have a choice but to deal with it."

"Maybe that's a good thing." Rowdy hiked a shoulder. "You don't date, Morg. You act like you're married to the school. You have unfinished business and it's time to finish it, one way or the other."

Morgan grunted and kept his mouth shut.

"Would you look at that?" Rowdy whistled over the bellowing of cattle. "Pest is lookin' good."

Morgan turned to see Jolie hopping from her Jeep.

"Yeah," he snapped. "Tell me something I don't already know."

Rowdy chuckled, crossed his arms and leaned back against the corral to watch Jolie. Morgan shot him a glare, not fond of that glint in his brother's eyes.

"I thought you said you were all right," Rowdy said.

"I'm not in the mood, Rowdy."

"Touché. Don't get me wrong, I'm on your side. You got a real raw deal, but maybe that was all she had to give you at the time. Like I said, this could be a good thing."

"Maybe I don't want to discuss this right now."

Rowdy chuckled. "Like I said, *touché*. Got to go get myself a hug." Pushing off the fence, he strode toward Jolie, who had stopped to talk to their dad. Tucker, the eldest of the McDermott boys, was the county sheriff. He'd been talking with Nana, and now they all headed Jolie's way.

Morgan scrubbed his scratchy jaw—it had been a long night delivering a new foal, he hadn't had much sleep and this morning he'd missed church. He was *not* in the mood for this.

"Hey, pest," Rowdy drawled, using his pet name for Jolie. "You're looking good, but a little on the thin side. You not eating out there, making all that money having your picture taken in that yellow banana of yours?"

"Rowdy!" Jolie exclaimed. Rowdy laid an arm across her shoulders and hugged her as if she was his long-lost friend.

"Jolie." Tucker greeted her with a hug, too.

Morgan almost got lockjaw, grinding his molars watching, his dad grinning as though he'd just reunited the family.

Ten thousand acres of West Texas ranch lands suddenly didn't feel big enough. This "reunion" was enough to make a man ride off into the sunset and never look back.

"Hey, Morgan." Chet, one of the top hands, called from the cattle pens on the far side of the barn. "Got a sec?"

A couple of years younger than he was, Chet had grown up on the ranch as a foster kid and had stayed on. Like the other fifteen cowboys who worked for the ranch, he knew Morgan's history with Jolie…and Celia. There had been no teasing so far, and that fact alone told him they all thought he was on shaky ground now that Jolie was back.

It was embarrassing.

"I hear you fainted yesterday," his dad said as Morgan hit the fast track across the corral toward Chet.

He'd had Jolie's fainting spell on his mind since it had happened. Something was up with her, and he figured the last place she needed to be was running up and down this arena trying to throw a yearling on its back with her bare hands. Of course she lived in a world where she took her life in her hands every time she got into that kayak of hers and plowed through raging white water *and* over ridiculous waterfalls that weren't meant for humans to fall over, much less charge over on purpose.

And to think he'd been the one to introduce her to it. Little had he known she would fall for it and become one of the best. When he'd taken her kayaking as a kid, it had been slow, easy river runs, nothing life-threatening—

He stopped his thoughts in their tracks.

Jolie wasn't his concern anymore—hadn't been since the day she'd walked away, choosing kayaking over him.

"What's up?" he growled, reaching Chet.

Nudging his Stetson off his forehead, Chet met Morgan's look with frank brown eyes. "Thought the love and admiration was about to start piling up knee-deep to a giraffe over there," he drawled sarcastically, then pointed at one of the steers.

"This 'un here's got a bad leg. Thought you'd want to pull it from the event."

That was no-nonsense Chet. Said what he wanted and moved on. Morgan almost grinned. Chet wasn't one to get in another person's business—giving him his support by saying what he just had meant a lot to Morgan.

Morgan studied the limping steer. "Yeah, take him out."

"Will do, boss." Chet nodded to one of the other cowboys working the gate to open it up. He and Morgan flanked the steer to send him through the gate, and one of the other cowboys herded him toward a separate pen.

"Time to get ready for some fun."

Chet nodded. "Sounds good to me."

Watching him head off to gather the men, Morgan knew Chet had his back. That was more than he could say about his own family. Although maybe his brothers' affection for Jolie could come in handy. She might not want to tell him about the fainting episode, but that didn't mean she wouldn't tell Rowdy or Tucker. Regardless, Morgan was determined to find out what was going on, whether Jolie wanted him to or not.

Chapter Five

The familiar scent of dirt and cattle filled the air as Jolie tried hard *not* to watch Morgan. It was an almost-impossible feat—the man had gotten only better-looking in the past six years. His black hair curled out from under his hat, just whispering against his blue button-down. The color made his eyes look darker than ever. And he was in his element as he strode back and forth inside the arena with Rowdy and the other cowboys getting everything set up for the mugging.

"I got trampled by a cow one time. That's why I'm afraid to go out there," Sammy was saying to Jolie. He'd been shadowing her since she'd arrived at the arena. Something about the kid spoke to her, and she wondered why he'd gravitated toward her. She couldn't help thinking that it was the fear eating him up that had drawn him to her. Maybe on a subconscious level he recognized a kindred spirit of sorts.

Because she had fear eating her up, too.

And it irritated the dickens out of her. So much so that despite almost no sleep, she'd dragged herself out of bed and made it to church on just one cup of coffee. Her night had been awful, to say the least—just plain terrible.

It had started with thoughts of Morgan—specifically, the feel of his arms around her and the beat of his heart in her ear. Those sensations kept her awake half the night. When she'd finally fallen asleep, the nightmares arrived. Why, oh, why had she thought coming home would help ease them?

They hadn't eased one iota.

Instead, they'd come as hard as ever, if not more so. Always the same, she was trapped in a raging vortex, upside down and fighting to make it to the surface. Always ensnared and struggling for her life.

Somewhere in the wee hours of the morning she'd given up trying to sleep and lay covered in sweat, tangled in sheets and worn-out. In the month since the accident, this had become the norm. Usually she turned to her Bible, searching for comfort and peace. Even though peace had been elusive, she knew God and only God had brought her up out of that watery grave.

A person would think that if she knew *God* had yanked her out of that murky water, there would be no reason to be full of fear from her toes to her roots—but she was. And she didn't know what to do about it.

"You're scared?" According to Morgan, Sammy was prone to exaggerations so she wasn't sure what to make of his remark about being trampled, but she certainly recognized fear when she saw it. And it was like a flashing red beacon in his eyes.

He nodded. "Scared bad."

"That's totally understandable. Did the cow hurt you very badly?"

His gaze slid left, then back toward the four-foot-tall steers. "Broke my leg. My dad, he took real good care of me, though. And my mom." He paused, gulping. "She cried, it scared her so bad." He sighed wistfully. "They loved me so much they hated to see it happen."

Heart *slam!*—Jolie was suddenly desperately grateful for her parents' love and affection. She wanted to hug the child close—and at the same time do bodily harm to his parents for giving him up.

"I'm sure they did." Jolie wondered if he even realized he'd said "loved" in the past tense. "You remember that anytime you need to talk about them, or anything that scares you, you can come to me. If you want to," she added.

A half smile appeared that was one day going to make female hearts stop.

What a cute kid. And what a tough road he'd traveled. As had most of these boys.

A steer broke from the pack at the end of the arena and ran full tilt down the inside of the fence right in front of them.

Sammy's head swung fast as he followed the black blur. Then immediately he turned back to her. "Are you really going to get out there?" he asked, his brows bunched in concern.

Jolie bit back a laugh. After all she'd faced in her kayak, a few half-pint cows didn't scare her. Not that she'd dare tell Sammy that.

"You bet I'm getting out there!" she exclaimed. "It's fun. If you learn how to do it right, even small people can flip a steer." He didn't look convinced at all. "You can do it, Sammy. It's all in the technique."

"We're going in two groups," Morgan called. Joseph clamored over the rail and jumped from the top rung to the ground. Instantly five more boys bailed over the rails and sauntered to join Joseph.

Jolie sure hoped she still had it—she hadn't run around an arena after a steer in years. It hit her that if she hoped to get Sammy to participate at all today, she needed to go in the first group and lead by example. She climbed the fence and dropped to the ground on the other side.

"No!" Sammy yelped, grabbing hold of her

shirt sleeve through the railing as if he feared he would never see her again. "Please don't go," he implored her.

"It's going to be all right, Sammy. I promise. You'll see, sugar," she urged.

Adrenaline was flowing through her, a feeling she relished. She gave Sammy's hand one last reassuring pat, then pulled away. She had never let fear hold her back—until the accident. But today, there was nothing inside the arena that remotely frightened her.

Matter of fact, she felt more alive than she had in a long time. Pure fun was what she called this.

It had been too long.

With big, goofy grins, the boys were whooping and waving her over. She jogged their way, smiling.

"Count me in on this one," she called to Morgan. She rubbed her hands together, joining the boys behind the line that had been drawn in the dirt. Mentally she went over the names of the boys in the group—Joseph, Wes, Tony, Caleb and Micah, who was sixteen with rusty-brown hair, a lean face and eyes the color of well-washed jeans. They were all grinning from ear to ear as they looked at her.

Jolie clapped Caleb, the youngest, on the shoulder. "Hey, aren't you Mr. Braveheart," she teased, and his grin widened to touch his ears.

She was just starting to enjoy herself when she looked at Morgan. The man's scowl told her he wasn't happy with her at all.

So what else is new?

"You sure you want to do this? It's been a long time, and yester—"

Jolie cut him off. "I'm fine, and I'm sure. Let's get this muggin' goin'!"

"If she can ride those rapids, I bet she can mug a puny five-hundred-pound steer." Joseph grinned and spat a sunflower seed husk to the ground.

"Why, thank ya, Joseph," she quipped, gloating a little at Morgan.

He frowned at the teen. "Maybe you need to tend to your own business."

Joseph chuckled. "You sure been ornery the last few days, Morg."

"Yeah," Wes agreed. "Real grumpy."

Morgan's scowl deepened. "May I have a word with you?" he asked through bared teeth. Wrapping his hand around her biceps, he started walking her away from the group.

Once they were a good distance away from everyone he let go of her arm, leaving her skin tingling from his touch. She felt a rush of disappointment but wasn't sure if she was disappointed that she'd felt a tingle or that he'd removed his hand.

"I can do this if I want to, Morgan McDermott." Here was one of the problems that had prompted her to pack her bags six years ago—the man was pushy.

"You passed out yesterday. That's not like you. I've thought about it all night and I've decided that there must be something wrong. You going to tell me what that something is?"

I've thought about it all night. He'd had her on his mind—the knowledge sent a shaft of joy straight to her heart. She continued to glare at him, though, because she'd never liked his bossing her around. It was all coming back to her now. Once he'd put his ring on her finger, he'd started trying to dictate her life—tried to wrap her up and keep her safe. It was out of concern, but she was not a china doll and refused to be treated as one.

Even if she felt broken right now.

"I did not pass out. I got a little faint is all."

"You would have hit the floor like a rock if I hadn't caught you."

"Maybe, but—"

"Jolie, I'm not kidding. You come back here after all this time, and you aren't kayaking. You nearly died—yeah, I know you didn't elaborate on that, but Nana is my grandmother, so I'm informed. I know what a close call you had. I'm not blind and I'm not stupid, Jolie. There is something wrong with you and I want to know what it is."

The man was impossible. "It's none of your business."

He loomed over her, his scent filling her senses. "I'm responsible for everyone out here and if you have some kind of condition, I need to know about it. You were hired on to this ranch without my say-so, but guess what? That makes you my business, especially if whatever's going on affects your job."

So his interest in what was wrong with her was because she *worked* for him. There was nothing personal about it. Nevertheless, she caved under that blue-eyed stare, blurting out, "I'm having trouble sleeping ever since the accident. I'm having a few nightmares."

"Nightmares," he repeated, clearly startled. Then his expression softened. "I guess that's understandable after what you went through."

Jolie suddenly wanted to tell him more, but was aware that all eyes were watching them as they stood practically nose to nose. This wasn't the time or the place. And now that she thought about it, she didn't want sympathy from him.

"I'm dealing with it," she huffed, "which is why I'm taking some time off. Now, can we get this done?" she asked.

"Fine, do it," he snapped. "Only, and I mean *only,* if you're sure you won't be passing out and getting trampled."

"Such a sweet thought," she replied, syrup dripping from her words as she crossed her heart. "I promise."

She spun and jogged back to the boys. Energy surged through her—for now, she was alive and unafraid, and Morgan McDermott couldn't tell her what she could or couldn't do.

She gave high fives to the boys.

"Let's do this," she said before turning her attention to the midsize steers milling about in a huddle. She took them all in and zeroed in on her pick, a hefty black angus that had some challenge in his eyes. Sure, there were a few mild-mannered ones milling around, but she'd never taken the easy route.

"Just so y'all know, I'm in it to win it," she warned.

"Win it," Wes said in comical disbelief.

"Win it," she clarified. Their disbelief was all the challenge she needed. She'd always liked having something to prove.

"Here you go, hotshot. Be my guest," Morgan said, issuing his own challenge as he handed her a rope.

Jolie stuffed the tie rope in her back waistband and gave the guys a grin just to egg them on because they were looking at her as if she'd lost her mind.

"All right," Morgan commanded. "This is our

version of a muggin' competition. All of you will go at the same time and first man—*person*—to get the steer by the horns and to the ground is the winner of this group. Once we have the winner established of this go-around, then one of you will tie its legs and be timed on that. We'll do the same with the second group, and the overall winner will be determined by time. Remember, we'll have a team roping in a couple of weeks and you'd better be practiced up on your roping and tying by then, because I'm bringing out the real steers." This information won huge grins and a ton of chatter.

"Everyone behind the line and we'll get this show started. Get set," Morgan called, "go!"

It was on. Dirt flying, steers running, cheers threatening to lift the roof off the building, Jolie and the five boys ran out into the arena. Jolie focused on her target—which was heading for Denver, by the looks of it. Anticipating his movements, she raced after him. When he spun, she dived for him—and landed face-first in the red dirt.

Sputtering the bitter, gritty dirt, she was on her feet in a flash. Hands out to either side, she waved the steer back when it would have broken left. Scrambling for traction, she broke right, then lunged again…and grabbed him.

"Gotcha, big boy," she grunted, locking her elbows around the steer's blunt-tipped horns. Instinct from years on the ranch kicked in. One arm locked around the horns, she grabbed the animal's jaw, dug her boots into the dirt and twisted the steer's head as she leaned back on her heels. Once she felt his weight shift she hung on, pulled harder and let herself fall back into the dirt. The steer came with her, landing on his side. Only then did the riotous yells and cheers begin to register.

Holding the angry steer's horns to her chest, she waited for someone to come tie its legs. A shadow blocked out the overhead light and Morgan grinned down at her.

"I reckon you haven't lost your touch after all," he drawled.

Looking up at him like this felt so familiar, like when they were teens and this was a normal part of their weekly routine. The steer squirmed, reminding her that she still had it by the horns. Thankfully Joseph raced up and had three legs tied in seconds.

Sliding from beneath its head, Jolie stood and dusted off her backside. "If you ask me," she said, her poker face in place as Rowdy joined the group, "that was kind of slow."

That got a grin from Morgan. She grinned right back at him, and for a moment the tension between them eased and she felt her heart pick up the pace.

Rowdy jogged up and nudged her arm. "Not too shabby, pest. For a girl."

"A girl who had her moments of glory beating you both a time or two."

"I'm impressed," Wes said, wiping sweat off his forehead with the back of his arm.

"You did it!" Sammy exclaimed, elbowing his way through the group and grabbing her around the waist, hugging her tight.

"Hey, I told you I would." She returned his hug. A warm feeling expanded in her chest like a hot air balloon, lifting her spirits. Beaming with gladness, Jolie met Morgan's hazardous indigo gaze... and *whoosh,* just like that, all coherent thought evaporated right there under the big lights.

Morgan was rocked by the attraction buzzing through him as he watched Jolie. It was as if they'd been swept back to the past and the world was right again.

He was also more than a little startled by the enthusiastic way Sammy had just latched on to her. His thoughts were stumbling all over themselves as her dancing green eyes locked onto his.

Clearing his throat, he tried to clear his brain and turned his gaze to the kid.

Sammy connected with Jolie on a level that he hadn't come close to doing with anyone else. Morgan could practically see the kid's heart on his sleeve. And it immediately reminded Morgan that—no matter what he'd been feeling toward Jolie just minutes before—her being here was a mistake.

Oh yeah, a big mistake—of gargantuan proportions.

The kid needed stability—he did not need to fall for Jolie, then have her exit his life in a few short months. But Morgan's hands were tied. Jolie was the kind of person who drew people to her—no doubt about it. What could he do now? It was clear that it was already too late—Sammy was attached with a capital *A*.

"Morgan, did you see Jolie?" Sammy yanked on his sleeve to get his attention, too young to realize that Morgan hadn't taken his eyes off Jolie for even a second while she was out there.

"I saw. She was born to be a cowgirl." His observation came out before he could stop it. Born to be a cowgirl riding a horse—and ended up riding river rapids. The thrill was clearly much more exciting out there taming white water in places he couldn't pronounce much less compete with.

"I learned everything I know from Morgan, so do as he tells you and you can't go wrong."

Her glowing eyes settled on him, drawing him like some poor moth to a flame. After all that had happened, he could still get lost in those gorgeous eyes of hers.

"Ha!" Joseph exclaimed, blessedly drawing Morgan's attention. "Morg taught me and you *still* beat me."

Jolie's laugh tinkled like wind chimes. "The steer has to cooperate, too, you know. That handsome hunk of a hairy dude wanted to be caught by me, I think."

"Well, duh," Wes drawled. "Who wouldn't?" That brought hurrahs from all and big goofy grins that were becoming commonplace around Jolie.

Jolie laid a hand on her heart and smiled at the boy. "Aw, that is so sweet."

She was a born dazzler. Morgan realized that in all of her wordplay with the boys, she'd still somehow managed to make them feel good about themselves, even though she'd beat them fair and square. He liked that, and appreciated it.

But what he didn't like was that he felt the shield he'd built up around his emotions slipping a notch as his admiration for her returned full force—he was feeling pretty dazzled himself.

Nope, he didn't like that. Not at all.

She hadn't even been back three days and he was already starting to think she was great again. He scrubbed the back of his neck, catching the half-amused eye of Rowdy.

Shaking his head, Morgan turned and headed toward the exit. While they prepared for the next groups muggin', he needed to put some distance between him and Jolie.

Some poor sodbusters just never learned.

Chapter Six

You can't go home again.

The words echoed in Jolie's head all the way back into town after the steer mugging. She'd never expected to come back to the sleepy little town she'd grown up in on that day six years ago when she'd hit the gas and aimed for the horizon. She'd left in a haze of confusion and tears, torn between two worlds. Now, here she was, amazing as it seemed, about to start teaching at Sunrise Ranch.

The boys on the ranch had instantly won a spot in her heart—and school hadn't even started yet. It felt as if she'd known them longer than two days. She was as attached to them as they seemed to be to her, and she knew it made Morgan edgy.

Everything about her made Morgan edgy, it seemed. But it sure had been nice to get a genuine smile out of him after she took down that steer. She'd felt that smile clear down to her toes. It had been hard to concentrate after he'd stalked out of the arena, but she'd done it and tried her hardest to convince Sammy to try, even saying she would go and help him, but he'd refused. She hadn't tried to force the issue—hopefully time would help him.

Time would hopefully ease the tension between her and Morgan, too.

Jolie pulled into the vacant spot in front of the three-story Dew Drop Inn. The old redbrick structure had originally been a dance hall saloon back in the 1800s. It had had a whole host of other aliases through the years, too, including funeral parlor, boardinghouse and restaurant. It was said to have welcomed many famous folks—and just as many infamous folks—inside its doors at one time or another.

It had been boarded up for years and fallen into terrible disrepair before Mabel Tilsbee bought it and poured her soul into it. And for over thirty years now it had been the Dew Drop Inn. Black porch posts held a second-story balcony, and Mabel kept two pots overflowing with ferns on either side of the ornate double doors with leaded glass insets and heavy brass fixtures.

Inside, wooden floors were covered with rugs that had been worn down over the years but still held a lovely charm and gave the place a welcoming feeling. For Jolie, the inn was home until she found a place to rent or decided to take the small house at the ranch Randolph had told her went with the job.

The decision was complicated by Morgan's being at the ranch, of course. She wasn't sure it was a good idea to be out there—around him—all the time, especially because it was obvious he didn't want her there. But even so, there had been moments—breathless times—when electricity crackled between them.

"Whoo," she whispered, just thinking about it. Even though Morgan had shut it down almost as quickly as it had happened, there was no denying they'd both felt it. And as a result, she was pretty certain he wouldn't welcome her moving out there, encroaching on him all the more.

It was a dilemma.

Swinging her legs from the doorless Jeep, she paused to stretch her aching back—taking a steer down by yourself did tend to strain muscles—and take in the rest of the town she'd left behind.

It had just two main roads that intersected, and smaller tree-lined roads that led to old-fashioned homes with spacious yards. She remembered it as the Mayberry of her youth. The newspaper office was on the far end of town, along with the hardware store and the barber shop. A church bench sat on the sidewalk between the two businesses, where the older men of town gathered to fix all the world's problems. Chili Crump and Drewbaker Macintosh, whom she'd hugged at church that morning, were occupying the bench at the moment. In their mid-seventies, they'd taken the place of Snoot Pickens and Sargent Hanes, two characters who'd both passed but whose legends lived on in the tall tales of many.

A slight breeze fluttered over Jolie like whispers from years gone by. Yep, she was sure she'd been the topic of conversation on that bench many times—she could just imagine how it had been after she gave Morgan back his ring and hit the trail.

Poor Morgan. She hadn't really thought about what he'd had to endure after she'd broken their engagement. She'd mostly been thinking about her own pain, and her frustration that he couldn't support her decision to pursue her dream.

She swallowed, the breeze still whispering in her ears. Regret for the pain she'd caused settled like a rock in her stomach.

It was payback time—she was certain she was once more the hot topic on that bench, and everywhere else in town. She'd prepared herself for that when she'd decided to come home. But giving them something to talk about was a small price to pay to make things right between her and Morgan, to apologize for hurting him—something she had to keep reminding herself she was here to do. Apologize and heal—that had been the plan, but the feel of his arms after she'd fainted had taken her off track and confused her reasoning.

She wondered how Morgan felt about being in the spotlight, which she was certain she'd put him in when she'd rolled into town. Folks meant no harm, but Morgan was a pretty private person who'd already had way more attention than he'd ever wanted, thanks to her…and Celia. If she had to guess, she'd say he was less than overjoyed that she'd come home and put him back in the hot seat.

Scanning the rest of the town, her eyes came to rest on the Spotted Cow Café. Vibrant red geraniums overflowed at the entrance, and the bright yellow door stood out like a welcoming beacon. She'd been the one who'd come up with the idea to paint the door lemon pie–yellow all those years ago. Jolie's stomach growled as she looked at it. Clearly, the door did its job, and did it well.

Behind her the string of bells on the Dew Drop Inn's door tinkled merrily. Jolie turned back toward the inn.

"Well, I'll be! If it ain't Jolie Sheridan! Hon, it's about time you came back home!" exclaimed Mabel Tilsbee, rushing from the building. The owner of the Dew Drop Inn engulfed Jolie and hiked her up in the air. Arms clamped to her sides and her feet dangling at Mabel's shins, Jolie felt her body shake in the breeze. Mabel had always had a soft spot for Jolie. She'd also been the one who'd told Jolie that she'd never be happy if she lived with regrets.

"I am so happy you're here!" Mabel cried as she squeezed the life out of Jolie. "Goodness gracious, this is the best surprise ever. When I got back into town a few hours ago and I found out you had checked in, I couldn't believe it!"

"It's good to see you, too," Jolie gasped, trying to move her arms. Mabel started jumping up and down—for a woman in her mid-sixties, she was as strong as a moose.

"Mabel, come on now, let the poor girl go," Ms. Jo barked from behind Jolie. Mabel obeyed her friend and released her. Feeling like a dishrag wrung dry, Jolie grabbed the porch post for support.

"Thanks," she wheezed. "I heard you were on a mission trip to Haiti."

"God was good to let me go. And good to let me come home." With her hands on her hips, Mabel stared at Jolie, grinning with her whole face. "Jo, ain't she a sight for sore eyes? I've been keepin' up with you," she said, not stopping long enough for Ms. Jo to answer her question. "And I saw that horrible accident. Just *terrible*. It was awful thinking of you trapped under that raging water. It's a miracle you're alive. A pure miracle, and don't you forget it. God's got plans for you, hon—that's what it is. Your shirt got caught under there on something, didn't it?"

Jolie nodded, her stomach turning over. It should have been a common roll maneuver that she'd made in the water thousands of times. But her shirt caught on a wayward limb beneath the water and everything went wrong.

Jolie's pulse grew shallow and she feared another fainting spell. It was maddening to feel so stinkin' weak. "I'm thankful to be alive." She smiled and tried to put a good face on it, hoping they wouldn't see through her.

"And here you are," Ms. Jo said, her knowing eyes catching everything. "Home to have Mabel do ya in right here on Main Street."

"Hush," Mabel scolded. "I was just excited to see her."

"That'd be a reason to squeeze the poor girl in half."

Mabel hiked her chin, gave her friend a warning look, then returned her attention to Jolie. "So how are you? Jo told me you were having some problems from it."

Of course Ms. Jo would have confided in Mabel. Maybe she'd said something to Nana, too. Well, there was nothing she could do about it now.

"Some." She cringed. "You know, it was scary, I'll admit, and I, well, I thought it was time to take a breather." She looked from one friend to the other. "And the truth is, I'd been missing the place, and everyone..." Her voice trailed off.

Mabel nodded, her expression empathetic. "Jo told me you're working at the ranch. Land's sakes, that was a shocker! How's that going, you bein' out there and Morgan, too?"

Mabel never had been one to dance around the elephant in the room. She just walked up to it and grabbed it by the trunk.

"He looks fine—good as ever." Boy, was that ever an understatement! "He's not too happy to see me, as you can imagine. So how have you been?" Jolie asked. Time to change the subject.

"As ornery as always," Ms. Jo grunted.

Jolie chuckled. "You still keeping Nana and Ms. Jo in line?"

"*Phassh*—me being the ornery one? Those two are the ones who can't be kept out of trouble."

"That's exactly what Nana said about you," Jolie teased, thinking of her visit with Nana. She was sure that Nana had kept her two friends in the loop about everything after that visit, probably because they were all worried that Jolie was going to break Morgan's heart again. Of course the man had shields of steel up—his heart was in no danger whatsoever.

"Where's the fun in staying out of trouble?" Mabel asked with a smile.

Jolie chuckled—it felt so good to see her old friends. It had been strange growing up and not really knowing girls her own age. She'd had the boys at the ranch, and all these ladies—her mother's friends—whom she'd thought of as grandmothers.

A big white ranch truck rumbled into town and slid into the slanted parking space just in front of them. Nana smiled and waved out the open window, her navy eyes luminous in the early evening sunlight. "Hey, there, gals. Y'all ready? Hey, Jolie girl."

"As we always are, Ruby Ann," Ms. Jo said.

"We're heading up to weed the flower beds at the church. Come with us," Mabel urged.

"Yes, come," Nana said, bobbing her hot-pink straw cowgirl hat with a peacock-feather hatband that matched her eyes. "No sense spending the evening up in that room alone. And I brought snacks." Those were magic words, because even though her lean figure wouldn't show it, Nana was a master in the kitchen, rivaling Paula Deen with her mouthwatering concoctions.

"Did you bring that spice cake I love for my welcome-home gift?" Mabel asked, winking at Jolie.

Jolie's heart warmed at their inclusion, her mouth watering when Nana said that she had indeed brought the famed spice cake.

"Sounds like a plan to me," Jolie drawled, feeling happier than she had in a while. The only thing that would have made this moment better was if her mother were here, too. Her folks had moved closer to Houston a few years back, to take care of her grandmother, and she didn't see them very often anymore.

"No way am I passing on that cake and y'all's great company." She looked down at her dusty clothes. "I've already swum in the dirt today, so why not dig in it?"

"That's my gal." Ms. Jo took her arm. "Come on, then, let's get this horse to a gallop."

Clucking and yacking away, they piled into Nana's ranch truck and headed out. *Maybe you can go home again.* The thought jingled through Jolie like a catchy tune as she settled into the backseat with Mabel, who was eyeing the spice cake in the wicker basket on the seat between them, temptation dancing in her eyes.

They drove past Chili and Drewbaker sitting on their church pew, Nana tooted her horn.

"Honkin' at your boyfriend, Ruby Ann?" Ms. Jo teased, hiking a brow at Nana.

"Ha!" Nana declared, chuckling right along with the rest of them. "That Chili is barking up the wrong tree when it comes to this ol' gal. But I do love to tease him."

They broke into more chatter after that, and

Jolie felt good realizing that after everything she'd been through and all the ways she'd changed, Dew Drop was still the warm, wonderful, welcoming place it had always been.

There was comfort in that, and despite her tangled thoughts about Morgan, Jolie settled in for an enjoyable evening with the girls. Maybe hanging with these wise friends would give her some much-needed clarity.

Monday morning arrived with the resounding confirmation that Morgan hadn't just dreamed Jolie was back in town and teaching at the ranch. Like a bad headache pounding on the back of his eyes, she'd stayed on his mind all night after she'd taken down that steer and won the heart of every boy on the ranch.

Even the grown-up ones.

It went without saying that he wasn't in the best of moods when he parked in front of the chow hall. As luck would have it, Jolie came striding out of the building, a cup of coffee in her hand.

Setting his resolve, he climbed from his rig and tipped his hat at her. "Mornin'," he said, taking in the excitement in her eyes despite the dark circles she'd tried to hide with makeup.

"Good morning. It's wild in there." She motioned toward the chow hall. "I thought I'd go get my head on straight before they show up."

The sudden need to pull her to him, to feel her pressed against his heart, again slammed into him, looking at those circles under her eyes. The woman needed some rest. She'd said she was having nightmares—how bad were they? Obviously bad enough to be damaging.

"Sounds like a plan. They'll be over there soon enough and then all bets are off for the day. If you have any trouble, I'll be in my office most of the day."

Her smile put a catch in his breath. "There will be no trouble. I promise—though I haven't taught since student teaching, I'm a whole lot less gullible. It'll be fine."

Giving him a wink, she headed down the plank sidewalk that ran the length of the chow hall. He just stood there, like a fool, unable to move.

At the end of the sidewalk, she stepped onto the gravel, paused, turning, then gave a hesitant smile. "Thanks, Morgan."

He watched her go, her long cinnamon hair loose today, swinging like waves of warm spice tea midway down her back.

His jaw tightened. It took him a minute to catch his breath and pull his gaze away. He was one messed-up cowboy—that was the long truth of it all.

The chow hall was buzzing as he strode inside. Excited conversations were easy to pick up on as he headed toward the buffet table—"Jolie" this, "Jolie" that. Their new teacher filled the airwaves.

Not only had she successfully beat Joseph in the mugging—something they all aspired to do—but they were also excited about her kayaking, just like he'd suspected. Yep, it was more than clear they thought she was pretty awesome.

But would they still think she was awesome when she headed off into the sunset, leaving them all behind, standing in the dust?

A sudden poke in the ribs halted his downward-spiraling thoughts. Turning, he found his grandmother holding a spatula in her hand.

"Those eyebrows of yours are going to grow together if they get any closer. And that frown is never a good sign this early in the morning."

Morgan grunted. "Mornin', Nana. It sure smells good in here."

Nana's cheeks were rosy red from the kitchen heat. Tilting her head to one side, she crossed her red-sleeved arms over an apron that proclaimed, *Cooked with love—so hug me!*

"At least you noticed." A teasing undertone matched the twinkle in her eyes. "I wasn't sure you were even with us. Saw you talkin' to Jolie out there. If her being back has got you this shook up, then I'm not sure you're going to make it till the end of the semester."

"Nana."

"No one *heard* me. Now, really, are you okay?" Her Texas drawl was thick as the syrup the boys were fighting over at the end of the buffet line.

"Just concerned for the boys."

"They're doing fine. Stop worrying." She looked over at Sammy and B.J., whose syrup tug-of-war had gotten a little out of hand. "We'll talk about this later," Nana said, then turned her attention to the boys. "Hey, fellas, hold your horses! Do y'all think that syrup is the last syrup on earth?"

The boys halted in their battle, blinking at Nana in confusion, still clutching the syrup bottle between them.

"Well, don't just blink at me like a couple of owls. Answer my question like gentlemen. Sammy, what do you think? Is that the last bottle of syrup on earth?"

The kid swallowed like he had a biscuit stuck in his throat. "I don't figure so."

"Ma'am," Nana reminded him.

"Ma'am," Sammy added quickly.

"And what about you, B.J.—what's your answer?"

The younger boy cleared his throat. "Ma'am, Ms. Nana, it probably ain't. Only it's the only one I see."

Nana put her hands to her hips and her lips twitched at the corners. "You are both right. There is a lot more syrup in the kitchen, so I don't think you have anything to fight over. Thank the good Lord for your blessings and share that bottle or you'll both be eating your pancakes with no syrup at all."

Sammy was the first to let go. "Yes, ma'am. Are you sure there's enough?"

Morgan patted Sammy's shoulder. "There's plenty, so no more fighting."

"Sammy started it," B.J. offered, dousing his pancakes. "But he's new and ain't learned we got it good here."

Nana met Morgan's gaze with grateful eyes. He knew that it meant so much to her to be here for these boys and all the others who'd come through the foster care program to live here with them. He felt the same way. But he had his work cut out for him with Sammy.

He had to get the kid acclimated to the ranch. Small things like fighting over syrup didn't bother Morgan. But struggling to fit in did. He'd seen the look in Sammy's eyes as he'd let go of the syrup. Fear laced everything the boy did. Something about Sammy seemed different, but Morgan just couldn't put his finger on it.

Maybe Jolie would be able to help with that. The notion struck him as totally counter to what he'd been thinking since she'd arrived. He was still worried about her leaving—more so since seeing how the boys, especially Sammy, had taken to her.

But he knew he had to ease up. Fact was, Jolie was here and there wasn't anything he could do about it. Except pray that she did more good than damage before she left—and that his heart was still intact when she went.

Chapter Seven

The week flew for Jolie. She and the boys settled into a routine, though it did take some getting used to. Jolie wasn't teaching just one or two
subjects, or even one age group. She was teaching
all subjects to sixteen boys in grades one through
twelve, all at varying skill levels—even those in
the same grade.

She had every available teaching tool at her
fingertips, though, and access to whatever she
needed. The purpose of the private school was
to give these boys a step up when it came to aca-
demics. Some of them had had such terrible home
lives before coming to Sunrise Ranch that they
either hadn't gone to school much at all, or their
grades were far below passing. Morgan's mother
had dreamed of not only giving boys the opportunity to live and experience life on this beautiful ranch, but also to see to their spiritual needs

and provide the chance for them to thrive in all aspects of life. The boys Jolie had gone to school with had gone on to become doctors, lawyers, businessmen, ranchers, rodeo champions—the list went on. There were even a couple of preachers in the mix, and a missionary, too. Lydia's vision had been a blessing in so many ways, and this week Jolie had gotten to experience it from the other side of the desk.

She was tired, but her spirit felt peaceful. She'd come to the decision that she needed to move into the farmhouse that Randolph had offered. Maybe if she settled into a real home for a few months it would help ease the nightmares and she could get some much-needed rest. Despite the lingering worry that Morgan might have a problem with her moving to the property, she was excited to make the move that evening.

Friday had come quickly. She was cleaning off the chalkboard prior to heading to the inn to grab her meager belongings. The creak of the front door had her looking over her shoulder, to find Morgan.

Immediately her pulse skipped as it had on the mornings she'd run into him briefly at the chow hall. Each time she'd been unable to gauge what was going on behind those deep blues of his.

Her nerves jangled, and it felt as though butterflies had taken flight in her stomach.

"Hey," he said, closing the door. He crossed the room in a few quick strides, coming to stand beside her desk with his hat in his hands. "Are you done for the day?"

The butterflies fluttered more. Morgan McDermott still had the ability to shake up her world. It was maddening—the man should be outlawed. Dressed in worn jeans and a loose turquoise button-up shirt with rolled-up sleeves showing off his corded forearms…Morgan was all cowboy.

"Yes," she forced herself to answer, trying to get her focus off just how handsome a man he was. "And I might add that my first week as teacher has been a success in my book. I *loved* it." She pushed on, ignoring the butterflies. "It felt so good reaching for ways to ignite those curious minds." Wrapping her arms around her waist, she tried to find the right words to express her feelings. "Your mother, she had such vision, Morgan. I'm just so glad to have this opportunity."

She thought she saw shock flash in his eyes, but the shield he seemed to wear when he was around her clicked into place almost instantly. Except for the mornings she'd run into him in the chow hall, he'd stayed clear of her since the mugging. The connection she'd felt between them—if only for a moment—had disappeared just as he had.

"I've heard from the boys that you are one cool teacher."

"Ooh," she cooed, giving him a teasing grimace. "I know it had to hurt you to hear that. Worse having to *repeat* it."

That actually won her a smile that tickled her insides—and suddenly she was remembering being kissed by Morgan.

As if she'd ever forgotten it.

She'd been kissed a few times over the years by the men she'd dated, but there hadn't been many, and their kisses had been like cola without the fizz. No one had ever appealed to her—or affected her—like Morgan. Her gaze shifted to his lips and her pulse paused. She leaned slightly toward him, drawn by an invisible cord.

"The boys expressed what I've been worried about from the minute I learned about this deal you and my dad worked out," Morgan said.

Jolie prayed for patience with capital letters. Looked as if there was no reason for her to be thinking about Morgan McDermott's kisses after all.

"Morgan, come on. This bad attitude…" She let her words trail off. She'd had little sleep, leaving no patience for this.

"I'm just worried—"

She pinned him with a glare and cut him off. "I *get* that you are worried that I'm going to run off and they will feel abandoned. But I'm here to help them, not hurt them. I've signed a contract for the semester and I plan to honor that."

Clamping his mouth shut, he said nothing, instead absentmindedly tracing a finger across the front of her desk. Despite her anger, Jolie shivered, thinking of his fingers tracing her cheek as they had so many times, so long ago. When he glanced up at her, his expression was less guarded.

"Look, I'm sorry. I didn't come here to fight. I've been watching Sammy ever since the calf wrestling and I think you're helping him," he admitted.

Had she heard him right?

"I came to tell you that I'll do whatever I need to do to help you help him," Morgan continued. His amazing blue eyes softened—he was actually conceding.

"G-good," Jolie stammered. She thought about trying to apologize again, telling him that she hadn't meant to hurt him. But she knew he would only deny that she'd hurt him in the first place. "That's the way it should be. Our past, what happened between us—"

"Is the past," he said firmly.

"Yes. We should still be able to help these boys even though we once had feelings for each other and it didn't work out."

What else could she say? She'd just come up

against one wall after another with him—he'd made it clear there was no sense in rehashing old history that he had no desire to revisit. So she stopped trying. For now.

They stared at each other as if both trying to figure out where they went from here. He raked his fingers through his black hair and she could almost feel the sensation on her skin.

Slapping his hat on his thigh, he nodded, then strode out the door. On the steps he turned back toward her.

"I hear you've decided to move into the farmhouse." Topic changed. "Do you need help moving?"

"No, I'm fine. I didn't bring much with me, and your dad told me it was semifurnished."

"Yeah, it should be okay to get you by till you leave at the end of the semester. If you decide you need help, call and I'll bring some boys over to lend a hand."

Jolie rubbed her temple, watching Morgan stride away into the distance. Oh, what a tangled web they'd woven.

She missed him. She'd not only given up her fiancé, but her best friend, too. Had she chosen the wrong road that day?

The question was irrelevant—she'd had to leave. She just wished it hadn't cost her Morgan's friendship. She'd hoped that coming here to apologize would give her back her friend.

A soft bump and then a creak sounded from the back storeroom. She headed to investigate and found the back door standing open. Someone hadn't closed it properly, she thought with a smile. Kids.

Deciding it was time to be practical—no more drifting back to the past—she locked up and headed out. She had a house to move into and a man to boot from her thoughts.

Good thing she'd worn her riding boots today.

"Guys! Hey...guys," Caleb huffed when he finally made it to the horse stable where the other boys were tending to their horses. "Sammy..." He paused, taking a deep breath. "I think Morgan likes Jolie!"

Joseph spun around, the cool-down brush he'd been using on his horse still in his hand. "Whoa, slow down, slick."

"Yeah," Wes urged, putting a hand on Caleb's shoulder. "Breathe, dude, before you keel over."

Caleb gulped air, feeling as if his eyes were going to pop out he was so winded. He needed to tell this, to make them understand!

"Now, what were you saying?" Wes asked after Caleb had sucked in a couple more huge gulps of air and calmed down a little.

"Okay," Caleb said slowly, looking around the group, trying to harness his excitement. "I was over at the school, and I heard Morgan and Jolie talkin'."

"And?" Joseph urged.

"And guess what? I think they used to have a thing."

"A thing?" Sammy asked. "What's a thing?"

"Yeah, what thing?" Wes asked.

Caleb grunted, impatient for them to get it. "You know, a *thing*. For each other. Back when they were young."

Caleb noticed Joseph and Wes look at each other all serious.

"You sure about that? Like, what did you hear?"

"Jolie, she said— She was talkin' to Morgan and said, just because they used to like each other and it didn't work out, that shouldn't stop them from helping us."

"Well, what do you know." Joseph crossed his arms and got that look in his eyes that told Caleb he was thinking something over.

"Swweeet." Wes grinned.

Joseph looked thoughtful. "You know Morgan's been like a dad to us for a long time and he's never been sweet on a girl."

"Well, there was that woman we saw him with once in town." Wes hooked his thumbs in his belt loops. "We never saw her again, so I figure that didn't work out so good."

Joseph nodded. "Yeah, he never talks about anyone."

"I heard he got left at the altar or something one time and it gave him a broken heart," Tony offered. "I'm just sayin', you know, like, do you think it coulda been Jolie?"

"Naaah, she wouldn't do something like that," Wes scoffed.

"I wonder, though." Joseph's eyes widened. "I heard Nana saying she left six years ago, then I got here not long after she left. And, you know, back then we didn't see much of Morgan."

Caleb waved his hands. "I ain't much on knowing what love looks like. I can tell you that Jolie looked real sad, though. And well, Morgan, he kinda looked weird, like he'd just swallowed some nasty cough syrup. Then he told her that that was the past and it should stay that way."

Wes whistled. "This is good. I feel *romance* in the air."

"That'd be cool." Joseph's grinned at Caleb as all the other kids started talking.

"You mean like if they fell in love," Sammy said, looking weird, too.

"But," B.J. piped up, "you said Morgan wanted it to stay in the past and he looked all mad."

"You'd have to have seen Jolie, the way her

shoulders were all hunkered down like she'd just lost the rodeo or something. She was sad. That's all I know, though, because I got out of there. Fast."

"Sounds good to me." Wes wiggled his eyebrows.

"Yeah." Caleb grinned. "I think it would be neat to see Morgan with a girlfriend. Oh! She's moving into the farmhouse, too, and Morgan said something about how it would be fine till she left at the end of the term."

"It'd be like having a mom," B.J. said.

Caleb heard the wish in his voice and knew what he meant. Morgan and his dad were like their dads—they were the ones involved in running the foster care program. The house parents were great, but they were more like grandparents than dads. It would be nice to have a mom around the ranch.

"Yeah, until mine comes back to get me," Sammy said. "I like Jolie."

Caleb felt bad for Sammy. They all knew his parents weren't coming back. He'd find out eventually, just as they all did. "Then it's done." Grinning from ear to ear, Joseph looked at everyone. "So here's what we're going to do."

Good. Joseph had a plan. He always did—the boys counted on that.

"What are we gonna do?" Sammy asked, and Caleb nodded because he wanted to know, too.

"Whatever it takes." Wes cocked an eyebrow at Joseph, who laughed.

"Yeah, that's about it. We're gonna make those two spend as much time together as possible." Joseph winked at Sammy. "Short Stuff, if you like Jolie, we're gonna make it so she sticks around."

Tony, who was tougher than all of them put together, frowned. "My sister used to love this old movie about some twin girls who did all kinds of stuff to get their divorced parents back together. I think my sis thought it would work on our parents. There wasn't any saving that train wreck, though."

"See, that's the thing. If Morgan fell in love with Jolie, then she might stay and we'd have a cool teacher. Maybe then she'd teach us to kayak, too." Wes had been talking a lot about kayaking. He craved adventure and wanted to ride bulls, only that was the one thing on the ranch the boys weren't allowed to do.

"You did good, Caleb," Joseph said, clapping him on the back. "Real good."

Caleb grinned, feeling as if his chest was going to explode. "You really think we can do this?"

Wes and Joseph hiked their eyebrows at each other before looking at the rest of them.

"We're gonna give it our best shot," Joseph said.

"And that's a promise." Wes had a twinkle in his eyes that meant one thing: they were going to have fun doing whatever it was they were going to do. That twinkle *was* a promise.

And hopefully it was a promise to get Jolie and Morgan back together so Sunrise Ranch could feel even more like a home, with a dad... and a mom.

Chapter Eight

Jolie eyed Salty, the black mare she was about to ride. She hadn't been on a horse in years and hoped she didn't embarrass herself.

"You sure are taking your time getting in that saddle."

Morgan walked up beside her looking all-too-good in his beat-up cowboy hat and checkered shirt. His jaw was scruffy with a five-o'clock shadow and there was some challenge in his eyes as he studied her.

"I'm about to climb up there. I'm just wondering if you could have given me a bigger horse to ride." Salty was huge—at least sixteen hands tall and very broad.

"She's a good horse. Not as salty as she used to be." His lips hitched into a grin. "You can handle her and you know it."

"If it's like riding a bike, then yes, I'll be just fine."

He turned serious as he studied her. "You look worn-out, Jolie. Are you still having nightmares?"

Lately, Jolie had been fighting hard against the urge to try to knock down the walls that Morgan had put up between them. She knew she *wished* there were no walls between them. Wished she felt free to talk to him. But would that be a mistake? If there was no wall she might fall for him all over again, and where would that leave her… them? But despite her uncertainties, when he looked at her with such concern, she knew she was fighting a losing battle to keep the wall up between them.

"I don't want to talk about that right now," she replied. "I'd like to hop on this horse and see if I still have what it takes to be a cowgirl."

"Uh, yeah—you're being a little too humble. You're a natural-born cowgirl and that doesn't ever leave a person."

She gave a discordant laugh. "My composure is a bit shaken, so that's all the more reason to hop on this baby and join this roundup. The boys were pretty persistent in getting me to come along. Sammy truly wouldn't take no for an answer."

"That's the reason he's sitting up there on Cupcake looking like he's about to toss his cookies."

She laughed. "Poor kid. The good thing is he's doing it, and that is a really big step for him. If helping in this roundup gets him to push himself, then I'm all in."

Morgan tipped his hat at her. "Good for you. Load up. You sure you don't need any help?"

The twinkle in his eye caught her off guard for an instant. Was he teasing her, or…flirting? Seeing the old Morgan for a second dumbstruck her. "I think I can manage. Do *you* need a helping hand?"

He laughed at her offer, shot her a wink and strode off with his cowboy swagger. Watching him swing into the saddle, a sigh escaped her. Berating herself, she jammed her boot into the stirrup, grabbed the saddle horn and hoisted herself up with ease. It felt like old times. A sense of excitement washed over her—this was going to be a good day.

Only after she grabbed the reins did she notice the boys watching her. Maybe it was her imagination, but they'd sure seemed interested in her past on the ranch this week during class. They'd asked all kinds of questions, even some about kayaking. She'd been happy to have made it through those without falling on the floor again.

She'd been able to put off their push for kayaking lessons, but that wouldn't last forever—the boys wanted to learn. She hoped she could eventually find her way toward teaching them.

Along with all those questions came some about growing up on the ranch. Even though she hadn't told them everything, she had given them small peeks into her life. And her life on the ranch couldn't be explained without stories of Morgan. They'd been inseparable as kids, long before he'd noticed her as a teenager. Long before she'd begun to panic that if she stayed at Sunrise, she would never find out who she really was and what she wanted out of life.

Long before she'd fallen in love with the feel of conquering a raging river, and long before she'd made the mistake of falling in love with Morgan, threatening her dreams of seeing the world one river at a time.

The boys were definitely getting to her. There was no way on earth she could look at those grins and tell them she didn't want to hang out with Morgan all day. So she'd agreed to come, and now she was suffering the consequences by having to corral the pitter-patter of her heart when he was near. No doubt about it, she was wrapped tightly around their wily fingers.

Giving them all a thumbs-up, she was rewarded by a grin from Sammy. B.J. giggled and Joseph returned the thumbs-up, then tipped his hat, copying Morgan. The kid was determined to walk in

Morgan's boot prints. Jolie couldn't blame him—Morgan was a good, good man.

"Let's roll," Morgan called. Jolie took a deep breath, and off she went to spend an entire day with Morgan. She just hoped her heart could handle it.

A couple of hours later, Jolie rode over beside Sammy and Morgan just as Joseph charged after a steer that had cut and run for the gully.

"Catch it, Joseph!" Sammy yelled, startling the steers around him and making his horse jump.

Jolie's heart skipped some beats but regulated when Morgan grasped the reins of Sammy's horse before she bolted.

"Easy, Sammy." His deep voice rumbled with gentle concern that pulled at Jolie's heart strings. "Don't go yelling like that and yanking on your horse's bit. You'll scare her. Okay, son?"

"Yes, sir." Sammy's knuckles were white as he clutched the saddle horn. "I got excited. I sure wish I could ride like Joseph."

"You will someday. But until you're more confident, you'll have to remember to take it easy when you're out here in the middle of a bunch of cattle."

They all watched Joseph racing through the tall grass and around scraggly mesquite trees in pursuit. Whipping his rope from the saddle, Joseph had his loop instantly twirling circles above his head as he chased the steer.

"He's really good," Jolie said, watching the rope land in a graceful arch around the runaway's head.

"Awesome!" Sammy exclaimed in a loud whisper.

"He's a natural," Morgan agreed. "Joseph took to cowboyin' like a duck to water. Kinda like someone else I know. She just had more duck in her than cowgirl."

Jolie tucked a stray strand of hair behind her ear as she took his half-teasing, half-serious words into account. "Funny. But there is some truth in that."

He nodded. "Believe me, I know."

Better than most. Even though he didn't say the words, Jolie heard them loud and clear.

All morning she'd been glimpsing the old Morgan, but now his shields slid back into place.

"I guess you do," she said. It was all she could say, because they both knew it was the truth.

Their gazes caught, like magnets pulled to each other. Jolie wanted to say so much to Morgan—

"Are you gonna teach us to kayak?" Sammy's question broke the moment—and it was a good thing, too.

"I'm not sure, Sammy. Like I said in class I'll have to see how things go."

"What things?" he persisted. "Wes said it looked real fun. We watched you on the computer and it was cool."

It struck her that he'd said teach *us* to kayak. He was getting braver.

"It's very dangerous." She forced herself to remain calm. They were simply *talking* about kayaking, she reminded herself. She wasn't in the water, wasn't near the water....

She wasn't under the water fighting for her life, finding the thrill of the ride not so thrilling when she held it up against being alive.

Sammy patted Cupcake. "Wes said I was too much of a scaredy-cat to ride a rapid."

"That wasn't nice of Wes to say," Morgan interjected, his tone saying he wasn't pleased with Wes. "He's a lot bigger than you and he likes doing things that are risky. You have to do what's comfortable for you, Sammy. *Not* what someone else wants you to do."

"That's right," Jolie said, relieved that the conversation was heading away from kayaking. "We're so glad you wanted to ride a horse this morning and help with the roundup. However, if it was something you really didn't want to do, then we would have respected your choice."

Sammy looked serious. "My momma was going to buy me a horse when I got older—I mean, she's *gonna* buy me a horse. She's probably trying to get the money to do it right now. So—so I need to learn to ride so I can be ready."

Jolie didn't know what to say. Maybe his mother *had* told him she was going to buy a horse. And what right did Jolie have to tell him he might never see his mother again?

Morgan shifted in his saddle. "It's good for you to learn to ride. It will help you join in with the others. Now, ease on over to the outside of the left line and stay on the outer edge. That'll help keep the cattle moving forward and not out. If a stray busts loose, let Joseph or Wes handle it. Got that? Today, your job is just to get used to the saddle and the cattle."

Sammy let go of the saddle horn and took the reins. He nodded, looking intently at the cattle. "I'll try."

"You'll do fine. Just do as I ask and stay safe. Okay?"

"Okay, Mr. Morgan."

Jolie smiled at him. "I'm so proud of you, Sammy. You're doing great."

Sammy's eyes widened as if he'd never heard a compliment before. "Thanks. I've been praying about my fears just like you told me. 'When I am afraid, I will trust in you, O Lord!'" As he repeated the verse Jolie had taught him, he finished as if he were a fire-and-brimstone preacher.

Jolie laughed and Sammy, grinning, tapped Cupcake with his heels and headed off.

Jolie watched him go, pride swelling in her as if he were her own child.

Morgan eased his horse closer to hers as they started moving with the cattle, keeping Sammy close by. "What's the real story on why you won't teach the boys to kayak?"

Jolie had known this was coming. She'd known it ever since she'd passed out.

"I have reservations about teaching them is all."

"I've figured that out. But something's going on here that isn't right. Like I said in the arena, you leave your career, you're having nightmares, you look like you haven't slept in months. You get faint at the mention of kayaking—yes, I noticed exactly what we were talking about when that happened. And now you avoid even talking about teaching the kids the very thing that makes you tick."

His expression had hardened as he spoke and his words were matter-of-fact. It was as if he had placed her inside a glass jar, and he was on the outside looking in without emotion.

She hated it.

And the realization that she hated it hit her like a cannonball.

"Like I told you, I'm having a little trouble."

"And?" he prompted. He'd always had a way of pulling the truth out of her if he wanted it.

"I'm afraid—" She'd no more gotten the words out when they heard shouting at the front of the cattle drive. Another steer had broken loose from the pack and was heading for the hills as hard as it could run. This time it was Wes who took off after it, his rope spinning in the air. Suddenly his horse reared straight up, then began bucking wildly. Wes dug his heels in and hung on. He kept his hand on the reins and fought to control the animal that had suddenly turned into a bucking bronc.

The second the ruckus began, Morgan spurred his horse forward, as had Joseph and Rowdy. Jolie knew instinctively what was in the grass before she saw the rattler strike out at the horse's legs.

It was *huge*—its head was as big as her fist!

The horse bucked far enough away that the snake missed its target. Morgan tugged his rifle from its holder and fired before anyone else could get close.

He didn't miss his target.

Morgan had always been steady with his aim and a sure shot, just like his dad and brothers. It was a known fact out here sometimes it took a bullet to protect the herd. Or the kids.

"Yee-haw!" Wes yelled. Getting his horse under control, he whipped his hat off and grinned as if he'd just won the bronc-busting event at the

National Finals Rodeo. She remembered Wes mentioning he wanted to ride bulls, but it wasn't allowed on the ranch. Even though she completely understood why the ranch wouldn't put the guys in danger like that, she wondered just how good he might be if given the chance.

Morgan's gun was back in its sheath before the smoke cleared and Jolie breathed a sigh of relief, sending up a prayer of thanks. It had been a very close call. If Wes hadn't been as good a rider as he was, he'd have been on the ground with the rattler and things could have been really bad. Of course to him, it was all a great adventure.

She remembered being that way. Before.

Jolie let the idea of God's goodness and protection wash over her. She knew in her case He'd been there for her, but she still couldn't seem to let go of her fear. She wondered what it was going to take to find her courage again.

She rode up beside Sammy, who'd halted his horse and sat frozen, watching the scene play out in front of him.

"You okay?" she asked.

His smile took her by surprise. "That was *awesome!* Did you see that? Did you see how Morgan shot that snake?"

Jolie chuckled. "Yes, I guess it was pretty awesome."

In the distance Morgan put a hand on Wes's

shoulder and grinned. Now that everyone was safe and sound, Jolie had to agree it was like a scene straight out of the movies. The way Morgan had charged to Wes's rescue—he protected the boys in his care as though they were his own flesh and blood.

He *was* awesome.

Snared by his gaze across the distance, her whole being seemed to hum. Her breath caught and she suddenly felt lost. Why had she really come home? Was it to apologize to Morgan? Or was it to find out if she'd made a mistake leaving in the first place?

And the biggest question of all: Was it possible that she was still in love with Morgan McDermott?

Chapter Nine

Morgan nearly had a heart attack when Wes's horse spooked. Standing there talking to the boy, he gave thanks that the snake hadn't bitten the horse, and Wes hadn't been thrown to the ground.

"That was some great riding you did," Rowdy told Wes. "You can be proud of that. No doubt about it."

"Yes, you can," Morgan added. "That right there shows why it's good to be prepared with your skills. And God had His eye on you, too. Don't forget that."

"I won't, sir." Wes's wolfish grin faded for a moment. "I was ridin' and I was prayin' at the same time." His smile popped back in place. "I was prayin', 'Good Lord, get me out of here!'" He chuckled as only Wes could, and the rest of them did, too.

After the excitement, Morgan didn't get to finish his conversation with Jolie. He and Rowdy split up, each riding the perimeters of the herd, away from the boys, watching for any other rattlers. When they made it to the last watering hole, it had been a long day. They still had a way to go, but the longest part of the drive was done.

The guys were tired and hungry and the cattle were thirsty.

Nana and her "truck wagon," as they'd named her version of the chuck wagon, were a welcome sight. The bed of the truck was rigged with all the essentials to fix a meal out on the range, and Nana also towed a barbecue pit behind the truck. This morning she'd started them off with a hearty breakfast in the chow hall, but they'd had only jerky and water in the saddle for lunch. The delicious smell of roasting meat and baked beans wafted through the air as Morgan dismounted.

"Want me to take your horse to the river for water?" Sammy asked. Morgan noticed he was riding with a little more confidence than he'd shown earlier. Riding all day could do that.

Morgan handed over his reins. "Thanks."

"I think Jolie's sick," the kid said, worry in his tone. "She didn't look like she felt good when she got off her horse. Caleb took it to the river for her."

Morgan looked up and saw Jolie trying to hide a limp as she headed toward Nana. "Thanks for the heads-up, Sammy. I'll check on her."

Sammy grinned. "*Yes!* I mean, good. That'd be a *real* good idea."

Morgan watched the kid lead the horses toward the river, a little confused but mostly amused by the kid's over-the-top reaction. Then he headed toward Jolie. He knew she'd bitten off more than she could handle today with this long drive. She was in great shape, no doubt about it, but there was a difference between riding a rapid and riding a horse all day. A shorter drive to start on would have been better. But she'd let the boys talk her into coming today, even knowing what it would cost her. The thought that she would do that for them—well, it did his heart good. Real good.

"Sore?" he asked, striding up next to her and grabbing a paper cup to pour himself some of Nana's sweet tea, which was a blessing all the way down.

Jolie cringed. "Just a little."

Nana clucked her tongue at her. "Honey, I'm not going to say I told you so, but I will say you're probably not going to be walking tomorrow. A long salty soak tonight might save you."

"Oh yeah," Jolie groaned. "I may soak all night."

Morgan's hand tightened on his cup. Laughing in the face of pain was pure Jolie—the Jolie he'd fallen for. He halted that line of thought and shoved it out of his head.

Massaging her thigh, she crinkled her nose, grinning at him. "There are just some muscles that are only used when riding a horse."

"Yup." Morgan fought being drawn to that grin with every ounce of strength he had. "But I have to say you've been a real trouper about it. Sammy's worried about you, though."

She clapped a hand to her forehead. "He saw me ease out of the saddle. I tried to throw my leg over the horn and hop off, but the leg just wouldn't cooperate. It was pretty pathetic."

Nana handed her the plate she'd fixed as they were talking. "Take this over yonder beside the river and hang your toes in the water while you eat. Take a load off."

Jolie took the plate. "I wanted to help you, Nana."

"You will do no such thing." Nana shooed her with her hands. "You've been doing your part all day. This is pretty self-serve for everyone and little work on my part. Now go." She shooed Jolie again. With a grateful look, she headed not toward the river but away from it, going to a stand of trees where the shadows of the evening settled.

Nana quickly stacked another plate high with

brisket and beans and thrust it into Morgan's hands and ordered, "You go with her."

His boots dug in, drawing a stern look from Nana and leaving him no choice but to go. Crossing the grass, he caught some of the boys watching him.

"Enjoy," Rowdy said with a smirk plastered on his face.

Morgan didn't bother to reply to Rowdy's teasing—he was too focused on continuing his conversation with Jolie. She'd been about to tell him why she wouldn't teach the boys to kayak, and what exactly she was afraid of. He'd been thinking about it all afternoon.

Joseph crossed his path before he got to Jolie. The kid was fighting a grin and an odd glint lit up his eyes as he shot Morgan a thumbs-up.

What was that all about?

Continuing on toward Jolie, he caught sight of Caleb, so busy watching Morgan that he tripped on a log and fell flat on his face in the dirt. Jumping up, the lanky boy dusted himself off as he grinned at Morgan.

Something wasn't right here. They were all looking too…happy. Watchful.

He sat down beside Jolie, then set his glass of tea between them on the flat rock she'd chosen.

"I'm thinkin' Nana is right. I'm going to be

in a world of hurt in the morning even with a salty soak."

Morgan stabbed a piece of brisket. "I'm sure you're used to being pretty beat up after a river run."

"So right," she answered, rolling her eyes as she scooped up a small forkful of beans and chewed. "These are so good."

He watched her enjoying her food for a couple of stretched-out moments and suddenly he felt like a goldfish in a very small aquarium. Glancing around he caught the boys watching him, although they immediately became very busy when they saw him catching their curious gazes.

What was with all the watching?

Ignoring them, he cut to the question he'd been turning over in his mind all day. "You were saying, before Wes tangled with the rattler, that you were having some trouble and that you were afraid." Jolie didn't take the bait and start talking. Quietly he continued. "What are you afraid of, Jolie? What's got you so tied up in knots that you're struggling with nightmares?"

She toyed with the meat on her plate, finally expelling an exasperated breath. "Okay, I'm only telling you this because we used to be…good friends. And I know you're going to pester me till I tell you and even pull the boss card, if needed."

"Yup." His mouth lifted at the corner—she knew him too well. "Right on both counts," he agreed.

"So here it is—the ugly truth of it. I can't bring myself to get back into my kayak."

What?

She couldn't have startled him more if she'd slapped him. She'd lived and breathed kayaking from the day he'd first introduced her to it when she was twelve—she'd already been after him to teach her for a year. He knew how dangerous it was when the water was up and had refused to take her out, but she finally convinced him, and they'd played around with the small rapids during the dry season, when the river had been low and slow. He wasn't into crazy thrills—he'd used his kayak more for fishing—but he'd taught the kid a few things. Nothing fancy, because he didn't know anything fancy. And he warned her to steer clear of the rapids when the rains came.

The next summer when the river was up, she sneaked down to the water and experimented on her own. He'd been hotter than molten lava when she told him she'd taught herself how to roll—which was no small thing—and several other tricks of creek kayaking.

But what could he do? There had been no stopping her. She'd had no fear of the water and she'd felt invincible.

Until now.

Staring into her clouded eyes, he realized he'd not had any idea how badly her brush with death on that river in West Virginia had affected her.

He studied her face. "I knew it was bad," he said, quietly. "But to make *you* afraid of the water? I can't grasp that."

She gave a humorless laugh. "Yeah, unbelievable. The girl you couldn't keep off the water is now afraid to go near it." She released a heavy sigh and rubbed her temples. "I can't get things straight in here. My head is so messed up. I'm in jeopardy of losing my sponsors if I don't get back out there soon."

Like the quick snap of a whip, anger ripped through him. "Don't they understand what you've been through?"

"I'm a professional. They pay me to compete with their logo on my shirts. I'm a billboard to them, and when I'm not on the water or doing press for an upcoming competition, they're not getting their money's worth out of me. It's understandable."

"*Understandable?* Yeah, I understand. You nearly died! They should have some sympathy for that."

"They do, to a point. I have to be back by Christmas, ready to shoot a commercial and test a new kayak for my biggest sponsor. We have to leave the country to shoot it in a warm climate, so they have to start making arrangements."

He had to admit that her life was interesting. She grew quiet, staring at the river that was just barely visible from where she'd chosen to sit. "If you're afraid to get in the water," he asked gently, "how are you going to train?"

"I'm still weight training, and I run each day before work."

"But you have to be in the water. You have to stay conditioned to it." Even he knew that jumping back in without being sharp would be suicide.

Jolie put her fork down. "I'm not sure if I'll ever be able to get back in the water, Morgan. I—I *lost* something when I was pulled under and I couldn't come up. I left part of me down there. I've had close calls before—that's part of the sport. This, this was different. It's like I lost my heart beneath the water."

Her eyes were huge, haunted. And he reacted on instinct as much as anything else when he slipped his arm around her shoulders and tugged her into hug. She responded by laying her head on his shoulder. "It's going to be all right, Jolie. Coming here, getting away from everything was probably a good idea. Distance sounds good to me."

It hit him that he could run with this. If he wanted her back in his life, then he could milk this for everything it was worth—and get her to stay here on the ranch.

His own thoughts startled him. Did he want to do that?

He still had feelings for her—he couldn't deny that any longer. He might have buried them deep, but right now they were pounding at the steel plate encasing his heart.

Could he finally have what he'd wanted six years ago? Could he talk her out of trying to go back to life on the water?

His conscience pricked. This wasn't the way he'd want to be with her, no matter how tempting the option was. It wasn't honorable, and that was what he'd promised God he would be.

"It's going to be all right. You're the toughest girl I know, and I've never seen anything keep you down or hold you back."

She straightened, lifting her head off his shoulder. "Thanks for believing in me. I'm just not sure if I want to continue." Her beautiful green eyes shimmered. "I came back to reevaluate my life. And I'm not sure, Morgan, but I think I might have made a mistake when I left here six years ago."

A *mistake?* Morgan stared at her, shaken by the emotions richocheting inside him. His heart pounded as he tried to form a coherent string of words. None came. She *thought* she'd made a mistake when she'd handed him back his heart—did she get that? Did she get that she'd been holding his heart in her hands when she'd held that ring?

He shot to his feet. "I have to check the horses," he managed to say with reasonable calm. Then before he could say anything stupid, he strode away.

There were moments in a man's life when the best course of action was to keep his mouth shut.

This was one of those moments.

Chapter Ten

Jolie's words were on Morgan's mind the rest of the week. After she'd dropped her bombshell, he'd gotten as far away from her as he could get.

And he'd stayed clear ever since.

Actually, he'd stayed clear of pretty much everyone. Because there were times a man couldn't hide how angry he was.

Four days after the drive, his dad met him coming out of his office.

"All week you've been about as ornery as that stallion we sold last year. What's bothering you?"

"You brought her here," he snapped, scowling at his dad. "What do you think?"

Randolph raked his hand through his hair in frustration. "Look, I know this is a tough situation. Nonetheless, I'm trusting God that it'll work itself out."

"That's mighty good of you," Morgan grunted,

feeling no better for his father's answer. *He* was the one who'd done this to him; *he* should be the one to fix it.

"Morgan." His father's voice stopped him as he started to leave. "You're going to need to forgive her, you know. For *your* sake."

Morgan kept on walking straight to his truck, started it up and drove. He just needed to *go*.

Forgive her? His dad had no idea what Jolie had said to him. She *thought* she might have made a mistake. A *mistake!* So, what if she hung around here, he let her back into his heart and then— boom!—she realized that the water was pulling her back? Where would that leave him?

Right back where you were when she left the first time.

After what seemed like forever, he ended up at Tucker's office in Dew Drop.

His brother had chosen to run for sheriff after his tours of duty in Afghanistan with the marines were done. There wasn't much happening in the tiny town, but there was still a need for the law since the county was fairly good-size. He had several deputies and Tucker led them well. He was steady as a rock and the brother Morgan went to when he needed good solid advice. Rowdy was more reckless—and the last thing he needed right now was reckless. Morgan entered the sheriff's department and went straight to Tucker's office, knocking on the open door. Tucker was pouring himself a cup of coffee. "Hey, Tucker, got a few minutes?"

His brother grinned and held up the pot. "You are right on time. Want a cup?"

"Do you have to even ask?" He walked in and took a seat in one of two hard-cushioned chairs. Tucker filled two black mugs and handed him one before taking his seat behind the desk.

"How's the situation going out there?" he asked, not one to beat around the bush.

Morgan knew he meant Jolie. "Is it that obvious why I'm here?"

Tucker hefted a shoulder. "You have that deer-run-over-by-a-semi-truck look. But then again, I'm trained to be observant." He waved at the wall of credentials behind him and gave Morgan a wiry grin before taking a sip of his coffee. "Talk to me before you explode."

Morgan told him, in confidence, some of what Jolie had revealed to him. He needed Tucker's black-and-white view on things. Even before he'd gone into law enforcement, Tucker had always had a clear view of the world around him.

"That's a tough one," Tucker said, a slow whistle escaping him. "It must have really messed Jolie up if she's thinking that way. Trauma has a way of cutting deep. Changing a person."

Tucker had experience with this—he'd seen lots

of action on hostile soil and lost comrades during an especially brutal attack. He had a slight limp from the bullet that had sent him home, and scars that he didn't talk to anyone about. Not even Morgan.

"She's scared and she's not sleeping well. Still, when the boys aren't asking her to teach them to kayak, she's herself. Well, almost. But I don't know if I can—or want to—try again."

Tucker nodded although he didn't interrupt.

"But if I did, I could talk her straight into thinking quitting was the thing to do. Tucker, this fear could guarantee that she stay here on the ranch."

"Sounds like it." Tucker's brows met over serious McDermott blue eyes. He frowned. "You'd have it made."

Morgan set his coffee on the desk, stood up and crossed to the window, where he stared out at the main street in Dew Drop. From here he could see the Spotted Cow Café on the corner. When they were teenagers he'd bought plenty of pie there just so he could tease Jolie while she worked. She'd loved it. Life had been perfect then. He'd believed they had a future stretching before them.

"I'd be lying if I said the thought wasn't flip-flopping around in my head, and that'd be pretty pathetic." He swung around as Tucker let out a gruff laugh.

"Yup. So what are you going to do? No, what do you *want* to do?"

Morgan's eyes narrowed. "Hey, you're supposed to be giving me some advice, not acting like a shrink."

"You're doing fine on your own. So?" Tucker pressed.

Morgan shook his head, hating what he was about to say. "She needs to get back in that water or she's going to regret it for the rest of her life."

"I agree. Sounds like she needs help from a friend."

Was he that friend? Dropping his head, Morgan felt his chest squeeze tight. When he looked up, he met Tucker's watchful eyes. "That water is what took her from me in the first place."

"Yeah." Tucker's eyes shadowed and he seemed lost in thought for a moment. "Life comes in circles sometimes. This might be rough."

Morgan just nodded, letting the truth settle in on him.

"You can handle it. Morgan, she came back here for a reason. She could have gone to her family in Houston, but she came here. That says something to me." Tucker looked down into his coffee cup for a few seconds, and then back up at Morgan. "When I was out there—when things were at their worst and I thought I was going to die before anyone could get me out—all I could think about was coming back here. Coming *home*. It wasn't just the ranch. Don't you get it, brother? Jolie came home. Maybe she doesn't even know why, but she came. Give this to God and see where it goes. You only live once. Maybe you need to take a chance and have no regrets."

Morgan knew Tucker was right. But that didn't mean doing what he suggested was going to be easy.

In fact, it was probably going to be the hardest thing he had ever done in his whole life.

Days had gone by since the cattle drive and Jolie felt at loose ends since Morgan had walked away from their conversation. The boys had tried several times to get her to join in on other activities with Morgan, but she'd always managed to have something else to do, enabling her to make an honest excuse. The last thing she wanted to do was make Morgan uncomfortable again.

It hadn't taken any gifts of discernment to figure out he hadn't liked what she'd said. The man had jerked to attention and stampeded to the farthest corner away from her—and he'd stayed there.

She didn't blame him really. She was confused herself. She hadn't even meant to say what she'd said—the words had just come out, like they had a will of their own.

But it had just felt so right, sitting there with him like old times. There had been such comfort in being with him, in telling him what she was going through.

And then she'd gone too far.

Exposed too much.

Well, at least now she knew that her being back at Sunrise Ranch hadn't softened his heart to her at all. It was good information for her to have.

So this morning, she decided she'd throw herself into teaching to distract herself, and it was the perfect day for it—it was science day, and she was teaching the boys how to make a volcano.

"A volcano!" Sammy exclaimed when Jolie told them what they were going to do.

Not ever having taught science—or ever thought she would have to teach science—Jolie had been a little intimidated by the subject. But she was actually enjoying the class. She told them they were going to build the volcano with just a two-liter bottle of diet soda, sand and water. And they jumped right in, sculpting the wet concoction around the bottle, which not only resulted in the volcano but in a few muddy teens as well.

After it dried, Joseph poked it. "Hey, that does look good. I hear they just foam a little, though."

"That's why we're going to add these candies to the soda. I read online that it will make things a little more exciting," Jolie said with a wink.

"Really? What's it going to do?" Sammy asked, intent on the project. He'd become Jolie's personal helper, and the happiness it seemed to bring him helped her heart.

Smiling at them, she opened the Mentos candy. "Now, I'm ready to show y'all what happens when these two chemicals are combined."

"Let 'er rip!" Caleb yelped. He was so excited to see the eruption that he could hardly hold still.

"Stand back, everyone," she said, looking around the room. If anything, they all crowded closer.

Wes backed up, giving her a wink. "Bombs away!" he called.

Joseph gave her one of his thumbs-up and chuckled, "Let 'er rip."

The younger kids giggled with glee as she poured the entire tube of candy into the mouth of the volcano. It erupted instantly—spewing everywhere! Foam and gunk hit the ceiling and splashed down on everyone. Jolie yelled and the boys whooped in delight.

And at that very moment, Morgan strode into the classroom.

"What is going on?" he yelled above the laughter of the boys.

"It exploded, Morgan! Look!" Sammy yelled, pointing at the ceiling and wiping liquid from his face.

Morgan looked up just in time—a glob of foam fell right smack in the middle of his forehead. Eyes flaming, he wiped it off with his shirtsleeve and glared at her. And with good reason. The room was a mess.

He'd avoided her all week, so why had he picked *today* of all days to show up?

"I thought the volcano was supposed to spew a *little*," she said. "I had no idea it was going to erupt like Mount St. Helens."

Just great. He was going to give her the worst-teacher-ever award. She knew this just made him think of the mishap during her student teaching.

Hair dripping, she looked around the room. The boys stopped laughing and watched her warily, as if worried she was about to cry. She took in their expressions, and suddenly Jolie couldn't help it—she laughed.

Yes, she might look like an inept fool to Morgan, but this *was* funny. She laughed harder. The kids looked at Morgan and to her surprise, his lip twitched and then he, too, began laughing. And then the boys joined in.

When the laughter died down, Jolie slipped her arm around Sammy's shoulders, giving him a hug. "Now we have to clean up this catastrophe."

"We'll help," Caleb offered.

Jolie grabbed paper towels and began wiping the sticky soda from the computers. Thankfully, she'd had sense enough not to set the volcano too close to them and the soda had only splattered on the keys.

"So, were you trying to trump your classroom adventures as a student teacher?" Morgan's voice was warm with teasing and his eyes warmer as he looked at her. But the tingle that raced up her spine was the warmest of all.

"Just trying to keep things interesting."

He chuckled. "Always."

She stopped scrubbing computer keys and he stopped wiping the desk. Funny how that simple word affected her—*always*. What would *always* be like with Morgan? She'd given that up with him and yet she'd never stopped thinking about it.

Standing with him so close, feeling the warmth of him and smelling the scent of his woodsy cologne, she began wondering full throttle about him, about feeling his arms around her and his lips against hers....

Great, Jolie. Just great.

"You almost missed all the fun, Morgan." Joseph broke into her daydreaming.

"Almost," Morgan drawled, looking at Joseph. "Thanks for inviting me to come to the show. It was a bit more exciting than you'd said it was going to be."

So that's why he was here.

"If your teacher would read her instructions

a little more closely, maybe things wouldn't get so crazy."

"That would be boring!" Sammy defended her, and everyone agreed. "I didn't even jump when that foam blew out of there," he continued, big eyes beaming and smile flashing.

"And that's saying something." Joseph gave him a teasing push on the arm. "You're comin' around, short stuff."

Goodness, Jolie loved these boys. In just a short few weeks they'd dug deep into her heart as if they'd been in her life forever. How had that happened?

This feeling must be embedded in Morgan even more deeply, she realized.

"Well, I guess I'd better get back to work," Morgan said, making no move to go as his gaze latched on to hers again.

She felt breathless.

She also felt the boys' full attention on them. Morgan must have, too, because he broke for the door, snagging what was left of the volcano experiment on his way out. "I'll toss this in the back of my truck and put it in the Dumpster. Unless you want to use it again." He held it toward her with a half grin.

She smiled. "You might want to save it. That volcano will probably become part of Sunrise Ranch legend. It could be valuable someday."

When he chuckled, she said to the boys, "Clean up a little more, fellas. I'll be right back."

And she followed him outside.

Morgan tossed the volcano in the back of his truck and then turned to face her as a soft breeze sent wisps of hair splaying across her face. To her surprise Morgan lifted his hand and gently brushed them off her cheek. A wave of emotion made her heart race and suddenly she was thinking about kissing him…and wondering if he was thinking the same thing.

His eyes darkened as he caressed the strands of her hair between his fingers. Butterflies fluttered inside her chest—no one had ever made her feel the way Morgan did with just such a simple touch.

"I better go," he said suddenly, letting go of her hair and reaching for the door handle. "Hold it down in there," he added with a wink, then climbed into his truck and drove away.

Jolie didn't move as she watched him go. She was unsure exactly what she was feeling…but it felt like hope. Could it be that there was a chance for them? Was she crazy to even think it?

As she turned to head back into her classroom, she was startled to see the windows full of grinning faces.

Unless she was mistaken, she wasn't the only one wondering if she and Morgan had another shot at love.

* * *

Morgan entered the stable, on his way to take a look at the new foal. It was quiet and sunlight filtered in through the windows, giving the stalls a glow.

The foal was a beauty. He was lanky—all legs with a sleek body that promised one day to be a beautiful cutting horse. If he was as talented as his daddy, they might have another champion on their hands. Rowdy had won the title on the foal's daddy two years in a row.

"He's looking good, isn't he?" Rowdy said, coming from the barnyard.

"Yeah, he looks just like Pep." Pep's bloodline was famous and a good building base for the ranch.

"Good ol' Pep, he knows how to mark 'em. Now if we could just get a few of his colts with some of his talent, we'd be in the money."

Though Rowdy grinned, Morgan knew he was serious. On a ranch the size of Sunrise, they pursued multiple avenues that could generate revenue as well as give the ranch a reputation for quality in every way. It also gave the boys exposure to different aspects of ranch life, and different possibilities for their future.

"Jitterbug's going to do us proud. You know he is," Morgan said, hanging his elbows over the stall gate next to his brother.

"He'll do. So, how's it going with Jolie? Y'all sure were looking cozy at supper during the roundup."

"We were just talking."

Rowdy studied him. "You going to throw in with her again? Forgive and forget and see where it goes?"

Morgan studied his boots. He'd almost kissed Jolie. But he was a grown man with responsibilities—he needed to have a clear head, and he wasn't sure he could do that around her.

Tucker had told him to give it to God and have no regrets.

Today he'd been tempted to do just that.

"I'm just asking," Rowdy said when Morgan remained silent. "I'm not sure I could do it in your situation. I like Jolie—always have—but that was harsh the way she led you on like she was going to marry you and then the minute she got the offer to join that kayak team, she jumped ship and bailed. My question is, can you ever trust her again?"

Bingo.

Morgan rubbed his jaw—startled by Rowdy's unexpected advice. Instead of being reckless it was on target with Morgan's thoughts. "She's here to teach the boys and work out a few issues she's had since the accident. I'm not going to kid myself into thinking she's sticking around this time. I'm not throwing in with her."

But I am going to help her get back in the water.

Rowdy slapped him on the shoulder. "Be careful."

"It's under control, but thanks for being in my corner." Morgan hadn't thought Rowdy was in his corner, and it felt good to know differently.

"What are brothers for?" With that, Rowdy sauntered out of the stable and disappeared into the bright sunlight. Morgan turned back to the foal.

Can you ever trust her again? Rowdy's words echoed in his head—and his heart. Truth was, he couldn't. He didn't.

And that was the answer he'd been searching for. The attraction was obviously still there, but without trust, it didn't matter.

He was going to help Jolie get back in the water because it was the right thing to do. But it didn't mean he'd give her his heart on a platter again.

Morgan had a good life and he'd come to enjoy it. If it got lonely sometimes, so be it, because finding a woman to share his life had proven to be more trouble and heartache than he ever wanted to risk again. First Jolie and then Celia—though truth be told, Celia had hurt far less than Jolie. Still, he'd opened up to both of them, bared his soul and let them into his life—and they'd both left.

Nope, Morgan wasn't ever going to trust a woman with his heart again.

He would help Jolie, and ensure that she moved on at the end of the semester. And it would be the best thing for both of them.

Chapter Eleven

Gulping air into her burning lungs, Jolie leaned forward and grasped her knees. She'd been doing sprints for thirty minutes and was covered in sweat, her muscles on fire. She'd let herself get out of shape in the month since she'd arrived at the ranch, and now she was paying for it.

Straightening, she wiped her brow with her fingertips and continued to breathe heavily. The hill she stood on was steep—pure torture, and excellent for a workout.

She smelled the sweet scent of pure country air. It was hot air—even though it was now September, the temperature still hovered in the low nineties—but it was Texas country, her country, and she'd missed it.

She hadn't told Morgan the whole truth last week when he'd asked her how she was staying in shape. She'd exercised a bit, but not like she needed to in order to be in ultimate physical condition to hold her own against the rapids. Her endurance had to be in top form. If it wasn't, it could mean life or death.

Embarrassed by her half truth, she'd begun a rigorous exercise routine the very next day. She'd needed to work out her frustrations over how Morgan raced away from her when she'd told him she thought she'd made a mistake in leaving six years ago. That the workouts helped her to feel more like herself was an added bonus.

The feel-good endorphins were definitely working their magic, and she needed them. Until today, she'd thought there was no hope for Morgan and her. But standing beside his truck earlier, he'd thought about kissing her—she'd seen it in his eyes. And she'd thought about kissing him. Thinking of that moment sent shivers through her.

Heading through the woods toward the farmhouse, she made herself think of everything she had to be thankful for instead of thinking about kissing Morgan. Being alive was top of the list, and coming home to the ranch, and meeting the boys. And Morgan was up there, too.

Since she'd been back, Jolie realized a bunch of things, including the fact that she'd felt adrift even before the accident, as if caught in a backwash. What had driven her for so long had come to mean less and less, and things she'd put on the back burner had begun to tug at her.

In the beginning of her career, it had been different. Driven by the need to conquer as many rivers as possible, she'd been hard to stop in those first four years. Regrets over how she and Morgan had parted always trailed her, but her desire to be the best female professional kayaker in the field overshadowed her regrets.

Not so these last two years—things had begun to change. When her friends and competitors began slowing down, getting married and beginning families, she'd become restless. And sad. It took two for her dream of a family to become reality. Her love life had dwindled to almost non-existent after she gave up dating, which had been nothing but disappointing. And she'd begun to really regret her past...and regret hurting Morgan.

After the accident, she'd known she couldn't run from it any longer. She'd told herself she was coming here to make amends, but now she knew she was here for more than that. Much more.

So here she was, her entire life in flux, so full of unrest that she was confused. And so full of longing, she was toying with fire.

The white wood and cheerful red shutters of her house came into view through the trees. Nothing fancy, but homey. And after being on the road so much, homey was exactly what she needed.

Stepping onto the back porch, the loud rumble of a diesel pickup signaled she had company. Going to investigate, she rounded the corner just as Morgan got out of his truck looking tall, dark and dangerous for her heart. Jolie sent gravel flying skidding to a stop.

She knew after a workout in scalding heat that she looked like a red lobster. Still, her pulse jumped despite her sweaty self.

"Jolie," he said, his eyes moving over her, probably taking in just how terrible she looked. "I was on my way to check some mares close to foaling and the boys told me I should see if you wanted to go." He grinned. "Just for the record, *I* thought you might want to come, too. I know you used to love the baby crop."

Jolie clapped her hands together. "Oh, Morgan, I would love, love, *love* to see the babies—are there any running around yet?"

"A few." He chuckled.

So the boys had sent him, but Morgan had thought it was a good idea. If she'd been wearing any boots, that fact would have just about busted them clean off her feet. "I'm a mess. Can you wait while I change?"

"You're fine. I mean—"

"Are you kidding? *I* don't want to be closed up in a truck with me right now, so I'm pretty certain you wouldn't want to, either. Give me ten minutes. Okay?"

"You got it." Following her to the porch, he sat down on the old wicker rocker that had been there when she moved in. "I'll be right here," he said, looking up at her with those blue troublemakers. Jolie almost tripped over the doorstop.

Her mind going wild, she raced into the house. Morgan had come for her. Heart pounding, she made quick time in the shower, not even giving the water time to warm up. Then she proceeded to sling clothes all over the place in search of the right thing to wear. The clock was ticking when she finally decided on the fourth shirt she'd tried on, along with the second pair of white shorts. Slipping her feet into her sandals she hurried to yank her wet hair into a ponytail, put on some moisturizer, a hint of mascara. Finally she gave herself a nod in the mirror, noting the tint of pink from the sun.

Or was it from being flustered?

With a minute to spare she raced from her room and ran hard into an end table with her knee. *Ouch.*

Through the screen door, she glimpsed Morgan fingering his Stetson between both hands, studying the hat like it held the secrets of the universe. Her heart clutched as he raked a hand through his ruffled hair and took a deep breath.

Was he nervous?

The very idea sent a tingle zipping through her. It was a good feeling to know she wasn't alone in this.

"All done." She pushed open the door, forcing herself not to sound too breathless, too eager. "Ready if you are."

Who am I kidding? she thought when Morgan looked up at her with those perfect blue eyes. *I'm not ready for this. I'm not ready for this at all.*

"Great, let's get this show on the road," Morgan said, jumping up from the chair. A little shaky in the knees, he caught the scent of her freshly washed hair. Whatever she'd used made him dizzy it was so sweet.

Get a grip, he told himself. He was in trouble and he knew it. Better to get this over with. He turned and headed for his truck, then remembered his manners and hurried back to open her door for her.

"I am so excited," she said, looking up at him like she had at the school the day before. Her eyes were so luminous he could practically see his fool face in their reflection.

He gave a stiff smile and put his hand on her elbow, assisting her into the truck. His fingers tingled as he touched her soft skin. Hurrying back around the truck, he slid behind the wheel. He'd never been happier that truck manufacturers had started making trucks bigger—he needed as much space as possible between him and Jolie.

Driving down the lane, the trees hung over the paved road like a canopy. It was a beautiful, sun-dappled section of road that he loved. And apparently so did Jolie.

"I've always loved this part of the road. When I was in Kauai, I saw a road with magnificent canopy over it. It's been painted and photographed an unbelievable amount of times. Every time I drove it, all I could think about was this little stretch of road in Texas and how much I'd loved it."

He glanced at her. "I didn't know there were any rapids in Kauai."

She shook her head. "I was there for a promotional event. My sponsor also makes rafts and wanted shots of me on the Na Pali Coast rafting. I *loved* it there—it was so gorgeous. And I got to swim with dolphins—one of the cool perks of my career."

"It sounds great." What else could he say? She certainly wasn't going to get that kind of perk here on the ranch. All the more reason to be cautious. In the end, he was certain Jolie would pack her bags and go back to the life that took her all over the world and let her swim with dolphins.

"It *was* great," she said. "And yet, Morgan, it's so good to be home." Her voice wavered slightly.

They cleared the tree canopy, turning into the drive that led to the mares. When they stopped, she quickly pushed open her door and hopped down, as if to get away from what she'd just admitted. "Let's see these mommas and their babies."

Sliding from the truck, he followed her to the fence where she studied the mares and their rounded forms.

"They are beautiful." She pointed out some of her favorites, talking a lot about each one. She was as nervous as he was, he realized. "You always did have a great eye for a good horse."

They were standing close again, as if drawn to each other. "Thanks," he croaked, his nerves getting the best of him. "It's just a talent God gave me."

"Well, we all have different talents. Yours is definitely cattle and horses."

And hers was riding a river in a plastic banana, as Rowdy always called her kayak.

"You have a wonderful talent with the boys, too, Morgan. They love you so much." She turned so that she was facing him, leaning her shoulder against the wooden fence post. The sunlight sparkled off her drying hair in a way that he liked.

"I try." It was the truth—he really did. "We've had some great kids come through here. I thought about leaving a few years ago, then decided instead to take on more responsibility and become involved. It's been a blessing to me."

In more ways than he could ever tell her. When his life had crashed around his feet after she'd left, he'd jumped into his relationship with Celia too quickly. After that had fallen apart, he'd almost left Sunrise. But deciding instead to be more involved with the ranch had been a turning point in his life, and the only way he could describe it was to say that he'd found his calling.

And now he would help her get back to *her* purpose in life so that he could continue on with his own. Maybe even take a chance on love without being on the rebound this time.

"And you've been a blessing to them," she said, breaking into his thoughts. "I think of Sammy and how lost and alone he must have felt when he came here. But you and this ranch, and Nana, and Randolph and Rowdy and everyone here… you're rebuilding his life, and the lives of all the boys. You know that, don't you? You're putting a new foundation of love beneath their feet." Her voice broke and it touched his heart.

He couldn't speak.

"Morgan," she said, her eyes brimming with sincerity, "I have to thank you for letting me stay. I love being a part of all this." When he still didn't say anything, she turned back to the horses and pointed at a very pregnant chestnut mare. "I predict she's next. What do you think—tonight?"

He forced himself to disengage from her and look at the mare. "I might have a good eye for horses, but you're the one who always had the eye for due dates. We'll see if you're right. I'll have Pepper bring her into the stalls just in case."

Opening the gate, he led the way into the pasture. Jolie spent the next little while patting and talking to all the mares. Morgan stilled his heart against how much he loved seeing her with the horses on Sunrise Ranch. He reminded himself that this was not her dream.

"Oh, what a sugar you are," she said, laughing when a gentle bay tried to nibble at her ponytail. Each mare she talked to got some sort of encouragement along with a gentle, loving touch of her hand.

It made Morgan more jealous than he wanted to think about.

About ten horses later, he realized visiting the mares had been a bad idea. Clearing his throat, he decided, purely for self-preservation purposes, that it was time to talk about getting her back in the water.

"Can we go over there to that tree? I'd like to talk to you about something."

Curiosity lit her eyes. "Sure. Lead the way."

Pushing old memories from his mind, he led

the way to the tree, checking for snakes before letting her sit. She placed her palms on the trunk behind her and leaned back to study him, her lanky legs crossed.

"Shoot. Tell me what's on your mind."

"I want to make you a proposition."

"Oh really? And what would that be?"

Dinner and some stargazing.

"I want you to listen to me before you jump in."

Cocking her head to the side, her eyes narrowed. "Sounds a little sketchy."

Morgan sat beside her. "I've been thinking about what you said, about being afraid of going back in the water. And also that you may have made a mistake when you left."

She inhaled a shaky breath and looked away.

"Jolie, I'm going to be honest with you. I don't want to get into whether your leaving was a mistake or not. I've moved forward—things change." Her shoulders stiffened. "But what I do know is that you've never shied away from a challenge. Fear has never defined you. If you don't get back in that water, I think you will regret it for the rest of your life. And you can't live with regret like that."

Jolie blinked several times, looking solemnly at him. "You know, it was fear of regret that drove me to leave all those years ago."

"Yeah," he forced himself to say. "And I understand that now. I'd be lying if I said it hadn't hurt back then. But you did what you had to do. And now you have to do it again."

She looked at her hands and then into the distance before finally looking back at him. This evasiveness wasn't like her, which gave him more insight into what the accident must have done to her.

"I've been thinking. Soul-searching. I'm not sure I want to continue kayaking."

"That's just fear and you know it," he said. "What about the guys? They are going to hound you until you teach them, you know."

She bit her lower lip, thinking. "I can't talk to them about the accident."

"All the more reason to just get back in the water and do it. Where's the girl I knew?"

She gave a humorless laugh. "I don't know if you've noticed but I'm not that girl anymore, Morgan. I'm almost twenty-eight years old."

"I've noticed." Oh yes, he had. "Look, you couldn't have kept up your competitive edge if you didn't still have the drive that you had before."

"Maybe I *don't* have that edge or that drive anymore. Maybe that's the problem. Did you think of that?"

"I don't believe it," he said gruffly, not liking the defeat he was hearing. "Not you."

She stared at him unsmiling. Seconds ticked by.

He fought off the urge to pull her into his arms and tell her that he would keep her safe. "Here's my proposition," he said instead.

A furrow appeared between her brows. "Shoot."

"I take you to the river and we work on your getting back in the water. No one has to know. We can get you over this hump and on with your life."

"Why are you doing this?" Anger tinged her words.

"So you can help the boys. And get back to the life you love."

Her eyes flashed. "You just won't believe—"

"No, I won't, Jolie," he snapped, losing patience. "You're afraid. And I don't want you here just because you're afraid."

Now he'd done it. The truth was out and he couldn't pull it back. Well, so be it.

She stiffened. "I see." She stood up and paced a few feet away from him. With her hands on her hips, she kept her back to him as she contemplated her situation. Finally, she swung around about as angry as a wildcat. "I'll do it, for the boys. I'll show them that letting fear keep you down isn't what we do. That God will help overcome. I just hope He gets with this program soon."

"That's okay with me." He knew she was still hot at him but holding it in check.

"So, when does this start?" Her hand was on her hip, her chest heaving with anger.

Feeling drained, he stood. "How about tomorrow afternoon? The boys have chores after school, so that's a good time to get away. I'll pick you up around four, if that works for you."

"Fine." Jaw clenched, she turned and stalked back across the pasture.

That was his cue—the conversation was over. She was not happy with him, but at this point, he didn't care. He was doing what needed to be done. Because the sooner she got back in the water, the sooner she got out of here. And the sooner she got out of here, the better it would be for both of them.

Chapter Twelve

The sound of the rushing water set Jolie's nerves on end. Before the accident, it had made her adrenaline pump and her energy level skyrocket. Now she was terrified by the sound, and by the thought of stepping into the swirling water and climbing into her kayak.

She'd had to push her anger at Morgan aside this morning so she could teach class. But last night she'd fumed at the high-handed attitude he'd had when making this proposition. For him to *assume* he knew what was best for her was irritating beyond comprehension—he didn't have a clue.

Okay, to be fair, he *was* right about the fact that the boys would hound her until she was forced to tell them the truth, and she didn't want to admit she was afraid. Especially not to Sammy—what a hypocrite she would be. So that was why she'd finally agreed to do this.

Before the accident, Jolie had really been afraid only once in her life, and that had been the day she'd handed Morgan back his engagement ring and driven away from him. God had given her the strength to do that—to reach for something more in her life, to dare to go beyond the boundaries of what was comfortable.

God was going to have to give her the strength to do the same here.

Only, right now she felt nothing except the cold edge of panic. Palms as wet as if she'd been dipping them in the river, her heart racing with anxiety, she marched down the path behind Morgan.

What am I doing? The question echoed in her mind.

Fighting came the answer, pricking at her like a thorn.

Jolie hadn't faced the possibility that her real reason for taking a break from kayaking was fear—it was easier to make it about needing to set things straight with Morgan. But the idea that Morgan could be right about her fear *bothered* her. More than she wanted to admit.

She was scared spitless, as Chili Crump would say. Both he and Drewbaker had fought in two wars and yet they both said crawling off in that yellow banana she rode over waterfalls would scare them spitless.

Long ago she'd thought they were just teasing her. Now she understood exactly what they'd meant.

"Are you all right?"

Morgan stopped a few feet ahead of her. She hadn't even realized she'd halted in her tracks until he'd turned around.

They were on their way to the spot where he'd first taught her to kayak.

"I'm fine," she lied, catching up to him.

It wasn't as if she was the first person this had ever happened to. Her friend Rita had gotten tangled upside down a couple of years ago and hadn't come back to the sport yet. She was a ski instructor in Colorado and guiding white river rafting expeditions in Tennessee. At least she was able to get on the water in an eight-man raft. Jolie hadn't so much as gotten her big toe back in the water.

"You don't look fine," Morgan said gently, studying her face.

So much for his not seeing her terror. Tears were welling way down deep, threatening to surface.

"Come on, talk to me, Jolie. Tell me what you feel. It didn't used to be hard for you to talk to me."

"I'm fine." She passed him on the trail. "I really am." *Liar, liar, pants on fire.* Her heart pounded, threatening to explode.

"No, you're not," he snapped, storming toward her, eyes blazing.

"Morgan McDermott." She swung around, glaring at him. "Stop telling me how I feel." Angry at herself for being a wimp, and at him for forcing her to do this, she lashed out. "How *dare* you!"

Tramping down the path, she could practically feel Morgan breathing down her neck. Despite her defiant spirit, her steps faltered the closer she came to the water, and her knees weakened. Her mouth went dry and her stomach hollowed out.

Crazy. This is crazy...and embarrassing. When she came to a sudden halt, Morgan slammed into her.

Grasping her arms, he kept her upright on the steep incline. His touch tempted her to throw herself into his arms, to bury herself in the security she knew she would find there.

Instead she forced herself to continue toward the sound of rushing water.

You don't have to do this! the wimp inside cried out to her.

Right. She was finished with kayaking anyway, wasn't she? Teaching full-time was the new plan. So she didn't have to be bullied into this. Panic gripped her like a choke hold and she spun, intent on fleeing.

Instead she found herself pressed against Morgan's hard chest, looking up into his dark eyes so full of concern.

"Whoa, take it easy," he urged, his tone softer than she'd ever believed possible.

Shaking her head, she backed away from him as though he was a hot frying pan.... The rest of the saying slipped her mind as his hands wrapped around her arms and his calm eyes searched hers.

She had to tell herself to breathe or she'd have suffocated right there as Morgan gazed into her very soul. "I—" *Breathe.* "I'm going back. I don't need to do this. It's ridiculous." The rush of the river seemed to get louder. She pulled away, trying to free herself from his grasp, but he held on tightly.

"Jolie, you can do this. Come on, babe. You can." His voice was full of compassion. "I know what happened to you must have been horrifying. But I also know you, Jolie. You can overcome this."

Swallowing cotton, she shook her head. Humiliation was the worst. Blinking fast, she fought off tears. *Please, no crying!* She hadn't cried at all since the accident—she'd held it at bay, even at its worst. Now a tear slipped from the corner of her eye.

The tenderness on Morgan's face made things worse. The pad of his thumb brushing the salty drop aside did her in as the tears she'd refused to cry for so long began to spill from her eyes, one by one.

"Don't cry, Jolie," Morgan said tenderly.

"I'm not," she denied.

His eyes twinkled but he didn't laugh. "Whatever you say."

She dropped her head to his chest and flat-out lost it.

If Morgan hadn't already figured out the seriousness of Jolie's situation, he clearly knew it now. Jolie wasn't a crier. He'd seen her get dragged and stomped by steers that would make a man cry, and she'd only gotten mad. She might look delicate, but she was cut from tough stuff. The fact that her sobs were soaking his shirt and her shoulders trembled in his hands shook him to his core.

"I'm sorry, sugar. I didn't mean to make you cry." He gently placed his hand on her head and stroked the length of her silky strands. "You don't have to do this today."

As she rested her head on his chest, he was certain she could feel his heart thundering away.

"No," she said in between sobs. "You're right, I need to do this, but as mad as it makes me...I can't...seem to make the last step into the water. I can't even make it *to* the water." Her eyes sought his. "I honestly think I'll pass out before I get my toe in the water. Isn't that a twist?"

Even though the last words were an attempt at humor, there was nothing funny about the situation. "If you make progress every day, it will happen."

"What will? Me passing out?" She attempted a grin.

He didn't. "No. You'll eventually get in the water, and then get in the kayak…"

She took a deep breath, finally getting a handle on her tears. She nodded, the hint of a smile still quivering on her lips. Morgan's heart stopped and every cell in his body went on alert as he stared down at her. She blinked—once, twice—and her lips parted. He felt her heart quicken against his own.

"Morgan." It was a mere whisper and it drew him like honey as he lowered his mouth to hers.

Instantly the years slipped away and it was just like it used to be between them. He hugged her close, wanting to feel the warmth of her against him. When her arms slipped up and around his neck his knees nearly crumpled beneath him.

Trouble. The tiny word wedged its way into his head.

This was supposed to be all about getting her back in the water so she could leave to pursue her passion, passion that wasn't for him.

She will *leave. She has to.*

Pulling away, he heaved a breath as they stared

at each other. The world slowly tilted back into place. "Are you feeling better?" he croaked.

A twinkle lit her eyes and he was glad he'd helped put it there, if nothing else.

"How could I not be?"

He found himself pushing her hair behind her ear, his fingers lingering, sliding down to her nape. She trembled at his touch and it took every ounce of his strength not to lower his lips to hers again.

"We'd better get back. We'll do this again tomorrow if you want—I mean, we'll try to get you in the water. Not—" He shut his mouth before he said anything else.

"Yes, you're right. If I'm ever going to be able to look at myself in the mirror again, I need to be able to conquer this. Tomorrow is a deal."

"No, wait. We're taking the boys out to build fence right after you let them loose tomorrow. I forgot." Understandable that he'd forget—his brain was fuzzy after kissing Jolie.

"Sure," she said, moving a step away from him. "I remember the boys mentioning that. They asked me to come along. I told them I graduated from fence building a long time ago."

Morgan chuckled, seeing that just the idea of not having to get in the water tomorrow was a relief to her. "You never thought you'd be back here teaching, either."

"True. But believe me when I tell you that stringing barbed wire in hundred-degree weather is *not* on my bucket list."

He wanted to ask her if kissing him again was. Afraid of her answer, he kept his mouth shut.

They headed back down the trail, and he talked sense into himself the whole way while clanging warning bells continued to go off in his head. They'd kissed once, and based on the way he'd reacted, he knew it could never happen again. Because if it did, he was a goner for sure.

Chapter Thirteen

"Aw shucks, Jolie, do we have to learn to cook?"

Jolie had to fight the urge to scoop B.J. up in a big hug. "Cooking is a skill that even boys need to learn."

"We'd rather be ridin' and ropin'," Sammy groaned, trudging along beside B.J. They were trailing the rest of the boys, making their way across the pasture toward the chow hall.

"You'll both live. Nana, Ms. Jo and Mabel are excited to teach you. I want you two to be nice to them and appreciative of the time they're spending to do this for you."

Sammy squinted up at her in the sunlight. "You been tellin' me not to lie, Jolie. If I tell them I'm likin' it, then that'd be a big fat lie."

Jolie almost fell over in a heap of laughter.

"Me, too," B.J. added. "I ain't but eight. Don't that make me too young to fiddle with a stove?"

Anything to get out of cooking or baking.

"Believe me when I tell you that you will be well supervised." Both boys' frowns practically dragged in the dirt under their feet.

Nana was holding the door open for them when they finally got to the chow hall. "Well, boys, glad you could join us," she said, a grin in her voice.

"Do we have to do this, Nana?" Sammy asked, as if he was going to get a different response from the one Jolie had already given him.

"Yes, you sure do, little man. And by the time we get through today, I bet you'll both be the fried egg kings."

"Eggs," Sammy said in dismay. "You mean we ain't even cookin' cookies?"

"'Aren't' cooking," Jolie corrected. She was his teacher after all.

Nana hooted. "You're cooking pies *after* you learn to cook something that'll actually put nutrition in your system."

Meeting Nana's laughing eyes, Jolie shook her head in dismay. "The other guys seemed excited about coming. I thought that was a little surprising, but these two, they take the cake."

Nana hustled them along toward the kitchen. "The other boys have been through this before and know we have a good time in the kitchen. These two ruffians weren't here last year."

Jolie thought back to when she'd gone to school on Sunrise Ranch. "We didn't cook when I was here."

Nana dipped her chin. "Randolph wouldn't hear of it. Thought it was for girls. That man." She shook her head and rolled her eyes as if to say he'd been stuck in the dark ages. "I've since changed his mind. I convinced him that many of these boys might have to cook for themselves one day and need to know the basics. And, well, then he saw firsthand with his boys. Not a one of my grandsons has a wife to cook for him yet and I had to help them all out with what goes on in a kitchen. You'd have thought those handsome cowboys had two left hands when it came to knowing the first thing about working a kitchen."

Jolie got a comical image in her head of Morgan elbow-deep in dishes with pots overflowing and the stove on fire. "I struggled a bit myself when I went off to college." She chuckled. "My poor mom didn't think I was ever going to eat anything except cereal and power bars."

The gloom hanging over Sammy's and Jake's heads was almost visible as they trudged into the kitchen several steps ahead of Nana.

"What in the world is wrong with you two?" Ms. Jo demanded in her no-nonsense voice, a twinkle in her eye. She had her fist on her hip, her gray head cocked to the side and a get-your-attitude-straight look on her face. Jolie grinned.

The boys were young but they came up to Ms. Jo's shoulder. When they didn't smile, she whipped her crooked pointer finger out and hiked her brow at them. Jolie knew they were in a heap of trouble—trouble that would be good for them in the long run.

"I didn't just ask that question to the air, boys. We're going to have ourselves a mighty fine time in here baking and cooking, so I'd surely like to see a little enthusiasm. You only get out of life what you put into it."

Sammy's eyes were big as saucers. "You ain't gonna whip us, are you?"

Ms. Jo's thin brows practically banged together and her eyes flashed with indignation. "*Whip* you? Why would I want to go and do that? I know for a fact that once you dig your fingers into the pie crust I'm going to teach you to make, you are both going to want to bake pies for a living because you're going to have so much fun."

"Fun. Cooking?" B.J. looked far from convinced.

Joseph had already tied an apron around his midsection and came striding over, his ever-present grin on his face. "Come on, little slowpokes, get your aprons on and let's get this show on the road. I'll show you my skills from last year."

Ms. Jo winked at the cute teenager. "Now that's a great attitude. B.J. and Sammy, right?" she asked and they immediately nodded. "Y'all go with Joseph here and he'll get the two of you all set up. Do you trust me?" B.J. nodded instantly, but her question clearly startled Sammy. His expression was guarded. "Trust is something earned, son, and I'm aiming to earn your trust so remember what I've said. Deal?"

Sammy thought on it. "Deal," he finally said. There was no doubt in Jolie's mind that Sammy would be watching everything Ms. Jo did. And when it was all said and done, he'd have a verdict.

And a very tasty pie to call his own.

Who knew cooking could build trust in a little boy who really needed a good experience in that department? As they walked off, Ms. Jo pivoted to her. Nana and Mabel, who'd been across the room handing out aprons, came over to join them.

"So, how are things?" Ms. Jo asked without so much as a blink of the eye.

"Things?" Jolie pretended ignorance.

"Now, Jo, easy does it," Nana chuckled.

"Easy does it, my foot," Jo balked. "I've been waiting for a little news and haven't seen hide nor hair of her."

"That makes two of us," Mabel harrumphed. "And I've had to put up with Jo's constant complaining because you've been AWOL. It's enough to make an old woman crazier than she already is!"

Jolie laughed. "Y'all knew exactly where to find me, so don't think I'm feeling sorry for you." She hoped the boys would return and they'd have to turn their attention to the baking at hand, but the boys were fighting over who was going to have to wear the apron with the big strawberry on it, and there was no telling how long that was going to go on. "I haven't been AWOL. I've been working."

Ms. Jo's brow cocked. "Is that all?" She sounded suspiciously like she wanted something more than that to be going on.

"Yes, that's all. And exercising—keeping my training up takes time, too."

"And going on roundups and birthing colts, too."

Nana was not helping the situation.

"Sounds like fun to me," Mabel cooed. "It is so romantic on the trail—once you get past the dirt hanging in the air and the heat. And the sweaty horses. On second thought, maybe the trail isn't a place to foster a budding relationship."

"Budding? Who said anything about a budding relationship?" The words were out of her mouth before she could clamp a hand over the traitorous lips—she hadn't intended to talk to them about any of this at all. "The last time I checked, you three were all against my starting anything up with Morgan." The words were hissed quietly so that the boys wouldn't overhear.

"True," Ms. Jo said. "However, there have been a few indications that maybe we were a bit hasty being protective of our boy."

"We're all set," Joseph called.

Praise the Lord for the intervention!

Joseph and Wes had lined up the motley crew like they were about to compete on the *Iron Chef* television show.

Jolie grinned. "Look, ladies, the boys are ready to cook."

"Bake," Ms. Jo corrected.

"Cook," Nana said, giving Jo the eye. "Eggs and sausage are necessities."

Ms. Jo gave a snort. "Depends on who you ask."

"Then I guess it's both bake and cook," Jolie chirped, escaping from the interrogation huddle. She had a terrible feeling that things were just about to start heating up.

The thing was, she hadn't seen much of Morgan since their kiss. They'd agreed to meet again and attempt to get her in the water, but it hadn't happened. She'd gone home and immediately gotten cold feet. Obviously Morgan had, too, because he hadn't called yet to reschedule the date. And that had been fine with her.

At least she'd kept telling herself it was fine. But just thinking about the feel of his arms around her and the heat of his kiss made her cheeks warm.

So far the only good thing that had come of the day beside the river was that her nightmares had eased up. And that was probably just because thoughts of Morgan were keeping her from sleeping in the first place. But that was a piece of info that she and she alone was privy to. And she planned to keep it that way.

Morgan was late. On purpose.

"You better hurry up," Rowdy teased as he threw a leg over his horse and jumped to the ground, his spurs jangling on impact. "We don't want to let the pies get cold."

Morgan deliberately took his time getting out of the saddle. When Nana overheard the boys begging him to come join their cooking class, she'd basically demanded that he and Rowdy sample the food with the boys. He'd groaned, knowing full well that the boys had an agenda—they were always trying to get him and Jolie in the same room. Knowing he was going to have to face Jolie for the first time in a week scared him.

He'd arranged his every move over the last few days with the sole purpose of staying out of her range. And with good reason. She was far more dangerous to him than he'd ever suspected. He'd naively thought that what she'd done to him would insulate him from the feelings that he'd had for her; he'd thought his heart would be protected. And then he'd gone and kissed her.

And completely messed up his world.

One wrong move and he was mincemeat.

Rowdy was having a lot of fun teasing him. The slug was supposed to have his back, not enjoy watching him hotfoot it across coals without his boots on.

"Payback is going to be sweet, just you wait, little brother."

"Hey, I don't have anything on the burner right now, so don't get your hopes up." His lips curved into a lazy smile.

"I wouldn't get too smug if I were you," Morgan warned, striding past him. "I'm a patient man."

Rowdy's chuckle followed him as he headed toward what he was certain would be a circus— with him as the main attraction. He knew Nana had keyed in to the fact that he was avoiding Jolie. She had asked him a time or two where he'd been hiding out at lunch—he might as well have admitted his guilt flat out. All the more reason for her to join forces with the boys to get him here today.

And she had backup—Ms. Jo and Mabel would be watching his every move, expression and twitch.

He was doomed.

And Rowdy wasn't helping him at all.

The last thing he needed was everyone in that room realizing what a vulnerable spot he was in. A rock and a hard place would have been better than this—at least he'd have had somewhere to hide. But no such luck.

Steeling himself for what was to come, he shot the good Lord a plea for help, pulled open the door and stepped into the center ring under the glaring spotlights.

"Morgan, look what *I* did!" B.J. yelled, instantly alerting Jolie and everyone else that Morgan had entered the room.

"Hey, I'm here, too," Rowdy clowned, pretending to be hurt, following Morgan into the kitchen. The room seemed to shrink with the two tall cowboys in it.

The instant Morgan's gaze sought out Jolie, all the air disappeared. Jolie dropped her metal spatula on the stainless-steel worktable, splattering meringue everywhere—including on Sammy—before it clattered to the floor. Every eye turned her way.

"You kinda like him, don't you?" Sammy whispered, blinking through globs of fluffy white meringue on his eyelids.

Jolie gasped, as much from having splattered

the kid with pie topper as from his keen observation. "Why would you say that?" she whispered, concentrating on cleaning the sticky stuff from his face with the skirt of her apron.

He squinted as she held his chin. "'Cause you get all nervous when he's around. That's what happens in all the gushy movies."

"No, I do not like him." She scrubbed harder.

"At all?" Sammy asked, looking confused now.

Guilt slid over Jolie. She stopped her scrubbing so she could leave some skin on the poor kid's cheek. "Yes, I do like Morgan. As a friend," she added quickly.

Nothing more.

"Well, you're pink right now and they do that in the movies, too, when they like the guy a lot."

She was about to ask him when he had time to watch all these gushy movies, but Morgan was coming their way.

"B.J.'s pie looks great. How does yours look, Sammy?" he asked, his eyes landing on her for only a moment before turning to Sammy. She wondered what was going on behind those pools of blue as her pulse cartwheeled through her body and memories of his kiss played havoc on her senses.

"We're about to put it in the oven. See?" He proudly pointed at the chocolate meringue pie. He'd been helping Joseph and finally decided to make his own, so they were running late on getting his into the oven.

"That looks mighty tasty." Morgan placed his hand on Sammy's shoulder. "You did a fine job."

"I didn't want to at first. You know cooking ain't for boys. But Nana showed us how to cook egg-and-sausage breakfast tacos so us boys won't starve when we go off to college."

Morgan chuckled. "She taught me the same skills before I went off myself. It came in real handy. And pie making—now that would have really come in handy for a college man."

A grin spread across Sammy's face. "I liked it. Jolie helped me and she did good. Till she dropped her spatula when you came in." He leaned toward Morgan. "And she turned kind of pink. You know what that means, don't you?"

Heat stung Jolie's cheeks. "Hey!" She gently tugged on Sammy's ear and he laughed mischievously.

"You tell me what it means, Sammy," Morgan teased, crossing his arms.

B.J. was suddenly glaring at Sammy. "You aren't supposed to say anything," he hissed in a low whisper that caused Sammy to grimace.

"Oh yeah, I forgot." He looked contrite, but then the words came flying out of him in a rush. "When a girl turns pink, it means she likes a boy. And when she drops stuff, too."

Morgan took in her hot cheeks, which she was certain were fire-engine red. "So I guess that means you better go tell Rowdy she likes him."

Both boys looked confused. Jolie was relieved—instead of being embarrassed, she found the scene touching. In their minds, the boys were just trying to help out the clueless adults.

"Morgan." B.J. spoke carefully as if explaining something to a two-year-old. "She likes *you*."

Sammy shoved him. "You weren't supposed to *say* it!"

B.J. glared at him. "*You* did and Morgan had it all mixed up!"

Rowdy sauntered over, bringing Ms. Jo and Mabel with him. Nana came from the other side of the room with the older boys trailing her. Jolie suddenly wanted to crawl into a hole.

"Did I hear my name? Morgan, what's up? You walk in and the kiddos start to fight?"

Ms. Jo didn't miss a beat. "You two looked like you just choked down a live cat for lunch. And I'm not talking about B.J. and Sammy. Jolie, why are you so pink? If I didn't know any better, I'd think you're a little flustered."

She did not need this. She really, really didn't. Fighting a river was easier than this.

"Do you feel well?" Mabel chimed in. "Maybe you have a fever, honey. Maybe Morgan needs to take you home."

"Good idea," Nana chimed in. "Morgan, why don't you take poor Jolie home."

"Whoa!" Jolie boomed, stopping the chatter erupting around the room. She knew a hoodwink when she saw one. "There is *nothing* wrong with me. I certainly don't need to go home. Now, weren't Rowdy and Morgan invited here to taste-test these goodies? Because I'm in the mood for pie!"

It was one thing for her to be having thoughts about Morgan. It was altogether another thing for this entire room of folks knowing it!

Thankfully Mabel led the boys away to set up for the tasting. Only problem, that left her standing alone with Morgan. "That was awkward—talk about being on the hot seat," she said, forcing herself to look at him.

"Is that what that was? Felt more like a frying pan." He chuckled.

Jolie's traitorous thoughts went straight to thoughts of the kiss beside the river. His gaze dropped to her lips and she knew he was thinking about it, too.

"I'm sorry I haven't gotten back to you about us going back to the river," he said.

"We better get over there before they start up again." Jolie knew this was not the time or place to discuss what had happened between them. Besides that, she wasn't sure at all what to say about that day…which was exactly why she'd been avoiding him. She'd been a disaster that day. It was embarrassing, and the fact that she'd been so distraught that she'd thrown herself into his arms and cried like a baby—that was the worst.

Chapter Fourteen

On Monday morning a few days after the pie fiasco, Jolie drove up to the schoolhouse to find the boys huddled in the front yard in deep conversation. The instant she stepped out of her Jeep, they busted apart, looking like guilty puppies that had just torn up her flower beds. Something was up.

"Hey, guys." She strode over to them as if she suspected nothing. "How are y'all today?"

"We're good." Wes grinned, excitement glistening in his pale green eyes. The teen looked more like a grown man than any of the kids, even Joseph, though he wasn't as tall. He was muscular and serious, unless he was thinking of an adventure. He was ready to finish school and get into college on the roping team. Life on the ranch had been good for him.

"How are you?" he asked her, stuffing his hands into his pockets. "You doing okay?"

She wasn't sure what to make of his line of questioning. Did she hear concern in his voice?

"Yeah, how are you?" Sammy asked as all the other boys chimed in.

"I'm fine, fellas. What's with all the worry?" She looked at Wes and then Joseph for answers. "What's going on?"

Wes shifted his weight from one scuffed boot to the other. "Well, I, ah, I was surfing the Net last night looking at your YouTube videos," he added. "And well, we've looked at it before, all the amazing stuff you can do in a kayak. It's really cool seeing you coming down those rapids and over those sixty-foot falls. It blew me out of the water. You're awesome, Jolie. But, man…" His words trailed off…worry filled his eyes.

Dread filled Jolie.

"We came across your accident." Joseph was the one who said the words, his lips tight with concern. "We hadn't seen that. You almost *died,* Jolie." He raked his fingers through his too-long hair, reminding her of what Morgan did when he was upset. "It was bad."

Bad didn't begin to tell the story.

"It was," she said, trying to figure out what else to say but coming up empty.

"People were screaming on the video," Wes said, "going crazy when they thought you weren't coming up. Then your kayak came loose and it seemed like forever before you surfaced."

Jolie's stomach rolled. Inhaling slowly, she counted to ten, fighting hard to keep her nerves steady. Falling apart in front of the boys twice was unacceptable to her. She was stronger than that.

Please, God, hold me up. Take me past this moment when I'm unable to hold myself up.

She searched for words of assurance for the boys who were so concerned that most of them couldn't speak. Their care steadied her.

"What happened?" Sammy asked, touching her arm. "How did you live through that?"

"By God's grace, Sammy. By God's hand." It was true. "Only God could have given me the extra air it took to be under the water all that time. There are things in life that can only be explained by God's interventions, guys. And me surviving my accident was one of them."

"I don't see how you can get back in your kayak after that." Coming from Mr. Thrill Seeker himself, Wes's words startled her.

"In all honesty, guys, it's time for me to come clean with you. I *can't* get in my kayak. I came here to try and get my head on straight, but the thought of getting back in the water is rough. I'm trying, though. It's just taking some time."

"That's why you haven't been too keen on teaching us," Tony said.

"That's why."

"It's kinda like getting back on a bull," Wes said. "Only, a bull is more controllable than a river."

Jolie's nerves had calmed down a bit and she found Wes's words compelling. "Why do you say that?"

"Well, you can study a bull, know its habits and in some manner, predict his moves. A river, like the one you were on..." He hiked a shoulder, his brows crinkling skeptically. "You have no way of knowing what's beneath the surface. If that log hadn't come downstream from somewhere and lodged in that spot, then you'd have done your roll, come out of the water and finished that run. No preparation could have saved you from that log being there."

Jolie knew his words were true to some extent. Her training was similar to a bull rider preparing for the arena. However, there was always the element of surprise.

"I think that's the way it is in life, too. We have to prepare and then give it to the Lord. That's what I did. I'm going to get over this and move forward, with God's help. And the time I'm spending here with you good-looking cowboys is helping me do that."

That won her some grins. Looking around at the group—at "her boys," as she'd begun to think of them—a lump formed in her throat and she ached with love of them. They were helping fill a spot that desperately needed filling in her soul.

"We like you being here," Sammy said, slipping his arm around her waist. "I'm glad you didn't die in that water."

She gave him a reassuring smile. "Me, too, because I'd have missed being here with you."

Sammy's expression was so full of hope that it stunned her. This child needed her.

The thought cut deep through Jolie. No one had ever needed her. Not like this. Yes, her team members needed her for her skills, and the points she could bring them. But the way Sammy needed her was different. He needed her for security, for support…for the love she could give him.

Thank You, God, for bringing me here.

She closed her eyes momentarily, the prayer filling her soul. Looking about the group, she realized that there were others who needed her, too.

Excitement surged through Jolie. She needed to talk to Morgan—to tell him what she was feeling. To share this new emotion with someone she cared for.

With the man she loved.

Morgan leaned back from his desk, weary from reading all the legalese that came with running the ranch. Taking in sixteen wards of the state did not come without an overabundance of paperwork. Keeping the ship running required staying on top of the forms that needed to be filled out. He'd taken on that part of the business when he'd signed on as partner with his dad.

Rubbing his eyes, Morgan was actually glad to have the office to hole up in for now. With Jolie being everywhere he was, it was hard to keep his head straight. Hard to keep his distance. Hard to stop thinking about kissing her.

That had been a gargantuan mistake on his part. Then, after the fiasco in the kitchen with the "spectators" watching their every move, he'd felt like even more of a fool than he had when he'd kissed her.

A man had to have a backbone.

Especially with an audience watching.

A knock on his door had him looking at the clock on the wall—nine-thirty. It had gotten late. "Come in," he called, expecting to see his dad, his brother or just about anyone other than Jolie.

So much for hiding out.

"Hi," she said, moving just inside the door. "Do you have a minute?"

Nope, all out of minutes. "Sure. I was just doing paperwork."

She glanced around his office, taking a few more steps into the room. "I like your space. It's you."

The walls had heavy, rich paneling. He had a cowhide rug on the floor, and Western art on the walls as well as pictures of boys with their animals at the county fair. Some of them holding championship banners and some were not. The projects weren't about the winning—they were about the experience of seeing something through. While Jolie's gaze had taken in the entirety of his office, it was the pictures of the kids that she had focused on.

"Thanks. I enjoy looking at those photos and seeing on their faces the satisfaction of a job well done."

Smiling, she perched on the edge of the leather chair across the desk from him. She wore jeans and a pale yellow blouse that caused her cinnamon hair to look darker and her emerald eyes to glow like jewels. They seemed less weary today, more alive. He hoped she was sleeping better.

He realized he was going to have to find some strength to handle being alone with her, or risk losing his pride.

"I thought we needed to talk. About several things. For starters, I need to apologize for falling to pieces down by the river. I—" She shook her head and closed her eyes briefly, drawing his attention to her long lashes against the warm golden skin of her cheeks. His gut clenched, remembering the soft feel of her skin.

"I'm not used to being so emotional. I'm sorry you had to pick up the pieces afterward."

"I should have kept my mouth shut and let you deal with your problem in your own time."

"No," she said. "I mean, you did the right thing making me try and face up to my fears. I'm glad I at least took a step toward the problem. Even though I ran away."

He cleared his throat. "I'm sorry I kissed you when you were…in a rough spot."

It's out there where it needs to be. Now move past it.

"About that. I'm sorry I threw myself at you."

That took him by surprise. The woman had been in a world of hurt. "I didn't see you do anything except need a little support. I was glad to give it."

Their gazes held as relief came over her face.

"Okay, then, we'll mark it up as 'I'm not sure what that was' and move on. Deal?" Her smile was warm.

"Deal."

"So, we need to discuss the boys."

The boys? "What's up?" he asked, trying to recover from the effect her smile had on him.

"The boys have been looking at videos of me competing. They finally came across the accident."

He should have known this would eventually happen. "What was their reaction?"

"Of course it scared some of them—all of them, actually. They wanted to know how I'm doing. I told them the truth—that I was having trouble. And they all understood. I told them I was trying to get my nerve back, that I'd come here to do that. Morgan, they were so sweet. I have to tell you that they've touched me deeper than I ever dreamed they could."

"They have a way of doing that." He took in his office for a moment. "That's why I'm here."

"I told them with God's help, I'd get back out there. I just wanted to tell you, and to thank you for trying to get me out there. I was a little miffed at you for pushing me. Maybe that was one of the reasons I got so…intense. I mean, when you're angry, it ups your emotions, so that could explain my anxiety."

"Were you mad at me the day you passed out?"

She frowned at him. "Okay, so maybe I'm just overly sensitive to the thought of getting in the water."

"That'd be my thought on the subject."

"Time will help. Anyway, I wanted to come and tell you what it means to me to be sharing time with the boys. Thanks for letting me be here."

What was he supposed to say to that? She was still leaving eventually, and they were still going to suffer because they'd all bonded to her. What did she expect that was going to do to them? "You're welcome." It was all he had.

Awkward silence filled the space between them. "Okay, then, I guess that's all I came to say." She stood to leave.

Say something.

Everything knotted in the pit of his stomach.

She headed toward the door. At last, impulse drove him out of his chair, skirting the desk in three strides. "Jolie—"

She'd spun at the same moment. "Yes?"

They stared at each other. Here they were *again*.

"I'm glad you came by. I've been swamped with paperwork that needs to be filed this week. So I've kind of been scarce."

She chuckled. "Well, that's a relief. I thought you'd been avoiding me."

"That, too," he admitted and smiled, loving her laugh. "Is there something else on your mind?"

"I'm thinking Sammy is better. We had a long talk today. That video gave me the opportunity to talk to all the boys, especially to Sammy, about how God is with us even in the bad times."

"Thank you for talking with him. Time will make everything better. Time and love."

Jolie's eyes brimmed with unshed tears. "Well, that is one thing the boys get here, that's for certain. Y'all are doing a great thing here, Morgan, and I'm proud to be a part of it. I've never been needed like I feel I am here. Today it hit me that I'm actually making a difference."

She got it. That dug deep into Morgan's soul. "Pretty cool feeling, isn't it?"

"It is. Well, I guess I better go and let you get back to work. Good night, Morgan."

"Good night, Jolie," he said. She was already heading out the door. He watched her cross the waiting area and push the door open. She didn't look back as she closed it behind her. The click of that door cracked like a gunshot in his head.

Jolie was falling for the boys and the boys had fallen for her. Raking his hand through his ruffled hair, he realized it was trembling.

So much for holding it together.

Jolie drove through the gate, headed toward her temporary home, her mind spinning in so many directions she wasn't sure what to think about first.

Morgan had looked tired but heartbreakingly handsome as always. She'd wanted to ask him more about his day, ask him how he'd been doing since he'd kissed her. Maybe kiss him again…

Nope, she was definitely not going to think about that. Pushing her hair out of her face, she was glad the top was rolled back on her Jeep—

she needed as much fresh air clearing out her muddled brain as possible.

Her mind shifted to Sammy. She wanted to do more to make Sammy feel comfortable on the ranch; something that was special, and would involve the other boys, as well—something to give them all a sense of ownership in this ranch that was their home. What could it be?

She would seek the advice of Ms. Jo and Mabel. Nana, too.

Maybe she'd just ask the boys if they had any ideas about something they could do. Like maybe a festival. Maybe a reunion? Something they could enjoy…something that would keep them—and her—busy.

Something fun. Something different.

Something they could call their own.

Something that would let Morgan know she was serious about being here at Sunrise…serious about working with him.

Chapter Fifteen

When Jolie asked the boys the next day at school what kind of event they'd like to hold at the ranch, they took hardly a second to think about it. In fact, she was so startled by their quick response that she wasn't sure they'd understood what she was asking. But they had, and their answer was clear as day: they wanted to have a fishing tournament on the big lake.

"Wow, that was the quickest consensus I've ever seen among you fellas! Have y'all had fishing tournaments before?"

"Us older guys have." Wes grinned. "But it's been a while."

"We hear them talking about how fun it was all the time," Caleb interjected. "And Mr. Macintosh—you know Mr. Macintosh and Mr. Crump? Well, they have done some funny stuff."

"Yes, I know Mr. Macintosh and Mr. Crump.

And I'm sure they do have some stories to tell," Jolie said, smiling as she thought of the town pot stirrers.

So it was decided that they were going to put on a fishing tournament and invite the town of Dew Drop to participate. The boys figured they'd charge a small fee and donate the money to the church's youth fund. Jolie thought this was an excellent idea—she was proud of the boys for wanting to donate to a good cause.

"What about you around the water?" Sammy asked.

She told him that they'd picked a good event, and it would be one more step toward getting her in the water. She didn't add that it wasn't the calm waters of the lake that shot her blood pressure sky-high—it was the raging sound of rapids.

By the end of the day Jolie had a plan and was pleased with how excited the boys were about the fishing tournament. They were even saying they could start having it every year. She liked that— loved it, in fact. It was exactly what she'd been after—an idea of their own that would tie them to the ranch in a special way.

Now she just had to run it by Morgan, but she was sure he would be all for it.

"Are you going to come work cattle with us?" Joseph asked, as they were all exiting the building. To her surprise, instead of racing off and claiming freedom, they lingered.

"I hadn't thought about it," she said. "I really need to see Morgan."

"Oh, then it's your lucky day—he's gonna be with us," Joseph drawled in his best Morgan imitation. "Come on. We're gonna vaccinate and tag 'em, and brand some, too."

Sammy grabbed her arm. "Come on with us. *Please.*"

Jolie could do nothing other than agree when the boys took her arms and pulled her along to the barn. Saddling up her horse, she listened to the excited chatter filling the stables as all her boys saddled up, too. Jeans were a staple on the ranch and she wore them to work most days, so at least she was prepared for this spontaneous change of plans. Slipping her foot into the stirrup she boosted herself into the saddle. It creaked beneath her weight as she settled into it, and joy settled into her.

She was glad the boys had insisted she come.

Riding out of the barn with the guys, Sammy came up beside her on Cupcake, his control better than it had been. "Goodness, you're looking like a regular old grizzly cowpoke. Awesome job, little man."

He grinned proudly. "I don't even need any help anymore. Joseph or Wes or Mr. Pepper have to cinch the saddle up for me usually, but I got under there myself today."

Sammy's pride in his accomplishment put a smile on her face that was so big it nearly hurt. "You're a regular cowboy now, Sammy."

"I know, and who woulda thought it? I mean, I never even saw a horse except in pictures before I came here. And now I'm a cowboy."

Jolie laughed. The sun was bright in the indigo sky as it beat down on them. As beautiful as it was, it couldn't begin to compare to the joy that filled her watching Sammy snap his bootheels against his horse's belly, urging it into a trot to meet Wes and Joseph at the head of the gang.

Thank You.

The prayer of thanks eased out of her. And as she rode out with the boys, looking like a posse from an old Western, she conversed with the Lord all the way, thanking Him for the blessings in her life, for the renewing of her spirit, which she hadn't even realized needed renewing, and for the way He took bad situations and made them good.

One of God's many promises whispered through her mind. *I will never leave you or forsake you.* It was true.

By the time they made it to the corral where the cowboys were working a huge herd of cattle, she'd finished praying and moved on to a loud, excited conversation with the boys about all their plans for the fishing tournament.

Life was good.

The instant the men came into view, Morgan—unmistakable in the way he sat in his saddle, so erect and proud—broke from the herd and loped in their direction. His straw Stetson tugged low over his penetrating eyes, his face covered in a sheen of perspiration and dust, he looked rugged and powerful. He set Jolie's pulse galloping as he took his hat off, smiled a welcome at the boys and rode straight to her.

"This is a nice surprise." A gorgeous smile cut across his tanned face—a smile just for her, cutting deep into her heart.

"The boys hijacked me and wouldn't take no for an answer." She grinned back at him. Mercy, mercy, mercy, she was going to have to hug each and every one of them for it, too.

Life, Jolie realized as Morgan spun his horse and took up beside her, still grinning, wasn't just good—it didn't get any better.

It was a scorcher of a day, although September was racing by faster than a wild mustang charging for open pastures. Morgan knew it would start cooling down over the next few weeks, but for now, summer was stretching out and taking everything it could get.

Jolie didn't seem to mind the heat as she worked right alongside the boys and men. She'd been branding and tagging with Sammy, encouraging him the whole time. Watching her made his chest feel tight.

She looked up from where she had a knee on a calf, holding it so Sammy could brand it.

The faster summer went by, the sooner she'd be gone.

The sooner he'd be safe.

The sooner he'd miss her again.

The caustic scent of burning hair signaled that Sammy had been successful.

"Great job!" Jolie exclaimed the instant Sammy had done the deed and she let the calf up to jog away. Sammy had been worried about hurting the calf, and Jolie had explained that God had made cattle's hides thick for a reason. After that, the boy had had no problem wanting to learn the age-old trade of cattle country. Now, he was grinning from ear to ear.

"I did it!" he yelped, giving Jolie a high five. "You're one good cowgirl, Jolie. Let's get another one."

"Send out the signal and Wes will cut one from the group for us."

Sammy whipped off his hat and whooped and Wes nodded his way, lifted his rope and sent a loop flying through the air. He and Joseph were bringing in the calves while the younger boys helped the ranch hands minister brands and vaccines, ear tags and whatever else the calf needed. Jolie had jumped right in there, not minding the grime that went with the job.

She was a tough cookie with a soft interior— and he had a weakness for cookies.

Morgan struggled with wanting more from Jolie every moment he was awake, and even while he was asleep. After seeing her last night, he'd had a very restless night.

"You sure do look like a man in need of a little distraction," Rowdy said, drawing up beside him. Morgan hadn't even realized Rowdy was riding over from where he'd been overseeing the action on the far side of the corral.

"What's that supposed to mean?" he grunted, not happy that he'd been lost in thoughts about Jolie—and even more unhappy that he'd been caught.

Rowdy laughed. "Morg, you're in la-la land."

His eyes narrowed to slits. "The sun is in my eyes."

What a stupid thing to say, McDermott! It just made the goofy grin on Rowdy's face get goofier.

"So, you've got it bad again, haven't you?" he asked, turning serious.

"Last time I looked I felt fine. Didn't know I had anything."

"You know what I'm talking about." He thumped his heart with his fist. "Right here, looks like to me. I'm not sure how to react to it, either."

So his brother was a wise guy with eyes of a hawk. "Okay, so I'm a little messed up."

"A *little*. You better shore up those leaks in the dam if you don't want everyone who looks at you to know you're 'a little messed up.'"

Morgan rubbed his jaw, stubble stiff against his fingertips. "I've got my feelings cinched up tight, Rowdy. She's going to leave again—there is no doubt in my mind that she will, come December. And I'll be a big part of getting her ready to do that." Morgan took a moment to look at her before he went on. "I've been praying about this and I know that she's meant for bigger things. She's reaching a multitude of folks out there. Last night I saw a video of her at a children's hospital, encouraging kids who have stars in their eyes over her. A kid's mother took the video and posted it because Jolie went there without an entourage or a camera crew. She went because she wanted to. She's the real deal, Rowdy. Too much ability to be here wasting away on a ranch in the middle of Texas."

Rowdy shook his head. "Don't belittle what you do here on this ranch with these kids. You're not wasting away doing what you do, are you?"

"No," Morgan denied emphatically. "I love

every minute of making sure the boys get what they need."

"Then why should it be any different for Jolie?"

"It's not the same. Here she'd have no spotlight and no chance to do the work she does, inspiring people. It's just not the same." And it wasn't.

Nope, come the end of this term, she'd be gone, and he'd have helped her get back out there where she belonged. It was time to head back to the river. And this time, she was getting in.

Chapter Sixteen

"It was awesome today!" Sammy gushed, pulling a feed bucket over to where the fellas were gathered at the back of the stables, covered in dirt, their faces streaked with sweat. He'd had more fun today than ever. And Jolie had hugged him and been so excited for him.

"Sammy's right, that was awesome. I *loved* it. But, so, what do y'all think?" Caleb asked, looking at Wes and Joseph.

"I seen what y'all been talkin' about," B.J. said, rocking on his bucket, his face still red as an apple from all their hard work. "Morgan, he was watching Jolie a bunch. Does that mean he loves her?"

Wes was chewing on a long piece of hay and he pulled it out of his mouth and grinned. "It's a start. I was watching him, too, and he's got it bad."

"Got what bad?" Sammy asked. "Love?"

He pointed at Sammy with his hay. "I think so, my man. I think so. Don't you, Joseph?"

"I hope so. We've been trying hard to get them together on the quiet, and they seem to like each other most of the time. But I'm not sure about all the time. That worries me."

Tony hung his leg over the rung of the stall. "Then we just got to try harder. Keep it up, man. In them romances, love takes time. Morgan don't look at anyone else like he looks at Jolie. Don't forget the day by the truck after the volcano. They were seriously thinking about kissing. You all know it."

"And Jolie was all pink in the kitchen," Sammy reminded them. "Remember?"

"Love's about more than just wanting to kiss or turning pink," Joseph said. "But I agree with Wes—let's keep finding ways to get them together. This fishing tournament is going to fit right in. Can y'all keep on keepin' this a secret? Everyone raise their hand who thinks we should keep trying to help Jolie and Morgan fall in love."

Everybody raised their hand, and Sammy and B.J. grinned at each other.

"Good," B.J. said. "'Cause I want Jolie to be my mom. Even if she is scared of the water. I don't care about that. I can still love her just as good. You can, too, right, Sammy?"

Sammy nodded, his insides feeling all funny

thinking about it. He knew he could love Jolie, but he wasn't real sure she—or anyone—could ever really love him. If his parents didn't stick around... He stopped himself. His parents would come back—they would. But until then, it would be nice to have Jolie and Morgan be his ranch parents.

"Yeah, B.J., I can love her, too," Sammy finally said.

Two weeks after they'd come up with the idea of the fishing tournament, Jolie headed to the newspaper office in town with the official advertisement in hand.

Since they'd first thought of the idea, the tournament had morphed into a really big day—it wasn't just about fishing anymore. There were going to be all sorts of competitions and events. And the boys also wanted to add a little arena fun for the kids who didn't want to fish.

They'd decided to have the tournament the week before Thanksgiving, which didn't give them long with the weeks flying like they were.

As she pulled up in front of the newspaper building, Chili and Drewbaker were sitting on the church pew outside.

"Stupendous idea about the fishin' tournament, Jolie. Folks are talkin', excitement is abuildin',"

Chili commented as she closed her door and stepped up onto the sidewalk.

"That's the truth." Drewbaker sliced off a sliver of soft wood from the elaborate bird he was carving. "I even heard we're having a competition on who's got the most decorated boat. Whoever thought about decorating a boat?"

"Well," Jolie chuckled, "that came from Nana, actually. She thought it would add a little something to the pot to have a bit more competition. She thought she'd put you fellas on the spot with decorating."

"Sounds like something she'd do." He scratched his chin with the knuckles of his hand, holding his knife. "I bet ol' Jo and Mabel are gonna have a doozied-up dingy."

"Don't you know it," Chili grumbled. "I 'spect they're already patting themselves on the back in congratulations on winning that part of the tournament."

Jolie saw the competitive wheels turning behind the two men's watchful eyes. "Well, you know them, I'm sure they have big plans."

Drewbaker squinted, drawing his bushy brows together, his face the picture of a man who loved a good contest. "I hear there's a paddle rule. No motors. I'm thinking y'all need to renege on this no-motor policy. Maybe give the teams whose ages add up together to be more than, say, a hundred and twenty-five, the opportunity to use a trolling motor."

Jolie laughed. "Boy, you've got this all figured out, don't you?"

That won her a hoot from Chili. "When two old codgers like us are fighting for our lives with the young studs you've got out there on the ranch, then you betcha we're getting things figured out. This takes strategy."

"And I can tell you're good at that."

Two wide, mischievous smiles spread across their faces. Jolie loved that everyone was having a good time with this, and she was thrilled that folks wanted to help out the kids. Many ranches around had offered the use of their boats because they knew that the ranch wouldn't have enough for all the boys to be on the water at the same time.

Morgan had teamed the boys up so that those with less experience had someone more experienced in the boat with them. Morgan himself was competing with Sammy and Jolie was very thankful for that.

Wes and Joseph had been disappointed that they hadn't gotten to team up together, but they made her proud by being good sports about helping out the younger fellas. Plus now they had their own competition going—Jolie was holding her breath to see which of the two would bring in the largest bass.

"Don't you be giving away any secret tips to the likes of them," Ms. Jo hollered from across the street. She'd come outside and was glaring their way with her fist on her hip.

"I'm not, I promise," Jolie called.

"Hey, you just stay over there and let the woman talk to us all she wants about this," Drewbaker returned. "Y'all are goin' down."

Chili hooted again. "Like a lead tank."

Jolie shook her head. "Boys, you do know Mabel and Ms. Jo fish together out at Patrick Lake all the time. They even have an alligator they've named."

"We know. That don't mean we're scared of them."

"Surely don't, Drewbaker," Chili agreed. "It surely don't."

Jolie excused herself before she got into any more trouble, and made her way to the newspaper office to drop off the ad. A little while later she was headed back home with plans to work out. She nearly drove her Jeep into the ditch when she saw Morgan's truck parked in her driveway with him leaning against the tailgate, boots crossed at the ankles and a long strand of grass sticking from between his teeth as he waited with arms crossed. Her pulse skittered to life as if it had been dead to the world until right now.

"Well, hey, there, mister," she said, hopping from her Jeep. "You sure are lookin' lazy all propped up by the tailgate."

A slow smile eased its way from one corner of his lips to the other beneath the shade of his hat.

Her toes curled and her stomach tilted.

"If you think I need something to occupy my time, then you need to give me something to do," he drawled.

"Hold on to your hat, bucko, or I just might do that." Not in any of the ways that were flying through her mind, of course. No hugging or kissing the cowboy. Nope, none of that.

"Sounds like a plan. Or if you don't have one, I'll tell you what mine is."

"I'd be willing to hear yours," she said, slamming the door. She strode to lean against the tailgate beside him, forcing herself to be at ease. His husky chuckle did nothing to help settle her butterflies.

"I'm here to see if you'd like to go down to the river for a rematch."

She gave him a grimace. "Talk about messing up a perfectly good afternoon."

He leaned so that his shoulder was pressing against hers. "I come in peace. You realize it's been nearly a month since we tried this? You're sleeping better, I think."

"That's true. Not always, but for the most part I am. The nightmares are only a few times a week now instead of a few times a night."

"So don't you think it's time to push yourself some more?"

Jolie took in some air—it was time to tell Morgan about the decision she'd made. "Morgan, maybe we should talk."

He shifted to face her, still leaning against the tailgate. In the past few weeks they'd worked together to get the fishing tournament in order and they'd relaxed around each other somewhat. Jolie was certain that Morgan felt the anchor load of attraction that she felt, and had always felt. And yet they'd never mentioned the kiss they'd shared on the banks of the river again, not since the night in his office.

She thought that was probably the way he wanted it.

There was still a no-trespassing sign on his heart, and she was trying her hardest to mind the sign. But she knew it was useless. Her heart belonged to Morgan McDermott, even though she'd trampled his years ago. What Ms. Jo, Mabel and Nana said was true—Morgan had never been the same after her. It hurt knowing what she'd done to him.

She was praying that time would heal the wound between them. God could handle this, even if she couldn't.

"I decided last week that I'm retiring from competition."

Morgan looked like she'd hit him with a soggy fish, he looked so shocked. "That's a mistake and you know it, Jolie. I've told you before you would regret doing something rash like that. You'll always know you let fear have its way with you. What kind of example is that?"

His words were what she'd expected, to a degree. "I didn't say I wasn't getting back in the water. But I don't want to compete anymore." She took a deep breath, preparing herself to reveal the next part of her decision to him. "I want to be here on the ranch. I'd like an extended contract."

"No."

For a moment, Jolie wasn't sure she'd heard him correctly.

"Haven't you been pleased with what I've been doing?" she asked.

He looked torn for a moment and she felt her heart sink. She'd been working her hardest, trying to do a great job because the boys deserved it. She'd also wanted to prove to Morgan she could do it. She'd been hoping for a firm "You've been doing a great job, Jolie," but that was most definitely not what she was getting.

"Well, that was eye-opening," she said. "Not sure what you expect out of your teachers, but when a girl gives it her whole heart and that's not good enough, that's pretty rough. Especially when I know I've been doing a knock-out job— the boys' grades and their attitudes reflect that."

"There is no denying you've done an excellent job. But this is about you, Jolie. I won't be a part of your not doing what you need to do."

"Excuse me, you don't know what I need to do and what I don't need to do."

"That so?"

"That's so." They'd moved within inches of each other, which is what always happened when they argued. How it happened was beyond Jolie, but it always did.

He searched her eyes. "I know you," he said, his breath warm against her skin, sending a shiver racing down her spine.

She shook her head, both to clear it and to deny what he was saying. "Not so. Or you'd know being here with these boys means the world to me. Being here…with *you*." There—she'd said the truth. It was barely audible, but she'd said it. "It means the world to me, Morgan."

He lifted his hand and it hovered for a moment, then gently touched her hair. Like a featherlight kiss, his gaze rested on her lips, making her step toward him.

"No." The word flew from him as he stepped back, breaking the pull between them. "I won't let you do this. You love what you do. You're afraid to admit it, though, and I won't let you use me and this ranch as a crutch."

"I *love* you, Morgan." It was true—she'd never stopped loving him. She was certain that what she felt for him now was the love of a grown woman who knew her own mind. "Coming back here and being near you, seeing the man you've become, watching you with the boys and witnessing the dedication that you have to them and this ranch, it just makes my heart ache with regret that I wasn't here to help build this with you."

Her heart felt swollen inside her chest.

Morgan's eyes flashed. "This would never work, Jolie." Grabbing his hat, he tore it from his head and slapped his thigh. "This will not work," he said again, and in one swift motion he pulled her into his arms and covered her mouth with his, stealing her breath. Jolie could feel the years of loss in his kiss, in the iron clasp of his embrace as he crushed her to him. And she returned his kiss with all the regret of lost years and the joy of homecoming. She trembled in his arms and was glad to have them for support. Her heart thundered in time with his and when he suddenly broke free and backed off, it felt as if a part of her had been ripped away.

He glared at her, swallowing hard as if there was a boulder lodged in his throat, his chest rising and falling. "I watched you leave once and had to pick up my heart." His voice was gruff. "I tried to be fine with it. Even thought I was in love with Celia. But she called me on it the night before we were to marry. Did you know that? She didn't marry me because she realized I was still in love with you."

She shook her head. "I knew the wedding had been called off, but I didn't know why. I'm not sure anyone did."

Are you still in love with me now? she wanted to ask, only the words wouldn't come. His glare held them off like a shield.

"She was right. But Jolie, I picked up my life and I've moved on. I was happy finally. And then you came back." He shook his head again, and bent and picked up his hat from the ground where it had fallen, forgotten in the midst of their embrace.

"I won't be renewing your contract, Jolie. You need to get back to the life you love. I'll help you all I can, but I can't do this—I can't go backward."

She couldn't breathe, couldn't speak as she

watched him stalk to his truck and slam the door behind him. He was already halfway out of the driveway before she could move.

Numb, she walked to the porch and sank to the step, too dazed to do anything else.

Chapter Seventeen

He'd really done it this time. He had completely lost his mind.

Yes, sir, no doubt about it, he was a raving lunatic. Why else would he have been fool enough to kiss Jolie after she fired a bombshell right at his heart?

Crazy—therein lay the problem.

Crazy *and* a fool.

Now he knew what had been wrong all along. There was obviously something in his brain that was broken when it came to Jolie.

He didn't like it one bit.

But he didn't have a clue how to fix it.

Gravel spewed behind him as he drove like the lunatic that he was down the road leading to his house. He'd built the place with his bare hands the year after Jolie left. He'd put a lot of sweat—and yes, tears—into the house. It had been a refuge away from the eyes of everyone in Dew Drop. Driving into the yard, he was relieved when he saw the stone-and-log fortress—home. It was sturdy. It had clean lines and hard edges. Just like his heart.

His grandmother kept telling him it needed a woman's touch to soften it up—some flowers, and a couple of trellises of roses and morning glories.

It was fine like it was, he'd told her.

He walked in through the heavy door that he'd made himself from the oaks in his woods, with hand-sanded planks and bold, strong hinges that were meant to last a lifetime. Strong, dependable, reliable.

Slamming the door behind him, Morgan's steps echoed as he walked straight through the empty house and out the back door onto the deck that overlooked the river.

Had he built this house to keep her memories at bay? Or had he built this house on the crook of the river to remind him of her?

The question slammed into him the minute the sound of the flowing water reached him.

Grasping the deck railing, he glared down at the river twenty feet away. His life had been in order. It had been settled.

And now this.

I love you.... Her words reverberated through his thick skull. *Coming back here and being near*

*you, seeing the man you've become, watching you
with the boys and witnessing the dedication that
you have to them and this ranch, it just makes my
heart ache with regret that I wasn't here to help
build this with you.*

Regret. He knew a thing or two about regret.
He closed his eyes and prayed for God to throw
him a lifeline.

Part of him clamored to go back and tell Jolie
he wanted her here. However, he'd learned that
love was about letting them go. It was about helping Jolie do what she was meant to do.

He wasn't giving in to any weakness this go-
around. Because if he gave in, if he opened his
heart again and then she left, he knew the pain
would be worse than the first time.

No. Girding up the door was the best thing.

But the kiss. His pulse kicked up like a buckin'
bronc just thinking about that kiss. How was he
ever supposed to forget it? He couldn't and he
knew it.

When she left…at least he'd have the memory.
But it was going to take everything he had to stay
strong and let her go.

Jolie went through the week—which was blessedly busy—on remote much of the time, but to
her surprise, she was able to enjoy the boys' excitement in getting ready for Saturday's fun.

Focus, Jolie, she kept telling herself. *Focus on the fishing tournament, on keeping sixteen boys in line, on putting Morgan's rejection on the back burner.*

The boys weren't the only ones who were excited. Nana, Ms. Jo and Mabel had prepared all manner of goodies for the occasion with help from Edwina, T-Bone and many others from town. No one would starve come Saturday—that was for certain.

Dew Drop and the surrounding area had been invited and a huge number of folks were going to turn out. Thirty-two teams had applied for the tournament, which was a great number—not too many and not too few. The boys had been figuring out how to decorate their boats and for the most part, they had kept it simple, not wanting to distract themselves from the main goal, which was to hook the biggest fish.

Many of the boats had forgone the decorations completely, because it had been optional, but some were done up in style. There were boats with umbrellas, including one that had an inflatable palm tree sitting next to the trolling motor, which, of course, would remain off because they had to use paddles. Another had an American flag flying. Sammy and Morgan had mounted a set of sun-bleached cow horns on the front of their boat and Sammy was proud of it. She'd laughingly offered to put a big red bow on the horns for added decoration. Horrified, they'd declined her offer.

Morgan had been around some, keeping busy with the boys and keeping interaction with her to a minimum. She was fine with that. She still wasn't clearheaded about what had happened between them. She'd told Morgan she loved him, and he hadn't said it back. They'd shared the kiss of a lifetime and she'd felt certain his whole heart had been in that kiss, and yet instead of telling her he loved her, he'd refused to let her stay. This really confused her, and by the end of the week it was becoming increasingly hard to focus. Best bet was to do as they were doing and let it steep— for now.

But it was not a foregone conclusion that they were done. Oh no, not by a long shot.

Saturday dawned, cooling off at eighty-five degrees—perfect for Texas in November. As up-and-down as the weather was in the fall months, it could easily have dawned at sixty degrees and wet. God had given them a beautiful day, though, and for that Jolie was thankful.

The lake area was beautiful, too—a steep hill sloping down to a picturesque lake surrounded by large oak and cedar trees. Upon Jolie's arrival, a group of deer lifted their heads from eating acorns beneath the oaks and raced for cover within the nearest stand of trees. She took a moment to enjoy watching them before driving the rest of the way down to the dock.

It wasn't long before things started rolling. The boys' boats had been carried down the night before and sat ready to slide into the lake, palm trees, cow horns, flags and umbrellas included.

Rowdy, Tucker, Randolph and most of the cowboys who worked on the ranch showed up to help direct people and offer assistance where needed. They were also in charge of the arena event, which the boys had decided was going to be a cow-dressing competition. Jolie could only imagine the fun the kids were going to have treating cattle like Barbie dolls.

Nana and Ms. Jo were unpacking a truckload of goodies and Mabel was setting up the drink station, with the help of several of their friends from church. Jolie realized early into this fundraiser that the folks of Dew Drop were just as generous with their time and money as they'd ever been. A feeling of peace filled her—it was nice to belong here.

She only wished Morgan felt it was nice for her to belong here, too.

"Where in the world are those two loudmouth whittlers?" Ms. Jo asked about thirty minutes before it was time for the boaters to put in. The grounds were crowded with folks milling around and kids running and playing. Everything was set—everything except Chili and Drewbaker. They hadn't shown up yet.

"I don't know. This isn't like them, is it?" Jolie asked, checking her watch one more time.

"Not on your life. Those two are usually first responders when it comes to being on time."

Ms. Jo's words were barely out of her mouth when a honking horn drew everyone's attention. Drewbaker's dusty blue, sixty-something Ford pickup topped the hill, heading slowly down the big slope toward everyone. Both men were grinning as everyone gaped at what they were pulling on the flatbed trailer behind the truck.

It was a round metal watering trough, about six feet across. It had two folding chairs sitting in it with a cooler in the center. On the edges they'd mounted fishing pole holders, and several poles stood at attention.

"Heavens to Betsy, what is *that?*" Ms. Jo snapped, marching to meet them as they eased to a halt.

"Here we are, secret weapon in tow," Drewbaker said jauntily as he climbed from his old truck with a grin.

Chili's cheeks were pink with excitement and cheer as he hurried around the front of the truck to where a crowd had gathered, studying their contraption. "Ain't she a beaut?" he bragged.

"She's a beaut, all right," Ms. Jo snorted. "Secret weapon—ha! I'll have to see it to believe it."

"Does it float?" Wes asked, sauntering up, eyeing the contraption with interest.

Drewbaker's mouth dropped open. "Does a dog wag its tail? Sure it floats!"

"But will it tip over?" Joseph asked skeptically.

"Well, now, there's an interesting possibility," Chili chuckled. "Me and ol' Drewbaker might just be takin' ourselves a little bath if it tips one way or the other." He tugged out two life vests and held them up. "Just in case."

Morgan stepped through the crowd, brushing past Jolie as he went. The woodsy scent of his cologne teased her senses. *Unfair,* she thought.

"Fellas, I'm not sure what to make of this, but I have to say I'm interested in seeing what happens when y'all climb in it."

"How do you get it in the water?" Caleb asked.

"Yeah," called a few people in the crowd.

Good question. Because the trough wasn't on a regular boat trailer and there was no curve to the bottom, she assumed they would have to get the boys to carry it down to the water.

"If we could get a little assistance," Drewbaker said. Climbing up on the flatbed trailer, he began gathering the fishing poles from their holders. He handed some to Sammy and Caleb and B.J., who had raced to help.

Drewbaker then lifted the fold-up chairs out and handed them off to a couple of boys, and the ice chest, too. When the boat thing was empty, he had Morgan, Tucker and Rowdy help him and Chili lift it to the ground, then tip it on its side and simply roll it down the hill to the end of the dock. Once there, they turned it upright and eased it into the water.

"Well, I'll be," Jolie murmured.

Chili used a rope tied to the handle to secure it to the dock. Now all that was left was their managing to get in the thing.

Ms. Jo and Mabel watched with squinted eyes.

"I have to give it to the old codgers, it's original." Mabel chuckled, shaking her head.

"They'll probably drown themselves before the day is done," Ms. Jo retorted. "Come on, Mabel, let's go show these fellas how it's done."

And so the day began.

The tournament was officially started with the wave of a flag, and everyone jumped into their boats and pushed out into the water ready for battle. Everyone, that is, except Drewbaker and Chili. They eased into their circular contraption very carefully, keeping their weight evenly distributed, grinning the whole time. Once in their seats they pushed off from the dock.

Drewbaker gave a salute, and to the amazement

of everyone watching, they floated out onto the lake like a dream!

Nana paused beside her. "I don't know about you, but I have a feeling the boys will vote that funny dinghy the winner."

Jolie chuckled. "If those two get dunked in the lake, it's a sure winner."

Nana's eyes widened. "I wouldn't put it past those two to do something like that on purpose if they aren't having any bites today."

A sudden squeal from the lake had them both zeroing in on Sammy and Morgan.

"I got one! I got one!" Sammy called. Morgan was sitting beside him in the small two-man boat, calmly showing him how to reel in the fish. Once he got it reeled in, he waved his pole in the air, the small fish dangling above their heads until Morgan grabbed it and took the hook from its mouth.

"That's good for both of them." Nana tilted her head to the side. "Morgan has been preoccupied and fairly irritable this week—more so than anytime since you got here. You wouldn't know anything about that, would you?"

Not wanting to discuss their situation even with Nana, Jolie hesitated. "Let's just say I might know something about it, and I don't know how to fix it."

Nana gave her a sympathetic smile. "This is what I was afraid of. I remember the first year after you left. I couldn't help Morgan with the pain, and I had to watch him work through it in his own way. 'He heals the brokenhearted and binds up their wounds'—I clung to that verse for Morgan, Rowdy and Tucker after their momma died. And I did it again for Morgan after you left. I knew he didn't love Celia." She shrugged. "I couldn't tell him that, though. Thankfully the poor girl had the gumption to realize it herself and do something about it." Her kind eyes looked steadily into Jolie's, and Jolie couldn't speak. "This can't be easy for either of you. I've been praying God's will—and you know He does have one. Even if we don't understand it. God's got a plan, Jolie."

Patting her on the arm, Nana headed toward the goody table. Jolie took a deep breath and studied Morgan from a distance. Sammy was keeping him busy, fidgeting on the boat seat and hooking his shirt almost every time he tried to cast his line. Morgan patiently worked with him.

Dear Lord, what is Your plan for my life?

"Please tell me," she whispered in the slight breeze. It was the first time that Jolie could remember actually asking God that question.

Morgan was trying hard not to laugh as Chili and Drewbaker were having a terrible time with a leak in their tub.

"They're biting better on your side," Chili said, poking his buddy in the shoulder with the tip of his pole. "And it's time for you to bail water and me to fish."

"Hang on to your horses. I think I have a bite," Drewbaker grumbled, keeping his fishing pole steady over the water.

Morgan and Sammy had been hearing bits of the fellas' conversation off and on all morning. It was entertaining, that was for sure. Fishing was normally a quiet sport, but not today on this lake. When a kid caught a fish, he whooped and his boat rocked with excitement—Morgan was glad he'd insisted on life vests. When a grown man caught a fish bigger than his neighbors', he whooped, too, and taunted them with his catch.

"I sure am liking this fishing," Sammy said, grinning when he pulled in his third bass of the morning. Holding it up proudly, Morgan chuckled.

"That's because you're whipping the pants off me."

Sammy shrugged. "I got the moves."

"Yeah, I guess you do."

"Hold on to your hat, Chili, I've got a bite! A big-un, too," Drewbaker yelped excitedly, drawing everyone's attention. His line stretched out and he began reeling in his catch. It was a fighter and the bass did a flip out of the water.

"Whoa, Nellie! That's a big-un," Chili said, halting his dipping. He shot to his feet in excitement, making the tub rock with force. It would have been fine except Drewbaker's chair tilted when Chili slammed back down in his seat. Hanging on to his pole, Drewbaker rode his chair as it slid with the rocking tub. To Morgan's surprise the tub stayed afloat as Drewbaker managed to get his good-size bass into the tub without bashing his buddy.

"I thought for sure they were goners," Sammy said, laughing.

Morgan was thoroughly enjoying fishing with the boy. Sammy was doing well in general, and seemed more settled now. The fact that he hadn't freaked out over the thought of the tub tossing the two whittlers into the lake was a good sign, too.

"Catch him," Drewbaker demanded, drawing their attention again. Chili was bent over, grasping at the bottom of the boat. "What's going on now?" Morgan called to the duo.

"The fish got loose in the bottom of the boat!" Chili yelled.

Drewbaker looked up, over the edge. "There's so much water, he's swimmin' and thinkin' he's found a new home. We can't catch him!"

"You two need to just take that contraption to the shore right now," Ms. Jo demanded. "Serious-minded fisherwomen can't even think straight for all y'alls lollygagging and jammer-jawin'!"

Sammy grinned at Morgan, his big eyes bright. "This is the most fun I've had since I got here. I sure am glad I'm with you."

If that didn't get to a man, Morgan didn't know what would. "Kiddo, it's the most fun I've had in a long time, too."

It wasn't lost on him that all of this had been Jolie's idea. She was a good teacher, with an eye for making things special for the boys. He had to admit it—she would be a blessing to the program if she were to stay.

The question was, could he handle it if she did?

Chapter Eighteen

The fishing tournament was a success. The boys could not stop smiling and teasing each other after they got back on dry land. And they were thrilled with the results of the boat-decoration contest—it was no surprise when Jolie counted the votes from the jar and announced that the galvanized tub had won unanimously.

Jolie loved seeing everyone have a good time. Kids were running around playing kickball, and people were visiting and catching up while Morgan and his men unloaded the young cows for the cow-dressing contest. She felt a rush of pride that her boys had made this day happen, with a little help from her. And from Morgan.

She and Morgan made a good team.

Pushing the thought from her mind, she went over to help organize the kids into six different groups—there were about seventy in all, in a vast range of ages. After they were organized, she lined them up around the temporary arena Morgan had hauled in for the occasion. She put Sammy in a group with Wes and several kids who were his age and younger—she hoped he would feel like the leader of the younger ones.

"Jolie, can you help?" Rowdy called to her. Climbing through the portable railed panels of the temporary corral, she crossed to where the cowboys were gathered around Morgan. His gaze landed on her and he lifted his chin in greeting.

"Your job is to pick a cow, stay by her and help out if needed. The object of the game is for the kids to dress the cow using the clothing they have on. Your job is to make sure no one takes off anything they shouldn't."

"Seriously?" Jolie asked. This was a new event for her.

Rowdy chuckled. "You'd be surprised just how inventive kids can be during a cow dressing."

"I hope we don't end up with a bunch of streakers running around."

"It will be fine," Morgan assured her, speaking directly to her for the first time that day. They had spoken a few times during the week, but their conversations had been quick and strictly about business. His eyes were distant, the wall between them firmly in place. Jolie looked away, not wanting him to see how much this hurt her.

"Okay, take your places. Two men to an animal," Morgan said. Cowboys scattered instantly.

Jolie didn't move quickly enough and to her dismay ended up beside Morgan and his cow.

Of all the luck.

Looking about as happy as she was about their situation, he continued giving instructions through a megaphone. "Okay. Here we go. Dress your cow."

Like a flood of ants attacking a bowl of sugar, the kids came over the railings of the arena and headed straight for the cows. The teams had to wrestle the cow to the ground, then dress it. Laughter and hooting erupted as the clothes went flying—kids stuffed colored socks on cows' hooves, stripped off long-sleeved shirts and tried to pull them over the cows' front legs and wrapped shirts around the animals' necks. By the time Morgan blew his whistle, the animals were running around with clothing flopping everywhere.

Everyone was laughing hard by the time it was over, and kids were jumping up and down with excitement. When Jolie met Morgan's eyes, she knew he was thinking the same thing she was: they'd done a good thing.

And for today, she was satisfied with that.

"Good job, Jolie." Morgan tipped his hat at her.

"Thanks. I was glad to do it." She pinned him with a steady look. "We make a good team."

Before Morgan could say anything else, Jolie turned and headed for the goody table. She needed some chocolate chip cookies to keep her mouth busy—the last thing she wanted to do right now was say too much.

With any luck, Morgan McDermott would spend some quality time thinking on what she'd just said.

When Jolie returned home from three days in Houston for Thanksgiving—where she'd been forced to answer endless questions from her parents about being on the ranch with Morgan—she headed straight for Randolph's office. She'd loved her visit with her family, but she'd missed the kids and she'd missed Morgan so much it hurt.

Driving up to the office, she was relieved to see that Morgan's truck wasn't there.

She entered the small lobby. Randolph's door was open and she rapped gently on the door frame to get his attention.

"Jolie," Randolph said, standing and waving her inside.

"I know I've done a good job," she said after explaining why she'd come.

Randolph, who looked so much like an older Morgan, leaned back in his chair. "You've done a fantastic job, Jolie, but Morgan is a partner in the ranch. He has a say in who will teach the boys on a full-time basis. If Morgan isn't on board, I can't give you the contract. I'm very sorry about that."

She'd known what he'd say, but she had to at least ask. In her heart of hearts she knew this was where she belonged. She'd been praying, and listening for God's will, and she had to see if He would open a door through Randolph.

Forcing down her disappointment, she rose. "Thank you for everything. I understand." Turning, she headed for the door.

"Jolie," Randolph called, his deep voice stopping her. "'Many are the plans in a man's heart. But it is the Lord's purpose that prevails.' That's Nana's favorite proverb."

"Yes, I've heard her quote it before."

"God's will is at work in your life. Remember that."

The words hit deep. "I will." She left, offering him a smile on her way out that probably looked as sad as it felt.

She hoped God let her in on the plan soon. Because she felt as if her life was here, on the ranch with the boys, and with Morgan. Without it, she had no idea who she was or what she was supposed to do.

Or how she was supposed to handle letting go of Morgan a second time.

* * *

"Something is wrong with Jolie," Wes said, looking at the group assembled around him behind the stables. He'd called the meeting because it was time to do something.

"Yeah, she's been quiet and real distracted this week." Joseph had his boot propped on the corral rung and was tapping his fingers on his knee. "I think she's worried about not being able to get in the water."

"Yeah," Wes agreed. "I heard her talking to someone about an advertisement she's supposed to shoot over the Christmas holidays. And she didn't look too happy when she got off the phone. It sounded like she's got her back up against the wall."

"She doesn't have to do it if she don't want to, does she?" Sammy asked.

"She's a professional kayaker," Wes stated. "She gets paid to do these ads. Her job is on the line, I think."

"But what about her being our teacher? And our ranch mom, like y'all told me?" B.J. asked.

The guys all looked at each other with uncertainty.

"Look—" Joseph pulled his boot off the rung and stood straight "—we want Jolie to stay, but she's got priorities. She's got to get past this bad thing that happened in her life. It's kind of how we've had to do it a little bit. I mean, we've each had some bad stuff—we know how hard it is to get past it."

Sammy looked sad. "Will she come back to us if she gets back in the water?"

"I don't know, Sammy," Joseph said.

He and Wes stared at each other for a long moment. Wes knew Joseph hated the look on the little kid's face as much as he did. And the other boys', too. They had to do something and they both knew it.

"Sometimes a person doesn't know what's in front of them till they face their fears."

"How do you know that, Joseph?" Sammy asked.

"I don't know. I heard it in a movie. It sounds right, though. I'm thinking Jolie and Morgan have this thing going on. Y'all have seen how they've been lookin' at each other lately."

"Kinda mad," B.J. said.

"And sad," Sammy added with a sigh. "When one isn't looking and they don't know we're watching."

"Yeah," everyone agreed at once.

"Couldn't Jolie teach us and still compete in kayaking?" Tony piped in.

"Maybe." Wes thought hard. "I'm just not sure."

Panic lit Sammy's face. "I don't want her to go."

"None of us do," Joseph said.

"Isn't there something we can do?" Caleb asked.

"Yeah." Tony stepped up. "We have to do something."

"We can pray that she stays," Joseph replied, perking up.

Sammy looked down at the dirt. "If we're good, maybe she'll stay."

Wes raked his hands through his hair, his heart hurting bad. He knew prayers didn't work. He'd prayed hard for his family not to fall apart, but God didn't always listen to prayers. He knew he couldn't tell the little kids that, though. They'd already been through enough, and it wasn't easy being a bunch of misfits that nobody wanted.

"Hey, you guys start praying. Me and Joseph will come up with something. Meanwhile, fellas, keep your ears and your eyes open. Anything you see or hear that could help us with a plan to get those two together, you tell us. If we get them to fall in love, then I betcha Jolie will stay."

Joseph and Wes looked at each other over the little kids' heads as they began to pray, hoping against hope that Wes was right.

Chapter Nineteen

A cold wind blew in from the north right after
Thanksgiving. It matched the chill in Jolie's heart.

Blinking in the wind, she urged her horse to
pick up speed as she rode across the open range.
She needed the feel of the wind in her hair and the
thunder of hooves beneath her. She hadn't been to
the river's bend since she'd gotten back, and she
had to go, even if she didn't want to.

Too many memories were there. It was where
Morgan had asked her to marry him. It was where
she'd said yes. It was there, on the banks of the
river, that they'd fallen in love.

Today, feeling lost and confused, her time on
the ranch almost up, she'd suddenly thought that
if God was going to give her answers, maybe she
would be able to hear Him at the river's bend. Or
at least maybe she would be able to think clearly.

Nearing the curve in the gravel road leading to

the river, she slowed her horse and rounded the corner at a slow trot.

Her heart stopped at what she saw. A log-and-stone house sat where she'd once dreamed of a having a home—and Morgan's truck was parked in the drive.

He'd never said a word.

Heart thudding, she slowly climbed from the saddle, tied up her horse and walked to the front door. It was beautiful, and looked hand-crafted. She ran her fingertips across the smooth surface, then, taking a fortifying breath, she knocked. Her heart pounded and her head was spinning with questions.

She'd never thought to ask where he lived. She'd never dreamed…

When there was no answer, she found herself walking around the beautiful house to the back—she had to see what it looked like. She halted when she saw the deck. It was exactly as she'd dreamed when she was seventeen—built on the edge of the steep hill with a beautiful view of the river below, and the setting sun. Morgan stood with his back to her, his elbows resting on the deck railing, a mug cupped between his hands.

Walking up the steps, she stopped on the last one.

"Morgan," she said, barely audible over the gentle sound of the river. It struck her then that she hadn't hyperventilated or freaked being close to the water. It had been part of her plan, coming here, hoping this would be the place she could make peace with her past—all of it. But she hadn't planned on finding this.

At the sound of his name Morgan straightened and swung around. "Jolie."

He took her breath away. He was the only man who'd ever made her feel the way she felt now, and the most handsome man she'd ever seen.

"You built our— A house. Here."

He set his mug on the railing. "I always said I was going to build a house here."

"Yes, you did." She stepped up onto the deck and walked past him to the railing. "It's still as beautiful as it ever was."

White foam rolled over the rocks at the river's curve. She braced her shoulders and forced herself to look at the rushing water curling over the rocks.

"Why?" she asked.

The question was simple. Why had he built this home, here, where they'd sat on the grass and dreamed young dreams together. Turning to him, she searched his guarded eyes.

"I built this house here because it wasn't just *our* dream, it was also *my* dream, Jolie. Just because you left didn't mean I had to stop dreaming. I wanted a house here on this spot and so I built it."

She crossed her arms, a conscious effort to shut out the pain this confrontation was causing. Was pain the only thing they had left to give each other?

"Y-you did a good job," she admitted, studying the house's lines. "It's a beautiful place."

He looked at a loss for words at her admission. "Thanks," he said curtly. "So why are you here?"

"I came to see the bend. To think…about things."

"You didn't know my home was here?"

She shook her head.

"It's a good place to think. That's what I do best out here."

Her stomach felt like it was turning upside down doing airscrews, which used to be her favorite kayak trick. She knew it was time to just lay her cards out on the table and come clean. "Morgan, I wish you'd give us a second chance."

"There is no us anymore."

Fire flamed inside of her. "You wouldn't know it from that kiss—"

"Not fair, Jolie. That was a mistake."

"I think you're afraid of us. I think you're just as afraid of letting me back in as I am of getting back in that water."

She expected him to deny it. He didn't.

"Maybe." His eyes were hard and as dark as a moonless night sky. "We've been over this."

"No. We've been over the fact that you won't

let me teach here because you think I need to go back to competing. What we haven't been over is that you won't open your heart to me and admit that you still love me."

She held her breath. Of all the brazen assumptions to make, she knew this could be the most presumptuous. When he said nothing, she somehow found the strength to continue.

"You think it's so easy to tell me to get back in that kayak and do what I love, yet you won't risk—"

"I don't have to risk anything, Jolie. I'm fine the way I am. You're not."

"You don't know what I am."

"Jolie, I've told you before and I'll tell you again. I will not give you a place to hide."

She started to tell him it wasn't his responsibility either way, that if she wanted to quit kayaking, that was her choice. But she couldn't have that conversation with him again—she just couldn't.

"Have you told the boys you won't be coming back?" he asked. "They need to know, and it needs to come from you."

"No, I haven't. I was hoping…" One look in his eyes told her there was no point in finishing that sentence.

"I'm not renewing your contract and that's final."

She stared at this man she loved, this man she

didn't understand. That was that; it was done. She'd done everything except beg and she wouldn't do that. Not that it would have done any good anyway.

"I'll tell them, Morgan." She turned and walked to the steps.

"I do love you, Jolie. Always have, always will. There just is no *us* anymore. You don't get to always make the rules. You don't get to just walk out when you want and then walk back in when you want."

She glanced over her shoulder, wishing—regretting. "You're right," she managed, then walked down the steps. What more was there to say other than asking if he'd ever thought about forgiving her—but he'd probably thought of that and rejected it. Asking him would feel like begging, and she just couldn't do it.

It was time to move on—yes, time to figure out a plan for her life and move forward.

This was over.

Morgan was elbow-deep in paperwork when Randolph walked into his office the next morning and laid a form on the desk.

"Jolie's official application."

"I told her I'd never hire her."

"She told me that when she dropped it off at the house yesterday morning. She said she still wanted to make it formal. She wants this application in her file."

"Why?" Morgan rubbed the bridge of his nose. She'd dropped the application off before she'd ridden out and discovered the house. And him. Before they'd talked yesterday evening. "I won't change my mind."

Exasperation lined his dad's brow. "I know you were hurt, son. I guess I can admit that after watching the two of you together these last few months, I'd hoped there might be a chance for reconciliation. But that won't happen if you aren't willing to take a chance. Son, let go of your pride if you love her and fight for this relationship."

Morgan pushed back from his desk and stood. "Do you think watching her go again is easy? Because it isn't. Dad, the *easiest* thing I could do would be to sign a new contract and let her stay. But I won't do that."

"Morgan, when your mother died, I didn't have a choice but to let the Lord have her. And I'll admit I was angry about that. Some people in this life get miracles—we didn't when it came to your mother. And when Jolie left you, it was one more time in your life when you didn't get the miracle. I hated that, son. But this time, you're getting the chance to have it. Now you just have to take it."

Morgan glared at his dad. "No." He couldn't be more plain than that.

"Then you may lose her forever. Are you really prepared for that? I think in the back of your mind you hoped she'd come back some day. That's why you built that house where you did, and that's why you haven't moved on and found someone else."

"What ever happened to 'when you love someone, let them go'?" His jaw jerked as he spat out the question.

His dad looked sad. "'If they love you, they'll return,'" Randolph said, finishing the quote for him. "What do you think is happening here, Morg?"

"The boys are going to need support after today," Morgan said, closing the door on the topic of him and Jolie, and moving on to what counted. "She's telling them she's leaving."

"They're resilient. They'll survive. It will be hard, though. They've bonded with Jolie like nothing I've ever seen."

"And that was what I was afraid of all along."

His dad pinned him with sharp eyes. "Morgan, you're harder than even I realized." Randolph turned and left Morgan to himself.

It had been all he could do not to go after Jolie yesterday when she'd left his home, telling himself one more time that this was for the best. If he gave her any kind of encouragement, she'd stay. And he would always be afraid—yes, he admitted to himself that he was afraid—that she would regret walking away from kayaking.

His dad believed Jolie coming home was a miracle, that all Morgan had to do was reach out and accept it. But Morgan was more afraid of seeing regret in her eyes down the road if she stayed.

And he was more afraid of that than losing her.

Miracle or no miracle, Jolie regretting coming back to him was the one thing he couldn't live with.

Chapter Twenty

Jolie knew it was time to tell the boys that she wouldn't be around next year. They needed time to adjust to the idea. And so did she.

So the last thing she was expecting was to walk into a classroom decorated for a party. There was a large sign that said "We love you, Jolie!" covering the projection screen. Colored ribbons from the storeroom dangled from the ceiling fans, whipping around as the two fans turned.

"Surprise!" the boys yelled when she entered, all smiles as they surrounded her.

"What's all this?" she asked, her hand on her heart as she looked around at her classroom. It was a sight she'd never forget.

The smaller boys were all talking excitedly. "Hold on, buckaroos," Joseph said, laughing as he calmed them down. When they quieted, he grinned his lopsided smile. "We wanted to make sure you knew how much we appreciate you being here, coming on at the last minute to take on a bunch of ragtags like us. You didn't have to do it but you did."

"Yeah," Wes said, looking a little worried. "It's good to be appreciated. We just wanted you to know."

Jolie bit her lip, tears brimming in her eyes. She sucked in a hard breath. "Thanks," she croaked like a frog. "You have no idea what this means to me."

That had all the boys beaming. They looked so proud that her heart clutched in her chest and she had to close her eyes.

"This is the sweetest thing anyone has ever done for me. And I mean that. And you are not ragtags. You are the kind of kids a woman could call her own—and I do. I want you to know that."

Their smiles faded, and she knew they could hear the sadness in her voice.

"I need you to sit down. I have to tell you something."

"Not that you're going to leave," Sammy blurted out, panic in his eyes.

Jolie hated this. He'd recently lost his family and now he'd formed an attachment to her and *she* was leaving. What would that do to him?

"Yes, I am. I have to. I'm sorry. Listen, Sammy, everyone, there are just some things that can't be changed. But my leaving has nothing to do with all of you. I have loved every minute of my time here since the first day I hopped out of my Jeep and saw you standing there. I love all of you."

Wes and Joseph looked down at the floor, not meeting her gaze.

Dear Lord, help me.

"If you loved us, you would stay." Sammy's brown eyes held unshed tears, his chin trembled and his voice was a faint whisper.

Jolie went to her knees in front of him. "I can't stay."

"Why not?"

How could she tell them Morgan hadn't renewed her contract? They would resent him, and that would be terrible because they had to have a good relationship with him. She had to preserve that no matter what.

What Morgan was doing, he was doing out of a misplaced concern. At least that was the assumption that was getting her through this.

Morgan was trying to do what was right for her.

The realization slammed into her as she looked into Sammy's dear face. This wasn't about not forgiving her…it was about doing what he believed was right. Jolie's heart raced at the realization.

Trying to grasp this new information she continued, "This was always a temporary position. You knew that, Sammy. All of you did. As much as I love being here, I have commitments that I have to keep."

And it was true, she did. Morgan had been right about that.

But you can come back...?

The words whispered through her. She heard a horn honk outside and she smiled. "It's going to be all right, guys. I promise. Sammy, it will be okay. Don't be afraid. Okay?"

He nodded. "Okay."

She hugged him tightly, then stood. "I didn't know y'all were fixin' things up for a party—it goes to show you great minds think alike because I was planning on having one myself. If I'm right, that horn is Ms. Jo and Mabel out there with a truckload of homemade pies. I ordered them for an end-of-term celebration."

"Awesome." Wes jumped up and headed to the door. "I'll help bring them in."

Jolie chuckled. "Y'all have worked so hard, you deserve it."

Ms. Jo's pies could make anyone smile, and she sure hoped it was true today as she watched the kids race outside to help, including Sammy after she'd urged him.

Glancing around the decorated room filled her with determination. No way could she just walk away. There had to be another alternative. And she planned to find it.

* * *

"What do you mean you can't do anything about it?" Ms. Jo demanded a few hours later after Jolie let the kids head out early for the day. She'd managed to turn the day around somewhat, though Sammy had remained quiet. He'd participated but kept asking her questions that told her he was still worrying. She just prayed that time would help.

"Yes, who does Morgan think he is making you leave if you don't want to?" Mabel snorted. "I tell you what, I was miffed at you for what you did to him, but now I'm equally miffed at Morgan. That man needs a knock upside the head, if you ask me."

"Whoa, there, aren't you two the ones who were telling me not to get any ideas? To just be friends?"

"Well," Ms. Jo snapped, "what else were we supposed to say? We didn't want him to get hurt any more than he already had been. We were just trying to be cautious."

"That being said," Mabel added, swiping another forkful of leftover coconut pie, "I agree with Jo. Who is he to tell you you have to leave?"

"He's the guy holding the teaching contract."

Ms. Jo and Mabel gaped at her.

"What?" she asked, bewildered.

Ms. Jo glared at her with impatience. "Who

says just because you don't work at Sunrise that you have to leave Dew Drop?"

The door crashed open before Jolie fully processed Ms. Jo's declaration, and Caleb rushed into the room. "Jolie, come quick. We can't find Sammy. He ran away!"

Some of the boys had stopped by the office and told Morgan Sammy was missing, so he was already on the phone with Tucker when Jolie and Caleb came racing out of the schoolhouse, Ms. Jo and Mabel hotfooting it behind them. They all hurried toward him across the pasture.

Tucker had told him that he'd be there in a few minutes. Morgan had never been happier that his big brother was the sheriff of Dew Drop County. And Rowdy and Chet were on their way with their group, too.

"Caleb said there was a note," Jolie gasped, grabbing his arm as she arrived.

He handed her the note, and his gut clenched watching Jolie, her eyes glistening while she read the words Sammy had painstakingly printed out on a piece of white notebook paper.

Jolie, I'm going to make you proud enough of me that you won't leave.

"What does this mean?" She blinked hard, fighting off tears.

"I'm not sure. He's got a plan, it sounds like.

We'll find him," Morgan assured her. "Tucker and Rowdy and the men are on the way. Dad, Pepper, Wes and Joseph are already out there on the roads leading out from the ranch."

She bit her lip. "Okay. We'll find him," she said as if to herself.

Clare and John, Sammy's house parents, hurried from the chow hall with Nana, clearly worried.

"He's crazy about you," Clare said, squeezing Jolie's arm. "He's just come alive since you showed up. Well, all the boys have, actually. They were devastated that you're leaving. But this…" Her words trailed off and she dabbed at tears.

"Leaving, that's the stupidest thing I've ever heard," Ms. Jo snapped, shooting Morgan a stern look as she and Mabel joined Nana in giving Clare some comfort.

Morgan tried not to think about his part in this—not right now. Now he had to hold everyone together and find Sammy. His gaze locked on Jolie. "We'll get a search up once Tucker gets here. We'll find him," Morgan told her again, wanting to give her a hug and ease the alarm in her eyes. But Jolie crossed her arms and nodded once, as if to block him out.

He couldn't say he blamed her.

Jolie fought to stay in control as the sound of Tucker's siren in the far-off distance signaled they would soon be taking action. But it wasn't happening fast enough for her. She needed to do something soon or she'd go crazy.

"Caleb," she said. "Who was the last to see Sammy?"

"Me. We were going to play in the hay barn, but he said he had to do something, so I went with Tony instead. We decided to go see what he was doing and found the note on his bed."

Tony piped in. "We took it down to Ms. Clare right when we found it."

"Do you guys have any idea where he might have gone?"

They all shook their heads. Jolie felt helpless as Tucker's SUV pulled into the yard and came to a quick halt. Turning off the lights and siren, he stepped from the vehicle and strode their way. Even though his aviation shades hid his eyes, the hard set of his jaw said he was taking this seriously.

"Tucker, glad you're here," Morgan said, looking just as grim as his brother.

"Any word?" Tucker asked, pulling his shades off, looking from Morgan to Jolie.

"None so far," Morgan answered.

Jolie wrapped her arms around herself. "Tucker, if he's walking off the property, the guys would have found him by now. A little kid like him couldn't have gotten far on foot in less than an hour."

"True. We'll start searching the ranch. But we need some facts first."

"These three were the last to see him." Morgan placed an arm around Caleb's shoulders. Jolie found herself wishing his arm were around her instead. "They came straight to us when they found the note."

"Do you have it?"

"I do." Jolie thrust it at him, anxious for his trained eye to see it. She watched as he read it, meeting Morgan's gaze for a brief moment. "Any hints in there that we're missing?"

"Sounds like he has something to prove. Any thoughts about that?"

"He's been better about being scared," Caleb said.

Just then, Randolph drove up with Joseph and Wes from scouting the roads. Randolph shook his head as he strode toward the crowd. He, Morgan and Tucker went off and had a discussion, and Nana came and put her arm around Jolie.

Within minutes cars began to arrive full of folks from town, like Chili and Drewbaker. Walter Pepper and the other ranch hands came soon after, having had no luck searching the immediate area. More law enforcement with a team of search dogs was on the way. Within the hour they had a full-blown search going.

Jolie had been going over her conversation with Sammy from that morning, and the note he'd left. Her gut was trying to tell her something…he'd asked her where she was trying to kayak and she'd told him about the trail behind her house that led down to the river where she had been going to picture herself getting in the water. She'd confessed that she hadn't been able to get in so far though. Surely he wasn't trying to prove—Jolie halted in her tracks.

Proud enough of me that you won't leave.

Spinning around Jolie searched for Morgan. He was getting on his horse on the other side of the pasture, about to start a mounted search. Racing toward him, Jolie had never been so happy to be in shape in all of her life. He spotted her and rode out to meet her.

"What's up, Jolie?" he asked as he brought his horse to a halt.

"I think he might be at the river behind my house. I think he's going to kayak."

"Seriously?"

Jolie nodded. "He wants to make me proud. Maybe he thinks if he can do what I can't, I won't leave."

Morgan's brows knitted beneath his straw Stetson. He held a hand out to her and pulled his boot from the stirrup. "Come on, let's go check it out."

Jolie didn't waste time. She reached for his hand, rammed her boot in the stirrup and let him hoist her up behind him. They were heading toward her house almost before she got her arms around his waist. Jolie clung to Morgan, her heart racing with hope as they galloped across the pasture.

"You sure you can face this? Do I need to get someone else to help me?" he asked over his shoulder.

"I'll handle it," she said with no hesitation. If they found Sammy in that river current—she prayed he hadn't done such a foolish thing, but if he had—he would need her. "I'm the best person for this."

"That's my girl," Morgan said. His words dug deep—it had been a long time since she'd been his girl. A long, long time.

Too long.

This wasn't the time to think about the past between them, but as they rode, memories crowded in alongside the worry for Sammy. Like a kaleidoscope of past, present and a future yet untold, everything shifted in and out of focus, bringing new images to her mind's eye.

When they made it to the cabin, Jolie's heart stopped as she looked at the spot where her kayaks sat. "My yellow kayak is missing," she said grimly. "He's out there, Morgan."

"Looks that way," Morgan said.

"I need to grab my gear." She jumped from the horse, raced inside the house and grabbed her backpack from where it rested in the corner, forgotten. Inside it was her kayaking gear, and her rescue ropes. Outside again, she went straight for one of her other kayaks, hoisted it to her shoulder and without waiting for Morgan she hurried to her Jeep and stowed it across the backseat, not bothering to attach it to the roof rack.

Morgan helped straighten it and then hopped in as she cranked the key and rammed the gearshift. "Hang on," she warned, and punched the gas. Wheeling through the backyard and onto the faint trail, she cut through to the clearing.

When they hit the steep hill, the Jeep's wheels left land for a moment as they surged forward, soared through the air and hit hard before racing downhill.

They didn't say much as they scanned the land while they drove, hoping to find Sammy before he made it to the water.

How long had he been gone?

When they made it to the trail that led to the water, Jolie jerked the Jeep to a halt and grabbed her kayak.

"I can carry that for you," Morgan offered.

She shook her head. "I always carry my own load."

It was part of the sport—her kayak was as much a part of her as her arms. "It's okay," she assured Morgan over her shoulder. "Thanks for the offer."

She jogged down the path where she'd had her meltdown that day that had ended in the kiss she couldn't forget. Morgan didn't ask her if she was all right again—he just jogged beside her and kept up. They topped the hill, bending down to miss a couple of low-slung tree limbs. She could hear the river now, the rush of rapids downstream from where they would put in. It was an ominous sound to Jolie. Her heartbeat became erratic and her skin clammy.

Thinking of Sammy, she never slowed down, refusing to give in. She was going in if Sammy needed her. No question about it.

Bursting through the last of the trees she headed straight down the embankment, scanning the water anxiously. And praying hard.

Her heart stopped. "There!" she shouted, spotting him on the far side of the river clinging to a tree branch, just past the first set of rapids.

Instead of holding him under, the vortex had spat him out when he'd slipped out of his kayak. She thanked God for that.

And for giving her a window of opportunity to get to him.

But there was no way to get down the rocks to Sammy. Going through the rapids was the only way.

She'd have to hold the kayak in control while maneuvering to him. And once she had him, they'd have to make it through the worst rapids together in a one-man kayak.

"You can do this, Jolie." Morgan's penetrating eyes told her he had faith in her. Even having seen what a basket case she'd been, he had faith.

Her head was swimming. "You better get downstream and be ready in case you have to grab him," she advised as she started moving again. Morgan would know the spot she meant— it would be his only shot to grab Sammy if she missed, or if Sammy lost his grip on the tree before she got to him. If they both missed, the river would sweep him into the worst section of the rapids. His only chance then would be in God's hands.

Jolie prayed.

Glancing over her shoulder she saw Morgan racing down the path. He'd be standing between two large rocks in a shallow section that had a slippery fast current, just bypassing a pool of calm water to the right, perfect for a takeout.

At the water's edge, Jolie fought her demons,

thinking only of Sammy. She was in the kayak within seconds—no hesitation, paddle in hand and moving. She found her line in the water quickly and set herself up to hit the rapid perfectly. She took the first set with no problem, a warm-up for what was to come.

Keeping her line, she set herself up for the second set of rapids, this one was the money spot, as they called it in competition, the one that counted...

This one's for Sammy.

The water was cold as it washed over her, the current swift, strong from the rain they'd had up north two days earlier. She prayed God would keep Sammy's strength up, and thanked Him for giving her the ability to do what needed to be done to save him.

She took the rapid, a mad vortex of powerful, churning water with the means to pull a person down and not spit her out until it felt like it. She wished for her yellow banana—her old friend—but this kayak would have to do.

She cut through the rocks with skill honed from hard work and God's gift...and then she maneuvered a perfect roll, dipping head-first beneath the surface then rolling out and flipping the kayak into the air. The move required strength as she twisted her body, forcing the kayak to alter its course. She landed it perfectly and with a swift push of her paddle was right next to Sammy beneath the tree.

Jolie held the boat still with the paddle against the rocks behind him. She reached with her free arm, muscles burning from the effort, and she got him. His eyes were huge, glazed with fear, his lips purple from the chill.

"Y-you came for me," he gasped, clinging to the limb.

"I'll *always* come for you," she declared, voice hoarse with emotion, knowing it was true. "Let go of the tree," she urged against the roar of the water. Thankfully, Sammy was thinking clearly enough to respond with a nod and do as he was asked. He took her hand and she pulled him toward the boat. It was hard to do, since she was having to use the paddle to hold the boat steady and keep them out of the current. If she wasn't careful she could be swept away from him. "You have to climb up by yourself, Sammy, okay? I can hold you steady, but you have to climb on your own."

There was no place for him except on top of the kayak in front of her, with his feet on the stern. This wasn't a normal situation—it was a tricky balancing act. God's hand and His alone steadied the boat as she held off the current with one hand on the paddle. She felt her strength waning—she knew she wasn't going to last much longer.

"When you get up, lean back against me, hold on to the deck line and keep your feet on the kayak in front of you. Can you do that?"

"Y-yes, I can." Even though his teeth were chattering, there was power in his voice now. Jolie was so proud of Sammy as he scrambled up the kayak and eased into place.

"We're going to make it," she told him as he leaned against her. "Hold on, buddy, here we go," she said, and let the current have them, sweeping them back into the dangerous flow.

Chapter Twenty-One

Morgan prayed harder than he ever had in his whole life as he watched the rescue. Jolie was amazing—her strength and skill awed him as she held it all together and came through the last set of rapids with Sammy in front of her. Once it was clear they'd make the trip without flipping, he moved to the calm pool where he knew she was headed.

Morgan steadied the kayak, then took Sammy into his arms. The boy looked slightly dazed as Morgan hugged him hard, thanking God. "You're okay, little man," he said, looking into his tense face. Limp as a rag, Sammy nodded and rested his head against Morgan's heart. Jolie climbed from her kayak, her exhaustion evident in the way she moved.

"We need to get him to a doctor," she said, hoisting her kayak to the shore and leaving it behind as she assisted Morgan in getting Sammy up the steep incline to the path.

"I got them on my cell. An ambulance should be getting to the woods' edge soon."

Hurrying along the path, Morgan kept talking to Sammy as Jolie held branches out of their way. Sammy looked up at him, his eyes bright with tears. "I didn't mean to mess up. I tried to make y'all proud of me. I tried to make Jolie see that I could help her in the water so she would stay. You won't send me away now, will you?"

Morgan held him closer, and kept his pace. "Never. You're going to be fine, Sammy. We're not sending you anywhere—you are part of our family."

Jolie placed her hand on Sammy's head as they continued to hurry along the path. "I was scared for you, Sammy, but God kept you safe out there today. You're going to be all right. I'm crazy about you, don't you know that?"

And Morgan was crazy about *her*. Hearing her say those words to Sammy made his heart stop in his chest. It was going to be almost impossible to let her go.

She'd proven she could get back in the water, and she could do it with style. Jolie belonged out there—it was evident to anyone who saw her in action. After today, he had no doubt.

Sammy obviously didn't want to see her go any more than Morgan did.

But they would have to let her.

They were just coming out of the woods when the emergency vehicles came across the pasture with Tucker in the lead. It was like the cavalry was coming. Morgan had never been happier to see his brother in all his life.

Sammy had been through a harrowing experience and it was a miracle he'd survived long enough for Jolie to get to him. It was God who had held Sammy to that tree, no doubt about it. And it was God who was going to have to give Sammy—and Morgan—the strength to see her leave.

A few hours later, Jolie held a cup of coffee in her hands, letting the warmth sink into her bones. She wasn't sure the chill would ever leave her. Sitting on a bench on the porch of the chow hall, she watched the boys laughing and playing a game of football in the yard. Morgan and his dad and brothers were sitting together at the picnic table, talking to various people from town who'd come out to help with the rescue and then stayed to celebrate. Sammy sat on the bench between Morgan and Tucker, looking a little stunned that so many people had come to make sure he was safe.

Nana, Ms. Jo and Mabel were hustling around

making sure everyone had something to eat and drink. Everyone was so relieved that Sammy was safe that the rescue party had turned into a regular party.

Jolie's role as the hero was making her uncomfortable. She'd had to repeat to Tucker what she'd done, then defer to Morgan. Morgan had a version of the tale that was so full of praise she couldn't listen, but his version pleased everyone more than her clinical retelling of events had.

"I gotta say one thing," Edwina said, stopping beside Jolie, topping off her cup of coffee without bothering to ask. "You got some nerves of steel, Jolie. You done good savin' that boy. You know I ain't never made it no secret that I ain't got a lick of use for men. But Morgan's got himself some good qualities aside from bein' drop-dead gorgeous—yeah, I do have eyes." She gave Jolie a grin. "But truly, you could do a whole lot worse—believe me, if you were to meet Lester or Darin or even Marv—any of that bunch of losers I married—you'd have a clue how much worse it could *get*."

Jolie smiled, chuckling. Edwina had not been lucky in love.

"There you go. If my love life won't pull a chuckle out of you, nothing will. But honestly, maybe you need to rethink this leavin' thing. If that man looked at me the way he looks at you,

I might be tempted to dip my toe back into the matrimonial waters. Somethin' to think about." She winked and was gone, off to spread her cheer elsewhere.

If she only knew that this time, it wasn't Jolie who'd chosen a different life. It was Morgan.

Jolie looked over at Sammy, who had stayed away from her since they'd made it back to the ranch, sticking close to Morgan's side. It was as if he needed to shut her out.

And she hated it.

But there was a huge positive here—Sammy had come so far. He wasn't lying anymore, and he'd taken a risk today. However misguided his actions had been, he'd left his fears behind and tried to be strong. Jolie knew she'd had a part in his growth. Looking at him now, she was filled with pride of accomplishment like nothing she'd ever felt on the river.

Jolie had no doubts now about what she was going to do with the rest of her life. What she didn't know was how Morgan was going to handle it.

He thought he'd figured out the rest of her life for her.

But he was wrong.

Standing, she dropped the blanket on the bench and walked over to where he sat. "Morgan, may I speak to you?"

When he looked up at her and saw her serious expression, elation slid off his face and his eyes darkened.

"Sure."

Jolie led them away from the crowd, to the quiet of the stables. The smell of hay and feed greeted her, and from the cool shadows she heard the soft nicker of newborn colts. She slowly turned and faced an unsmiling Morgan.

"I'm staying, Morgan. I'm retiring from competition," she said quietly. "I know where you stand on all this, but I know what I want, and I know what's best for me."

"Jolie, I saw you out there today. You were magnificent. To leave that beauty and skill behind would be a waste. You are meant for great things."

She smiled. "Yes, I am. And so are you. Here on this ranch is where the great things happen. Watching these boys flourish, and loving them. This is the great thing I'm meant for now. This is what I choose." She studied his face as he stared down at her. "I'd like your blessing, Morgan, but I don't need it. My plan is to move to Dew Drop and get a teaching job at the public school, and volunteer on the ranch, if you'll have me."

Morgan had grown still. His jaw jerked and his eyes cut through her, searching for the truth. "I don't know what to say," he said. "I know for me the boys are enough. At least, it satisfies me. But you're going to regret—"

"I already regret, Morgan. I regret leaving you. I regret hurting you. Yet I know that God had a plan back then and it was meant to be. And now I know *this* is meant to be. So I'm here to stay, and I'm praying that at some point you will trust my love for you and let me into your heart again."

She stepped close to him and placed her hand on his heart. It was racing.

"I love you, Morgan McDermott, and you love me. You told me so. Can you let me back into your life?"

He didn't say anything, and her heart sank. She'd hoped if he knew she wasn't leaving it would change his mind. But as she stepped away from him, she knew her plan wasn't going to change one bit. Dew Drop was where she was supposed to be.

"I hope one day you'll be able to accept my being here, Morgan, and even let me help out with the boys. It would mean a lot to me." Jolie turned, not knowing what else to say. She'd made it to the double doors of the stable when his hand on her arm halted her.

"Jolie."

She faced him, framed in the doorway with the soft breeze in her hair. She knew she must look a sight after all they'd been through on the water, but she didn't care.

"Don't you know it would be easy to agree? The hard part is to let you go. I hope you understand that."

She lifted her hand to cup his strong jaw. "I do," she whispered, nodding. "I truly do. But this is where I *want* to be. Where I need to be. With you. And the boys. And no regrets. None."

She could see the war in his eyes, his beautiful, deep, fathomless eyes. His forehead crinkled and his jaw tensed as he struggled with the right thing to do. The right thing to do by *her*.

"You have to trust that what I say is true, Morgan. I love you, and if you open your heart to me I will never, ever leave you. Please trust me."

He nodded ever so slightly. His eyes calmed and a slow smile eased across his face as he turned his head to kiss her palm. His hand came up and took hers, and Jolie's heart cracked open with love. And hope.

No words were needed as his arms came around her and his lips met hers. "I love you, Jolie Sheridan. Will you marry me?" he whispered.

With tears in her eyes, she nodded. And behind them, whoops, cheers and clapping erupted.

"Well—" Morgan chuckled "—it's a done deal now. You're stuck with us. Because I'm not telling *them* any different."

Jolie looked across the grass to her boys. "Good. This is my *family,* and I'm not going anywhere."

Squeezing her hand tightly in his, Morgan looked at her with love in his eyes. "Then let's go make it official."

She smiled, her heart in full bloom. "Lead the way, cowboy. Lead the way."

Epilogue

"Hubba, hubba, come to papa," Wes croaked from the front pew where all sixteen boys were standing in the church.

Morgan would have gone over and thumped him on the ear if he hadn't been standing beside the preacher and thinking a more polite version of the same thing as Jolie entered the sanctuary on the arm of her dad. She was so beautiful that he could do nothing but hold her gaze and watch her walk down the aisle toward him. He'd been waiting six long years for this day.

After she'd convinced him that she wanted a life on the ranch with him and the boys, they'd wasted no time setting the date. Jolie had wanted to get married immediately, but they'd given themselves a month.

It was a cold day in January, with a fine layer of snow on the ground and the wind rattling the church windows. He'd hoped for a sunny day for Jolie, but she'd said even a blizzard wouldn't keep her from becoming Mrs. Morgan McDermott.

For Morgan, the sun had come out the moment Jolie said yes. He'd gotten down on his knees in front of the boys so they could see how it should be done. She'd laughingly agreed, and her laughter had filled every space in his heart.

He thanked God for bringing her back to him in *His* time. Morgan recognized that Jolie had needed the time away, and even though he wasn't real high on thinkin' it, he'd needed the time she was away, too. Although he'd loved her, he'd tried to corral her when what she'd needed was space to find her way and become her own person.

Now she could live life with him on the ranch with her whole heart and no regrets.

"She looks like a fairy princess," B.J. whispered so loudly the whole church heard him.

Morgan had to agree. To get a good view of her coming up the aisle, the two boys had moved over to peek around Wes, who was standing on the end.

Her long, white dress was soft and kind of sparkly as it moved about her. She practically looked like she was floating. Her eyes were shining with happiness and locked to his as the space slowly disappeared between them. Her lips trembled with a soft smile.

"She *is* a fairy princess," Sammy said, puffing his chest out. "She's ours and she's here to stay."

Joseph had moved up behind them. "Yes, she is, boys," he said quietly. "Now let's move on back to our seats and let the preacher marry her up with Morgan."

Beside Morgan, his best men—Rowdy and Tucker—chuckled.

"That'd be a good idea," Rowdy murmured low. "Because Morg here has been waitin' his whole life for this moment."

"You're up next, Rowdy, my man," Morgan heard Tucker tease their little brother.

"Me? Nope, that'd be you, big brother."

Morgan met his dad's steady gaze from the front row and they shared a moment, both thinking it would be interesting to see which one would be next.

The piano drew to a halt as Jolie and her father stopped in front of him.

"Who gives this woman?" the preacher asked.

"Her mother and I," Mr. Sheridan said, and placed Jolie's hand in Morgan's.

Jolie smiled that hundred-watts-of-pure-joy smile of hers, aiming it straight at him as she squeezed his hand, their eyes locked on each other. "I love you," she whispered, and as one they turned toward the preacher.

"This is gonna be *goooood,*" Sammy whispered.

"It already is," Caleb hissed.

"We got her for always now," B.J. said, his voice loud and clear, making the congregation chuckle.

Jolie turned and shared that killer smile of hers with the boys. "And I've got y'all," she assured them.

Morgan chuckled and cleared his throat. "Preacher, the floor is officially yours. Let's get rollin' so I can put a ring on her finger."

"At last," Rowdy said with a chuckle.

Morgan shot him a warning look—he hadn't forgotten that payback was owed to his little brother. And he was a patient man.

Jolie turned back to the preacher and nodded. "Okay," she said. "Make me the happiest woman in the world."

"Finally," Morgan grunted. Laughter rumbled behind them as the preacher proceeded to make Morgan the happiest man in the world. At last.

* * * * *

If you enjoyed this story by Debra Clopton,
be sure to look for the other
Love Inspired books out this month!

Dear Reader,

Thank you for joining me at Sunrise Ranch deep in the heart of West Texas. I have to say that I loved creating this new bunch of characters. As you can tell from reading this book, I wanted to keep you on your toes with them, so that you'll never know what to expect when you visit the ranch or the small town of Dew Drop and the Spotted Cow Café.

Just like my Mule Hollow series, I love never knowing what my characters are going to do next. So I'm busy working on the second story and having fun seeing what mischief everyone is getting into…stay tuned!

I so enjoyed telling Morgan and Jolie's story, and I hope you are looking forward to watching the other two McDermott brothers meet their matches later in the year.

The theme verse of this book, John 14:18, is one of my favorite of God's promises: I will not leave you comfortless—I will come to you.

I loved using the theme of comfort in this book. Sammy needed comfort, and Jolie and Morgan were there for him, helping him through his grief. Jolie needed comforting, and so did Morgan. For all of them, God was the ultimate comforter, and He put them all in place to comfort each other.

I pray that if you need comfort today, you'll bow your head and talk it over with God. He is there to comfort you, too.

Until next time, live, laugh and seek God with all your hearts!

Debra Clopton

Questions for Discussion

1. Morgan's mother's vision for creating the foster program at Sunrise Ranch was to share the beauty and blessing of this West Texas ranch with less fortunate boys who had no place to call home. How did Morgan feel about his mother's dream? What are his plans for the future?

2. Why did Randolph McDermott hire Jolie Sheridan when she'd hurt his son, Morgan, so badly?

3. Despite what he is feeling when he learns what his father has done, Morgan is determined to be a good role model for the boys of the ranch. What does this say about him as a man?

4. Why do the boys of the ranch react in such a heartfelt and wistful manner when they watch the mother horse care for her newborn?

5. Jolie has regrets despite the fabulous life she has lived and the adventure and success she has known. She is torn between two worlds—the one she chose and the one she left behind. Have you ever felt torn between two choices?

Did you pray for God's guidance in making the right choice?

6. How do Ms. Jo and Mabel react to Jolie's return to town? They love Jolie and Morgan and are not even thinking of matchmaking. Why?

7. Sammy is certain his family is going to come back and get him. Even in his time of need and distress, when his parents abandoned him, God was taking care of Sammy. What did God do for Sammy?

8. Putting his personal reasons for not wanting Jolie at the ranch aside, what is the main reason Morgan thinks her teaching the boys is a bad idea?

9. Jolie realizes, as she and Morgan have their first battle of wills outside the classroom under the oak tree, that God has given her a purpose in coming back to the ranch. She realizes she can help the boys. How does this make her feel?

10. When Morgan realizes he still loves Jolie and that she is afraid of the water, what is his reaction? What does he contemplate doing? Are you glad that he makes the choice to help her? Why?

11. Jolie is terrified of the water, and the night-mares haunt her. She is struggling and asking God to help her, but it isn't an overnight fix. Sometimes in order for God to help us, it takes time. Have you ever had to have patience while you waited for God to act?

12. When Sammy needs her, does Jolie hesitate? What does she do?

13. Why is helping Jolie get back into the water an act of love and sacrifice on Morgan's part?

14. Jolie is forced to take a stand when it comes to choosing to leave or stay. What does she realize when she has to make the choice on her own without Morgan's help?

15. Sammy thought if he was good, Jolie would stay. Like Morgan knew in the beginning of the book, he needed stability and commitment in his life, as did all the boys. When Jolie makes up her mind to stay, it's about more than her love for Morgan. It's about finding her purpose in life—what is that? Sometimes it takes a while to realize our purpose. Do you believe that God has a purpose for each of us? Have you asked God to help you find your purpose?

LARGER-PRINT BOOKS!

GET 2 FREE LARGER-PRINT NOVELS PLUS 2 FREE MYSTERY GIFTS

Love Inspired

Larger-print novels are now available...

YES! Please send me 2 FREE LARGER-PRINT Love Inspired® novels and my 2 FREE mystery gifts (gifts are worth about $10). After receiving them, if I don't wish to receive any more books, I can return the shipping statement marked "cancel." If I don't cancel, I will receive 6 brand-new novels every month and be billed just $5.24 per book in the U.S. or $5.74 per book in Canada. That's a savings of at least 23% off the cover price. It's quite a bargain! Shipping and handling is just 50¢ per book in the U.S. and 75¢ per book in Canada.* I understand that accepting the 2 free books and gifts places me under no obligation to buy anything. I can always return a shipment and cancel at any time. Even if I never buy another book, the two free books and gifts are mine to keep forever.

122/322 IDN F49Y

Name	(PLEASE PRINT)	
Address		Apt. #
City	State/Prov.	Zip/Postal Code

Signature (if under 18, a parent or guardian must sign)

Mail to the **Harlequin® Reader Service:**
IN U.S.A.: P.O. Box 1867, Buffalo, NY 14240-1867
IN CANADA: P.O. Box 609, Fort Erie, Ontario L2A 5X3

Are you a current subscriber to Love Inspired books and want to receive the larger-print edition?
Call 1-800-873-8635 or visit www.ReaderService.com.

* Terms and prices subject to change without notice. Prices do not include applicable taxes. Sales tax applicable in N.Y. Canadian residents will be charged applicable taxes. Offer not valid in Quebec. This offer is limited to one order per household. Not valid for current subscribers to Love Inspired Larger-Print books. All orders subject to credit approval. Credit or debit balances in a customer's account(s) may be offset by any other outstanding balance owed by or to the customer. Please allow 4 to 6 weeks for delivery. Offer available while quantities last.

Your Privacy—The Harlequin® Reader Service is committed to protecting your privacy. Our Privacy Policy is available online at www.ReaderService.com or upon request from the Harlequin Reader Service.

We make a portion of our mailing list available to reputable third parties that offer products we believe may interest you. If you prefer that we not exchange your name with third parties, or if you wish to clarify or modify your communication preferences, please visit us at www.ReaderService.com/consumerchoice or write to us at Harlequin Reader Service Preference Service, P.O. Box 9062, Buffalo, NY 14269. Include your complete name and address.

LILPDIR13R

LARGER-PRINT BOOKS!

GET 2 FREE LARGER-PRINT NOVELS PLUS 2 FREE MYSTERY GIFTS

Love Inspired® SUSPENSE
RIVETING INSPIRATIONAL ROMANCE

Larger-print novels are now available...

YES! Please send me 2 FREE LARGER-PRINT Love Inspired® Suspense novels and my 2 FREE mystery gifts (gifts are worth about $10). After receiving them, if I don't wish to receive any more books, I can return the shipping statement marked "cancel." If I don't cancel, I will receive 4 brand-new novels every month and be billed just $5.24 per book in the U.S. or $5.74 per book in Canada. That's a savings of at least 23% off the cover price. It's quite a bargain! Shipping and handling is just 50¢ per book in the U.S. and 75¢ per book in Canada.* I understand that accepting the 2 free books and gifts places me under no obligation to buy anything. I can always return a shipment and cancel at any time. Even if I never buy another book, the two free books and gifts are mine to keep forever.

110/310 IDN F5CC

Name	(PLEASE PRINT)	
Address		Apt. #
City	State/Prov.	Zip/Postal Code

Signature (if under 18, a parent or guardian must sign)

Mail to the Harlequin® Reader Service:
IN U.S.A.: P.O. Box 1867, Buffalo, NY 14240-1867
IN CANADA: P.O. Box 609, Fort Erie, Ontario L2A 5X3

Are you a current subscriber to Love Inspired Suspense books and want to receive the larger-print edition?
Call 1-800-873-8635 or visit www.ReaderService.com.

* Terms and prices subject to change without notice. Prices do not include applicable taxes. Sales tax applicable in N.Y. Canadian residents will be charged applicable taxes. Offer not valid in Quebec. This offer is limited to one order per household. Not valid for current subscribers to Love Inspired Suspense larger-print books. All orders subject to credit approval. Credit or debit balances in a customer's account(s) may be offset by any other outstanding balance owed by or to the customer. Please allow 4 to 6 weeks for delivery. Offer available while quantities last.

Your Privacy—The Harlequin® Reader Service is committed to protecting your privacy. Our Privacy Policy is available online at www.ReaderService.com or upon request from the Harlequin Reader Service.

We make a portion of our mailing list available to reputable third parties that offer products we believe may interest you. If you prefer that we not exchange your name with third parties, or if you wish to clarify or modify your communication preferences, please visit us at www.ReaderService.com/consumerchoice or write to us at Harlequin Reader Service Preference Service, P.O. Box 9062, Buffalo, NY 14269. Include your complete name and address.

LISLPDIR13R

ReaderService.com

Manage your account online!

- Review your order history
- Manage your payments
- Update your address

We've designed the Harlequin® Reader Service website just for you.

Enjoy all the features!

- Reader excerpts from any series
- Respond to mailings and special monthly offers
- Discover new series available to you
- Browse the Bonus Bucks catalog
- Share your feedback

Visit us at:

ReaderService.com

"GODDESS, WHY DON'T YOU LISTEN? HAVEN'T YOU KILLED ENOUGH?"

"Enough? What is 'enough?'" the Warlord said. "What payment for your evil? I tell you 'enough' is not yet, will not be until all are dead!"

The two Meiglans glanced at each other, well and truly frightened now.

"I will tell you how it was," the Warlord continued in a low, lethal voice. "Islands under swords, warriors killed, women raped, children dead. Herds slaughtered so people starved. Crops burned, so people starved. Fishingboats sunk, so people starved. For a hundred thousands of days, we remember. For such evil, no numbers of killings can be enough."

The two women traded looks, and one of them said, "I don't know what you're talking about. A hundred thousand days?"

"Your evil! Yours! No peace until you starve and die as we did! Until the *Azhrei* and all his lands and people starve and die!"

"That's insane! You can't mean this war is because of something that happened almost three hundred years ago, that we had nothing to do with!"

He whispered to her, their faces a breath apart, "You forgot us. But we remember. Your evil. Your magic. Our deaths. A hundred thousands of days. You do not remember. But you will. Before he dies, the *Azhrei* will know. Before I kill him and his evil magic for the Dragon, he will know. He will speak all lost names before I slice out his *faradhi* tongue, and he will see the truth before I carve out his Goddess-green, Goddess-blue eyes. . . ."

DAW Books Presents
the finest in Fantasy by
MELANIE RAWN

*Forthcoming in hardcover from DAW Books

DRAGON STAR: BOOK III

SKYBOWL

MELANIE RAWN

DAW BOOKS, INC.
DONALD A. WOLLHEIM, FOUNDER
375 Hudson Street, New York, NY 10014

ELIZABETH R. WOLLHEIM
SHEILA E. GILBERT
PUBLISHERS

First Paperback Printing, March 1994

19   18   17   16   15   14   13   12

DAW TRADEMARK REGISTERED
U.S. PAT OFF. AND FOREIGN COUNTRIES
—MARCA REGISTRADA
HECHO EN U.S.A.

PRINTED IN THE U.S.A.

For
Sharon Jarvis,
Sheila Gilbert,
and
Michael Whelan
for so graciously enduring
six books' worth of dragons,
Sunrunners, and me

CUNAXA Tuath
Castle

Tiglath

peruche

DESERT

Skybowl

Remagev

Stronghold

Vere
Hills

eep

ord

Faolain River

SYR

River

Catha
Hills

Sunrise

Water

The Long Sand

dorval

Radzyn
keep

Graypearl

Small
Islands

South

Water

AUTHOR'S NOTE

A summary of casualties, how they died and where, may suffice as a reminder of events in *Stronghold* and *Dragon Token*.

Killed

on Kierst	Latham of Kierst, his wife Hevatia of Isel
at Gilad Seahold	Segelin, his wife Paveol (sister of Edrel and Kerluthan), their son Edrelin
at Faolain Riverport	Baisath, his wife Michinida (parents of Mirsath and Idalian); Miral of Faolain Lowland, his wife Kemeny (parents of Karanaya), their son Gevnaya, his wife Pelida (Draza's sister); ✪Brenlis
at Goddess Keep	✪Oclel, ✪Rusina
at Tuath Castle	Jahnavi
at Stronghold	✹ ✪Morwenna; ✪Relnaya
at Swalekeep	Kerluthan of River Ussh; ✹ Branig
at Tiglath	Tallain; Birioc (Miyon's son); ✪Vamanis
in the Veresch	Lyela of Waes (Tallain's cousin); Rabisa of Tuath Castle; Feneol (Hildreth's son)

✪ Sunrunner	✹ Sorcerer

Died of wounds	Rihani of Ossetia
Died of natural causes	High Prince Rohan; Myrdal; Volog of Kierst; Narat of Port Adni; Siona of Tuath Castle

Murdered

at Balarat	☯Arpali
by Merida	Kostas of Syr
at Swalekeep	Halian of Meadowlord, his niece Cluthine; Aurar of Catha Heights; Rialt and Mevita
at the Ussh River	Edirne of Fessenden
at Einar	Camanto of Fessenden

Executed

by Mirsath	Patwin of Catha Heights
by Kostas	Patwin's daughter Izaea, his brother Othreg
by Meiglan's order	her half-brothers Duroth, Ezanto, and Zanyr; Birioc's Merida uncle Urstra
by Andry	Miyon of Cunaxa

Major characters surviving as of the fifty-seventh day of Winter, 737:

The Desert and Princemarch

☯ALASEN	of Kierst, Lady of Castle Crag.
☯ANDREV	Andry's son; Tilal's squire.
☯ANDRY	Lord of Goddess Keep. Maarken's brother.
☯ANTALYA	of Tiglath. Sionell's daughter.
BETHEYN	Formerly betrothed to Andry's twin brother Sorin.
☯CAMIGWEN	of Castle Crag (Jeni). Ostvel and Alasen's daughter.
☯CHAYLA	of Whitecliff Manor. Maarken and Hollis' daughter.
CHAYNAL	Lord of Radzyn Keep.

☯ Sunrunner   ✳ Sorcerer

DANNAR	of Castle Crag. Ostvel and Alasen's son; Pol's squire.
DRAZA	Lord of Grand Veresch.
EDREL	Lord of River Ussh. Norian's husband.
FEYLIN	Lady of Remagev.
⊙HOLLIS	Lady of Whitecliff Manor.
IDALIAN	of Faolain Riverport. Mirsath's brother; Laric's squire.
ISRIAM	of Einar (in Fessenden). Pol's squire.
✴JIHAN	of Princemarch. Pol and Meiglan's daughter.
⊙JOHLARIAN	Court Sunrunner at Faolain Lowland.
KARANAYA	of Faolain Lowland. Mirsath and Idalian's cousin.
KAZANDER	Battle leader (*korrus*) of the Isulk'im.
✴MAARA	of Feruche. Riyan and Ruala's daughter.
⊙MAARKEN	Lord of Whitecliff Manor. Battle Commander of the Desert.
MEIG	of Tiglath. Sionell's younger son.
MEIGLAN	High Princess.
MIRSATH	Lord of Faolain Lowland.
OSTVEL	Lord of Castle Crag.
✴⊙POL	High Prince.
✴⊙RISLYN	of Princemarch. Pol and Meiglan's daughter.
✴RIYAN	Lord of Feruche, Skybowl, Elktrap Manor.
⊙ROHANNON	of Whitecliff Manor. Maarken and Hollis' son; Arlis' squire.
✴RUALA	of Elktrap Manor, Lady of Feruche, Skybowl, Elktrap.
⊙SIONED	of River Run, High Princess.
SIONELL	of Remagev, Lady of Tiglath.
⊙TOBIN	of the Desert, Lady of Radzyn Keep.
⊙TOBREN	Andry's eldest daughter.
VISIAN	Kazander's brother-by-marriage.
WALVIS	Lord of Remagev.

⊙ Sunrunner   ✴ Sorcerer

Dorval and Firon

✳ALDIAR	Yarin's distant cousin.
✳ALLEYN	of Dorval. Ludhil and Iliena's daughter.
✳AUDRAN	of Dorval. Ludhil and Iliena's son.
AUDRITE	of Sandeia, Princess of Dorval.
CHADRIC	Prince of Dorval.
✳ILIENA	of Snowcoves, Princess of Dorval. Lisiel and Yarin's sister.
LARIC	of Dorval, Prince of Firon. Chadric and Audrite's son.
LUDHIL	of Dorval. Chadric and Audrite's son.
✪MEATH	Court Sunrunner at Graypearl.
✳TIREL	of Firon. Laric and Lisiel's son.
✳YARIN	Lord of Snowcoves. Brother of Lisiel and Iliena.

Gilad and Grib

AMIEL	of Gilad.
CHEGRY	Master Physician.
ELSEN	of Grib. Norian's brother.
NORIAN	of Grib, Lady of River Ussh. Elsen's sister.
NYR	Princess of Gilad.
SETHRIC	of Grib. Elsen and Norian's cousin.

Syr and Ossetia

DANIV	Prince of Syr. Tilal's nephew; Pol's squire.
GEMMA	of Syr, Princess of Ossetia.
KIERUN	of Lower Pyrme. Pol's squire.
TILAL	of River Run, Prince of Ossetia. Sioned's nephew.

Meadowlord

CHIANA	Princess of Meadowlord.
RINHOEL	of Meadowlord. Chiana's son.

Kierst-Isel

ARLIS	Prince of Kierst-Isel.

✪ Sunrunner	✳ Sorcerer

| ✳NAYDRA | of Princemarch, Lady of Port Adni. Chiana's half-sister. |
| ✪SAUMER | of Kierst-Isel. Arlis' brother. |

Goddess Keep

✪ANTOUN	*Devri.*
✳CRILA	*Devri.*
✪DENIKER	*Devri.* Ulwis' husband.
✪EVARIN	Master Physician.
JAYACHIN	Waesian merchant; unofficial *athri* at Goddess Keep.
✪JOLAN	*Devri.* Torien's wife.
✪LINIS	*Devri.*
✳MARTIEL	*Devri.*
✪NIALDAN	*Devri.*
✳✪TORIEN	*Devri.* Chief Steward of Goddess Keep. Jolan's husband.
✪ULWIS	*Devri.* Deniker's wife; mother of Andry's son Joscev.
✪VALEDA	*Devri.* Mother of Andry's daughter Chayly.

HIGH WARLORD OF THE VELLANT'IM

✪ Sunrunner   ✳ Sorcerer

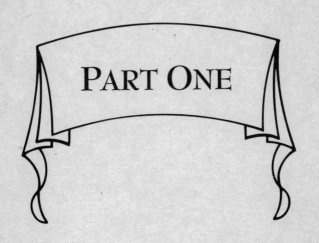

PART ONE

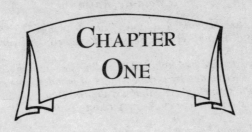

CHAPTER ONE

She *appeared without warning, balanced exquisitely on a carpet of sunlight, crowned in stars. When she smiled at him, all the sweetness and serenity that ever were shone from her face. Beautiful, of course—though he could not have defined the color of her eyes, or her hair, or her skin. She was all he had ever dreamed, many things he had never dared imagine, and she was here, with him, smiling. He reached out a reverent hand, hoping he would be allowed to touch her.*

"No," she murmured, her voice softly throaty, "not yet, my dear. All things in time."

Her starry crown brightened, pulsing in rhythm with his quick heartbeats, dazzling his eyes. He drew back slightly, frightened of power for the first time in his life. But he could not look away, for from that arc of brilliant light shot clear, fiery sparks, each expanding to a crystalline sphere. She juggled them easily, almost whimsically, all twelve in turn caught and then tossed high by elegant fingers.

Within each was a castle. Stronghold, Radzyn, Tiglath, Skybowl, Remagev, Swalekeep, Castle Crag, Balarat, Tuath, Goddess Keep—he knew those well, but two were strange to his eyes. He tried to follow their movements, tried to discern the patterns of wall and tower and court.

"Too fast?" she asked. Suddenly the spheres were suspended in midair, the two unfamiliar castles resting delicately on her fingertips. She held one iridescent globe out to him.

"The Feruche that was, before it was taken by Fire."

Yes, he recognized it now, from drawings. Not half so beautiful as the Feruche Sorin had created, and very much older.

She extended her right hand, and he saw a strong, soaring tower, surrounded by a trim village of wooden houses glowing with stained-glass windows, unprotected by walls.

"This was mine, before the building of the place you now hold."

And when he saw the crystal dome that was oratory and calendar and mathematical triumph, he knew that he looked upon the ancient Sunrunner keep on Dorval.

More. He looked upon the Goddess.

She was toying with the castle-spheres again. They rose and fell at the flick of her fingers. All at once she gestured, and they hovered in a straight line before her.

Stronghold fell and shattered.

And Tuath.

Feruche.

Remagev.

The castle on Dorval that no one living had ever seen.

"Wait!" *he cried.* "Not Radzyn! Please!"

"No. You have already paid for your home. But one other will fall."

Which one? Swalekeep—where Ostvel was, making Alasen a widow? Tiglath—to further break Sionell's heart? Castle Crag? Skybowl? Balarat?

Goddess Keep?

"I can't choose!"

"Have I asked you to?" *Her laughter was sunlight on diamonds. She began to juggle the remaining castles once more, swifter than his eyes could follow.*

"Then why—?"

"Because they are still in danger."

"You said I paid for Radzyn. How?" *He thought of Brenlis.*

The lovely features drew into an expression of shock. "Not with pain. I am not so cruel as all that. You paid with belief."

Of course. What other coin would Deity accept?

"Is it possible to do the same for—"

"Which one?"

As unable as he had been to choose a castle to destroy, neither could he choose one to save.

She was smiling again. Her eyes were green and then blue, black and then hazel and then gray. Her hair was spun sunlight—no, fiery red—no, soft brown—black—pure silver. She was his mother and Sioned and Andrade and Hollis and Brenlis and even Alasen.

"You see how difficult power can be. One more will fall. But which?"

She flung all the spheres up into the air. He watched helplessly, holding his breath, heart stopped in his chest. Higher, higher, seven glowing globes, shrinking to pinpoints of light that circled into a crown of stars. . . .

"Andry? My Lord, wake up." The voice was urgent, familiar. "Andry!"

He opened his eyes. Evarin; only him. "Where is she?" he muttered thickly.

The Master Physician sagged with relief. "About time you came out of it. Don't worry about Princess Alasen. She's on her way to Feruche. She should get there tomorrow sometime. I had a look earlier, while you were sleeping. Then this fever came over you like a summer squall, and it was all I could do to get a cure down your throat. How do you feel now?"

"Cold." Drenched in sweat, Andry huddled into a sopping blanket.

Evarin produced a dry one that reeked of horse. Andry found the smell comforting. He stripped off wet clothes and wrapped himself in the wool. Then he drank whatever Evarin gave him and lay back weakly.

A little Fire glimmered nearby, warming the darkness of a small stone shelter. "Where are we?"

"One of Lord Garic's way stations. Before you ask, we got here on horseback. Undignified, but there weren't any artists around to note the pose for a commemorative portrait, so—"

"Stop babbling and tell me what happened." Then, looking more closely at Evarin's face, he said gently, "You've got a fever, yourself. How's the leg?"

The young man shrugged. "It'll do."

"Where'd the horse come from?"

"*Your* horse, actually. He wandered back. You don't remember?"

"No."

"Well, you got a pretty nasty crack on the head today.

Your memory may play tricks for a while. Anyway, we heard hoofbeats, and you tried some whistle or other, and your stallion came trotting up—well, limping, actually. You took the stone from his hoof, and—you really don't remember?"

"None of it. But I'm glad you didn't have to do all the work yourself. I presume we got on the horse and started riding?"

"I doubt you'd call it that." He grinned tiredly. "Your father'd be appalled—or laugh himself senseless, one of the two, seeing us. And I'm babbling again, so I think I'll let *you* take the watch for a while."

"Yes, get some rest. Is there anything to eat?"

"Water and what was in your saddlebags." Evarin reached out and dragged the leather satchels over. "Dry clothes, too."

"Good. You lie down and sleep. I'll tend the Fire."

One moment Evarin's little blaze faded, and the next Andry called Fire to the same spot. The exchange was made smoothly; at least the injury to his head hadn't played foul with his gifts. The physician curled himself into another blanket and was asleep between one breath and the next.

Andry changed clothes, keeping the blanket like a shawl over his shoulders. It was bitterly cold, but his need for warmth had more to do with his guts than his skin.

"One will fall. . . ."

But which? Oh, Goddess, which one?

He took hard bread and cheese from his saddlebags and went to the shelter doorway. He had no sense of time; it might have been anywhere from just after dusk to just before dawn. There must have been a clear sky earlier, or Evarin wouldn't have been able to go looking for Alasen, but now only faint, milky luminescence showed where the moons lurked behind the clouds. The unusable light mocked him.

Which would fall?

Not Radzyn. She said he had bought it with his belief. He remembered his dreams of death and destruction. She had shown him what might happen, and he had believed.

Tiglath, then? Evarin, on their long ride before the disaster of today, had told him all he knew of events. The Vellant'im had sailed to Tiglath, attacked, been repulsed, and departed. Tallain had died defending his castle, but the castle still stood. They had tried to take it once. They had failed. There was no reason to think they might attempt it again.

Not so with Goddess Keep. Seven ships were in Brochwell Bay even now. But Torien and the other *devr'im* knew how to protect themselves. Prince Elsen of Grib was riding south with troops in answer to Torien's call for aid. The prince's sister Norian was on her way from Dragon's Rest with her husband, Edrel of River Ussh. They would provide more traditional defense than the spells used by the *devr'im*. With sudden wryness, he reminded himself that Jayachin was there, too—and nothing would prevent her from doing everything she could to uphold her own safety and her new position as unofficial *athri* of the refugees outside the walls.

No, it would not be Goddess Keep.

Castle Crag was too remote for the Vellant'im to bother with. But not, he realized with a start, for Chiana. It had always been her goal to rule there. Once she realized that no Vellanti or sorcerous help would be coming to her at Rezeld Manor, she might decide to fulfill her lifelong ambition. Ostvel was at Swalekeep; Alasen was at Feruche; all their troops and the levies from the surrounding Veresch were with one or the other. There was no one left to defend Castle Crag. Would it be the one to fall?

Perhaps Swalekeep. No, the Vellant'im had tried once there, too, and failed. There was no military profit in the place, anyway.

That brought him to think of Balarat, up in Firon and equally irrelevant in terms of securing the continent—which was obviously not the invaders' intention to begin with. Politically, however, the place presented dangers. Yarin of Snowcoves occupied the castle and held in custody the rightful prince's young heir. Regaining Balarat would present a pretty problem. But if it fell to Prince Laric, would that not be returning it to its rightful owner? This hardly constituted the kind of "fall" he felt sure the Goddess had meant.

Lastly, there was Skybowl. Something inside him quickened. A Desert castle. The Vellant'im had concentrated on such; it was the next logical place to seize on the way to Feruche, where Pol was; it was a place of dragons.

If the choice was his, then it would be Skybowl. The sixth and last to fall. It could not be bought back from the Goddess' claim, not even with faith. A battle would be fought there. Men and women would die there. Skybowl would go the way of Stronghold.

Andry knew all the castles of the Desert. He had visited them in childhood, before going first to High Kirat and his abbreviated service as Prince Davvi's squire and then to Goddess Keep, where he had always wanted to be. Stronghold was destroyed, as was Tuath; Radzyn still stood, though in enemy hands. Skybowl and Tiglath were held fast. And Feruche—

Of them all, next to Radzyn, Feruche was dearest to him. It was his dead twin brother's work, his legacy of beauty and strength. Sorin's very spirit lived within its walls and towers.

Stronghold and Tuath were gone. He had bought Radzyn's safety. Remagev was useless to the enemy, as was Tiglath now that the Merida were shattered. If it came to a choice between Skybowl and Feruche, there was no choice. Skybowl would be the sacrifice. The sixth and last offering to the Goddess.

No, that wasn't quite right. She was not so cruel, she had said so. Then why must another castle fall?

His head ached with it, his heart in turmoil. He gave it up, but for one clear decision: Feruche would not be the one to fall.

✳

Faint sounds intruded on his thoughts—familiar sounds that should have blended into his consciousness unheeded. What had this barren land done to him, that noises heard from childhood caught his attention as the strange noises of the Desert did not? The ring of steel on stone, the call of the master masons, the grunts of the slaves—all the sounds of the quarry that was his family's wealth. Good, solid granite with beautiful black graining, cut into smooth blocks to build homes and temples as far away as Kersau, the Island of the Blind. . . .

But those sounds did not belong here. Wind, the occasional clatter of sandstone pebbles, the whisper of sand underfoot—the Desert had its own music, and he had reluctantly learned to appreciate it. The cutting of stone, however, was as alien here as he.

Coming out of his tent, he fixed a cold gaze on the Flametower, all that could be seen of Stronghold from his camp. A single lifted finger brought a guard running, a horse trotting along behind. He mounted, galloped up the slope to the canyon, and bent his head as he went through the tunnel.

They were using picks on the cobbles of the outer courtyard. They were hacking away at the walls. They were gouging mortar from the foundation stones.

They stopped when they saw him, and knelt before him in their hundreds, proud of what they had accomplished.

He spoke very softly into the hush. "The priest?"

"In the gardens, O Most High," someone said to the broken cobbles.

"Bring him."

Someone else scrambled to his feet and, after bowing to him where he sat the stallion, raced for the inner gardens. A few of the others risked a glance upward. He ignored them.

The priest did not hurry. His strides were long with confidence, but he did not hurry. Nor did he bow. His voice was rich and smug.

"Since the Fire was chased away by your righteousness, lord, I have been thinking how best to drive the lingering evil from this place. After much prayer, the solution was vouchsafed me: bring the castle down around itself."

They had sent him another priest from Radzyn to replace the one who had met his demise at Skybowl. A very young priest. Only someone just out of Sanctuary would use a word like "vouchsafe."

Repressing a sigh, he let his gaze travel slowly from the gatehouse to the walls to the vast looming bulk of Stronghold. "That may take some time."

"It must be done, lord," the priest said firmly. "This is a source of the *Azhrei*'s power. It must fall."

It has been burned to a crisp—what more do you want? he thought. What he said was, "And had you considered the demons that might still lurk within?"

The young face glowed with sunburn and fervor. "The Father of Storms will protect us."

"Had you noticed," he continued as if the priest had not spoken, "how the Dragon Sign is everywhere here?"

"We are being careful to eradicate all of them."

"I'm sure you are." He paused, knowing this must be phrased exactly right. They were all listening, even though they pretended not to; it was not the first time he had faced off with a priest, and this pompous little half-beard was beginning to annoy him.

"I'm puzzled," said the High Warlord, crossing his wrists casually on the pommel of his saddle. "If Stronghold is razed, will the *Azhrei*'s power die?"

"No, he carries the taint and the sin with him. But—"

"If all Dragon Sign is defaced, will the *Azhrei*'s power die?"

"No, he will only call forth other dragons of his cursed Fire. But—"

"My lord priest," he said with respectful curiosity, "how will we rid this land and the Father's Sacred Dragons of the *Azhrei*'s power?"

"By killing the *Azhrei* himself, of course," came the impatient reply. "That is why we came to this horrible dead place where nothing grows because of the sins of—"

It may be why you *came,* he thought. "Then why?" He swept an arm wide. "What does it gain but sore backs and crushed sword-hands?"

Someone coughed, and in the sound was amusement.

Plump cheeks turned redder above the scraggly beard. "It is necessary."

"I don't see why. It seems to me that killing the *Azhrei*'s castle accomplishes very little, when killing the *Azhrei* himself would not only rid the dragons of his evil, but all the land and all its castles as well."

The priest's forehead congested with blood. "It is necessary," he repeated stubbornly.

You damned idiot! he wanted to shout. *You're using up their strength that should be saved for battle, and for a stupid superstition—for nothing!*

"As you say," he remarked instead. "Tell me, for you have studied things I have not, what would be the source of power in this place?"

"The Dragon Signs." Suddenly he looked halfway intelligent—and as if he wanted to cut out his own tongue for having fallen into the trap. It was tempting to offer him a knife to do it with.

The High Warlord continued, "Then perhaps if those were taken care of, this long and dangerous task of bringing the keep down around itself would *not* be necessary?"

The priest glanced around him. It was a terrible mistake. Not one face was to be seen, only bowed heads. But everyone knew he had searched for support; everyone knew his weakness as he realized that he was not the one who truly commanded here.

At least the fool knew when he was overmatched. "I hadn't thought of it that way. In my zeal—"

"—which is commendable," the High Warlord interrupted gently before the youngling could make an even bigger spectacle of himself. Authority had been established; humiliation was to be avoided. "You rejoice in the purity of your calling and the advantage of scholarship. I am only a warrior—ignorant of the deeper mysteries, too concerned with worldly things." He leaned down a little, as if wanting to speak confidentially. He could practically feel the hundreds sharpen their hearing on mental whetstones. "You know, I can't help thinking of their wives. Palms roughened by calluses of sword and shield are marks of honor, but very different from those left by working stone. These would not be pleasing to a woman's pride as a wife—or to her skin. And there are times when even the Father of Winds cannot howl as loudly as an angry woman."

No one dared even clear his throat this time.

The priest shifted his legs—between which there was lacking certain equipment essential to conjugal relations—and shrugged his shoulders. "Sometimes we priests forget the more practical and, as you say, worldly considerations."

"You are fortunate to be able to do so," he replied with good humor. "The Dragon Signs, then—and we shall see how it affects the power of this *Azhrei* who is steeped in sin."

The priest drew himself up proudly. "And when shall he steep in his own blood?" he challenged.

He supposed he was owed that, after the rebuke. "The vision was a true one. It shall be done when the ritual is completed."

"You are making plans to that end?"

He wished he knew where the deadfalls were at Stronghold; he would take significant pleasure in pushing the priest into one.

"I am." He raised his head to the Flametower. "You might start up there. Dragons sleep atop every one of those pointed windows."

Turning his horse, he rode from Stronghold. Out in the Desert once more, he gave in to impulse and urged the stallion to a gallop across the sand, far from the idiots he must suffer for his greater purpose.

He knew the priests were restless. It was their customary condition, and did not trouble him overmuch. But this matter of the Desert castles was irksome. The priests wanted so much to obliterate at least one.

It hadn't been necessary to forbid the destruction of Radzyn and Whitecliff; the priests had seized on their luxuries gladly. Remagev survived because the old *Azhrei* had fled it—and the traps inside were too numerous to risk. The priests had grumbled at that, but all he'd had to do was comment that anyone willing to brave the spells left behind was welcome to do so for the glory of his clan. Faolain Riverport mattered nothing to him. It was too new to be of importance. The Merida had demolished and burned Tuath Castle, forgetting all the subtlety of their origins in their passionate vengeance. As assassins, the only token of their existence was the broken glass knife left in a victim's heart. But as conquerors, they became as children smashing a coveted toy for spite.

Feruche mattered little, except that it now sheltered the *Azhrei.* And *her,* he reminded himself, reining in to gaze out at the empty vastness of her Desert. *She* was why he wanted Stronghold to remain standing. If the Storm Father was good to him, he would be able to see her, perhaps even touch her, before the ending. If circumstances were different, he would have named *her* as the prize, not the new *Azhrei*'s wife. But things were as they were, and in fact he was glad that *she* would not be in the charge of the priests.

Although, he told himself with an inner grin, it would have been a wonder and an education to see.

Turning, he saw the sun balance atop the Flametower. Soon it would glow through the topmost chamber, almost as if the old *Azhrei*'s fire still burned.

It did not. The young one's Fire would never be lit. Eventually he would leave Feruche and they would face each other in battle at last. And then, after the victory, the true prize would be taken.

Skybowl.

✳

Andry let Evarin sleep himself out. When the young man finally woke on his own at midmorning, hot taze and toasted bread and cheese were waiting for him. The physician ate, tended to his own and Andry's wounds, and pronounced them fit for travel.

"Elktrap?" he asked as Andry hoisted him into the saddle.

"I'd rather go straight on to Feruche if you can make it." Taking the reins, he started walking. Though Radzyn horses were strong, this one still favored his near foreleg a bit.

Just past noon they reached a shortcut Andry remembered from a map. No need to trust his memory, though; the trail was trampled down, clearly visible. Alasen had come through only yesterday. No subsequent rain or snowfall obscured the tracks.

A sluggish breeze began to stir halfway through a gray afternoon. Measure after measure, Andry put one foot in front of the other, ignoring the throbbing in his head, refusing to consider what was and what might be. Eventually he was unable to think past the next step. His body was beyond weariness, numb with cold; his mind found comfort in sodden exhaustion.

But what was permissible and even desirable for him was not allowed his horse. They might have continued by dark, a fingerflame lighting their way, but the stallion was exhausted and limping badly. So when the pale, stubborn glow of the sun was a fingerspan above the western crags, Andry called a halt.

Evarin stirred blearily in the saddle. "We there yet?"

"No. I have to build a shelter while there's light enough to work. You're tonight's cook. Surely all those years of brewing potions qualifies you."

Evarin rallied a little as he was helped off the horse. "Febrifuges and eye ointments aren't stuffed venison with mossberry sauce. I can boil water."

"That's more than Sioned can do." He settled his friend on a flat rock cleared of snow. "I know, I know, a princess isn't expected to cook. But she can't even brew a drinkable cup of taze. Speaking of which, here's a pot, and there's the snow. I'll be back soon."

Andry left the saddlebags where Evarin could reach them, tethered the horse, and started off into the trees. Snow would be thin on the ground beneath the gigantic pines, and he had every expectation of finding branches suitable for his purpose. He had collected nearly a dozen—needles still green, limbs still supple enough to bend—when he came upon a rabbit burrow. He'd never been much good at hunting large game, but he'd caught plenty of sand-nesting creatures in his childhood. Rabbits couldn't be much more difficult.

He was wrong.

Sighing, he cast aside the stick he'd been using in a doomed attempt to coax the bleating animal from its den. So much for rabbit stew tonight. But on his way back, lugging heavy branches, he had the good fortune to find a brave, bedraggled clump of wolfpaw growing around a tiny frozen pond. Everything about the plants, from golden-brown flowers to pulpy root, was edible, nourishing, and delicious when soaked in wine. Hoping Evarin hadn't drunk all of what he'd liberated from Pol's cellars, he crouched down to harvest dinner.

The pond was no more than a puddle, barely an armspan across, and the trees formed nothing resembling a circle. But all at once Andry sat back on his heels, breathing hard. The stones rimming the pool had been set there deliberately.

He'd heard of two tree-circles in his life: one near Goddess Keep, the other close to the ruins of Lady Merisel's castle on Dorval. He'd never even considered that there might be others.

Or that they might be used by the *diarmadh'im*. Stoneburners.

Was the Goddess here? Was this her place? Had it once belonged to her and been corrupted?

Only one way to find out.

He stripped off his gloves and pocketed them, and let his cloak fall from his shoulders. There was no question of removing the rest of his clothes; he wasn't suicidal and doubted that the Goddess wanted the Lord of her Keep to freeze to death. After closing his eyes for a few moments to steady his mind and his breathing, he gazed at the stone directly opposite him. It was larger than the others, upright in the frozen mud like an arm reaching for the sky. He would call Fire to it, let it cascade down to melt the ice, and then pluck a hair from his head to float on the freed water. . . .

But at the first glimmer of Fire, the stone itself turned to flame. Angry crimson burst head-high, then bled in a swift circle to ignite all the rocks. Andry flinched back and bade the Fire be gone.

It burned brighter than ever.

Within the circle, the sheet of ice reflected living Fire. Across the mirrorlike surface swirled furious shadows painted in red and yellow and orange. His hands shook as he tugged a single hair from his nape—startled to find it was a gray one—and let it fall onto the solid, unmelting ice.

Fire, Water, the Earth of which he was made. One more thing would finish the gathering of Elements—and somehow he knew that if he did not breathe Air across the pond, the flames would burn forever. This was a ritual that demanded completion. But for Andry, it was like being trapped in a dream, struggling to wake, desperately aware that until it was over there would be no escape.

It was not his breath but the Storm God's that blew across the ice and flames, scattering shadows. The pond was truly a mirror now—a *diarmadhi* mirror, not reflecting what was before it but revealing what was inside it.

And unlike the mirror he'd found in the Veresch, this one did not show the living. Every face he saw was the face of someone dead.

He knew them, had seen them since childhood or at *Riall'im* or in Fire conjurings that showed others how to recognize them. Halian of Meadowlord, the Parchment Prince; black-eyed Miyon of Cunaxa; hawk-nosed Kostas of Syr. Volog and Latham of Kierst, father and son, alike in features but not in the marks of age and rule. The brothers Edirne and Camanto of Fessenden, utterly unalike. And the youngest, and the most regrettable death: Rihani of Ossetia.

One after another the faces of dead princes appeared and were consumed in flames, just as the castles had been dropped and shattered.

The price of this war? The sacrifices? What might have bought their lives?

Kostas, assassinated by a Merida. Rihani, dead of wounds. Halian and Latham murdered. Volog alone had succumbed to natural causes. Edirne had been killed in an accident. Miyon's death had been an execution as far as Andry was concerned. He didn't know how Camanto had died—hadn't even been aware of his death, in fact, until now.

But if this was the tally of princes sacrificed to this war, where was Rohan?

Andry sat back on his heels, tearing his gaze from the empty ice-mirror to stare at the trees. Though they formed only an arc, not a circle, around him, they were easily identified. The one directly to his left was the Child; next to it, Youth. A flowering bush, naked now in winter, intervened between that tree and the one that must represent the Man. Beside it was the Father. And just to Andry's right was a massive pine that could only be the Graybeard.

Would there be any answer, in this place that seized Fire and gave it independent life to mirror the faces of the dead?

Long ago he had consulted other trees at the proper time. At Goddess Keep the pines formed an elegant circle around a larger forest pool with its rock cairn. He had asked his questions of all the trees—except the Graybeard. Not many had the courage to look into their old age until it was actually upon them. And by then questions generally lost their importance anyway, if one was lucky enough to be granted a placid finish to life.

Andry had the depressing feeling that his own old age would be as turbulent as his youth.

He shifted slightly, biting his lip. Then he plunged his bare hands through the Fire and into the ice, and faced the mighty tree.

The ice shards cut like crystal. Needles of pain drove into his knuckles, bringing a muffled cry to his lips. The Fire atop the standing stone flared once more, and in it he saw the face of a man.

No. The face of the God.

He was like unto the Goddess in that his terrible beauty had no specific feature. He was Rohan and Meath and old Prince Lleyn; he was Torien, Pol, and Walvis. He was Andry's father and grandfather and brothers and sons. Ostvel's gray eyes became Roelstra's leaf-green, Tallain's deep brown, and then a clear sapphire blue.

He was . . . Andry.

A voice smooth and hard as polished stone reverberated in his mind. *No one calls Fire here now. No one comes to see the faces of the dead.*

Andry caught his breath in an instinctive protest, then realized his foolishness. Everyone died. No bargain could be struck here—his faith for a life as it had purchased Radzyn.

You, the voice accused, *you are not of the Old Blood. You are afraid. Go. Return when you understand.*

The Fire died. The face that was all faces and none faded into the broken ice. The stones were only stones. Wind whispered in the pines, finding lonely echo in Andry's soul. He slid his hands from the water and stared at them as if unsure they were his. The skin was stung scarlet with cold, the nails blue.

It was a long time before his fingers warmed enough to use. He fumbled with his gloves, drew his sodden cloak back up around him, and pushed himself stiffly to his feet.

Evarin was nodding over steaming taze. He glanced up when Andry trudged from the wood with his branches and his pockets full of wolfpaw.

"I was beginning to worry, my Lord. It's getting dark."

"Yes," Andry agreed. "Very."

✳

". . . hundreds and thousands of them, more than anyone could ever count. But even with all those stars, people were frightened by the night. So they learned how to make torches, and candles, and lamps, but it wasn't enough."

The sound of Pol's soft voice stopped Sionell just outside the half-open bedchamber door. She waited, listening as he told an old, old legend; it had been one of her own favorites as a child.

"Now, as it happened, there were three sisters who had very special gifts. The eldest of them could speak with trees, and the second one could speak with clouds, and the youngest could speak with dragons."

"Like you," Jihan's voice said smugly.

"Well, not quite. Anyway, the sisters thought for a long time about the night's darkness and finally decided on a plan. The first asked the trees in the forest to fashion three boats. The second asked the clouds to spin themselves into sails. The third asked a few dragons to carry them on their backs far up into the sky, until the starry wind caught their sails. Soon everything was ready. Trees had built themselves into boats, and clouds were hung from the masts, and dragons hunkered down to take the boats on their backs, and the three sisters stood at the prows. Up they went, into the dark sky without sunlight, until the wind caught their sails. The dragons flew back home.

"Then the sisters called Fire to their boats, beautiful silver and gold that shone from the curving hulls and billowing sails. And just the way a candle makes a circle on a window-pane, the light glowing from the ships made great circles in the sky.

"Down below, the night was not so dark as it had been. The three sisters sailed their boats across the sky, and looked down from the prows onto the land, where people took heart that there was light in the darkness.

"But after a while they realized that they'd forgotten something. With the clouds as their sails, there was nothing for the rain and snow to fall from. Fields withered, and rivers dried up, and only the places where water came directly from the ground could still—"

"Like at Stronghold," Jihan interrupted.

"Yes, like the spring at Stronghold. But one or two springs, or even a hundred, couldn't water the whole world. So the sisters decided that part of the time, they'd have to do without their sails, so that the clouds could give the water a place to live before it came back down as rain. And that's why tonight the sisters are drifting through the sky in their curving boats, for their cloudy sails are somewhere making a home for the rain."

"And that's also why there's a lady at the front of every ship, isn't that right, Papa?"

"Absolutely right. Sailors and shipmasters call them the 'wary watchers' because, like the three sisters, they're always keeping an eye out for clouds."

"The sisters must have been Sunrunners," said a new voice—Tobren's. A predictable remark, considering who her father was, Sionell thought, then berated herself for the injustice.

"Or sorcerers," contributed Jihan.

"No, they weren't," Tobren stated. "They use the stars, not the moons."

"But Sunrunners get sick when they sail," said Antalya, and Sionell nearly marched into the room to demand the reason why her daughter wasn't in her own bed. Though recovering and no longer contagious, she was barely over her fever.

"So it can't be Sunrunners," Jihan said triumphantly.

"It's not Water up in the sky, it's Air," was Tobren's superior reply.

"Well . . . so what," Jihan muttered. "Papa, it could have been sorcerers, couldn't it?"

"Not being in a position to ask the three ladies, I really couldn't say. And I think it's time you settled down for the night. It's late and I thought we were only going to have *one* story, not four."

Once again Sionell took a step, intending to enter the room. Once again the conversation inside stopped her.

"I'm going to be a Sunrunner when I grow up," Jihan announced. "So is Rislyn. And so is Talya, and Meig, and Maara—and you, too, Tobren," she added.

Sionell's knees went a little weak. She'd known about her daughter, but—Meig? And how did Jihan know, anyway?

Pol's voice was even and easy as he said, "If so, you'd better follow Meig's example and get some sleep. Being a Sunrunner is hard work."

"No, it's not," Jihan said, encouraged—*As if that child needed any encouragement,* Sionell mused—by her father's acceptance of her statements. "See what I can do already, Papa?"

Pol gave a startled exclamation. Tobren cried out. *Goddess, what has she done?* Sionell thought frantically, and flung open the door.

The room was brilliant with light. A branch of candles over by the windows was ablaze—not just the wicks but the wax and the iron stand as well, perilously near a tapestry curtain.

Sionell sidestepped a chair and snagged the cloak draped carelessly over its back. The heavy, soft wool was enough to smother the flames.

Catching her breath, she turned around. Pol was struggling to untangle himself from children and coverlet on the bed. Tobren's face was white with shock; Antalya seemed only thoughtful and curious. Meig, bless him, was curled at the foot of the bed like a kitten, sound asleep.

Jihan perched on a pillow, hands folded demurely in her lap. "You didn't have to do that, Lady Sionell. I would have put it out myself."

"But not before you burned up half the room," Sionell responded. "It got away from you, didn't it?"

"Well, some," she admitted unwillingly.

Pol was on his feet now, looking down at his daughter with eyes of solid stone. "Jihan."

"Yes, Papa?"

That innocent little face, those sweet blue eyes beneath tangled golden hair. . . . Sionell knew precisely what was going through Pol's mind. Jihan needed a good scold and a bad scare, but not now. Not after what had happened to her mother and twin sister.

"Don't do that again," Pol said, not gently, but not as severely as he might have. "Give me your word."

"But, Papa—"

"Your word as an *athri* of the High Prince."

Jihan cast a quick glance at Tobren—almost defiant, almost sly. "I promise, my lord."

He nodded acceptance. "Well, then. Into bed with all of you." He scooped up Meig, who squirmed and snuggled against him. "Sionell, does anything short of a trumpet in his ear wake this child?"

"He'd sleep through thunderstorms. Hand him over."

She felt his forehead with her own cheek, relieved to find it cool. Four years old—and already identified as a Sunrunner? She held him more tightly to her breast, wondering dismally why her immediate instinct was to protect him from what he could become.

The three girls shared the bed. Once they were all settled, and Sionell had reassured herself of Antalya's well-being, Pol retrieved the scorched cloak and beckoned a maidservant down the hall to come keep watch over the children.

As the door closed, Pol murmured, "I brought the other children in to keep Jihan company. She's having nightmares. She's always slept with Rislyn in the room, you see."

"It's all right. I understand."

He touched Meig's tousled dark head and gave a rueful smile. "He insisted on joining us—and I think I bored him right to sleep."

"He's like that. Wide awake one moment, oblivious the next."

Pol sighed wearily as they started down the corridor. "I envy him. I thought it would work with the girls, too, but—it seems I can't even tell a simple bedtime story anymore without something outrageous happening."

"Did you know Jihan could call Fire?"

"Alasen mentioned it this evening when we spoke."

"And it doesn't worry you?" Sionell asked carefully.

Pol shrugged. "Jihan is what she is. She was bound to pick it up on her own one day. My mother did when she was only a little older than Jihan is now. There's power in her. I don't want her to be afraid of it like Alasen is." He paused before his own chamber door. "Ell. . . ."

Swiftly, she said, "Your mother is looking for you. Kazander's turned up missing, and you *know* where he's gone—or at least what he plans to do."

"Kazander—? Oh, good Goddess, that fool!"

"I'll go tell her you're on your way, shall I?"

He caught her arm. She froze. He let her go and looked anywhere but at her. "We have to talk."

They were at her door; she opened it blindly. "There is nothing to discuss. Nothing happened."

Eyes bruised beneath with exhaustion widened with shock. Not because of her denial; it was Meiglan in his eyes, not her.

"Ell, I didn't mean talk about—about *that*."

"No, of course not," she said mindlessly. "I'm sorry, I should've known—"

"I need you."

His quiet plea hit her all wrong. She held Meig defensively against her shoulder. "I have three children who need me. You don't."

"You don't understand. I have to know that you—"

"I don't want to hear this," she snapped, turning from him, furious. He had no right to claim anything from her. No right to start hurting her again. *No,* she told herself, *I'm the one who hurt me, all those years ago. It was never his fault. He was what he was.*

But what is he now?

This time his fingers shackled her forearm hard enough to bruise the bones. "I need you more than Tallain ever did."

And this time she gasped. "Don't you dare say his name to me!"

Meig grumbled in his sleep. She rocked him, glaring at Pol. There was no quick response of temper in his eyes. Bleak, vulnerable, his face almost broke her heart.

Almost. She would not allow it.

"I don't know what to do, what to say," he whispered. "If you want to pretend that it never—it would be best, you're right. But don't do this to me, Sionell. Not now, when I need—"

"Do this to *you?*" she echoed incredulously. "You selfish bastard! What could I ever do to you that you haven't already repaid me a hundredfold in advance? Damn you, let me go!"

To her surprise, he did. "I'm sorry," he told her, and in the next instant vanished down the hallway.

Composure shattered, Sionell sagged back against the wall. Her son curled against her; she buried her lips in his silky hair and closed her eyes.

Pol had been cruel, trying to claim her. She had nothing for him. Her children needed her. Their father was dead, their world forever changed. Jahnev was Lord of Tiglath now—at barely seven winters old. Antalya would be a Sunrunner one day—but who would teach her? Not Andry! And not Pol, either. Maarken? Sioned?

And what of Meig? Grubby, bright-eyed, full of mischief, secretly her favorite—was Jihan right? Was he gifted, too?

She thought of another child then. Two children, really. Meiglan was as gentle and innocent as Rislyn. She thought of them held captive by the Vellant'im, and wondered why Pol was not a shrieking madman.

Selfish, she'd called him. They were two of a kind.

Goddess help us, she thought wearily, and went to put her youngest to bed.

*

Pol stood in the middle of his bedchamber, wondering numbly how and why he was there. Certainly not to sleep. Restlessness had seized him as surely as exhaustion, fevered brain and tired body at constant war, with him as the battlefield and the casualty.

Meiglan.

Rislyn.

Chayla.

Sionell. . . .

Swords stabbing through iron bars at a caged animal.

He turned as if to escape the pain and saw himself in the wall mirror. Only his own tense face was reflected, his own sleepless eyes. But within that other mirror, a dark and dangerous image—caught? Trapped inside silver and glass, alive only in Fire, silent and helpless. . . .

He watched his own face in the mirror, thinking of that dark reflection. Trapped. Helpless.

Meiglan.

Rislyn.

Chayla.

Sionell. . . .

Oh, Goddess help him . . . Sionell. . . .

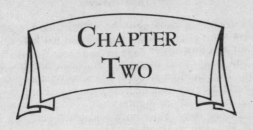

CHAPTER TWO

The only problem with sneaking into Faolain Lowland was the only thing that allowed Saumer and his troops to sneak in at all.

Rain.

He'd waited two nights for this storm that would obscure the army's movements. He could, however, have done very nicely without the deluge that obscured absolutely everything. He couldn't see more than a handspan from his nose. Torches were a sodden joke, and he didn't know much about conjuring a fingerflame. So he directed his people down an access tunnel dark as a Sunrunner's nightmare, listening to curses that told him feet had slipped on the ladder. A nice little shower to keep the Vellant'im in their shelters, some convenient concealing mist—that was all he'd wanted. Instead he sent his troops through an entry in the forest floor that reminded him forcibly of a rabbit hole, and huddled into a sopping cloak that weighed more than if he'd simply draped the wool around his shoulders while the sheep still wore it.

At last everyone was through the chimney Lady Hollis had described on sunlight—a thing Saumer was convinced he would never see again—and he began his own descent. As he reached up to shut the wooden covering, soil around it gave way. A silkweight of muck dumped on his head.

"Lovely," he grumbled, spitting grass, mud, and a few rocks. "Thanks."

But at least the torrents of rain were closed out. Sliding the iron bar home to lock the entry—Mirsath had had it opened a couple of days ago—he climbed down, jumping the last rungs to land in water halfway to his knees.

Havadi, Prince Kostas' captain and now Saumer's own second-in-command, was waiting, having already sent the rest of their people on ahead. "Lord Mirsath left a few dry ones for us, my lord," he said, holding up a lighted torch. "The passage is through there."

Saumer pushed mud-thickened hair from his face and eyed the darkness of the low tunnel uneasily. "Under the moat. We might as well have swum the thing."

They started off, following dim flashes of fireglow ahead and the sound of more swearing. The young prince tried to take his mind from the closeness, the cold, and his incredibly soggy self by concentrating on the torch Havadi held. Having only recently learned that he was *faradhi* like his aunt Alasen, Saumer wondered if he could sense anything different about fire. But he saw only a torch made of wood and pitch, and the flames were like any others he had watched in his life.

The sudden glowing quiver on the edge of his mind was made of another kind of Fire entirely.

Saumer straightened abruptly and bumped his head against the low ceiling. Havadi turned when an annoyed exclamation left his lips.

"My lord?"

Saumer was running his gloved fingers over the dripping overhead stones. "There's something here. Just above the rock. . . ."

"Um . . . yes. The moat."

"No, something *in* the moat." He heard what he'd said and blinked. "Why would I think a crazy thing like that?" But in the next breath he ordered Havadi to douse the torch. "The light's distracting me."

He stripped off his gloves in total darkness and blew on his hands to warm them. Searching with only his eyes, he saw no telltale fiery flicker. So he closed his eyes, and, biting his lower lip, explored the ceiling with his fingertips. The shining itched at his mind stronger here, weaker there. He followed its pull, all formless black-rainbow iridescence, and all at once snatched his hands back as if they'd been burned.

"Saumer! What is it?" Havadi grasped his arm.

"I don't know—but it's powerful, whatever it is." He

touched the spot again, gingerly, and again his fingertip felt burned. "How thick is this ceiling, do you think?"

"I don't know, and unless you want the moat flooding in to drown us, we're not about to find out." Flint struck stone, and the torch flared to life again. "Come upstairs, my lord, before you catch a chill."

"But—" He sighed. "Oh, never mind. I'll ask Mirsath about it when I see him. But I want to mark that place." He groped in his pockets and came up with a hoofpick. He jammed it into a seeping crack in the rocks near the source of the glow.

They continued down the tunnel, and the water dripping through from the moat began to rival the rainstorm outside. Saumer wouldn't have minded so much if it hadn't smelled so foul. Curiosity about that strange black-fire shimmer gave way to the pure and simple desire for a long, hot bath and clean, dry clothes.

They emerged at last into a circular room. The tallest staircase Saumer had ever seen spiraled upward, lit by torches and candles. A man and woman waited for them, prudently standing a few steps up from the ankle-deep water on the floor. Both were young, finely dressed, and had the look of family sameness stamped on their features.

"Lord Mirsath, Lady Karanaya," Saumer said politely, glad to stretch his backbone straight again. "Lovely weather we're having, isn't it?"

"Welcome to Faolain Lowland, your grace," Mirsath responded in kind, his eyes dancing with humor at the casual exchange of pleasantries. "I hope your journey wasn't too tiring."

Karanaya gave a snort. "Next you'll be asking after the comfort of your horse. At least one of us is practical here, your grace. Have some wine."

She turned, and from a candle-shelf took a crystal goblet footed in silver and set with gems. The deep ruby liquid in it steamed in the chill. Saumer drank gratefully as Mirsath remarked, "I notice you got out the princely guestcup, cousin."

"I hope I know what's due a Prince of Kierst-Isel, and a kinsman of the High Prince into the bargain."

Saumer handed the goblet to Havadi. "Here—warm your bones with this. As it happens, Lady Karanaya," he went on, "my horses are being well seen to. We left people to guard them, and as soon as this rain lets up a little they'll be herded to a safe place."

"After which we'll herd the Vellant'im to an *un*safe place," she finished with determination. "If you'll come with us, your grace. We've already had your people seen to, and now the most important thing is to get you dry and warm."

Saumer mounted the steps to get out of the water, wishing he could upend both boots; he was fairly sloshing his way up that daunting staircase. "Wet and warm would be better," he smiled at her. "I stink of your moat and need a bath. By the way, Lord Mirsath, when I was going through the tunnel, I—"

A rumbling from the black mouth of that very tunnel presaged a crash that shook the foundation stones. Havadi dropped the priceless goblet and raced up the steps, arms spread wide to shove the other three ahead of him. Karanaya stumbled against Saumer; he held her upright and dragged her with him as they fled the gush of rainwater and moat mud and shattered rock.

Saumer went to his knees on a riser, cursing, and looked over his shoulder. Debris-laden water surged eight steps below him, seven, six—then seemed to pause and consider, lapping flirtatiously at the next step. He caught his breath and sat down to watch, earning amazed looks from his companions.

"What are you—"

"My lord, we really must—"

"Prince Saumer, there's still danger from—"

"Just wait," he said, and closed his eyes.

Ah. There it was. He fixed it in his mind and scooted down the steps, heedless of his boots—full to the knees anyway—and the leaden drag of his cloak. Standing on the bottom step, chest-deep in smelly muck, he plunged a gloved hand into the gently rocking waves.

A few moments later he climbed back up to the others and opened his fist. In the stained and sopping leather rested a tear-shaped lump of filth. Saumer scraped the mud from it as best he could so they could see it. But he knew that Havadi, Mirsath, and Karanaya (who gasped in delighted recognition) saw only a black pearl, not its magical sheen of rainbows.

＊

"What I don't understand," said Mirsath to Johlarian a little while later, "is why *you* didn't see it before."

The Sunrunner gave a shrug. "Perhaps it's in the way of children—which Prince Saumer is when it comes to *faradhi* things. They see what's there, not what education and experience tell them to see. And I was concentrating on the fingerflame, my lord, while I was down there. That might have something to do with it."

Mirsath peered into the gaping hole in his hall floor, wrinkled his nose, and strode over to push the Dragon's Eye that closed it. "Well, *that's* lost to use, anyway. Ours or theirs." He watched the stone slide shut. "You know, it bothers me a little that Saumer was so smug. Totally unsurprised that the Tear should snuggle right into his hand."

"Again, my lord, like a child. Why *shouldn't* it happen that way? Reason and logic tell us it's absurd. Impossible. But it's the privilege of the young to believe that even if they leap into a midden, they'll come out holding a rose. Or a pearl." He smiled. "Perhaps the hand of the Goddess was in it."

"Don't start sounding like Lord Andry," Mirsath warned as they climbed the stairs. "Reason and logic tell *me* that the collapse of the moat had an even chance of washing the pearl either direction down the tunnel. It was luck."

"As you say, my lord. Good night, and sleep well."

The next morning they met in a room Mirsath's grandfather had rather pompously termed the Hall of Petitions. Because most consultations were done out in the fields or in the village, and rarely through so formal a method as a petition, everyone at Lowland simply called it "the office." They ignored the ranks of chairs posted along the walls and gathered around the fruitwood table that old Lord Baisal had fondly pictured awash in respectfully worded parchments pleading for his favor.

Saumer was bright-eyed and refreshed after half a night's sleep in a real bed—and a second hot bath before breakfast this morning. At Mirsath's request he explained the logistics of the Battle of Catha Heights while they waited for Karanaya. Eventually she arrived, dressed in a plain, high-necked gown of bright red wool. The Tears of the Dragon, all six of them bound in silver wire, hung from a short chain around her throat.

Johlarian watched Saumer carefully for reaction. The young man didn't even blink. He complimented Karanaya on the jewels; she thanked him prettily for retrieving the missing one; they settled down to business.

Or would have, if Mirsath hadn't asked, "Your grace, do you see anything now when you look at the pearls?"

"Certainly," was the ready reply. "Don't you, Johlarian?"

The Sunrunner concentrated. Then he stopped concentrating. He pushed all his education and logic aside, opening himself as he had not willingly done since the night some unknown woman had come in the guise of the Goddess to make a man of him.

The pearls began to shine.

Not as the single one had when he searched for it by Sunrunner means in the moat. Then, the lost gem had worn an angry greenish shimmer. Now all six were strangely serene, luminous, darkly iridescent.

"Gentle Goddess," he murmured. "The High Prince showed me what to look for, and the one of them alone—but all of them together—"

"It looks like you're wearing a black rainbow, Lady Karanaya," Saumer told her. "It spreads in a sort of burst over your head. Too bad you can't see it."

She fingered the pearls. "They're beautiful just as they are. Thank you again, Prince Saumer."

"No trouble," he answered with a grin. "As you saw. Now, let's see what kind of support we can give Prince Tilal when he arrives. The flood wasn't such a disaster after all, you know—I heard about the bath the Vellant'im took in the moat. Mud will keep them out as surely as water. I'm worried about that causeway, though. Can you show me the plans of the castle, please?"

*

The childhood accident that had crippled Prince Elsen of Grib made walking painful and riding a torment. This had not prevented him from climbing into a saddle for the journey to Goddess Keep when the call went out for help. Now, within sight of the great seaside castle on this fifty-ninth day

of Winter and the fourteenth of his journey, his long agony
finally caught up with him.

He had been thinking of it as comparable to childbirth.
Weak as his wife Selante was after two days of an exhausting and dangerous labor, she had found that final reserve of
strength that allowed their son to be born. Surely, Elsen
thought, surely if she could endure such wracking pain
through her entire body, he could outlast one knee.

It mortified him that the first glimpse of Goddess Keep
nearly toppled him from the saddle. He would dredge up a
last determination, he would endure the pain, he would ride
into the courtyard as a prince and not a cripple—

Whatever his mind's resolve, his body knew that respite
was close. His body wanted that surcease *now*.

"Your grace!"

When he fell, it was very slowly. His bad leg, foot twisting in the stirrup, gave a sickening crack. Oddly, it didn't
hurt at all. He didn't remember hitting the ground.

Elsen woke in darkness. He turned his head and then
turned it away from a sharp rectangle of light.

"Mama? He moved. I think he's awake."

He didn't recognize the young voice, nor the one that answered. "Hush now, Ondiar. We mustn't startle him. Your
grace? Prince Elsen? It's all right, you're with friends. My
name is Jayachin, and you're in my tent just outside Goddess Keep. No, don't try to move. I've splinted your leg and
your shoulder. You took a nasty fall."

He opened his eyes and squinted up at her. She was white-
skinned and black-haired, and very beautiful. "How
long—?"

"It's just gone noon. They'll be here from Goddess Keep
in a little while with a litter to carry you in."

"My people? Where are they?"

"Within the keep, your grace, and made more than welcome." She settled on a low stool beside the cot. "I had
them bring you here to rest and recover yourself before you
meet Lord Torien. A few of your guards are outside." She
hesitated. "Before I call them in, your grace, I must thank
you for your goodness in coming to our aid. I speak for
thousands driven from their homes who came to Goddess
Keep seeking Lord Andry's protection. But he is gone, and
Lord Torien refuses to do the necessary Sunrunner things

against the Vellant'im who wait to attack us. You stand between us and destruction, your grace."

She paused, as if giving him time to speak. When he did not, she went on, "They will land soon, your grace. They must be attacked. It is not enough to defend Goddess Keep—the battle must be taken to them. I've tried to find a way of teaching these people to fight, but they're farmers and townfolk, your grace, not warriors. And Torien impedes me at every turn. He thinks only of his vow not to kill. But I was made *athri* of these people by Lord Andry himself, and I cannot afford such qualms. Help us, your grace. Please."

A thoroughly uncharacteristic anger competed with the agony in his knee. Had his people come all this way only because the Sunrunners were squeamish? What in all Hells was the matter with them? He would not watch his army fight and die as Prince Tilal's had for the sake of a *faradhi* vow.

But he owed it to the *faradh'im* to hear their side of it. He said to Jayachin, "I will speak with Lord Torien."

She nodded and clasped her hands together. The gesture was oddly possessive, as if she held within her palms a promise of love or war.

He had no right to demand that the Sunrunners forswear their most sacred vow. He had come when they called for aid; it was his duty. He had never deluded himself about leading the charge, but at least he could have stood on the ramparts, urging his people to victory. Now he was worse than useless; long familiarity with pain told him it would be spring before he could so much as set his feet to the floor.

But he must do something to fight this horror that had overtaken the continent and killed High Prince Rohan, who had befriended him with letters and gifts of books. The demands of his own honor and his affection for a man he had never met were no less binding on him than the Sunrunner oath was to them. It was what they were.

But why should his people have to die for them? Or for him?

Later, after an unspeakable journey in the litter, he swam out of slow, hot waves of pain to hear voices discussing him.

". . . how he managed to sit a horse at all, with that leg," a man said.

"Yes," a woman replied, "but the break is the best thing that could have happened."

Elsen struggled to understand. How could his injury benefit anyone? Slitting his eyes open, he saw the pair standing at the foot of the bed he lay in. The man was tall, long-boned, about a dozen years Elsen's senior, his Fironese blood strongly proclaimed in his dark features. The woman was younger, delicately made with black hair and smoky-gray eyes.

She continued, "We'll have to keep him immobile for quite a while. It depends on what I can do with that knee. I'd like to find the fumble-fingered excuse for a physician who had the original setting of the bones. Goddess, what a mess!"

"Should we find Evarin on sunlight and consult him about proper treatment?"

"Torien—"

"I know, my love—you're wearing the same ring he is, and you're almost as good. But we're going to need his advice."

She replied grudgingly, "All right, yes. For now, we'd better just let the prince rest quietly, with no distractions."

Elsen closed his eyes again and tried to breathe around the panic in his chest. Unable to leave this bed, he would be unable to give orders. He wouldn't even know what was going on unless they told him. He had fought physical helplessness since childhood. This was worse. This was so much worse. It wasn't just him—it was all his people, who had followed their crippled prince because they loved him.

"I wonder," the woman mused, "if Jayachin was as clumsy with words as she was with her bandaging."

"Meaning what?"

"Meaning she had him alone long enough to say just about anything."

"Jolan! She's not that much of a fool."

"You think not? Well, just consider how lucky it is that Prince Elsen is here with us, and not camped outside with her."

"I see what you mean. Come, let's leave him to his sleep."

✳

"You realize, of course," Sioned was saying quietly as the children gathered in the Attic, "that this is a case of hiding the sheep after the dragons have feasted."

Meath gave her a shrug. "They have to learn."

"Granted." She leaned against the door frame and folded her arms. "I'd like to get Audran and Alleyn up here from Skybowl, too. And Jeni, if she can be persuaded to leave her dragon."

"You know we don't dare let any group smaller than an army ride anywhere. Not until Chayla's been found, and we can be sure we've cleaned out all the lingering vermin from the hills."

"I'd like to have them here all the same." Sioned nodded to the table, where five children stood behind chairs. At each place was a white candle rising from a small crystal holder. "Do you see the look on Tobren's face?" she went on in a murmur. "She knows as well as you and I that her father's not going to appreciate this at all."

"Since when have you ever worried about what Andry thinks?"

"Since I've had the feeling that we're going to need his help." Sioned ran a hand back through her short curls and moved from the door to the head of the table. "Good afternoon, *ellitev'im*," she greeted the children with a smile. "For those of you who don't recognize that word, it means 'little friends-in-Fire.' It's what every First Teacher at Goddess Keep calls young Sunrunners. Tobren, please tell the others what *faradhi* means."

" 'Silent knowledge'," the girl responded sullenly. Her grandmother had told her to be here, and so she was. But as Sioned had observed, she didn't approve.

"Exactly. And since none of you have much knowledge yet, you can do me a favor by taking to heart the *silence* part of it!" She smiled again, then looked at Meath. He stood at the other end of the table, waiting for his cue. "We'll begin with our rather *large* friend-in-Fire down there."

"This is the way Sunrunners greet each other before a lesson." He held both hands out before him, palms flat. "I am Meath, son of Keriv and Aldannaya, and my rings are six. Goddess blessing to you, Sunrunners."

Sioned gestured to Antalya, who stood at Meath's right. "Your turn."

Sionell's daughter blinked huge blue eyes and stammered, "I—I am Antalya, daughter of T-Tallain and Sionell, and I don't have any rings. Goddess blessing to you, Sunrunners."

Jihan was next. She spread out her hands and identified

herself by saying, "I am Jihan, daughter of High Prince Pol and High Princess Meiglan, and I'm a princess and the *athri* of Rosewall at Str—"

"Jihan." Meath spoke her name softly.

"But if we're saying who we are—"

"Your name, the names of your parents, and the number of your rings is enough," he replied. "We know who you are."

"Then why—"

"Because that's the way it's done," Tobren said sharply.

Across the table, Jihan gave her a look to incinerate stone. "I am Jihan," she said again, deliberately. "I am the daughter of Pol and Meiglan, and I have one ring. See?"

"It's not a Sunrunner's ring," Tobren challenged.

"All right! I don't have any rings! Goddess blessing!"

Sioned and Meath exchanged a glance of mingled amusement and exasperation.

Maara, like Jihan, was *diarmadhi*. Unlike Jihan, she was quiet and serious as she named herself the daughter of Riyan and Ruala, without rings, and gave the traditional ending.

Then it came Sioned's turn, and the first part of the greeting took her back more than forty-five years. She could almost feel Camigwen nearby—indeed, Cami's granddaughter stood right next to her. So strong were the memories that the last words, which honesty compelled her to say, tasted strange. "I am Sioned, daughter of Daniv and Riaza, and I wear none of my seven rings—"

This reminder was Tobren's limit. "This isn't Goddess Keep," she exclaimed. "We shouldn't be doing this at all— and especially not with *you!* You don't even wear your rings!"

Meig, four-year-old face poking around the ladder back of the chair he stood behind, wrinkled his brow. "Don't yell!"

Sioned sighed. "Hush, Meig. Tobren, you're right, of course. This *isn't* Goddess Keep. I *don't* wear the rings Lady Andrade gave me."

Meath stripped off all his rings and put them on the table. "Neither do I."

Tobren caught her breath. "Put them back on, Meath!"

"Will they make him a Sunrunner again?" Jihan asked, all innocence and gleeful blue eyes.

Sioned cast her a quelling glance. "All of you know why you're here. There are things you must learn for your own safety. It has been decided that Meath and I will teach you. If any of you choose not to participate—"

A soft voice interrupted from the doorway. "I am Alasen, daughter of Volog and Gyula, and I have no rings. Goddess blessing to you, Sunrunners."

She glided gracefully into the room to stand at an empty place between Meath and Meig. Her long, gold-lit brown hair was undone across her shoulders, and she was pale and hollow-eyed with weariness. She looked worse than when she'd arrived at Feruche yesterday.

"I need to learn how to use what the Goddess has given me," Alasen said, staring down at her hands. On the left was the ring Ostvel had given her in token of their marriage—the only one she had ever wanted to wear. "Will you teach me? May I learn with you?"

"You may," Sioned told her. "Will you join us, too, Tobren?"

"You know so many things we don't," Antalya contributed shyly. "We'll need your help."

Tobren was silent for a time. Then, reluctantly: "My name is Tobren, I am the daughter of Andry and Rusina, and I have no rings. Goddess blessing to you, Sunrunners."

Meig spoke the formula, looking bored. Alasen repeated it, completing their circle. Meath brought a candle for her from the sideboard, and when they all stood quietly behind their chairs once more, Sioned made a slow, graceful gesture. Her candle lit with a pure, golden flame.

"The next time we greet each other," she said, "we will each call Fire in turn. Yes, Jihan, I know you already can. And you, too, Tobren. You must wait for the others to catch up. Please sit down now. And while Meath gives you this first lesson, you must all remember that part of a *faradhi*'s name is silence."

If Jihan expected to learn spells—and if Tobren expected some revelation of Goddess Keep's secrets—it was a disappointing afternoon. Meath gave them a history lesson. After lighting his own candle, he began with the beginning of Lady Andrade's rule in the Dragon Year of 677—the year of Sioned's own birth, ancient history to everyone but her and Meath. He stayed away from politics and wars, merely recounted how Goddess Keep was governed, what a typical day was like, and what the basic duties and functions of Sunrunners were. He spoke of Sunrunners who resided at

Goddess Keep, those who were assigned to specific courts, and those who rode the princedoms as itinerants.

As he talked, faces appeared in Sioned's candleflame—not by her conjuring, but called up by memories and visible only to her. Camigwen, Meath himself, their other friends of the same age and level of training. Urival, striding around the keep with Ostvel hurrying at his side and making frantic notes on parchment scraps as he was taught the duties of Chief Steward. Kleve, who had roamed Princemarch and the Desert and Meadowlord for so many years, who had died so horrible a death. Crigo, setting off so proudly to become a court Sunrunner, lost to Roelstra and *dranath,* his death even more hideous. But the strongest vision was of Andrade: pale and stern and acid-tongued, and loving them all in her own arrogantly demanding way. Loving Rohan and Pol so much that she died trying to save Princemarch for them.

What do you think of all this, I wonder? Sioned mused as Meath began to detail the changes Andry had made. *Are we right in teaching these children? And Alasen—what about her? It isn't mind-hunger that brought her to learn, but fear. Not a good start. But I think Meath and I can cure her of it, show her that she needn't be afraid. . . .*

Jihan, now—there's not a quiver of fear in the child. Her mother and sister were taken in a battle she saw with her own eyes, but I'll wager she wasn't much frightened then, either. This is the best thing for her, I suppose—occupy her mind, give her something to do besides fret. But after what Sionell said about last night and the candle branch, she'll bear watching. . . .

Are you watching me, my Lady? Are you somewhere out in the Desert sky, with Zehava and old Prince Lleyn, cursing our stupidity?

Rohan, are you there, too? Am I doing what you would have done?

And what in the Name of the Goddess shall I do about Pol and Sionell?

It was near dinnertime when Meath finally dismissed his students. Sioned collapsed back in her chair with a grimace of relief.

"Goddess! What a group!"

"At least they all kept their mouths shut. Want some wine?" He handed her a cup and she drank gratefully.

"Sioned, I'm not sure we should include Meig in this. He's so young. And I think I just about sent him to sleep."

"Sionell wants it done. Frankly, I think she's wise to begin getting him used to *faradhi* things early. Did you notice how nervous Antalya was?"

He sat where Maara had been and sprawled long legs under the table. "That took me back a few years, I can tell you."

"More than I care to think about." She met his gaze with a slight smile. "Ghosts?"

"Cami, especially. And Mardeem—remember the way he sang? A voice to make the Goddess weep for the beauty of it. And Palevna—do you know that Andrev's her grandson? Her daughter Othanel was his mother."

"How about two more ghosts for the collection?" she said, her smile growing wider. "That great big lump of a Sunrunner lad, and a freckled red-haired stick of a Sunrunner girl.... Goddess, Meath, how did we ever get here?"

"They're almost all gone now, you know," he mused. "Those of us who shared lessons, the ones who came with you to the Desert. Just you and me, Hildreth and Antoun. I haven't talked with either of them in a long, long time. He's still at Goddess Keep, isn't he?"

"Yes. And a *devri* now, in case you hadn't heard."

Meath stared at her. "One of Andry's—?"

"Yes, one of Andry's." She lifted one shoulder and drank more wine.

"How do you know?"

"They had to train people to replace those who were killed. As you know, Antoun is extremely gifted—if extremely antiquated, like us," she added wryly.

"How did you find out that he's joined Andry's cause?"

"I have a source." She opened her eyes to their widest and most innocent.

"And that's all you're going to tell me."

"You know me so well," she purred.

Meath snorted.

She pushed herself to her feet. "I'm going to take a nap. The moons will set early tonight, and I'll be up all the rest of it on starlight."

"How's Hollis?"

"Pretending to be brave. Maarken thinks he has to hold

her together, and she's the same way about him, so they've both been lying to each other and everyone else for three solid days now."

"If only we'd taught Chayla—"

"If only she'd been interested in something other than medicine," Sioned reminded him. "All she wanted to learn was how to use a fingerflame to give her light to work by. It's nobody's fault, Meath. Oh, Maarken and Hollis think it's theirs, for not forcing her to learn how to go Sunrunning. Right now Chayla is probably damning herself for the same thing. But Tobren keeps telling us what we've been trained to think: *faradh'im* can only be taught at Goddess Keep."

"Something you ignore when it suits you."

"Who gave Pol his first lessons?" she challenged.

"At least I asked permission. You never bothered." He made a little gesture of apology. "That wasn't fair. You did what you thought was right."

"Not right, necessarily. Expedient. They aren't always the same thing." She paused, smiling again. "Meath, put your rings back on."

He stared at his naked hands for a moment, then quickly replaced the six circles of silver and gold. "Goddess—I didn't even feel they were gone!"

"I haven't missed mine in years. Jihan was right. You don't need rings to be a Sunrunner."

"There's a dangerous idea in that somewhere."

She almost laughed. "Somewhere? It's right out in the open! If any gifted person can set up a school for others of our kind, what need for Goddess Keep?" She started for the door. "Andry would call that a sin. Which is why it occurs to me more and more often."

Meath frowned his confusion. "But you said we're going to need him."

"Did I?" She gave him a curious glance over her shoulder.

"Sioned! Stop playing chess games with words!"

"Better words than lives—the way Andrade did," she answered with sudden vehemence.

"She's eighteen years dead. Don't mistake Andry for her," Meath warned.

Sioned tightened her fingers around the door handle. "No fear of that. He's worse. Andrade believed in what she did as a servant of the Goddess—the most important one, to be sure. But Andry, he believes in *himself.* He doesn't serve the Goddess—he thinks of himself as her lover."

"Sioned!"

"It's true and we all know it," she said, and shut the door behind her.

*

All during the afternoon, while two of her children began their paths to becoming Sunrunners, Sionell prowled Feruche. When she appeared in the kitchens for the third time, the cook had compassion on her nerves and kindly allowed her to help wash vegetables. As the sun vanished and torches were lit, Hollis arrived and was similarly provided with something to do.

It was absurd, really. Two highborn ladies, scrubbing and peeling and chopping as if they were servants. But it was good, honest work, it demanded their attention if they weren't to lose parts of their fingers to sharp knives, and it had the virtue of being useful.

Which was at the heart of each woman's unease. Uselessness.

"Ell, we're out of whitespice," Hollis said, up to her elbows in a cauldron about to be put on the hearth. "Will you run down to the storeroom for me, please?"

"Whitespice?" The cook sniffed disdainfully on his way past. "Better to bring up enough strong wine to get everyone drunk, so they won't taste this slop. Ah, Goddess, for the old days at Skybowl!"

The butcher, who stood next to Sionell shredding meat into a pot, whispered, "And now he'll treat us to the full list of his triumphs. Escape while you can, my lady."

Sure enough, the cook had launched into tender reminiscences of a rolled roast—featuring kid wrapped in lamb wrapped in venison, the whole of it covered in liver paste, baked in a pastry shell, and "crowned with the merest drizzle of berry compote that we made ourselves, for only a fool trusts an apprentice with a sauce. And it was stupendous. A masterwork, even for us. We created this marvel for the occasion of Lord Riyan's marriage. Such was its success that we were invited to prepare the Lastday banquet at the next *Rialla.* Still, even we cannot perform the same feats of artistry for three hundred as can be accomplished for a small party of, say, fifty or sixty, such as the time when we...."

Sionell escaped down the steep cellar stairs, a torch lighting her way. She recalled Riyan and Ruala's wedding feast very well; it set her stomach growling. Opening the heavy wooden door of the storeroom, she took a deep breath of the spicy air and immediately sneezed.

Her nose began to clog as if she had caught a cold. Quickly she located the canisters of whitespice amid boxes and barrels of taze, nuts, dried fruit, and other pungent seasonings that made her eyes water. Thanks to that madman upstairs, their meals were tasty, but it was tricky work feeding an army. While measuring out careful spoonfuls of spice, Sionell mentally tallied the sheep and goats in their courtyard pens, the dressed carcasses hanging in a coldroom deep underneath the castle, and supplies of flour and other staples. Elktrap was supplying Feruche as best it could, but fear of other marauding bands of Vellant'im had stopped shipments for a while. What was here would have to last until they were certain that no one else would be captured as Chayla had been.

Sionell pushed the big door closed with her hip, the torch in one hand and the bowl of whitespice cradled in her other arm. She wanted desperately to wipe her eyes and rub her itchy nose. Another sneeze echoed in the cool stone cellar. "Damn!" she muttered—and froze as footsteps not her own sounded softly in the far darkness.

Children, even ones caught playing where they shouldn't, would have made more noise. Anyone with a reason to be here ought to have seen her and spoken by now. Sionell placed the bowl at her feet, freeing her right hand for the long dagger at her belt. With fire in one hand and steel in the other, she told herself she could fight her way to the stairs and give warning.

She edged toward the stairs, trying to see into the dimness. Cisterns of water and barrels of wine formed a maze that began just within the reach of torchlight. Anyone could be hiding there.

But how would the Vellant'im know any of the secret ways into Feruche? Had they forced Chayla to reveal—

"Put up your weapons, my lady," said a mocking voice she recognized. "I'm not dangerous. I promise."

"Lord Andry?" She could have killed him then and there for giving her such a fright.

He stepped out from behind a cistern and bowed. "The same. You brandish fire as if you were a Sunrunner to command it, Lady Sionell. And I don't doubt you're capable of making at least a dozen good-sized holes in my hide with that knife. Can you do something else with it, please, besides pointing it at me?"

"How did you get in here?" She knew it was a stupid question the instant it left her lips, and answered it herself before he could do more than raise an amused brow. "Of course. Sorin shared the plans with you. But why have you come?" Another idiotic inquiry; how could he assert his power tucked away at Goddess Keep?

Andry sauntered forward, and now that he was fully in the light she saw his travel-stained riding leathers, the glinting of his rings and wrist cuffs. A dark stubble of beard shadowed his jaw and cheeks. New lines at the corners of his eyes were filled in with dirt, and there was a bruise on his left cheekbone.

"Well, for one thing, I came to see my daughter."

"And for the rest of it?"

"I'm not your enemy, my lady," he said softly.

"Not mine, no," she said just as sweetly.

His head jerked up a fraction. "You forget yourself, Lady Sionell. And you forget who I am."

Blue eyes met blue eyes squarely. "Not for a moment, my Lord. And because you are who and what you are, why all this sneaking around in the cellar? Why not ride up to the front gates? Unsure of your welcome, perhaps?"

"You don't like me, do you, Sionell?"

"No more than you like me, Andry." Her hand clenched on the knife hilt, thumb rubbing the amber chunk at its tip. It had been a gift from Tobin, who had taught her how to use it.

"Ah, well," Andry sighed. "At least you're not afraid of me anymore. You were when you were a little girl."

"Afraid of you? No. But I used to feel sorry for you."

That found its mark. "You *pitied* me? Why?"

Because you lost Alasen, and I came to understand how much that must have hurt. But you could have gone on from that, as I did, as hundreds of people do. Instead it made you bitter, and I have no patience for that.

"Oh, don't worry," she replied, "I don't pity you anymore, so you don't have to resent me." She put away her knife and retrieved the spice bowl. "When you're ready to come out of the cellar, you'll find Maarken with your father and Pol—if you dare face any of them."

"You don't fear me, and you don't pity me," Andry said. "You hate me."

"Wrong again," she told him. "What I feel for you—to be perfectly honest, I rather despise you."

Andry nodded, as if he had expected nothing less. The torchlight played over his coolly handsome face, revealing nothing of his thoughts. So his next words startled her badly.

"I was sorry to hear about your husband," he murmured. "He was a good man."

Sionell headed for the stairs, unwilling to let him see the tears that sprang to her eyes. Her husband, a good man whose memory she had betrayed. What had gone so wrong with the world that she could do such a thing?

"Shall I tell them you've arrived, or do you want to slink around down here a while longer?" she tossed over her shoulder.

"Actually, you might send someone with a litter. I left my Master Physician in the little chamber where this passage lets out. He wasn't up to the walk."

Sionell turned, gazing down at him from the steps. "You *did* want to sneak in, didn't you? Why?"

Andry shrugged. "The truths one overhears when one is not recognized are occasionally interesting."

"Oh, and here I've spoiled it for you."

"You're not sorry. Not that I expect you to be."

"In fact, I am. You'll hear the truth either way—it's just that now there'll be at least an attempt to polish it a bit. I'm sorry everyone will have to make the effort."

Andry smiled up at her. "Pol won't."

"For your sake? Certainly not. For Maarken's and Chay's."

She continued up the stairs. By the time she reached the main cellar door, she was shaking so hard the torch quaked in her hand. She did despise him, for being smug and powerful and for what his presence would do to a group of people already strung taut as the fine wire strings of a *fenath*.

Dousing the torch and leaving it on its shelf, she entered

the kitchens. "Whitespice," she said to Hollis, setting the bowl on the table.

"Thank you. You didn't have to bring so much, but—Sionell?" The older woman frowned, searching her face. "What is it?"

"Nothing. I'll tell you later," she evaded, turning for the door.

"It's not—oh, Goddess, is it Chayla? Have you heard—"

"Now, how would I learn anything down in the cellar? Don't be silly, Hollis," Sionell replied, trying to smile.

"Then—"

"It's Andry," she blurted. "He's here. Downstairs."

Hollis closed her eyes briefly, nodding. "Yes, he *would* come here," she murmured at last.

"He brought the Master Physician with him. I have to go warn Pol."

"Warn?" Hollis frowned. "As usual, Andry is condemned before he even says a word."

"He condemns himself," Sionell told her. "I know he's Maarken's only living brother, and I know you both love him. But he'll be nothing but trouble, Hollis."

"If everyone takes that view, we can be sure of it." Reaching for a towel, she wiped her hands meticulously clean. "Even if he were not my husband's brother and my own friend, I welcome the Lord of Goddess Keep because he can help find my daughter. And that's how I intend to present it to Pol. You can go tell Sioned and Tobin. Leave Pol to me."

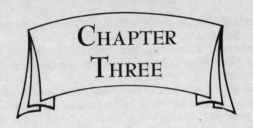

CHAPTER
THREE

Whatever words Andry had planned while on the road, however he had thought he might greet his family—and they him—after the horrors of the Autumn and Winter, all of it fled and none of it mattered when he saw his brother.

Maarken strode eagerly across the courtyard, arms held wide. For a moment Andry thought it was a trick of the twilight, that half-empty left sleeve. Then he glimpsed the white bandage and cried out.

"It's all right, Andry," Maarken whispered as they embraced. "Don't worry. It doesn't hurt and it's healing well. I'm even starting to get used to it."

He could say nothing but his brother's name, almost a moan of rage and pain. Why hadn't Sionell warned him?

The second shock came when Tobin hobbled across the cobblestones. Sunlight observation had distanced the reality. Andry looked down at the slurred ruin of his mother's beautiful face, heard her voice stumble over the two easy syllables of his name, and wanted to weep. He bent quickly to hold her, to hide his face and his anguish.

When he glanced up, his father was standing nearby. Chay was old now. This was his seventieth winter and there was no denying it. Even in muted dusk, the lines and gray hair and the strain of war showed painfully clear. As Maarken supported Tobin, Andry blindly sought his father's arms. There was strength in them still, but he was trembling.

"Andry. I'm glad you're home," Chay said simply.

He hung on as hard as he could, until he was sure he could face them all again without tears in his eyes. Drawing away, he caught sight of Pol in the great doorway of the castle. In some strange way, this was the worst of all. He'd coolly prepared himself to face his cousin, but the triple blows of his brother's maimed arm, his mother's infirmity, and his father's age unbalanced him. Pol's wife and child had been seized by the enemy. Andry had seen it happen. Pity—stronger than anything he had intended to feel—took him by surprise.

Odder still, Pol made it easy on him. It was the High Prince who descended the steps of Feruche, hands outstretched, to say, "You are well come, my Lord."

"Thank you, your grace," replied the Lord of Goddess Keep.

But somehow, by the time their fingers clasped and held, they were only Pol and Andry again. Each felt it, acknowledged it with a single glance, and let the other go.

"There's a lot to be said," Pol murmured. "But it can wait until you've rested. Tobren and Hollis are getting your old room ready for you."

His "old room," when he had only been in this castle once before in his life. But it was the room Sorin had made for him, everything in it selected with him in mind. Andry nodded, appreciating the subtle inclusion of him as part of the family.

"There *is* a lot to tell," he answered, adding wryly, "I'll try to sleep fast. Or maybe Chayla has something to keep me awake while we talk. I'm told she's getting to be quite the physi—" He broke off at the stricken look in Pol's eyes.

"Andry, the Vellant'im have her."

Something else Sionell had neglected to mention. "When? What's being done? Have you looked for her on sunl—oh, Hells, of course you have."

"Maarken can tell you on the way upstairs. Go on, you're exhausted." He began to move away.

"Pol." Andry waited until his cousin had faced him again. "About Meiglan—"

He shook his head violently. Raking back sun-bleached hair with an unsteady hand, he rasped, "No. Later. You can tell me later."

Andry and Maarken stayed silent by mutual consent on the climb upstairs. Tobren was waiting in his rooms, and burst into tears when she saw him. He held her and soothed her with paternal murmurings, but was grateful when Hollis took her down to dinner. The brothers were left alone.

"Just so you know, I'll tell you how this happened," Maarken said, holding up his left arm. "But I don't want to hear anything more about it. Ever."

Andry sank into his bath and nodded.

Maarken settled on the tiled edge of the tub, speaking in crisp, dispassionate tones. "It was at Skybowl. Pol and I were back-to-back, the way Father taught us. I don't know if the Vellanti got lucky or I got careless, but—" He shrugged. "Pol killed him. Then he cauterized my arm with Sunrunner's Fire—probably saved my life, according to Feylin. Instead of bleeding to death, I lost hardly any blood at all."

"I see," Andry replied numbly.

Maarken's voice changed then, took on a shading of bewilderment. "It really *doesn't* hurt—except when I think it's there. That happens with this kind of injury, I'm told. But it's odd, because it feels familiar, in a way."

"Kind of like the way you felt after you lost Jahni, the way I felt when Sorin died."

"Yes," Maarken said, relieved at being understood as few others could understand him. "It's losing part of yourself. They say the connection is much stronger with identical twins, and none of us are, but I can't imagine it could be any worse than it was for you and me. When I think of Rohannon and Chayla—" His voice nearly broke on his daughter's name.

Andry said quickly, "Is Rohannon all right? Where is he?"

"With Arlis. Safe enough for now. Chayla—" Maarken's jaw tightened. "That's what I regret about my hand. I want it back to kill them with."

He scrubbed intently at a foot so he wouldn't have to look at his brother. "This is the last time we'll speak of it, Maarken. You're still you. Still a Sunrunner."

"That's the other thing—and the strangest, really. Even when I don't feel the hand still there, I sense my rings. As if they're—I don't know, as if the power was somehow in them, not in me."

"It's special gold. Lady Merisel's work, or so the stories have it. I've seen Torien cast them, the way Urival taught him to do. But it's her power in the gold. Just because they're gone doesn't mean—"

"Yes, well, I can still work," Maarken said. "Losing her rings didn't affect Sioned, after all. But it's a weird sensation all the same." He handed over a green glass bottle of liquid soap. "Anyway, I'm not sure how much you know of where things stand, so I'll tell you all of it. If something comes up that you know more about than I do—"

"I'll interrupt as rudely as I ever did." Andry smiled up at him from under a headful of lather.

"As rudely as you *just* did!" Maarken's right hand suddenly rumpled his soapy hair. "Goddess, Andry, it's good to have you here. Between the Lord of Goddess Keep and the *Azhrei,* we can't help but win."

"Is that what Pol's calling himself now?" He kept the edge from his voice.

"Reluctantly. The Vellant'im use it all the time. They seem to think he's some kind of evil influence on the dragons, and—Hells, it's going to be hard to get this in order."

"Tell it any way you like, but tell it!"

✳

When Hollis opened the bathroom door, clean clothes folded over her arm, Maarken was still talking and Andry was still in the tub.

"You idiot, get out of there at once! The water must be stone cold."

Both men started. Maarken nearly lost his balance and had to brace himself on the sink to keep from tumbling into the bath. Andry grabbed a washing cloth and spread it strategically.

Hollis snorted and threw a towel in his face. "If you must be so silly, try hiding behind this instead of that little rag. You're made like your brother."

"Hollis!" Andry exclaimed, crimson-faced.

"I brought you something to eat. Dinner's long since over," Hollis went on, placing a pile of shirt, tunic, and trousers on a shelf. "In fact, the moons have almost set. Sioned wants to talk to you before she starts work for the night. *If* she does. The sky's clear over the Desert, but there may be clouds blowing over the hills."

"Work?" Andry echoed. He stood, draping the towel modestly around his hips.

"The rest of us take turns searching on other light," Maarken explained.

They were all silent while Andry used a second towel to dry off. Maarken started to help him with his tunic, then looked sourly at his left arm and gave the garment to Hollis.

"I can do it myself," Andry protested.

"Yes, he's quite grown up now, isn't he?" Maarken said with an attempt at a grin. "Feeds himself, talks in whole sentences—"

Distracting humor; Andry recognized it with an unexpected pang. *Rohan. I almost expect him to be waiting downstairs. . . .*

He made an effort. "And I even remembered to wash behind my ears."

"Clever child!" Hollis' smile was a very bad fit on her worry-drawn face. "Come along and show me how well you can use a spoon, little brother."

Andry tugged the tunic into place. "Whatever happened to the dignity of my ancestry and position?" He kept on with the game as he followed them into the bedchamber. "I'm thirty-eight, not five!"

Hollis produced a comb from the dressing table. "It's the hair. Grow some gray like the rest of us."

"Oh, but I have." Glancing to the door as light shifted there, he saw Tobren's small face peeking in. "And here's one of the reasons. Come in, heartling. Papa's clean and proper now, he won't ruin your pretty dress with the dirt of four princedoms—or is it five? I've lost track!"

He held her on his knee while he and Maarken devoured soup, bread, cheese, and wine. Tobren nestled against his shoulder, touching his cheek every so often as if to reassure herself that he was real.

"She's been taking good care of her grandmother, haven't you, love?" Hollis said. "And her grandsir, too, even though he thinks he doesn't need it."

"Now, *there's* a task," Andry smiled at his daughter.

Tobren eyed him narrowly. "Are you going to frown like he does when I let him and Granda Tobin sleep late in the morning?"

"Probably."

She gave a sigh, and he laughed.

"Papa? I know you're busy, but—" She squirmed a little on his knee. "I have to talk to you, please," she blurted out.

"Right now, if you like." When blue eyes the same color and cant as his own flickered to Maarken and then Hollis, he added, "But tomorrow morning might be better. We'll have breakfast together, just you and I. Will that suit?"

She nodded and jumped off his lap. "I have to say good night to Granda. You won't go away before tomorrow morning, will you Papa?"

"Of course I won't, sweetheart," he replied, hiding dismay as he realized how distant a father he'd been. He loved all his children, and they knew it. Tobren's assumption that she must make an appointment to see him, and her worry that he would leave without telling her, stung him.

When she had kissed him and departed, Hollis said quietly, "I can tell you what she wants to talk about. Sioned and Meath began giving the children lessons today. *Faradhi* lessons."

"So?" Andry poured taze. "It's for the best, you know. And they're both entirely competent as teachers. Excellent, in fact, if Pol is any indication."

"Don't start, please," she begged. "I can't bear it."

"I'm sorry."

She bit her lip, then burst out, "It's just—it almost kills me to hear you talk about each other. You both have the same note in your voice—"

"Out of tune?" he suggested. "Hollis, I promise you I'll make the effort. I'm not a churl. Neither am I Pol's enemy. Whatever conflicts he and I might have are meaningless compared to this war."

"But don't you see, that's what I'm afraid of! You're going to have to work together and we all know—"

"We may surprise you," he replied. Bringing her hand to his lips, he placed a gentle kiss on her palm. "For you, dearest lady, I will try."

His brother growled, "Stop trying to seduce my wife," and again they were all glad of the chance to smile.

But when Maarken went to tell Sioned that Andry would soon join her, Hollis stared Andry straight in the eye and said, "It's not for my sake. It's for his. He loves you both. He's loyal to you both. As your brother and a Sunrunner, as Pol's cousin and Battle Commander. Please don't make him choose between you."

Andry searched her eyes. At last he said, "I wish that just

once, just for one day, someone would love me the way you love my brother."

*

When Andry entered Sioned's rooms, she gave him a quick embrace, then stepped back and said, "Out, the rest of you. Go on."

Hollis, Maarken, Riyan, and Chay all opened their mouths to protest at the same time. Ruala, wiser than they, simply turned for the door, tugging her husband along with her. The others shrugged and followed.

Andry's brows arched. "You must tell me sometime how you do that."

Sioned grinned wearily. "I'm still a High Princess. Besides, I'm old."

"You? Never."

"For the rest of my life, my dear. Come sit down. I've wine and taze—"

"Thanks, but either would put me right to sleep." He took the chair opposite hers at the hearth. "Sioned, before anything else—"

"Please don't," she murmured, fingers wrapped around a cup of hot taze.

"I want you to know how we honored him at Goddess Keep that night."

"Antoun told me on sunlight. He and I have known each other a long time. I thank you for what you said in Rohan's memory, but I don't want to talk about him, Andry. It hurts too much."

"Forgive me."

"Nothing to forgive." She stared into the flames for a moment, banishing memory of other Fire.

Andry began, "I should tell you what happened with Meiglan."

"Alasen saw most of it. That can wait. We have things to do, you and I. Now. Tonight. I've been looking on starlight, but there's nothing. I should have thought of this when we first learned she was missing, but—" She shrugged. "I'm as stupid as the next person. My only defense is that it's not something we Sunrunners use often and I'm not very good at it. Pol might be able to do this, but he's in no state to make the attempt." She glanced up with a sardonic smile.

"Seems perfectly calm and rational, doesn't he? If a trifle abrupt. He's treading a sword edge, Andry, slicing himself with every step. Frankly, I don't think he's capable of what I have in mind. But you are."

Rising, she went to the table by the windows and returned with a wide, polished silver bowl half-full of water and a surgeon's knife.

"Chayla's," she said.

Comprehension gleamed in his eyes. "You're going to find her with a Star Scroll spell."

"No, *you* are."

He frowned. "Why not one of the others?"

"Maarken? Hollis?" Shaking her head, she set the bowl and knife on a low stool and hitched her chair closer to his. "They're on the same edge Pol is. Your mother's not strong enough, your daughter is untrained, and why should I use Meath with his six rings when I have the Lord of Goddess Keep with ten?"

"What about you?"

"As I said, I'm not much good at it." She hesitated, then decided to tell him the truth. "And it has to be *your* work."

Andry pursed his lips. "I can see where it would benefit me, to be the one to find her. But why should you make the effort for my sake?"

"It benefits the Lord of Goddess Keep," she corrected. "Chayla's uncle doesn't matter. It's *what* you are that means something right now, not *who*."

"It must be seen that I use my power on everyone's behalf," he interpreted.

"Seen by the Vellant'im," she agreed. "And by Pol." She smiled as startlement scrawled across his face. "Do you know what he keeps telling me? How much he needs me. But not as his mother. He needs the Sunrunner High Princess. Well, that dear lady is every bit a manipulative witch. She has to be. If you're the one to lead us to Chayla, then in spite of what he may feel for you personally, he'll have to acknowledge you're on his side and he needs you. It might be that once he gets that past his craw, you two will be able to work together as you ought."

"As long as I don't rub his nose in it," Andry said. "You trust me not to?"

"I trust that you love your home and family more than

you love your own pride," she answered forthrightly. "I'll allow you yours. Let Pol have his. That's all I ask."

"There's more, though. You learned from Andrade, there must be more."

"We both learned from Andrade—and very well, too, I'd say. Wouldn't you?" Sioned smiled briefly. "Rohan used to tell me that the difference between him and her was that although he used people, too, it was only to do what they would have done themselves anyway. What their own instincts would have led them to if only they'd thought of it first."

"As you're doing with me tonight. I like Rohan's way better." He smiled back. "What's the rest of it, Sioned?"

"All right, yes. There's something else." She leaned forward, fingers tightly laced. "When it comes time—and don't ask what I mean, I'm not sure myself—you're going to have to give over control to him." She saw Andry's shoulders stiffen. "He's High Prince," she insisted. "Unless you want to be, and I know damned well you don't, it must be his work. By doing what I hope you'll do tonight, he won't just take your gifts and use them—and he could, you know. He saw me do it at Stronghold. He's a quick learner. But for his own sake, he can't be allowed to do that. He must treat you with the respect you deserve."

"Allowing us both our pride?" Andry leaned back in his chair and crossed long legs. "Very well, then, I'll be just as honest with you. This elaborate emotional game isn't necessary. I promised Hollis that Pol and I won't carve each other up into little pieces. We'd be killing my brother."

Her turn to be startled, knowing she shouldn't be. As their love for Sorin had kept them civil to each other for so long, now their love for Maarken would do the same.

"Andry." She held the bowl out to him. "Find her."

His rings clicked softly against the silver as he cradled it in his hands. Sioned held the thin, curving surgical knife between two fingers, hoping not to leave too great a trace of herself, and slid it into the water. It very nearly vanished on the wide, flat bottom of the bowl.

Actually, she had lied some. Pol was perfectly capable of this—and, as it was a *diarmadhi* spell, he would be better at it than Andry. The rest, however, was true. She understood her husband's son and her husband's nephew as if they had both been born of her own body and blood.

Still, she wondered what Andry was going to say when he found out who and what Pol really was. Cami's mirror made that discovery certain. Ah, well; worry about it when it happens, she told herself.

"I'm not getting anything." Andry's brows nearly met over his nose with the ferocity of his scowl. "Damn it, I've done this before—"

She thought for a moment, then suggested, "Too many other kinds of light? I shut the curtains to moons and stars, but maybe the hearth is distracting you."

He glanced at the flames and winced. "You may have something there. It hurts my eyes." After a slight pause, he said, "It's not just fire, is it?"

"We're a little short on trees to burn." Obligingly, she doused the Fires of her making, from the candle branch near the bed to the hearth. A reflexive, wary glance at her hand in the darkness showed her no emerald glow pulsing in precise rhythm to her heartbeat. *That* was something she would prefer not to explain to anyone until she could explain it to herself.

But there was a glistening in the room now, coming from the bowl in Andry's hands. He had called Fire into the Water, and it lit her heart to pity for his tired face.

"There, that's got it," he murmured. "Much better. Now to focus on Chayla through her knife—"

All at once his body shuddered convulsively and he cried out. The Fire vanished from between his hands. Sioned relit the hearth instantly. Andry was shaking, sweat standing out on his forehead and upper lip.

Sioned snatched the bowl from him and put it on the rug. Quickly she poured wine and made him drink, then smoothed his hair and waited for sense to return to his eyes.

"Goddess," he whispered as color seeped back into his face. "I've never felt anything like that in all my life."

"What was it? Is Chayla in pain?"

"No—it was that damned knife." He looked up, a rueful twist to his mouth. "I know it should be something used often by the person you're looking for, but couldn't you have chosen an earring or a button? That thing's brutal, Sioned."

She sat down very hard in her chair. "Andry—it never even occurred to me."

"Me, either." He stared into the bowl at his feet. "It was the oddest feeling. Pain, as if the knife had cut into me, but—I don't know, gentleness, perhaps. Compassion. And a determination to heal, polished by knowledge. . . ." He trailed off, embarrassed.

"The things Chayla feels when she uses it? Yes, I see."

Gingerly he dipped thumb and forefinger into the bowl, lifting the knife by its handle. "If that's what's in her mind and heart when she works, I wonder she can't cure people by just touching them. Evarin will either be ecstatic to find another bred-in-the-bone physician, or else insanely jealous."

"He'll get over it," she said impatiently. "Are you sure you're all right?"

He nodded, turning the knife this way and that to watch Fire play on steel. "Remind me to gloss this spell in the margin of the Star Scroll. 'Never, ever use anything with an edge or a point.' You'd better note it in your copy."

"It's at Stronghold."

Andry frowned. "Burned?"

"No. But they won't find it. The Star Scroll isn't something one keeps out on a shelf. Besides," she added with a shrug, bending to retrieve the bowl, "what could they do with it? They can't use it. There's no danger to us if it's found. Not like Feylin's dragon book."

"Actually, they're rather the same. You obviously meant them to use her book or you wouldn't have been so artistic at Remagev—oh, of course I heard about that!" He smiled briefly. "You burned what you didn't want them to see—the truth. For all its vagaries, there's truth in the Star Scroll, too. And your copy is a clear one, without Lady Merisel's little confusions."

"What's your point?" she asked curiously. "There's not a spark of power in the lot of them. They can't use the Star Scroll."

"Let's say that there's a field bare one day and covered in grass the next. *You* don't find it remarkable because you know that seeds in the ground sprouted overnight. But if you knew nothing about seeds or the way things grow, the sudden appearance of grass would be magic."

Sioned frowned into the bowl on her knees. "Well . . . yes, I see what you mean. Finding out that there are spells and recipes and so forth behind what we do, that it isn't the hand of the Goddess working through us—"

"Never explain a mystery when keeping it a mystery is to your benefit."

She nodded agreement, disliking it on principle but admitting she'd put it into practice quite a few times. "Andrade would appreciate that. And she'd probably blister my ears for not thinking this through better. I'm sorry, Andry. When I tried to find something Chayla uses that's the essence of her, I naturally chose one of her instruments."

"The stronger the association, the more powerful the pull."

"Then you saw her?" she asked eagerly. "You found her?"

"The pain shook me up for a moment. Evarin will tell you I got a good knock on the head in the battle and I admit it scrambled my wits for a time. But what I saw is coming back." He closed his eyes, fist clenched around the handle of Chayla's knife as he concentrated. Voice soft, almost muffled, he began, "Dark. Thin starlight. Walking beneath trees, off the road, under cover. Hands free. Head bent, starshine on her hair. . . ." He paused, frowning. "Men watching her. One in particular—twice her size, something in his face I don't like. . . ."

"What about the terrain? Give me something I can use."

"Curve of the road around a gigantic pine . . . sheer drop just beyond where it clings to the cliff . . . cave half-hidden in the trees on the slope above. Faint light there. Horses tethered nearby. Four—no, five." He was silent a moment; Sioned held her breath. Then he opened his eyes. "That's all. Just the cave and the tree. I'm sorry."

"That might be enough," she mused. "Ruala and Riyan know this part of the Veresch—and if they can't identify it, their hunt master might." Leaning back, she cradled the bowl in her hands and considered for a time. "They haven't tied her up. They let her out for fresh air and exercise. They're not monsters."

Andry reached for the winecup, saying bitterly, "They want her alive and healthy to hold for ransom."

Something else to worry about when it happened. "Let's think about when they can travel. Not by sunlight, not by moonlight—why not by starlight? If they know about Sunrunners, they know we don't use it."

"Most of us, anyway."

"Most of us. But back to the point. When can they move? Only when there are clouds that blot out *any* kind of light."

Andry nodded slowly. "I've good reason to know the weather's been miserable. How much looking have you been able to do, and can you calculate how far they might have gotten during the time you haven't been looking?"

"Always assuming they need to eat and sleep like the rest of us, and which direction they're going—"

Andry's brows arched. "South, of course."

"Would they?" she challenged. "That's the first place we'd search."

"Where else would they go except to their High Warlord?"

"Oh, I don't doubt that. The question is how they'll get to him. . . ." She gnawed her lip. "Someone here *must* be able to recognize that tree and cave combination."

"And then?" he asked softly. "How do we get her back without risking her life?"

She decided not to tell him about Kazander. "That's for military minds."

"Which lets me out." Andry sipped at his wine. "I wish I'd paid more attention to your brother when I was his squire."

"Davvi? Good Goddess, he was no more a warrior than you are. Oh, Kostas did very well in the field, but not because his father taught him much beyond what happened in 704." She shook her head sadly. "Rohan hoped none of you would have to study war."

"Maybe if we had, we'd be doing better now. Speaking of study, I hear you and Meath are holding classes."

With perfect calm, Sioned replied, "Yes, we are."

His lips quivered with amusement. "Did you think I'd come roaring in here to forbid it? Sioned! Why should I make a fool of myself condemning something that's not only a practical necessity, but that you'd go on doing with or without my permission? It's much wiser to condone it. And I trust you won't mind if I give my official approval by doing some teaching myself?"

"I wish you would," she said honestly. "But watch out for Jihan. I think we've convinced her to hush up and listen, but that child's silences make me nervous. You never know what's going on behind them."

"I'll bear that in mind." Rising, he placed the knife and winecup on the side table and stretched from toes to fingertips. "That bath did me a lot of good—nothing cracks when

I move," he observed, though he rubbed at his sore shoulder as he spoke. "Shall I go talk to Pol now, or wait for tomorrow? Frankly, I've got the grandsire dragon of all headaches."

"That's one reason this sort of thing isn't done too often. Go to bed. Your Master Physician won't thank me for giving you a strain like this when you've had a bad bump on the head."

"I really ought to go see Pol," he said, his eyes solemn.

"He can wait until you're feeling up to it." She paused. "It was you who killed Miyon, wasn't it . . . Master Sorindal?"

"I didn't think Alasen would remember the name."

"She did—and the unfamiliar face that went with it. For a while afterward she thought you were part of Miyon's ambush, until she remembered what you called yourself. 'Sorin's shadow.' "

"I can feel him here," Andry replied softly, glancing around the chamber. "Does anyone else?"

"All of us, all the time." She watched him in silence for a moment. Then, because unexpected questions often brought interesting answers, she said, "I'm not up on shapechanging. Is it difficult?"

Andry was a past master at the verbal parry. Even with a throbbing head, no sleep, and the rigors of a desperate ride behind him, all he did was smile and say, "Not when you've practiced as much as I have the last thirty days. I think you'd find it intriguing."

She ruffled her own hair. "Not that I need much disguise these days. Half the servants at Skybowl and Feruche didn't even recognize me when I arrived."

He inspected her, a little smile dancing across his lips. "You know, I rather like it. You look younger."

"Looking and being aren't even in speaking distance of each other," she assured him. "Go to your bed, Andry. Sleep well."

"Good night."

When he was gone, she reached into a pocket and pulled out a small glinting bit of silver, an earring set with carved white sand-jade. She had searched Meiglan's room earlier but found nothing that was strongly enough hers to use. She had brought little with her from Dragon's Rest, still less on the flight from Stronghold, and packed almost all of it for the journey home. Only a lace scarf was left behind, and a horn comb used while she was here. But the lace had spent too much time in the weaver's hands, and Meiglan had probably used the comb on the girls' hair. Sioned would search again. If she found something, and if Pol could settle enough to work . . . well, they'd see.

As for the earring—she would use that herself, later, to find Kazander.

She had lied some about her own talents with this spell, too.

✳

It was said that the Isulk'im could hide in the wind. Tonight it was true. Twenty-one lean black shadows on black Radzyn horses galloped down a mountain road, the wind-roar in the trees muffling even the thunder of their hoofbeats.

Very suddenly, Kazander reined in. The rest stopped instantly. He turned his face to the sky, where clouds drew swift veils across the stars. Fine tremors shook his body and his eyes turned blank and blind.

In every mind was the same thought: *Ros'eltan*. The Black Warrior, to whom the Goddess spoke on the wind.

In Kazander's mind was Sioned.

Steady yourself, my lord. It's sheer luck that I found you. Every one of you is a shadow in the darkness. Don't try to reply—you're not a Sunrunner and this isn't a Sunrunner spell. Just listen. Chayla is being held forty-five measures from the crossroads ahead of you. Near a place where the cliff road curves around a giant pine, there's a cave almost directly opposite the tree. Ruala recognized it and was very specific. Chayla may still be there tomorrow night—they don't dare travel when there's light for us to work with. But if she's not, she won't be far and traces should be there to follow. Bring her back to us, Kazander. May the gentle Mother of Dragons shelter you beneath her wings.

Then she was gone.

He turned to his fellows, trembling now not with shock but with eagerness. A quick glance at the sky told him there wasn't much of the night left; even if he pushed his men and horses to the breaking, it would be well past daybreak before they reached the tree and the cave.

"Find us a place to sleep," he ordered Visian. "We reclaim

the lady tomorrow night. Our wise and powerful High Princess has shown me the way."

None of them thought he referred to Meiglan.

✳

Until she saw the glint of eyes in the firelight, Chayla thought they were all asleep. He had set a guard outside, of course—pacing footfalls counting off the moments of the night. Four and a pause, four and a pause, maddening as the drip of a water-clock in an otherwise silent room.

He was watching again. The others had stared—at her blonde hair, her blue eyes, her pale skin. He *watched*.

She shifted against the stone wall behind her, trying to find a place where rocks didn't jab into her spine. She was as far from them as she could get, as close to the fresh air as he would allow, unable to bear the stink of them. Distance from their odor, however, also meant distance from the only source of heat. After four nights of this, one would think she would stop being so silly. She was cold. She needed the warmth of the fire. It occurred to her that this was a stupid time to develop a squeamish nose—she who had been up to her elbows in blood, and sliced into putrefying flesh without a grimace.

What was happening to her was real now. All the time, not just in spurts. The cold was a fact, and her weariness, and trying to keep down the food they gave her. The bread was pungent with mold, the meat so highly spiced to disguise its age that tears streamed from her eyes as she gagged it down. It humiliated her to think they might believe she was crying. She supposed she was lucky they shared their rations with her at all.

Cold, exhaustion, stomach cramps, and the smell of their unwashed bodies. Those things were real. Sunlight was not; she hadn't seen any. Logical. They feared *faradh'im,* and so moved only when there was cloud cover, and even then kept beneath the trees. If the sun or moons threatened, they built shelters of branches or found caves. Tonight, with the wind blowing hard, Chayla assumed there were no clouds—but they did not travel under starlight, either.

She didn't know how far they were from Ivalia Meadow. The first two days had been real only in sharp jolts like pricks of a knife, and now that she thought back on them she knew what a fool she had been to succumb to shock. She was a physician, she knew the symptoms, she should have recognized them and dragged herself out of stunned lethargy.

But she hadn't, and now hadn't the vaguest idea of where she was. Twenty, fifty, a hundred measures in any direction from the meadow.

Not that knowing her location would have done her any good.

She wasn't afraid of him—of any of them. They hadn't touched her, had been almost polite. They gave her food and water, let her walk off her saddle-stiffness, allowed her decent privacy to attend to her physical needs.

That was the only time he didn't watch her.

The others only looked, fascinated by her strangeness. He was the one who searched beyond the color of her eyes to what might be found within. He was doing it now—catching her gaze, trying to reach into her. She bore it as long as she could, then turned her head away.

The guard came in quickly, nearly treading on her feet, and said something she didn't understand. On the other side of the small fire, he sat up, the blanket crumpling around him. Flames danced off the golden tokens in his beard. A question was asked, answered, and he stood and kicked his companions awake. A harsh order was given and they hurried out into the night.

Chayla scooted to the mouth of the cave. Fire-dazzled eyes saw nothing, but she heard horses, voices. Not even an instant's hope heartened her; they spoke the old language, or their version of it. Whoever these new arrivals were, they had not come to help her.

Levering her chilled body upright, she took a few bold steps outside. A hard hand grasped her wrist—the first time any of them had touched her since she had been seized in the meadow.

"Let go of me," she said without fear, and tried to shake him off.

But she was hauled down the slope to the road. Someone had lit a torch, and by its light she saw a score of riders on her grandfather's finest horses. Even after so long, the sight of that still made her angry. Goddess, how it made her angry.

She was released, and stood rubbing her wrist. She found him with her eyes, glared at him. He paid no attention.

"Faradh'reia," he said in triumph to another tall, bearded

man on a gray stallion, and then a word she didn't understand. *"Brenac."*

The rider leaned down, peering at Chayla. She wanted to
spit in his face when he began to laugh.

"Princess?" he mocked, and the others of his party chortled in response. A gesture brought forward another rider,
leading a dainty mare. *"Kir'reia!"* he announced.

The cloaked figure astride the mare looked up dully. The
child in her arms stirred. Chayla nearly strangled trying not
to gasp her recognition.

But Meiglan had seen her in the windblown torchlight.
Her eyes were black wells of terror. "Chayla?" she breathed.
"Oh, Goddess—no—"

"Chayla?"

This time when he stared at her, it was with narrowed
eyes. He repeated her name, then those of her father and
grandfather.

"Faradhi!" the mounted leader growled, and spat. All the
rest of them did the same. "No princess!" He flung an arm
toward Meiglan, who flinched, then struck his own chest in
pride of ownership. *"Kir'reia tir!"*

There ensued a discussion Chayla didn't even try to follow. Meiglan's cloak had shifted with her movement; one
sight of Rislyn's face told Chayla that the little girl was ill.

"Shut up, all of you!" she snapped, starting toward
Meiglan's horse. "They need my help, I'm a physician—"

He closed his fingers around her shoulder tightly enough
to break bones. "No princess!" he growled accusingly.

The newcomers all laughed. Their leader said something
else, and they rode away. Chayla struggled, hearing Meiglan
cry out her name. Then her voice was lost in the sound of
galloping hoofbeats and laughter on the night wind.

Chayla was dragged back up to the cave. "No! Turn me
loose! What are they going to do with her? Where are they
taking her? You're nothing but cowards, all of you, preying
on women and children—"

He flung her down before the fire and loomed over her.
"No princess," he said once more.

"No! I'm not a princess, damn you! But my father is the
Battle Commander of the Desert and my kinsman is the
High Prince, and they'll kill you!"

The words were brave and ridiculous, and she knew them

for what they were: the sound of her own voice to fling against sudden fear.

He paced the short distance to the rear wall and spun around, thrusting out an accusing finger. *"Diarmadhi?"*

Her answer was immediate and vehement. "Certainly not!"

Incredibly, he looked disappointed. She wanted to slice out her own tongue. She should have claimed to be a sorcerer. They shouted the word in battle, they were allied with the Merida, everyone said they were on the side of the *diarmadh'im* even though they worked no spells. She could have used her Sunrunner gifts, done something else they would consider magical—

Except that she knew nothing beyond how to call a tiny fingerflame. *"Light to see by, that's all I need,"* she'd told her mother. *"The rest can wait until I can be a Sunrunner as well as a physician. I don't have time right now."*

Oh, Goddess, why had she never found the time?

He was pacing again. Short, sharp steps, boot heels digging into the rocky floor. His finger suddenly stabbed into her face. She flinched back.

"Faradh'reia!"

"No! I'm not a princess! And I'm not *faradhi,* either! Do you see any rings, idiot?" She held up both hands, infuriated to see them tremble. Clenching her fingers, she repeated, "I am *not* a Sunrunner!" And felt, stupidly enough, that in denying what she was, she had betrayed her parents and her heritage and even her Uncle Andry.

He spat on the ground. Just when she thought he would stalk out in disgust, he stopped, firelight seeping wickedly into smiling black eyes.

Terror, lurking for four days at the edges of her soul, found her then, seized her by the heart and mind and claimed her for its own.

"No princess ... *no diarmadhi ... no faradh'reia,"* he murmured, and his fingertips stroked a dirty path down her cheek.

It was real now. All of it. Hideous and unrelenting and real.

✳

Sioned found Pol in his bedchamber. He had cramped his long body into a window embrasure, knees to chin, hair glinting by feeble candleglow.

"You look like seven kinds of Hell," she told him.

"No," he muttered. "Only three."

"Meiglan, Rislyn, and Chayla," she supplied. "I would have thought there'd be four."

He winced.

She hesitated, then said, "Waiting for the clouds to clear, I take it."

"They haven't. Not where it was important to look."

She didn't order him to bed. Sleep wasn't something anyone was familiar with these days. Standing beside him, she rested a hand on his shoulder and felt him shy as if touch hurt.

"Kazander will find Chayla tomorrow night," she said quietly, and when his head jerked up in surprise, told him what she and Andry had done.

Hope blazed in his face. "Then Meiglan—"

"Perhaps. I came to look through these rooms again. Did she leave anything behind that we can use?"

He searched the chamber with his eyes. "No. Nothing. I would have noticed it by now. There's nothing left of her here. . . ." Resting his forehead against his drawn-up knees, a shuddering breath sighed out of him. "I should have—"

"No, you shouldn't," she interrupted. "They took her for a reason. If it's to lure you out of Feruche to a battle you'd lose along with your life, then they'll be disappointed. Meiglan and Rislyn won't be harmed, Pol. Didn't you hear what Alasen said? That Miyon was adamant about it."

"Miyon is dead. What happens when they're taken to the High Warlord? I've got to *do* something, Mother, I can't just sit here and—Goddess, what are they doing to my wife, my daughter—"

"Stop it," she commanded, fingers clawing into his shoulder. "Nothing will happen to them. It's you they want. You've said it yourself, *Azhrei.*"

"But you can't risk *me*—and Meiglan and Rislyn are expendable!" He lurched to his feet, nearly knocking her down. "You never cared about Meggie, never wanted me to Choose her—"

Sioned remained silent as the accusations went on. It was not her he railed against; it was himself, and the new emotions that made mockery of that Choice. Meiglan on one side, Sionell on the other, and Pol snared between, paralyzed by guilt. Sioned thanked the Goddess he *was* paralyzed. Taking action now, when he could not think and all his emotions were dangerous, would be fatal.

A fire iron was seized like a sword, wielded viciously against the dying hearth. Sioned waited him out. When he set the poker back into place, it rattled with the shaking of his hand.

"I'm sorry." His voice was subdued. "None of that was fair, or true."

She said nothing.

"I don't know what to do, Mother." He spoke to the dim flames. "I can't ride out to find them if I don't know where they are. Walvis has sent people out from Skybowl to search. Everyone who can is looking for them when there's light enough. Ruala came close to being shadow-lost last night, did you know that? I'm doing all I can think to do and it's not enough. They have my wife, my little girl. What they really want is me. That's what I have to give them."

"On their terms? The sacrificial prince?"

"If necessary."

"Don't be a fool!" she exclaimed, her voice rough with fear.

He didn't hear her. "They're savages," he said to the fire. "Barbarians. If I offer myself, if my death would satisfy them so we'd be left in peace—"

"It wouldn't. You know it wouldn't." She shook her head, still surprised not to feel the weight of her hair, to feel instead the swift tousle of it around her cheeks and neck. "We don't have any evidence that it would. We don't even know who these people are!"

"Don't we? What about their battle cry?" He turned suddenly to face her, his body like a rope yanked taut. "Mother—what if I reveal myself as *diarmadhi?* What if I claim to be something besides the *Azhrei?*"

"Andry would love that, wouldn't he!" she snapped. "Not to mention all the people who believe with him that sorcerers are evil! What would you do, Pol, proclaim yourself rightful ruler of the Vellant'im, a prince of savages? Even if you succeed in taming them, who would accept a High Prince to whom the enemy bows down in homage instead of in defeat?"

For a moment he looked as if he might argue. But then all the tense energy drained out of him and he bent his head. "You're right, of course."

Sioned's knees went a little weak with relief. She sat on the window seat and folded trembling hands in her lap. "I understand, Pol. You're looking for anything that will get Meiglan and Rislyn back. But you can't offer yourself in their places, and you can't make some wild claim that might or might not work."

"Then tell me how, High Princess."

"I don't know," she replied, damning her helplessness.

"That's not the answer I need to hear."

"It's the only one I have."

He began to pace, but not with the usual supple quickness. Each step was heavy, almost hobbled. "So we wait like Father always did, and see what solution presents itself? This isn't politics, Mother, it isn't someone's scheme of power. These are the lives of my wife and child! I won't be pushed until the only way out is of Vellanti making!"

She bent her head. There was nothing more to say and they both knew it. After a time Pol stopped pacing and looked down at her.

"You were up all last night, and now most of this one," he said colorlessly. "Go get some rest."

Sioned pushed herself to her feet. At the door she paused with her fingers on the dragon's head handle. "Pol, this *is* about power. They didn't take your wife. They took the High Princess."

"She's not like you," he answered in a muffled voice. "She's too—"

"Gentle? Sheltered? Not like your ruthless mother—*either of them?*" she snapped. "Meiglan ordered her own kinsmen executed without blinking an eye. The action of a High Princess—brutal and necessary. Just like me. One of the few real privileges of the position and its power is to do what you have to in order to make the world the way you want it to be."

"Oh, and I can do that by waiting for other people to force me into actions I never chose?" He laughed bitterly.

"You can do it by not acting before you know what will come of it! Let's say they made a ritual sacrifice of you— let's even say they were satisfied and sailed back where they came from! Who would be High Prince then? Andry? He's got the bloodline and he's got Goddess Keep and all the Sunrunners behind him. Is his world of rituals and sins the one you want to make for your children?" She flung open the door. "You just think about *that* for a time, High Prince!"

✳

Jihan began screaming sometime after midnight. It was dawn before Pol soothed her back to sleep.

Her cries still echoed in Pol's ears as he climbed wearily to the battlements—like his father, seeking a dragon's perch. His dragon curled in the sand far below him, not appreciating this change in position. Usually it was Azhdeen who looked down on Pol.

There was light enough to weave, to communicate. Pol didn't use it. How could he ask the dragon to fly the morning sky, searching for Meiglan and Rislyn—who were with those who would kill Azhdeen and call themselves glorified?

Yes, I'd risk even you if I thought it would do any good, he thought, watching the tentative sunrise shine on golden hide. *I doubt you'd understand. Hatchling dragons are lost all the time. As for females—if one leaves, there are always others—*

He balked at that thought and shook his head at the injustice. *No, because Meiglan and Rislyn are part of me, you'd want them back as much as I.*

"But there's nothing I can do," he said aloud. Just to hear someone say it. Frustration choked him, but he forced himself to repeat it. *"Nothing!"*

They were searching every way they knew, everywhere they could think to look. But the Vellant'im weren't stupid. They knew to stay out of usable light. They knew their safety was in darkness and clouds.

Azhdeen roared, wings spreading wide. Even without a connection between them, the dragon was sensing emotions that confused him. Pol hesitated a moment too long in turning for the stairwell—

—rage—fire—kill—talonrip—bastards—bloodclaw—fury— Meiglan—rendflesh—swordthrust—Rislyn—hatchling—avenge defend KILL—

The dragon's shriek deafened him. He was lying on his side on the stones, twisted, his hip and shoulder bruised. He pushed himself upright, gulping air, sick to his stomach as he realized how easily he could have tumbled over the ramparts to the Desert below.

Azhdeen was skyborn, still bellowing his fury—and Pol's. A primal emotion; familiar. Of human guilt and fear and pain, he understood nothing. Pol sat there in mute bewilderment, bereft of the rage that had kept him functioning. In the clear soft light of dawn, he sat there on the cold stones and cried.

✳

There was a point beyond which the brain refused to sustain its connection to the body. Chayla had seen it happen a hundred times. Pain simply stopped registering as the mind sought protective oblivion from the unbearable. Chayla had watched for it, knowing she could set broken bones, clean the worst wounds, ply suturing needles as necessary without worrying about the patient's agony. But once the mind reawakened, pain returned tenfold, as if avenging itself for the denial. Capable physicians gave pain-killing drugs before that happened.

She didn't remember when her mind had abandoned her body. But there was no soothing, numbing potion to ease the rejoining—although memory efficiently provided the names of several suitable to her need, according to a purely professional evaluation of her injuries.

The inventory was not all that bad, really. No broken bones, though the ribs were badly bruised. There were more bruises and some torn muscles along back and shoulders. Weals on breasts and thighs. A cut lip that had nearly stopped bleeding. A mild throbbing at the back of her head where it had struck the ground hard. Not much blood there. Not much blood at all, except—except—

She shied away from the specific pain that had called her mind back into its battered shell of a body. The physician calmly noted what had been done and gave assurances that it would heal. But Chayla could not acknowledge what the pain meant.

A cold breeze wrapped around her naked skin. She wished it was water, enough to wash away the filth, enough to float forever in silken cleanness. She remembered how in childhood at Whitecliff even the sight of the sea from her windows made her queasy. Now she wanted to plunge herself into endless water and have a Sunrunner's honest excuse to vomit.

She forced herself to sit up, push matted hair from her face, open her eyes. The fire had gone out, and she was alone. Morning seeped through the green weaving of trees at the mouth of the cave. She drew on her clothes, wrenched muscles protesting every movement. Her shirt and tunic and trousers weren't even torn. Why should they be? He weighed at least twice what she did, and was three times as strong.

Her clothes stank of him. Her skin felt of him. Her mouth tasted of him and her own blood. There was no part of her body that did not bear his imprint.

She didn't want to wash in an ocean of water, she wanted to drown in it.

Sliding along the wall to the entrance, she peered out at what little she could see of the world. A thin forest of evergreens, a road below, a great sentinel pine, a canyon wall beyond, western crags painted by dawnfire.

Had she expected the world to change? That the sun would hide in shared shame, the sky wrap itself in mourning gray, the rocks bleed in sympathy?

Was this what awaited Meiglan?

She drew back into the shadows as two of the Vellant'im strolled by. One of them was *him*.

"No *reia*, no *diarmadhi*, no *faradhi*," he said, ticking off the words on his fingers, and laughed as he finished with, "No *brenac!*"

Dully, she waited for the meaning to come to her. It took a long time. When it did, she bit her lip and shuddered.

Woman-child, he'd said. *Virgin*.

Oh, Goddess.

My father will kill you—and my grandfather will tear apart what's left and feed it to the carrion crows.

She told herself she had enough Fire to kill him. To kill them all. She was a Sunrunner. Her parents were both powerful Sunrunners. Her uncle was the Lord of Goddess Keep himself. She could do it.

She searched for rage enough to lend her strength. All she found was numb weariness. The time for it had come and gone. Killing would not undo what had been done to her last night, again and again and—

No. I won't remember. I won't!

The physician remarked that once more her mind was choosing to abandon her flesh—not from pain this time, but from loathing. She curled against the rock wall and closed her eyes, willing her brain and body to separate.

It was very hard. There were so many bruises, so many memories in her flesh that moaned of their hurt, like feverish children crying for their mother. Her mind rejected them. Their whimperings slowly faded away. The last thing she thought before she thought nothing more was that perhaps, if she was very lucky, she would never have to listen to them again, never have to fit herself back inside her body again at all.

CHAPTER FOUR

Prince Tilal held a debate with himself all the way from High Kirat to the mouth of the Faolain: sneak up on the Vellant'im or march in as if he owned the place? (Well, his nephew Daniv *did* own the western bank of it.)

The victory at Swalekeep argued the direct approach. Surely word had spread; mere sight of Ossetia's dark green banner with its golden wheat sheaf ought to scare the enemy witless. He was well aware, however, that he owed that triumph not to superior numbers or his own skills as a commander, but to a ruby-eyed dragon token stolen from the enemy's ally, Prince Rinhoel.

Tilal was still weighing probabilities thirty measures from the sea. He must decide soon. Now. If only the sky would clear and allow Andrev to scout ahead for him. Riders searched as far forward as they dared. No one was sure where or whether the Vellant'im lingered along the river. Burned farms and unharvested fields offered nothing to live on, but Riverport might still be garrisoned and the enemy seemed able to supply themselves with food and drink out of thin air.

He worried the problem and his lower lip until both were raw. Slink in by night and slit throats? Surge over the coastal hills and slaughter them in open battle? Be bold or be sneaky? Challenge them or trick them?

But Tilal had seen too many of his people wounded and killed. As he wobbled between various plans, fighting them out in his mind and unable to accept even the most optimistic estimate of casualties, he learned something about war.

When a commander's first concern became his army instead of victory, he was very likely to lose that army in defeat.

As it happened, the decision was taken from him. On the morning of the sixtieth day of Winter, the storm that had bellied up the river and provided cover for Saumer to enter Faolain Lowland drew its last wispy veils north. Andrev used the clear sunlight immediately, and within moments reported that a battle was already going on.

"There's a lot of fighting onshore, my lord. But—you'll never believe this—Prince Amiel's flag is raised on two of the five ships in the bay!"

"Amiel—?" Tilal swung around and stared southward as if he could see this marvel with his own eyes across the intervening measures. "Goddess help him! You're right, Andrev. I *don't* believe it!"

"The ships the Vellant'im still hold are going after the other two. They're heading out to sea at a good clip."

Tilal frowned. "Where do they think they're going? Oh, never mind. I know you don't know any more than I do. All right. As I understand it, his 'army' consists mainly of physicians. Young idiot! How in Hells did he take those ships?" Turning to Chaltyn, he said, "There's no time for anything pretty. Fifteen measures at a hard gallop, and then hack our way through them."

"Very good, my lord."

"No, *not* very good at all. But at least we may surprise them."

They did.

The fight was over by noon, with nothing elegant about it. Vellant'im gathered along the bay turned their backs to the sea and fought even as they were driven into the surf. Some of them died hip-deep in saltwater. But most of them did die. The beach was so soaked with blood that the sinuous tracery of driftwood and shells marking the wave line was obliterated for a full measure of its length.

Tilal learned three interesting things that afternoon when he and Amiel finally met over a belated meal along the rocky shore. First, Nyr was pregnant. Amiel announced this before anything else, and as if no one had ever accomplished such a thing before.

"Congratulations," Tilal said politely. "I understand your enthusiasm, but perhaps we can discuss your dynastic triumph after you've told me what in all Hells you thought you were doing by stealing those ships."

Amiel blinked. "Didn't I tell you?"

"No. What you've said thus far is, 'I'm glad to see you, my lord,' 'Thank you for your help, my lord,' 'I hope you weren't injured, my lord,' and 'My lady wife is expecting a child, my lord.' " Tilal grinned. "Pull up a rock and sit down. You can tell me the rest of it now that the really important news is out. Andrev, some wine to toast the next prince or princess of Gilad. Oh, your pardon—Amiel, you don't know Lord Andrev, my Sunrunner and squire. It was his sighting of your little seaside party that brought us here at speed."

"Lord Andry's son?" Amiel's hazel-brown eyes popped. He recovered himself in good order and nodded acknowledgment of Andrev's bow. "I've your skills to thank, then, for sparing my people more hurts. I'm in your debt."

"Not at all, your grace."

"Where's your lady, anyhow?" Tilal asked as he settled down to eat.

Amiel pointed. "See that hill? I told her to stay put until I came for her." Then he sighed. "Which, of course, means she'll be down here before Andrev has sliced the bread."

The second piece of news held a great deal more fascination for Tilal. It seemed that after picking up troops from the beaches of the Pyrme and the mud of the Catha delta, the dragon ships had been anchored in Faolain Bay for several days to wait for all the remaining troops to march back downriver.

"I learned this from one of the physicians—a Fironese who can make himself understood without being suspected of anything but an odd accent. He talked to one of their sentries last night—"

Nyr arrived then, to be duly greeted and congratulated. She seated herself on a convenient rock, cushioned with a soft woolen blanket, and thanked Andrev with a lovely smile as he gave her food and drink. Amiel paused to admire her, then mentioned where he was in the story.

She smiled innocently. "Have you said yet how our physician got away with impersonating a Vellanti warrior?"

Amiel grinned. "To give this devious woman her due— seven days ago she ordered him to stop shaving."

"I approve of devious women," Tilal replied. "Beards

aren't too fashionable anymore, but they can be useful. Go on."

"Well, he heard that they'd wait one more day for some clan or other—they organize themselves into kin groups which are further divided into sections of forty-five, according to which island they're from and which of about fifty different warriors they claim as their primary ancestor, and—"

"One more day?" Tilal prompted.

"Huh? Oh—yes. So I knew that if we were going to steal the ships, we'd have to do it today."

"Then the ones we pushed into the sea this morning—"

"—are mainly the ones who destroyed Riverport and marched up the Faolain. The ones from the Pyrme and the Catha are on those three ships we missed." He frowned. "They're chasing our two right now, aren't they?"

"Andrev?"

The boy was silent for a time. Then he met Tilal's gaze. "There's a good wind, and they're good sailors. They've passed the headland into the channel between Radzyn and Dorval, my lord. If Prince Amiel's ships can lose them among the Small Islands. . . ."

"Yes, but that leaves three ships full of the whoresons to land and march up to Stronghold."

That was the third item, and the most momentous. The Fironese physician had learned that, according to the High Warlord's vision—"That was the word he said the man used, my lord, a 'vision' and not a battle plan"—all surviving Vellant'im would soon be at Stronghold. To what purpose, the physician hadn't dared ask for fear of giving himself away.

"How many to a ship?"

"About three hundred. The two we took were for the ones they're expecting, and empty of all but the crew. So we simply stole a couple of longboats by night and—"

"Excellent," Tilal interrupted, thinking that he'd have time to hear the whole story when the bards made it into a ballad. Until then, he had other things to do. "Andrev, how many ships are off Goddess Keep?"

"Seven. Prince Arlis sank the others in Brochwell Bay."

"He did?" Nyr asked eagerly.

"When?" Amiel seconded. "How did it happen? We've been completely without news since we left Medawari."

"I'll tell you all of it soon," Tilal promised. "Let's call it ten ships of three hundred each, added to the troops at Radzyn and Stronghold—"

"And those on Graypearl, my lord," Andrev reminded him.

"Goddess, yes, I'd forgotten. Well, when they leave, at least poor Ludhil can come down from the mountains and take his island back." He did some rapid calculations—and had to pause for a bracing gulp of wine.

"Pol's in trouble," he said at last. "I make it at least three thousand, possibly more, all converging on Stronghold."

"How many does he have at Feruche?" Nyr asked in a whisper.

"If he's lucky, seven hundred."

Amiel's windburned face paled. But it was only a moment before he earned Tilal's admiration by saying briskly, "You know, I haven't been to the Desert in years. Nyr, my love, how do you fancy a look at Radzyn Keep?"

✳

Andry had been talking almost without interruption for quite some time. His throat was dry as he said, "So I thought Miyon must be on his way here, to lie his way out of the implications of what he did. I didn't realize what he was really up to until it happened."

Pol shrugged and hooked a finger at Kierun, who immediately poured more taze. "You did what you could, Andry. And that was plenty, believe me. I can't tell you what a relief it is to be rid of him."

Andry nodded his thanks to the squire. At the beginning of the conversation, the boy had eyed him the way a colt eyes a hungry dragon. Now, at nearly noon, when most of the tale was told, evidence that the Lord of Goddess Keep made mistakes like anyone else had obviously eased Kierun's mind. Andry noted it with an inner smile.

"What I don't understand, though," he went on, "is why he didn't go to Rezeld. I was convincing enough with Chiana and Rinhoel. Why didn't Miyon join them as my Merida impersonation bade him do?"

"I suspect he saw something Chiana didn't." Pol tilted his chair back on two legs and propped one booted foot on the table. "Did your host at Swalekeep tell you how Tilal got the Vellant'im to march where he wanted them to?"

"He was a fine gossip, but tavernkeepers aren't privy to military secrets."

Pol delved a hand into a trouser pocket and produced a little green-glazed ceramic dragon. "This is from my father's collection at Stronghold. Maarken found them on corpses after the skirmish he fought on his way from Remagev." He tossed it to Andry, who sat a quarter of the way around the table. "They're made of various materials. Gold and silver indicate someone important. Safe-conduct passes, essentially. You're damned lucky Chiana and Rinhoel are fundamentally idiots. If they'd asked, and you hadn't been able to show them one of these, they would have killed you."

Andry turned the token in his fingers. "So Miyon knew I wasn't who I said I was. I wonder why *he* didn't try to kill me."

"Presumably, you had a superior—of whichever faction—to report to. If you didn't. . . ." Pol shrugged.

"Why wasn't I told about these?"

"Because no one could find you. Who knew you'd traipse around enemy-held countryside from Ossetia to Princemarch?" Pol was smiling, shaking his head. "Cousin, you're the same breed of crazy I am. Probably why we don't get along."

Andry had to laugh. "At least you drag an army along in your wake. Me, I get stuck with a lame-legged physician. How's Evarin feeling, by the way? I didn't have time after breakfast with my daughter to look in on him."

"Maarken played tyrannical Battle Commander and ordered him to stay put. His intent was to hobble around tending the wounded."

"He's better, then." Andry paused. "Pol, I have to thank you for what you did for Maarken."

"Oh, yes," Pol replied bitterly. "I did a lot. I didn't see the bastard in time to prevent—"

"I used to watch you practice at swords, you know," Andry interrupted. "You were only fourteen but already good. Maarken wouldn't have had you at his back if you weren't. You aren't to blame for what he lost any more than I am for what you lost."

Pol was quiet for a long time. Then he drained his cup and said, "Goddess, aren't we tender of each other today? Sorry about this, thank you for that—does it make you as uneasy as it does me?"

"Yes," he answered candidly. "But we haven't gotten to the difficult parts yet, have we? We've stuck to what's already happened, the things we can't change. We do share the same kind of insanity, cousin—neither of us crazy enough to fight over a bone that's picked clean."

"The meat lies elsewhere." Pol agreed. Over his bent knee he regarded Andry with clear, blue-green eyes. "Well, shall we carve it—or each other?"

Andry took his irritation by the throat and strangled it. Calm and composed, he said, "I made a promise to Hollis, for Maarken's sake. You'll hear no dissent from the Lord of Goddess Keep unless what the High Prince plans would harm the Sunrunners."

"For Maarken's sake," Pol agreed.

They regarded each other for a time in perfect understanding. Both knew how binding their promise was—and how fragile. They had been brought together by tragedies. They shared immediate common goals. But sooner or later one of them would make a chance remark, and all the old enmity would boil up again.

And if it came to the point where Andry's power rivaled Pol's—

"When I rode in," Andry heard himself say, "I half-expected—and don't hear this wrong—but I kept looking around for Rohan."

Grief flickered in blue-green eyes. "So do I. They say 'High Prince' and I keep looking for my father. You were lucky, in a way, when you took over Goddess Keep. People have been calling you 'my lord' all your life."

"Yes, but it was a year before I connected that note in their voices with the Lord of Goddess Keep, and still longer before I stopped listening for someone to say 'Lady Andrade.' "

Pol smiled—his father's wry and charming smile, but without Rohan's gentleness. "It's Hell having to be a grown-up, isn't it? Do you remember when we were children, and the only thing we worried about was whether we could get somebody clever to be our dragon? Which reminds me, whatever you do, *don't* let Jihan cozen you into that, or anything else!"

"I hear from Tobren that she calls Fire rather enthusiastically."

"Meath says he'll teach her not to burn the castle down."

"Perhaps a lesson from the Lord of Goddess Keep would help."

Pol's head tilted curiously. "You'd teach her? And the others?"

"You mean so far in advance of when tradition says they ought to learn?" Andry shrugged. "I've been thinking about that for several years. Why should we wait to show Sunrunner children what they are, what they can do and become? But there are very good arguments on both sides. If they learn young, they're easy with what they are. They grow up knowing—the way you grew up knowing you were to be High Prince."

"And now that I am, it's not easy—but I understand what you mean."

"Your mother is a case in point, about knowing she was a Sunrunner. She didn't—or, rather, she knew but didn't dare say anything. Her brother's wife didn't exactly appreciate the prospect of a Sunrunner in the family."

"Yes, but my late Aunt Wisla's appreciation of becoming Princess of Syr *because* of the family Sunrunner was truly profound," Pol remarked, and all at once Andry understood what differenced him from Rohan: cynicism.

"Pol, how many children hide and deny what they are because they're afraid? That weighs heavily in my mind, and it makes me want to find these people as young as possible. But—"

"But then there are the ones like my Jihan—power to spare and very little restraint in using it." He paused while Kierun filled his cup again. "Doesn't that argue for teaching them the ethic while they're young?"

"Of course. But it's a long process, you know, and forcing them to grow up too soon isn't a wise move. I look at what this war has done to Tobren, how hard it is to make her laugh. . . ." He shook his head. "Teach them early and impose Sunrunner discipline on them, or wait until they've formed their own discipline of their own choice? It's an interesting problem."

"And yours," Pol said with obvious relief. "Let me know how you feel about it once you've spent some time teaching Jihan. I'm betting you'll come down on the side of waiting.

A hatchling like that is a handful enough without adding Sunrunner training to it."

It was no time for Andry to reveal that he knew Jihan was no Sunrunner. In fact, he had every intention of teaching the child; the *diarmadhi* taint would be countered by proper *faradhi* disciplines, as it had been in Riyan and Torien and several others. The younger the better, as far as such people were concerned.

But he kept all of it from his face and eyes, and chuckled instead. "I admit the prospect of being knee-deep in precocious children is an appalling one. They'd bring the walls of Goddess Keep down around our ears."

"Speaking of which—what do you think the Vellant'im are waiting for? I mean, their ships are just sitting off the coast, staring at the towers."

Andry grunted. "I hope winter fog wraps them closer than a Giladan wool blanket and they all ram into each other and sink. Whatever they come up with, Torien can deal with it."

"He knows how to work the *ros'salath?*" There was nothing but honest curiosity in the question.

"Certainly."

"I'd be interested in your opinion of what we did at Stronghold," Pol continued. "Maarken told you some of it, I'm sure, but he wasn't included in the working. Ask my mother. Between you, you should be able to figure out a way to use it more effectively."

"We?"

"Me." That smile again—but this time instead of cynicism there was the gleaming of a dragon's teeth. "But you expected that, Andry."

"Yes, I did." He leaned forward, his ten rings and wrist cuffs shining as he flattened his palms on the table. It was like surcease from chronic pain to feel them against his flesh again. "I will do all I can, and that includes protecting my brother from anything you and I may disagree about. But I will not be ordered. And *you* expected *that,* Pol."

"Certainly," he echoed. "We understand each other, my Lord."

"We do, your grace."

On this note of not-quite-sweetest harmony, Meath entered the room without bothering to knock. His graying hair was windblown as a boy's, his eyes alight and nearly hidden by the width of his grin.

"Your firstborn's filial duty to you, my Lord," he said to Andry, then turned to Pol. "Andrev has just told Hollis, who's just told me, that there's been a battle fought and a victory won at Faolain Bay. Prince Amiel took two Vellanti ships, and the other three turned tail and ran for the Small Islands. Prince Tilal's cousinly compliments to the High Prince, and do you want him to start for Radzyn Keep now, or take care of the pestilence at Lowland first?"

Pol's foot slipped off the table and his chair nearly toppled. "Radzyn?"

Andry had more immediate concerns. "Is Andrev all right?"

"Perfectly. Even if he weren't, they're with Prince Amiel's little army of physicians. Twenty or thirty would swarm all over him if he even stubbed a toe. Well? What's your pleasure, my prince?"

Having recovered himself, Pol was almost laughing. "By the Goddess, I'd forgotten how good good news can feel! My congratulations to Prince Tilal and Prince Amiel—who deserves to be taken over somebody's knee. I thought I taught my squires to be more sensible than to risk their lives in silly adventures like stealing ships. Don't you go getting any ideas, Kierun," he added, wagging a finger in the boy's direction.

"No, my lord." Kierun's mist-gray eyes brimmed with mischief. "Not yet, anyway."

"Goddess, why am I afflicted with other men's sons?" Pol moaned. "At this rate, I'll have to sire a dozen of my own to avenge myself on their fathers!"

"Perhaps I should lend you my younger boy," Andry drawled. "Joscev is only seven, but already the plague of the schoolroom."

"The true family spirit, eh?" Meath grinned.

"Goddess help us," Pol sighed. Then, more intensely, "Meath, have Tilal sit tight for a day or two, as unobtrusively as possible. I have something in mind that may spare giving those physicians something more to do. Tell him to camp on both sides of the river and wait."

Andry frowned, trying to envision it. Then he smiled, almost fondly. "You're going fishing and he's the net."

"Absolutely. The problem is to get the fish to swim in the right direction. But I think I know how. And I need you in order to do it. We'll have a little talk with Johlarian at

Faolain Lowland. With the full force of the High Prince and the Lord of Goddess Keep behind the order, not even the acquisitive Lady Karanaya will refuse to give up her black pearls to the enemy."

Andry sat forward. "The—what are they called? Tears of the Dragon? Why?"

"That's what the Vellant'im are after. As I understand it, they used the sale of them to get into Riverport, fully expecting to reclaim them. But Karanaya rode off with all six, so they besieged Lowland. My mother scared them off with her Fire dragon, but now they're back. And they still want those pearls." He rose and began to pace. "There's something very odd about them, Andry. Johlarian didn't see it until I told him how to look—he's competent at his work but not especially powerful. If Karanaya's within sunlight, I want you to take a look at them and tell me what you see."

"Odd in what way?"

"You'll find out." He swung around on his heel. "Meath, have Hollis convey all this to Andrev. Do it now, before Tilal gets restless and starts to move."

The Sunrunner bowed slightly. "At once, my prince. But you know how disappointed young Saumer will be if there's no battle at Lowland. There's one other thing. Tilal believes the Vellant'im will gather soon at Stronghold. He estimates their probable numbers at three thousand."

Andry gave a low whistle. "Thank you for not telling us that first!"

"It's why he wants to go to Radzyn and take out as many as he can," Meath explained. "But if he's right—"

"Then in a short while the only people still in danger will be us," Pol finished. "From Kierst-Isel to Dorval, everyone else will be free of them. That's good. That's very good."

He actually sounded happy about it. Andry blinked. "It is?"

Pol gave him a smile. "Of course. It's good for the other princedoms, obviously. It's good for the High Prince and the Lord of Goddess Keep, too. Also obvious if you think about it a moment."

Andry did, and decided he would have preferred a less life-threatening way to demonstrate his power.

"And it's good for the rest of us because it's *very* bad for the Vellant'im," Pol went on, looking feral again. "They'll

all be in one place. We won't have to go chasing them down
to destroy them."

Cautiously, Andry asked, "Has it not occurred to you that
we might—"

"No," the High Prince said fiercely. "It has not. And part
of your job is to make sure it doesn't occur to anyone else,
either." He flattened his hands on the table, three rings—
topaz, amethyst, and moonstone—shining. "All right, then.
We'll work our trick at the Faolain if we can, then think
about how to kill three thousand Vellant'im."

"Goddess help us," Andry added, meaning it.

"I think she will," Pol told him. "She always struck me as
the kind of lady who enjoys a good show. Meath, after
you've seen Hollis, please find Maarken and Chay and have
them come here. There's work to do."

*

By the time Johlarian finished speaking—firmly and without
apology, as both Pol and Andry had instructed—Karanaya
was livid.

"No! I won't!"

Mirsath squared off against her in the sunlit courtyard.
"You *will*, if I have to rip those damned things from around
your neck!"

"They're mine! I won't give them over to that pack of
savages!"

Saumer, whose female relations were generally even-
tempered—or at least considered screeching beneath their
dignity—frankly gaped.

"Give those pearls to the Vellant'im and they'll leave us
alone!" Mirsath shouted. "I should've made you do it long
ago!"

"I'd like to see you try!"

Johlarian ventured, "My lady, it is the command of the
High Prince and the Lord of—"

"I don't care if the Goddess herself commanded it!" The
black pearls shimmered with her rage.

"My lady," Saumer said reasonably, "I'd much prefer to
do battle with them and rid Lowland of their presence that
way. But surely once they've been defeated, Prince Tilal will
find the pearls and—"

"Pol made no mention of it," she fumed. "Doesn't he understand that they're all I have left? This was my father's castle and it should be mine, but now it belongs to Mirsath. Idalian will have the rebuilding of Riverport as his lot, and I wish him joy of it. My family has nothing else to give me."

"But your prince does," Saumer pointed out.

"I may be a beggar, but I won't take his charity!"

The young man turned to the Sunrunner in bewilderment. Johlarian only sighed and shrugged. Mirsath wasted no time trying to comprehend his cousin. He advanced on her with one hand outstretched.

She clutched the gems around her throat. "No!"

Johlarian lifted one hand suddenly. "Wait." His eyes glazed over and Saumer felt a subtle tingle at the edges of his own thoughts. Goddess, to be able to do it so easily! War was currently very useful work, and he was good at it. But to be a Sunrunner. . . .

At length Johlarian looked sternly at Karanaya. "The High Prince commands it. He watches us even now, and the Lord of Goddess Keep with him."

"He spies on us!" she burst out. "That's what comes of having a Sunrunner for a prince! Rohan would never—"

"Rohan would have *asked*," Saumer blurted. "My brother Arlis knew him well, and from all he ever said about him, High Prince Rohan wouldn't have ordered—"

"But Lady Andrade *would*." Johlarian spoke from sure knowledge of that ruthless mind.

Mirsath shrugged impatiently. "I don't care if it's wrapped in silk or raw wool with thistles still in! You were given a command by your prince and Lord Andry. Hand them over!"

✳

Pol leaned against the frame of the sunlit window he shared with Andry and blew out a long sigh. "I thought she'd *never* give them up."

"Interesting woman," his cousin remarked.

"*You* can say that—you're not her prince," Pol retorted. Then he sighed again. "I do her a disservice. She stood on the ramparts of Faolain Lowland and pretended to summon a dragon—didn't even flinch when one appeared. Courage and stubbornness made her do it. Unfortunately, they also make her somewhat difficult."

He rested his head against carved wood, watching Andry

stare down at the kitchen garden. Servants were planting seeds. Pol thought this showed a remarkable optimism. Did they continue the usual seasonal progression in serene certainty of the harvest—or in defiant hope?

"Andry?"

"Mmm?" He didn't glance around.

"You surprised me just now."

"Really?" A tiny smile twitched the sensitive mouth.

"I thought you'd bargain your help for getting your son back."

Andry said nothing.

"For Maarken's sake, then?" Pol asked softly.

"Mainly Andrev's," he answered softly. "He'd never forgive me. Of course, *I'll* never forgive Tilal. But that's unimportant, compared to my son's pride."

Pol moved away. "You're welcome to sit in with your father and brother on the military part of it if you like. It's your neck, too, after all."

"So it is. But I don't have any training in such things."

"Nor I." He slouched into a chair. "Oh, I'm all right once I'm in the middle of a battle, but the real work of planning it . . . actually," he confessed with a brief smile, "it bores me. All I ever do is tell them what's going on, let them know my idea, and let them work out the specifics."

"And while they do, you'll go search for your wife and daughter." Andry approached slowly. "They won't be harmed, Pol."

"I wish I could believe that. The Vellant'im have never taken hostages before. Why now? And why two women and a child?"

"Ransom. I'm told you're the price." He hesitated, and then said something shocking. "Would they settle for the Lord of Goddess Keep, do you think?"

It took Pol several moments to recover. Had he really so misjudged Andry all these years? Or was this a ploy for greater power? The noble Lord of Goddess Keep offering himself to the enemy's wrath—only to work some magical scheme that would save himself and everyone else, too?

Switch identities, and there was his own rather nebulous plan.

"We really are far too much alike," Pol said with an honest smile. "I appreciate the thought, Andry, but if either of us proposed to exchange ourselves for the captives, our beloved parents would take us over their collective knees."

"And take turns blistering our asses?" Andry grinned back and shook his head, clean light gilding his brown hair. "No, too crude. Your mother and my brother would simply fry our colors for us on sunshine. Well, then, what else? Have you thought of using your dragon in some way?"

"Have Azhdeen fly over and scare the Vellant'im?" He shook his head. "They're more likely to kill him. Dragons *don't* scare them anymore." But Meiglan was terrified of them, even of Azhdeen. His Meggie . . . what were they doing to her and Rislyn?

"Those pearls," Andry said abruptly. "I understand what you mean."

Pol felt his thoughts being dragged in a new direction. He made an effort and caught up. "It's no wonder they want them back—but why risk them at all?"

"Do they really know what they are?" Andry countered. When Pol frowned, he went on, "Mirsath and Karanaya don't see it. Johlarian has to concentrate and know what to look for. Saumer spotted it at once. But there's no evidence that any Vellanti has perceptions comparable to a Sunrunner's—or a sorcerer's."

If you only knew. "The pearls are priceless in and of themselves. You saw how beautiful they were."

"That has something to do with it, yes."

Pol said nothing, knowing that his cousin wanted to be prompted and damned if he'd give him the satisfaction.

Andry gripped the finials of a dining-table chair. "You have the Star Scroll, but not the histories. Pearls are mentioned only once. Lady Merisel preferred diamonds and emeralds." He smiled slightly. "Her description of what she wore to a victory banquet goes on for half a page. But there's only one instance when she wore pearls—shaped like teardrops and glowing like black rainbows. They must be the same ones."

"How many?"

"She didn't say. Enough for earrings and a necklet, anyhow. She loved jewelry and always wore at least that much, and usually rings and bracelets and sometimes a circlet as well. She called it her one weakness—and I think it's probably one reason Sunrunners wear rings."

"Could be. When did she wear the pearls?"

"It's part of what made me remember. She visited the Desert once—and only once, she hated the heat—and was entertained at Stronghold by a distant ancestor of ours. It was a Dragon Year. That's what she said she came for. She'd never seen a dragon, so they rode out to Rivenrock to watch the hatchlings claw out of the caves."

"But you think she had some other purpose for the visit?"

"She always did." He snorted. "Hells, she could have given Andrade lessons. But I don't know what she had in mind this time. She didn't say, and I can't connect anything that happened later to the Stronghold visit. Anyway, that night she wore the pearl earrings and necklet."

"So they were hers," Pol mused.

"And you're wondering why I didn't claim them myself, for Goddess Keep."

Pol laughed softly. "Oh, cousin, this feels much more natural, doesn't it? You've just repaid me for what I said about Andrev. No, I don't wonder any such thing. First, the pearls are useful. You've as tidy a mind as anyone I've ever known, and if they gain us a castle's safety and a few hundred captive Vellant'im, then they'll have done their work. Second, it seems to me that Lady Merisel herself would be pleased by the trick. And third—" He grinned. "—Tilal *will* get them back, you know. We can argue about who owns them then."

The Lord of Goddess Keep offered brief laughter like a man paying a tax. "I wonder how much luck I'll have prying them out of Lady Karanaya's clutches."

"It'll be fun to watch you try." Pol rose. "Let's go see what's keeping Chay and Maarken. If I can't do anything myself, then I might as well exercise my privileges as High Prince and tell everybody else what to do."

CHAPTER FIVE

Pol was huddled over maps with Maarken, Chay, and Andry when the Attic door burst open, propelled so hard that it rattled the cabinet crammed in behind it.

"Papa, Papa!"

Jihan raced across the room and grabbed his arm with both fists. The pen in that hand dragged a thick black line across a map of the Veresch spread on the table.

"Papa, it's Linnie, she's hurt!"

The four men exchanged quick glances. Pol dropped the pen and took his daughter's shoulders. Her blue eyes were huge and wild, her cheeks so sickly pale that the freckles stood out greenish-yellow like bruises. "What is it, sweetheart? What's the matter?"

The two other twins in the room came to her at once, kneeling on either side of her. Maarken spared a glance for Pol, but Andry wasted no time on someone who could never understand. In a soft voice he asked, "What does it feel like, Jihan? Something you can't quite see from the corner of your eye?"

She shook her head violently. "No! I *felt* it—all hot and achy and scared, and they won't let her sleep—they just keep riding and riding, and it's cold and hot all at once—"

"Jihan," Andry said firmly. "Tell me what you're feeling right now."

She froze in Pol's gentle grasp. After a moment she shook her head again, frustrated, tears welling. "Papa, she's not there anymore!"

"Of course she is, darling," he said, gathering her in his

arms. Her head burrowed into his shoulder. "It's just the feeling that's gone. Rislyn is still there." But his gaze met Andry's, begging for reassurance.

"She'd know," Maarken mouthed silently. Andry nodded confirmation. They rose to their feet, looking only at each other now, twins who knew what it was to lose a twin. Pol rocked Jihan, trying to soothe her, watching his cousins. All at once Chay spoke behind them.

"Rislyn's a Sunrunner, too."

Pol frowned his confusion. But Andry was nodding, and Maarken bit his lip before nodding, too. Then he understood: neither Sorin nor Jahni had been gifted. Both Rislyn and Jihan were.

"So the connection is stronger?" he asked, finishing the thought aloud.

"Probably." Maarken hesitated, then went on, "Andry, do you think—?"

"Could be."

Pol was following them now—a bit belatedly, most of his concentration on the shivering child in his arms. He walked over to the windows to give Maarken and Andry freedom for a whispered consultation.

"Shh, it's all right," he crooned. "You and Rislyn are very special, did you know that? You're twins, like Chayla and Rohannon are twins, and both Sunrunners just like them, too. That means you have a special bond with each other. You've felt it before, haven't you?"

She nodded against his shoulder, sniffling. "Little bit. More since Granda Sioned and all the light at Stronghold."

He could feel his cousins listening even as they spoke to each other in low voices. "And you can tell when Linnie's happy, or upset—"

"Or cold, like in the stone house." She raised her head, sniffling, no longer crying. "I can see colors, too, if I try really hard in the sunshine."

"Can you see mine now?" He moved into the wedge of light coming through the window. She smiled slightly, touching his hair.

"You're all kinds of colors, Papa. More than Princess Alasen—and all swirling around through each other." She wriggled around in his arms and looked at Andry. "I saw him, too, just before Mama—and Linnie—" She trembled again and he held her closer.

"Shh. It's all right, sweetheart. We'll find them." He paused, meeting Maarken's eyes. The older man nodded. "In fact, I think you might be able to help us."

Jihan came up with the obvious very quickly. "I don't know how to go Sunrunning. Are you going to teach me?"

"Not just yet," said the Lord of Goddess Keep, with an easy smile. "But you know what, Jihan? I think I'd like to see *your* colors on sunlight. May I?"

She nodded shyly, clinging a little tighter to Pol. Andry came to them, standing with them in the sunshine. After a moment Jihan gasped softly in wonder. Andry caught his breath, too. Pol was tempted to enter the weaving, but did not. Not just yet.

"My lady," Andry said at last, "you will make a fine, strong Sunrunner one of these days."

"I know," Jihan agreed proudly, and Pol hid a smile.

"But you have much to learn, and I'll enjoy teaching you some of it," Andry went on. "For now, if you can, I'd like you to think about your sister for me."

"You mean find her on sunlight?"

"No. Just think about her."

Pol said, "Think of Rislyn's colors, and how she might be feeling right now." A quiver coursed through her, and he smoothed her hair. "It's all right if you don't want to, love. And it's all right if you can't."

"I can do it." She closed her eyes, delicate pale brows knitting over her nose. Pol sensed Andry thread the sunlight around her, so gently and unobtrusively that even he was impressed by the subtlety of Andry's touch. Pol did enter into it then, sliding himself into the loosely woven fabric, watching the colors that skirted each other with exquisite precision.

All at once Jihan stiffened and cried out. The sunlight unraveled so swiftly that Pol was momentarily blinded. Jihan was crying again, sobbing against his shoulder. Andry took several steps back out of the sunlight, looking stunned.

"Papa! Papa! It *hurts!*"

Frantically he tried to soothe her, rocking her, whispering, holding her to his heart. But she shook as if her small bones would shatter. At last he gathered up bits of light and wove sleep around her. She resisted for a moment, then seized on the refuge and went limp in his arms.

"What in all Hells did you *do?*" Chay demanded.

Andry, still shaken, managed, "It—it wasn't me. It was her. She connected for just a moment—I know that much. But having me there seemed to intensify it. She wasn't feeling Rislyn's fever at a remove—she was feeling it as if it were her own."

"Fever?" Maarken asked.

"Rislyn must have caught what the other children have," Chay said. "Did *you* see anything? Any indication of where they are?"

Andry shook his head. "I just felt the fever. I'm sorry, Pol. I shouldn't have put her through that, just on a chance that it might work."

"We had to try it," he muttered. "I'll be back in a little while." And he left the room, his sleeping sorcerer-child cradled in his arms.

✳

Chayla spent the day within the cave—sometimes sleeping, sometimes simply curled around herself, around the body she loathed. She could hear them outside, sheltered from Sunrunner eyes amongst the trees, arguing with each other. But not with him. She did not hear his voice at all.

They left her alone.

She had resigned herself to the fact that by now her brain had taken up permanent residence inside her body again. Being a brain—and an intelligent one, at that—it thought and kept on thinking. Sleep was her only escape. Given a choice between waking thought and sleeping dreams, she settled on the former. At least she had a little control over it. Not much—every time she moved there was a new ache to remind her—but she could consciously distract herself. Dreaming, she was at the scant mercy of her own mind.

Thinking, then, she found distraction in the cave around her. It was not a place of dragons. No claw-gouges on the walls, no ground-up shell shards or marks of ancient flames on the ceiling indicated past use as a hatching cave. The chamber had been carved by the river many hundreds of years ago on its slow, inevitable course between mountains, pushing at softer rock until it collapsed. Though Water was the Storm God's Element, caves had ever been the special places of the Goddess. Wombs of the Earth, where dragons—creatures of Air and Fire—were born.

Long ago, during the conflict between Sunrunners and Sorcerers, *faradh'im* had met secretly in caverns. Perhaps even this one. For a moment she imagined her ancestors crouched around Fire, plotting the destruction of their enemies. *They* had faced people with powers as great as their own. How ashamed of her they would be for allowing these savages to defeat her.

Outside, they seemed to be trying to decide what to do with her now, with no one winning and thus nothing being done. Every so often one of them spoke the names of her father and grandfather; she wondered what they thought the Lord of Radzyn and the Lord of Whitecliff could pay in ransom, with both rich holdings in Vellanti hands. But she doubted they wanted gold or anything else. She was worthless to them now.

Did they speak instead of what Maarken and Chay would do to them if they were caught? A fearsome vengeance, exacted by redoubtable warriors—and for nothing. She was not a princess, not a Sunrunner, not *diarmadhi*, not a virgin. Not anymore.

"My father will kill you. . . ." There were two things wrong with that. Her father mustn't risk his life—and why must she rely on him? She could kill them herself. She was no weak and timid woman to wring her hands and beg some big, brave man to protect her. There was Fire in her. She could kill them herself.

Practically speaking—the physician in her thought in cool, reasoned practicalities—if she didn't get all of them at once, the ones who remained would kill her for a *faradhi* witch.

That was a remarkable thing, really. She didn't want to die. It would have been very easy to accomplish. She was a physician. She knew exactly how to get the work done with a minimum of pain and fuss.

But why should she? *He* was the one who deserved death for what he had done. And with that small spark of anger that she had even for a little while wanted to die, she began to live again. Only a little, and reluctantly at first. Yet she was alive, and meant to go on being alive, if only to see *him* dead.

She was a physician, as inevitably as Andry had become Lord of Goddess Keep—a Sunrunner forbidden to kill with the gifts. But he had. She was a physician, dedicated to preserving life, who had just rediscovered her own in the fierce need to kill.

She wondered wearily if being an adult was to glimpse, every so often, the Goddess smiling behind her hand.

The Vellant'im would die, and before she returned to Feruche. There must be none left for her father to risk himself in killing. But Maarken—gentlest and most civilized of men—Maarken's rage would be the greater for being deprived of its primary object. He would ride out to slaughter the rest of them for what one of them had done to his daughter.

So he must never know.

She pushed herself upright, leaning back against the rock wall. No one must know. Not for the shame of it, but for their lives' sake. And she had better start practicing her portrayal of scared-but-unharmed former captive right now.

It was dusk outside; astonishing. It had taken her a whole day to come to one obvious conclusion. She was disgusted with herself.

Rising and righting her clothes, she yanked on her boots and strode outside into the gloom. The Vellanti guarding the cave blurted with surprise and grabbed for her. She eluded him with a swift step and an icy glare.

"I want food and something to drink and I want it *now*," she snapped. "Food, you imbecile!" She pointed to where the others were crouched around a tiny fire, roasting some hapless bird caught for their dinner.

The guard gestured her back into the cave. She ignored him and marched to the clearing, and forbade herself to tremble as *he* turned to look at her.

A slow, secret, almost reminiscent smile began on his face. "Princess," he said mockingly, and his flame-shadowed gaze ran over her body.

Fury took her unawares, part fear and part anger and part hatred that this worthless carrion could have made her want to die. She imagined him eaten by Fire, screaming as it licked at his hair and clothes and beard.

And the flames circled by stones on the ground leaped in response.

The men tumbled backward, crying out. She stood perfectly still, knowing she had betrayed herself as *faradhi*, but curiously satisfied. He scrambled to his feet, and there was fear in his eyes. Goddess, how satisfying that was, to see *him* afraid of her. She began to understand a certain kind of power, and called the Fire higher.

Behind her, without warning, a gurgling choke of pain. Before her, lean black shadows drifting through the twilight. All around her, swift death.

Chayla stood still as a stone. Nothing touched her but the silent breeze of the shadows' passing. She watched him, held him with her gaze and would not relinquish him, the way legends said the dragons—and Lady Andrade— captured souls with a single glance.

A sword point burst like a small silvery flame below his breastbone. The steel gleamed, blood wiped clean by his skin and shirt. The blade was withdrawn with a wet, sucking sound. She watched him, keeping him alive through the sheer force of her eyes, wanting him to feel himself mortally pierced by that swordthrust. Violated. Rent asunder.

His lips parted in agony. No sound came from him, no cry. Only blood, leaking from his mouth as terror leaked from his eyes. He knew he was already dead. Chayla smiled.

She chose to let him go then. He fell on his face in the dirt.

Behind him where he had toppled stood Kazander, in black from head-cloth to boot heels, his teeth sparkling white as he smiled at her.

"My lady!" He gave her a bow and a flourish of his sword. Straightening up, he glanced once around the clearing, to the cave behind them, the road and the huge pine, barely visible now. Visian approached—she had trouble recognizing him, so alike were all the shadows around her— and saluted, brow-lips-heart.

"My brother, not one lost."

"Truly the Mother of All Dragons has watched over us this night." He sheathed his sword. "It helped that they are stupid—and most of all that my lady called Fire. The Goddess guided your gifts. You've taken no hurts?"

"None." There: the lie successfully told for the first time. "But I–I'd like to go home now, Kazander." Suddenly she began to shake, hating herself for it. Any moment now she'd start crying, and that would make him ask questions, and she hadn't told the lie often enough yet to make it completely natural. . . .

"At once. Visian!"

A horse was brought, and she suffered Kazander to lift her

into the saddle. Her knees wouldn't work. She kept herself from flinching as his hands circled her waist—not because a man touched her, but because what *this* man touched nauseated her. Surely he would smell it on her body, sense it in her flesh.

He settled her on her horse, then paused and looked up with searching eyes. "They did you no harm? None?"

"None," she said once more. But the saddle chafed the welts on her thighs, and it took all the strength she had left to meet his gaze calmly.

Nodding, he mounted his own horse and led her down to the road. There were black-clad Isulk'im everywhere. So many, risking their lives for her. It shamed her; it shamed her greatly.

"Kazander?"

"My lady?"

"Thank you."

He was shocked. "It is I who must thank *you,* my lady, for your Fire that made so easy the killing of the enemies of our prince."

"Pol!" Chayla's heart gave a sick thud. "Oh, Goddess—Kazander, I saw Meiglan yesterday! The Vellant'im have her and Rislyn!"

Visian heeled his horse over to them. "My lady, this cannot be true, they would not dare—the High Prince's wife and daughter—"

Kazander said through his teeth, "How did this happen?"

"I don't know, how could I know?" Memory of Meiglan's stricken face swirled in her mind. "It was yesterday morning, not quite dawn. They—"

"Riding south? To Stronghold?"

"I think so. They must be, mustn't they? To the High Warlord."

He nodded shortly. "Visian. Take my lady and eight *ros'eltan'im* back to Feruche. Tell the High Prince that I will reclaim what was stolen from him."

"There are at least twenty of them, maybe more," Chayla exclaimed. "I can ride back alone. I don't need—"

Kazander smiled. "Your courage is surpassed only by your beauty—and your stubbornness. Six of us will ride with you just the same."

"Absolutely not! I forbid it!"

"Six," he repeated dangerously, his smile gone.

"One," she shot back. "Or the instant we're out of your sight I'll order them to follow you and—and call Fire to their horses' backsides if I have to!"

Kazander chewed the ends of his mustache, eyeing his brother-by-marriage. "You are half an army in yourself when you put your sword to it. Guard her."

Visian's shoulders straightened proudly. "If any dare to threaten the lady, I will become five hundred swords."

Kazander reached into the breast of his tunic and extracted a thin, beaten gold circlet set with pale stones. "You know who I would have wear it."

The younger man bowed his head reverently and tucked the coronet against his heart. "Yes, my lord and my brother."

With a final nod, he wheeled his horse around and gave an order to form up for a long, hard ride. Chayla suddenly felt alone, bereft.

"Kazander!"

"My lady?" He turned in his saddle.

"Be careful." She reached for the right words, and found them in the tradition of the Isulk'im—his people that once had also been hers. "May—may the Goddess fold you in the shelter of her wings."

He paused a moment, then touched his fingers to his heart. "Your life is my life, *Zabreneva*," he murmured for her alone to hear.

And then he rode away, a black-garbed man on a black horse, vanishing into the night.

✳

Tobin was long since in bed, scolded there gently but sternly by her Namesake granddaughter. Shortly before midnight, Maarken left Andry's room for his own to take over the moonlit watch from Hollis. So it was in that curious suspension of time between midnight of one day and dawn of the next that father and son spoke, and were silent, and spoke again as the need occurred.

Family things, most of them. Tobin's illness. Maarken's injury. Brenlis and Rusina, mothers of two of Chay's grandchildren, dead at Vellanti hands. The children themselves: Chayly, Joscev, and Merisel, safe at Goddess Keep. Tobren, growing up too fast. Chayla. Rohannon, sailing the Dark Water, a Sunrunner on his feet because of *dranath*. Andrev.

"He won't come back to me. I can't order it of him."

"The contract was freely made between him and Tilal," Chay replied. He stared into flames that burned without need for fuel.

"Was it like this for you? When all I wanted was to become a Sunrunner?"

"Some. You never openly defied me. You just got everyone else to do your arguing for you." He smiled briefly. "But it taught me something I should've learned long before that. Denying a person's true nature is struggling against a sandstorm. It can be done, but it's a fight every step of the way, using energy better spent elsewhere. We are what we are, Andry. We become what we must."

They spoke of other men's sons—Rihani, who was dead; Saumer, who was discovering his abilities as a *faradhi*. Dannar, Ostvel's son who might have been Andry's (though neither said that aloud). Kierun, Sethric; Daniv, now Prince of Syr. Jahnavi, killed defending Tuath Castle. Edirne who had died in a senseless accident; Camanto, murdered by a sorcerer. And Tallain.

"Except for Rohan, that's the worst of all," Chay murmured. "I'm glad Rohan didn't have to bear the hurt of it. We loved him as if he were our own blood."

Andry's turn to speak to the Fire. "Tallain was more like you than I am. More like Rohan than Pol is."

Chay canted a curious look at him. "How so?"

"Pride without arrogance, honor without ostentation, laughter without mockery—his strength came from himself, not from power. A truly noble man. He . . . he always reminded me of Sorin."

"You view yourself and Pol rather harshly."

"So does he. We've spent years denying we're anything alike. But we are each other's mirror in many ways. I look at him and recognize parts of myself. What I am, what I might have been—what I have no wish to become. It's the same for Pol when he looks at me." He shrugged. "We're very frank about it."

*

Sionell was less than frank with Alasen when the latter came upstairs with breakfast for two, intending a private talk. Separated in age by twelve years, the women knew each other as parts of the vast interlocking kinweave spread across the continent: relations and friends of Rohan or Sioned or both. They met every three years at *Riall'im,* exchanged occasional letters, and liked each other well enough. But they had never been enough in one another's company to know each other intimately, or to become close friends.

So it was that Sionell took some time to recognize Alasen's tactics, but immediately thereafter knew what they maneuvered her toward.

"I don't know how Hollis does it," said the princess as they settled to the meal. "She goes about her duties, tends to what Ruala has no time for—not as if nothing had happened, but as if it can't be allowed to interfere with any life but her own."

"Meiglan's example," Sionell replied. "I'm told that when she got to Stronghold, she insisted on continuing the children's lessons, making life as regular as possible for them. She did the same here. It does help. It's at least one hand grasping something firm."

"Goddess, this taze is strong enough to fell a dragon! Perhaps a little honey to sweeten it. . . . Maarken is just as grimly occupied with military matters. But while there's much to be said for routine, it's rather mindless, isn't it? The hands are busy, and part of the mind, but the fear is still there. And in spite of all their pretending, neither sleeps at all."

She paused, stirring another dollop of honey into burning, bitter taze. *Here it comes,* Sionell thought.

"As for Pol—he looks dreadful. Sionell, you don't think he'll do anything insane, do you?"

She tore a piece of bread into crumbs. "There are plenty of people ready and willing to tie him down if he tries it."

"Yes, but he'll have to be untied eventually, and then he'll just figure a way to avoid us. What he needs is to be convinced that he can't risk himself."

"Sioned is very good at convincing."

The princess snorted inelegantly. "My children haven't listened to me since they were five winters old. Have yours?"

"Meig's only four, but I can already see the signs," she admitted.

"Well, then. We really can't keep the High Prince locked up for his own good. He's always been stubborn. One can't *tell* him anything. Someone has to tell him without telling him, if you catch my meaning."

Sionell dipped a spoon into her bowl of hot grains, making patterns in the raisins that sweetened the mix. How much did Alasen know? Or did she merely suspect? No one had breathed a word; no one had so much as cast a speculative glance in Sionell's direction. She had guarded her own feelings well enough. Pol was another matter, but she dismissed the idea that he was childish enough to reveal through look or speech what had happened that night. That wild, mad night when he had said he loved her. . . .

No, Alasen could not know. She must be remembering Sionell's girlhood infatuation, believing love enough was left to make her make the effort.

Resenting it, Sionell said with deliberate purpose, "He won't hear it from Andry, that's certain."

Alasen didn't even blink. "I agree. It must come from someone who cares for him—but who doesn't have any political motive. To almost everyone here, he's not just Pol. He's the High Prince."

"The Sunrunner High Prince," Sionell agreed pleasantly.

"Exactly. Much as we love him for himself, *what* he is never escapes our minds. It has to come from—"

"Jihan," Sionell interrupted, tired of the dance. "It's cruel, but we can use his own daughter against him."

Alasen was genuinely surprised. But she seized on the idea quickly. "Jihan. You know, I think you're right. After she tried to find Rislyn—yes, that's the way to do it." She rose from the table. "I'll go talk to Sioned and see what she thinks. As you say, it's cruel, but it'll work."

Sionell met the Kierstian green eyes calmly. "Who you were considering," she said, "was me."

"Yes," Alasen replied. "Forgive me."

"No need. That was all a very long time ago."

"As it was for me," Alasen murmured. "Or so one must remind others. Tiresome, isn't it?" She smiled and left Sionell to her untouched breakfast.

In the event, it had nothing to do with Jihan. Or Sionell, either.

Maarken and Riyan were having it out with Pol in the sunlit courtyard. A fine highborn disdain for the astonishment of the servants led them to conduct a shouting match in full view of anyone who cared to watch. Grooms to guards to maids who gaped from the windows, they all watched as their lord, their Battle Commander, and their High Prince fought like hatchling dragons.

"Have you lost your wits? 'Seems to be their purpose'—you'd throw your life away on a 'seems to be'?"

"There's no guarantee they won't just kill you and march on us anyway! I forbid it!"

Sioned and Alasen arrived, drawn by the noise, just as Andry took up position on the castle steps to watch. He waved them to seats near him, saying, "All we lack now is my father, who can yell louder than any of them. Happily, he's sound asleep and his windows overlook the Desert."

Tobin, however, was up and about. She and Hollis emerged from a storage shed, the latter holding a parchment inventory. The instant Tobin was within sunlight, she halted her limping progress and scowled in ferocious concentration. All three arguing men abruptly fell silent.

"Well, *that's* a relief," Sioned remarked.

Andry nodded. "Nice of them to conduct the battle out here, where she's free to be eloquent. Look at Maarken's face! Takes me back to our childhood."

"Can't you stop them?" Alasen asked Sioned.

"Why should I? Pol and I had this discussion before, as I told you. Evidently he didn't listen to a word I said." She gave a shrug and sat down beside Andry. "I'd make a wager, but it's obvious Maarken will win and none of you would take the bet. I rather miss the late Prince of Cunaxa that way."

Alasen was still standing, dividing a bewildered stare between them and the three men, who were still mute as Tobin used sunlight on them. "They're making fools of themselves!"

"Just so," Sioned told her. "And right out in public, too, where it'll do them the most good."

Andry eyed Sioned sideways. "Them, or the rest of us?"

"All of us," Alasen said suddenly, comprehension quickening her voice. "They get it all out of their systems. Pol shows he's willing to sacrifice himself, which appalls everyone. Hasn't anyone thought to remind him that if he dies, Jihan becomes High Princess?"

Sioned grimaced. "Yes. It doesn't seem to have made a lasting impression."

"So you're going to trust that Maarken and Riyan can argue him out of it—"

"—with a good deal of help from Tobin," Sioned added. "Whoops, she's given up on them. Look."

"Not given up," Andry corrected. "Had her say!"

Tobin had turned her back on them and was stamping across the courtyard for the main steps. She caught Sioned in a sunweaving and fumed, *Children! And yours the worst of the lot!*

You think I don't know that? Come sit down and be comfortable. We're likely to be here quite some time, for all your efforts.

The volume had decreased fractionally, but the fight raged on. Maarken was gesturing with both arms, instinct to hide the left one forgotten. Tobin settled awkwardly on the stair, helped by Andry and Alasen. Hollis hovered near Maarken, the parchment twisted in her hands. Her anguish sobered Sioned. Reaching out on sunlight, she said, *Come away, my dear. This had to happen.*

Sioned, make them stop! Please! I can't bear it!

She rose, well and truly worried now. Andry followed her to where Hollis stood trembling.

Pol caught sight of him. "Well?" he challenged, flushed beneath his tan. "What has the great Lord of Goddess Keep to say?"

Sioned held her breath. Andry merely shrugged.

"Whichever I choose—go or don't go—you'll think I'm trying to gall you into doing the opposite for my own purposes. Being damned whatever he says, the Lord of Goddess Keep says nothing."

Pol stared at him for some moments. Then he burst out laughing. "Beautiful! Perfect! Andry, what would I do without you?"

Incredibly, they grinned at each other. Hollis sagged with relief. Maarken looked chagrined; Riyan, suspicious. Sioned sighed in disgust and opened her mouth to order them all into the keep where they could discuss this as if they were rational adults.

"Open! Open the gates to the Lady Chayla!"

Sioned was the quickest. She caught Hollis as she lurched on her feet, held her up while Riyan and Pol performed the same service for Maarken. Every eye in the courtyard and watching from windows above fixed on the massive gates as frantic guards fumbled with heavy iron bars and hauled the gates open.

An Isulki warrior, all in black on a black horse, rode in first. Right behind him, drooping over her horse's lathered neck, was Chayla. Dirty, exhausted, alive. She slid from the saddle into her uncle Andry's arms and looked both surprised and annoyed when she fainted.

✳

". . . and so we came to the place of the tree and the cave, and waited in silence and secrecy for nightfall, and killed all the Vellant'im."

Visian never paused in all his long tale—not for interruptions, for no one else spoke, and not even to moisten his throat with wine. He had humbly declined all comforts offered—bath, fresh clothes, food, even the chair Pol himself pulled out for him at the oval table—until he said his piece.

But now that the recital was nearly done, he swayed a little on his feet. "Forgive me, your grace," he said, fingers clenched around the chair back. "There's not much more to the telling—only that we rode all night, and that Lord Kazander and my brethren now seek the High Princess and your daughter."

Pol nodded. "A few questions, my friend, and then you'll give yourself over to my squire's care—and no argument," he added as Visian opened his mouth to protest. "You'll only have to tell it once. We'll explain to Lord Maarken and Lady Hollis while you're resting."

"How did you know where to look?" Ruala asked.

Sioned answered for him. "Because I told Kazander what Andry saw."

"Chayla," Pol added succinctly.

Andry narrowed sharp blue eyes in Sioned's direction. "But I thought you said you couldn't—" he began, then subsided.

"Yes," she agreed. "That's what I said."

"Couldn't what?" Sionell frowned, as confused as Ruala and Meath. Neither did Pol fully understand, and he cast a suspicious look of his own at his mother.

Sionell persisted. "But how did you know where she was? And how did you tell Kazander about—"

"Sunrunner means." Sioned folded her arms on the table. "Visian, does he know where he's looking?"

The young man was bewildered. "Did I not say that part of it?"

"No, and that means you're half-asleep on your feet," she told him. "Answer this and then go to your bed, you foolish boy."

A blush stained his skin the color of strong taze in crimson crystal. "I'm sorry, your grace. I forgot to say what the Lady Chayla told me. Those who stole the High Princess and her daughter rode by two dawnings ago. They—"

"Chayla saw them?" Pol's voice was strangled.

"She did, your grace," Visian affirmed. "Whole and unhurt, though afraid—as is easily understood. Upon seeing the Lady Chayla, the newcomers scorned those who had taken her, and rode away south to where the High Warlord befouls the sands outside Stronghold."

"So much we guessed, about where they're going," Sionell mused. "But do you think Kazander will be able to catch up with them?"

"If anyone can," Ruala said. "But why were they—what did you call it?—scornful about Chayla?"

"Theirs was the greater prize," Visian said bitterly. "The Lady Chayla is not a princess herself, merely the granddaughter of one."

"Worthless, compared to my wife and daughter," Pol added in the same tone. He gestured to Kierun. "See Lord Visian to his room and make sure he stays there."

The young Isulki's eyes widened at the title. "Your grace, I—"

Pol arched a brow. "Even had you not done us this service—and don't talk to me about your duty—in Kazander's absence you're the leader of your people here. I suppose you won't allow me to make you an *athri*. You Isulk'im have no walls but those of your tents. But I can give you the authority. Kierun, push him, trip him, or have Meath carry him, but put Lord Visian in his bed."

Despite exhaustion, Visian was very much on his dignity. Meath proved unnecessary. When the warrior and the squire were gone, Pol rose, shoving his chair back so hard it toppled to the carpet. "What they want, they can have."

"Damn it!" Ruala exclaimed. "What's wrong with you? Didn't Riyan and Maarken convince you? You *can't!*"

"Everyone in this castle wails the same damned tune!" he snapped. "I'm tired of listening!"

"You haven't *listened* to a single word!" Ruala got to her feet, squaring off against him across the length of the table.

"Which of you listens to *me*? It's my fault they were taken—"

Sionell's voice was cool acid. "And what do you think will happen once you've sacrificed yourself?"

"That's not for you or anyone else to say!"

They had at it for some time. Sioned didn't even hear them. Sacrifice. Dragon sacrifice. . . .

Of course.

The Vellant'im would do exactly what the legends dictated. It was why they'd seized Chayla, why she had been rejected as worthless, why Meiglan and Rislyn—

The virgin princess, the pious invocations, the sacrificial murder by ceremonial knife, the whole barbaric, superstitious, brutal, *meaningless* ritual. . . .

They would do exactly what Feylin's dragon book told them to do. The book Sioned had left them at Remagev: facts burned, legends intact.

She had left them *instructions!*

Her heart pounded insanely, nearly throttling her. She had shown them how to kill. If not Chayla, then—

No. Kazander would find them, as he had found her. Sioned could not imagine him failing. Besides, Meiglan had borne two children, she—

But Rislyn.

They wouldn't kill a child. They couldn't.

Pol's wife and daughter had been taken to draw Pol to battle. It must be that. It had to be that. They wanted the *Azhrei*. Nothing anywhere told of a little girl being used as the sacrifice, all the stories were about older—

They wouldn't kill a child.

But if the Vellant'im *did* believe the superstitions, they'd need a virgin of royal blood. Not a child—please, not a child!

Jeni?

She was not a princess any more than Chayla was. But did the Vellant'im know that—any more than they had known with Chayla?

She rose to her feet, and the others fell silent. She was aware of Meath's worry-dark eyes searching her face.

"Enough, all of you!" Sioned told them, the words splinters of ice. "Try what you like, Pol—the gates will not open to you and no one will show you any other way out of Feruche. *By my command.* I am still a High Princess. And *I* say you will stay here until *I* say you may leave."

Pol got as far as "How *dare*—" before Sionell deliberately knocked over the pitcher, startling them all. The red wine stained the table like flowing blood.

Sioned left the room. Out in the corridor she sought a window overlooking the Desert. There was light enough and to spare. She twisted it with swift, expert turns of her mind and sent it to Skybowl.

There was no gentleness in the way Sioned grasped Jeni's colors. The girl fell to her knees in rough lakeshore sand, two hundred paces from her dragon.

Hear me, child Named for my childhood friend. This is a command of the High Princess Sioned. Never again venture outside the keep at Skybowl. Not even to the lake. Do you understand?

Yes—I—Goddess, it hurts!

I mean it to. Obey me, Camigwen. It may mean your life.

But my dragon—Lainian will—

The Vellant'im no longer fear dragons. Stay within the keep. Swear it!

I swear, your g–grace. Please, I can't breathe— Colors trembled and frayed with pain.

Sioned eased her grip. *Forgive me. But you must understand that you are in danger. You specifically. If they can, they will take you the way they took Chayla, and this time we may not be so lucky as to get you back.*

Then she's—

Yes. Returned to us safe and unhurt.

But why did they want her?

Because she is like you—a young woman descended from princes. I know you don't understand. It's not necessary that you understand, only that you obey me. Tell the others about Chayla, and that Kazander rides to find Meiglan and Rislyn. But this promise must be kept between us. There's no reason to alarm anyone if you have a care for your safety.

But Lainian! How do I talk to him? I have to be near him to share colors.

Talk to him from the walls. Do anything you like, as long as you don't go outside. Not a single step, not a fingerspan.

I promise, your grace.
Go back inside now, Jeni. Hurry.

She waited to make sure the girl did as told, then returned to Feruche. Meath stood at her elbow, watching her with a frown.

"Where?" he asked.

"Skybowl. I didn't think Pol had told them, and I was right."

Meath caught and held her gaze the way Andrade used to. She glared back irritably. "Oh, stop it!" Hurrying to the stairs, she climbed quickly, heading for Chayla's room. Meath followed. "And don't hover like Elisel does, either!"

He paid no attention to the rebuke, merely opened the door for her. Within the antechamber, Master Physician Evarin was resting in the depths of a soft, upholstered chair. He tried to rise and sank back down with a rueful smile.

"Your pardon, High Princess," he said, flicking a finger against the bandage around his leg. "No one ever told me Feruche had so many stairs."

"How is Chayla?" Sioned asked.

"Her parents are with her—sitting on either side while she sleeps, counting every breath. There's no need for it, of course. A strong girl, like all her breed. Bruised in spirit more than body. But that will heal now that she's back with her family, and safe."

"Meath, go in and share Visian's telling of it. I'll be there in a moment." When the bedchamber door closed behind the Sunrunner, Sioned took a step closer to Evarin. "You're good, my lad. You're very good. But there's something foul wrapped in those sweet words. Out with it."

The physician, caught off guard, abruptly lost the confidence of his accomplishments and looked exactly like the twenty-two-year-old youth he was.

"Quickly," Sioned insisted. "It will go no further than me."

Gulping, he tried to pull his professional dignity together. "Your grace—I didn't want to tell her parents—"

"Tell me, instead."

Dark head bent, he began. "I came up earlier, to tend the children. Andry carried her into her room—I saw him running along the hall with her, heard him shouting for me. She was unconscious. Lord Maarken and Lady Hollis were still below. Andry put her on the bed and took off her boots, her tunic. She was shivering and her hands were like ice. We had to get her warm."

He shook his head, absently rubbing his leg above the bandage. "First I saw the bruises on her shoulder. A strong hand—Goddess, I could almost see the fingertip swirls imprinted on her skin. Her tunic and shirt were torn, and—oh, your grace, the bruises and welts, and—and marks of *teeth* on her breasts—"

"No," Sioned breathed. "No."

"Andry got a nightdress to slip over her head and hide her wounds, saying that if her father saw, he would be neither to hold nor to bind. When she was covered, I pulled her trousers off and saw the blood. That was when I knew."

She stumbled against a wall, staring down at him.

"I was brewing simples when I was seven winters old," he murmured. "People came to me for healing when I was thirteen. I've seen all manner of illness and injury, young as I am—but I've never before seen this. And I never even knew anyone among all the physicians at the Giladan school who'd seen rape!"

"No," she said again.

"We heard the others here in the anteroom. Andry went to his brother, kept him back for a moment so I could make sure there was nothing for her parents to see. She was asleep by then, so it was only a matter of reassuring them and hoping her sleeve didn't slide down to show the bruise on her shoulder. Those on her arms are easily explained. The rest . . . are all too obvious."

"No." It seemed the only word her lips were capable of forming. Her thoughts grated against each other, groaning and screaming.

Evarin's voice dwindled to a whisper. "They raped her. Not just once. Many times."

The words repeated again and again between her ears, behind her eyes, throbbing down into her chest and belly until she begged them to become meaningless sounds, not words, not pictures, not memories.

Not just once. Many times. Raped not just once. Many times. Not just once—

"They violated a Sunrunner, Lord Andry's own kinswoman, one of the Goddess' *faradh'im* chosen to receive her gifts of light and power. They will be utterly destroyed for their sin."

—many times. Many times. Raped not just once but many
... many ... many. ...

Evarin waited for her to speak, grieved that he had to tell
her but glad the knowledge was not just his and Andry's.
Men knew horror at this crime, anger, pain for the woman's
pain. But all physicians were agreed that the best help for a
victim was the comfort and counsel of other women.

He knew this woman's history—who did not?—and
though she had never been raped, High Prince Roelstra had
attempted it. He thought he saw remembrance of it in her
eyes. The black centers were so huge that all the bright
fierce green was nearly obliterated. She was white to the
lips, and for a moment he thought that she would slide to the
floor in a faint. Then she gathered herself together. Her steps
were slow, as if she must order each one from a body that
had forgotten the knack of it, but by the time she reached the
door she was steady enough.

"Your grace?"

If she heard him, she gave no sign.

"Lady Chayla will heal," he said gently. "With help, and
time, and in the safety of Feruche—"

The castle's name sent a spasm through her, shoulders to
knees. She braced herself against the door with both hands.

"Your grace?" If she fell, as she looked near to doing, she
might injure herself—and his wounded leg made him helpless as a child for all his physician's skills. He called her
name, thinking it might reach her. "Sioned?"

Her head turned so swiftly he thought it would snap on
her neck. And in her eyes that were black in her face that
was the color of bleached silk, he saw that whatever her
memories were, they were of madness.

"Andry!" he shouted, struggling to gain his feet.

She ran then, stumbling and blind.

"Andry!"

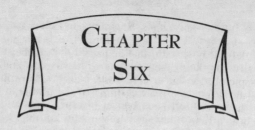

CHAPTER SIX

"I couldn't stop her," Evarin said for the third time. "I couldn't even move! She must be found, my Lord. The look in her eyes—"

"But what caused it?" Maarken asked.

When a swift glance passed between the physician and Andry, Meath tensed. Whatever had been said, it wasn't something they wanted Maarken to know. He touched the younger man's shoulder. "We'll find her. Take care of Chayla. Go on, go back in to her. It'll be all right."

Meath wasn't particularly subtle about closing the bed-chamber door. In fact, he leaned back against it as if to keep Maarken separated from whatever knowledge Andry didn't want him to have.

"Tell me," he ordered softly.

There was another silent exchange before Evarin said flatly. "Chayla was raped—and I beg the Goddess that her parents never find out. I told the High Princess because it's said Roelstra attempted the same crime. I thought she would be able to help the girl." He shook his head and finished miserably, "I didn't know she'd—I'm sorry."

"Roelstra. Yes, that must be it," Meath lied, his veins running with ice. "It's no fault of yours, Evarin. People look at her and see only strength. We forget sometimes. . . ."

Andry nodded. "We'll find her. But as quietly as possible. There mustn't be a general alarm. Meath, take the lower floors. I'll take the upper. Enlist whoever you think wouldn't frighten her."

"Or be frightened *by* her," Evarin added. "What was in her eyes—I never want to see anything like that again."

Meath left them, grateful that he hadn't been forced to ask specifically for the nether regions of the castle and thus rouse suspicion. He had a very good idea of where Sioned was, and he wanted no one but himself to find her.

But as he descended the stairs—wanting to take them two and three at a time, prevented by knee joints that weren't what they had once been—he changed his mind. Riyan stood on a landing with his steward, talking over some detail of running the keep. Meath waved the man away and took Riyan aside.

"Find Pol. Bring him downstairs to the cellars. Hurry."

Black brows knitted together, accenting the tilt of his eyes—eyes just like his mother Camigwen's, she who was dead these thirty-six years. As he grew older Riyan grew to resemble his father more and more, but for those beautiful Fironese eyes. Sorcerer's eyes. "Meath, what is it? What's wrong?"

"Sioned is ill. That's all I can tell you for now. No, don't ask me anything else," he warned. "And don't talk to anyone but Pol. Find him!" Meath kept going down the stairs, ignoring Riyan's worried call of his name.

In the kitchen, casual inquiry confirmed that the High Princess had indeed come through and disappeared down the cellar stairs. No importance was attached to it; she must have behaved normally, then—or passed so quickly that no one noticed what Evarin said was in her eyes.

Meath was almost certain of what she remembered, and it was not Roelstra.

He paused at the first landing, summoning a tiny fingerflame to light his way. He listened for her footfalls. Silence, but for the faint scrabblings of mice. His own steps sounded unnaturally loud, his heartbeat even louder.

In the Feruche that had been, this staircase had descended to the dungeons.

Musty, pungent smells wafted upward, stinging his nose. He paused again when he reached a wooden floor braced by massive iron beams stretching from wall to wall, support for storage rooms containing staples and spices and huge crates of bottled wine. The stairwell continued and he began to think it endless, this wide stone spiral down into the dark.

It was colder now. Still there was no sound but his own

boots, his own heart, his own breath. Fire hovered at his shoulder, showing him the next few steps and the blackness below them, around and around in a slow descending circle, the rich spice-scents lost now in the chill.

He climbed down past another storage floor, this one for meats that must be kept cold. The great hooks for hanging sides of elk and deer were empty. With so many to feed, an animal slaughtered was an animal eaten that same night.

At last he reached the bottom. Sioned was there, huddled in a corner. Meath's fingerflame, the only light, reacted with a flutter as he realized she had come down all this way in absolute dark.

She didn't look up as he approached. Her face was ashpale, her eyes black and empty, but for all of it she seemed strangely calm. He had seen that expression before, during the seasons at Stronghold while she waited for Pol to be born: doing nothing, thinking nothing, feeling nothing.

He glanced around. Great cisterns bulked into the darkness, water for times of drought. More crates of wine aging to maturity were stacked among them. Nothing else. No cells, no doors, no iron bars, no reminders of the Feruche that had been. Yet she was here, as he had known she would be, and as he stepped carefully near he saw that her eyes saw no farther than where the walls of a cell had been.

"Stay with her," Rohan had told him. But where she had gone now, no one could follow. Meath must bring her back.

He crouched down a few arm-lengths away from her. The fingerflame settled in midair, close enough to illumine her face but not within her self-circumscribed range of vision.

"Sioned."

His voice was soft, steady. She didn't hear him.

"Sioned, look at me."

Her eyes did not blink. For a moment he wasn't even sure that she was breathing.

"It's Meath, dearest. You know me. Look at me. You're safe, Sioned."

She stared at nothingness. It seemed he must follow her into her prison after all. Rising, his knees stiff with the cold, he eased closer, bringing the light with him.

It caught in her eyes and she flinched. The fingers of her right hand began rubbing at her left, rubbing at Sunrunner rings that were no longer there. She had told him once that she could still feel them, like scars. If she kept chafing her fingers this way, blood would flow and there would be scars.

"Sioned, listen to me. No one's going to hurt you. You're safe."

She watched the light, trembling, fingers convulsively moving—skin rasping against skin, bone grinding against bone.

He had only made things worse. He knew where she was—but how did he find her? How did he bring her back? He knelt within touching distance and sat back on his heels.

"Sioned, please. Look at me."

She looked, and saw him, and screamed.

✳

The shriek echoed up from the cellar depths. Pol clattered the last fifty steps at a run, bracing himself with a palm slapping the wall when he stumbled. Riyan was behind him, the torch he carried casting wild shadows in the gloom.

Meath slumped helplessly near Sioned, who had wedged herself into her corner as if she wanted to hide within the wall. She cried out again and wrapped her arms around her head as Riyan's torchlight washed over her.

Meath spasmed upright. "Get rid of that, damn it! She thinks you're here to attack her."

Riyan blanched and extinguished the Fire. He said nothing, but his gaze begged to be told why.

Pol thought he knew. "She's back at the old Feruche, isn't she?" he asked Meath, who nodded, dull-eyed with misery.

"Chayla was raped. Maarken and Hollis don't know—and don't tell them. But Sioned learned it from Evarin, and—" His head bent again. "Being here in this castle was always an act of defiance for her. This time the memory won."

Chayla. Fifteen winters old. Raped. Pol couldn't face that; not yet. Not with Meiglan in enemy hands. He watched his mother for a few moments, unable to equate this cowering, terrified creature with anyone he had ever known. "Wh—" His voice caught and he cleared his throat. "What can we do?"

"Wait for her to come back to us. Hope that she does."

"Do you mean she's remembering when *she* was—" Riyan could no more say the word than Pol could. He looked as if he would be sick. "I didn't know. That—that Ianthe had done this to her."

The sound of his voice, or perhaps the sound of that name, brought her head up. Her fingers twisted, stilled. Squinting into the dimness, she whispered tentatively, "Ostvel? Is that you?"

Riyan flung a shocked glance at Pol, who nodded. Taking a deep breath, Ostvel's son went to her, crouched down, took one of her hands. "Yes, Sioned. I'm here."

Her smiled was sweet, radiantly youthful. Pol saw her again as she had looked when he was a little boy. An instant later, that woman vanished behind a bewildered frown. "But . . . you shouldn't be here. He's not born yet, it's not time to take him from her."

"I've come to take you home."

Her eyes sought the darkness beyond the fingerflame, wary and searching. "It's not time yet. And you mustn't stay. They'll find you. They were here just a moment ago, I can still smell them—"

"There's no one here but us."

She shook her head. "No! They were here. They leave me shut in the dark except when they come and—and—" She clutched his shoulder with her other hand, peering at him. "Ostvel? Why are you here? It isn't time yet. Hurry, you must go before they come back and find you—"

"We'll leave together, Sioned."

Pol held his breath. Her mindless terror was gone. There was sense of a sort in her eyes, anguished concern, knowledge of why she was afraid. But her worry was for a man who wasn't even there, from a time before Pol was born.

"No, Ostvel. I must wait until she lets us go, and then I must wait for the child. We'll come back, don't you remember? You and Tobin and I. We came to Feruche and he was there in the cradle and—and you—"

Suddenly her features contorted and she went for his face with fingers like talons. Riyan struggled to grab her wrists before she clawed his eyes out.

"*You!* Damn you for stealing her death from me! It was *my right* to kill her, not yours!"

Pol heard this in stunned unfeeling shock. He'd always thought Ianthe had died in the Fire. They'd allowed him to believe it.

"Sioned, stop it!" Meath slid forward. He held on to one arm, Riyan to the other. "Sioned!"

Her eyes found him, flaring with new rage. "And *you!* Watching me, all that time—sneaking across the sunlight, too much of a coward to speak openly! But I knew it was you, I felt you *watching* me, spying on me for Andrade—"

Meath turned his face away.

"Sioned!" Riyan snapped, catching her attention again. "That's not true and you know it. Listen to me! Ianthe is dead. You're free. We have to leave now, and take Pol home."

"Pol?" Her face crumpled into confusion with the pull of memories back and forth in time. One instant she had already lived it; the next, it had not yet happened. "But how do you know what I'll Name him? It was at Skybowl. . . ." Memory solidified for her and her eyes softened, her voice almost dreamy. "You remember, Ostvel. Nothing but the Desert and the stars . . . you and I and Tobin, and him so small and new . . . but I felt the power in him. Goddess, what a Sunrunner he'll make, and what a prince—you can't feel it, of course. I know Tobin did. When I gave him his Name, and the stars with it . . . and when—when I used the st–stars to—" Horror flooded her face. *"Rohan!"*

"No, it's all over, he's—" Meath choked on the rest. He couldn't do that to her. Not even to bring her back could he give her that lie. Rohan—safe, waiting for her at Stronghold—Rohan was dead and Stronghold was a blackened gaping ruin.

"Rohan!" Sioned's voice had changed, trembling now with joy. She freed her hand from Riyan's grasp and held out both arms, and the smile that curved her lips now was one of transcendent love.

She was looking straight at Pol.

"Rohan—oh, please, take me away from here, take me home—"

Pol couldn't move. He felt the contours of his own face as if they had become a stone mask, and he within made of malleable flesh, invisible behind the carved semblance of his father.

Sioned caught her breath. "Don't you see, it doesn't matter that it was Ianthe! She'll bear the son I couldn't give you! Please, don't look this way, beloved! I don't care that you were with her. She'll give us your son, just as I saw in the Fire—" She broke off, and her fingers began to chafe madly at each other. "Midwinter, Rohan," she continued feverishly. "She told me so—laughing, she was laughing as if the victory was hers. But it's not. It's mine. She'll bear your son and then she'll die."

His knees would no longer support him. He put out a hand to brace himself on Meath's strong shoulder.

His mother was begging him now—begging Rohan. "You told me once that you couldn't bear looking at a child that didn't have me in his eyes. Don't do that to him, Rohan. Please, beloved. He isn't hers, he's yours and mine."

Her arms formed a cradle against her breast. He realized with a jolt that it was himself she held in memory. Himself, newborn of a woman they had all hated, who had died by Ostvel's hand.

"He's innocent. If it's guilt you want, we can both carry it. Blame yourself and blame me—but not him."

When he stayed mute, tears formed in her eyes. Green eyes, the color his own turned sometimes in certain light.

"I know you don't want to touch me. What they did to me—I remember it all, every hand, every—she watched sometimes, I'm sure of it. Watched and laughed. But it doesn't matter. There's Pol. I would go through it all again, to have him in my arms like this. Won't you look at him? Please?" She held the invisible child up for him to see. "He's nothing like her. There's only you in his face, in his eyes. Rohan, *look* at him!"

He could endure no more. Sinking to his knees, he wrapped his arms around her and rocked her as if she were the child. She whispered his father's name and began to cry very softly, still holding her memory of a baby to her breast.

After a time she wilted against him, senseless with exhaustion. He lifted her, appalled at how light she seemed, how fragile.

"Will she—" Riyan couldn't find words for it. He gestured helplessly.

"I don't know." Meath pushed himself to his feet. "Take her upstairs, Pol," he said in a voice like death. "Riyan, go up ahead of us. Make sure there's nobody to see."

"How? What do I say—" He stopped, swallowed hard, and nodded. "I'll think of something."

Meath lit their slow, silent way back up the stone spiral. Pol climbed, a dull mindless agony clutching his chest. In the kitchen, they immediately saw how Riyan had cleared the room: Sunrunner's Fire still blasted from the main hearth as if a hatchling dragon had exhaled down the chimney.

"It was just the cook and a couple of maids. I didn't singe anybody," he explained as he let the flames die back. "They didn't even know it was me. I hid behind the door. Take her up the back way."

It was Meath who went ahead then, to tell Andry that Sioned had been found. Pol followed Riyan up the narrow well of the servants' stairs, lit by tall, thin windows like arrow-slits. It wasn't much past noon; the sunshine hurt his eyes. He had expected it to be night, as lightless black as the cellar below.

Alasen and Tobin were waiting in Sioned's bedchamber. They asked no questions, merely removed the outer layers of her clothing and put her to bed. When Alasen moved to pull the curtains, Pol said, "No. Don't let her wake in a place where there's no light," and Tobin's eyes filled with tears that told him she understood. All of it. She always had.

Pol hadn't. Not all of it. Not until now.

"We'll take care of her," Alasen told him.

"Yes," he answered, and went away.

He wanted solitude. He wanted to hide. But just down the hall from his own chamber door he saw Sionell. Her name left his lips before he even knew he had spoken. She hurried to him, searching his eyes. A soft, wordless exclamation escaped her and she urged him into the privacy of the anteroom. He moved unsteadily, chafing his hands as his mother had done, to hide their shaking.

"Pol."

She touched his arm, the warmth of her palm branding his skin. Turning, he reached for her blindly.

"She thought—she thought I was Father—Goddess, what Ianthe did to her—"

"Hush." She surrounded him with her arms and her strength.

"She was raped, over and over again—I knew it had happened but I never—she thought I was Father, spoke to me as if she saw him, not me—what will it do to her when she remembers he's dead?"

"Pol, no. You mustn't."

But he couldn't stop. "She said she'd go through all of it

again, it didn't matter because—because of *me!* Ell, what *am* I that she would say such a thing?"

"Her son. Not Ianthe's. Don't you know that by now? Pol, look at me."

He lifted his head. Her eyes were dark with grief, yet the quiet certainty in them touched a place in his soul he had never known was there.

"Your father was Rohan, and your mother is Sioned. They had the making of you—they and all the others who taught you and loved you. Who are you to doubt such love and trust? *They* know who you are when they look at you—and it's the son of Rohan and Sioned they see." All at once she smiled a little, and brushed the tousled hair from his eyes. "I told you all this a long time ago. Why do you make me keep repeating myself?"

"You . . . believe it," he said, not quite a question.

"Yes. And you'd better, too. I really am getting tired of saying it."

She offered her arms again. He and she fit each other like seal and matrix. Gradually a subtle peace seeped through him. Suspicious of it at first, soon he relaxed into it and closed his eyes. This was something new in his experience of Sionell. The challenge of her he had often seen; her anger, her intelligence, her pride were all familiar to him. He had always known that passion was in her, and when he had awakened it the other night—

But he had never thought that he would find such sweet tranquillity in her arms. She was as close to him as his own heartbeat. He listened to their slow, twinned breaths and was at rest.

"Can you tell me now what happened?" she asked softly.

They sat on chairs in the anteroom, close together but not touching. Yet he felt her all along his body—not with desire, but as if her presence was his second skin—warm and supple and protective. That strange, gentle quiet stayed with him even through the pain of what he must say.

"I don't know what Riyan told the others," he finished. "I'll have to ask him and Meath so we can get our stories straight. Maarken and Hollis mustn't know what really caused this."

Cautiously, she asked, "Is it fair to keep it from them?"

"Think what Maarken would do if he found out Chayla was raped," he countered, shaking his head. "I agree with

Andry and Evarin. If Chayla wants her parents to know, that's her choice. Not ours."

"Yes. All right." Sionell gazed at her folded hands for a long moment. "Pol ... about Sioned. She might remember nothing or everything. But if it's as you said, and she's kept this locked in for so many years—"

"Not just that. She's always said she didn't recall much of the last part of that year. That maybe she'd been a little mad."

"She's remembered now. She lived it again."

Pol frowned. "And survived it? Is that what you mean?"

"I hope that's how it will be. She was afraid to remember, and didn't. Couldn't, perhaps. But now she has, and it didn't destroy her."

He mulled this over, and at last nodded. "I can't be there when she wakes up. She might think it's Father with her again, not me." Pausing a moment, he ventured, "Ell, it was—I felt as if I really was wearing his face for a time."

Her head tilted, sunlight glowing in her dark red hair. "It's a face very like his, but it's your own. With you inside it."

"Yes, but—I felt trapped. Into looking like him, being him. And I'm not. Everyone expects me to be as wise and clever as he was, and I'm not."

She regarded him with patient blue eyes, deep-set in the pale triangle of her face. "You know, that's about as stupid as thinking that everyone expects you to be like Ianthe. You're forcing me to say the same things again. All that changes is the name. You're not Rohan. People don't look at you and see him. For one thing, you're a lot taller," she added with another small smile.

He felt his lips curve hesitantly. Thank the Goddess for a woman who could make him smile in spite of everything.

"And for another," Sionell added deliberately, "he was losing this war."

Pol stiffened in his chair, his serenity shattered. This was the Sionell he knew. He wanted the other one back.

"I loved him as if he were my second father," she went on. "But he was fashioned to make peace. Have you realized yet how angry you are with him for not teaching you how to make war?"

He was too exhausted to rise and pace and shout at her. Too exhausted to deny it. All he could do was nod.

"It wasn't his fault, Pol. And it doesn't make you less

than he—or more, for that matter—that you're getting rather good at war. You hate it as much as he did. But where it made him sad, it makes you furious. That's what people see in you, the power of your anger. And that's why you'll win."

He shrugged his irritation, aware that his interviews with Sionell always did this to him. "I'm not my father. I couldn't be if I tried, and I intend to stop trying. Is that what you want to hear?"

She sat back, looking smug.

He scowled, understanding her now. "You are an impossible woman. You know that, don't you?"

She gave him an unrepentant smile. "My prince, I rejoice in it."

"Do you *always* have to make me angry?"

"Yes—when you use it to accomplish things, instead of ripping up yourself or someone else with it." She stood. "Go get some rest. You look like you need it. I'll talk to Riyan and Meath. And don't worry too much about Sioned."

"You didn't see her today."

"No. But she lived through it once in reality, and once again in memory, and survived both. Do you know anyone else who could?"

✶

Sioned slept until early evening. Pol had ordered that no one who had known her back then should be near when she woke, so the first face she saw was Alasen's. She frowned a little, then sat up and stretched. Alasen brought her a bowl of soup kept hot over the bedchamber hearth. As she ate, she asked about the children—including Siona, who had died several days earlier. Alasen replied that everything was fine and there was nothing to concern her. She went back to sleep.

She woke again around midnight. This time it was Sionell who sat with her, reading by the considerable blaze of two candle branches. Pol had been specific about that, too. The two women were quiet for a long while. Then Sioned's eyes filled with tears.

"Rohan is dead," she murmured, as if saying it for the first time. Her Namesake held her close while she wept, and stayed with her through the night.

In the early morning of the next day, Pol was in Meath's

room, talking with him and Riyan. A knock at the door turned their heads; the entrance of their topic of conversation made them start guiltily.

"Oh—all of you together," she said, nervous and trying to hide it. "I wanted to—I said and did some terrible things yesterday. I—"

"Mother, it's all right. You were—"

"More or less insane. Yes, I know. Please don't interrupt, Pol. I need to apologize." She looked at Riyan. "I thought you were your father, as you know. I'm sorry I came at you like a raving madwoman."

Riyan bit his lip. "You're all right. That's all any of us cares about."

"Thank you," she said, and the quiet, bruised gallantry of her manner cut Pol's heart in pieces. She faced him next, hesitating, fingers moving at her sides and then stilling as if she recognized the action.

"Pol . . . I'm afraid you learned things yesterday that you shouldn't have. It's true that your father couldn't look at you—but you mustn't blame him. He hadn't seen you in Fire the way I—all he could see was Ianthe, and what happened to both of us at the old Feruche."

"Mother, you don't have to—"

"Yes, I do," she insisted. "I want you to know that the first time he looked at you, he forgot everything except that you were his son, and mine. From that instant onward the rest didn't exist." Again she paused, glancing at Riyan and then away. "Ostvel . . . did what he did. But you have to understand why. It was the same reason he tossed a knife to Lyell of Waes so that he and Kiele could die quickly, before Andry's Fire killed them." She shrugged. "Andry was a long time forgiving him for it. So was I, about Ianthe. But to Ostvel, it was very simple. We mattered and he didn't. He kept their blood from our hands by taking it onto his own. But the truth of it remains that Ianthe died because of me. I just—I don't want you to look at Ostvel any differently because of it."

Pol made himself say, "No. I won't."

At last she turned to Meath, who had risen when she came into the room. Her head tilted back so she could look into his face. Her lips parted, but he forestalled her words with a gesture.

"Don't."

"I have to," she repeated.

"No." And he started to leave his own chamber.

"Meath, please!"

He stopped, his back to her.

"I'm sorry," she whispered. "You must know that I never believed what I accused you of yesterday. When you watched over me, it was for my own sake. I always knew that. And I remember that it comforted me, feeling the nearness of a friend. Will you forgive me for what I said?"

"For the Goddess' sake, Sioned! Stop it!" he rasped, swinging around. "It kills me to hear you—"

"I'm sorry," she said again. "But I had to." She drew herself straighter and ran a hand back through her hair. Pol was startled to see how much of it was stark white. "I won't talk about any of it again. Can any of you tell me—I don't like to intrude, but—is Chayla awake? Do you think she'd see me?"

✳

"*Thank* you," Chayla said, sighing her relief as the door closed behind her parents. "They mean well, but they've been staring at me as if I'll disappear if they don't. You won't scold if I get out of bed, will you, Sioned?"

"Of course not."

The girl threw back the covers and went immediately to the window. She opened the casement and gulped in several deep breaths of fresh air, then sank onto the embrasure seat with one foot tucked under her.

"They treat me like a hothouse flower," she said wryly. "Too fragile for air and sunlight. But I swear I'm perfectly fine. Sore from riding so far so fast, but otherwise—"

Sioned, still feeling a bit fragile herself, nodded noncommittally and tried not to hurt too much for Chayla. She looked made of sunlight, sitting there in the window, clothed in a white lacy shift and her unbound golden hair and the brightness of the morning. Fifteen summers old—one could not count winters when faced with this shining girl.

"Is there any word of Meiglan?"

"None. Chayla. . . ." Sioned pulled a chair from beside the small hearth and sat down. But she couldn't think how to begin. "Has Master Evarin been to see you?"

"Yes, and told Mama I'm fine—which she doesn't believe from him any more than she does from me."

"What did he say to *you?*"

"Nothing. Just physician-talk. As equals," she added with a pleased smile. "I'm glad he's here. I can learn a lot from him. And he doesn't speak to me as if I were a child and my only experience was setting a bird's broken wing. He used to, you know, when he was younger than I, and—"

"Chayla," Sioned murmured, staring down at her hands.

"Is something wrong?" Her eyes sharpened. "It can't be me, I know as well as Evarin does that my bruises and scrapes will heal. Is it Meiglan?"

Her heart cringed. "No, I'm sorry. It's just—"

"Please. Tell me what's the matter."

Sioned stared at the emerald ring on her finger. "I was a captive, too, you know. In the castle that once stood here. You've heard the story, I'm sure. I could never bear to think of that time. I was afraid of it. But it's better to face what one fears. Even the things that are too terrible to remember."

"Oh, Sioned!" Hands warm with sunlight reached to enfold her own. "I brought it all back—I'm sorry!"

"Don't be, heartling." She clasped Chayla's fingers and searched her clear blue eyes. For someone who had felt queasy at the very sight of the ocean when a child, Chayla's eyes were ironically the exact color of a sunlit sea. "It was like lancing a wound, painful but necessary. The poison of it is gone and I'm all right now. And so shall you be."

The girl went very still.

"You mustn't do what I did," Sioned told her gently. "You mustn't build a wall. Keeping it intact will use up your strength. It will never be the past. It will always be *now*. You'll probably dream about it, as I did at first. But the dreams must fade on their own—not because you force every memory behind a wall. Do you understand, Chayla?"

"I think so," she said after a time, and for an instant Sioned thought she would talk about it. Chayla's next words negated that hope. "I hadn't considered bad dreams. Thank you for warning me."

Sioned gathered herself, her own memories clawing at her mind. But the poison was gone. Not the pain, not yet. Perhaps never. But she had known worse. She was no longer afraid—not for herself. For this bright-haired girl made of sunshine.

"Chayla . . . if you want . . . if it's something you can't tell your parents or anyone else . . . I know what it is to—to be frightened that way."

She was caught in a fierce hug. "Thank you. You're very good to me. I'm sorry all this reminded you."

Coward, she accused herself as she stroked Chayla's long hair. *But I can't force her to tell me. I just can't. Not even for her own good. No, I'll just keep an eye on her, and if she seems to be all right, then—*

I "seemed to be" for over thirty years. But it was waiting for me. Always waiting. . . .

"My dear," she began.

Chayla pulled back and sat again in the window seat. "You mustn't worry, Sioned. I'll be fine once I'm not reminded every time I move." She smiled, rubbing a shoulder ruefully, and Sioned's heart broke.

Courage or denial? Sioned had argued Rohan into rebuilding Feruche, which could be construed as bravery—but the castle formed visible walls to match those inside her. Tangible denial. At least Rohan had been honest about it; he had never set foot inside this keep. Not for lack of courage, but because he could not deny what had happened to them here.

I'll keep an eye on her, she told herself again. *That's all I can do for now. Maybe she's stronger than I. The young are more resilient. More prideful, as well. And maybe she's right, and the memory of it will fade naturally once all the bruises are gone. I might do more harm than good by forcing her to talk about it now.*

A pretty excuse.

✳

War or no war, and perhaps especially in time of war, castles must function. The usual deliberate rounds of stewards, cook, master of horse, guards commander, and all the other retainers who oversaw a keep's daily life must be maintained. Sometimes Riyan found his conferences with his servants comfortingly normal, and sometimes so unreal that he was tempted to pinch himself awake. But it was an obvious fact that rigid routine soothed. While no one was fooled into believing life was as it had always been, still the appearance of it was there: something of order to hold fast against chaos.

But it was still like walking with one leg injured—a sure and easy step, then a painful limp.

The Lord and Lady of Feruche customarily met over the noonday meal in their joint office—a trick borrowed from Rohan and Sioned at Stronghold, with a similar pair of desks facing each other. From Feruche, their main seat and favorite castle, they governed the substantial triangle of mountain and sand, Princemarch and Desert, formed by their three major holdings. In fact, their lands were only a little smaller than the whole princedom of Isel, though not as populous.

Some concessions to the unsettled times were necessary, but abandoning the daily conference was not one of them. Ruala had complained the other day that the only time she ever saw her husband was at noon and in bed. Today, after sharing the reports of various stewards and deciding that hunters must be sent out to find what deer and elk they could, the pair fell silent and gazed at each other for long moments. Finally Ruala began to laugh.

"You'd think we'd each forgotten what the other looks like!"

"Ah, so *that's* why you gave yourself a little tour of me last night in the dark!" He grinned.

"I'd like to try it sometime when I can actually see you."

"I miss having the time to look at you," he said, abruptly serious, gazing wistfully across the expanse of polished fruitwood. A thin streak of white hair twisted from her left temple back to the knotted braid at the crown of her head, delicate lightning in a starless night sky. This was the only difference between the woman she was and the woman he had first seen nine years ago at Elktrap. Her fine, pale complexion had defied Desert sun and wind; there wasn't a line on her face, not even around green eyes that made him think of secret forest glens. "I really do forget sometimes how beautiful you are, Ruala. Why don't we lock the door, clear off the desk, and make good use of the daylight?"

"The mother of your children deserves better, my lord!"

"Oh, all right, the rug, then. It's s–soft. . . ." The plural suddenly clubbed him over the head.

"Damn it, this isn't how I planned to tell you." She sighed her regret. "It's an insane time for it, the middle of a war, but we've waited and hoped for so long. Just please don't behave the way your father always did with Alasen, as if she were made of glass—"

"Stop right there," he commanded. "What are you telling me?"

The corners of her mouth tucked into a crooked smile. "Take a guess. You can count. Permission to use your fingers if you have to."

"Ruala!" He wanted to leap to his feet and seize her in his arms and dance her around the room. His legs did not cooperate. "Why didn't you tell me?"

"I just did." She peered at him. "Riyan, are you all right?"

"You're pregnant?"

"Well, yes. Sometime around early summer, or so Master Evarin says."

His jaw dropped halfway to his lap. "You told him before you told me?"

"He told *me,* yesterday morning. Don't ask how he knew when I didn't know myself—or at least I wasn't sure. And don't act so injured! I would've said something last night if you hadn't fallen asleep so fast."

"I'm sorry," he said reflexively.

"Don't mention it."

They spent a while staring at each other again, a little bewildered, before an arch of Ruala's brows brought a twitch to Riyan's lips, and all at once both were laughing again.

"Well, well," came Pol's cool voice from the doorway. "If it's that funny a joke, tell me at once. I could use a good laugh."

Riyan sobered on the instant, feeling a little guilty for his joy. Ruala did not share the emotion. She smiled at Pol, saying, "Only the joke every wife loves to play on her husband when telling him he's going to be a father."

"Really?" Pol's eyes lit, chasing away moodiness. "But that's marvelous! What do you think—boy or girl this time?"

"How should I know?" she retorted. "How does any woman know? Men!"

Pol grinned and went on, "Congratulations, Riyan."

"Thank you," he said, a bit helplessly. "I'm wondering how I'm going to tell my father, though. No Sunrunners at Swalekeep."

"Oh, leave that to me." Pol made a casual gesture. "I've been meaning to have a talk with Princess Naydra anyway."

Of course. Lallante's daughter, as Pol was Lallante's

grandson. She might not know how yet, but weaving light was her birthright as much as it was Pol's and Ruala's and his own. *Diarmadhi,* all of them, as his daughter Maara was, as the new child would be. Heirs to starlight, and sorceries, and mirrors—

"Pol," he said urgently, "does Andry know about that mirror?"

"Mother of Dragons—I'd forgotten all about it!"

"Not surprising," Ruala commented.

"Riyan, find a place for it, a room where we can work undisturbed."

"Work?" he echoed, bewildered.

"It has a purpose," Pol said grimly. "I'm going to find out what it is."

"If Andry learns we have it, he'll learn that only *diarmadh'im* can see into the thing—and then he'll know about you."

"What if he does?" Pol shrugged. "What can he do? Denounce and execute me for a wicked, sinful sorcerer? I'd like to see him try it. Besides, he seems to have mellowed. We have a rather good understanding between us now."

"Lady Merisel decreed that any of their mirrors must be destroyed," Riyan warned. "And you know he takes her words as though they came straight from the Goddess herself."

Pol walked slowly past the bookshelves, one finger brushing the spines of fine tooled leather printed in gold. "If it comes to *diarmadh'im* against *faradh'im,* then we'll lose everything, Riyan—including this war. Andry will have to understand that. If he doesn't—" Again Pol shrugged. "He's proud and stubborn, but he's not an idiot."

"No, he'll just wait until after we've won," Ruala warned. "You'll give him a reason to condemn you publicly. And if he succeeds with the High Prince, none of us will be safe." She put a hand over her waist. "Damn it, I don't *want* to see him as an enemy to my children! But if he makes himself into one—" She paused, then shook her head. "Grandfather was right. We're safe only when we hide what we are. Andry mustn't find out about that mirror."

"He won't," Pol assured her. He leaned a shoulder against the window frame. "But we can't go sneaking about or Andry will be sure to notice."

Riyan shrugged. "So hide it in plain sight. It hung in the

hall at Skybowl for thirty years and nobody ever saw anything but themselves in it."

"We can't put it right out in public like that. We need a place we can work in—undisturbed and unremarkable."

Ruala toyed with a stick of blue sealing wax. "We haven't had dinner in the Attic since Andry arrived. Would that do?"

"Perfectly. He'll only notice that you've added a decoration—"

"—and what more natural than a mirror that belonged to my mother?" Riyan finished. "Some of us usually linger in there after dinner anyway, and it's convenient for strategy sessions. Yes, that will do very well indeed."

"The Attic, then," Pol agreed.

Riyan hesitated. "Maarken will never lie to his brother."

"If Andry doesn't know what to ask about the mirror, he can't question. And if he doesn't question, Maarken won't have to lie."

"But—"

"Then Maarken will just have to choose," Pol said softly. Glancing out at the courtyard, he added, "Chayla's up and about. I'm surprised she was kept from her patients this long."

Another secret, Riyan thought. And this one must be kept even from his wife. Did secrets define people, make them who and what they were? Pol's had. Chayla's might. And what was the real secret of that mirror?

Pol turned for the door, then turned back. "Oh, I almost forgot what I came to tell you. All the patrols have returned, and it's the general opinion that the mountains are clean of Vellant'im. They've covered every square handspan for fifty measures around. So I think we can send to Elktrap for supplies and let the hunters go about their work without too much worry."

"Good. We need the food." Ruala got to her feet, and Riyan couldn't help looking her over for signs. She made a face at him. He grinned, abashed. Catching the byplay, Pol laughed at them both.

But there was an edge to it, as there had been to every word and look since Meiglan's capture. No, Riyan amended as he tidied his desk, since Rohan died. All the easy grace of speech and manner had vanished. Lean, tense, all angles, Pol had become a living sword.

Riyan found himself hoping that he didn't carve himself up along with their enemies.

CHAPTER SEVEN

At about the same time Sioned was watching the Desert sun glow in Chayla's hair, Tilal was watching the dismal Syrene rain drizzle outside his tent. The message from Pol had been received yesterday on what proved to be the very last glimmer of light.

"It's supposed to be getting better," he groused to Andrev, shaking his head at the offer of more mulled wine. "Hints of spring, sun waking the flowers, that sort of weather. Come to think of it, slosh out some more of that. I might as well get drunk at my leisure. Goddess knows, there's nothing else to do around this miserable swamp."

Andrev obediently poured. Then he withdrew to stand beside the closed doorflap, silent until his lord chose to speak again. Tilal appreciated that. In fact, he was more and more impressed with the boy. There was a quiet self-possession about him unusual in one his age: a quality of watching and listening that had nothing furtive about it, only a desire to learn. He didn't run riot like most children—making noise simply to be making it, heedless of anything but themselves. Tilal wondered if this was an acquisition of his status as a squire, along with the dark green Ossetian tunic and wheat-sheaf badge, or if he had always been this way. He reminded Tilal of Rihani at that age.

Ah, Goddess, his firstborn, his boy. . . .

I should be with his mother right now. We ought to be together, Gemma and Sioneva and Sorin and I.

There wasn't even anyone to drink with. Amiel was out in the rain, slogging through ankle-deep mud to check on the troops. Nyr sat and shivered in her tent—not that Tilal would have given more than a thimbleful of wine to a pregnant woman anyway. His own commander, Chaltyn, had joined Amiel. There was only Andrev, who was much too young to understand or appreciate the uses of a dozen cups of wine.

Still, Andrev was definitely an asset. What had been a slap in Andry's face had turned out to be Tilal's best luck of this whole bloody war. He'd gained squire and Sunrunner both in this towheaded boy whose eager smile revealed a crooked front tooth that made him look even younger than he was.

But Tilal had come to value Andrev for more than his abilities. He had grown fond of Andry's son—though except for the Sunrunner part of it, he considered him more as Chay's and Tobin's grandchild and Maarken's nephew. He was pleased by the glimpses of the man Andrev would one day be, and even more pleased that he would influence the forming of that man. Andry's son he might be by blood and Sunrunner gifts, but Tilal would teach him the ways of people outside the insular little world of Goddess Keep, the work and duties of the great lords and princes who were his ancestors.

"Your grace! Prince Tilal!" Amiel burst into the tent, nearly knocking Andrev aside. "Ships, my lord—out in the bay with boats rowing ashore!"

"Ours or theirs?" Tilal put his wine down. Incredible how the young Giladan prince could neglect to mention the most important things first.

"Ours!" Amiel reported triumphantly. "The ones we stole!"

"Excellent!" For more reasons than one. Not only did he have an idea about using those ships—he must remember to reward whoever was in charge for sheer brilliance in bringing them back—but finally he had something constructive to do. "First make sure they really *are* on our side. The Vellant'im aren't above a few tricks. Once you've settled that question, we're going to take a little boat ride." He grinned. "Andrev, stop trying to look the stalwart. Would I do that to you?"

"Don't worry about me, my lord," the boy replied gamely. "I'll do what my cousin Rohannon does—find myself a corner and a bucket!"

"You won't have to. I need my Sunrunner on his feet and able to use the light—if we ever see any again. Come on, let's get to it. We have a lot of work to do if we're going to improve on Pol's scheme."

Amiel rubbed his chin. "How so, my lord?"

"He wanted us to march up the Faolain and attack them on their way down the river. I'm not inclined to bestir myself to march that far in this muck. So the Vellant'im are going to come to us."

Amiel's hazel eyes, the lashes long and curling enough to be envied by any woman, blinked wide and then crinkled at the corners as he laughed. "I like it! Oh, I do like it!"

"I thought you might. Go find out if they're really our people, and then come back here with Chaltyn and your own captain."

When Amiel was gone, Andrev ventured, "My lord? I think I understand about getting them onto the ships, but you don't have to risk any of your soldiers in an attack. I can do it."

Tilal opened his mouth, then closed it again and stared long and carefully at his crooked-toothed squire, son of the Lord of Goddess Keep.

✳

There was a full complement of highborns in the Attic that night. Riyan kept waiting for someone to remark on the mirror, hanging now above the hearth between two candle sconces. The space had formerly been filled by a framed tapestry square depicting Feruche in spring splendor, rising from flowers more properly found in the forests of Syr. This now decorated the wall above the sideboard. It didn't quite fit there, just as the mirror didn't quite belong above the hearth, but unbalancing Sorin's design was secondary to hiding the mirror in plain sight.

But no one said a word about it as they stood around the room waiting for dinner to be brought upstairs. People sipped wine, talked of this and that, and generally behaved as if this were any other family dinner. Riyan began to get nervous. Surely somebody had noticed. He was about to say something himself, just to get it over with, when Kierun and Dannar flung open the door. Two burly menservants carried in an immense silver platter of sliced roast venison. In great half-moon bowls around the meat were most of the usual accompaniments: vegetables, thick-crusted loaves, hot and cold fruit compotes, cubed cheeses, and such salad greenery as the kitchen garden afforded in late winter.

"Well!" said Alasen as the platter was hefted to the sideboard. "I see somebody had very good luck in the hunt today."

"Goddess in glory," Evarin breathed reverently. "Andry, will you look at this? When I think of what we ate on the road, this is almost painful!"

"Two helpings of everything, Master Evarin?" Dannar asked with a grin.

"Three," he said happily, and limped over to the table, seating himself with knife and fork at the ready in his fists.

By mutual agreement, nothing was discussed that might disturb the digestion. Everyone had had enough of tense, silent meals; everyone remembered what had happened the last time Chay had sought to get some conversation going. So everyone did his or her part in the conspiracy of civility. Certain names were not spoken; certain events were not referred to. Riyan, presiding at the head of the table, could almost believe it really was just any other family dinner. Almost. For though sixteen chairs were occupied, he still thought of family and friends who were missing. So many faces he would never see again—

And that one face that would appear when Fire was called to unlit candles beside the mirror. The three-lobed crystal lantern hanging over the table glowed with traditional flames, but he couldn't help the feeling that those strange dark eyes watched. He glanced involuntarily to his left, where the mirror tilted slightly forward above the hearth.

"Don't worry, it looks lovely there," Sioned told him, leaning forward to speak around Evarin and Chayla. "I'm glad you brought it up from Skybowl to be properly admired. I meant to tell you that when we first arrived."

"A beautiful piece, my lord," Evarin commented.

Maarken asked Andry to pass the salt.

"It belonged to Riyan's mother, my childhood friend Camigwen," Sioned explained. "I suppose she's long forgotten at Goddess Keep."

"Not at all, your grace! I have her to thank for the stillroom, in fact. It's a marvel of logic. And someone told me it was her good, clear hand that copied the simples books from the scrawls of former physicians."

"Her project when she was quite young. Doubtless you've found her spelling an entertainment in itself."

"More wine, my lady?" Kierun inquired of Tobren, who sat between Riyan and her father.

"Watered," Andry said firmly, reaching for the pitcher.

There, Riyan thought; the mirror had been commented upon and the subject neatly turned in Sioned's inimitable style—though he'd have to remember to choose a date for its appearance.

At Riyan's end of the table, Chayla and Evarin predictably talked medicine while Meath engaged Tobren and Andry in reminiscences of Goddess Keep then-and-now. Sioned became as quiet as Tobin, directly across from her, but Riyan had the feeling that a whole conversation was going on between them in total silence. Which was impossible with the sun down and the moons not yet risen, and the windows too far away to give light from either in any case. But the impression lingered all the same.

He heard only a little of the talk at Ruala's end, but snatches of sentences indicated that topics ranged from children (whose were the most rambunctious: Pol's, Sionell's, Alasen's, or Maarken's; Chay finally settled it by snorting that he defied anyone to present pestilential sons to match his) to Alasen's hilarious description of Princess Chiana's private bathroom. At Pol's and Maarken's urging, Draza refought the Battle of Swalekeep using condiment dishes, winecups, and cutlery.

Every so often Riyan caught his wife's eye, and once caught her glancing over at the mirror much as he had done. Toward the end of the meal, while the two squires cleared away empty plates before taze and the sweets arrived, Chay turned to Pol.

"It's getting dark in here. Make yourself useful."

Pol gave a start, then gestured with his right hand. From the tall swirls of wrought iron in the corners to the pair of sconces flanking the mirror, every unlit candle in the room flared to life.

"Much better," Chay said glibly. "I was embarrassing all these pretty women by squinting at them. And at my age, all I can do is look."

Tobin turned her head and arched an eloquent brow.

"Well, mostly," he amended, grinning.

The gathering broke up slowly. At last there were only six left: Pol, Sioned, Meath, Riyan, Ruala, and Chay, who rose to his feet and cast a sour look at his nephew.

"I won't stay for your discussion—I wouldn't understand it. But you should know that there's very little my son the Battle Commander doesn't tell me."

"So you deliberately had me light the candles," Pol murmured.

He snorted. "That piece of pious fraud about when that mirror got put on the wall—as if I hadn't seen Riyan unload it as if it was worth more than every bolt of silk that ever came through Radzyn port."

"Nothing gets past you, does it, my lord?" Sioned asked sweetly.

Eyes dancing, he accused, "Sunrunner!" and she laughed.

When he was gone, she turned to Pol. "You were a little flamboyant about it, you know. Have fun?"

"Absolutely. There's nothing in the mirror for Andry to see."

Riyan took his cup and moved to a chair facing away from the mirror. "Well, *I* can, even though I haven't looked—but I can feel him watching us."

"Like somebody's ghost," Ruala agreed.

"Well, my lady," Meath said, "you're the only one who can tell us anything about it."

"It's not much," she apologized. "I've been trying to remember what my sister and I used to pretend to read when we were little. Grandfather despaired of teaching us anything. Neither of us had the makings of a scholar. And the scrolls were mainly histories, like stories you tell children at bedtime. All imagination and no substance."

"You were both very young for such knowledge," Pol said. "Maybe he thought the way we're having to think now, with Jihan. Learn it early so it's part of you and you don't get knocked over by your own power later on."

"Maybe. But I wish now that I'd paid more attention." She finished off her taze and stared into the empty cup. "I remember that the way to use any mirror was to call Fire, but Rossana and I experimented with every mirror at Elktrap, from the ones in our pockets to the big one in Mother's dressing room. Not a glimmer." She smiled. "We were very disappointed."

"I'm not surprised your grandfather didn't keep any around," Riyan said. "They sound risky things to have, for a *diarmadhi* who didn't want to be known as such."

Pol rose and approached the hearth. "Have you looked into this one yet? No? Then come tell me what you see."

She joined him; they all did, even though Sioned and Meath would never see any reflections but their own. Ruala's head tilted back, and she gazed into the mirror—and her milk-white complexion turned the color of ashes.

Riyan put a hand around her waist to steady her. "What is it, love?"

"I–I *know* him," she breathed. "He looks like my father!"

"Your father died of Plague the year after you were born," he reminded her gently. "You were too young to recall his face."

She shook her head violently, backing away from the mirror. "Grandfather liked to draw. He did that picture of you and me the day we married, remember? It was to match a portrait of my parents." A shaking finger pointed to the face in the mirror. "He looks the way my father looks in that portrait. Thinner, and a little older, and his eyes are unhappy, but I tell you the face is the same."

Sioned had pulled a chair out from the table and sat down in it, hands clasped quietly in her lap. "An ancestor," she said. "You may be looking at the face of a man who lived when Lady Merisel lived."

Shaken, Ruala asked, "But if that's true, why did the mirror belong to Camigwen?"

"Possibly she was of the same family."

"Of *diarmadh'im*," Pol added.

"Or," Sioned went on, "possibly someone in her family was an enemy of this man, and kept the mirror as a token of victory."

Meath peered up at the glass, then shook his head. "Nobody but me in there. Pol, you can see him. Does he look like Riyan?"

Pol studied the proud face, moved again by the ancient, patient sadness. "Only around the eyes, like most Fironese." He glanced at Ruala. "No resemblance to you at all. Your eyes are green, not dark brown or black, and don't tilt upward." Those eyes glared at him, and he added hastily, "I'm not calling you a liar, you know I'm not. It's just an observation—"

"You never met my twin sister," she snapped.

"No," Sioned told them, "but *I* did once, when she was about twelve or so. Your grandfather brought her to a *Rialla*. You were sick and had to stay home. Rossana could have been Camigwen's daughter—Fironese to her eyelashes." Rising, she glanced at Meath and finished, "We're useless here. It's time to relieve Hollis on the watch, anyway."

The three *diarmadh'im* were left alone with the mirror—and the man inside it. Ruala refused to look at it again. Riyan and Pol exchanged helpless shrugs.

"What do we do now?" Pol asked. "Ask him questions?"

Ruala straightened abruptly and started for the door. "If he answers, I don't want to hear it. Good night."

She slammed the door. Riyan whistled softly, a low, descending note. "This has really upset her. She's not usually like this."

"Pregnant women are notoriously unpredictable," Pol replied idly. "Shall we start?"

"Start what?"

"Damned if I know."

✳

Long past midnight, weary and discouraged by an utter lack of success, Riyan stripped and fell into bed. Ruala wasn't there, but he didn't worry much; she was probably helping in the search for Meiglan. He curled up beneath the velvet quilt and was immediately asleep.

The next morning, however, they heard him all the way downstairs when he read the note left on his wife's pillow.

> *Gone to Elktrap for Grandfather's scrolls. Back in a few days.*

Nothing more—but enough to make him shout for servants, soldiers, and a horse.

A short while later, down in the courtyard, his guards commander informed him that Lady Ruala had ridden out a little after midnight with a contingent of twenty—under his strenuous protests, of course, but she *was* sovereign lady here. Riyan strangled the urge to strangle the commander.

As he was about to order a troop of his own to ride out

and bring her back, he felt familiar and cherished colors dance around him on the morning sunlight.

Riyan, don't you dare.

He was so angry he couldn't form coherent thoughts.

I'll be perfectly safe, she went on. *It's not very far. Pol told us yesterday that the hills have been scoured of Vellant'im. And we need Grandfather's scrolls or we'll never know what that mirror really is.*

Damn all strong-willed, independent, intelligent women—especially when they were right.

Very well, then, she told him, sensing what he would not say. *I'll talk to whoever's in the light whenever I can. I hope it's someone who'll condescend to talk to* me.

Ruala—

But she was gone from his thoughts as surely as from their castle, and all he could do was stand there like a fool.

✳

Tilal rested his back against a tree overlooking the Faolain River, watching a dragon float its stately way to its own death.

His army, made up of his troops and Amiel's, had shadowed the great ship along either side of the river, and would wait here until the Vellant'im came down on it from Lowland. Midmorning, he guessed, taking a swig of water from a skin, and he squinted at the shadows cast onto the river by trees on the opposite bank. A while yet to relax and contemplate his advantages in this coming battle that he hoped would be no battle at all.

Lovely, having half an army of physicians at his disposal. For one thing, what they lacked in fighting technique they made up for in sure knowledge of the vulnerabilities of human anatomy. He'd inspected the Vellanti corpses at the mouth of the Faolain and the precision of the death-wounds impressed even him. No flailing about with a sword, hitting anything they could; they seemed to approach each kill with surgical deliberation. Thrusts to the neck cut directly through the vital artery; those to the heart, up and under the leather chest-armor and between the appropriate ribs as if the blade had eyes. Few trained warriors tested in a dozen battles were more efficient.

The physicians were *not* trained warriors, of course. The

fever that came over most of them had nothing to do with the veteran soldier's battle-lust that banished all fear. They fought as they did because they were terrified and wanted out as quickly as possible. Young Chegry, who attended Princess Nyr, had admitted as much to Tilal on the ride here.

"Some really do like it, my lord," he'd said, "but most of us are scared to death."

One would have thought that men and women dedicated to healing injuries would balk at inflicting them. Some did, of course. They were the ones who stuck to their trade and stayed out of the fray. But it surprised Tilal that so many turned their knowledge to taking life instead of preserving it.

After further consideration, he decided it was entirely understandable. They had homes and families; they were part of the princedoms like everyone else, battling the Vellant'im who had despoiled the lands. Tilal himself didn't much like slashing his way through a hundred bearded savages all bent on killing him, but it had to be done.

He thought again of Rihani—as capable as any man and more so than most, but in the end too sensitive for the brutality of war. Brooding over his son's death in the empty days at High Kirat, Tilal had come to understand that it had not been the festering wound or the sickness in his lungs that had killed Rihani. He had warred inside himself, and lost.

There were people who would consider Rihani a coward and a weakling. His inability to adjust to the horrors of what he had been forced to do would have been seen by some as a flaw in his character. Tilal knew he had only been born into the wrong time, a civilized prince in a world of barbarians.

Like Rohan. But Rihani had lacked the toughness that maturity had given Rohan, which allowed him to survive the battles he fought within his own soul.

Chegry had interrupted Tilal's bitter musings by saying something else about the physicians: that not only did they know where to strike for a quick kill, they also knew what enemy thrusts to avoid at all costs. "That's why we haven't lost many, my lord. We know which way to turn to keep a blow relatively harmless. Our technique may not be pretty, but it works."

"But you're frustrating the spit out of the Vellant'im," Tilal smiled. "You don't play by the rules and you don't make the usual moves. You don't waste energy by engaging them in swordplay, but wait until you can get in a really good hit. You don't have the decency to stand there dazzled by their brilliant maneuvers, but slide out of the way however you can. 'Pretty' belongs in the practice yard to impress girls, Master Chegry."

The third advantage to their presence was morale. The usual ratio of battle physicians to soldiers was along the order of seventy to one. In this army, it was more like ten to one. This produced a certain serenity on the part of the regulars, who knew their wounds would be treated almost immediately, with a correspondingly greater chance of total recovery.

So, as Tilal presided over the west bank of the Faolain and Amiel over the right, it was a remarkably cheerful army that waited for the Vellant'im to sail downriver into the trap.

They would have been downright festive if they'd known what that trap really entailed.

Tilal glanced at his squire, and even though the plan had been set firmly yesterday, felt it incumbent upon him to voice the usual caution about using his gifts to kill.

Andrev looked surprised for a moment, then shrugged and replied with a circumvention worthy of his father's highly flexible reading of the *faradhi* ethic. "All I'll be doing is calling Fire to whatever will catch on board the ship. The sails and hull won't—they learned that at Graypearl and Radzyn. But there should be other things to work with."

"Not their clothing."

"No, my lord, of course not. Just whatever's around them." He shrugged. "Even if they get singed by accident, they'll be free to jump if they want."

The river was cold and ran swift and high this time of year, but it was probably possible to swim for shore—where the army would be waiting. Fire or sword: no choice at all, really. Tilal's conscience didn't bother him. He'd seen Maarken set Fire to bridges across this very river—in truth, not so very far from this spot—back in 704. It hadn't done Maarken any irreparable moral harm. But as Andrev's lord, as a prince, as a fond substitute parent, and as a man who had lived with Sunrunners much of his life, he'd had to mention the Sunrunner vow. Especially to a boy who was the son of the Lord of Goddess Keep.

"Soon now, my lord," Andrev murmured a few moments later.

"Really? Has it gotten that late?" He sat up a little straighter, peering upriver. "Can you see them?"

"On what little sunlight there is since the mist cleared. The ship is about two measures off, carrying a full load of Vellant'im."

"Ha! Then Nyr's idea about beards worked."

"Yes, indeed." Andrev grinned. "I didn't know the Fironese were so hairy! Torien must have to shave twice a day!"

"Well, our little group of them have been working on theirs for three or four at least. Smart lady, the Princess of Grib. I'm going to enjoy doing business with her."

"Oh, you mean after Prince Velden dies and Prince Amiel inherits."

Tilal's voice was bland as milk. "And do you really think Cousin Pol will let an obvious incompetent remain as ruling prince? Don't be too surprised if Velden suddenly decides he's earned a peaceful retirement and hands things over to Amiel."

"Then Prince Cabar had better give us some help, too," Andrev said. "And Prince Pirro, and—my lord, what's Pol going to do about Rinhoel?"

"Whatever it is, there'll be a long line of those eager to hold his cloak while he does it." He eyed the boy. "You, on the other hand—what would you like to do after this is all over?"

"Continue in your service, my lord," Andrev replied promptly. "If you want me, that is."

"I have no complaints," Tilal assured him. "But what about after that? You could do just about anything, you know. There are plenty of holdings throughout Pol's lands. As his kinsman and a great-grandson of Prince Zehava, you could take your pick. Do you see yourself ruling a castle?"

"I'm not sure." The squire shifted uneasily. "I think—my lord, you won't tell anyone, will you?" When Tilal shook his head, Andrev went on, "I think my father wants me to be Lord of Goddess Keep."

He squelched the urge to say, *No, really? I hadn't guessed.* "What do *you* want, Andrev?" Then, ashamed of himself for pressuring the boy, he added immediately, "Well, how should you know? You're only thirteen. But a Sunrunner for all your scant years. Where's that ship now?"

"Coming, my lord. Coming!" Andrev grinned at him. "You're starting to sound like my little brother Joscev!"

Tilal growled, instantly spoiling the effect by laughing. Goddess, he was looking forward to this. Not a hundred killings, nor a thousand, nor five times a thousand would bring back his firstborn, but it was going to feel very, very good to kill all the same.

He sat forward, elbows on splayed knees, and fixed his gaze on the bend in the river, half a measure away. A stand of trees and the four burned cottages tucked beneath them formed a screen to prevent the Vellant'im from catching sight of the ambush. Unhappily, Tilal's view was obscured as well. But he had Andrev—and all at once the boy jumped to his feet.

"Easy," Tilal cautioned, amused that suddenly the impatience was all on the squire's side. "Tell Chaltyn to send word down the line."

Tilal pushed himself to his feet, sliding deeper into the cover of the trees. Timing, he told himself, it was all in the timing. He and Amiel must hold their people back or be seen too soon. Andrev could not begin his Fire too late or the river's speed would carry the ship out of range. Except for the one who spoke something akin to the barbarians' language, Amiel's four bearded Fironese must all be high in the riggings, out of danger.

Many of the Giladans and Tilal's own Ossetians had experience with ships, and gave the Fironese physicians intensive instruction. The major problem of impersonation had been solved when a rich merchant's daughter from Graypearl had offered her gold bracelets. They had been a gift from her Chosen when she left Dorval to become a physician. From each tiny link of the chains hung small, delicate golden beads.

Her eyes filled when she handed them over; she knew not whether her lover still lived, and the bracelets might be all she would ever have to remember him by. Tilal and Amiel promised her that every bead would be retrieved and remade into twin wedding necklets, and beside every one of them would be an emerald—gem of healing—added by them.

After the bracelets were taken apart with thin surgical probes, the beads were threaded through Fironese beards. They were too small to match the Vellanti version, but at a few paces the impression was good enough. Closer, things became riskier. Which was another reason why the majority of the men had been told to climb the riggings and stay there.

Andrev reported what Tilal had hoped: Vellant'im on board, all serene. Now, if only everyone else stuck to their timing. . . .

The ship appeared around the bend in the river. Tilal caught his breath. He heard Andrev come back to his side, felt the boy tremble with eagerness. The laden ship rode low in the river, more beautiful than a vessel that had brought such death and destruction had a right to be. But beautiful it was. The dragon head rose and dipped with proud majesty, the sails spread like wings about to sweep down and lift the ship into the air. He stared at it, thinking that whatever else these savages were, they had a thing or two to teach the shipwrights of Einar and Waes, Port Adni and Sandeia. The masts were as tall as towers. To stand in the nests atop them would be—

He saw it at the same time Andrev gasped. "There's no one up there! Not in the nests or the rigging!"

"Take a closer look at the deck. Tell me what's going on!"

It took only a moment. "They—they have Prince Amiel's man, my lord. With a sword to his throat."

"What about the others? Can you see them?"

"No—no, my lord. There are so many of them with beards—"

"Chaltyn!"

The commander was beside him at once. "My lord?"

"We're in trouble," he said grimly. "Andrev says they're holding our man at sword point. They must've been found out. The other four may be dead."

The ship was within easy sight now. On the short upper deck the crush of Vellant'im parted, and Tilal had an all-too-clear view of the Fironese physician and the two men who held him captive. His hands were pinned behind him, his head wrenched back by the hair. The blade shone at his exposed neck.

"Why did they let him live?" Chaltyn whispered.

"What?" Tilal turned from the infuriating scene.

"They've killed everybody else they could get their hands on. Why not him?"

"How in Hells should I know?"

"Maybe—" Andrev hesitated. "Maybe they want him as a hostage. Or to tell them what he knows about us."

"Or maybe they know that we value every life," Chaltyn said.

"Maybe, could be, perhaps—hush up and let me think!" Tilal ground his teeth. "Right," he snapped with sudden decision. "They want to talk to us. That's why he's alive. He understands both languages."

"Son of a—" Chaltyn glanced at the boy and swallowed the rest. "I'll go," he said.

"No, you won't," Tilal replied, and strode out of the trees down the steep slope toward the river. "Damn it," he muttered to himself on the way, "why is it *nothing* ever happens the way it's supposed to?"

Sailors more expert than Amiel's collapsed the sails with enviable swiftness. A moment later the anchor splashed into the river. The current tugged at the ship but could not carry it any farther. It rode just out of arrow-shot of where Tilal stood.

"All right, you whoresons," he grunted. "Here I am. Talk to me."

"My lord!"

Unaccented except for the lilt of a mountain-born Fironese, the voice belonged to the captive.

"I'm listening!" he yelled back.

"My lord, I am to tell you that you are to—to surrender!"

Tilal drew in a deep breath and used it in laughter that echoed off the opposite shore.

"They say they don't want to waste their time fighting, my lord! There's a big battle coming up at Skybowl and—" He blurted with pain, as if his captors had decided he spoke too many words for the content of their message.

"Tell them that if they want us, they can come ashore and take us—if they can!" His mind was a torrent: *Skybowl? Why? When? Three thousand of them—if these make it, which they won't—but how can I work it without losing that man's life? And what about those stupid pearls?*

As if hearing his internal question, the voice shouted, "My lord, they have told me to say that with the Tears of the Dragon, they are invincible and you have no hope!" He spoke faster now, his words racing Vellanti patience. "They number one hundred eighty, some wounded—the pearls are carried by the one with a horn at his belt—he wears a badge with a wheel device—*ahhh!*"

Tilal winced in sympathy. He knew the sound of a fist in the belly when he heard it. "Tell them there's another army waiting for them at the mouth of the Faolain! Their own ships have fled! Tell them that *they're* the ones without hope! And tell them that if you're harmed, I'll cut off their balls and then let them *live!*"

There was no reply. He narrowed his gaze, then cursed and pulled Rihani's long-lens from his belt. Senile at forty-five winters, not to have remembered it earlier. Yet as he put it to his eye and found the upper deck, he wished he hadn't. The physician was on his knees now, curled over. There was a second sword now, one at his back joining the one still pressed to his throat. The man's head lifted. His right eye was swollen nearly shut, and blood smeared his lips and chin. Tilal took an involuntary step back; the dark eyes seemed to be looking straight at him.

"My lord!" the call came, weaker now. "The others are dead. There's only me! Tell Lord Andrev to call his Fire *now!*"

And on that word he lurched back onto the swordpoint. Agony was there and gone so swiftly in his face that Tilal cried out and dropped the lens. He didn't need it to see the man fall forward onto the deck, the sword embedded in his spine. *Physician—he knew the quickest way to die—*

"Andrev!" he bellowed. "You heard him! *NOW!*"

Fire sprang up from the physician's corpse. And at last things began to happen as Tilal meant them to.

✳

Andry was strolling with Tobren in the maze garden when the little girl half-stumbled against him. He caught her, started to speak—and felt colors swirl around her, bright with triumph. He'd seen them many times before, though never in sunlight; the mirror he'd shattered had been a useful way to discover a Sunrunner's colors, and perhaps such teaching had been its intended function. He knew Andrev because of it, and hesitated only a moment before weaving himself into the glowing skeins that linked his offspring.

—we got them all, Tobren, either our swords or the river

when they jumped and tried to swim! It was hard, calling Fire like that, but—

The rush of words ceased. Andry spoke gently into the silence. *It's only me, son. Goddess greeting to you, Sunrunner. I take it you won the battle?*

Father? Uh, yes, we did, my Lord. We didn't lose many, only fourteen. I called Fire to the ship—well, to the physician who'd died, because I thought he'd want to be burned instead of the river getting him—was that right?

Very right. How is Prince Tilal?

Fine and unhurt. Prince Amiel twisted his ankle on a rock underwater, but he didn't even notice it until later, he was killing so many of them.

Tobren asked, *What about you? Are you all right?*

Not a scratch. Andrev sounded aggrieved. *Prince Tilal has me guarded so close that I never get the chance to get scratched!*

And a good policy it is, Andry said. *You're his Sunrunner as well as his squire.*

Another silence, while a living rainbow spun around them. At last Andrev ventured, *Father, I know you didn't want me to go with—*

We'll talk about that some other time. For now, be assured that I'm proud of you, Andrev. You've done your duty to your lord and to Goddess Keep. That's what counts in the end.

The boy's colors shone. *Thank you, Father! I'm trying my best. Oh, I almost forgot! Prince Tilal says to tell you we got the pearls back. He went himself to look at every single corpse that washed up onshore, and for a while we were scared that the man holding them might've washed downriver. But we found them, and now he wants to know if he should give them back to Lady Karanaya or keep them.*

Hmm. Hang on to them for now. There seems to be power in them—

Is there ever! I held them in my hand and they almost burned!

Do they? That's intriguing. Bring them with you to the Desert, then. Are you going by boat or on foot?

Prince Amiel's taking the ships. Prince Tilal's going to march, thank the Goddess!

Andry and Tobren laughed, and she said, *You're luckier than Rohannon! He's still with the Kierstian fleet, Uncle Maarken says, going to Snowcoves!*

What's Tilal got in mind? Andry asked.

Just a moment, please, Father. I want to ask him and make sure I've got it right.

They waited, he and Tobren. She was leaning against his side, as easy and trusting as her colors woven around and through his.

You're not mad at Andrev anymore?

I never really was, darling. At Tilal, yes, for not sending him back to us at Goddess Keep. But I was thirteen once, you know—hard as it may be for you to believe it!

She laughed again and the light danced around her. He rejoiced in her golden beauty of amber and topaz lit with luminous moonstone white. Jihan had been very different—all deep, intense colors, edged in onyx, a pattern of mystery and dark power. But perhaps that was only his distaste for *diarmadh'im*—

Father? Tobren?

Still here.

Tilal says this: Amiel is going to Dorval to pick up Prince Ludhil and his troops, because we're going to need them. Even with those we got rid of today, there should be something like three thousand to march on Skybowl—

Skybowl? The light tilted wildly around him as he remembered the Goddess' crystal globes.

That seems to be their plan. It had something to do with the pearls, and the High Warlord, and a ceremony. Nobody here knows what or why.

Pol said that Skybowl is the best place for a battle, Andry mused. *And I have pretty much the same feeling myself. So we'll all meet there, one way or another, shall we?*

It looks that way—unless Prince Pol wants us somewhere else. From what you say, he doesn't. I'll tell Prince Tilal that. We'll bring the pearls with us. Maybe we can draw them out of Radzyn or somewhere and make them fight for them, and kill a few more so there won't be so many at Skybowl.

Leave military management to those who understand it, Andry warned. *You're a Sunrunner.*

Yes, my Lord. Chastened, Andrev paused before continuing, *Is Princess Meiglan found yet?*

Something else glinted on the edges of Andry's mind, something that made the correct sum out of Skybowl, pearls, Meiglan, Chayla, and ceremony. He couldn't quite grasp it.

No, Tobren was saying sadly. *Lord Kazander—I've told*

you about him, the crazy one who likes Chayla—he's gone after Princess Meiglan, and Jeni at Skybowl says Lord Sethric of Grib is doing the same.

The Desert's a big place, even just from Feruche to Stronghold, Andrev worried. *Does anybody know where to look?*

We've all been searching on light. But there's nothing to be seen. They're being very careful how they move. Chayla saw her a few days ago when they rode by, but that's the last anybody knows of her.

Andry entered the conversation again. *We'll let Pol know what you've told us. Congratulate Tilal and be sure to give him my thanks for taking good care of you whether you like it or not!*

I will, Father.

I am proud of you, my son, Andry finished, and withdrew to let the children say their own farewells.

He held Tobren closer, concentrating on that elusive equation. No, it was gone now. When she returned, looking up at him with a smile, he smiled back and took her with him to find Pol.

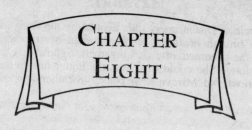

CHAPTER EIGHT

Of all the people searching for Meiglan that day, only one saw her.

Those trained in Sunrunner arts kept watch by any light they could weave. One of them used the stars. Kazander and Sethric and their soldiers had no such help, and had to seek with unaided eyes. The Vellanti High Warlord repeatedly scanned the terrain around Stronghold, and, like all the rest, often swore sharply in frustration.

But one person saw her—not unaided, but not with the aid of sun or moons or stars. Meiglan was found as Andry had found Chayla and Sioned, Kazander.

Thanys tucked herself inside a shelter made of her cloak and a blanket, supported by a few branches. It was evening, and damp beside the little stream she'd been following all afternoon. She had tried this spell several times during her journey, without success. It had been a very long time and her gifts were rusty. But now she called on the deepest part of herself, power buried and denied as her distant kinswoman Lallante had rejected what she was. And she did it with the help of *dranath*.

It grew wild in the Veresch. She had seen a patch of it today as her horse limped over the crest of a mountain pass. The animal's lameness would not heal without rest, but there was no time for that. Better to make a few measures each day than none at all.

Thanys mixed the herb with stream water and drank. The cup was clouded with milky sap that warned her the *dranath* was too fresh and therefore dangerous. She drained the cup nonetheless. Distant memories evoked by the flush of intoxication brought a dark fire, like that in her mother's eyes when she dreamed of regaining their rightful place in the princedoms. She could even feel the hotter lust in the gazes of Mireva and Mireva's unspeakable father for the same thing—though they had done more than dream.

But their purpose had never been hers, any more than it had been Lallante's. Thanys let the recollections run their course and fade. Then she evoked the memories of Meiglan, for it was Meiglan she sought this evening, out of the distracting light of the setting sun, the rising moons, the first pale stars.

She cradled the silver bowl of water in trembling fingers. Meiglan's wedding necklet coiled within like a diamond snake, the great pendant amethyst rattling. Thin, nearly invisible smoke misted across the Water when she called Fire to it, and she exhaled slowly. When the vapor turned white, she nodded her satisfaction. It had been a very long time, but the power was still there.

The first glimpse she had was of Pol. Thanys waited patiently for impressions of him to swirl away, unsurprised that he should appear at her conjuring. He was the one Meiglan thought of and dreamed of every time she saw this necklet, touched it, wore it, unclasped it from her throat to lay it tenderly away.

Eventually Pol was gone. Thanys had no interest in where he was or what he was doing. He didn't need her; her lady did. Observation by more usual means had shown Jihan and Princess Alasen at Feruche, but not Meiglan or Rislyn. Thoughts of her ladies in enemy hands shuddered Thanys' heart so she could hardly draw air into her lungs.

The whole necklet chittered against the silver now. The smoke vanished. Water rippled with Thanys' own quivering. She stilled herself, concentrated, and at length white smoke drifted across smooth Water again.

She saw Meiglan.

The High Princess slumped on a horse picking its weary way across a sparsely wooded hillside, along a trail no wider than a bookshelf. One bad step in the evening gloom and she would be lost down the rocky slope. It didn't seem as if she cared one way or the other; her hands hung limply, her head drooped, her spine bent with exhaustion.

Her head turned then, slowly, to look over her shoulder.

The hood fell from her hair and face. Although Thanys could not see what she stared at, the anguish in her eyes was unmistakable. Straining to expand the vision, the watching woman had a fleeting blink of a look behind Meiglan. A huge man rode just behind the High Princess, sword arm crooked up toward his body. A strange posture for one of these accursed dark-bearded warriors—but perfectly natural for a father holding a child.

A child with sweat-dulled fair hair.

The warrior glanced forward at Meiglan, and the small nod of reassurance he gave was even stranger. Thanys recoiled from his eyes that seemed to look directly at her. The spell reacted to her fear: necklet writhing into mimickry of the twisting road, vision expanding, distancing her from the riders. She was borne on a cloud of white smoke, sobbing aloud as the hills receded dizzyingly. The living map on the Water's surface diminished as she rose higher and higher—as high as the clouds, as the moons. She would never find the Earth again—

Thanys flung the silver bowl away and collapsed into a heap. The sky was alive with mocking stars before she stopped shaking and lifted her head.

She had found them. It meant nothing. Who could she contact, who could she tell? Who would listen to her pleas for help in rescuing Meiglan and Rislyn?

Not the *diarmadh'im* who opposed Mireva's faction; even had she known any, they wouldn't believe her. Not her own kin; they would only laugh and shrug and say that Meiglan was worthless, and Pol deserved to suffer for murdering Ruval.

Not Pol, or whichever Sunrunner was on duty at Feruche tonight. They all thought the Vellant'im allied with the sorcerers. Perhaps they were; she had been too long from the councils of her kind to know. But if she revealed what she was—and she would have to, for this spell was not one worked by Sunrunners and there had been none of their kind of light to work by in the dusk—it was worth her life. And that would not help her lady.

Besides, who could ride fast enough to reach Meiglan before Meiglan reached Stronghold?

Thanys began to weep as she realized that Meiglan *would* reach Stronghold, no matter what was done or not done. Her wild upward flight had shown her that those hills were perhaps half a day's ride from the empty castle and the encampment below it. Tomorrow night at the latest, her lady would be brought to the High Warlord. No one could reach her in time.

✴

In this, she was mistaken.

Lord Sethric of Grib and Lord Kazander of the Isulk'im rode the same narrow hillside track not ten measures from where the Vellant'im halted for the night. They were certain their quarry *would* stop, once the sun went down and the moons came up. The Vellant'im knew Sunrunner ways. Staying beneath the cover of trees when they could, hiding themselves when the land did not provide shelter and the light was good—it was the sole explanation for the Sunrunners' inability to find them.

The two young men had met the previous evening. Perhaps "met" was the wrong word; they very nearly came to blows. Sethric's troop was abruptly and silently surrounded by black-clad men on black horses. Swords sang from scabbards before Sethric recognized the smiling dark face from the mock battle at Remagev and several battles in earnest since. He called to his people to hold, and greeted Kazander with admirable self-possession.

"Welcome, my lord *korrus,*" he said pleasantly. "Lovely night for a gallop, isn't it?"

Kazander nodded enthusiastically. "It is, my lord of Grib, it is indeed! All one lacks is a lady to share it with."

"My thought precisely, my lord."

But the lady they encountered that night was not the one who needed finding. She appeared on the road before them as suddenly as moonlight slicing through a cloud, holding up both hands that glistened with *faradhi* rings.

Sethric's first thought was not *What in all Hells is a Sunrunner doing here?* Instead: *So will Jeni's fingers shine one day, with tokens of what she is that I am not and can never be. . . .*

Kazander had no such notions to distract him. He sprang down off his horse, as spry as if he'd been in the saddle only for the afternoon and not six whole days. Striding forward, he bowed and saluted the Sunrunner woman.

"Lost, strayed, or stolen, you are safe now, my lady," he

said gallantly. "I am Kazander, unworthy one who leads the Isulk'im. My noble companion is Lord Sethric of Grib, knight, accomplished warrior, and generous in honoring me with friendship I return in gladness and trust."

The woman blinked at this speech. So did Sethric, not so much at the praise but because Kazander called him a friend, and really did sound sincere about all of it.

"My name is Valeda," the Sunrunner said at last.

Kazander's fingers fluttered like a bird's wing, brow-lips-heart. "*Devri* to Lord Andry, mother of his daughter Chayly, and powerful *faradhi* of many rings. You were not lost, then, for such as you cannot become lost. You have not been stolen. But why do you stray so far from Goddess Keep?"

Valeda seemed to need a moment to recover after each recitation. This time she was quicker, and more blunt. "We could stand here all night exchanging our credentials and pretty words, but that wouldn't do Princess Meiglan any good."

Instantly the *korrus* abandoned his flowers of Isulki eloquence. "Have you seen her? Where?"

"I'm a Sunrunner. We're supposed to see things."

Sethric gestured at the moons. "On that light? Your pardon, my lady, but—"

Valeda gave him a wry smile, as unexpected as it was attractive in her rather severe face. "No magic for you, eh? Trail-signs aren't difficult to see if you know what you're looking for. I found theirs. Then I found *them*—damned near walked into a sentry, if you must have the truth. The important thing is that the High Princess and her Vellanti escort are ten measures away, right over that hill." She pointed. "A little while and *you* would've galloped smack into them, with predictable results."

"So you came to find us," Kazander interpreted.

She nodded and pushed back the straggling ends of her dark blonde hair. "You don't happen to have anything to drink, do you? My horse and I parted company about fifty measures back. He got homesick for Radzyn in the middle of the night and took most of my gear with him."

Sethric immediately handed over his waterskin. "You've been two days on foot through these hills?"

"Only one," Valeda replied laconically. "I don't waste time."

"I guess not," he said, impressed that she had come so far

in a single day through tough country on foot. After waiting politely for her to drink her fill, he asked, "Are they riding fast?"

"They're camped, and not all that carefully. It's not far to Stronghold, after all, and nobody's found them yet."

"We must give thanks to the Goddess that you did, my lady," said Kazander.

"Oh, it's one for the bards to write songs about, all right." She handed back the waterskin. "But we haven't put the finish to it yet." Surveying the troops gathered around in the moonlight, she addressed a slim young woman astride a big gelding. "Will that gray brute of yours mind double weight?"

The soldier slapped her horse's neck affectionately. "Oh, no. Rabenel likes Sunrunners. Lord Maarken trained him from a hatchling." She held out a hand. "Up you come, my lady. He's no silk pillow, but he'll spare your feet."

"This is fine." Valeda settled herself to ride pillion.

"Thank you, Hestiba," Sethric said, not *quite* pointedly. Valeda gave no sign that she'd heard. He exchanged glances with Kazander, who shrugged, gathered his reins, and remounted.

"All right, then," the Sunrunner continued, pulling leather gloves over her hands and her nine telltale rings. "Let's get moving—and quietly. We'll want the advantage of surprise."

"Indeed," Kazander said mildly. "My lady, I am pleased we could offer you a horse to ride, however uncomfortably. But it would be even more useful for you to ride the moonlight and tell the High Prince where we are and what we plan."

She shook her head. "Once we've succeeded."

"Please do it now," he replied, with utmost courtesy and with steel in his voice.

"Understand this, my lord *korrus*. I go Sunrunning when, where, and as I see fit, and take orders from Lord Andry alone."

"Order?" He was all innocence. "Respectful request, my lady!"

Whatever she might have answered was cut short when the gelding jumped and sidled, nearly spilling Valeda into the dirt. "Sorry," Hestiba murmured, sounding contrite. Sethric knew better.

So did Valeda. She scowled, her lips tight and her jaw

clenched. But a moment later she wore the expression that had become familiar to Sethric since Autumn, the expression most Sunrunners wore while working.

Kazander still looked as guileless as a child. Hestiba winked at Sethric; others of the company were grinning, and Isulki teeth shone especially white above black clothing in the gloom. They had all sobered by the time Valeda returned; this Sunrunner might be prickly of temper, but she *was* a Sunrunner, and due proper respect.

"There's cloud cover across the approach to Feruche," she said.

Sethric wondered if she was lying. Kazander seemed undisturbed, and after a moment the younger man understood why. Telling Pol mattered little; authority had been established and everyone, including Valeda, knew it.

"Later, then," Kazander responded with perfect calm. He and Sethric signaled to their people, and they started off to find Princess Meiglan.

A silent way down the road, Sethric asked, "Did you have any trouble finding us, my lady?"

"I knew where you'd be." Valeda shifted her hold on the back of Hestiba's saddle. "Intercepting you before you stumbled into the Vellant'im was the problem. They're about half a measure either side of the camp."

"In fours or eights?" Kazander asked. When she gave him a startled look, he explained, "That is their habit when posting guards. I have observed this from Remagev to Skybowl. So I say again, my lady: fours or eights?"

"Eights. All on foot. You should be able to kill them quickly enough, if you're quiet about it." She paused. "Which you Isulk'im will undoubtedly be. I've read about the Black Warriors."

His turn to look startled. But he said nothing.

Sethric waited for her to ask questions about what had transpired since she'd left Goddess Keep. Eventually he wanted to kick himself for stupidity. She was a Sunrunner; what the others knew, she would know. Hells, she probably knew more than he did. Pol had recently taught Jeni to do more than listen passively on sunlight, but her colors were not yet widely known and so she did not receive news as readily as other *faradh'im*. And what was there to know, anyway? He had his task to perform. That was all he needed to think about.

Now, however, with a Sunrunner riding next to him, he wanted to hear about his family. His cousin Elsen, crippled as he was, had surely reached Goddess Keep by now. Word was that Norian and her husband Edrel weren't far behind. The Goddess herself couldn't match Norian for fury when she really made the effort. He wondered if Elsen's courage would finally cause Prince Velden to bestir himself from Summer River. If it didn't, Pol would find some way of making him sorry he hadn't once this was all over. Perhaps Cabar of Gilad would now do something as well, for his son Amiel was fighting Vellant'im in the south. It was possible that Cabar's daughter, married to Elsen, would argue both cautious and frightened princes into action. Sethric hoped so. Pol was going to need all the help he could get.

But most of all he wondered how Valeda had come so far through such perilous country without getting herself killed. He decided this was the question he wanted answered most of all, and so asked it.

Her answer was very simple. "I'm a Sunrunner. And up until last night, I had a good, strong Radzyn horse."

"Still, you were lucky."

"The Goddess watches over her own." She almost smiled. "If we have the sense to keep our own kind of watch, of course."

"Silence," Kazander snapped, and held up a hand to call a halt. Sethric heard nothing unusual. Valeda's eyelids drifted shut and the moonlight shone on her blank face for some moments before she shook her head.

"Nothing."

"That you can see," Kazander appended. "I feel them. Like death waiting outside the tent of my mother, many years ago." His fingers moved in the air, and his nineteen black-clad warriors gathered around him. Sethric and the rest were pushed gently but firmly away. No words were spoken, and Sethric wasn't close enough to see what further signals Kazander gave, but in the space of three breaths all of them but the *korrus* had melted into the night.

"Ride on," he said into the emptiness between himself and Sethric. "Keep alert. My lady, watch as you can. They are near, I feel them. May the Mother of All Dragons fold you gently in her wings." He saluted and became as invisible as his companions.

Valeda glanced around, amazed. "Where did they go? How did they do that?"

"Silence," the young man told her, then gave a few swift orders of his own, wishing for the kind of communication Kazander had with his people. He sensed nothing, but his spine itched anyway and his palm ached for the hilt of his sword.

They rode on. No one talked now, not even in low voices. Only one moon remained above the ragged black trees on the ridge, veiled in clouds and then clear, the light flirting with perceptions. That bush, was it a crouching man with sword ready to kill? And the strange bend of that tree trunk just down the slope—every boulder, every hollow of ground, might hide a secret in its shadows.

"Stop."

It was barely a whisper, heeded instantly. Valeda slid from Hestiba's gelding. "He's right. They're close," she said, with more breath than voice. Drawing up the hood of her cloak to cover the shine of her hair, she moved to the side of the trail where the tree-shadows were and picked her way silently down the hillside.

Sethric dismounted. Eighteen of his group did likewise, swords hissing softly free in the uncertain moonlight. The other six stayed on horseback, and would wait here to cut off any escape. That was the idea, anyway. New to this kind of warfare, he was discovering that he much preferred open battle in open country. All this sneaking about in the dark roiled his stomach and knotted the muscles between his shoulder blades.

Like Valeda, he sought the shelter of deeper darknesses as he went, gliding from one patch to another like a child jumping from puddle to puddle after a rain. The rustle of garments was painfully loud. He convinced himself that the sound was exactly like wind playing with leaves. The trail leveled out just as the last moon set, making darkness of everything.

No, not everything. In that gulley just up ahead was the faintest glow, screened by a stand of scrub pine. Sethric froze.

Valeda crept to his side and leaned close, her breath tickling his ear. "The moons are down, they may leave shelter. I'll do what I can."

Days ago, some stray shower had soaked to silence the

dry leaves and needles littering the ground. Not a branch snapped, not a footfall was audible as Sethric and his eighteen soldiers stole through the pines toward the light. From the thin cover of a scraggly trunk, he squinted down into the hollow. The Vellant'im were getting what rest they could. Thirty or so dark heads—pillowed on the ground, leaning against trees, bent over cups of some hot drink that boiled in a pot on the fire—contrasted sharply with the gleaming fair hair of Meiglan and her daughter. They huddled back from the others, the child cradled in the woman's arms. Meiglan was not afraid; she was too exhausted, too much in shock to feel anything. Sethric suddenly pictured Jeni in her place, and just as suddenly knew that when he returned to Skybowl he would tell her how deeply he loved her. Life was too uncertain to deny feelings. He might lose her or she him, and there might be no future at all—reasons enough to love her as much as she would let him *now*.

A tall, powerfully built Vellanti whose beard was thick with gold tokens glanced up at the moonless sky and rapped out a command. Instantly the hollow was alive with movement. Men rose and stretched and finished off their drinks; some went to bring the horses around. It was only when one of them came roaring back into the camp shouting *"Enel'im! Enel'im!"* that Sethric realized what Kazander had done. The word was a familiar one, though seldom used in the plural like this.

Kazander had done what his people did best. He had stolen their horses.

Sethric almost laughed aloud. He watched the chaos down below for some moments as the leader bellowed orders in a rage and men scurried to catch the wayward animals. Meiglan sat in the middle of it, seemingly oblivious as she stroked Rislyn's forehead and tried to get her to drink from a cup. Sethric decided that when four or five more Vellant'im had gone to look for the horses, he would attack.

But their commander was no longer shouting. He called out one word. The warriors who remained in the clearing took up position with their swords, circling Meiglan in a wall of steel.

Sethric nearly gave his own order then. But Kazander was nowhere to be seen, and that worried him. His eighteen were overmatched. So he waited.

And waited.

And nearly laughed again as, when no one arrived to do battle, the leader was made to look like a nervous fool.

The Vellant'im lowered their swords, raised them, peered around into the night as if the dying fire could pierce the shadows of the trees. At length the commander swore—the tone was unmistakable, even if the words were incomprehensible—and ordered them to sheathe their weapons.

Sethric reminded himself to congratulate Kazander. The enemy were now convinced that the horses had simply wandered off. Those responsible for such carelessness would pay dearly if their commander's expression was any indication. His face was congested with anger and humiliation as he paced before the fire, snarling—probably about the time and trouble needed to catch the accursed Radzyn *enel'im*.

But Kazander had decided the time was now. And Sethric was only a heartbeat behind him.

They had talked it over yesterday, agreeing that if the Vellant'im had wanted to kill Meiglan, they would have. They wanted her alive and in the possession of the High Warlord. So whatever happened during the fight, she would not be harmed. This knowledge gave their swords a certain freedom as they converged on the Vellant'im from all sides—twenty men in black, eighteen more wearing the badges of Skybowl and Remagev and Radzyn Keep, and one whose tunic boasted the white candle of Grib.

As he shouted *"Azhrei!"* and fought and killed—this feeling much more familiar than skulking through the dark—Sethric sometimes caught a glimpse of Meiglan. She was curled as small as she could make herself, protecting her daughter with her body, while warriors clashed and shouted around her. He tried to fight his way to her, blocked at every attempt by what seemed a wall of bearded men. The nearest he got to her was when a fallen Vellanti caught him a vicious slice across the back of one thigh with his sword, and he lurched forward, toppling flat on his face two arm-lengths from her.

Sethric was lucky. The enemy thought he was dead. They paid him no more attention than they would a fallen log. Which for a time he resembled, lying strengthless and nauseated by the agony of what he knew must be a slit hamstring. His right leg was useless—and might remain so the rest of his life.

He vowed to get what use he could out of the rest of his body and began to drag himself toward Meiglan. Keeping hold of his sword while plowing through the dirt on his elbows took up most of his attention. He didn't see Kazander coming until the man practically stepped on his outflung sword, barely missing the fingers that grimly hung on to it.

"The princesses!" Sethric called out. "Get them out of here!"

Startled by his voice, Kazander parried a slashing sword barely in time. He bent, trying to haul Sethric to his feet.

"No! Leave me! See to them!"

He was ignored. His right leg dangled, unable to support him, but with the left one under him and his sword as a cane, he was steady enough—if totally defenseless.

"Go!" Kazander ordered, swerving to avoid one Vellanti and skewering another who was making for Sethric. Whirling furiously, he stepped toward Meiglan—at the same time the Vellanti leader ran toward her from the other side.

Neither man touched her. Sunrunner's Fire sprang up in a neat circle, encasing her in a tiny castle of flames. She screamed, huddling tighter around her daughter. The Vellanti couldn't reach her—but Kazander couldn't, either. They glared at each other through the Fire, and Sethric couldn't tell which was the more surprised, or angrier.

Valeda's work, of course: both a brilliant move and a mistake. The enemy still on their feet ran to find the Sunrunner, screaming *"Faradhi!"* as they stormed up the hill. Their abandoned opponents raced after them. Sethric was knocked down again and groaned as his leg twisted under him. Gritting his teeth, he straightened it out with both hands, half-blinded by pain. He used his sword to lever himself upright once more and looked around.

If his leg hadn't hurt so much, and if there hadn't been so many fallen bodies, he would have laughed: the precipitous mass flight had emptied the clearing. As it was, he shivered with dread. Remaining were only himself, the cowering figures within the flames, and two warriors who began a dance of swords and cunning that would end in death for one.

Sethric leaned heavily on his own sword, cursing his helplessness. Kazander was smiling. He did not engage in direct play; instead, his blade flickered out like a dragon's tongue to tease the Vellanti. After a moment Sethric saw what he was up to. The Isulki carefully, almost gently, coaxed the enemy commander away from the princesses. Sethric took one slow, limping step, then another, then another. He was close enough now to feel the heat of the Fire—but there was no heat.

His brain balked at that. The flames were real. He could see them, was close enough to touch them.

But the air was chill. There was no sharp crackle, no smell of burning, no smoke, nothing of real fire but the sight of flames.

Illusion, conjuring, trickery—an image of fire but not its substance—

No! It was bright and red-gold and, by the Goddess, it *was* fire—

He told his brain to shut up and leave him alone, and reached through the flames with his free hand.

Reason told him he should be writhing in pain, his arm immolated to the elbow. But he wasn't even singed. His heart tried to leap out of his throat. He swallowed it back down and grasped Meiglan's shoulder.

She looked up, and in her eyes wild, dark reflections blazed. Between her and him was Fire. Swaying, nearly losing his balance, he again told himself that it had no heat, no substance, it wasn't *real*.

"Your grace, hurry! The flames won't hurt you! Get up!"

She caught her breath on a sob and shook her head violently. Sethric tried to pull her to her feet, but he was too precarious on his own.

"Your grace, please!" He glanced around and saw Kazander keeping the Vellanti busy enough, their swords ringing now in the cold night, Firelight flashing off steel. "Meiglan! Touch it! Look at my hand! It can't hurt you!"

But the fingers that ventured toward the flames were those of a child, small and trembling, one of them wearing a delicate emerald ring. Rislyn's face was flushed with sickness, and her green eyes were only half-focused, but she almost smiled, as if recognizing the Fire as something of her own. Her fingers stroked it wonderingly.

Sethric grabbed her hand. Her slight weight was easy to lift. Her mother cried out again and thrust her at Sethric, up through the flames. Whether an act of blind trust or total desperation, it was done and he had the child safe in his arms.

"Take her!" Meiglan screamed.

Weak and feverish, Rislyn was terrified by the loss of sheltering arms. She clung to Sethric, crying for her parents and her sister.

"Hush now, it's all right, it'll be all right." Sethric held her awkwardly against his left hip. His voice wavered between gentleness and urgency, a mad fluctuation like a string going in and out of tune. "But you must help me, Rislyn, we have to hurry—my lady, your grace, for the love of the Goddess, it won't hurt you! It didn't hurt her! Shh, it's all right, Rislyn, your mama will come with us. Meiglan, get up!"

"Mama!" the little girl pleaded. "It's not bad fire, Mama, please!"

Meiglan gathered her legs under her. "Take her! I'll follow! I'll—"

The Fire vanished.

Sethric knew what that meant. "Kazander! They've got the Sunrunner!"

The *korrus,* fighting for his life now against a man half again his size, yelled something. Sethric heard great crashing sounds in the scrub now. Any moment the chance to escape would be lost. Without the sword in one hand to prop him up, he had no hope of walking more than one pace. But with Rislyn in his other arm, he was out of hands to drag Meiglan to her feet. The High Princess tried to stand and couldn't; tried again; failed again. And then he saw why. They had hobbled her ankles.

"Kazander!"

Gloved fingers clamped around Sethric's shoulder and his stomach lurched. But the voice shouting at him was female, and familiar.

"Here—mount up! Take the girl and ride like all Hells! Hurry, damn you!"

Somehow the Sunrunner had eluded everyone. She snatched the sword from Sethric's right hand and replaced it with the reins of a black Radzyn mare whose ears were laid flat with anger. Rislyn was no weight at all, but Sethric's balance was so fouled by his useless leg that halfway into the saddle he almost collapsed. Valeda shoved his right leg over the horse's rump and Sethric saw stars. And then, miraculously, he was seated, the child snug at his side, the reins in his hand.

"Go!" the *faradhi* yelled.

He turned his head, hoping she would push Meiglan up

behind him. She had knelt beside the princess, fingers scrabbling at the rope around her ankles. But there was no time. He saw shapes of men and horses in between the trees, converging on the clearing once more.

"Valeda! They're—"

She looked up, the rope dangling from her hand. "Get out of here!" she screamed at him.

And as he accepted that she was right, and he must at least get Rislyn to safety, he saw something that made the Fire's unreality seem as natural as breathing.

Her face changed.

Blue-gray eyes shaded to brown. Strong, handsome features softened to wistful delicacy. Dark blonde hair paled, curled in an unruly cloud around her face that was no longer her face.

It was Meiglan's.

Sethric heard a guttural cry of *"Diarmadh'im!"* behind him that snapped him out of his entrancement. Clutching Rislyn to him, he dug his heel into the mare's ribs and fled.

*

Valeda cursed under her breath as Sethric finally rode away, damning him for taking so long about it. Then again, it wasn't every day one saw such things. And the astonishment scrawled across his face had served her as a mirror. She had succeeded.

No, not quite. She yanked the cloak from the High Princess' shoulders and exchanged it for her own. Confusion enough, if she was lucky. Then she stripped off her gloves and stuffed her rings into them, clenching small, white, unfamiliar hands around them for an instant before throwing them into the forest as far as she could.

What else? Necklet? Earrings? She checked quickly, relieved to find no jewelry that might give away the game. The clothes were almost right—both of them were dressed in brown riding leathers of standard design, though her own were of lesser quality. She thanked the Goddess that Meiglan was evidently a practical sort of woman who did not ruin really fine clothing by wearing it on a long journey. Besides, what man ever truly noticed what a woman wore unless he had given it to her or had plans to remove it?

She ran through the list Evarin had established of possible

troubles in this spell, and decided she had taken care of everything that could be done on such ridiculously short notice. During the long ride from Goddess Keep she had amused herself by working the spell on occasion, barely able to hide her smiles when at a farmhouse in Syr she had been welcomed as a man. That had been difficult. Men moved differently than women—something about the set of the hips that affected the balance of the body. But she had succeeded in her guise. Taking Meiglan's shape was much simpler. And, by the expression on the High Princess' face, copying her demeanor would only be a matter of acting afraid.

Not that she had to act. Valeda knew what these barbarians did to Sunrunners. It was why this madness had been her only hope, once she had escaped their discovery in the forest.

But she had not heard Meiglan's voice. As the clearing filled with battling warriors again—all avoiding the two women who huddled together in unfeigned terror—Valeda drew both their hoods up and took Meiglan's face between her hands, whispering urgently.

"My lady, I know what it's like to see your own face in a living mirror. I'm sorry for the shock. But it's necessary. My name is Valeda, and I'm a Sunrunner of Goddess Keep. You know of my daughter, Chayly, who is also Lord Andry's daughter, grandchild of your husband's aunt. So in some small way we are kin. I will help you all I can, but you mustn't be afraid of me."

The first kind voice she had heard in many days slowly got through Meiglan's fright. She touched a finger to the face that was her own, then snatched it back. "You—how did you do this?" she breathed.

A lighter tone than mine, softer, not as deep. "It would take too long to explain. I—" She was jostled against Meiglan as someone stumbled into her back. Righting herself, she kept her head bowed and her shoulders drooping and said, "I must tell you two things about it, though. I can't do any other Sunrunner work while this is taking up all my power. And this face will become my own when I sleep. If we don't win free, and if we're taken to the High Warlord, then we must be constantly together and neither of us can sleep at the same time. Do you understand?"

Meiglan gave a jerking nod. "But we will be freed. Lord Kazander—"

"Of course, of course," Valeda soothed. "I only told you in case the worst happens."

"But why would you—Andry has no love for my lord."

"Andry is Desert-born, and Lord of Goddess Keep. He—"

Hands dragged her up, set her on her feet. She hadn't noticed the sudden quiet. Meiglan was hauled up to stand beside her, and clung to her arm. Valeda curved her spine a little more to make the three fingers of difference in height less noticeable, and looked around.

Bodies littered the hollow. One of them sprawled half across the campfire, his clothes smoldering. Valeda was pleased to see it was the commander. It might be easier to deal with underlings, those who were accustomed to obey rather than think. She had originally thought to take on the shape of a Vellanti, but aside from the problem of movement, she knew it was a poor leader who did not know his own men—even though they all looked alike to *her,* with their beards and their fierce black eyes.

They were not fierce now. They were stricken.

She bit back a smile of satisfaction. There was no reason to smile in any case. Rislyn was free—but there was no one left to help her and Meiglan.

One or two men approached, then shrank back. Someone came into the clearing saying something about the horses being found. Valeda had heard enough of Jolan's old-language poetry to discern most of the words, even if they were snarled instead of sung. The talkative one stopped in midstride when he saw the doubled image. He and all his fellows stared at the two women and at each other, utterly at a loss.

Suddenly one of them wiped his sword clean on a black Isulki cloak and marched up. Valeda knew what he was about to do and flinched back. So did Meiglan, but for a different reason.

The twinned reaction stopped the Vellanti, but only for a moment. He grabbed Meiglan's arm—proof enough that no one could tell the difference—and brought up his blade.

Another man cried out in protest, talking rapidly. The first paused and turned his head, the sword a handspan from Meiglan's skin.

Valeda held her breath, concentrating on putting the words together in her mind. Then she had it—and nearly sagged with relief.

The man had called out, *"No! Unmarked! Priestlaw!"*

He spoke again, coming forward with eyes that dared not look at the two women. *"No! No blemish, no fault! It is law! Priests will know which is false!"*

*"But—*faradh'im *die of steel!"*

"Choose wrong, you *will die! Think, my brother!"*

The sword wavered. Meiglan's arm was released, and the blade returned to its scabbard. Meiglan half-collapsed against Valeda, breath sobbing in her throat.

The horses were brought. Several of the Vellant'im began to stack the dead for burning. Meiglan whispered, "Is Kazander there among them? Is he?"

Valeda shook her head helplessly. "I don't know. I can't tell."

And then they were lifted onto horseback, and led away into the night.

✳

Kazander's fate was also in Sethric's mind. He rode due north without regard to the terrain, certainly without heeding whatever trails might appear before him. Rislyn had long since fainted, or slipped into fever. He couldn't tell, and he couldn't stop to help her. *Feylin,* he kept thinking, *I must get to Feylin at Skybowl, she'll know what to do. Skybowl. North. Hurry.*

His leg didn't hurt now. He could feel nothing below his right hip. He was beginning to get dizzy, and knew it must be from loss of blood. Earlier, he'd sensed the leg sliding against saddle leather and reached down. The blood was still flowing, incredible amounts of it. He slowed the horse and used his belt knife to cut a length from one rein, and tied it around his thigh as best he could. But he must get to Skybowl, to Feylin, who would know what to do for him and for the unconscious child.

He had no idea how long he'd been riding. He kept expecting to hear Kazander's voice behind him, calling him to a halt, telling him that the High Princess was safe and everything was all right. But perhaps they would meet at Skybowl. Feylin was there to scold his carelessness and heal him and say that he would have the use of his leg again in perfect health. And Jeni was there. He would tell her, he swore he would, and if she said she loved him, too, he would go down on his knees in thanks to the Goddess who had let one of her Sunrunners care for him, a mere younger son of a younger son—

—and probably a cripple for the rest of his life, like his cousin Prince Elsen.

Goddess, he felt strange. Light-headed, shapes moving closer and then darting away, his face clammy, his hands loosening on the reins. . . .

No. Mustn't fall asleep. Must ride. North. Skybowl. Feylin. And Jeni—

"My lord?"

His head snapped up. "Kazander?" he muttered thickly.

There was an odd hesitation. "Here with us, my lord, and twelve of our Isulk'im, and ten of your own from Skybowl. Here, let me help you—"

"Skybowl," Sethric repeated as hands eased the child out of his arms. He was cold now where she had been.

"Yes, my lord. Careful now coming off your horse, we'll want to bind that leg a little better—"

"Meiglan?" he asked, trying to focus on the dark face at his knee. Hands coaxed him down, ready to help him. " 'M fine," he mumbled. "C'n ride. . . ."

"After you've been bandaged, my lord. Lady Feylin will lop off my ears to cast in silver for wind chimes if you lose any more blood. Come, my lord—"

"Feylin . . . Skybowl. . . ." There was one more word that went to the formula, and as he frowned and groped for it, he felt himself topple slowly from the saddle. But that didn't matter; someone caught him, and he had found the word.

"Jeni."

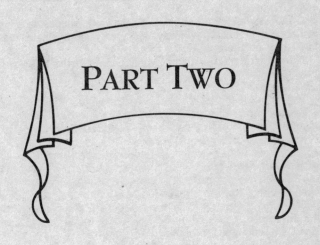

PART TWO

CHAPTER NINE

Edrel, new Lord of River Ussh, was aware that his Chosen lady had a temper. No one would think it to look at her. She was blandly blonde, sweet-featured, with big, soft blue eyes and a gentle smile. But, in fact, one of his most cherished memories was the sight of her confronting her father, eyes flashing and cheeks afire with a fury of determination.

Prince Velden of Grib had forbidden his daughter to marry a mere younger son. Prince Velden had changed his mind. Norian in a rage was about as dainty as an exploding furnace.

And she had been smoldering ever since they'd left Dragon's Rest.

Edrel had been waiting fifteen days now for the blast. Nothing. At length he understood: she was not one to vent her anger at any but its true object. On the morning of the sixty-fourth day of Winter, that object became visible over the crest of a low hill: Goddess Keep.

The troop they had started with had been augmented during their ride through Grib. Those unable to come in time to Prince Elsen's summons now joined his sister and her new husband. It was therefore a respectable army—seventy-one mounted warriors, over a hundred archers, and at least that many brawny farmers carrying wickedly sharp scythes—that marched through the morning mist.

Edrel thought his wife would ride faster now, grimly intent on a chat with those who had compelled her crippled brother to this journey. Norian surprised him. She slowed her mare to a walk, regarded Edrel with a frown, and said something completely irrelevant.

"Your hair's gone white. Did you know that?" She pointed to his right temple. "Just a few threads, but I swear there are more every day."

He ran a hand reflexively back through his hair and shrugged. "Just a coincidence. It runs in the family."

Norian shook her head, braids like pale rivers of gold across her shoulders. "It's something else the Chief Steward of Goddess Keep will pay for, along with every measure my brother had to ride—and the rest of us, too."

"I've been meaning to talk to you about that," he said as their horses ambled down the hill. "Let's see how Elsen is doing first, get his ideas and impressions. We ought to know everything before we say anything."

Norian considered, then nodded. "Yes. Besides, it's this Torien person who should be admitted to *our* presence, not we to his." At the expression on his face, she began to laugh. "There are uses to being born a princess, love!"

"I know." He grinned back. "I spent years curing Amiel—he started out an obnoxious little beast, you know."

"It's not a disease, knowing what your rights are," she complained. "And you ought to learn a bit of it. You're *athri* of River Ussh now."

"And you're my lady," he said firmly. "Which means that until we do summon Torien to explain himself, I'll do the talking. No," he added, raising a hand half to warn her, half to placate her, "a Princess of Grib you may be, but I learned politics at Dragon's Rest, where lessons are slightly more subtle than your father's. You can carve up Torien at your leisure once I've found out what I need to know." He paused, grinning again as fair brows drew together over her nose. "Just please don't sharpen your tongue on me for practice!"

"Oh, very well. But keep those Sunrunners out of my way."

He said nothing in reply. He couldn't. The awkward village of tents and lean-tos lay before them, hollow and empty as a drained winecup. Mist slunk low and furtive, like cats stalking field mice.

"Did the Vellant'im attack? No," Norian answered her own question, "there aren't any bodies, and no smoke to mean they've been burned."

"I'm not sure what this is, but I'm damned sure I don't like it."

He led the way through the silent sprawl, his stallion's hooves shredding the thin mist like silken lace veils. Pots still simmered on fires. Items lay scattered about as if abruptly abandoned—a child's toy here, a water bucket there. Outside one tent a box of razors and scissors and brushes had overturned near a rickety stool, as if a barber had been interrupted in a morning's work.

Edrel reached for his battle helm. "Norian. Get back."

They hadn't been married long, but they'd been married long enough for her to know he did not give orders on whim. She reined her horse around and cantered away.

Breathing no easier, he rode toward the closed gates of Goddess Keep. His army formed up around him, eight across and forty deep, mounted soldiers in front.

"My lord?" whispered their elected commander, son of a minor *athri* from near the Grib-Meadowlord border. "Do we attack?"

How in Hells should I know? There's not a sound coming from the place, not a single sign of life. There may not be anybody in there to fight.

"Not yet. Let's see what's going on in there first."

As he guided his horse up the rise, someone within the keep cried out. A child, calling in panic for his mother. Edrel flinched. One little boy left alive of all the hundreds—no, thousands, by the look of that village—at Goddess Keep?

Another voice, loud and strong, shouted angrily. Edrel waited for the man to finish, then stood in his stirrups and yelled up to the walls.

"Open! Open to the Princess Norian of Grib!"

There, he thought, momentarily amused, she'd have great fun teasing him later for his quickness in learning the uses of her rank.

Silence again. Several faces appeared above the walls, and in due course the gates were unbarred and pushed open.

Edrel simply gaped. The great courtyard was packed. Men, women, children, Sunrunners and not, were crammed like sides of meat in a coldroom after a hunt meant to feed a castle all winter. A narrow path opened for him, straight to the main stairs, where a curious scene presented itself.

A woman stood on the bottom step, her long black hair spilling down the back of her white cloak. A row of angry *faradh'im* spread behind and above her at the doors. With defiant shoulders and proud head she confronted the throng, one arm flung out to point at Edrel.

"You see? The Goddess heard me! I begged her to come to our defense against the Vellant'im, and she has provided a whole army! And it was *my* work, not these cowardly prating Sunrunners'! *Mine!*"·

Edrel didn't know what it was he'd stumbled into, but nothing here convinced him to put up his sword. He cursed under his breath as his wife nudged her mare through the crowd to his side. Norian was flushed and furious, and every whit the princess.

"Where is my brother?" she demanded of the Sunrunners. "I've come to see Prince Elsen of Grib, and I will see him *now!*"

There were nine *faradh'im* lined up before the tall doors. In the middle was a tall man of about forty winters, dark skin and hair and eyes proclaiming him Fironese. At his right was a woman several years younger, whose delicate moonlight-and-midnight beauty did nothing to distract from the righteous rage in her gray eyes. Instinct told Edrel that these were the pair to deal with. There were four more men—one of them resembling a respectable-sized tree, and one of them very much older than the rest and deeply troubled in a way different from the others—and three women, of whom two were quite young. All were undoubtedly formidable enough in their calling, but, with Andry gone, the two in the middle held the power here.

So these are the devr'im, Edrel thought. *Lords and Ladies of light, as Andry would have it. Who's this woman in front of them, and what has she done that the little gray-eyed one looks ready to kill her?*

The Fironese took a half-step forward. "Princess Norian? Then you would be Edrel of River Ussh. I am Torien, Chief Steward of Goddess Keep. This lady is my wife, Jolan. Please be assured that Prince Elsen is receiving the best of care from our physicians. He—"

"Is he injured? What happened?" Norian asked anxiously.

"Nothing, my lady. No battles. His leg was troubling him, but is healing."

The woman beside him—Jolan—spoke up. "You'll want to see him at once, of course. Your people may rest outside the keep."

"Arrayed to defend us against the Vellant'im," interrupted the white-cloaked one who had claimed the Goddess' favor.

"I see no threat here," Edrel said. "Do you expect one soon? Is that the reason for this in-gathering of—"

"This does not concern you," Jolan replied sharply. "It is a matter for *faradh'im.*"

Torien gestured. "Antoun, please escort the princess and her husband to her brother's chamber."

"Go along, my lady," Edrel told Norian. "I'll be there shortly."

She searched his gaze for an instant, aware that no one else must see her hesitation. Edrel gave her a tiny smile and a nod. He might need her authority as a prince's daughter—but she needed to see her brother. She dismounted and tossed her reins to a nearby Sunrunner, who looked startled at this demotion to groom.

Norian climbed the stairs; the older man met her halfway, bowing slightly as he placed a hand lightly at her elbow. "Your grace," he said, "I talk with Prince Elsen often, and he will be very glad to see you."

Edrel thought he heard something beneath that. But although Norian gave Antoun a gracious enough nod, her attention was for Torien.

"You are the one who authorized the summons?"

"I am, your grace."

"I'll speak with you later."

Jolan turned to stone, only her furious eyes alive. Norian ignored all of them—especially Jolan, though Edrel didn't know how one ignored one person in particular when ignoring a crowd in general—and accompanied Antoun inside.

Not knowing what he had interrupted, besides some transgression on the part of the white-cloaked woman, Edrel explored the anger and tension around him and decided it would be best to break it—if he could.

"I don't mind saying, Lord Torien," he began pleasantly, "that my troops could do with a hot drink. Any chance of it?"

The usages of hospitality were the last thing on Torien's mind. Jolan frowned more deeply.

"It would be best to remove yourself from the courtyard for the time being, my lord," she said. "Things of importance are being done here in which you have no part. Your soldiers will have to wait."

Edrel felt thousands of eyes on him and didn't much like it. Did Pol feel this way when he was on display at a *Rialla,* and everyone looked to him for solutions to impossible problems? Well, first he had to discover what the trouble was.

Nothing if not direct, Edrel asked, "What things?"

"I have done what no one else dared to do," said a voice at his knee. He glanced down. The accused woman had abandoned the bottom step and now stood next to him. Her proud and lovely face was raised to him, but she truly spoke to the crowd. "I freely admit it, my lord. The Vellant'im hover offshore, preparing to attack us. I prayed to the Goddess in her grove nearby, and she answered me by sending you and your army. And now I am blamed for it, for—"

"For violating the circle and the spring, which are sacred to Sunrunners alone!" Jolan exclaimed. "You admit your sin without shame or contrition! Master Jayachin, you are judged—"

"*Lady* Jayachin," she flung back, "*athri* of Goddess Keep by Lord Andry's own order! None can judge me but him, or the High Prince!"

"In matters of the High Prince's Writ, that would be true," said Torien. "This is different. It is a sin against the Goddess."

Edrel wanted no part of this. He wished he'd gone upstairs with Norian. He wished even more fervently that he'd arrived tomorrow. But he was the nearest thing to a representative Pol had here, and he knew his duty to his prince.

Taking a determined breath, he asked, "What exactly did you do?" It was not a question destined to find favor with the Sunrunners, but he needed knowledge and time to think up what to do with it.

"I will tell you, my lord," Jayachin declaimed, moving away from him so she could be heard from one end of the courtyard to the other. She drew the white cloak around her, lifting her head so her voice would carry. Edrel had to admire her command; he thought Pol would, too.

"This morning at dawn I rose after a sleepless night, and in gazing at the first light of the Goddess' Fire I suddenly knew what I must do. I walked alone to the circle of pine trees in the forest, on the cliffs where Sunrunners go when they wish to speak with the Goddess. It was cold, and the mist was everywhere, and many times I almost lost my way, but the Lady must have guided my steps, for I found myself facing the circle of mighty pines, with the small Water and rock cairn within."

More substance and less art, if you please. Edrel shifted impatiently in his saddle. "And then?" he prompted.

She didn't break verbal stride. "Even in the morning chill, I knew that I must not approach so sacred a place except as the Goddess made me, so I removed all my clothes. And I was no longer cold, for the sunlight came through the trees to warm me with the Goddess' own Fire. I knelt beside the pond, and as I begged the gentle Lady for her help, I also begged her pardon for coming into this place that the Sunrunners say is only for them."

Uh-oh, Edrel thought, appreciating the dig for what it was. He snatched a glance at Jolan. Here, too, he realized with a start, was a woman who would unleash her fury only on the one who had caused it.

Jayachin spread her arms wide, the white cloak unfolding. "At that moment, thirst came upon me, even though I had sipped a little wine before I left my tent. The Water before me looked soft and sweet, and my thirst increased—and I felt the Goddess guiding my hands into the shape of a cup, and I gathered Water in them, and drank."

She had probably told some of this before, but evidently this part was new. The courtyard hissed with gasping breaths. Edrel, having spent years serving one of the three most powerful Sunrunners now living, knew all of it to be dramatic embellishment, if not downright lies. The *faradh'im* knew it, too. But the common folk did not.

Jolan's words were shards of ice. "For this alone you deserve punishment."

Jayachin whirled, white cloak and long black hair flying. "For daring the grove, and the Water? Why? I was sent there by the Goddess herself, I firmly believe it! And after I had drunk of the sweet Water, I beseeched the Lady for help—as none of *you* have done that anyone can tell! And now look—here is that help, come in response to my prayers!" She pointed at Edrel once more, a wild gesture that made his horse's ears lay back. "An army has come, and we will be defended against the barbarians who have raped our lands and made us homeless! The Goddess heard me, and has saved us!"

"You're not *faradhi*," Torien said calmly. But Edrel, feeling the turn of the crowd's mood in favor of Jayachin, heard an undercurrent of fear in his voice. "You are not chosen of the Goddess. The circle is forbidden to you. The Water is forbidden to you. The Goddess cannot speak to you as she does to us."

"I never said she spoke," Jayachin retorted. "Not in words. The presence of Lord Edrel with his army is answer of another kind!"

This is a very dangerous woman, Edrel told himself. And she had put him in an impossible position. If he took her side, which Torien's pompous edicts and Jolan's pious mouthings tempted him to do, he would be undermining the authority of Goddess Keep and all Sunrunners—not to mention aiding and abetting what he knew to be a lie. But if he asserted that his arrival was only a fortuitous coincidence, he would be allying himself with this new idea that *faradh'im* were set apart by more than their ability to weave light. What had Torien said? *Chosen of the Goddess?* He didn't like the sound of that at all. After so many years with Pol, he had no awe of Sunrunners and scant regard for Lord Andry and his innovations. Who spoke for the Lady? Who could speak *to* her? Who would judge whether a Sunrunner told the truth about it?

And just what was a "sin," anyway?

Yes, a *very* dangerous woman, with dangerous ideas. Jolan obviously thought so, too. And Edrel saw in her frost-gray eyes that she did indeed intend to punish Jayachin. Perhaps even to kill her.

Torien was speaking again. "Lord Edrel has come here—safely, thank the Goddess—after a long journey from Dragon's Rest that began many days ago."

"Yes," Jayachin agreed. "But he arrived *today.*"

Jolan was having none of this petty nattering over what to her was an irrelevancy. "And if he had ridden a little faster, he would have come last night, before your sin! *That* is the issue here, and the judgment is clear. By your own unrepentant admission, you have entered the sacred circle. You are not *faradhi.* Your words are lies. The Goddess did not listen to you, she did not even notice you—except in anger that you dared a place that is for her chosen Sunrunners alone." She paused—no stranger to dramatic effect either, Edrel noted—and used her sharpest blade. "Otherwise why would a Sunrunner, a *devri* of Lord Andry's own choosing, be warned and go to the circle this morning to discover you there, and raise the alarm when she witnessed your sin?"

The young woman flanking Jolan called out, "I saw you by the dawn's light! I woke early with a feeling of dread in my heart and went to the forest to ease my fear by consulting the Goddess!"

"And all of you know what happened after," Jolan continued. "Linis came running back to Goddess Keep. Deniker and Nialdan returned with her, and found Master Jayachin coming from that sacred place, ready and willing to tell everyone of her sin."

Edrel could almost hear Pol's snort of disgust. If it was a sin to take a walk in the forest, everyone was guilty but those who lived in the Desert. As for Linis' "dread," that had the same smell as Jayachin's supposed thirst.

He cleared his throat. Jolan shot a look of icy daggers at him. "Lord Torien," he said deliberately, further infuriating her, "I understand that she did something offensive. Surely she meant no harm by it."

"Do you expect me to *apologize?*" Jayachin exclaimed. "I won't! I acted in accordance with the charge Lord Andry himself put upon me—to guard the safety of the people outside the walls, whose *athri* he made me!"

She had claimed the authority of the Goddess, and now she was claiming Andry's. Edrel felt as if he stood between a Merida with a poisoned glass knife on one side and a Vellanti with a hungry sword on the other. Support Jayachin and her lies to keep the Sunrunners in line, or take the Sunrunners' part in their self-righteous arrogance—and *their* lies—to curtail Jayachin's blatant ambitions?

In the end, he didn't have to make the choice. Torien raised both hands, his rings glittering, and his voice rang out in the morning chill.

"This woman admits and even boasts of entering the tree-circle and drinking of the Water there. She claims that the Goddess answered her pleas, using Lord Edrel's appearance here as 'proof' of the truth of her words. She claims the sanction of the Lord of Goddess Keep and of the Goddess herself.

"But what she has really done is lied. The Goddess heard nothing from her, and saw only the sin of her entry into a place sacred to the Goddess and her chosen *faradh'im*, and warned one of us with feelings of fear and misgiving. Lord

Edrel came here today by the Lady's gracious guidance—not at this woman's command. This woman has no standing at Goddess Keep, which is in my guardianship in Lord Andry's absence.

"The only truth here is her sin. She has defiled the tree-circle and its Water. She has thus defiled the Goddess' chosen Sunrunners, and the Goddess' intention that they alone should come to the circle.

"And for sin against the Goddess, the punishment is clear."

Edrel had thought himself ready for it. Death had been in Jolan's eyes from the beginning. But he had thought a sword, or perhaps Sunrunner's Fire, would be their weapon, and was preparing himself to leap from his horse and snatch the woman to relative safety. Whoever he sided with, whatever she had done, she didn't deserve to die.

But he had forgotten what the *devr'im* had done here that had so enraged Prince Tilal, the wall of horror that had surrounded Goddess Keep.

It could surround a single person, too.

Nothing changed from one heartbeat to the next. Torien, arms still upraised, did not move. The men and women around him on the top step did not even close their eyes.

Jayachin screamed.

Edrel's horse leaped as if lightning had exploded in his hooves. The stallion bucked and lunged away from Jayachin, nearly trampling a girl who was slow in getting out of the way. Edrel clamped his knees tight, fighting to control the terrified animal. He felt a little of it himself as his horse skittered to the other side to avoid a small boy who broke free and ran for Jayachin.

"Mama! Don't hurt Mama—"

People pressed back, crying out, hollowing the courtyard where the white cloak had crumpled to the ground. Jayachin was on her knees with her arms wrapped around her head, shrieking. Her son had collapsed in a small, writhing heap an arm's length from her.

The stallion reared. Edrel was nearly unseated. He yanked the reins and the horse came down on all fours, immediately leaping, slamming into someone else. When he hit the cobbles again, he kicked out with his hind hooves. Edrel was tossed forward, out of the saddle, and the last thing he knew was Jayachin's scream following him down into darkness.

✳

"I blame myself," Antoun said dully, staring down at his beringed hands. "I knew what was in her mind to do. I should have stayed. I might have stopped it from happening."

"How?" Edrel resisted the impulse to rub at a bruise on his shoulder. Norian was finally convinced that he would live, but it had taken most of the morning to do it. He had been unconscious only for a few moments—only for as long as it had taken Jayachin's heart to give out from the extremity of her terror. He had been groggy for some while after, but, aside from a cut on his head and a few aches, was perfectly fit.

Now they sat in Elsen's chamber, a snug and even luxurious guest room directly above the library, with a view through two narrow windows of the southern cliffs and the sea. The weather was typical of Goddess Keep in winter: early fog giving way reluctantly to stubborn sun. Clouds massed out to sea like Vellanti ships gathering for war. It would rain tonight, perhaps even this afternoon, but in this room the threatening chill was warded off by a seascape tapestry on one wall and a good-sized fire. Elsen's bed was set before the hearth, a book-laden table beside it. Antoun had drawn up chairs for himself and Edrel, while Norian sat cross-legged at the foot of her brother's bed. It was a pose that brought back memories for both of them, of long days when, bedridden, he had taught his little sister to read. She had remarked on it earlier, while they all pretended to eat.

But now they spoke of other things, in quiet voices though not in whispers. Antoun had reassured them that no one would think anything of their sharing the noon meal with him, and even less of his joining them. He looked in on the prince rather often, and as Norian's commanded guide and a *devri*, no one would suspect him of disloyalty. For as they talked, a thing left unspoken became clear to all: that they were conspirators.

Elsen set his winecup aside and hitched himself a little straighter in bed. Addressing the Sunrunner, he said, "My friend, you are no more to blame than Edrel. If either of you had interfered, Jolan might have killed you, too. For 'sin,' " he finished bitterly.

"That's something I don't understand yet, but we'll leave it for later," Norian said. "I want to know precisely what happened and why."

"Precisely?" Antoun shrugged, gray eyes bleak as a mourning cloak. "I don't doubt that some of Jayachin's story was true. She tried various schemes for provoking a battle—shaming Torien into it, into killing the Vellant'im at a distance. She also tried to worm her way into residence within the keep. Nothing worked, so she violated tradition by entering the circle."

"She had plenty to say to me when I arrived," Elsen put in. "Enough to make me suspicious of what these Sunrunners might have in mind—which could be just what they did to Prince Tilal's army."

"They won't do it to ours," Edrel growled.

"That's why I'm glad my new little brother is here," the prince smiled. "With me laid up in bed, they could issue any order they liked in my name. But now they have you to contend with, a man knighted by the High Prince, and lord of a great holding in his own right." He patted his sister's hand where it rested on his arm. "You've done very well by all of us, Norian."

"It wasn't my intention to do well by anybody but me," she replied, amused. "But it does seem I have excellent judgment."

"I'll remind you that you said that, someday when you're ranting at me for one thing or another," grinned Edrel. "New big brother, you're my witness."

"Rant? I would never have such bad taste! That knock on the head must've addled your wits."

"Long enough to miss what really happened after," he answered grimly. "I suppose they took Jayachin for burning, but what about her little boy?"

"As it happens, you're wrong," Antoun told him. "They took her body to the cliffs and threw it into the sea."

"Unburned?" Norian looked sick.

" 'As she liked Water so much,' Jolan said, 'Water and its creatures shall have her.' I don't know about the boy. Someone probably took him back outside when the rest of them left." He pinched the bridge of his nose between thumb and forefinger, closing his eyes. "Ah, Goddess, why didn't she go home to Waes when she could?"

Elsen looked surprised. "In Waes she was just another

merchant. Here, she was an *athri*. We ought to find out about the child, though. Whoever takes guardianship of him takes control of whatever wealth the family left, too." He shifted again, and Norian was instantly ready with pillows. "No, I'm fine. My rump gets sore, that's all. One thing I'll give these Sunrunner physicians, they're healing my bad leg for me. It hurts less now than ever before in my life. And they say I'll be able to walk on it without pain, maybe even without a limp."

"The only thing I've found in their favor thus far," Norian said. "If it's true—and I beg the Goddess that it is."

"True enough, my lady." Antoun smiled. "I've heard them discuss him, as I've told Prince Elsen before. They're quite excited, actually. He's a real challenge. All they ever get to treat here are cuts and scrapes and the occasional broken bone—and the inevitable winter colds, of course."

"They made quick enough work of my cracked head," Edrel admitted. "I'm curious about the *faradhi* girl—Linis? How did she happen to go out to the tree-circle this morning?"

"Oh, that." Antoun poured himself more taze. "My lady? No? It's a little strong for some, I know. Linis is pregnant, or so she hopes. She and Martiel have discovered each other as woman and man, not just as *devr'im*. She went this morning to consult the Mothertree. That simple."

"But revised by other needs into that story about waking up filled with dread." Edrel declined the offer of taze. "You Sunrunners are nothing if not creative in your thinking, and quick with it, too."

Elsen frowned. "Don't class Antoun with them. I've said he can be trusted."

"But you didn't say why," the graying *faradhi* reminded him.

"That's yours to tell, my friend."

"So it is. And I'll tell it now, so there's no misunderstanding." Settling himself with hands folded, he began, "I was here at Goddess Keep, twenty-two winters old and four rings to my hands, when Lady Andrade commanded Sioned to the Desert. Meath, Hildreth, and I are the only ones left of those who went with her. And a journey and a half it was, too," he added with a reminiscent smile. "Of us three, Meath went to Graypearl, Hildreth eventually came to rest with Pol and his dragons, and I stayed here. When Andry became Lord of

Goddess Keep, many of us who had learned our craft from Lady Andrade grew impatient and angry—as Hildreth did— and asked to leave, either to be court Sunrunners or to ride the princedoms—as Hildreth did."

"But you stayed," Norian said.

Antoun nodded. "I stayed. Not because I agreed with Andry's changes and ambitions, but because Sioned asked me to."

Edrel felt his jaw hang open and quickly shut it. Every so often at Dragon's Rest he'd heard Pol wonder aloud— sometimes irritably—just how Sioned got her information about Goddess Keep and what went on there. Now he knew. This aging, plain-faced, clever Sunrunner, friend of her youth, was her source.

And Lord Andry didn't have a clue.

"I haven't seen her in, oh, it must be twenty years now," Antoun mused. "But of course I can see her, and she me, whenever we choose. And we do talk quite often on sunlight." All at once he laughed, and they all had a glimpse of the young man he had once been. "I can tell you it was the shock of my life when Andry made me one of his *devr'im!*"

"Was the High Princess—um—able to appreciate the irony, then?" Elsen ventured.

The *faradhi* sobered at once. "She knows now, of course. But when it happened. . . ."

"Rohan," Elsen murmured.

"Yes."

Norian paused a moment before asking, "You're loyal to Sioned, not Andry?"

"To Lady Andrade," he corrected. "To her teachings, and those of Lord Urival. During his last years here he helped me escape Andry's notice, mainly by telling me to keep my eyes open and my mouth shut whenever Andry changed something. Don't mistake me, I'm not arguing with everything he's done. The physicians, for instance." He nodded at Elsen. "There have been good things that have come of his rule here. But others . . . this idea of sins against the Goddess. . . ." He sighed. "No. My loyalty is to Andrade, and to her hope that Goddess Keep and High Prince would clasp hands, not raise fists."

After a time Edrel got to his feet and went to the windows. The sea was a deep gray-green, painted by the wind with whitecaps like miniature shifting mountains peaked in snow. The Vellanti ships were to the north, hovering in Brochwell Bay, waiting for they alone knew what. He couldn't even imagine them, although they had been described to him several times. Dragons plying the waves, wings outspread, carrying death on their backs.

Not turning, he said, "Fists will be raised here, you know. From what little I've heard, they've had more than enough chances to land and take Goddess Keep, as they failed to do the last time. You Sunrunners can't burn them in their ships because their ships don't burn. The oath not to kill with your gifts doesn't seem to apply anymore. You'll protect Goddess Keep—and, presumably, the people outside the walls—if they land and attack. But they haven't." He swung around. "Antoun, what in all Hells are they waiting for?"

✳

The bright noon sunlight seized Andry's mind so powerfully that he stumbled against his brother's shoulder. Maarken caught him, said something Andry didn't hear. The voice in his mind and the colors swirling around him obliterated all other awareness.

Andry, thank the Goddess I found you! Listen carefully— there's not much time. Meiglan and I are being taken to Stronghold. She's all right, shocky, but all right. I'm wearing her face. We'll be safe so long as nobody sees me asleep or while I'm Sunrunning. I don't know yet what they want of her—as soon as I can, I'll find out and tell you. But I need to know what you want them to know. Quickly, Andry—they let us have some privacy for a wash, but we'll have to go back soon.

He didn't even have to think about it; he and Maarken and Sionell had just been discussing that very subject. *Skybowl. Whatever happens, convince them to go to Skybowl.*

Why?

I saw it. The Goddess showed me that one more castle will fall. It has to be Skybowl. For military reasons, Maarken and Pol agree, though they don't know about the vision. Say whatever you think will persuade the Vellant'im, but turn their minds to Skybowl.

I'll try. And I'll tell Meiglan.

He tried to catch his breath after the lightning exchange.

Valeda, you said you're shape-changed to Meiglan? Why? What happened?

The Isulki and that young Gribain tried to free her. I think they got away with the little girl, I'm not sure. But I couldn't escape. So I threw my rings away—better that and wear someone else's face for a while, than have them wear my rings in their beards.

Goddess! his mind began to reel again. *You're not injured? Meiglan?*

Unhurt. So far. I'll speak to you when I can—perhaps by the moons, I don't know. But don't try to reach me. I tried this spell a few times on my way here, and found out that I can't do any other work while caught in it.

Valeda, be careful. Here, let me show you my brother and his wife. If you can't find me, try for them. He built their patterns, first Maarken and then Hollis, with elegant speed and skill, and sensed her fix them in her mind.

Thank you. Now I don't feel so alone. She paused and he felt her colors tremble. *Andry, I'm frightened. These people, I don't know what they want, what they'll do with us—*

Abrupt silence.

Valeda! he cried into it. But the light had cleared of her colors. She was gone. He swayed against his brother, gasping.

"Andry? Are you back with us? Sionell, get him some water—"

"I'm fine," he managed, and leaned against Maarken's strong shoulder.

"No, you're not. What happened?"

"It—it was Valeda. She's with Meiglan—wearing her face—they're being taken to Stronghold. We have to find Pol—"

"Not just yet." Maarken half-carried him to a mounting block and made him sit down. "Ell? Where's that water? Oh—thanks. Drink," he commanded, spilling chill liquid down Andry's throat. "Again? All right. Deep breaths now. Easy."

The courtyard of Feruche came into focus around him again. His brother's worried face, Sionell nearby, servants eyeing him askance. The great Lord of Goddess Keep, shaking and weak as if he'd never felt the touch of sunlight before. Andry straightened his spine and cleared his throat of fear.

"I'm all right."

"You're such a rotten liar," Maarken observed, smiling crookedly. "Drink some more water, calm down, and tell us what you heard."

Lord of Goddess Keep or no, it was a relief to do what his big brother told him. He sipped more water, waited for his racing heartbeats to slow, and drew in a breath.

"There was a rescue attempt. They seem to have gotten away with Rislyn, but not Meiglan. Valeda was caught, too. We all know what the Vellant'im do to Sunrunners, so she shape-changed into Meiglan. Evidently it's working so far. But it'll fade when she sleeps, and she can't work anything else while working the spell."

"Shape-changed?" Sionell whispered. Andry looked up, and saw equal astonishment in Maarken's eyes.

"It's something some of us have learned how to do," he explained. "I've used it myself on occasion."

Maarken chewed his lip. "At least the Vellant'im will be confused for a while as to which of them is really Meiglan. I don't want to think what will happen if Valeda slips."

"She won't," Andry said. "She knows what she's doing." *I hope.* Pushing himself to his feet, he continued, "We'll have to tell Pol, and warn Jeni down at Skybowl that Kazander is on his way, with Rislyn if we're lucky. Oh— Skybowl. I told Valeda to convince the Vellant'im to march there."

Sionell folded her arms. "Don't you think you should consult Riyan before you give away his castle?"

It was what they had been arguing about before Valeda's precipitous Sunrunning. Maarken said, "We've explained why it's the best place to fight them. We can sneak a whole army in and they won't be any the wiser until we land on them like a dragon on a stray lamb."

Andry stayed silent, the castles globes whirling in his memory. One more must fall. It must not be Feruche or Goddess Keep or any of the others. Skybowl was his choice. Thank the Goddess that Maarken and Pol agreed with him— even if they didn't know what the castle's ultimate fate would be.

Sionell gave an annoyed shrug. "I'll go find Sioned so she can warn Jeni."

"Do that," Maarken agreed, and as she returned to the keep his glance seconded Andry's own thought: she didn't want to be anywhere near Pol when he found out what had happened. Andry didn't blame her.

✳

Sioned was duly informed, and the afternoon lessons for Sunrunner children left to Meath. Sionell returned to her own room, there to sit at the window with one of Jahnev's shirts to mend, taking only a few stitches before she flung the garment to the floor.

It seemed forever since she'd felt anything for herself. For others, yes: for Chayla, Sioned, Maarken and Hollis, Chay and Tobin, Meiglan and Rislyn and Jihan. Each name in her mind brought its measure of horror, fear, pity, anguish. But apart from loving her children and grieving that they had lost their father, she dared risk none of her own emotions.

She wasn't *really* avoiding Pol. For one thing, it wasn't possible. He was everywhere at Feruche. Her own duties—the wounded, the Tuathis and Tiglathis, her children—took her in a fairly restricted round, but he was likely to appear around any corner. She couldn't afford to let the sight of him affect her, and so she allowed nothing to affect her.

It was easy during the days. Other people demanded her time, her thoughts, her feelings. It was even easy at night, when she fell into bed too tired to think or feel. The bad time was morning, when she half-woke and turned to reach for a familiar, comforting body.

The worst of it was that she never knew which of them she sought.

One man she would never see again; the other, all too visible. One of them her own husband, the other Meiglan's.

What kind of person was she that she had done this to herself, to Meiglan?

To Pol?

No. Whatever had been done, he was responsible for his part in it. Enough that she should bear guilt for Meiglan. For herself. For Tallain. . . .

It wasn't loving Pol that she feared. She didn't want to know what she felt for him, because it might turn out to be hate. But even that would be bearable compared to the other thing lurking inside her. Because what truly frightened her was the anger.

Not at him. At Tallain. For leaving her. For sending her

away by means of a trick and a betrayal, sending her away to be safe, while he fought and died.

How could he have done that to her, knowing how much she loved him?

How *could* he have left her alone with this madness that had caused her to do what she had done seven nights ago?

She could hate Pol—and herself—because they both deserved it. But her anger was directed at Tallain. It shamed her, this rage that cut into her vitals, at times so deep she could scarcely breathe. It edged her voice in broken glass and made her want to shatter everything from the wine goblets on the dinner table to the arrogance in Pol's eyes.

She knew it was wrong and wicked and appallingly selfish. If Tallain was here, she would have begged his forgiveness on her knees. Worst of all was knowing he would only stare, lift her up into his arms, and tell her in honest anguish never to kneel to him again.

But he was not here. Damn him for not being here.

She wanted to cry. Couldn't, of course. She'd never had any practice in a loved and sheltered childhood, so she'd never learned how. Oh, once or twice in frustration and hurt over Pol's indifference, but no more than that. Surely this terrible Autumn and Winter should have taught her how. All the losses, all the defeats, all the deaths. Her brother Jahnavi, his wife Rabisa, their daughter Siona. Lyela. Rohan, Tallain. . . . Surely all those she had lost deserved their tribute.

The tears that burned in her eyes now and would not fall were not of grief or even of rage. She thought of Meiglan—gentle, innocent, betrayed Meiglan—and was bitterly ashamed.

But not even for Meiglan could she weep.

What kind of person was she, that she could do these things and feel these things and not cry?

*

When Andry and Maarken left his chamber, Pol sank onto the pillowed seat of the window embrasure and put his face in his hands.

Rislyn. Safe. Probably, anyway. Soon she would be at Skybowl, with Feylin's skills to cure the sickness Jihan had sensed, and Audrite's soft voice to soothe her terrors. Rislyn would be safe.

Meiglan. . . .

Sionell. . . .

The one name brought with it the other nowadays. And each brought with it a fist to crush his heart.

He had faced down enemy princes' schemes, his father's wrath, his own half-brother's sorcery. He had stood in the sand with his dragon at his back and faced a Vellanti army.

He could not bring himself to face Sionell.

He knew he should talk to her. Quietly, in private, where they would not be interrupted. Women talked out their emotions, vented their hurts and angers with words. Most women. His mother did; Tobin did. Meiglan—never. He would have thought Sionell the type who expressed herself as impulse took her; if it included a fist to his jaw . . . well, he was prepared for that. Would have welcomed it. Anything but this terrible silence.

Was she sparing him, or herself?

She had been kind the other night, when his mother had slipped into the past. She had been brutal several nights before, revealing to the others who and what he was. And between times she had been silent.

It might never have happened. They might never have made love. He was beginning to think that for her, love had had no more to do with it than when a mare allowed a stud to mount her.

No. She loved him. She must love him. No woman was capable of such passion without loving the man she gave it to.

Used it against?

Oh, Goddess, why wouldn't she *talk* to him? Scream, rant, rave, knock him out, run him through, tear his heart out with words she knew very well how to use like Chayla's surgical knives—

Anything but this terrible silence.

But as often as he resolved to break it, equally often he knew he could not. He was too afraid that breaking it would break his heart.

And Meiglan? What about Meiglan?

Soon she would be near Stronghold, and the Vellanti High Warlord would have her guarded as the prize she was. Thank the Goddess for Valeda and her strange shape-changing spell. Perhaps she could take some of the brunt of it from Meiglan. For there would be questions, and demands, and angry words.

Meiglan. . . .

Sionell.

His wife, his mistress. Goddess, what a horrible thought. Was he turning into his grandfather? How many mistresses had Roelstra acquired in his fifty years? Or his blood-mother—now, there was a woman who didn't waste a moment in bedding whatever man she wanted. Four sons by four different men, and who knew how many lovers between.

Pol had already made a good start, before his marriage. He remembered them all—he wasn't *that* much of a churl—and there had been quite a few. From Graypearl to Stronghold to most of the manors and keeps in Princemarch and the Desert, on visits to Syr and Waes, and at Dragon's Rest before Meiglan—

Was he turning into his grandfather?

Sionell as his mistress? The very concept nauseated him.

But what would he do once Meggie returned to him, if he still loved Sionell with this helpless gnawing ache?

He wanted the past back. He wanted his father and his placid life at Dragon's Rest and his friends and family all around him and his own turn at being High Prince a hundred years away.

No going back. The past was as dead as Rohan, as Tallain. As dead as, sometimes at dawn when he hadn't slept and the fresh new sunlight pierced his eyes, Pol wanted to be.

No going back. They were dead and he was alive. High Prince. All of it was his responsibility. His to solve.

Meiglan.

Sionell.

Goddess help him, he loved them both.

Chapter Ten

Idalian had been lying flat on his back in bed, staring up at the blackness of the ceiling, since nightfall. And black it was in his chamber: curtains drawn, candles snuffed, hearthfire quenched. Black was an appropriate color. It fit his mood, his hopes, his anger, the night outside, and that strange boy Aldiar's eyes and hair. Idalian was sick and tired of black. Well aware that if he tried to do something about it he might just be courting the eternal blackness of death, he thought it all over one last time.

"All right, that's it," he muttered, and rolled out of bed.

He'd lived in this chamber for years. He didn't need light to dress by. He didn't stumble over furniture or rug nap as he took up sword and knife. Knives; Aldiar's had developed a wobbly grip that Idalian had offered to fix. And fixed it now was, as good as ever. Sharper than usual as well. He slid it into his boot top, pulled his trouser hem down to hide it, and snatched up his cloak.

The garment was heavy Cunaxan wool, black as the rest of his clothing. The color might as well help him, after depressing him all Autumn and Winter. He'd debated on white so he could vanish into the snow, but decided he could just as easily become a rock and fool any watchers that way. Besides, after he got past the fields around Balarat, it would be mostly forest all the way to Snowcoves. Forests draped in white, of course, but better to be a shadow.

Black helped, too, getting through the castle hall to Tirel's rooms. There was no guard; where would the young prince go? How could he escape? Idalian thanked Yarin for his overconfidence and abruptly damned his own when a servant went by at the intersection not thirty paces away. Idalian melted against a stone wall, holding his breath. Safe. He opened the door of Tirel's chambers and slipped noiselessly inside.

Pausing to watch the child sleep for a moment, he had yet another ache of doubt. No use in it; if they stayed, Tirel was dead one way or another. When the attack came, he would be killed if Prince Laric lost, or killed the instant Prince Laric looked to be winning. Idalian had no choice.

And if they both died out there in the winter snows? Trying to get through this country in this season on horseback was foolhardy enough. Idalian proposed to do it on foot—at least until he could beg, borrow, or buy a horse. He shouldered misgivings aside. No use in them. He'd made up his mind.

By the light of the bedside candle, he gathered black clothes—easy enough, as it was Firon's color and Tirel had plenty of shirts, tunics, and trousers to turn him into a shadow, too. Idalian chose the heaviest wool, and with his belt-knife cut the Fironese badge—a red shell on a black field outlined in silver—from a tunic. Placing the clothes at the foot of the bed, he bent over Tirel and whispered his name.

The boy grunted irritably and turned over, snuggling deeper into the blankets. Idalian's throat tightened when he saw that the pillow was damp; Tirel had cried himself to sleep, too proud to call for him.

"Tirel. Wake up now. Come on." He put a hand on the thin shoulder.

He started awake, flinging back the covers with a soft cry. "No!"

"It's only me," Idalian murmured hastily. "Tirel?"

Sinking back into the froth of pillows, he knuckled his eyes. "I thought it was Uncle Yarin."

Come to kill him in the middle of the night, when there were no witnesses. Idalian cursed himself for not continuing the habit of their seclusion for "disease," when he'd slept outside in the antechamber. Tirel had had no bad dreams then.

"No, just me," he said again, smiling for the boy's sake. "How would you like to get out of here?"

Tirel bounced up onto his knees on the mattress. "Really? You're not fooling with me, are you, Idalian?"

"No, I'm not fooling. We're leaving tonight. It's midnight, the moons are down, and I've had enough of this. Well? Want to come with me?"

"Do I!"

"Put these on, then. And be quiet about it." He gestured to the clothes. Tirel pounced. Idalian suddenly took his shoulders in both hands and looked down into the bright gray eyes. "Listen to me first. You must do everything I say, without question or argument. If I tell you to run, run until I say stop. If I tell you to be still, turn to stone until I say it's all right to move again. This isn't a game, Tirel. It's our lives."

The child nodded solemnly. "I understand. I won't even talk unless you say I can. Promise."

"Thank you, my prince. Now, put your clothes on and let's get out of here."

The nightshirt was off and the undertunic was on before Tirel asked, "How are we going to do it?"

"Just do as I tell you to." He hesitated. "And if we're caught—"

"We won't be."

"If we *are,* tell them I said I'd hurt you if you didn't come along with me quietly."

"Idalian!"

"No arguments, remember?" He held out the black wool shirt. "Put this on and hurry up."

The boy was silent until his boots were on and he stood ready to go. "Idalian?" he asked in a small voice.

"Yes?"

"Shouldn't we do something with the pillows? Make it look like I'm still in bed?"

"Do you honestly think it would do any good?"

Tirel sighed. "No. If somebody came in it'd be to talk to me, not to see if I'm asleep. I'm sorry. I won't ask any more dumb questions."

"It wasn't dumb. But I've thought about all of this. Trust me."

Nodding, he pulled his hood up to shield his face. "Let's go."

There were a few tense moments on the way downstairs, glimpsing servants and Lord Yarin's guards here and there.

But it was very late, and nobody was looking for a pair of black-cloaked shadows in the hallways and stairwells. Idalian stopped in a side corridor near the kitchen and leaned down to whisper in Tirel's ear.

"I'm going to go get us something to eat on the way. Stay here."

"No! Don't leave me all alone." Tirel clutched at his arm, gray eyes wide. Reluctantly, Idalian nodded, and they sneaked down the stone floor to the kitchen entrance.

No one was about, except for a boy about Tirel's age who shared the space before the hearth with a few cats. All were sleeping soundly, curled up together near the warmth of the low fire. No meat roasted overnight on spits, so no one would come in to turn or baste or otherwise interrupt Idalian's foraging. Quickly, efficiently, having planned this out in his head, too, he took an empty grain-sack from the hook near the pantry door and filled it with fresh loaves, fistfuls of dried fruit, a small jar of honey, a sizable wedge of cheese, and dumped a container of candies in for good measure. He knew his charge's love for sweets. Finished, he turned to smile success at Tirel and found himself face-to-face with Nolly.

The cook's eyes were as round as her moon-round face. Idalian knew her for a sympathetic friend, but he couldn't help a defiant glare. She looked from him to the sack to the prince, bit her lips between her teeth, and nodded. Gesturing for him to follow, she tiptoed past the slumbering kitchen boy, heading for the garden door. She opened it, glanced around, and beckoned them to her.

"Hurry," she breathed. "This way's safe. Take the path to the gate, go right ten paces, and slip through the chink in the fence where rabbits got in last summer. You'll both fit."

He hadn't planned on that route, but now saw that it was better than going through the pleasure gardens. The herb and vegetable beds, swathed in snow, were closer to the postern gate he intended to use, and would avoid the courtyard entirely.

Tirel stood trembling in the doorway—unafraid, eager, like a hawk anticipating free flight. Idalian put a hand on his shoulder.

"Thank you, Nolly," he whispered. "Prince Laric will hear of this."

"It's best to get the boy out of this castle. I only wish

you'd told me so I could have something ready for you.
Goddess keep you both, and send you safe to our true prince
at Snowcoves."

Tirel looked up, his hood falling back. "My father is
there?"

"By the time you arrive, my lord, he will be. I heard Lady
Vallaina's maid gossiping with the second steward, all aflut-
ter with the prospect of a siege here. Thank the Goddess,
you'll be safe with your father."

Idalian drew in a breath of cold midnight and grasped
Tirel's gloved fingers. "Take care, Nolly."

It was a short run to the fence, a tight squeeze for him
through it, and six quick paces across the slushy path between the stables to his left and the courtyard to his right.
He had a bad few moments just inside the postern turret
when heavy footsteps overhead warned him a guard was
climbing the spiral wooden steps to the upper wall. Idalian
waited until the sound faded, then slid open the bolt of the
outer door.

"Ready?"

Tirel's nod was felt more than seen, and more emphatic
with urgency than fear. Idalian knew there would be another
difficult stretch between the gate and the nearby trees. If the
guards happened to look down. . . .

He gathered himself, hoisted the sack of provisions over
his shoulder, and got a tight grip on the boy's hand.

"All right. Run!"

❋

Back inside the kitchen, Nolly's plump figure and round,
kindly face were nowhere to be seen. Instead, someone
young and thin and angular gave a deep sigh, raked black
hair out of slanting black eyes, and muttered, "At *last!*"

❋

At dawn Feylin and Walvis were rousted out of bed by
Daniv, who burst into their chamber at full cry.

"Hurry—wake up, please, my lady! Come quickly, they're
hurt!"

Feylin jumped out of bed and grabbed a robe. "Who and
how bad?"

Walvis, groggy after spending half the night walking the walls with Chadric, raised up on his elbows and blinked at the young man. "Vellant'im—? What—?"

"Sethric and Kazander," Daniv said, rummaging in a wardrobe for something for Walvis to put on, as if he was a lowly page instead of the Prince of Syr. "And Princess Rislyn—she's very sick, my lady, Jeni's frightened. She sent me up here for you. She says you must hurry."

"Done," Feylin said, knotting her loose hair around itself to keep it out of the way. She slid her feet into low shoes and swooped down to pick up her coffer of medicines. "Walvis, I'll need Audrite. Come on, Daniv, don't just stand there."

On their way downstairs, she questioned Daniv about the wounds. He didn't know much, only that they were plentiful and some of them serious. Outside, in the blue-gray dawn's light thin as milk skimmed of cream, she had to stop and catch her breath. Of all those who had gone with Sethric and those who had been with Kazander, not more than twenty remained. All needed help getting down from their horses, limping or half-delirious with fevered wounds or too sodden with exhaustion to walk unaided.

Jeni called out to her. Daniv was right; the girl was badly frightened, her voice high and thin. She knelt on the cobbles with Rislyn in her arms. Sethric wavered on his feet nearby, supported by a black-clad Isulki whose own stance was none too steady. Feylin looked him over swiftly, found nothing worse than a few rents in his clothing, and sighed with relief that here was at least one who wouldn't need her skills. He squinted into her face, obviously trying to find something familiar about this wild-haired woman in nightgown and robe.

"Go on, get cleaned up before you fall over," she told him. His whole face relaxed then; he had recognized her voice. "I'll take care of Sethric."

"My lady," he rasped, "Lord Kazander—"

"I'll see to him, too. Go on." She prodded him out of the way. "Daniv, get your shoulder in there for him to lean on. That's right." Sethric's curly head drooped with weariness, his spine with despair.

" 'M all right," he mumbled when Feylin bent to inspect the leather strip tied around his leg.

"Oh, of course you are," she told him, careful to keep her voice sharp and sarcastic. If she altered her usual pattern and spoke as gently as her worry wanted her to do, he would know something was wrong. And it was. She pried off the makeshift bandage and set her jaw. The slash across the back of his thigh, open and still oozing blood, cut deep enough to sever muscles damned near to the bone. Unstitched for a day and a half, it would have to stay that way and heal from the inside out; she couldn't draw the edges together into a natural dressing without doing more damage than the long ride had already caused. She didn't want to think what it must have been like for him, weak with blood-loss, clinging to the saddle, one leg dangling useless and crudely bandaged. Goddess only knew what the strain had done to the muscles. With luck and care, he would heal, but the scar would be thick and heavy, without suppleness, and probably give him a lifelong limp.

Twenty winters old, with his whole life ahead of him, Feylin thought. *Goddess, what is this war doing to these children?*

At least Sethric was still alive. Not like her own son. Not like Jahnavi. Or Tallain. Or Tilal's boy, Rihani.

"Daniv, get him up to bed. Clean the wound, Jeni—you know what to do, you've watched me and done it before yourself. Look lively now. Give Rislyn to me." When Sethric looked at her all muddle-eyed, Feylin snapped, "Are you *trying* to bleed to death? Go on!"

"K–Kazander," he managed, before swaying to one side. Daniv caught him. Feylin swept Rislyn up into her arms. Jeni, white to the lips, rose and between them the two young people half-carried Sethric into the keep.

Feylin immediately felt Rislyn's convulsive shivers. Her skin was dry, water-starved, giving off waves of heat like a shimmer-vision on the Long Sand. At Feruche the children had come down with silk-eye. Feylin had lost her granddaughter Siona to it, another child sacrificed to this damned bloody war. But this was different. It might have started as the familiar childhood disease, but had become something else.

She held the little girl in one arm against her hip and with the other hand tried to turn her head from side to side. Rislyn moaned feebly. Feylin called out for Audrite, frightened now. Rigidity in the neck muscles, high fever, spasming tremors, heart shaking within the small body—

"Audrite!" she cried again, and a moment later the princess was at her side. Disheveled, barefoot, wearing a cloak too short for her over her nightgown, looking twenty years younger than her age, Audrite gave a soft exclamation at the sight of Rislyn.

"Take her upstairs. Wash her down with cool water—but first get some milk into her. Goat, sheep, mare, it doesn't matter what kind. All the milk she'll take. Hurry."

She transferred the child to Audrite's arms. Rislyn whimpered as her head was moved, cradled by a gentle hand to the long, loose hair at the princess' neck. "What is it? What's wrong?"

"Later," Feylin said. "Do as I say. At once."

She turned, not wanting to watch them go, not thinking what she might have to tell Pol about his daughter. But what she saw next was the worst of all.

Kazander.

She knelt where they had placed him atop blankets on the stones. Wrappings went all the way around his chest, but the bulk of the bandage was at his back. She eased him half onto his side. Middle ribs, right side—not the heart, Goddess be thanked—but by the sound of his breathing his lung had collapsed. And the blood at his mouth—bright blood, the brightest in the whole body.

He was awake. Incredibly, through the pain and an impossible ride and with only one lung working, he was awake and aware. He even smiled.

"You foolish boy," Feylin chided, a lump in her throat. "Look at all the trouble you've put me to." Over her shoulder she called, "I need a litter!"

"Lady," he said with no voice at all.

Reaching into her medical chest, she said, "What I'm going to do to you will hurt like all Hells—not that you don't deserve it for being so silly. I'll be sticking a tube right in the same spot the blade went in and then I'll expand your lung again so you can get air enough to tell me how beautiful I am, you honey-tongued liar. But for now I want you to get this past those cactus spines on your upper lip." She slipped a tiny pill past the blood and his teeth, and watched as he labored to swallow. "Don't worry. It'll dissolve on its own. You don't have to choke it down." She had seen enough of such wounds this year to know he had already swallowed enough blood to choke a dragon.

Two guards arrived with a litter. She helped them slide

Kazander's limp body onto it, talking all the while, watching as the drug took effect and his eyelids drifted closed.

"You really are the most impossible man," she told him as she walked beside the litter toward the keep. "What am I going to do with you? Here I was all set to give in and run away with you, and off you gallop on some mad chase through half the Veresch. I don't know what ails your wits, but a good swift kick in the head wouldn't come amiss. Or, considering where you keep your brains, a boot in the ass would work much better." She paused. He was drowsing now, the pain gone. Only then did she allow herself to smooth back his hair. "You sleep, dearest," she whispered. "I'll take care of everything."

By midmorning she had reinflated his lung, checked on Rislyn, made sure Sethric was in bed where he should be, and tended all the other wounded. Only then did she realize she was still in her nightgown—and with blood all over it, too, and even in her hair. Wearily, she started back to her rooms for decent clothes.

Her husband came toward her down the stairs. She didn't know why it happened, why the mere sight of him suddenly collapsed every defense she had. But everything fell in on her then. Jahnavi. Tallain. Siona. Rohan. Kazander and Sethric and Rislyn and poor Meiglan and all of it, all of it.

And in the rubble of her thoughts one thing remained intact: it might have been Walvis, it so easily could have been him—

Silently, he held out his arms. She clung to him and sobbed until she had no tears left.

✳

Sethric emerged from sleep with a feeling of drowsy contentment. Warm and clean, he floated on some silky-soft cloud that wrapped all his bones and muscles in a hazy glow. He didn't want to move ever again.

But he had to move. He must hurry. Back to Skybowl— never mind the pain, the cramps in his hands around the reins, the knotted leather around his thigh (was it time again to loosen it so blood could flow and he wouldn't lose the whole leg—no, they couldn't stop, they must go on) and what about Kazander and Rislyn and—

"Jeni!"

But there was no sound. He *couldn't* move. The muffled sleepy glow snuggled in around him. He struggled against it, and all he managed to do was slit his eyelids open.

Jeni. No mistaking the sun-streaked brown hair cascading down her back, the graceful curves of waist and hip revealed by the belted green-velvet robe. But there was a hand smoothing that hair, and an arm circling that waist, and she was trembling as she huddled into someone's comforting embrace.

The head bending gently to hers lifted. Sethric blinked, meeting Daniv's intense turquoise eyes. *So that's how it is,* he thought; *she's decided, and it's not me.* Well, who could blame her? Daniv was strong and intelligent, handsome and brave. Though not even seventeen, he had proved himself in battle and under siege, and had been squire to High Prince Rohan. He had all the makings of a fine man and a wise Prince of Syr. A loving husband. Sethric saw the needing way Jeni held him. *They'll be happy. Good to each other. I'm glad.*

And the rotten thing about it was that he *was* glad—in a bittersweet sort of way. Anger would be more appropriate, wouldn't it?

Daniv's brows had met over his nose in a puzzled frown. Then his mouth stretched from one side of his face to the other in an irrepressible grin. He turned Jeni around by the shoulders. There were anguished shadows in gray eyes that went wide as she looked at Sethric. Daniv gave her a little push toward the bed—and she stumbled, sat down abruptly as if her knees couldn't hold her, and clasped Sethric's hands as if she would never let them go.

He stared from one to the other of them, bewildered. Daniv was still smiling, and in fact looked vastly pleased with himself, as if he'd just done something very clever. Jeni looked ready to cry. The young prince backed away to the chamber door, his watchful anticipation changing to exasperated impatience.

"Go on, you idiot!" Daniv exclaimed at last, opening the door and sliding halfway through before delivering his parting shot. "Kiss her!"

The door slammed.

Jeni flinched.

Sethric gaped, not understanding at all. Then comprehension flooded in, brighter than the noonday sun.

Jeni kissed him.

*

They were brought into the Vellanti camp, escorted on foot through the sand to the tent of the High Warlord. Trembling; clenching teeth to keep back whimpers of fear; holding each other's hand for support, if not comfort, for of comfort there was none.

Stronghold bulked still behind its natural walls of rock. The Flametower rose as proud as ever. Blackened now, scarred by Fire—yet somehow undefeated. Unpossessed. Sioned had seen to that. She had burned every stone and stick and stitch of it. Still, Rohan's Fire was gone, as dead as he was. Only the Goddess knew whether or not Pol would ever light his own flames to burn across the Desert night.

Earlier in the day, the two women had been allowed a few moments' privacy to wash away some of the dirt and stink of the road. The cursory daubing with torn cloth soaked in water from a skin only made each long for a real bath. Oddly enough, it was this murmured confidence from one to the other that put each by way of liking her double. For it struck them both as incredibly silly after all that had happened, wanting to loll in a bath in the middle of the enemy camp. They'd returned to their horses feeling better, a state that lasted only until they reached the Vellanti enclave outside Stronghold. There, wrists free at last, they stumbled on foot through heavy sand, watched by what seemed thousands of black eyes above black, gold-speckled beards. Fingers sweat-moist and shaking, each woman tried in her own way not to be afraid.

Meiglan—the real one—remembered dragons, and how she had always hidden her terror of them from Pol. If only she thought of this High Warlord as one more dragon, she would be all right. The fear was the same. She couldn't help feeling it, but she could hide it. She could. She must.

The other Meiglan remembered Lady Andrade. She had known and feared the formidable old woman half her life. Born in 700 at Goddess Keep of two Sunrunners dead in the next year's Plague, she'd had her skills tested and her first rings bestowed by Lady Andrade, shaking almost as much as she did now. But she'd hidden it, as they all had.

Walking toward the large silken tent, the two Meiglans kept their composure by thinking of their separate dragons.

"It's Lord Chaynal's, from Radzyn," one of them whispered.

"I recognize the colors," the other murmured, and pressed her companion's fingers. They had managed a few words now and again since last night, and enough after Valeda's Sunrunning to share the essential information about Skybowl. But there was so much of the one that the other didn't know. They'd decided to dole out what was necessary to keep these people guessing, but knew they must rely on silence as much as they could without endangering each other.

All the world seemed unnaturally bright, with the clear, piercing sunshine of a crisp winter day. But not even the breeze could disguise the stench of too many men and too many horses who had stayed in one place too long. As they made their way through the center of the camp to that large sky-blue wool tent, a silence fell around them so that the only sounds were the *shussh* of the slight wind and the echoing rasp of their steps in the sand.

The tent flap was pushed aside for them, and they entered. A tall, lean-limbed man sat with his back to them at a carved fruitwood desk, like any merchant or *athri* or prince tending his affairs. But the desk, the chair he sat in, the silver pen he dipped into a fat red jar of ink, the parchment—all of it, down to the rugs on the floor and the sheets on the cot—belonged to Andry's father. All except for the singed pages of a book stacked inside a half-burned leather cover by the man's elbow. Barely visible in gold leaf on the spine were enough letters to tell them what it was and who it belonged to: Lady Feylin's book on dragons.

The two women exchanged glances. Both had heard the story of how at Remagev all but the legends had cunningly been burned to terrify the Vellant'im when they found the book. Again, Sioned's doing. But as the pen was replaced in its stand and the long frame unfolded from the chair and turned to face them, neither woman thought this was the kind of man to be terrified by anything.

Perhaps they had expected him to be striding about his camp like the conqueror he had come here to be, snarling commands and ordering vicious punishment for the slightest infraction of warrior discipline. Perhaps they had thought he would be fierce, or fiercely ugly, with a thousand gold tokens in his beard and eyes even a dragon—or Lady

Andrade—would cringe to meet directly. Whatever they might have anticipated, it was not this darkly elegant man, no older than forty-five winters, whose black eyes held both sharp interest and sardonic merriment and whose face was as clean of whiskers as on the day of his birth.

"Welcome," he said in their own language, his voice deep and sonorous. "High Princesses," he added wryly, looking from one Meiglan to the other with no hint of anger. Then he gestured and spoke a single word that one woman understood and the other didn't. The guards bowed and left the tent. "Please sit," their host invited, indicating two chairs near the desk. "A long ride tires. Sit and rest. Wine for your thirst?"

Neither woman spoke or moved.

The High Warlord smiled, revealing a shining set of large, straight, white teeth. "Lady—and Lady," he said, evidently relishing the irony, "a princess sits in the presence even of enemies. I ask, please."

When they remained standing, he shrugged and turned the desk chair around to take his ease. He had made himself utterly at home in this stolen splendor, as if he had owned it always—and yet it was like a fine cloak he could discard at will without missing it at all.

"Two High Princesses," he mused, still smiling. "One real, one not. My choice, clear as mud." Leaning forward, he propped his elbows on his knees, hands clasped loosely between them, and scrutinized each face in turn. "One *faradhi,* one not."

One pair of dark brown eyes stared straight over his head, unflinching. The second pair glanced wildly about the tent, as if seeking escape. The High Warlord watched, plainly fascinated. Then he rocked back in the chair and began to laugh softly.

"Two *Kir'reia'im!*" he chuckled. "My wish, given by the Father of Wind and Rain! He laughs, so I laugh also. My asking was not—ah, what word?—precise? Yes." He wagged a finger at them, sleeve falling back from a broad, shining armband. "Have care in wishes, Lady—and Lady. I forgot to wish for one with firegold hair and one of dawn-cloud. *Kir'reia* Sioned, *Kir'reia* Meiglan." He grinned widely, enjoying the joke his god had played on him for not being specific. "Now—two of one!"

The women shifted closer together. At last one of them quavered, "Wh–what do you want from us?"

Still he laughed.

The other, voice equally tremulous, said, "If any harm comes to us, the High Prince, my lord and husband, will slaughter you and your people, every one."

"Let us go," pleaded the first. "Leave our lands in peace."

And the other cried, "Goddess, why don't you listen? Haven't you killed enough?"

His laughter stopped. Again he sat forward, hands fisted now on muscular thighs. "Enough? What is 'enough'? What payment for your evil? I tell you 'enough' is not yet, will not be until all are dead!"

They glanced at each other, well and truly frightened now.

"I will tell you how it was," he continued in a low, lethal voice. "Islands under swords, warriors killed, women raped, children dead. Herds slaughtered, so people starved. Crops burned, so people starved. Fishing boats sunk, so people starved. For a hundred thousands of days, we remember. For such evil, no numbers of killings can be enough."

They traded looks again, and one of them said, "I don't know what you're talking about. A hundred thousand days?"

Rising, he stood an arm's length from them, black fire in his eyes. "Your evil! Yours! No peace until you starve and die as we did! Until the *Azhrei* and all his lands and people starve and die!"

"That's insane! You can't mean this war is because of something that happened almost three hundred years ago, that we had nothing to do with!"

"That," he whispered to her, their faces a breath apart, "is why we come—to remind you. You forgot us. But we remember. Your evil. Your magic. Our deaths. A hundred thousands of days."

"But it wasn't us!" the other woman exclaimed.

He glanced at her. "You do not remember. But you will. All names that were lost to your evil will be spoken. And remembered." He stepped back. "Before he dies, the *Azhrei* will know. Before I kill him and his evil magic for the Dragon, he will know. He will speak all lost names before I slice out his *faradhi* tongue, and he will see the truth before I carve out his Goddess-green, Goddess-blue eyes."

"No!" she screamed. "No!"

Instantly he drew a knife from his belt and plunged it into

the other's heart. She gasped, falling to her knees, hands clasped around the hilt embedded in her chest. And a terrible thing happened, that made the second Meiglan scream again. Delicate features became stronger, sterner; the cloud of curling fair hair turned to longer, thicker waves; eyes paled from brown to blue-gray.

Meiglan knelt and yanked the knife from Valeda's breast. But removing the iron, deadly as poison to *faradh'im,* ended only one kind of pain. Blood soaked Valeda's hands, leaked between her fingers that clutched the wound as if trying to hold her life in. She looked up at Meiglan, infinite agony and infinite pity in her eyes.

"I'm—sorry," she managed.

Meiglan plucked helplessly at her sleeve, touched the face that was no longer a mirror, whispered, "No, you can't—please don't—"

Valeda coughed blood. "My daughter," she said, slumping. "Chayly—and . . . Andry . . . tell. . . ."

"Yes," Meiglan said, "yes, I'll tell them, anything you like—oh, please—"

". . . that I'm . . . s–sorry . . . and . . . love them . . . oh, Goddess," she whimpered, and folded around herself, and died.

The High Warlord wiped his knife on Valeda's cloak. Quite dispassionately, he said, "She spoke as a High Princess. You spoke as the *Azhrei's* wife."

Meiglan looked up, stunned almost to senselessness. He loomed over her, black eyes very bright in his Desert-tanned face. Then, with amazing care, he bent and helped her to her feet.

"We honor wives. Not princesses."

CHAPTER ELEVEN

Arlis turned weary, red-rimmed eyes on Laric and said, "I'm going back by land if I have to walk every measure on my own two feet."

The older man shrugged in rueful apology. The first thirteen days of their sail north had been simple enough, even pleasant—if one didn't think too much about what they'd have to do once they reached Snowcoves. The ragged coastline was close on the west; to the east, south, and north, though Rohannon had kept careful watch, no Vellanti ships had appeared. Even as it grew colder, and the wind acquired icy teeth, clear weather and relatively smooth sailing had been their lot. Laric had warned Arlis about floes that would clog the sea, and gigantic mountains of ice as impassable as the high Veresch, but Arlis hadn't believed him.

Now he did. After a day and night and half a day again of weaving his flagship on a perilous course, he believed, all right. The other ships followed, captains gnawing their lips bloody just as Arlis had, squinting against the white sunlight glare by day and peering into eerie greenish-black glow by night. They trusted him to lead them safely through, but all of them—and their crews and the soldiers, too—knew what would happen to wooden hulls if a misjudgment brought them too close to one of those monstrous icebergs. Guessing which could be approached and which must be avoided was Laric's work.

And he had done it very well. There remained only a cape to be rounded, and then the castle and town of Snowcoves would appear, nestled in a protected cove. Now it was Rohannon's turn.

His supply of *dranath* had run out last night. He'd doled it out carefully, taking only what he hoped was enough to cure his seasickness, for Arlis didn't need him as a Sunrunner. But these fourteen days had been hard going, especially whenever he thought of his father's horror at what he'd done. Perhaps he had already become addicted. He thought not; his mother had been fed small doses of the drug for quite some time, and while her withdrawal from it had been agony, she had survived. Rohannon hadn't taken as much as Hollis, or for as long. And at least he'd gotten some use out of it. But he kept hearing Maarken's voice in his head, thick with fear.

Well, what was done was done. Soon he would be on land again. With the *dranath* wearing off now, and his stomach queasy, he longed for ground underfoot instead of planks—and perhaps at Snowcoves someone had stockpiled the herb against a day when the Plague might return, and he could borrow some, just a little, just enough to—

Rohannon listened to what he was thinking—no, what his body was urging, for it had nothing to do with his mind—and shuddered.

"Too cold for you, Desert-born?" Arlis asked, ruffling the boy's hair fondly. "Well, I'll tell you something. It's too damned cold for *anybody* up here. Thirty-five days till the end of winter—you'd never know it, would you? I think my bones have turned to icicles."

"Mine, too, my lord. We're safe enough now, aren't we?"

"Enough. At least my poor ship isn't the needle anymore, with the others a string of thread, stitching our way through this." Arlis gestured to the bleak seascape, where snow-shrouded ice-mountains floated in uncaring majesty. "Now all we have to do is weave Laric's princedom back together. And to that end I need you to weave the sunlight for me."

"At once, my lord."

They were still out of sight of Snowcoves, not having sailed around the cape. It was too much to hope that no one knew they were coming, though; Rohannon had seen a *diarmadhi* ritual in the forest near Balarat, so it was taken for granted that eyes had watched their progress. But if the sorcerers thought Arlis and Laric helplessly limited to what their own eyes could see, they were mistaken.

What Rohannon saw now was a daylight version of what he'd watched on starlight fifteen nights ago. There had been no new snow since then. The streets were shoveled more or less clean, but perpetually running with meltwater. Rainy Swalekeep, built on mostly flat ground on the Faolain River, had perforce an excellent drainage system; in the Desert, nobody bothered. They didn't worry about it at Snowcoves, either. Built on a slowly rising hill, the upper levels drained right down the streets to the docks and the sea. It made for slick, dangerous footing, but people mostly stayed on the sidewalks if they ventured from their homes.

And venture they did, despite the cold, during the scant time the sun shone these short winter days. All the shopping, visiting, moving of goods, and other daily commerce Rohannon had observed in other places—Radzyn Port, Einar, New Raetia, Zaldivar—was carried on as if this were a warm spring day. Children romped outdoors while parents gossiped in open doorways. Rohannon admired the hardiness of the people of Snowcoves and felt vaguely humiliated by his own reaction to the cold—until he realized these people would be as miserable in his native climate as he was in theirs.

Yarin's flag flew over the keep in solitary arrogance. Laric's should have been there, too. If anyone had protested, if anyone was nervous at their *athri's* usurpation of their prince's power, there was no sign of it on the streets of Snowcoves.

But within the keep itself, Rohannon saw much to intrigue him. The soldiers, all in Yarin's colors of white and yellow, did not drill in anticipation of a fight. They merely trod off the paces of their watch without seeming at all interested in whether or not the castle required their guardianship. They sat about the courtyard, walked the walls, gamed with dice or chessboards, meandered through the gates on their way to or from town. It was very odd, and Rohannon said so when he returned to the ship.

"They must know we're coming," Arlis said, worrying a raw place on his upper lip where the cold had cracked the skin. "Damn! Are they so confident that they don't need to mount a defense?"

Laric stood with his spine against a mast, arms folded, wind blowing thick brown hair back from his face. "How many did you count, Rohannon?"

"Only about fifty, my lord. But there are probably more within the keep, staying warm. Very few on the town streets at all."

"And on the ships? Guarding the docks?"

"I didn't think to look. Excuse me a moment."

"Take your time," Arlis said wryly.

A short while later Rohannon was nodding. "There are only a few people on the docks, my lord. But four of the ships ride low in the water and the sails aren't wrapped and stowed the way we always do at Radzyn for winter harbor."

"Ready to raise them, are they?" Arlis mused.

"Against their prince," Laric added, his cheeks red with more than cold.

"I saw something else, my lords," Rohannon said. "The holds are all open to the sunshine. From the size of the ships, and counting the ones within range of light, I'd say there are about fifty soldiers on each of those ships."

"Where is Yarin *getting* these people?" Laric exclaimed. "Two hundred ready to sail, at least another hundred in the keep. By the Goddess, I'll cut him to pieces with my own sword!"

They were beginning to get used to such vows from the bookish prince, so neither made any comment about it. What Arlis said was, "So they *do* know we're coming. They've hidden themselves. Rohannon, did you see any beards in the lot of 'em?"

"None, my lord. I would have said."

"That you would. My apologies." Arlis reached into a pocket for salve to rub on his bleeding lip. "All right, then. I want you to look for me once more, and this time into the castle windows if you can. Laric, is there any place Yarin might use as a prison?"

After a moment's thought, he nodded. "Try the west side, a building that used to be a stable. The roof caved in from snow last winter. Yarin lost a lot of good horses that I bargained with Chay at this year's *Rialla* to replace, the more fool I. The roof's back on, but the horses were all moved to the older stable at the east gate. If I needed a jail, that's where I'd put it."

One last foray on sunlight, a lengthy one this time as Rohannon tried every window on the western wall. High and wide, placed to spare courtyard and castle the usual horsey smells, the windows were recessed to make arrow-shots more difficult (although it was only a stable, and in time of war empty of horses). But the angle was also wrong for the morning sun to penetrate. So Rohannon sought around the other side, approaching from the east after fixing the location in his mind.

He was very lucky. Two servants crossed the courtyard, staggering with the weight of a cauldron of porridge that swung between them. Another followed with a sack, presumably of bread. Guards who had formerly lazed about snapped to the alert, swords drawn, as the stable doors were unbolted and the food taken in. Rohannon found a gap in the slats of the projecting roof, slid down the thin shaft of sunlight, and hovered at head-height a handspan inside the open door.

He saw what Arlis had hoped he'd see: all the soldiers, servants, and townsfolk loyal to Prince Laric were stuffed into the stalls and tack rooms of the stable. He withdrew quickly and opened his eyes. He didn't need to say anything, only nodded.

"Right," Arlis muttered. "I'm betting that these shipboard troops aren't really trained soldiers at all, but *diarmadh'im* siphoned down from the Veresch for the occasion and suited up in Yarin's colors. Same for the ones inside the castle—though they may know a bit more about what to do with a sword."

"Don't underestimate mountain folk," Laric cautioned. "I've seen them drop a wolf at two hundred paces with a single arrow."

"I don't doubt it. But a *single* arrow, cousin." He smiled, then swore as his lip cracked again. "They're independent, not given to the kind of discipline and concerted effort needed in a battle. If they'd been inclined to work together, we would've heard from them long before this. Our own troops, on the other hand, have been tested in battle and not found wanting." He paused. "It's your holding, of course, and I'll be guided by your wishes. But I have an idea or three, if you'd like to hear them."

✳

All Sethric had done was kiss Jeni back. Nothing else. Weariness and weakness, he told himself, had nothing to do with it. How could it, when life seemed ready to explode within him at the touch of her mouth on his? No, it wasn't his wound or the loss of blood or the long ride to Skybowl that made him keep his hands to himself (mostly). It was the thought of her parents, and her youth, and honor, and ... and. ...

But, oh, her lips were sweet, and her hair soft, and her fingers tender as they cradled his face, and her smile filled with shy wondering joy. ...

He was dreaming with his eyes wide open when she came into his room next morning. Feylin had already been by to look at his leg. Jeni brought breakfast for two. Seating herself on the bed, with the tray between them, she acted as if this was the habit of more years than either of them had been alive.

But they were only halfway through the meal when Walvis poked his head in. Apologizing for the interruption, he asked Jeni if she would do him the favor of apprising Pol of the news.

"Oh—I completely forgot! I was going to do that first thing!"

"I think you can be forgiven," Walvis answered, casting Sethric an amused glance. "For myself, I don't mind at all. I won the bet!" And he was back out the door before either could do anything more than blush.

Sethric watched Jeni perch comfortably in the window seat in full sunshine. For a few moments he indulged in more waking dreams, admiring the straight line of her back, the highlights in her hair, the pretty profile limned in white-gold. But as completely with him as she had been earlier, so now was she gone. Her body was present, her thoughts elsewhere.

He had never been exactly *jealous* of Daniv. Not of a friend. Nor even of that dragon of hers. But now he began to wonder about his own character—for he suddenly could not bear to have the sunlight take her away from him.

The High Prince's caution repeated in his mind, words about getting used to her being a Sunrunner. But how in Hells would *he* know anything about it? In that marriage, Pol was the Sunrunner. He never had to watch while eyes that had gazed softly on him turned blind to his very existence. He never had to wait while mind spoke to mind in a manner forever beyond his understanding, using words he would never know unless he was told about them.

Sethric wanted to look away from her where she sat all aglow with morning sunlight. No, he didn't *want* to—he wished he *could* look away. The sight of her was all he had left of her. Jeni—voice, smile, thoughts, feelings, all that was Lady Camigwen of Castle Crag—had left him.

But she *was* here. He had that much: the knowledge that with him was where she wanted to be. She would come back, and it would be to him. Not to Daniv or her dragon. To *him*.

By the time she sighed quietly and rose from the window seat, Sethric could smile and welcome her back to his side.

Jeni nestled close for a moment, there within the curve of his arm. Then she drew back slightly, her cheeks pink, her gray eyes straying to his mouth as she said, "I have to go talk to Walvis. I—"

Sethric nodded. "But you'll come back."

"Yes." She seemed puzzled. "Of course."

He kissed her to seal the bargain—not only with her, but with himself.

✳

Morning lessons had just begun in the Attic when Sioned came in, smiling a smile that caused Meath to falter in midword. He looked quickly at Riyan, then at Andry. Neither understood the reason for that dangerous glitter in her eyes any more than he did. But though they were all three grown men, and Meath Sioned's elder by four years, each struggled to hide automatic *I don't know what I did, but whatever it was, I'm sorry!* expressions.

"Good morning!" Sioned greeted the children brightly. "And too pretty a morning it is to sit like lumps inside while these boring old men drone on. I'm declaring a holiday. Go on, out! Into the gardens, all of you!" She lowered her voice to a conspirator's murmur. "And if you ask him *very* nicely, perhaps Meath can be persuaded to be your dragon."

He cast her a sour glance. She replied with another sleek and lethal smile.

The children took instant advantage of the suggestion, tumbling from the room. When Andry and Riyan made as if to rise from their chairs at the table, Sioned spoke again.

"No. *You* stay."

They sank back down.

Meath shut the door behind him, thanking the Goddess that he was well out of it.

Sioned got right down to it. "What do you know of a woman named Jayachin?"

Riyan frowned slightly. "Sounds familiar, but—"

"It should," Andry said. "The *Rialla* of 719? Black hair, white skin—"

"Oh."

Sioned tapped her fingers impatiently on the finials of a chair, then gripped them as if they were her temper. "What about her, Andry?"

He shrugged. "A merchant from Waes, now living outside Goddess Keep."

"Wrong."

"I beg your pardon?"

"*Not* living. Dead. Yesterday—by means of the *ros'salath.*"

For just a moment his muscles tensed, as if he'd spring to his feet and challenge her physically. She watched him consciously relax and lean back. "I have always," he said lightly, "admired your sources of information. Better than mine, in this instance."

"You don't use the stars much," she retorted. "It's a prejudice you might consider overcoming."

"Thank you for the advice."

Riyan shifted as if to stand and go. Sioned spared him a single glance. He subsided. "I'm sorry she's dead. You've known since last night?"

"Since the last stars before morning. I don't get much sleep these days."

"No, indeed," Andry commented, still unruffled. "The Goddess has but two eyes. High Princess Sioned has—how many is it? Dozens? Hundreds?"

"Thousands, for all you'll ever know of them." She glared across the width of the table at him. "Would you like to hear about it?"

He made an idle gesture. "Of course."

"She went to the tree-circle. She was seen there. Brought back. Subjected to what your Chief Steward and his wife would probably term a trial. Condemned—and then murdered."

"Executed," Andry corrected.

"Murdered," she repeated. "For something called a 'sin.' By a spell forbidden—"

"—except in defense of Goddess Keep," he interrupted. "Torien and Jolan have my complete confidence. Considering what she did, they'd have no choice but to condemn her. They have the authority to—"

"To kill her by driving her mad? Dear Goddess, Andry, what have you made the Sunrunners into but murderers?"

He met her gaze, head tilting upward, a little smile teasing his lips. "And are *your* colors clean of blood, Sioned?"

"That's enough," Riyan snapped. "Andry, ask your people what happened. Wait until he knows the specifics, Sioned, before you condemn." Fisting one hand on the table, he said fiercely, "This is *my* castle and I won't have it made a battlefield—especially between *faradh'im!*"

Sioned opened her mouth, closed it again. "You're right. I ask your pardon, my lord."

She meant it, but she also meant it to make him uncomfortable. She used titles on her own *athr'im* only on formal occasions or when she wished to remind certain of them that she had changed their wrapping cloths back when they were squalling infants.

Riyan met her stare for stare, then rose. He went to the door and opened it, standing beside it in silent and obvious invitation to get out.

Sioned left first. She didn't much care if Andry thought her emphasizing her precedence or if he thought her fleeing from further contention. She sought the battlements and the sunshine, on the Desert side of the keep where she would hear no children laughing in the gardens and no soldiers drilling in the courtyard. Leaning a shoulder against a high stone crenellation—solid for defense, yet delicately balanced for beauty—she gave up fighting the wind's playful tousling of her hair and stared at the Long Sand.

Confronting Andry had been a mistake. She'd known that even as she stormed up the stairs. But after hearing Antoun's horrifying account of Jayachin's death, imagining what it must have been like, realizing what Andry had done in creating his *devr'im*—

"I wouldn't have done it if you'd been here to stop me," she murmured. "If I'd said nothing, he wouldn't know to tell Torien to keep alert for a spy. Oh, I can hear you saying that—now. When it's too late. But I couldn't be silent, can you understand that? A working of madness, used to kill—and for what? A 'sin.' Not even Antoun could really explain that one.

"And what have I done to *him,* you'd ask. No, you never did. He offered to be used. Not during Andrade's time— although I found out a thing or two back then as well, that she didn't think I knew. But since then ... we both used him. He wasn't doing anything he wouldn't have chosen to do on his own. That was always your justification, wasn't it? Only now he's in danger. Him and Edrel and Norian and poor crippled Elsen, riding to Goddess Keep's defense when they need no defending except from themselves.

"That's why I had to confront Andry. I had to. He doesn't see it. But you always knew, didn't you? Power once used is easier to use again. And again. Until using it becomes its own justification, and *not* using it is impossible. But he'll never understand that.

"Does Pol? He did once. He was scared into it, nine years ago, fighting his half-brother. But this is different. This war is different. Using power is not only possible and justified, it's essential, and not just to save his own life. What will he do with it? With that mirror, if Ruala finds out at Elktrap how to use it ... with his *diarmadhi* heritage. . . ." She glanced down at her clenched fist. "And with this, if it turns out to be a thing of power. . . ."

The emerald was just an emerald, gleaming in the sunshine just as it always had. But in darkness it glowed and pulsed in precise rhythm with her heartbeats. Blooded, like a sword.

"I've killed," she whispered to the sands far below, to the sky above and the wind between. "With my gifts, my power, I've killed. I've been blooded—my colors, the way Andry said. No more killing. I don't want any more death to come of my kind of power—or Pol's, or Andry's." She sighed. "Is it only that I'm old? Is that why I'm so sick of death, because I'm afraid of my own?"

With both hands she scraped the tangled curls back from her face, held her head between her hands as she stared up at the bright blue sky.

"You know, I don't much like being alive without you," she said.

✳

Andry nearly bumped into a cloud on his way to Goddess Keep. Pausing, he cursed himself roundly for behaving like a four-ringed Sunrunner who barely knew how to weave light. Anger made for haste, and haste made for carelessness, and if he didn't watch it he would become shadow-lost—and *then* what would become of them all?

Detouring around the cloud, he was halfway across Grib when something tugged him back toward Feruche. That made him even angrier. But the insistent colors would not go away, so he returned—and found that the presumption and the colors were his elder son's.

Annoyance vanished instantly. *Andrev? What's wrong? Where are you?*

Everything's all right, Father, I'm sorry if I startled you. We're on the way to Radzyn—only we have to go slow so we don't get there before Prince Amiel and Prince Ludhil sail in from Dorval.

From—? What's going on? Why didn't Tilal do what he was told?

He said Prince Ludhil would be furious if he wasn't in on the kill, what with being trapped up in the hills all this time, so Prince Amiel took one of the ships to Graypearl. They thought he was friendly! It was beautiful! He sailed right in and Prince Ludhil came down with all his fighters and the Vellant'im were smashed between!

Andry tried to envision it—a dragon ship unloading arrows instead of bearded warriors; a sudden attack from the rear while the docks swarmed in confusion; the two forces pinching the Vellant'im like a dragon's talons. *Sounds risky—but beautiful, you're right! Serious casualties?*

Not as many as we were afraid of. They'd already sent most of the troops at Graypearl across to Radzyn. I guess they'll go up to Stronghold from there.

Only Tilal plans to stop them.

Yes. Prince Amiel and Prince Ludhil are loading their own people on board ship right now. I'm to keep an eye on them to make sure we all get to Radzyn at the same time.

You've done good Sunrunner service, then.

The boy's colors glowed. *It's my duty, Father, nothing more,* he said, as expected. Then: *But it's wonderful to be in the middle of it! Not the fighting, Prince Tilal won't let me, but to be able to watch everything, and know I'm the only one who can report back, that I'm my lord's eyes—*

So you like being a Sunrunner, do you? Andry asked, amused. *Well, you should. It's what you were born to do.*

It feels that way, Andrev admitted shyly. *And born to a sword is what Princess Iliena looks like, can you believe it? I saw her this morning, fighting right alongside her husband!*

He tried to picture the forty-year-old mother of two arrayed in armor, her dark Fironese—*diarmadhi*—face nearly hidden behind a helm. Of all the women he could see in the pose, Iliena was among the very last. But people did what was necessary, he supposed. And one couldn't fault her courage.

Then something occurred to him. *Did they fight back? Against a woman, I mean. And all the other women in Ludhil's group.*

Yes. No such luck as Rohannon had on Kierst-Isel, Father. By the way, is he all right? Where is he?

In Firon by now, I should imagine. Goddess, all the reports from all over the continent—it's a wonder I can keep track of where I am! I assume you're also here for news, so I'll give it to you. Chayla was found—but you knew that, didn't you?

Yes. Prince Tilal told me to ask about Princess Meiglan.

They still have her. But we got Rislyn back. She's at Skybowl now. They're undoubtedly taking Meiglan to Stronghold, so be careful what you do there. A wrong move and they could kill her.

Tilal says that if we work it right, he'll march up from Radzyn with Amiel and Ludhil, you can come from the north, and we can smash them outside Stronghold.

No. At Skybowl. It must be Skybowl. He had the impression of mental fidgeting. *It's my decision, and Pol's. Tilal can push them north all he likes, but the final battle must happen at Skybowl.*

I'll tell him. But I don't know if he'll do it that way. He's been a little strange lately. After his son died, it was like he didn't see or hear anything. He just sat with Princess Danladi for days. Then we started to march again, and now sometimes it's like he has a fever. He said yesterday he'd like to line up all the Vellant'im and kill them one by one with his own sword, but so they'd die as slowly as Rihani did.

I understand. Others feel the same. And I know how I'd feel if anything ever happened to you. But the Goddess will keep you safe. There's work for you to do far beyond being Prince Tilal's Sunrunner squire. And now I think you'd better go back. All this weaving of light has tired you.

Not very much.

This is your father you're talking to, my lad, and the Lord of Goddess Keep knows weary colors when he sees them. Go on. I'll tell the others what you've told me, and come to you tomorrow with further orders for Tilal. And tell him I said to take good care of you.

Oh, he does. Too good. I never get to do anything really interesting. Well, except the Sunrunning, of course, but just once I'd like to stick my sword into a Vellanti. For Brenlis, and Oclel and Rusina.

I . . . understand, Andry said again. *But leave the swords to the soldiers. And consider this: that by doing what only you can do, you're helping more than anyone with a sword.*

I guess so. You take care of yourself, too, Father.

I hear and obey, my lord Sunrunner.

Laughter echoed down the light. Andry relaxed back in his chair, smiling. It had taken Andrev's defiance and his own anger to do it, but somehow they were closer now than they had ever been. It was the gift of *faradh'im* to each other, this communion. The gift of the Goddess.

He spent a few moments resting, breathing in the scents of turned earth and a few stubborn flowers in the kitchen garden, letting the sun warm him. Gradually his pleasant mood faded, for he had yet to do what he had come out here to do. Gathering himself, he once again spun sunshine in the direction of Goddess Keep.

✳

"I think that finishes it. Anything else?"

Odd, Jolan thought, *how the same words can be so different.* Andry had said on sunlight what Torien now said aloud to the *devr'im,* but Torien's genuinely concerned inquiry was a world away from Andry's impatience.

The upper balcony emptied of everyone but Jolan and her husband. *Such good little peasants,* she told herself, *hearing and obeying the orders of the great Lord of Goddess Keep. Do this, do that, keep an eye on Edrel and Norian, too bad about Jayachin, you did the right thing—patting us on the head like kittens who've caught their first mouse.*

"Jolan?"

She shrugged Torien's arm from her shoulders. "He should be *here*."

"He has duties to his family in the Desert."

"His duty is to us!"

"As ours is to him," Torien reminded her.

She laid her hands flat on the balustrade stones, glaring down at the gleam of silver and gold on her fingers. "We'd follow him on sunlight or on foot or any other way he asked, just for the asking. But he doesn't ask, Torien. He doesn't *want* us to follow. Why did he create us, out of his vision of this war, if not to follow and support him?"

Standing beside her, watching the bustle in the encampment below the keep, he neither touched her nor spoke for a long while. At last, with a weariness that alarmed her, he said, "I feel very much alone. Not in my heart—you're always there, love, Goddess be thanked for it. It's in my mind, in the part of me that's a Sunrunner. I've yoked and shackled the *diarmadhi* in me ever since I found out about it. But when the Sunrunner is silent, sometimes I hear the sorcerer whispering."

"No, you're wrong," Jolan protested, taking his arm in both hands. "I hear the same thing and there's no *diarmadhi* blood in me at all. It's not disloyalty to Sunrunners or to Andry—it's being abandoned like this. He should be *here!*"

"His vision is larger than ours. We see only Goddess Keep. He sees—"

"—the chance to beat Pol."

"It might have begun that way," Torien admitted. "I don't think that's very important to him now."

"Maybe I'd feel better if it was," she muttered.

"You're not make any sense, dearling."

Oh no? she thought, and did not say out loud. *At least if he was behaving as the Lord of Goddess Keep, I'd know he still gave a damn about us. He's become Chay and Tobin's son again, a son of the Desert. A lord of the Desert. And all we good little peasants can do is wait for him to find time for us.*

"I feel alone, too," she told her husband.

Torien encircled her with both strong arms. "But not in your heart?" he murmured into her hair.

"Never," she replied. "I'd follow Andry wherever he asked—but only if you were there with me."

✳

"But didn't she tell you what we ought to do?"

Antoun shook his head. "My lady, you must not expect too much just yet. The High Princess has her own difficulties. I'm sure that once she consults with her son, she'll contact me again with advice."

Frowning, Norian tapped a finger against the spine of a shelved book. Her brother had sent her down to select another volume for him to read, knowing that Antoun was usually in the library during the early afternoon. It would not do for any of them to be seen overmuch in his company, especially as he was one of the *devr'im*. He would either be questioned for information about their discussions, in which case he would have to lie even more than usual, or someone might question why he was so often in attendance on the Gribain prince, his sister, and her husband. They would have to be very careful and very clever to keep most of their encounters "accidental."

Norian didn't much like having to wait on Sioned's convenience, and said so. The Sunrunner arched a brow at her.

"What choice do we have, my lady? We could provoke a conflict with the Vellant'im, and see hundreds killed—and not just by them, but as Jayachin died. You and your husband could withdraw to prevent your troops' being used in that fashion, but moving your brother risks the healing of his leg. No, we must do as High Prince Rohan always did, wait, and see how events shape themselves. When the time for action comes, we will know it."

"I don't enjoy feeling helpless, Antoun," she said.

"No more than anyone. But have patience. The Vellant'im are waiting for something, too. I don't know what, but perhaps that's something Sioned can find out for us so we may plan accordingly."

"And if she can't? If she's just as ignorant as we are by the time they finally attack?"

Antoun said nothing for a moment. Then he climbed a stepladder, making a great deal of noise. Norian stared up at him as if he'd gone mad.

"My students ask me the damnedest—your pardon, princess—but the *damnedest* questions sometimes, which send me to the most obscure volumes—which are invariably in a place where I must risk life and limb to reach—ah! Look out!"

He purposely spilled a few books from an upper shelf. Norian jumped out of the way.

"Will you be so kind, your grace, as to help me pick those up?"

Norian finally caught on. "Oh, of course." She knelt and he clambered down to crouch beside her, complaining about his age and infirmities.

"If there's anything to learn, Sioned will find it out," he whispered. "Trust her. I have, for all the forty-five years I've known her."

And with that Norian had to be content, for just as Antoun again began his imprecations against his over-inquisitive students, a boy of about sixteen came around a corner of the shelves and said, "Everyone all right? Oh, Princess Norian. The very person I came to fetch."

Antoun frowned up at him. "Kov! Did you grow up all alone on a mountaintop in the Veresch, then, with no one to teach you manners? You do not 'fetch' a princess!"

The boy turned pink to his earlobes. "I—I'm sorry, I didn't mean—"

"It's all right, Kov," Norian said, rising with a heavy book in her hands.

"Begging your grace's pardon, and mindful of your grace's generosity, but it *isn't* all right." Antoun pushed himself to his feet. "Not everyone becomes a Court Sunrunner, but we all learn how to be polite. The first thing you do, Kov, is bow to her grace. Then you ask her pardon for imposing yourself on her. Then you introduce yourself. Then you say that so-and-so wishes to know if she would be so kind as to spare a few moments. Go on, say it."

Kov gave an abrupt, awkward bow. Staring at his ringless hands, he stammered, "Your g–grace, excuse me for interrupting. My name is Kov, and I was sent b–by Lady Ulwis to ask if you and your husb—I mean, if your grace and Lord Edrel would honor her and her husband by dining with them tonight." He looked anxiously up at Antoun.

The old Sunrunner smiled with perfect benevolence. "Excellent. All the proper forms observed. The bow could use a little work. But I know you've never addressed a princess before in your life."

Norian almost missed her cue—a quick glance—so intent

was she on watching Kov's reaction. But the boy found nothing unusual about such wholehearted approval following so closely on the heels of such irritable severity; evidently it was Antoun's habit.

"Yes, very prettily done," Norian said, smiling. "My father's pages rarely do it so well. Please tell Lady Ulwis that we'd be glad to accept her invitation, and thank her for it, please."

Antoun snorted. "Never heard a princess say 'please' to you before either, have you? *That's* manners, Kov. Remember them. Run along with you now." As he gave another bow, Antoun smiled again. "*Very* good!"

When Kov was gone, the Sunrunner leaned wearily against the bookshelves. "A recent arrival, who's become Ulwis' pet. I hope she doesn't have his man-making night—he's so cow-eyed over her he'd see through the spell in a moment."

"His what? I don't understand."

"Never mind. Just be careful around him. He pops up all over the place on errands for Ulwis or Deniker, and repeats everything he hears to them."

"What are they like?"

"Deniker comes from Gilad Seahold. But don't count on any righteous anger at its destruction that could be turned to Pol's advantage. He's Andry's to his toenails. Ulwis is another matter. She had a son by Andry—and didn't want to. In love with Deniker, you see, but too proud to say it. She ignores young Joscev—and wrongly, for he's a likely lad."

"So she has a grudge? Will it be useful?"

"No," he said flatly. "You don't understand the kind of loyalty they give Andry as Lord of Goddess Keep. But another thing about Ulwis—she's Cunaxan, and Merida stock, although she'll deny it to her dying breath. If you want to end an uncomfortable conversation, bring up this puzzling connection between the Vellant'im and the Merida. It won't make her love you, but it'll turn the talk quick enough."

"But why do they want to dine with us?"

He shrugged. "Jolan wants to sound you out. Her actions of the other day didn't exactly meet with your approval, so she assigned Deniker and Ulwis to do the work for her."

"It's all so obvious, once you explain it." Norian clutched the big leather-bound volume to her chest. "Antoun . . . I understand court intrigues, but—"

"You're shocked to find it goes on at Goddess Keep?"

"A little. I always thought—I mean, I've always been told that things are different here."

"So much for the purity of our calling." He smiled, but she was like her brother in that her sense of humor was nearly inoperative when she was upset. "Don't worry. Edrel will do just fine. He was Pol's squire, with the opportunity to watch him—and Sioned and Rohan as well. And they were better at it than anybody. Even Lady Andrade used to say so."

She frowned. This was an aspect of her new husband's position that she hadn't considered before. Norian had grown up a princess—but Edrel had grown to manhood at the court of the High Prince.

Except for the honor of it, and the importance of the connection, she wasn't completely certain this was a desirable kind of training. So she was not comforted when Antoun finished, "If he's listened to even half of what he's heard over the years, he'll know how to handle Ulwis and Deniker."

✳

Following Draza's example in describing the Battle of Swalekeep, that evening Andry refought that morning's events at Graypearl using the Attic table as a battle map. He had to do some guesswork, of course, but was pretty sure he had the basics right. And until Ludhil and Amiel told their version in person, Andry's would have to serve.

Odd to think that soon now—in ten days, perhaps twenty—the two princes would indeed have a chance to give a firsthand account. They would land at Radzyn tomorrow or the day after, with Tilal attacking from the east, and if all went well would march for Stronghold and push the enemy up toward Skybowl. And *then* let the Vellant'im call on the sorcerers for help as they were ground between two armies like grain in a mill.

Ten days, fifteen, twenty—it had become difficult to remember a time when the war was not being fought. It was nearly impossible to conceive of its being over. But it would be, and before winter's end.

"I make it twelve days," Chay said. "Two to clean out Radzyn, two more to rest. Three to march to Stronghold. We may have a problem there. If the High Warlord refuses to budge—"

Maarken shrugged. "Let's say for the sake of argument that they move. We'll figure that out later. I'd call it four days to Stronghold, Father, Radzyn will be a hard fight and they'll want to take it slow."

"All right, four days. Add another four to push them up to Skybowl, a day for the usual insults and feints, and one more for the battle."

"Fourteen days until all this is over?" Riyan shook his head. "I don't believe it."

"No more do I," Andry agreed. "A lot can happen in a single day—as we've seen over and over since Autumn—let alone in fourteen."

"We'll plan on that anyway, and revise as necessary." Chay drained one goblet of wine and poured himself another. "Sioned? You haven't had much to say about this."

"Is my opinion something you need to hear?"

The acidic comment gathered all their attention. Pol took stock of her pose—relaxed, casual, completely deceptive.

"I think you intend to tell us anyway," he said.

"Oh, it's not much. Only this. *What are the Vellant'im waiting for?*"

She rose, distributed a smile all around, and walked out.

"Goddess, but I hate it when she does that," Chay remarked. "Picked it up from Rohan." He gave a long sigh. "Very well, my ladies, my lords, and my prince. Any of you care to try an answer to that?"

Hollis looked down at her half-finished dinner. "I think it's another way of asking what it is they want."

"And as they haven't been considerate enough to tell us," said Sionell, "we're still where we were to begin with."

"Not quite." Maarken reached for the taze pitcher, stopped, and made an annoyed sound. "Damn it! I'm going to put a bell on it, I swear, to keep me from doing stupid things like that!"

Sionell poured for him. After nodding his thanks, Maarken continued, "We know they're here partly because of the dragons. We heard what they yelled when they came for Pol. And didn't Visian say that he threw Birioc's head at the High Warlord outside Rivenrock? So they're investigating dragons. It's got something to do with them."

"They attacked the rivers and Kierst-Isel to prevent anyone from coming to our aid," Riyan said. "That part of it's over. Anyone who's going to help is already in the field. The rest are sitting tight like the cowards they are."

Hollis glanced up. "And now Tilal says the Vellant'im will converge on Stronghold. That must be why the High Warlord is waiting. He needs the rest of his forces before he can move."

"Perhaps," Andry mused. "But what about the ships off Goddess Keep? Personally, and I admit I'm prejudiced, I think that's what Sioned was talking about. What are *they* waiting for?" He picked up the fork he'd used to represent a line of Vellanti ships in harbor and speared a cube of cheese. "They've timed everything rather carefully, don't you think?"

Draza spoke up for the first time. "Not everything, my Lord. They couldn't know how long it would take to march on Swalekeep—or that they would lose."

"Forgive me for saying it," Chay murmured, "but Swalekeep didn't matter. Nor Kierst-Isel, nor Waes, nor any-place else."

Pol nodded. "If they'd really wanted New Raetia, for in-stance, if it had been essential, they would have kept at it until they won. But they didn't."

"And Goddess Keep?" Sionell asked suddenly. "Did they change their minds?"

"Not at all," Andry said. "Lady Merisel's histories speak of Sunrunner armies—or at least of Sunrunners in arms along with regular troops. I think we were meant to be bot-tled up, the way Roelstra trapped Lady Andrade in 704."

"And because they're back at Goddess Keep, that's a clue that something big is about to happen?" Chay nodded, paused for a sip of wine, and continued, "All these other things were to keep everyone else busy. Nothing truly mat-tered but the Desert."

"And not even all of it, Father," Maarken said, sitting straighter. "They were herding us to Stronghold. They didn't even bother with Tuath themselves, but let the Merida take it. And they turned around and went back to Radzyn once they knew they wouldn't be able to take Tiglath. But Tiglath wasn't important."

Sionell stiffened. "Then it was for nothing?"

"No—Goddess, no!" Maarken exclaimed. "If Tallain hadn't stopped them, they would've trapped us here at

Feruche and we'd never get the chance to meet them at Skybowl! Sionell, I never meant—"

She gestured helplessly. "Forgive me. It's just—"

"Skybowl," Pol interrupted. He stood, began to pace, nervous energy crackling along his muscles. "We won't have to lure them. We won't have to intercept them before they can march on Feruche."

"Explain yourself," Chay snapped.

"Radzyn was taken but not destroyed—too useful as headquarters. They followed us to Remagev—herding us, as Maarken says. But they didn't destroy that, either. Stronghold—Mother did that. But what did they want? What were they after? Look, we've never even heard of these people, we don't know who they are. Lady Merisel never mentions them in her scrolls—does she? Andry?"

The Lord of Goddess Keep shook his head.

"All right, then." Pol found himself in front of the mirror. He turned to avoid looking at it, even though no spell of light had called forth that strange, compelling face. "She *did* write about Sunrunner armies. One of the first places the Vellant'im went was Goddess Keep, to destroy you if they could. They didn't, so they left—but now they've returned, and they're waiting for whatever it is the High Warlord is going to do. They must be afraid of what *you* might do when the time comes—things that haven't been done in fifteen or sixteen generations, since Merisel's time."

He paused, trying to control the fever of ideas. "I'm muddling this. Does anybody see what I'm getting at? All of our Desert castles are old, but none predates Skybowl. They didn't really want Stronghold, except that that's where Father was. He's dead—so they came after me. The *Azhrei*. They could've followed us up here. They didn't. They don't care about Feruche. It's Sorin's creation, too new to have any history. But Skybowl is the single most identifiable keep anywhere. It's a place of dragons, even more than Stronghold. Threadsilver Canyon is where they used to mate."

"And?" Chay prompted when Pol stopped for breath.

"We don't have to worry about getting them north. They'll march on Skybowl whatever we do. Hells, they already did! And they'll go back, with everything they've got this time."

"Why?"

Of them all, only Sionell was not caught up in the flood of his words. "Why?" she demanded again.

Pulling in a deep breath, he replied, "Because Skybowl is where the dragon gold is."

CHAPTER TWELVE

Arlis was subtle only as a sailor. He had coaxed and cajoled his ships through miserable seas and vicious battles, coming at times within a fingerspan of disaster but always slipping free. He had skill as a sailor, and even grace. As a prince, however, and a warrior, he was simple, direct, and lethal.

Laric, listening to Arlis' ideas and contemplating his friend's probable effect on his princedom, decided he had something else in mind for Snowcoves.

In the late afternoon of the sixty-fifth day of Winter, Arlis ordered his ships into harbor at Snowcoves with every soldier on board lined up in full battle gear—and full view of the town. The setting sun behind them made the sails loom like dark, uplifted wings. The light suddenly sliced a wicked glint through the gloom: the polished steel tip of a single arrow shot from the flagship, quenched in a wooden pole. It was taken down by trembling hands (so Rohannon reported, trembling himself with the need for a stronger dose of *dranath*) and the attached letter read aloud to the astonished and growing crowd.

> *To the good and loyal people of Snowcoves, from Laric of Firon, your prince, greetings.*

("I have to assume they're innocent," he'd said as they worked out the wording over the noon meal. "If they think they'll be punished, they'll be too afraid to do anything. I'll sort out the blameless from the guilty later.")

I understand that recently, to your shock and dismay, the peace of Firon has been compromised by the illegal and injurious actions of the traitor Yarin, formerly athri *of Snowcoves and, to my regret and my dear wife's shame, my own brother-by-marriage. I know that this treachery was not your design. I know that the castle which hitherto protected your lives and property is now occupied by servants of the usurper. I know that those who attempted to resist are now imprisoned within the castle. I know that Yarin has seized Balarat and even now threatens the life of my young son, Prince Tirel. I know also that troops are hidden in various ships in the harbor, waiting their chance to take up arms against me.*

("In other words," Arlis grinned, "you know everything! And what you don't know, they'll assume you'll know, and deal with it anyway. Brilliant, Laric!")

("I try," the prince replied modestly.)

Good people of Snowcoves, this cannot but be as intolerable to you as it is to me.
Prince Arlis of Kierst-Isel, my cousin and stalwart friend, who has had much more experience in matters of war than I, having lately destroyed many ships of the Vellanti fleet in battle on Brochwell Bay, believes that a fight is necessary to remedy this situation.

("Do pardon my making you out a bloodthirsty savage who can't wait to start lopping off heads.")

("My dear cousin, I don't mind in the least. What a lovely reputation I'm getting! I can hear the bards now, singing my prowess. Besides, you're the one who has to rule here afterward, not me.")

But I am of different mind, for although he may know the ways of war, I know the ways of the people of Snowcoves and of Firon. Our way, yours and mine, is peace.
I know that by dawn tomorrow, my belief in you will be demonstrated, and my princely cousin will receive an education.

Laric

Clouds blew up after the letter was delivered, so
Rohannon could not have seen what was happening even if
he'd been in any shape to look. At dawn, Arlis and Laric
went up on deck, leaving the Sunrunner in abject misery below.

"I am ready to be educated," Arlis announced.

"There is your lesson," Laric replied, and pointed to the
banner flying over the keep: a red seashell on a black field,
edged in gold.

It turned out to be true. The people of Snowcoves,
whether or not they had participated, resisted, approved, or
bewailed Yarin's treachery, had remedied the intolerable situation. There had been some fighting within the walls of the
keep, until those imprisoned in the stables charged the doors
and joined the fray. But there had been no blood spilled in
the town at all. As for the soldiers on board the ships—they
were dead enough. The vessels had been cut loose from their
moorings by night after holds were nailed shut and hulls
hacked open below the waterline.

As he sailed in, Laric lifted a palm to acknowledge the
welcoming cheers of a populace which, if not precisely loyal
to their last collective breath, was smart enough to do the
necessary for self-preservation.

"Listen to them, Arlis. You'd think I'd come to shower
them in gold coins."

"Enjoy it. Their relief is genuine—and so is mine."

Laric replied lightly, "And so will poor Rohannon's be,
after he's gotten some sleep!"

"I'm serious," Arlis insisted. "I'd be yelling your praises
with them if you'd let me. You're the only one of us to defeat the enemy without a scratch to any of his people. I wish
I could say the same."

"It was mostly your idea. And they did all the real work."

"Don't be so damned modest. I only suggested that we
sail in and let them know our strength. The letter was your
doing—the perfect use of power without using it at all. Rohan would've loved it." He was quiet a moment as they
came alongside masts rising like drowned, denuded trees.
"Of course, whoever did *that* work will need three days to
thaw out. Hell of a season for a swim."

Laric peered over the side. "I must remember to have the
harbor dredged come spring. It's cold as a meat locker down

there now, but when things warm up the corpses will rot and kill the lobsters."

✳

It was Sioned's favor to Arlis that his brother Saumer was not present for Tilal's ship-sinking festivities on the Faolain. He had asked that Saumer be protected—not an easy thing to impose on a seventeen-year-old youth eager to prove himself yet again at the warrior's craft. But she managed it. Saumer was asked (not precisely ordered, but who dared disobey the Sunrunner High Princess?) to stay at Lowland and do what he could to secure it—not from any further incursions of Vellant'im, but from the results of his own entrance. The collapse of the moat had flooded the underground tunnel with a noxious, possibly disease-bearing muck. Somehow the castle must be protected from it, and the moat repaired.

Just how to accomplish this was left to any imagination fertile enough to devise a plan. The stench proved inspirational.

Karanaya, with fine disdain for back-breaking work she wouldn't have to do, said that the only course was to bail out the whole mess by hand. Johlarian agreed with the bailing, but thought some sort of pump could be arranged. Saumer had no opinion at all except that he resented missing the action downriver. Various of his soldiers and Lowland's citizens proposed other plans: wait for the spring sunshine to dry it; cut drainage channels; fill the passage with rubble to mix with the mud and eventually form a kind of cement; or give up entirely and move to what shelter was left at Faolain Riverport. It was Mirsath's outrageous proposal that finally solved their problem.

"You're *faradh'im*," he said to Johlarian and Saumer. "Use Fire."

They stared at him as if he was out of his mind.

"We can't build a fire of the regular kind," he added a bit testily. "We couldn't control it. The whole keep might go up. But if you concentrate enough heat down there, it'll turn into an oven, and—"

"I'm a Sunrunner, not a baker!" Johlarian exclaimed.

"For the next few days, you're a baker," Mirsath told him.

For the next few days, he was a baker. So was Saumer.

At first the effort was ludicrous—half a moat's worth of slush would not evaporate on command. But after the second evening, it was seen that the level of water had gone down appreciably. They kept at it, wringing with sweat as foul-smelling steam billowed up the access stairs. Every window and door at Lowland was flung open to let it escape. Karanaya, who had elected to wait out events in a tent set up in the burned fields, reported that the keep looked like a gigantic double boiler bursting at the seams.

It worked. It took them five days of constant Fire, but it worked. Johlarian and Saumer took turns keeping it stoked, pausing only to eat a little and sleep less. The flames burned white-hot noon to midnight and midnight to noon. Down below, iron fixtures melted and stone walls turned black, but the water gave over sovereignty to Fire.

Both Sunrunners collapsed for a full day when it was done. When they woke, late in the afternoon of the sixty-sixth day of Winter, it was to Karanaya's news that Prince Tilal had sent a courier to tell of his victory in the south. He had not, however, remembered to return her pearls.

The people of Faolain Lowland could now work on repairing the moat—and, if Mirsath chose, the underground passage—without fear of disease or further landfalls, for mud had been baked into brick. His duty to his hosts done, his commission from the High Princess fulfilled, Saumer left at dawn the next morning, ostensibly to reclaim the Tears of the Dragon and deliver them to Karanaya. What he really wanted was to get out of there as fast as his horse could carry him while clouds obscured the sun and no more orders could come from Sioned.

He marched east at the head of the army of Syr, which now seemed to consider him its prince as well as its commander. In truth, he had to keep reminding himself that these were not his people and he was only delivering them to Prince Daniv. When Mirsath sent him off with the parting gift of a pennant in Kierst-Isel's yellow and scarlet, he waited until he was out of sight of the keep before ordering it rolled up and tucked away. It was only a little flag, nowhere near the size of Kostas' turquoise banner that led the march, but it embarrassed him.

Still, for all intents and purposes, these *were* his people. He had fought beside them at Catha Heights, led them to River Run where they'd stood vigil together at Kostas' pyre, and taken them all the way to Faolain Lowland. Now they would follow him into the Desert.

At noon, with the river long behind them and its rich green farmland fading to scrub that heralded the endless sand beyond, Saumer asked Havadi to call formation. The captain did so and the army of Syr—sadly depleted since Catha Heights—gathered to hear him. He pointed to the distant golden haze.

"That's where we're bound next. The Desert. Skybowl, where Prince Daniv will lead you against the Vellant'im in a battle that will be sung about when your great-grandchildren are great-grandparents. It'll be a long march, but as dreary as the Desert is, there's one absolutely *beautiful* thing about it. The blessing of the Goddess on your good prince, for summoning us where we can march in dry boots!"

✳

At about the same time that the shouts of Syr's troops for Syr's prince were soothing Saumer's conscience, Riyan's was bothering him not at all. The Lord of Goddess Keep technically commanded the loyalty of all Sunrunners, before even their princes. But while Riyan's prince did occupy second place with him, it was not because Riyan was first and foremost Andry's man. He was his wife's.

So he had no trouble doing something about Andry on the afternoon of Ruala's return to Feruche.

After five long days, Ruala was finally back from Elktrap Manor. She had no sooner embraced and kissed Riyan than she whispered in his ear, "Meet me in the Attic as soon as possible. But do something about Andry first."

It was afternoon, and the children's daily lessons were over, so that excuse was unavailable. But as Ruala deserted him for a quick wash upstairs, he saw Evarin limping across the courtyard from the infirmary and had an idea.

"Lord Evarin!" he called out, approaching with a friendly smile. "How are you today?"

"Walking," Evarin answered with a cross between a grin and a good-natured grimace. "Can I be of service, my lord?"

"Now you mention it, yes. There are some wounded down in the garrison below the castle—are you up to a short ride down and back?" He lowered his voice to confidential tones. "And could you take Chayla with you? She's working much too hard, climbing down there and back—if she hears your opinion on their progress, she'll be easier in her mind about them and take a little more time to heal her own hurts."

Evarin was nodding intently. "From what I've seen, my lord, she's a physician born and takes no one's word but her own. Still, it's worth a try. She's thinking of everyone else so as not to have to think of herself."

"That's how I see it, too," Riyan agreed. Then, as if an afterthought, "You know, Andry might need the same medicine. It would do him good to get outside the castle walls for a while."

"May I say that you wouldn't have made a bad physician yourself, my lord?" Evarin smiled. "If I mention Lady Chayla, he'll be sure to come. He's very fond of her."

Andry thus conveniently disposed of for the remainder of the afternoon, Riyan wandered his castle, casually extending invitations to several who had an interest in the mirror, and at last made his way up to the Attic.

Ruala had waited for his arrival to start. Pol and Meath had taken the mirror from the wall and were propping it against a chair, with a table on either side arrayed with candles.

"Andry's down at the garrison with Evarin and Chayla," Riyan said as he took his seat at the head of the table. "With luck, they'll be gone until dinnertime."

"Then let's hear what Ruala found out," Pol said. "Is this all right? Can everyone see?"

They could. The mirror was in full view of everyone—Sioned, Meath, and Pol sat on one side of the table, with Ruala at one end and Riyan at the other.

"I read everything I could find about mirrors," Ruala began. "It wasn't much, actually. I'd hoped for more, but. . . ." Scanning her notes briefly, she paused for a sip of wine. "There were four different types of mirror, each very difficult to make. It involved spells and calling Fire at different times for different reasons—none of which are detailed in anything I read. The first kind of mirror was called *kenida*, which means 'glass voice.' It was used when there was no light to work with, not even the stars. One large mirror was made, and smaller pieces cut from it—hand mirrors for a dressing table, pocket mirrors about the size of a palm. The pieces were tuned to their users and whoever made the original mirror. If someone who owned a shard died, the mirror and the rest of the shards continued to function. But if the maker died, every piece became useless."

"*That's* a relief," Sioned remarked wryly. "I was beginning to wonder if the next time I glanced into my pocket mirror, the thing would talk back to me!"

"It wouldn't, though, because you're not *diarmadhi*," Riyan said.

"Not necessarily," Ruala told him. "Of the four kinds, this is one of two that could be used by Sunrunners. *If* they knew the proper spells to make the mirror—or to tune one of the shards."

Pol had been taking his own notes. "I'd say that probably only the most powerful would have them," he said. "And 'powerful' is usually interchangeable with 'important,' which would be the leaders and their essential commanders. However, I think we can assume that Mother's right. There couldn't be any such mirrors still functioning. The people who made them are all dead. Go on, Ruala. The second kind—?"

"I think that's what Mireva used on Chiana." She hesitated. "I don't mind telling you that going through those scrolls gave me the strangest feeling. It's been so long since I read them, and my sister and I weren't much interested anyway. But in spite of really needing to know about mirrors now, the scrolls are still like stories told to children at bedtime. I don't half believe most of it, any more than I did when I was ten."

"At ten, you're excused by youth," Sioned observed. "At your age, by adult skepticism."

"Maybe," she replied with a shrug. "Anyway, this second mirror is called the *kazniradi*."

Pol glanced up in mid-scribble. " 'Long window knowledge'? Kind of clumsy."

"Very, until you understand what it was. The *kazniradi* was a portable window. Some had names—Glass-trap and Ice Window were the most famous."

"I don't much like the sound of that."

"And with good reason." Ruala ran a finger down the parchment page to find her place again. "They were cast for general power, not a particular person. Anybody could use them. When the proper conjuring spell was worked, you could see whatever was within range of the mirror. They tended to be rather large and beautifully framed for display in useful places—main halls, meeting rooms, audience chambers, bathrooms—"

"Excuse me—*bathrooms?*"

Ruala laughed at Meath's involuntary question. "We may assume a certain prurient interest. . . ."

Meath grinned back. "Oh, Goddess—Morwenna would have *loved* it! She'd make a list a measure long of men she wanted to watch lolling naked in the tub!"

"*Two* measures," Sioned corrected straight-faced.

Pol chuckled, too, recalling the Sunrunner's cheerfully lascivious nature. Before leaving Goddess Keep, her favorite duty had been the man-making night—no duty at all for her, but lusty delight. He hoped he wasn't blushing; he had received the benefits of her tutelage himself.

And he refused to be distracted by speculating on what Sionell had thought of the results.

"Anyway," Ruala was saying, "the trick was getting the mirror to where you needed a distant window to be. If someone wanted to lug it along for you, fine. There'd be plenty of people who'd agree to having a *kazniradi* around so the sorcerers could see what was going on. But if someone was given the mirror unawares, a spell of suggestion or even compulsion was set so the mirror would be taken along. That's why I think this is the sort used on Chiana. Of all the things she took with her to Rezeld from Swalekeep in 728, that triple-mirror from her dressing table made no sense at all."

"How was it used?" Pol asked. "And did you say that anybody could use one?"

"No, sorry. I should have said 'any sorcerer.' You called Fire, then conjured an image of the mirror itself so that Fire reflected in its image. It was kind of complicated."

He frowned. "Didn't any of the scrolls include the proper spells and how to work them?"

"You have to remember that basically these were textbooks. People studied them to learn about mirrors or history or *dranath* or whatever—but the specifics were given word-of-mouth only. Riyan says it's the same at Goddess Keep. The dangerous things aren't written down."

"Pol!" Sioned rapped her knuckles on the table. "Stop counting all the mirrors you've ever seen for future experiments. You wouldn't know what to do with them and you'd probably end up frying your brains." To Ruala she said, "You were about to tell us about the third mirror?"

"Uh—yes. This is the other one Sunrunners can use. I remember that one because it had such an evocative name: Shadowcaster. *Dalaaji* in the old language. When you called Fire, it showed you various people when you spoke their names, and whether they were *diarmadhi, faradhi,* halflings, or without power at all."

"The *aleva?*" Sioned asked.

Ruala nodded. "The colors that some of us can see if we try very hard, and others can't see however they try—but Jihan sees with no effort at all."

"Interesting," she said mildly.

"The mirror sounds rather useless to me," Meath said. "But doubtless one of you clever, devious minds will understand its purpose."

"Thank you." Sioned winked at him. "I can tell you right off why it was a good thing to have. Suppose you have a great many enemies. Suppose some of them you knew to be gifted, but others you weren't so sure about. This was a sure way of telling who could cut you down with a spell and who couldn't, despite any claims to power."

"Yes," Pol agreed. "But it would also be good for culling those of impure blood. Like Sunrunner rings burning on a *diarmadhi*'s fingers when sorcery is worked nearby. That was Lady Merisel's warning. This kind of mirror would be another."

"Andry had a *dalaaji,*" Sioned murmured.

"What?"

"He found it on one of his little purifying raids into Princemarch. Took it back with him to Goddess Keep and for all I know called out every name in the genealogy of all thirteen princedoms." She met Pol's gaze levelly. "So don't assume he doesn't know about you, although he couldn't have the slightest idea how it happened."

Meath was shaking his head. "With that *and* the warning of the rings, he could purge where he chose."

"Not anymore. He smashed it. I don't know how or why."

"Your informant wasn't specific?" Pol asked.

She gave him the little smile she used when he became irritable over her eyes-and-ears at Goddess Keep. "No. He—or she—knows a great deal, but not everything. Still, the mirror no longer exists." She poured herself a cup of wine. "What was the fourth mirror, Ruala?"

For a moment she didn't say anything, merely stared down at the parchment. Riyan half-rose from his end of the table, a worried frown on his face.

"Are you all right? It's a long ride from Elktrap, especially in your condition—we can go on with this later if you want to rest."

"No, love, I'm fine. Really." She glanced up briefly. "It's just that I remembered this one the moment I saw the name again. I'd deliberately forgotten because it's so horrible. It was called *daltaya*. Shadowcatcher."

All of them cast furtive glances at the mirror propped against the chair nearby. Whose shadow was caught inside?

Ruala continued in a dull voice, "I copied the whole entry on it—the only one I found in all Grandfather's books. It scared the *diarmadh'im,* too. There were no notes and no instructions. Only the mirror's name and this." She read aloud.

> *Unless you have cast a mirror yourself, or know its origins from the first grain of sand that made the glass to the last featherweight of silver or gold that made the frame, never call Fire within its sight. Only* faradh'im *are safe with any mirror. Your* diarmadhi *blood is your weakness, most of all with the* daltaya. *You will not die—and that is the horror of it. Shadowcaught, you* cannot *die.*

Pol shivered. "Then the face inside it—"

"Is the shadow of someone who once lived?" Riyan gulped. "I can't believe—Goddess, it's not possible!"

"Can't believe, or won't?" his wife asked softly.

"Either. Both. You're right, it *is* horrible. Besides, how would they do it? Catch someone's shadow—"

"How would they make any of the others?" Pol challenged. "Our good friends the Fironese crystallers may have whole books devoted to the subject that they haven't used since the *diarmadh'im* ruled, books they've forgotten they even have. Now that Laric has taken Snowcoves back, I may ask him to conduct a search."

"No," Sioned commanded. "Not unless it's to find such books and burn them."

He stared at her. "But—the knowledge—"

"You regret not knowing such horrors?" she snapped. "All those really creative ways by which persons of power can murder each other?"

"Of course not! But it's not the mirrors. It's not power that's intrinsically evil—as you and Father kept telling me most of my life! What I regret is that so much knowledge has been lost. Look at Lady Merisel's Star Scroll—or her histories, for that matter. Think of all we can learn! There's so much that she knew and we don't."

"I hardly count the demise of deadly mirrors and spells as a loss."

"You're deliberately misunderstanding me."

She made a dismissive gesture. "If you want deliberate, how about what Merisel did? Why bury those scrolls? If no one knew how to work such spells, no one *could* work them. She was trying to ensure peace—or at least the more usual forms of war and death."

"Yet she wrote them down," he shot back. "Not even she could swallow losing all of it forever."

"Oh, yes, she wrote them down—and put them in code! That way, only the truly dedicated powerful would have the patience to figure it out. And somebody that dedicated—"

"—would be that much more dangerous," he finished, annoyed but willing to concede the point. "All right, all right. But I wonder more and more often whether one should be more admiring of or appalled by that woman."

"Wise and long-sighted, or a meddling and vicious tyrant?" Sioned lifted one shoulder as if shrugging off a cloak. "Probably much of both, like the rest of us."

"You're too modest," Meath said softly, and she glared at him.

Ruala brought them back to the subject. "If this mirror is indeed a Shadowcatcher, and I feel certain that it is, then whoever's inside it must have been a deadly enemy of the *diarmadh'im*. Which is insane, because these mirrors were fashioned by sorcerers against other sorcerers. Sunrunners can't use them, and can't be caught in them."

Riyan's eyes flickered to the mirror. "So this man, whoever he is, can be nothing other than *diarmadhi?*"

His wife nodded. "I may be reaching a bit, but I think we may be able to call up the face of one of the most important sorcerers who ever lived. And I'd go even further than that.

I'd say he was a traitor to them, and allied with Lady Merisel."

"Ruala, my dear, you *are* reaching," Sioned told her. "We're not even really sure when it was made."

"Oh, but we are," Meath said.

Everyone turned to him. He rose and slowly approached the empty mirror.

"I was the one who dug up the Star Scroll and the histories—and never think that at times I wish I hadn't. At the old Sunrunner keep on Dorval where I found them, a level below the oratory tiles, there were plenty of carved decorations still clear enough to trace."

He touched the silver frame delicately. "I had a little talk with Princess Naydra a few days ago. She says Ostvel is as bewildered by this thing as we are. But he also says that it was never set in any other frame, that this is the original as far as he knows. And he's right—because I saw this pattern in at least five places at the old keep.

"Three were of stone, and at one time arched over doorways. One was small, and cast in silver, broken on the floor as the lintels were. There were bits of glass where I found it, so it must've been a mirror at one time. Princess Audrite had the silver fixed and used it to frame the little plaque at the entrance to the rebuilt oratory at Graypearl. Sort of a dedication, to mark our renewed consecration of the calendar, she said at the time."

He paused, then finished, "The fifth was on the floor tiles of the chamber where I found the scrolls."

"Meath—" Pol began.

"Hush," said his mother.

The Sunrunner stood before the mirror. Starting at the left where the surmounting curve began, he traced it with one finger to where the pattern finished on the other side of the mirror.

"All along here, the same order of leaves and apples intertwined. It was done in color, glazing work as fine as anything I've ever seen. Each tile fit together as if there were no seams. After I cleaned them they glowed, even after so many years. At intervals—here, and here," he pointed to the frame, "there were jewels—not real ones, of course, but bits of glass in colors of ruby and sapphire and emerald and so on."

Turning to face them, he finished, "The identical pattern. It doesn't appear anywhere at Goddess Keep—which

Merisel built and ruled for who knows how long. Granted, I haven't traveled as extensively as some of you, but I've never seen the pattern anywhere else, nor heard of it, nor found it on anything made since the Sunrunners left Dorval. That's why I nearly fell over when I got a good look at this frame—and why I know it's the original, and dates from those times, and *means* something."

There was a brief silence as they all gazed at the mirror with renewed awe—and more than a little horror. Ruala said it for them.

"To think . . . that a shadow was caught inside . . . hundreds of years ago . . . and he's been there ever since. . . ."

"I still don't believe it," Riyan said, but much less certainly now.

"Meath." Sioned's voice was hushed. "You said it means something. What?"

"I don't know." He came back to his seat and would not look at the mirror again. "I'm not sure I want to know."

"If only he could speak," Pol mused. "If he's really inside that Shadowcatcher, he might be able to tell us—"

"What he knows about killing?" Sioned asked sharply.

"No," he answered. "How to set him free."

CHAPTER THIRTEEN

Parchments were piled in five groups of varying heights on Ostvel's desk: fix-it-now, this-can-wait, taken-care-of, too-depressing-to-contemplate, and don't-make-me-laugh. A sixth collection, just delivered, waited on a chair nearby: not-yet-sorted. It was twice as tall as any of the others. Ostvel glared at it. Had he been a Sunrunner, the whole stack would have ignited. But he wasn't, so it didn't, and that meant he had to do something about it.

Since just after dawn he'd been doing things about the mess Meadowlord was in. He'd damned well had enough for one day—and the creak of his muscles as he pushed himself out of the chair agreed.

A spectacular sunset drew him to the balcony. The sky had been misted all afternoon, not an honest cloud to be seen. Now a yellowish glow seeped through trees etched black against a white-gold sky. He watched, expecting brassy brightness to intensify through orange to red. But the heavens surprised him. Delicate pink washed over the haze, deepening to rose and finally to vivid purple thinly veined in gold and blue, like some exotic marble ceiling. With the first star, a breeze blew up. All the misty clouds vanished and the sky was abruptly alive with stars.

He rather pitied Sunrunners, for they tended to look at light as either usable or too risky to weave, forgetting to appreciate its diverse beauty. Then again, they also saw colors he never could in patterns he would never comprehend. Still, he supposed it was the old story about describing a rainbow to someone blind from birth. He didn't really miss something he'd never known.

Caught outside without a cloak, Ostvel shivered. He lingered long enough to see torches lit in the gardens and lanterns at intervals along the low wall. Then he went back indoors, casting another sour glance at the desk.

"Too old to fight, too young to shove this on someone else's shoulders," he muttered. Goddess, what it was to have a sense of duty.

Few crops had been planted in the south this year, even where the Vellant'im had never set foot. Much of the populace of Gilad, Syr, Ossetia, and Grib had taken refuge within their lords' or princes' keeps. Most of the rest were too frightened to go out into the fields. Without winter crops, there would be no food come spring. Ostvel was enough of a farmer to know that the land would be the richer for a respite from the plow, but that wouldn't feed hungry mouths.

War and famine were brothers who were never separated. The second followed in the wake of the first as the moons chased each other across the night sky. But not this time. He had sworn it, as his last gift to Rohan. No one would starve this time.

So he had done his best to make of Meadowlord a vast breadbasket. Once Pol drove the enemy out, Ostvel would be ready with caravans of carts, fleets of barges, anything that would carry food to where it was needed. And he wouldn't even charge the other princes for the privilege of eating.

He told himself he should be feeling very noble these days. His efforts would feed thousands; he had put Chiana's treasury to good use; he had calmed most of Meadowlord; he'd done his duty by these people and his prince.

All he really felt was tired. And lonely. He missed his own castle. He missed his children. He missed his wife.

Sinking back into the desk chair, he opened the top drawer and pulled out a velvet pouch. He smiled a little as a dozen translucent milk-white moonstones tumbled into his palm. Chosen from Chiana's extensive hoard of loose gems, they would be set into bracelets for his wife and daughters. He might as well get something out of this besides backaches and eyestrain. Of course, there were many who expected him to plunder all Meadowlord for his own gain. This honestly puzzled him. He would do no such thing—and not be-

cause of any special morality or honor. He simply had no
personal interest in wealth. To Ostvel, private money existed
for only one purpose: to buy pretty things for his girls.

Goddess, but he missed Alasen.

"My lord? Why are you working in the dark?"

He straightened and rose as Princess Naydra entered the
chamber. "Oh, I'm only sitting around feeling sorry for myself," he told her with a smile. He reached for the tinderbox
on the desk.

Naydra gestured. Every candle in the room lit, one after
the other, from wall sconces to the branch on the desk.

Ostvel laughed. "Been practicing, have you, my lady?"

"It's easier than it was," she admitted. She sat in a chair
near the hearth, where a fire was kept going all day for
warmth. Budding trees and hesitant flowers had hinted recently at spring, but the wind was still cold.

Ostvel joined her after placing another log on the fire.
"How is Palila?"

He had asked the same question the last thirty evenings.
Naydra's reply was always the same: a sad shake of her
head.

"She does what she's told—sleeps, eats, bathes, dresses—
but she says nothing. Oh—she did react a little this afternoon when Polev showed her his drawing of a dragon. But
it was only for an instant."

"It'll take time." He said that every evening, too. "By the
way, I got another request for an audience from one of
Halian's daughters today—I can never tell them apart, can
you? I put her off. I wanted to ask if you know what her
problem is before I receive her. The last time, whichever it
was of them wasted half a morning with complaints."

The princess looked annoyed. "I've *told* them not to
bother you! It's probably just more of the same. You have
more important things to do than listen to them moan."

"I don't know what's wrong with them. They're leading
the same lives they always led. And they don't have to contend with Chiana. For that alone they ought to be singing my
praises."

"I suppose it has something to do with the illegality of
your authority here," Naydra mused. "Perhaps they think
they ought to be running things."

"If they want to, they're welcome." Suddenly he grinned.

"All those three know about food supplies is that when they want food, it's supplied!"

"They'd starve before they'd peel an apple with their own dainty hands." Naydra leaned forward to warm her hands at the fire. "My lord, I, too, had a request for an audience today."

"Who from?"

Not looking at him, she replied, "They didn't ask for me. They asked for the *Diarmadh'reia*."

Ostvel sucked in a breath. "Did they, now? What did you tell them?"

"I had the page say that I would consult you."

"Where are these people? How many came? Where from?"

Naydra got to her feet. "With your permission, we can find that out together. They refused to leave, it seems, and have been waiting since late afternoon."

"Then let's see what they want."

She arched a graying brow. "Please don't take this amiss, my lord, but—you've been working a long day."

"Well, I'm tired, but this has woken me up quite nicely, and—oh." He saw her gaze indicate his wrinkled shirt and scuffed boots. "Give me a little while, then, to make myself presentable. Where should we receive them? You're a princess, you know about such things."

"The Green Harvest Room would do. It's large, but not oppressive."

As opposed to what? he thought as he went up a flight of stairs to his chamber. The huge hanging lamp that gave the Green Harvest Room its name was a monument to Chiana's always intriguing taste: hundreds of silver tendrils flared wildly around pendant green crystal globs evidently intended to look like grapes. The thing was bigger than a canopied bed. When fully lit, it hurt his eyes. Still, he supposed Naydra was right. The grand audience chamber was even worse, with its square measure of garish carpet—he swore the Giladans commissioned to weave it must have been color-blind or heavily bribed—and walls painted with an improbable stag-hunting scene, featuring Chiana in properly sylvan garb.

Ahead of him he saw Polev kicking his way sullenly up the staircase, and paused to call to the child. "Come help me get dressed. I have to look important to greet some visitors, and I don't have a squire to advise me."

He made a game of it—deliberately choosing a red shirt, purple tunic, and green wool trousers—to see Polev's face wrinkle up in consternation. He tried to spend some time with the boy each day, at first for Rialt's and Mevita's sake but soon for Polev's own. He was a funny little thing, quick-witted and affectionate, though initially shy of the great Lord of Castle Crag. As Polev's half sister Mistrin had been with Ostvel and Alasen for three years, Ostvel had claimed a foster-kinship that pleased the child. He understood that his parents had gone away and would not be coming back, but Ostvel wondered sometimes if he really believed it. At not quite five years old, who could say whether or not a child comprehended death?

"How about the orange shirt, then?" he asked, and Polev made another face. "Goodness, but you're a picky squire! I'll leave it all to you while I go have a wash, or we'll be here all night before you think I'm pretty enough to receive guests."

"Who's coming?" Polev asked as he rummaged through Halian's clothes. Ostvel didn't much like wearing a dead man's garments—they didn't fit very well, for one thing, and were too luxurious for his tastes—but his riding leathers were too plain. "Is it Prince Tilal? Or somebody from the Vellant'im?"

"No, Prince Tilal is in the south," Ostvel said from the bathroom, "and the Vellant'im are a thousand measures away. I don't exactly know who it is."

"Can I come, too?"

"I think you'd be very bored."

"I'm *already* bored!"

Ostvel scrubbed himself dry with a towel, pausing to sigh softly at the gray hairs that now vastly outnumbered the brown on his chest. Sixty-four winters. Goddess, what an age.

"Is this all right?" Polev appeared in the doorway, holding a blue shirt in one hand and a violet tunic in the other.

"Fine." He smiled at the boy in the mirror. "Did you know those are Castle Crag's colors?"

Polev nodded. "My sister made a cloak for my wooden knight with blue inside and purple outside. Can I go to Castle Crag and see Mistrin? Please?"

"Not just yet."

"Why not? That's where everybody else is going."

"Are they?" Ostvel asked idly, rubbing his chin and deciding the morning's shave would do.

"Palila told me."

His fingers froze in mid-rub. Finding the boy in the mirror again, he asked as casually as he could, "Is that what she said?"

"She doesn't talk to anybody else. They *watch* her. If anybody watched me like that, I wouldn't talk either."

He reminded himself to discuss this with Naydra, and said, "It does seem rather rude. What else did she tell you?"

"She heard her mother and Rinhoel fighting about where to go. He said Dragon's Rest and she said Castle Crag. But Prince Pol would kick them out of Dragon's Rest and your soldiers wouldn't let them into Castle Crag, right?"

"Right."

"I don't like Chiana," Polev stated. "She wasn't nice to Mama. And she was *glad* when Prince Pol's father died. She didn't smile or anything, but I could tell. I don't like Rinhoel, either."

"There is very little about them to like," Ostvel agreed. "Well, let's get me properly dressed, squire, and then you're off to bed. No, no arguments, now. If you're good and go to sleep when you're supposed to, then tomorrow I'll take you into town with me to the shops."

Polev eyed him. "I'd rather ride my pony."

"Riding it is, then."

It was considered bad form to bribe children, but Ostvel had always found it highly effective—depending, of course, on the bribe.

A short while later, Ostvel was seated in a large chair, Naydra at his side, waiting for the delegation to be announced. Every third candle in the great hanging monstrosity was lit, dripping white light spangled with green down onto the grapevine pattern of another enormous carpet. Ostvel agreed with Alasen: every rug at Swalekeep should be picked apart and the wool returned to its original owners, except that no self-respecting sheep would wear such awful colors.

But as their guests arrived and accorded him bows almost as deep as the ones they gave Lallante's eldest daughter, he forgot about his surroundings.

Of the nine, four were men and five were women. They ranged in age from about twenty to over seventy, and in coloring from fairest blond to darkest Fironese. Their clothes were plain brown and blue and tan wool, but all wore some sort of pendant jewel dangling from the right earlobe—everything from emerald to moonstone, each different. A few seemed to be related, and the young woman who spoke in response to Ostvel's nod might have been his first wife's sister.

"Our duty to the *Diarmadh'reia*," she said in a voice with crisp edges and oddly liquid vowels. "And to the Chosen of my kinswoman, Camigwen."

"Kin—" He broke off and cleared his throat. "Welcome. On behalf of the High Prince, and the Princess Naydra, and in memory of my late wife, welcome."

"I share more than the look of her," came the reply, with an acknowledging smile for his startlement. The nose was a little too long, and the mouth a little too wide, and Cami's sharp intelligence was in this woman a brittle wariness, but the resemblance was still enough to shake his heart. "I share a part of her Naming. Mine is Camigina. I have the honor to speak for my people. May I proceed?"

"Please. And please sit down," Naydra invited with a graceful gesture. "May we offer you some refreshment? Hot taze, perhaps?"

"Thank you, we have no thirst."

Ostvel knew by the phrasing that the common language was not the first one she had learned. He wondered where she grew up that was so isolated that people still used the old tongue for everyday matters.

The nine arranged a half-circle of chairs, Camigina in the middle. She settled the folds of her dark blue skirt to hide mud-stained boots and folded her hands in her lap. Heavy lashes drooped over black eyes as she began to speak—no, to chant.

"These are the generations by which I claim kinship. Camigwen was the daughter of Camlen who was my grandmother's sister, both daughters of Rossan, son of Rosmeril, daughter of Rezev, son of Haldric, son of Merisen, daughter of Merith, daughter of Aleron, son of Ruala, daughter of Rosmeril, daughter of Rualyn, son of Lord Rosseyn."

After the sixth name Ostvel was lost—until he heard the name "Ruala." The name of Riyan's wife, whom they knew to be *diarmadhi*. He was barely over that shock when the final name was pronounced, in a tone of sorrow different from the regular cadence of the others. Lord Rosseyn, who had been friend to Lord Gerik and Lady Merisel?

Lord Rosseyn, a sorcerer?

Riyan's—and possibly Ruala's—ancestor?

Camigina wasn't finished. Eyes still closed, she chanted, "And these are the generations of the *Diarmadh'reia*. Lallante, daughter of—"

"No," Naydra interrupted. "Thank you, but you must understand something at the outset. I am honored by your regard for me, but it is not a title I wish. Nor do I desire to hear my—generations."

Camigina opened her eyes. "As you wish, your grace. But the fact remains that you are the last of your line. Your sister Ianthe's sons are dead. Your sisters Pandsala and Lenala died childless. Please believe that we mourned with you the death of your own son many years ago. He was precious to us, as you are. For as the last, you are the *Diarmadh'reia*, and we are yours to command for the good of all our people."

It hovered in Ostvel's mind that if anyone could claim that title's masculine version, it was Pol. Son of Ianthe, grandson of Lallante, descendant of—of whom? Rosseyn again?

This was water deeper than he wanted to dip a toe in—let alone go swimming.

"May I ask why you are here?" he interposed.

"There have always been those of the *diarmadh'im* who scheme for the return of power squandered and lost those generations ago. They were the ones who used her grace's line, or tried to. Mireva, of bitter memory, who was regrettably your grace's own kinswoman, escaped our watchfulness until it was too late. We give thanks to your Goddess, to the Father of Wind and Rain, and to the Nameless One that Prince Pol was strong enough to defeat them. And," she added with a nod to Ostvel, "that your own son, whom I am proud to name kinsman, had a hand in their defeat."

"Then—you oppose this faction," Naydra murmured.

"Branig spoke to you of us, your grace?" Camigina asked.

"Very little. Enough to make me curious."

"Enough to gain our entrance to your presence tonight," she interpreted with another of those smiles that wrung

Ostvel's heart. "Branig was the brother of Perchaya." She indicated a fair-haired girl three chairs down from her.

"I'm sorry for your loss," Naydra said. "Your brother was a brave and noble young man."

Perchaya whispered her thanks, staring down at her hands.

"We keep watch," Camigina went on. "We have not enough eyes to see in all places at all times, but certain people require observing. Chiana was one. There are others it would not be safe to name to you now. Forgive me for this silence, but we have known nothing but wariness and fear for so many generations that even now, in the presence of the *Diarmadh'reia* and Camigwen's Chosen, we must be cautious."

"I would say," Ostvel remarked, "that you've done everyone great service over those generations. The High Prince will want to thank you for it. You know, I'm sure, that he is opposed to persecution of *diarmadh'im,* despite the events of nine years ago."

"We know this, and are grateful. But still we are cautious. You do not know the risk." Camigina brooded for a moment, then glanced to either side. The other eight nodded as if giving permission. "After Lady Merisel's time, when we still fought because we had always fought, even though against Sunrunners we must always lose the fight, we contended against each other. It has endured that long, yes, the differences between Mireva's people and ours. Differences that led to many deaths. You outside the circle of burning stones never knew. Our battles were not as yours, with sword and knife. Our battles were of the mind. The gifts. Perhaps even the soul—or, no, *for* the soul of what we once were. Still, we kept each other in check, until Mireva. That was a mistake. The marriage of Lallante to Roelstra was *their* mistake— saving your presence, your grace," she added to Naydra.

"But why now?" Ostvel asked. "Why are you here?"

"Because the Princess Alasen on her recent travel said *Diarmadh'reia.*" Another smile, wry this time. "Your wife is a subtle woman, your grace."

He noted the error in his title but pushed it aside as unimportant. "So you've come to offer . . . ?"

"What help is needful." She bit her lip and a yearning look came into her tip-tilted eyes.

"How may we help *you?*" Naydra asked, reacting to it.

"It is not for us to ask anything of the *Diarmadh'reia.*"

"Then ask it of me," Ostvel said. "I speak for the High Prince." *Who's in a much better position to grant favors, seeing as how if you knew about him, you'd call him the* Diarmadh'rei. *Goddess, Sioned is going to have a fit.*

Camigina shook her head. "Not of you, your grace. For it is you who hold what once we built."

It was the second time she'd mistaken his status, and the second time he ignored it. "Castle Crag," he murmured. "You want Castle Crag."

"Not for ourselves," one of the men protested in the slurring accents of the mid-Veresch. "We wish only to see it again, to walk there freely. You don't understand. It is Mireva's line who want it for their own again. That's why there was Lallante. They desire to walk there as princes. They will try to take it however they can."

Ostvel looked at Naydra. "Sound familiar?"

She clenched her fingers in her gown. "Chiana may be on her way there now."

"We saw no sign of it," Camigina assured him. "But if it is possible—indeed, even if it seems impossible—she will try to take it. She will be their tool again, as she was before. And she will no more know it this time than she did the last. She will take it unless she is taken first."

He'd come into this room half-inclined to give orders for a march on his own castle. Now he was positive of it. *Right up the Faolain—she won't leave Rezeld until she's sure no help will arrive—but if Camigina's right, help will arrive, and damned soon. I can cut her off, make sure she doesn't get within a hundred measures—but against an army of sorcerers? Because that's what she'll have, even though she won't know it.*

He got to his feet. "My lady, you have told me exactly what I needed to know. My troops and I will set out by tomorrow noon." He spared an internal wince for what long days in the saddle would do to his aging bones.

Camigina rose as well, and the other eight with her. "We will be ready."

Ostvel blinked. "You—?"

"Shall we allow you to encounter them unprotected?"

"I'm going, too," Naydra said.

"Princess—" Ostvel began.

"It is settled," Camigina announced, reminding him even more forcibly of his first wife. "More will join us along the way, once we send out word on the stars. You will have enough and more than enough to counter them, your grace."

If there was a flaw in his character, he reflected wryly, it was that he rarely—if ever—said *no* to the women around him. He smiled at Camigina. "I thank you for the dignity, but I'm nothing grander than a 'my lord.' "

Perchaya glanced up in surprise. Then she smiled shyly at him. "Didn't you know? You will rule many long years as a prince before you die."

"Oh, no," he said firmly. "Not a chance."

Camigina gave a low chuckle. "Heed her, your grace. She is that rarest of all of us, *diarmadhi* or *faradhi*. She is *urkazria*—in your speech, a lady with long sight."

"I don't doubt her gifts," he replied politely. "But I'm not going to be a prince. Pol wouldn't dare."

Perchaya only shrugged and smiled.

*

A tent had been brought from Radzyn for Meiglan's comfort, a pretty little folly of white silk that Chay and Tobin used when they wanted to spend a few nights away from home. Ten paces across, with a bed, washing stand, two chairs, and a beautiful standing brass lamp arranged on a Cunaxan rug that formed the floor, it was a haven of privacy only at night. By day, the sounds of the camp intruded and she could always see the shadows cast by the guards marching round and round the tent.

They had also brought clothing—Tobin's, for they were much of a size. A gown or two, shirts, trousers, boots, nightwear; the High Warlord seemed intent on making her feel herself his guest instead of his captive. For two days now he had come by morning and evening to inquire after her comfort as sincerely as she would have done had he been given rooms at Dragon's Rest.

She said nothing. She could not put out of her mind—and must not, lest she become unwary—the sight of his dagger in Valeda's breast and the feel of Valeda's blood on her own hands.

There was nothing to do. Nothing to *be* done. She spent the days curled on the bed or in one of the chairs with Valeda's cloak wrapped around her, gaze numbly tracing the brilliant red flowers on the carpet. She was caught in a paralyzed balance among terrors: for Rislyn, for Pol, for herself. She could do nothing about any of it. Vaguely, she wondered why anger sparked in her at this helplessness. Surely her years with her father should have accustomed her to the feeling.

But between then and now had come her marriage, and being a princess, and the examples of Sioned and Tobin and Sionell and all the rest. She was not a child anymore. She was the High Princess. Had she not ordered executions and seen them carried out? Did she not have power?

She had none. Not here. Only the name he called her kept her safe. *Kir'reia.* It wasn't even her true title, it sounded harsh and alien to her ears. She was the High Princess. But not here.

They had just taken away her evening meal—thin slices of fresh venison in a sauce too spicy for her tongue—when the High Warlord's voice asked permission to enter. She said nothing. He parted the tent flap and for once he did not look concerned for her well-being.

"Outside, *Kir'reia.*"

Meiglan pushed herself up from her chair, knees trembling. Was he going to kill her now? If so, she told herself, straightening her spine and lifting her head, she would die as the High Princess.

He held the white silk aside for her. She stepped from the tent into the cool night air, where the cookfires could not compete with the brilliance of the Desert stars. Nor could the sharp odors of food overwhelm the smell of blood.

"My lady. . . ." Thanys whispered. She lay on sand soaked dark with her blood.

Meiglan fell to her knees. "No—oh, Goddess, no!"

Thanys' lips moved, and Meiglan leaned down to hear. "Rislyn . . . safe. Skybowl." She coughed, a sickening gurgle deep in her throat. "I s–saw. . . ."

"Saw?"

The woman's fading eyes sought the stars. Meiglan understood. *Diarmadhi.*

"Thanys? No, you mustn't—please, not you, too!"

The head cradled in her hands lolled, and the eyes swallowed all light into darkness. Meiglan watched the only kind memories of her childhood die.

"Butcher!" she screamed. "Murdering son of a whore!" Utterly beside herself, she lunged for him. He caught her easily by the waist, but she twisted and shrieked her rage, shredding her nails on his clean-shaven cheeks, pounding her fists into his face.

"Forgive me," he murmured, and slapped her.

Stunned but still conscious, she felt him lift her and carry her back into the tent. He placed her on the bed, covered her with Valeda's cloak, and stood over her for a moment.

"*Azhreia,*" he murmured, smiling a little as he touched his scored cheek.

If she'd had any strength left, if the world had not spun around her in shades of white and red, she would have torn his eyes out.

He lit the lamp and left her then, leaving behind him the sound of a soft chuckle. Unable to move, she lay there and wept silently until her eyes were burning and no more tears would come.

It was a very long time before she could roll onto her side and sit up. Her fingers were damp and sticky. Blood. Oh, Goddess, when would there be no more blood? She tottered to her feet and went to the washing stand, immersing her hands in the tepid basin. Delicate red swirls imitated the most beautiful of Desert sunsets. She shut her eyes.

Valeda's cloak, thrown around her own shoulders during the shape-changing, was on the rug. She picked it up, wrapped it around her once more, and wedged herself into a chair. Valeda was dead, and Thanys, and soon she would be, too. They were all going to die.

No. Not Rislyn. Thanys had said she was safe at Skybowl. The terrible constriction around Meiglan's heart eased a little. Her daughter would be all right. Lady Feylin was at Skybowl, and Lady Feylin was so clever. Rislyn would be all right.

Until the High Warlord attacked Skybowl, and everyone died.

He had talked about the castle yesterday. She had said nothing. Now, suddenly, the word filled her mind. Skybowl. Pol had said—and Valeda had said—it must be Skybowl. That was where the battle must be fought, the battle that ended this horror once and for all. Skybowl.

But why? Of all the places on the continent, why that particular one?

Meiglan pulled the cloak tighter, dragging the hem up from the floor to tuck around her feet. She was alone, she had no one to help her, no one would come—Goddess, please, no one else must come here and die!—so she must think all of it through for herself. She had learned from the best. She had watched and listened and Sioned had even approved of her forays into politics and the great chess game princes played with each other.

It was nothing compared to this. But she was the High Princess now. She had better begin acting like it.

Skybowl. Dragons. Pol. Herself. Somehow they all fit together, by way of the High Warlord's thinking.

She must learn why. Only he knew. None of the other Vellant'im could speak to her in her own language. He was her only source. She must learn why from him. She must—

Her fingers flinched away from an unexpected lump in the heavy cloak. Returning to it, she lifted the material closer to her face and by the soft glow of the standing lamp inspected it.

Vertical stitches were sewn at intervals intersecting the long horizontal one that hemmed the cloak. She explored the little pockets with her fingers. In each, stitched closed, separate so they wouldn't rattle against each other, was a coin. She counted six, distributed all the way around, judging by their size that they were of generous denomination. There were six empty pockets as well; Valeda had used those coins to buy food or lodging on her journey.

Carefully, Meiglan picked at the stitches and took out all the coins. They were bright and chill in her palm, all gold. She had enough money here to buy—

To buy what? Her freedom?

Initially excited, Meiglan despaired once more. What could she possibly do with a few gold coins?

She put them in a pocket of her trousers, then thought better of it and slipped them into her bodice. They warmed with the warmth of her breasts. Secret still, hidden away—useless but oddly comforting, for they were the coins minted by Rohan with Desert gold, with Dragon's Rest pictured on one side and Stronghold on the other.

She picked up the cloak again, staring at the hem. Valeda had been clever in her hiding place.

Meiglan could be, too.

But instead of coins—

What?

Parchment. No, it would crackle. If it was found, they would kill her.

They were going to kill her anyway.

But if she succeeded, if she could send word to warn Pol once she found out from the High Warlord his reasons for Skybowl, and hide the letter in a cloak's lining, and—

No, it was hopeless. She would need a reason to ask for parchment and ink, fabric and needle and thread. She could say that she needed something to keep her hands busy, like the dutiful wives the Vellant'im evidently admired; that might do for the sewing. But writing materials? Never.

Even if by some insane chance she *did* get her hands on all her needs, how would she get the finished cloak to Pol? And if it reached him, how could she expect him to know that there was something to look for?

As surely as Pol had been meant to be a prince, Meiglan had been meant from birth to be a pawn. She could not change that. Strength and brains and cunning belonged to the other pieces on the board. She supposed she was fortunate to have survived as long as she had. The Sunrunner Valeda had been clever with her coins, and died. Thanys had been *diarmadhi,* and died. Princes and warriors and even a dragon had died in this endless game of war.

Meiglan was a pawn, and pawns were always sacrificed. Somehow, she had simply been overlooked. Until now.

✳

Pol was on his way across the courtyard to the stables, intending to ride down to the garrison and do—well, something. It was part of his job as High Prince to show himself, even if he was of no other particular use. His father had taught these people too well. Never do yourself what others can do better and faster for you. They attacked their tasks with fervor so that he didn't have to. Goddess, what he would have given for just one knot to untie himself.

A knot that *could* be untied, he amended. There were plenty of the other kind available, and he could feel every one of them tightening around his throat.

Killing was so easy. Quick, clean, relatively little risk to a capable fighter—especially one whom his fellow warriors were determined to preserve at the cost of their own lives. *What makes me so damned important?* Pol asked himself, knowing the question for the absurdity it was. *He* wasn't important at all. It was the High Prince who mattered. The *Azhrei*.

To Hells with all of it. A fast gallop into the Desert would clear his head. It had been his father's happy capacity to turn problems over to those most able to solve them, and otherwise occupy himself until the time came for decisions. Pol needed physical action, physical escape.

"Don't you *dare* speak to me that way!" came a shrill voice from just beyond the garden wall. "I'm a *princess!*"

Pol winced. He'd gone through the same stage at around age eleven or so, an exalted sense of his royal dignity turning him into an unbearable brat. Sionell had never allowed him to get away with it, he remembered with a faintly pained smile. *Oh, Sionell . . . why was I so blind?*

But Jihan was different. This was not the foolish arrogance of a spoiled child; it was a terrified grasp for something familiar, something of substance to replace all that she had lost. Everything she knew was gone: her mother, her sister, her adored grandsir, her home, her safe and settled life. Her father had no time for her. No one did—except when they taught her about being a Sunrunner, and even then the lessons were not up to her expectations. Everyone had changed. Strained faces and sharp voices surrounded her, and she was at the mercy of whatever the adults decided to do with her. Take her from Dragon's Rest, from Stronghold, from Skybowl, from Feruche—she must go and do whatever they told her. And to a proud, intelligent, willful child, this was intolerable. Scant wonder she seized on her royal status as the only thing that still made her special, that hadn't changed.

Sighing, he abandoned his planned ride and started for the garden gate. The standard remedy would not work on Jihan. She didn't really deserve it, anyway. She wasn't being a brat simply because she could; she was hurt, scared, and alone.

His hand was on the latch when another voice, cool and even, stopped him. "Are you quite finished, Jihan?"

Andry? Pol stiffened.

"I'm a princess! Princess Jihan! You're supposed to call me 'your grace'."

Knowing now whom she addressed, Pol was more tolerant of the manner of it. Still, the words reminded him uncomfortably of stories he'd heard about Chiana before she'd married poor stupid Halian—insisting on "your grace" even though Roelstra's other bastard daughters were styled "my lady." He'd worried that he was becoming like his grandsire. Was heredity really stronger than upbringing?

"I know you're a princess," replied Andry. "I'm Lord of Goddess Keep. So what?"

"What do you mean, 'so what'?" she demanded.

"I mean that either or both of us could've been born in a hut in the high Veresch, and nobody but our families would ever have known our names, and what's more, nobody would've cared. But you know what else?"

"What?" Jihan asked suspiciously.

"I'm very glad I was born to my parents. And I'm even glad your parents had you." There was a grin in Andry's voice now. "Otherwise who would I have to argue with over what a Sunrunner your age should know?"

Jihan started to laugh.

Pol stood on the other side of the wall, dumbfounded.

"All the really interesting people won't fight with me," Andry went on, sounding aggrieved. "Your grandmother, your father, my brother Maarken, my parents—and I could scarcely have a good fight with Meig, now could I?"

"He's a pain," Jihan agreed. "But, you know, you're not so bad after all. I just don't see why I can't learn—"

"Do I tell you how to be a princess?"

"No—but you tell me how to be a Sunrunner. How *not* to be a Sunrunner," she grumbled.

"Because I know how and you don't. Not yet. You're the one who wanted lessons, if I recall correctly."

She paused only a moment before coaxing, "If you asked, I'd give you lessons on how to be a prince."

"Thank you, no!" Andry laughed.

"Why not? Granda Sioned says you've already made yourself Prince of Goddess Keep, and Papa says—"

Pol opened the gate very quickly before Jihan could quote him. What *had* the child overheard? He was positive he didn't want to find out. Pasting a smile on his face as he pretended surprise at catching sight of them, he sauntered over.

"Good afternoon, my lady, my Lord," he said pleasantly, noting at once that Andry wasn't fooled at all. "Isn't it time for you to clean your room, Jihan?" Leaning down, he said as if he didn't want Andry to hear, "That's a roundabout way of telling you I want to talk to Lord Andry alone."

She gave him a disgusted grimace. "Why didn't you just say it, then?"

"Your father is giving you lessons in being a prince," Andry said smoothly.

"That's right," Pol affirmed. "Now, if I wanted to be high-handed about it—instead of just clumsy—I'd order you upstairs and you'd complain and then I'd have to be nasty. This way, I've told you I want you to leave while at the same time giving you an excuse."

"What if I don't want to leave?" she challenged.

"Then I order you anyway," he replied with a shrug. "It's a tough job, being a prince."

"But you don't *have* to be nasty about it," Jihan scolded.

"I quite agree. Therefore—I hope you remembered to tidy your room this morning, Jihan." He grinned down at her.

She made a face, then said, "I did, but I'll leave anyway. There! Are you happy now?"

"Completely." He caught her up in his arms and gave her a kiss.

"Papa? Can I ask him something?"

"Let's find out." He turned to Andry. "My Lord, may she ask a question?"

"Of course."

"Why did you have on somebody else's face that day?"

Andry's brows vanished into his hair. "I beg your pardon?"

"It didn't fit."

He cleared his throat, and Pol toyed with the idea of sending his daughter to Goddess Keep for training, just for the sheer amusement of watching Andry try to keep up with her.

"Umm . . . I suppose it didn't. What did you see?"

"Your colors were all fuzzy, like they were trying to hide and couldn't."

Pol bit his lip at the expression on Andry's face, then had pity on him. "She can see them if she tries. She'd just been telling Alasen about hers, so I'm told, when you happened by."

"Oh." Helplessly. Then, making a quick recovery, Andry said, "So you were already trying to see colors?"

Jihan nodded. Her forehead wrinkled a bit and her lips pursed, and then she said, "You're very bright in the sunshine. All red and purple and gold."

"Stop showing off," Pol chided, and hugged her before setting her down. "Go along with you now."

Giving them a pert bend of the knees, she scampered to the gates and vanished. Andry blew out a long breath.

"*How* old did you say she was?"

Pol laughed. "I know what you mean. Does she give you much trouble at lessons?"

"Less than I expected, actually. It's only the impatience. By the way, how does she do that? Did you teach her?"

"No. She just does it. Like calling Fire. Goddess help us when she learns the rest of it."

"Mmm." Andry gestured to the path away from the wall, and they began walking. "What did you want to talk to me about?"

"I rather thought you might have things you wanted to say to me," Pol answered quietly.

"Oh. About being Prince of Goddess Keep, you mean." He shrugged. "I know what Sioned thinks of me. She's wrong, but I'll never convince her with words."

"Your actions haven't been all that comforting. What happened with that Waesian merchant—"

"—was not my doing," Andry interrupted. "Although I approve of Torien's decision, never think I don't. I knew the moment I met Jayachin she'd be dangerous."

"Then why make her your *athri?*"

"Because of the very qualities that made her dangerous, of course. She was proud, ambitious, and clever. I don't know any better recommendations for being a leader, and that's what I needed at the time."

Pol listened to the fine gravel crunch beneath his boots for a few moments, then said, "She stood between you and the people outside Goddess Keep the way you stand between common folk and the Goddess. An uncomfortable height, Andry. I'm surprised you don't get nosebleeds."

The Lord of Goddess Keep said nothing.

"If I understand you, then the idea is that only Sunrunners have the attention of the Goddess. Anyone who claims otherwise is a liar."

"Anyone who claims otherwise sins against the Goddess," Andry said flatly.

"By questioning your exclusive right to the truth?"

Andry paused at the entrance to the maze. "Some years ago your mother sent me a young girl who turned out to have extraordinary gifts. She knew things days in advance of their occurrence. She was never wrong." His fingers circled a wayward branch, drew it through like a veil through a ring. "But it was an odd sort of sight. Things that seemed trivial on first consideration—a birth, a riding accident, a vision of herself at her old home in Syr—but which turned out to have important implications. For instance, she saw Meig's birth before it happened. I don't know why. But mark it, he'll have something important to do someday. It'll be interesting to see what."

He glanced up, saw Pol's impatience, and let the branch go. "Back in Autumn she saw herself at her parents' home. Word came that her brother was ill. She left, and on the journey heard about my mother. I thought that was why she'd had the seeing. I was wrong. What she saw was her last moment of life, I think, before the Vellant'im killed her. It was a warning that what I'd seen in dreams was about to happen. We just didn't know how to heed it."

"She had visions, and you had dreams," Pol said. "What's the point? That no one but Sunrunners can do so?"

"Have you ever heard of anyone else who could?" He gestured to the maze. "Do you know of anyone else who can thread sunlight to find their way to the Goddess? We're special, Pol. You can't deny it. We *do* stand between ordinary people and the Goddess. She put us there. Anyone who tries to usurp that place, especially with what we know to be lies, sins against the Goddess herself."

Pol gaped at him. "You really believe that, don't you?"

"Of course. Don't you?"

"I believe that what you're doing is wrong! Can't you see that? Once you put yourself above others, soon they'll be praying to *you,* not the Goddess! Or is that what you want?"

"And your way is better?" Andry snapped. "You and Rohan—with Sioned's able help, I might add—taking power that once belonged to the other princes and *athr'im* and gathering it into your own hands as High Prince? Soon they'll be obeying you and no one else. And that, cousin, is what *you* want!"

"It's not the same!" Pol cried. "How can you accuse my father of doing anything but for the good of all the princedoms? The laws that were different from one place to another, the mess trade was in, the petty wars—he never used his power for his own gain!"

"*He* didn't, no."

Andry let the implication hang there, dark as a blood-drenched knife.

Pol shook his head violently. Everyone thought that only their combined strengths could defeat the Vellant'im. But how could he join hands with a man who would make himself little less than a god?

Then he remembered something. Something to use against Andry.

"Do you remember Mireva?" he asked softly. "Do you remember that she told us we'd work together the day dragons sailed the sea like ships?"

Andry snorted. "Are you claiming the gift of sight for the *diarmadh'im?*"

"Sight, dreams, prophecy—call it whatever you like. Believe it or don't, as you like. But mark *this,* cousin. You will work with me, fight beside me and not against me, and do as I tell you to do with your gifts at my command—or by the Goddess as she truly is—"

Breath hissed between Andry's teeth. "You risk much, High Prince."

"You risk more. Do you think you could oppose me and win?"

"I don't have to win. All I have to do is survive. It's not me they're after. It's you." Contempt curled his lips into a thin smile.

"Tempt me, Andry," Pol murmured. "Right here, right now."

The sunlight began to thicken with power—deep, bright, fatal.

Before it could coalesce and possibly—probably—destroy them both, it was shattered by a voice beloved by each, the one voice they would obey.

"Pol!" shouted Maarken. "Pol, come quickly! It's Jihan!"

CHAPTER
FOURTEEN

They took the back stairs three at a time, Pol in the lead. Halfway up he heard his daughter's cries and increased his pace. Maarken knew nothing more than that Jihan had been with him and Chayla in the library when she began to tremble and then to scream.

"I couldn't get through to her on sunlight," Maarken panted as they turned a narrow landing. "Damn you for whatever you were trying to do to each other!"

Pol didn't even glance over his shoulder. Andry said, "Never mind that—it won't happen again. Was *she* within sunlight?"

"This time of day the whole room is filled with it. She—"

Pol sprinted down the corridor. He could hear Jihan's words now—crying for her mother, for him, for Rislyn.

Sionell stood sentinel at the library door, and her expression of stark fear crumpled when she saw him. He nearly collided with her; she steadied him with both hands, then gripped him more tightly to keep him back.

"Chayla's trying to give her something to calm her down. Wait until she—"

He wrenched free and darted around the central table to the window. Jihan cringed into the tapestry pillows of a large chair, her blue eyes nearly black, her face ashen and streaked with tears. Chayla knelt beside her, offering a little ceramic cup that the child didn't even see.

Pol reached past Chayla to take his daughter into his arms. He rocked her, murmured to her, stroked her sweat-damp hair. Fine tremors shuddered through her small body, and all at once she gasped out, "Papa! Oh, make it stop, please, Papa, please! Make it stop!"

"Shh, shh," he crooned. "It's all right. I'm here now. Make what stop, heartling?"

"The c–colors—they're all gone—Papa, I can't see!"

He wove sunlight around them both—and cried out when the whole world went black. Only Andry's strong arm around his shoulders kept him upright, brought him back to awareness of his body—brought back his sight.

"She's caught in—something—I don't know—it's all blind—"

"Get Sioned!" Andry called over his shoulder.

Pol sucked in a deep breath, holding Jihan tighter. "I'm here, love, I'm here," he said shakily. "It'll be all right. We'll make it stop. Don't cry, my darling, Papa's here."

Chayla sidled around behind him, trying to coax Jihan into drinking. "Just a little, and you'll feel better—"

"No," Andry said. "Her mind must be clear."

Pol's eyes sought everything in the room and everything outside it—all the lamps and chairs and rugs on the floor and the pattern of plain brown tiles between them, the books someone had dropped, the fierce bright gold of the dunes and the limitless Desert sky. The memory of blackness, the knowledge that Jihan still saw nothing but that blackness, thundered through his body and left him weak—and hungering for the sight of things. *Any* things.

He heard Sionell's voice, and then Sioned's, and soon his mother was beside him, her hands cradling Jihan's head. A few moments later, his daughter went limp in his arms.

He rubbed his cheek to her hair and met his mother's gaze.

"I've . . . untangled them," she said slowly. "Wait." She turned so the sunlight was full on her face and for the first time he could remember, the strain of Sunrunning showed. When her lips parted in a soundless moan, his heart stopped.

"Goddess," she whispered. "Jeni says—she says Rislyn's fever was bad, there were seizures—infection—" She looked up, tears luminous in her green eyes. "Pol, Rislyn is blind."

"No."

He didn't recognize his own voice.

"Jihan must have been trying to find her, the way she tried before—even Sunrunning, perhaps—" She smoothed

Jihan's bright hair. "Oh, sweetheart, little one, what it must have done to you—"

"You've separated them?" Andry asked.

She nodded. "She'll sleep for a little while—I made sure of that. When she wakes, make sure it's in a bright room with plenty of things to look at. What she'll remember is—is her sister's blindness."

"No," Pol said again.

"Put her to bed, Pol," said his mother. "Go on. Maarken, Sionell, help him."

They coaxed him to walk. He clasped Jihan tightly to his shoulder. Dimly, he heard Sioned still speaking behind him.

"Chayla, how did this happen? It wasn't silk-eye, you told me it doesn't work like that. It was only a fever—children get them all the time—" Her voice broke.

"Pol," Maarken said at his side, "do you want me to carry her?"

He glared at his cousin through tears.

"All the time," Chayla echoed hollowly. "And we use what we have to treat them, and they recover. But Meiglan had nothing. Oh, Goddess, if only they'd let me help—talk to her for just a moment, tell her what she might use—"

"Don't," Sioned ordered. "Jeni says Feylin is blaming herself as well and I won't stand for it from either of you."

"Pol's rooms are closer," Sionell said to Maarken. "Come on, Pol. This way. Jihan will be all right."

Jihan, yes. But Rislyn?

✳

Somehow, he was in his own chambers. Somehow, they had pried his arms loose from around his daughter. They had found a chair for him, put it beside the bed where she slept. He thought Maarken might have said something, or that Sionell replied. He wasn't sure, and didn't care. He didn't take his eyes off Jihan.

His eyes that could see. Rislyn's never would again.

It could have been years before he heard his own voice speak again. That strange, hard, remote voice.

"Everyone but me."

There was a rustling sound, as if someone had given a start. "What?" asked Maarken. "Pol, what did you say?"

"Everyone but me," he repeated. "You, Father, Tallain, Jahnavi, Rialt, Mevita, Kostas—"

"Pol. Stop it." Sionell again.

"—Rihani, Volog, Latham and Hevatia—"

"Pol!"

Shocked, Maarken said, "They're dead. I'm not."

"You paid." He stared at his daughter's pallid face. "You and more whose names I know—and whose names I'll never know. One way or another, you've all paid. Chayla, Meiglan, now Rislyn and Jihan—everybody but me."

"Maarken. . . ." Sionell whispered.

"Yes."

Pol felt sleep begin to stitch itself around him, and fought back furiously. "No! I have to be here for her when she wakes!"

"You have to be *sane,*" Sionell told him harshly. "Maarken, do it!"

The arms that caught him as he toppled were Sionell's.

The face he saw when he woke was Sionell's.

"Jihan—" He struggled to sit up.

"With your mother and Hollis. She woke up, and she's all right. Stay put. Drink this." She put a cup to his lips.

"Drugged, of course?" As his mouth opened, she deliberately spilled wine down his throat. He coughed.

"No, as a matter of fact." She sat back in the chair he had been in earlier, and drank from the goblet herself. Her hair, backlit by the late-afternoon glow through the windows, shone like dark fire.

"Find a Hell and rot in it," he snarled.

"Been in one, thanks. Several, now that you mention it. Oh, not to compare with the ones you've made for yourself, but the tour convinced me I like it better here."

"With me?" He gave an unpleasant laugh. "When it snows on Radzyn Keep!"

"Or floods on the Long Sand," she agreed. Her tone changed. "You hurt Maarken very badly, you know."

"It was all true."

"Not with what you said—that just confused him, then made him angry. I'm talking about what you and Andry did, or tried to do. I'm not very clear on it, frankly."

"Andry said it won't happen again. I think he might even believe it. But it will." He leaned his head back and closed his eyes. The darkness made him open them again at once, to stare at the carved wooden beams of the ceiling. A beautiful room, exquisitely detailed, warm and elegant. The tapestry had been rehung on the wall. No evidence.

But how could Sionell be in this room again?

"Why are you here?" he asked rudely.

"To make sure you're all right. It was your mother's idea."

"Goddess forbid it should be because you give a damn about me."

"You are without a doubt the most self-centered man who ever drew breath." But the observation was mild, without rancor. "Even when you anguish over what other people have lost, it's always in relation to you. They paid, you haven't. I'd like to know what in all Hells you think you did that was so wrong you had to lose your father, so many of your friends—"

"Don't try to be compassionate, it doesn't suit you."

"Compassion? Not really," she said calmly. "Curiosity, maybe. I'm wondering when you'll think you've paid enough. When you're dead, too?"

"Get out." But then his hand reached for her of its own accord. "No—stay. I'm sorry."

She didn't touch him. Neither did she leave. "We've all been hurt, Pol," she said, and now her voice was soft. "No one escapes. Even those who try to keep out of the war— Pirro of Fessenden lost both sons, Halian of Meadowlord lost his life. It's not your fault."

He didn't answer directly. "It's just that everything has always been so easy for me. . . ."

"Killing your half brother was *easy?*"

"That's not what I meant. My father used to say that you have to wait for a course of action to present itself, until you had to do the only thing you *could* do. Events were in control. He was helpless, really. Forced to do things. That's how I always saw it."

He glanced at her then, saw her face, serious and attentive. She listened to him with her mind—but not with her heart. Not the way Meiglan did. Then again, would Meiglan have understood what he was trying to say? He wasn't sure he understood it himself.

"I wanted to use whatever power I had—Sunrunner, Sorcerer, prince—to control events. Keep them from controlling me. I saw Father as helpless, only using power when he was forced to."

"But the more you've tried, the more everything escapes your grasp."

"Exactly. And I think I know why, now. There was nothing missing in my life, you see—everything was easy, all the decisions made for me. Dragon's Rest isn't mine the way Feruche was Sorin's. My father built it, other people ran it for me. All I had to do was live there. It was the same with my whole princedom. I made the decisions, but—do you know what I'm talking about?"

"Go on."

"And then there was Meggie." He saw the merest tightening of her lips, regretted it. "She was something else that just *happened* to me. She was so different from the rest of you. I was *supposed* to love her—Miyon arranged it, and Mireva—and I knew all that and loved her anyway. No control. So there I was with my position and my palace, a wife and children I adored, a life that suited me perfectly—and I didn't have to work for any of it. All of it was so easy. It just fell into my lap."

"Nothing missing in your life," she repeated.

"I didn't think so. I know better now," he said, unable to look at her anymore, staring at the pattern of the thin silken quilt across his knees. "It's what my parents had all their lives, after they met each other. Not the love. The passion. Commitment to a purpose. Always trying to create something better and finer—but using their power sparingly, because they knew how simple it would be to abuse it. That's something else that's always come easily to me. Mother would be happy to hear me say this, because it's what she and Father warned me about for years. Power scares me. Looking into that mirror, that face trapped inside—that scares me to death. And it's something I could do if I knew the right spells. Andry can't. No Sunrunner can. But I could."

She was quiet for a time. Then, in a neutral voice: "These spells—do you *want* to learn them?"

"For a little while I did. Then I called Fire and saw him again, and—Goddess, Ell, they called that kind of mirror a Shadowcatcher. *Shadowcatcher,*" he repeated, repressing a shiver.

"You don't want to know," she murmured. "Neither would I. Does that make us cowardly, or wise?"

He glanced at her again and smiled slightly. "Both."

"I don't find that comforting."

"You think *I* do?"

"Pol? Are you awake?" Sioned came in, and arched a brow to find them in each other's presence without furious words lingering in the air. "Maarken said he had to be rather adamant about sleep-weaving. Jihan's asking for you, Pol."

He got up, found his boots, and pulled them on. "She's all right?"

"Chayla got some sort of potion down her, so she's a little groggy, but for now that's a good thing. I'll send dinner up for you both, and you can sit with her until she falls asleep again."

"Does she remember?"

"Yes. So do I. I wish I didn't."

"What was it?" Sionell asked.

"A strange combination of things—not really Sunrunning, because she doesn't know how." She folded her arms. "More as if she was attempting the eyes-and-ears spell without knowing how to do that, either."

"And there was nothing to see," Pol whispered.

Sioned changed the subject, saying to Sionell, "Meig and Jahnev and I spent part of the afternoon turning your rooms into a mountain fortress, so don't go in without a candle to light your way. There's a lot of furniture to climb over to get to your bed tonight." She paused, her gaze barely flickering to each of them in turn. "If you go to your bed tonight, that is."

Sionell and Pol both turned crimson with embarrassment. Sioned divided a serene glance between them and left.

"What in all Hells—" Pol began.

"No. Don't say another word." Sionell hurried out, leaving him to stand there in mid-sentence like a tongue-tied fool.

✳

"How *dare* you!"

The hissed accusation made Sioned turn on the stairs. She eyed her infuriated Namesake, who stood just above her on a landing.

"What did you mean by that?" Sionell demanded.

"What did you think I meant?"

"You don't know what you're talking about."

"Probably," she conceded.

"Nothing happened."

"If you say so, my dear."

Sionell hesitated a moment, then burst out, "You didn't used to be so malicious—or so cruel!"

"And is it kindness to let you gnaw at this 'nothing happened' like an animal chewing off a leg to get free of a trap?"

Sionell caught her breath. "Stay out of it, Sioned," she warned, and fled.

Rohan would have lectured her half the night for this little piece of interference. *But it's necessary,* she argued. *They're hurting themselves and each other. And Meiglan, too, if she ever learns about it—which she's bound to do when she comes back if they haven't resolved this.*

No stern voice spoke to chide her. With a sigh and a shrug, she continued down the stairs.

*

He did not come to her tent again until the second morning after Thanys' murder. Leaving the flap tied back for fresh air, he smiled and held up a bottle of cool wine and a pair of blue crystal goblets.

"Good drink," he told her, pouring out the almost colorless liquid. "From Radzyn," he added. "I commanded priests for these. You are *Kir'reia,* not a peasant."

Evidently the priests—whoever and whatever they were—had fulfilled the minimum of the order: Meiglan recognized the glasses as Tobin's second-best set, and the wine's label as an everyday vintage provided for guests who wouldn't appreciate a truly fine wine and wouldn't know the difference. Pol kept a few hundred bottles of it at Dragon's Rest for exactly that purpose.

"Drink, *Kir'reia.*"

She set the wine on the carpet beside her chair.

A little smile touched his lips. "You hate me. For the killings. Yet your people kill mine. That's war."

"A war you started," she observed, using Sioned's coldest voice.

"A necessary war. You hate, we hate—but ours is stronger, and we will win." He sat down in the other chair, sprawled out his booted legs, and regarded her for a silent moment. "You have daughters. No sons?"

If she said nothing, he would talk for a time and then leave. But she needed information. What Sioned had done for Rohan on light, she would now do for Pol by more ordinary means.

"No sons," she replied sullenly, aware that after so much silence, sudden chatter would be suspect.

"And you are so old," he marveled. "Past twenty, past twenty-five. With your years, our women have borne many sons. Five, six, seven. Were you injured in childing, then?" He paused, and corrected himself, "Birthing."

"No."

"Your husband no more desires you?"

Meiglan's head snapped up indignantly.

"Then he is the weakling, not you, to put no sons into your body?"

"Don't be absurd! You've met him in battle—he's no weakling!" She blushed furiously; this was not the sort of conversation she had imagined having with this man. "How many children do *you* have?"

He smiled proudly. "Of sons, eighteen."

Good Goddess. "And daughters?"

"They do not count. My five wives know their duty to me—all but the third, a bad choice. Only one son and four daughters, but the daughters have sons by their husbands, so I will not complain." He drank wine. "I will return and take more wives, if I find some worthy of my bed and my sons. Tell me why does the *Azhrei* not do this? Only two daughters—but you say you are well, he desires you, so what difficulty? What worth in a woman who does not have many children?"

"If that's all your wives mean to you, then I wonder you have any at all!"

He frowned in bewilderment. "I chose them. They are mine."

"And they had no say in the matter?"

"Why should they? I am who I am. Say to me now why women are in your armies, and fight with men."

"Why shouldn't they?"

"The strong should not risk strength. The old and the barren work, and free men for war and strong young women for bearing."

"That is not how it is here."

"You have many strange ways." He paused for a sip of wine. "Who among you has the most sons?"

She thought for a moment. "My husband's aunt gave birth to four."

"This is Princess Tobin, yes? Daughters?"

"No."

"I admire her. And other women? How many are their childings?"

"Four, sometimes five."

"All sons?"

"Not always."

He mused on this for a while. Meiglan retrieved her winecup and drank; her throat was getting dry from all this talking.

"It is clear," the High Warlord said. "Your people had few children, except when they mated with mine."

The goblet nearly slipped from her hand. "Th—they did?"

"Their men got sons and more sons from our women, and their women bore sons and more sons by our men." His jaw hardened. "When we find any left, we kill them, of course."

"But—it's not their fault they were born!"

"They show taint," he replied bluntly. "They are killed. As all who spin Fire shall be."

"Why?"

"You do not remember." His voice was soft, menacing. "But you will."

"Not if you don't tell me." She forbade herself to be frightened by his eyes.

"You ground our faces in dirt so we could not breathe. You chained our feet so we forgot how to run. You bent our heads with shame so we lost the sky." He drained the wine down his throat and rose. "Yes, our women breed until they die of breeding—but this thing they do with pride. They look on their tall, strong sons and know they are chains to bind *you*. And then we will go home, and breathe freedom at last, and run for the joy of it, and embrace the sky."

Meiglan said what she knew Sioned would have. "You will never succeed."

"No?" He smiled down at her. "You are my success, *Kir'reia*. Precious jewel of Princemarch, sweetwater spring of the Desert—what will the *Azhrei* not do to have you back, even if you have borne him only daughters?"

To have her back—? Wasn't he going to kill her? She pushed wild hope aside. "I was wrong. You *do* value your own wives—else you could not understand why my husband values me."

He looked startled, then gave a roar of laughter. "He would be a fool not to! You are a clever woman, *Kir'reia!*"

She lowered her gaze to her hands. Sioned was clever; so were Tobin and Hollis and Sionell. Meiglan was only beautiful. His own women must be stupid indeed if by comparison he found her clever.

"I wonder," he said suddenly, "what your sons would be like."

"One day I'm sure I'll find out," she replied, and her voice shook only a little. "But you won't be around to see them."

Laughing again, he took the bottle and his cup and left her alone.

*

"It's been twenty days." Chiana sat at the window of a miserably damp chamber that the hearthfire did nothing to warm, and said again over her shoulder, "Rinhoel, it's been *twenty days.*"

"Do you think I can't count?"

"You're drinking too much," she scolded.

"Is there anything else to do around here?" He finished emptying the pitcher into a cup—ceramic, and chipped into the bargain. Chiana ground her teeth. That common drudge Ostvel was drinking from her gorgeously expensive crystal goblets, eating off her exquisite gold plates, and sleeping between her cloud-soft silk sheets while *she* had to make do with glazed clay, dull pewter, and thin wool. Woolen sheets, for the Princess of Meadowlord!

She was positive that little bitch Avaly, who ran Rezeld, had all her fine things stashed away in cupboards somewhere and wouldn't share them. No one could possibly live like this all the time. It wasn't civilized.

And the clothes she had been given—Goddess in glory! Even if the Vellant'im did arrive today, how would they know her for who she was, dressed in such rags?

But they were not coming. She was sure of that now. Damn that lying son of a whore—he'd pay for this. They all would.

To her son she said, "You might try getting ready for our journey to Castle Crag."

Rinhoel almost choked. "In the snow? You complained to the skies for the ten or twelve days it took us to get here—and it's twice that to Castle Crag!"

"Where else is there?" she shouted. "Ostvel's in Swalekeep, we can't go back there! Pol still holds the northern Desert—and the Vellant'im hold the south! Is there anything to choose between them?"

"You think we'd be welcomed at Castle Crag?" he sneered.

Appalling, how closely he resembled his grandsire these days. "There are plenty left in Princemarch who still long for my father. You look enough like him to be his brother instead of his grandson. They'll look at you and see him. We'll send out a call as we march, to tell everyone that Roelstra's daughter and Roelstra's grandson are coming home."

"You've lost your wits, Mother," Rinhoel said.

"I want out of here, Rinhoel! The Vellant'im won't come, you know they won't! I can't stay here any longer—and I want Castle Crag! Ostvel's troops are all in Meadowlord, there's no one left to defend it! It can be mine—finally mine!"

He loomed over her, scowling. "*I* am the prince here, not you."

"Then act like it!" She snatched the cup from his hand and dashed it to the floor. "I *will* go to Castle Crag!"

"By yourself?" He laughed.

"Do you have any suggestions about where else we can go? Or do you intend to stay in this hovel and drink yourself to death because you don't have the courage to fight? Are you Halian's son, or mine?"

"I don't see that it's any honor to be either," he snarled. "Very well. Fine. We'll go to Castle Crag. I've got nothing better to do."

"What's wrong with you, Rinhoel? When we left Swalekeep, you led the soldiers like a true prince—"

"All fifty-two of them! What chance do we have with

fifty against Castle Crag? What's wrong with me is that I lack an army, a *real* army."

"The people of Princemarch will rally to you. Pol is a stranger, he's not of the true royal line. You are."

"That and a copper coin will get me a swig of ale at any filthy inn on the road to the Faolain."

Chiana nearly screamed with vexation. "Do you want to sit here and rot?"

"I've already said I'll go." He flung himself down in a chair. "What more do you want?"

"I want my son to be High Prince. I want him to believe that he *will* be High Prince. You'll see, Rinhoel. They'll flock to your banner, they'll march on Castle Crag with us—"

Someone perfunctorily thumped a fist on the door, then swung it open without waiting for permission. Avaly came in, glanced at the shattered cup on the floor, and frowned. Chiana rose, shaking with rage. The cold and the dirt and the shabby clothes were bad enough, but this woman's manners were the foulest thing about her. As the days passed, and no army of bearded warriors turned up, Avaly had abandoned courtesy along with belief in Chiana's claims.

"There's someone outside the gates calling for you, my lady."

"How many times must I tell you to address my mother as her grace?" Rinhoel demanded. "Well? Who is it? What do they want?"

"To speak with you." She shrugged. "They're not Vellant'im, if that's what you want to know."

"What I want to know," he said, advancing on her, "is not who they aren't, but who they *are*."

"I don't know. How should I know? You'd better go talk to them yourselves." She departed, leaving the door open.

Chiana picked up her cloak from a chair. The dark green velvet had been cleaned and from a distance would look as fine as ever, even if the gold embroidery was snagged in places. "If they're Pol's soldiers, or Ostvel's, then let me do the talking."

"Anything you like, Mother."

A frigid wind swept down the valley of Rezeld Manor, making an instant wreck of Chiana's hair. She stood on the walls with archers on either side of her and Rinhoel. Below were close on sixty men and women, all dismounted from decent-looking horses, none of them dressed for war and no banner with identifying colors whipping overhead in the wind. All her enemies were too much the honorable idiots to disguise their troops to trick her. She had no idea who these people were.

"We are the Princess of Meadowlord," she called down, shivering in the cold. "Say what you came to tell us!"

A tall young man stepped forward. "Only this, your grace—that we beg the privilege of following the true Lord of Princemarch, and of Castle Crag, and of this place and all others in this land—the noble grandson of Roelstra, the Prince Rinhoel!"

Her son let out a gasp. She slanted a quick look at him—*I told you, I told you!*—and leaned forward. "You are welcome, then—and all who believe as you do! Are there more?"

"Many more, your grace! Many more, who will join us along the way!"

She laughed in delight. But Rinhoel pushed her aside and shouted down, "And where do you think we're going?"

"Why, to Castle Crag, of course! To claim your grace's rightful place!"

"You see?" Chiana hissed. "It's already started! It just needed a little time for the word to spread—"

"I don't like it," he muttered.

"Don't be a fool!" Moving forward again, she cried, "The gates will open to you good people, and you may rest and refresh yourselves! You've come just in time, for tomorrow we begin our march to Castle Crag!"

They cheered down below. Chiana snapped an order to one of her own archers, who yelled at someone else to unbolt the gates.

"I don't *like* it," Rinhoel insisted as they made their way back down to the small courtyard.

"I don't care whether you like it or not! This is what we've been waiting for! I knew it would happen, I knew it! This is our chance, Rinhoel—no, more than a chance! A certainty! Twenty days from now, twenty-five, and you and I will be at Castle Crag!"

He accompanied her as she welcomed the new arrivals, and said all the right things, but there was a shadow in his leaf-green eyes that almost spoiled her triumph.

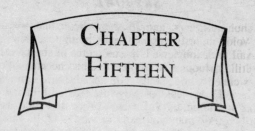

CHAPTER FIFTEEN

A troop of fifty was left behind to secure Snowcoves—mostly Pol's soldiers from Dragon's Rest, a reminder that the High Prince was Laric's kinsman and would not look kindly on any further difficulties. Nearly a hundred men and women from Snowcoves had volunteered to join the march to Balarat. Laric chose only thirty of whom he was absolutely certain: they were either kin to his own trusted retainers or had been imprisoned by Yarin's adherents—or both. The people of Snowcoves had fallen all over themselves declaring their loyalty. Except for those actually wearing Yarin's colors, no one could be found who admitted sympathy with his cause.

Laric merely shrugged when Arlis remarked caustically on it. "There are two sorts of people in Snowcoves. The crafters don't care who's in power so long as glass ingots come from the Desert and they're left alone to create. The merchants don't care so long as they can import the ingots and they're left alone to create profits. Yarin had a way of prying into their books in search of unpaid taxes."

"Have they always cheated, then?"

The older prince looked surprised. "Of course. So do the silk and pearl merchants on Dorval. I asked Grandfather about it once. He said if you let them be, they only hold back enough to make themselves feel clever at outwitting you. But if you go after them, they think up ways to hold back even more."

"Hmm. I'll have to remember that the next time my own grandfather complains about—" He stopped abruptly. "More than a hundred days, and I can't believe that when I sail home, Volog and my parents won't be there. . . ."

The sail back to Kierst-Isel was scores of snowy measures away. Still, Arlis was in a more or less cheerful mood as a halt was called while scouts rode ahead. Laric unhooked his wineskin from his saddle, and Arlis toasted him.

"Here's to drinking the New Year beside your own hearth."

"I'd better! It's thirty days to the New Year and only eight or so to Balarat." Laric squinted into the gray-white distance. The weather had held, insofar as the clouds did nothing worse than threaten, but those same clouds made Rohannon useless.

"How long do you think it will take to recapture Balarat?" Laric asked.

"Depends." Arlis took a long swig and recapped the spout. "It won't be easy, the way Snowcoves was."

"Then my tally of wins without having fought a battle will stand at two."

"Two? Oh—you mean that little dance you did with Edirne and Camanto on either side of the Ussh. Tell me, do you think Isriam is really Camanto's son and not Sabriam's? Because if it's true, and Pirro accepts him, Isriam may end up Prince of Fessenden one of these days."

"I'd be in favor of it. I'd rather have him at Fessada than wasted at Einar. Rohan had a good opinion of him as a squire. And it would be infinitely preferable to having Arnisaya as regent until her son comes of age. There's something a bit slimy about that woman."

"We'll see what Pol thinks after this is all over. In fact, I wouldn't be surprised if you had to leave Balarat fairly soon after you get it back again. All of us will have to gather to confirm him as High Prince—formally, I mean, with the oaths and all that—and figure out what we'll do about resuming trade and so on. Things have changed since the agreements signed at the *Rialla*."

"It seems a thousand years ago, doesn't it?" Laric mused. "If only I hadn't stayed at Dragon's Rest—none of this would have happened."

Recognizing the start of a *What if?* conversation—a complete waste of time as far as he was concerned—Arlis gave a hearty laugh. "Oh, but then I wouldn't have had the pleasure of freezing my balls off on this little trip through your charming countryside!"

Laric grinned back at him. "We'll have you and your wife to our Midwinter Hunt. You'll love it—we spend five solid days galloping around no matter what the weather, and at night thaw out before the fire having learned—if somewhat drunken—discussions about the forty-six different words for 'snow.' "

"I beg your pardon? Forty-six?"

"According to when, how, and where it falls, how long it will take to melt, the texture of it from dry powder to sloppy footing, if it forms good ice for the cold-cellars—need I go on?"

"Please don't," he begged. "You'd *have* to be drunk to discuss it! And don't invite us, either!"

The scouts came back with nothing to report but a gradual rise in the land that would slow them down. There was another route to Balarat that involved few hard climbs and several easy passes through the hills, but this was the most direct road. And it was no use being subtle; Yarin surely knew they were coming.

On this, the second day of the journey, they continued to make good time. There had been some neglect of the road—many farmers and village folk along the way had neither cleared the snow nor laid down salt. Laric frowned at that. One of his concerns was to keep as much of his princedom accessible during Winter as possible. There was nothing to be done about the upper reaches of Firon, but few lived there anyway and those who did enjoyed their isolation. When they came down from ice-field and mountain to sell the furs that were their livelihood, they wilted in sweltering summer heat—which on Dorval would have been called a chilly day.

The army stopped at noon for a meal and a well-deserved rest. A third of the troops were mounted, and took the lead to trample down the snow for those on foot. Arlis did not believe in sparing horses' legs in favor of human ones—horses might carry soldiers into battle, but they didn't carry swords or spears or bows. This march would be difficult enough on foot soldiers without exhausting them unnecessarily.

They had barely formed up again when scouts sent ahead came pelting back, yelling for Prince Laric. He looked around from checking his saddle girth to find two riders heading for him at a full gallop, snow fountaining with every hoofbeat.

"Good Goddess, Yarin's sent a force out to meet us," he breathed.

"If he did, he's not as smart as I thought," Arlis retorted. "He's better off inside Balarat. Let's see what's what before we worry."

The scouts leaped from their horses and ran to where the princes stood waiting. "My lord!" one of them cried. "Your son!"

Laric suddenly couldn't breathe. "Dead?"

"Oh, no, my lord! Here!" The woman—one of Arlis' own household guards from Zaldivar—gulped in air and smiled widely. "He and his squire—your squire, I mean—they left Balarat six days ago!"

Laric leaned his brow to his saddle, closing his eyes. The Goddess had smiled on him. Tirel was safe.

"Don't fall over," Arlis advised. "Come on, let's ride out to meet them."

Laric felt no shame that he had to be helped to mount. Any father would feel the same—weak with joyous relief, so weak he couldn't keep his hands from shaking. But as he crested the hill, and saw in the hollow beyond it a small black-haired boy on a large gray horse, he vaulted from the saddle and started to run, his legs working perfectly now.

A short while later, when he had heard the story (traded back and forth in garbled order between Tirel and Idalian), he finally reacted to his son's squirms and loosened his embrace. The army had caught up now and was marching past, smiling and saluting—and Tirel was very conscious of the picture he made. Laric smiled and rested his hand on his heir's shoulder as the volunteers from Snowcoves came by, cheering as loudly as they could.

"You didn't say where you got the horses, Idalian," Laric said.

"I—I'm sorry, your grace—I stole them."

"We *borrowed* them," Tirel corrected. "It was fun, Papa! In the middle of the night, sneaking into the barn and getting to know them first so they wouldn't be scared when we took them, we couldn't find the saddles at first and then a bridle broke and we had to find a rope, and it was almost daylight and the farmer almost caught us—"

Laric interrupted this breathless recital. "I hope you remember who you ... um ... borrowed them from, so we can pay for the use of the horses."

"Oh, yes, my lord," Idalian said earnestly. "I know exactly. Tirel wanted to do it the honorable way, and tell them who he was and let them help us of their own will. But I didn't think that was especially wise, in the circumstances." He cast an exasperated look at his charge. "It took me a while to convince him."

"I'm sorry," Tirel said, genuinely contrite. "I know I promised to do everything you said and not to question anything—but it just made me so *mad* to know I had to steal a horse like a common thief!"

"Well, don't make a habit of it," Arlis said, smiling. He looked up at the gloomy clouds overhead. "I hope this clears soon, so Rohannon can get word to Feruche that you're all right."

"Is that where Mama is?"

Laric shook his head. "She's still at Dragon's Rest with your new brother. Prince Arlis means that they'll send from Feruche to let her know." He couldn't help it; he caught the boy up in his arms again and hugged him tight. "We've been out of our minds with worry," he murmured into the thick black hair. "Thank the Goddess, you're safe."

"And thank Idalian, too," Tirel said loyally.

"But no thanks to Lord Yarin," the squire added. He turned to Arlis. "Your grace, pardon my way of putting it, but I'm so frustrated I could spit. What in all Hells has been happening?"

"It's a long story," Arlis answered with a sigh. "Let's find Rohannon and ride with him, and the two of us will try to get it straight for you."

*

It was early afternoon before Meiglan stitched together every scrap of her courage and demanded to see the High Warlord. The difficulty of getting her point across frustrated her nearly to tears. In the end, it was not her words or gestures or even the imperious tone of her voice that brought success; it was the High Warlord's simple curiosity about the source of the commotion at her tent.

When he was before her, she steeled herself and said, "I would ask a favor of you."

He canted his head slightly. "Favor? What is your need? You know that to walk outside is not permitted. As for food, it is made changed for you now—no spices." He ran his gaze down her figure. "No wondering that you are so small and have no sons, you do not make your health with good food. What can you want? All is comfort within this tent," he reminded her, gesturing. "More than all but my own."

"I have no complaints."

He considered. "No bath. There is not water."

"Within Stronghold there is," she said unwisely.

"And we carry it all here to you?" He snorted. "Or let you go there, to call up dragons from their sleeping stones?"

This made no sense to her, so she only shook her head. "I wasn't going to ask that."

"Not walking, not eating, not washing—what, then?" He gave an indulgent smile, the kind one would offer a child. "Ah, yes. A woman loves clothes. From Radzyn we take silks to make our wives smile. You wish other things to wear."

"It does have to do with clothing, but not for me." Meiglan consciously relaxed her hands that wanted to clench in tense fists. "You seem to know much about us. There is one thing you do not know, but you should—it has to do with what we must do when a prince is—when he dies."

"The burning? We know this. We share it."

"You send your dead to the sea. We send ours to the wind and the sky."

"And so?"

She had thought up her lies very carefully. He was no fool. Many times during the night she had despaired of making it all sound plausible—but then, toward dawn, she had remembered about Sioned.

"You seem determined to kill my husband. I've seen how many you are here, and you've said how many more will come." She met his gaze placidly. "In my lands, when a prince dies, his wife and daughters—if he's lucky enough to have daughters—use the time between his death and his ritual to sew a cloak for him. It's made of his color, and on it they embroider words recalling his great deeds in silver and gold thread."

"Yes! I understand!" He nodded vigorously. "So that when the cloak burns, his deeds are made into smoke and ash to rise on the wind with his soul!"

Meiglan thanked the Goddess for making this easier. She hadn't thought of it that way. "That's right. It's to remind the Goddess and the Father of Storms that he did many good things in his life, that he was powerful."

The High Warlord considered. "*She* must ache in her heart that this was not done for the old *Azhrei*."

There was only one *she* in the man's vocabulary; that had been obvious from the first day. He had talked of Sioned since, asking questions about her, praising her beauty and intelligence and strength (even though he regretted she had borne only one son). She fascinated him. Meiglan had no idea why.

"She made his cloak of her own hair," Meiglan said.

"Ah!" He reached within his shirt and pulled out a tiny leather pouch. From this he slowly extracted a long strand of red-gold hair, tied around the clasp of a topaz earring. Recognizing both, Meiglan blinked. "This was found by me," he announced. "Beside where he burned. I knew it hers, and his."

She said nothing as he tucked away his prizes.

"And now you wish for silk and thread? You wish to make a cloak for the new *Azhrei?*"

The corners of Meiglan's mouth lifted in Sioned's tiny, mocking smile. "No," she replied. "For you."

For a moment she didn't know whether he would laugh, choke, or strike her. Courage borrowed from memories made her go on.

"Your wives and daughters are far away. For all that I hate you for what you've done, you've treated me almost as a civilized man would. I should not like to see you burned without a proper—"

"Silent!" he bellowed.

Instantly four guards crowded into the open doorway of the tent. He spun on them and gave a guttural order. They withdrew.

"You will make this cloak!" he shouted at Meiglan. "But for *him!* You will sew onto it all the evils and crimes of your people done against mine! You will finish in seven days! In seven days I will send it to him and he will know that he will die!"

Meiglan cringed back, genuinely frightened. "No! I won't! He's not going to die!"

"He *will!* By the work of my hands! And by the work of *your* hands he will know it!"

He stalked out of the tent, calling commands that included a part of her name: *meig,* which meant *silk.*

She wilted into her chair, shaking badly. Seven days. What would happen in seven days? No, more—three days at least to get the cloak to Feruche, another three for the return of the courier. Unless he planned to begin the march within that time, and all his people converged on Skybowl—

—where Rislyn lay, fevered and sick—no, Lady Feylin was so clever, Rislyn would be all right.

Seven days? Ten? Pol would march from Feruche, how many days to Skybowl from Feruche? An army on foot moved more slowly than a rider on horseback. Two days to Skybowl from Feruche. Two days from Stronghold to Skybowl.

Twelve days? The eighty-second day of Winter?

Seven, ten, twelve, fifteen—her mind skittered, trying to make sense of how many and when. Pol had never been any good at numbers, either. . . .

She gave a start as shadows shifted on the tent wall; the guards had been doubled. Did they expect one woman to escape their whole army? She giggled, then clapped a hand over her mouth; the sound was not entirely sane. But something inside her went on laughing in honest delight, for he had not only sipped the wine, he had drained it to the dregs.

✳

Saumer's arrival had been anticipated by Tilal's sentries. He was escorted straight to the prince on the afternoon of the seventieth day of Winter, welcomed for himself as much as for the troops he brought with him. His reunion with the pearls, including the one he'd recovered himself, occasioned vast amusement: he pretended to be Lady Karanaya in the same circumstances, madly clutching the gems to his heart as he alternately gave thanks for returning them and railed that it had taken so long.

When their high spirits settled, Tilal brought out a map of Radzyn drawn from memory. Nyr held it for him, peering over the top as he detailed his plan.

Saumer, while not precisely battle-hardened, had fought enough engagements with the enemy to consider himself justified in saying, "I beg your grace's pardon, but—are you out of your mind?"

Nyr blinked wide eyes; Andrev boggled. Tilal only laughed.

"I'm hoping the Vellant'im will think so, too! It'll work. Now that we have you and Andrev both, it'll work just fine. Besides, Chay would roast me to a turn while Tobin basted me in cactus juice if a single stone of their castle gets chipped."

"Yes, but—"

"Take a little while to imagine it," the elder prince suggested. "Think how it'll look from their side of things."

Saumer tried it out in his head. "I still don't—"

"If you can't believe, then at least trust me." He rolled up the map. "I don't want to lose any more people," he added more seriously. "I'm fed up to the teeth with watching my soldiers die. Amiel agrees with me, and I'm sure Ludhil will, too. Get some rest, Saumer. Andrev will wake you at sunset."

Not that he slept. Not much, anyway. Over and over again he pictured the scene and his own part in it. As a warrior who had led an army, he had his doubts. As a Sunrunner who barely knew what he was doing, he had more than doubts.

Lord Andry's son arrived at dusk, as promised, to begin his lessons. They walked a little way from the camp, where bedrolls were being tied shut and armor was being donned— not in a hurry, but efficiently. With luck, everyone would sleep under Radzyn's capacious roofs tomorrow night. But between then and now lay a long night of Fire.

"From what you said about Faolain Lowland, Prince Saumer, you know how to burn things."

Andrev kicked at a rock beside the path—hardly dignifiable with the term, as it was merely a depression in the sand. This was not the true Desert, this coastal strip with goodish farmland a few measures away toward the sea, but even in the gloom Saumer could sense the bleak dunes.

"The cold sort of Fire is different," Andrev went on. "You just—I don't know, *think* it. Like this."

Saumer jumped as a tiny blaze appeared a few paces ahead of them. "It—um—certainly seems like fire," he said.

"But you can put your hand through it and not feel a thing. Try it."

"No, thanks. Let's see if I can manage it."

He thought about what a fire looked like, imagining a hearth back home at New Raetia. Red and orange and white-gold, flames licking upward, bending a little in a thin draft, leaping higher as they found fresh fuel—

Nothing happened.

"Nothing's happening," he told Andrev.

"Well, conjuring is hard," the boy admitted. "Some people aren't very good at it, even if they've studied for years." They paused on either side of his own cold Fire. "You just have to think about it really hard."

Once more Saumer tried, and once more he failed. "I don't think this is going to work, Andrev."

"We've only been at it a little while."

"But we don't have that much time. Maybe you'd better take the Fire part of it, and I'll join the regular troops."

"My lord says that you're to call Fire with me," Andrev replied stubbornly.

"I can't."

"That's not a word a Sunrunner uses—or a prince."

"Did your father tell you that?"

Andrev shrugged. "Are you somebody else who doesn't like my father?"

"I don't know him." Saumer was forthright about it. "But he's done things that—"

"He does what he has to!" the boy exclaimed, and the Fire blew higher and brighter with his vehemence. "Just like everybody else! If you're going to come to Goddess Keep and learn from him, you'd better start understanding that!"

"Settle down. Nobody's insulting him. But does everybody have to agree with him all the time?"

"Sunrunners do."

Saumer knew he shouldn't but he said it anyway. "You didn't, when you ran away to become Prince Tilal's squire."

Andrev drew himself up straight. "We're talking about Sunrunners. That was *family*—and not your concern."

He deserved the rebuke, but didn't acknowledge it. Not to a thirteen-year-old boy.

"Try cold Fire again," Andrev said.

By the time the combined armies—Syrenes, Ossetians, assorted soldiers from Princemarch, and Amiel's contingent of physicians—were ready to march, Saumer had succeeded only in frustrating himself and Andrev.

"No luck?" Tilal sighed. "Seems they'll get their beards singed after all." He turned to Nyr and Chegry, her attending physician. "I don't want to see either of you within ten measures of Radzyn until I send someone back for you. Is that understood?"

"Can't I watch?" Nyr complained.

"If you can turn into a *faradhi* in the next little while, you can watch," he told her. "Except for the fact that I chose tonight because the moons won't rise until nearly dawn."

"Men," Nyr announced, "are incredibly tedious. And bad-mannered, too. Andrev, take note and grow up nicer."

Close to four hundred men and women started for Radzyn, initially at a rather slow pace, for they paused now and again to gather up what scrub branches they could find along the way. It made for a messy and noisy march as every fifth person bundled the gleanings together with a rope. Long before midnight the foraging stopped and the bundles were tied to horses. When the army set off again across the sand, there was almost no sound at all. A few twigs rustled, boots shuffled softly, horses nickered—but no battle gear creaked and not a single bridle jingled. Everything had been oiled, muffled, or wrapped to stifle all sound.

At midnight the army began to split up into smaller groups of twenty and thirty each. These vanished into the Desert darkness. Tilal, surrounded by his own Athmyr guard, Andrev, and Saumer, took up a position on a hill overlooking Radzyn Keep at a three-measure remove. One part of his mind counted to itself, following the groups who had the longest walk. Another part worried for the two boys at his side and the hundreds of other lives that were his responsibility. Yet another reviewed his battle plans over and over, looking for flaws—and finding several. Still, his forty-five winters (Goddess, nearly forty-six now) had taught him that nothing was ever perfect before it started. Only afterward, when it was over and he had won.

And he *would* win. His heart was given over to bitter rage every time he thought about Radzyn, proudest jewel of the Desert, in the hands of the enemy. He had guested there a hundred times—as Rohan's squire, as the young *athri* of River Run, as Prince of Ossetia—and always as a loved kinsman and welcomed friend. To see the windows of its eight towers lit now by Vellanti torches was almost more than he could bear. It was worse than Stronghold—he knew it was gone but he hadn't seen it yet, and so did not have to believe. But Radzyn Keep was before him now. Had it been up to him, had it been his life alone, he would have gone through every room and slaughtered every Vellanti with his own sword.

"Think again, my lad! I won't have you getting blood all over my rugs!"

He swallowed sudden laughter at Tobin's imagined scold. Very well, then, he'd herd them all outside to the beach and kill them there, where the waves would wash away the stain.

If things worked as they should tonight, he wouldn't have to kill anybody personally at all. The sea would do it for him.

Pity. He owed them for Rihani.

Cunning against brute force, he mused, near the end of his counting and aware that those around him were restless. Saumer thought his plan insane. Nyr probably did, too, although she was too polite to say so. Amiel had been willing to go along with whatever Tilal told him to do. As for Ludhil—it would be interesting to see how Chadric's bookish elder son had changed after two seasons of living in the hills and raiding Vellanti camps.

Chadric's bookish younger son came to mind, and Tilal wondered briefly what was going on up in Firon these days. The last time Andrev had asked for news, none had been available. Clouds. Poor Sunrunners. He was glad he wasn't one.

Which led him to think of his daughter, Sioneva. Athmyr was locked up tight, the court Sunrunner gone back to Goddess Keep. But Andry knew how to reach Sioneva. If anything happened—

It wouldn't. Cunning against brute force, he reminded himself. The Vellant'im had done very well with the latter, but were sadly deficient in the former. Look how they'd lost at Swalekeep.

And Swalekeep hadn't even mattered. He knew that now. For that alone, every one of the whoresons deserved a slow and painful death. Swalekeep meant nothing to them. It had been a feint, just as Goddess Keep and New Raetia and Graypearl and marching up the rivers had been. Nothing mattered but the Desert.

So many dead. So much destroyed. It would take years to recover—for those who made it through this next year.

Ossetia had not been ravaged as Gilad and Syr and parts of Grib had been, but Ossetia could not feed everyone. And Tilal was damned if he'd give so much as a rotten apple to Cabar or Velden.

Ah, but that wasn't right. Neither of those princes would suffer in a famine. It was their people who would starve. And, truth to tell, their sons and daughters had shown courage and honor enough for ten of their craven fathers. Amiel had defied Cabar and come to war; poor crippled Elsen had done the same by riding to Goddess Keep (though he'd best watch his back, Tilal thought sourly). Elsen's wife Selante, Amiel's sister, had supported her husband's decision to answer the *faradhi* summons and shamed Velden into letting him go. And as for Norian of Grib—word was that she, too, was at Goddess Keep, helping her brother and furious with their father for his cowardice.

Tilal sighed softly. It seemed he'd have to help Velden and Cabar. How annoying. Then he cheered up; Pol doubtless had something exquisite in mind for them. Tilal could hardly wait.

An alarm sounded in his head, signaling that the current bout of waiting was over. No one had ridden back breathless and bloodied to tell of encounters with Vellanti sentries; no one stirred but the usual guards walking Radzyn's walls and towers. The night was quiet, serene.

That was about to change.

"Prince Saumer, Lord Andrev," he murmured.

The formality straightened them up in their saddles. "Yes, your grace," each replied.

"You have the map in your minds. Everyone should be in position by now." He smiled a little in the darkness. "Please try not to incinerate any stragglers, Saumer."

"I'll try, my lord."

They were on a hill to the west-southwest of Radzyn Keep. Between them and it were pastures empty of horses and a few barns probably just as empty. Tilal didn't dare risk that—Chay would run him through if he was wrong. Beyond the keep was the small port town, and he couldn't be sure who might or might not be in those buildings, either.

So, deprived of interesting things to burn, Tilal had organized his own little bonfires.

Andrev's work would be the hardest. All Saumer had to do was ignite one by one the piles of brush gathered for his convenience—the troops had been warned to back away a quarter of a measure after placing them, since the inexperienced Sunrunner would be working in the dark. Andrev, however, must augment those Fires with cold ones of his own, jumping from place to place, advancing ahead of the soldiers here, extinguishing the flames to move them to some other spot. Tilal's vision had been of an army of Fire marching in on Radzyn, bringing them out of the castle if he was lucky—and if he was luckier, they would panic and move down to the beach.

For at the first sign of Fire, Amiel and Ludhil would sail their two laden ships around from hidden shelter behind one of the Small Islands. It would take a little while, but soon enough they would appear in the harbor, and the Vellant'im would do one of two things: jump in their longboats and go out to them, or cheer the arrival and expect them to come ashore and join the festivities.

Either way, they would come out of Radzyn then if the Fires hadn't already brought them out. Reinforcements would make them think a victory guaranteed; if they had already been unnerved, they would want to escape. In the first instance they would be sorely disappointed. In the second, they would be shot down in their longboats from on board ship.

Tilal supposed it *was* crazy. But he couldn't retake Radzyn by brute force. He didn't have the troops for it. Radzyn was a formidable objective designed to daunt even the most determined commander. The Vellant'im had won the first time due to sheer numbers, and because Chay's duty had been to protect Rohan, not the castle. But Tilal could not throw soldiers against the walls until the walls came down; he'd be here until next Summer. And Chay really *would* kill him if he tried it—for colossal stupidity if nothing else.

So, cunning. And because cunning and insanity were close kin. . . .

He saw the first fires. Saumer's. Thirty of them, in an arc about two measures from the keep, they lit with slow, almost stately regularity. Tilal pulled out the long-lens from his belt and had another look at the walls. Yes, they'd noticed. He smiled.

Those who had stealthily left their bundles of brushwood and scrub had gotten well out of range. Tilal knew because none of the Fires sprouted smaller ones that moved. What he saw now, with the lens tucked away for the moment, was Andrev's work—flames the size of a small cottage seeming to break off from first one and then the other of Saumer's bonfires. They moved forward, shifting quickly and without pattern, and if Tilal hadn't known better he would have sworn they were being set by some invisible being that kept changing its mind.

They had *really* noticed within Radzyn now. Lights blazed all over the keep. Tilal chuckled to himself.

"We seem to have woken them up," he said. "Wait a while, Saumer, before you light the nearer ones. I want them to get the full effect."

Using the long-lens once more, he peered out to sea. No, not quite yet. Give it another little while. Amiel and Ludhil had stationed lookouts on the island to tell them exactly when to hoist sail, but it would take some time.

Timing, of course, was crucial—and would have been impossible without the astonishing revelation that Princess Iliena was a Sunrunner. Tilal wondered how Sioned had broken it to her in such a way that her understandable stupefaction was pushed aside in favor of making herself useful. Perhaps she had reacted as Sioneva had, with wonder and delight. Tilal hoped she hadn't been like Alasen, and afraid.

Well, that didn't much matter to him right now. Andrev had told Sioned, and Sioned had told Iliena, what was planned for this night. *Our web of Sunrunners spinning light gets bigger all the time . . . Hells, some days it must be hard for them not to bump into each other, the way Sioned and Maarken bumped into that dragon years ago. . . .*

Turning back to Radzyn, he caught his breath. The walls were crammed with soldiers now. Some large, bulky personage in white—a nightshirt, Tilal thought, until he saw the glint of elaborate gold embroidery on the robe—stood atop the tallest tower. He flung his arms up to the sky, gesturing madly.

"Saumer! Now!"

Fuel sneaked in even closer—the riskiest job, Goddess blessing that it had been accomplished without incident—began to light. Andrev's Fire leaped and danced all over the place, making it seem in the darkness and at a distance as if the arc of flames teased the castle.

Vellant'im poured out of the gates, swords aloft.

"Here we go," Tilal muttered. Giving the lens to one of the three Ossetians detailed to guard Andrev, he turned to Saumer. "Nice work. Let's go finish it before we can't see for the smoke."

The young man grinned from ear to ear. "At once, my lord!"

Saumer was thrilled by the prospect of a fight. Tilal was angry with the enemy for not succumbing to terror and fleeing. But his disappointment was premature—for it was not the soldiers of Syr and Princemarch and Ossetia and the physicians of the Giladan school that the Vellant'im fought. It was the Fire.

They cried *"Azhev'im!"* with one voice as they ran for the flames, swords slashing like scythes. Tilal could hear them even over his horse's hoofbeats and even at this distance. Hundreds and hundreds of them, racing every which way to battle the Fires as if they were alive. They showed no discipline, no cohesion—and the first one Tilal cut down didn't even have gold in his beard. Half of them weren't even warriors. Even fewer wore armor. Tilal didn't know who or what they were, and didn't care. He killed them as they ran. And run they did, intent on killing the Fires.

Too easy, he told himself, jerking his sword from yet another unprotected chest. Much too easy. Saumer was over there having himself a wonderful time, laughing uproariously and slicing off heads neat as melons on poles in the practice yard. No conflict there, Tilal thought; no misgivings, just honest enjoyment of battle skills. Not like his own Rihani.

He pushed the grief aside and reined in, pausing to lop off a sword arm that dared come too close to his horse's neck. The big Kadari beast kicked out with hind legs, making Tilal lurch forward in the saddle. He slapped the stallion's neck a good one, yanking his head around. Things were well in hand here. He wanted a look at the beaches.

Galloping to the end of the fiery arc Saumer had first set, he squinted out to sea through thin, drifting smoke. Nothing—nothing—*there!* Two full sets of white sails, just coming around the headland at a dangerous speed. He urged his horse up a rise, and yelped with delight as a stream of white-robed Vellant'im poured from Radzyn's seaside postern gates.

"Lovely, lovely," Tilal crooned. "Yes, get into the boats, you cowardly bastards—row like all Hells to where you'll be safe while others do your fighting for you against the Dragon Fires!"

When the sword got him in the side, all he had time to think was that Elsen at Goddess Keep wasn't the only one who needed to watch his back.

CHAPTER SIXTEEN

Pol watched as long as the sunset lasted. Meiglan sat just outside a small white tent, a length of violet silk spilling over her lap and the arm of her chair. Her fingers plied silver needle and golden thread rhythmically, swiftly, without mistakes even as the light began to fail. She paused only to run more thread through the needle, smooth the double strand between her fingertips, and knot the end with a quick twist.

He had seen her do this so often. So many quiet evenings in their chambers, while he read aloud to the girls before the hearthfire, her clever fingers had taken a million stitches in a hundred different patterns on silk and velvet and tapestry wool. He watched now as she gathered another section of cloth into her hands, bit off another length of thread, began another delicate golden wreath. She looked so young, fair head bent over her embroidery, fingers stitching in and out, silver and gold. Young and beautiful and so fragile.

He hadn't seen her since she'd left Feruche twenty-three days ago. He'd looked—Goddess knew, he had searched frantically on any light available—but until today she had been under cover of clouds, or trees, or this white tent.

Meggie, he called. *Meggie, I'm here with you, I'm here—*

But she would never hear him, never feel his presence on the waning light. Knowing that, he could tell her what he could never tell her aloud: *I'm sorry. Forgive me, Meggie, I didn't do it to hurt you. I would never hurt you.*

He knew he should leave. With each moment he must weave the thinning rays a little more strongly in order to stay. But he hadn't seen her in so long.

I love you, Meiglan. What happened had nothing to do with you.

The real Hell of it was that even if he did tell her, there would be no accusations, no blame, no anger. No matter what truths he told—or what lies—whatever he did or didn't do or say, she would always love him with the same undemanding trust. He would never see forgiveness in her eyes— because in her eyes, he could never do anything she would have to forgive.

It won't happen again. I swear it. I do *love you.*

She glanced up. Her face was thinner and very pale, yet oddly serene. Oddly secretive. She gathered up the little basket of thread and the rich folds of violet silk, and went back inside the tent.

Tracing the remaining light back to Feruche, he found his mother standing at his side, watching him.

"Meiglan?" she asked.

He raked wind-tousled hair from his face and nodded.

"I saw it in your eyes." As he turned for the stairs down from the battlements, she added, "No, wait a moment. Tell me what you saw."

He shrugged. "Meiglan. Sitting outside that white tent— you were right about that, by the way. Of course, you usually are."

Sioned ignored the bitterness. "Is she all right?" An instant later she shook her head. "I'm sorry. Stupid question. They've had her for—what is it, thirteen days now?"

"Fourteen."

"Pol—I'm sorry for what I said the other day. To you and Sionell. It was . . . malicious and cruel."

"Yes. It was."

"It's only that I love you—*all* of you."

"I know. Come inside, it's getting chilly."

They descended half a flight in silence before she spoke again.

"Do you sleep at all?"

"It's not really sleep—more like snuffing a candle."

"You get that from your father. He had the lucky kind of body that knew when it needed rest, and took it whether his mind liked it or not. A useful quality in a prince." She paused. "Tilal's inside Radzyn."

"What?"

"He attacked, if you can call it that, last midnight. Saumer wasn't clear on the details. Andry will have gotten more of it from Andrev, so we should hear most of the story over dinner." She took his arm and coaxed him to continue downstairs. "Tilal was wounded. But he's got at least a hundred physicians to fret over him, and Saumer didn't seem worried. There were very few losses, thank the Goddess. But the Vellant'im died almost to a man—in the pastures outside the keep and when they tried to get to the ships from Graypearl. Those ships, you see, were commanded by Amiel and Ludhil."

Pol took a couple of steadying breaths, excitement beginning to race through him. "Does Chay know?"

"I told him before I came up to find you." She smiled. "He looks twenty years younger."

"I don't doubt it. So there won't be so many thousands of them marching on Skybowl—if Tilal wasn't already a prince, I'd make him one for this!"

"Well, I'm sure you'll think of something appropriate to reward him for doing what he would have done anyway."

"Don't start," he warned, smiling down at her. "It's moving toward us now, Mother—we're going to win this. We'll meet them at Skybowl and slaughter every one of them—all except the High Warlord. *Him* I intend to keep alive for a very long time."

She said nothing. He sighed his exasperation and hugged her around the shoulders.

"I know, I know. I've got half the course ahead of me, and the worst of the jumps, before I get to the finish. But I'm going to win, Mother. You can feel it, too, can't you?"

"Yes." She smiled. "Yes, Pol. I can feel it."

They resumed their descent, and when they reached the lower corridor Pol said, "I kept asking myself what Father would have done. I kept getting no answer. Do you know, I never saw him with a sword in his hand except at ceremonies—and even though it wasn't the real one, the battle one, he hated the feel of it. I could always see that in his eyes. And when he handed me his own sword that day—I've been thinking that maybe that was his answer."

"And?"

"It's not. Not the whole answer, anyway. I've spent so much time being angry at him for never teaching me anything that's useful to me now that I forgot all that he *did* teach me. I worshiped him for being wise and kind and strong and everything a High Prince ought to be. What I kept forgetting is how his mind worked."

Sioned leaned her cheek to his shoulder as they walked down a hallway. "Not the sword, but the brain behind it."

"Exactly! And what I have to do is fashion a victory that will let me put that sword away again, just as he did."

She hesitated, then murmured, "I lost the sunlight when he died, Pol. It was so bright for so long. . . ." She sighed. "I've been living in shadows ever since. Sometimes, for that brief time, in absolute darkness."

He stopped walking and put both arms around her. "Don't think about it. That's all over."

"Yes. Over. And there's still light enough, you know." She touched his face, the scar on his cheek that was the near-twin of the one on her own. "It's hard for you, I know—having to light such darkness as this. But you do. More and more. And you *will* win, my son. By the stars I Named you for, you'll win."

*

The snowstorms had begun slyly, a sprinkling of fat, soft flakes in late afternoon. By sunset—or what Arlis thought might be sunset; who could tell?—men and horses were fighting a relentless white wind that thickened every moment.

Either his luck had run out or he had reached the regions where even the Goddess' sunlight bowed to the Storm Father. And it seemed the current whim was to bury a whole army in snow, presumably for the fun of it.

He didn't bother asking Laric where they were. Laric didn't know any better than he did. The world gradually darkened and night became a certainty instead of a threat. Arlis wiped his eyes clear of snow, peering over his horse's hanging head in search of shelter. Futile, of course; all Firon was one gigantic storm. And if he didn't find refuge soon, he would command an army of ice sculptures.

The tactics of the Desert were worthless here. Hunkering down in a cloak to form an air pocket until the wind died and one could dig out wouldn't work. Suffocation wasn't the problem. Freezing to death was. They had to keep moving. But every step was slower, costlier, more and more begrudged by the storm.

"My lord! Prince Arlis!"

He turned his head stiffly, trying to identify the white-shrouded rider at his side. Had Rohannon truly grown so tall recently? Maarken and Hollis wouldn't know him. Swirling snow cleared and Arlis felt foolish. It was Laric's squire who shouted for his attention. Which wasn't what it should have been; his brains must be freezing solid along with the rest of him. Prying icy cloth from his mouth and nose, he yelled back, "What?"

"There, my lord—" Idalian pointed ahead and to the left.

Arlis saw nothing, and said so.

"A light, my lord!" The young man got a faceful of driven snow and coughed. "I can just barely see it!"

"I can't—but lead on!"

Though it seemed forever, finally Arlis saw it, too. One light, then several, then a whole line of them like tiny candles in a distant window. How, in the Name of the Goddess, did they keep torches burning in this wind? He decided he'd ask some year when he was warm again and certain that his lips wouldn't crack and fall off like icicles.

A day past forever, someone bundled in clothing enough for an entire family appeared before him. He saw now that the torch was made of a steel rod supporting a small bowl of oil, surmounted by a glass shade to protect the flame. Nice, he told himself numbly; he'd order a hundred of them for windy days at Zaldivar.

"Only a little way to the village, your grace!"

He was fairly sure that was the message. It didn't much matter. Though it had occurred to him that these might be *diarmadh'im,* Yarin's kin and his own enemies, given the choice of being killed by the storm or being killed by sorcery, there was no contest. At least with the latter, there was the probability of getting warm first.

But how had this person known to call him "your grace"?

The village nested in the curve of a little hill. The wind was not so fierce here, nor the snow so thick, and he saw cottages and a communal barn. A small building off to one side looked like a hunting lodge. A very penurious *athri*'s hunting lodge, but he wasn't disposed to argue. If it had a hearth, he was prepared to adore it.

"We'll stable the horses with our animals! Come down now, your grace, come within!"

Sounded like a fine idea. A short while later he was walking through the lodge's door, and someone put a cup of mulled wine into his hand.

"Welcome to Pimanost."

He drank, completely missing whatever was said to Laric when he came in. The wine burned his tongue and the spice-laden steam made his eyes water. It felt glorious.

Laric's teeth still chattered. "Thank you for f–finding us. We're v–very grateful. But how did you know to look?"

Arlis tensed. This was the question that needed answering. In the warmth of the lodge—wood secured against the wind by brown daub, one large room and a half-loft above it for sleeping—he was beginning to sweat, and not just from the weight of layers of clothes.

There were six people present besides himself and Laric. Dark-skinned, dark-haired Fironese all, with tip-tilted black eyes. None of them answered Laric's question. Idalian, just now coming in the door with Tirel hoisted in one arm, did.

"You!" he exclaimed.

"Aldiar?" Tirel said, peering at a slight, thin-faced young person who brushed straggly hair back and shrugged.

The squire handed the child to Laric and placed himself protectively between them and Aldiar. "Don't believe a word he says, my lord! He's Yarin's kinsman, he's—"

"Would I have saved you from the storm only to kill you now?" The youth stamped an impatient foot. "I've been following you ever since you left Balarat. Who do you think kept that farm quiet so you could steal the horses? And a clumsy long time you took about it, too!"

Idalian started forward, fists clenched. Laric shook his head. "No. Let's hear him out."

Aldiar inclined his head as if this were the Princes Hall at Dragon's Rest, and he the High Prince. "Thank you, your grace. It's not very complicated. When Idalian and the little prince found you, I started back. But I saw this storm blowing up and I knew it would be a bad one. So I came here, hoping you would, too. When you didn't arrive. . . ." He shrugged. "I went looking for you."

"I'll just bet you did!" Idalian cried. "My lord, I've told you about Aldiar. He's *diarmadhi!*"

"So," said Laric quietly, "is my wife."

Arlis cleared his throat, judging it was time to intervene. "Whatever and whoever anybody is, *I'm* glad to be out of that storm. Aldiar, my thanks to you and the good people of

Pimanost. I confess I've never heard of it, but your 'hill of storms' is aptly named." He used the smile that had helped win him his wife, and it worked on these folk almost as well as it had on Demalia. Granted, they didn't throw themselves into his arms, but they did smile back. "With Prince Laric's permission, I propose to send you a hundred bottles of my best wine every year from now on to replace all that I'm going to drink in keeping warm." He held out his empty cup. "I'd love to make a start on it right now."

Wine was poured, and everyone gathered around the trestle table that dominated the lodge. Idalian placed himself between his princes and Aldiar, who noted it with another little shrug. The five other people were introduced—a brother and sister who were the village elders, plus their spouses, and a middle-aged worthy who was caretaker of the lodge. His wife was in the shed attached at the back, cobbling together a meal.

It was instantly clear that they considered Laric their true prince. It wasn't that none of them sat until he did, or that all of them bowed low when Aldiar named them. Arlis had spent enough of his youth determining which Kierstian notables despised him for being half-Iseli, and which Iseli for being half-Kierstian, to know sincere regard when he saw it. He sat among them with perfect calm, certain that he and his companions would not all be murdered in their beds this night or any other. Not by these folk.

This young kinsman of Yarin's though . . . Arlis watched him now and again as food was brought in and more wine poured. Fair-spoken, except when addressing Idalian, reasonable, with good manners and a definite presence about him, yet there was something about Aldiar that was not quite what it seemed.

The delegation from Pimanost shared wine with them for hospitality's sake, but politely declined to stay and eat. They told Laric that his soldiers and horses would be well cared for, accepted his thanks, wished him a pleasant night, and departed, disagreeing among themselves on how long the storm might last. Arlis heard estimates of anywhere from midmorning tomorrow to another four or five days. "Storm Hill," for certain. Sighing fatalistically, he cut another slice of herbed bread and washed it down with wine.

Aldiar was explaining that not everyone agreed with Yarin's actions, as had been demonstrated at Snowcoves. As he had tried to tell Idalian, he added with a disgusted glance in the squire's direction.

"You came to Balarat when he took it over," Idalian countered. "He set you to watch me by having me teach you knives and swords—"

"And you're as rotten as a swordsman as you are a horse thief," Aldiar shot back.

Idalian sprang up from the table, his temper as well as his muscles warmed by the wine. Aldiar jumped to his feet, hand at his belt-knife.

Which wasn't there.

"Looking for this?" Idalian taunted, holding up a fine, sharp blade.

"Give it back!" Aldiar demanded.

"Where do you want it—in your throat or in your guts?"

"Stop it!" Laric commanded. "Sit down, both of you. Idalian, apologize for your rudeness. And you, Aldiar, apologize for insulting skills you well know to be exceptional."

After a moment's defiance, each muttered something that might have been "I'm sorry" and sat down.

Laric said, "Idalian is my squire—and tomorrow morning will be made a knight in this hall, in front of as many as can be packed in here."

The young man's eyes widened in surprise.

Ignoring him, the prince continued, "Any insult to him is an insult to me. Is that understood?"

"Yes, my lord."

For the second time Arlis interposed. "If you're Yarin's blood-kin, then you're Prince Laric's as well, by marriage. And tomorrow he'll be in need of another squire."

Aldiar's big black eyes narrowed. "You'd do that, my lord? Take me on, knowing who and what I am?"

"I believe I would," Laric answered slowly. "Informally, perhaps."

"But, Papa," Tirel piped up, "there won't be an oath or anything!"

If Aldiar had a sense of honor, a formal swearing would engage it and breaking the vow would be punishable by the laws of Firon and the High Prince's Writ. If he didn't, then no oath would bind him. Laric was offering to trust Aldiar without any oath at all—a sign of faith that made Arlis nervous. Whereas keeping a sorcerer in sight was a very good idea, trusting him was a very bad one.

"However you like, my lord," the sorcerer was saying. "I will swear or not, as you please. Not because it means so little to me, but because I could not be more your servant than I am now."

Prettily said, Arlis thought. Perhaps *too* prettily.

Idalian was coming out of his shock. "My lord—I did nothing to deserve—I haven't been in a battle!"

"Neither had I," Arlis said cheerfully, "when the High Prince knighted me. Nor any of the rest of us, either."

"Getting my son out of Balarat was battle enough for anyone," said Laric.

"But—"

Tirel squirmed. "Oh, hush up, Idalian! If Papa hadn't, I would've! I'm a prince, too!" He eyed Aldiar. "You can be *my* squire, if you like. I'm too young for an oath to be legal. Did we tell you about that, Papa? The paper Uncle Yarin made me sign?"

"Yes, and you were very clever." He glanced at Aldiar. "Swear to my son, then, as your blood-kin as well as your future prince."

"Doubly binding," Idalian muttered, "not that *that* signifies." He buried his nose in his winecup.

Aldiar cast him a fulminating look, then responded, "If that's your wish, my lord, then I shall become Prince Tirel's squire tomorrow—or will that interfere with the honors accorded Lord Idalian?"

Arlis had had enough. "Speaking of squires, I seem to have misplaced my own. Has anyone seen Rohannon?"

"He's probably looking after the horses—a true grandson of Chaynal of Radzyn." Laric smiled.

Idalian bundled himself in his cloak and started for the door. "I'll go find him."

Aldiar stepped forward. "My knife?"

Faster than the eye could trace, Idalian whirled and flicked his wrist. Silver flashed in firelight. An instant later, the blade was quivering in the wooden floor a precise fingerspan from Aldiar's left boot.

"Your knife," Idalian said, and stalked out.

The sorcerer gulped hard and bent to retrieve his property. When he straightened, his face was almost—almost—bland.

"There's a lot to talk about," he said. "And plenty of time to do it in. This storm looks likely to last at least three days."

"And at Balarat?" Laric asked.

"They won't be going anywhere, either."

"What happened when Uncle Yarin found out we were gone?" Tirel asked.

"I don't know—I wasn't there. But I can imagine he wasn't all that happy about it." Aldiar grinned suddenly, his mouth stretching from one side of his narrow, beardless face to the other. "I hope he had a fit and choked on it."

"Me, too," Tirel declared. "You're not my squire yet, but could you please find me somewhere to sleep? I'm tired."

"You must be," Laric observed. "Actually *asking* to be put to bed! Aldiar, if you wouldn't mind—? We'll talk tomorrow."

The two boys climbed the ladder to the loft. Arlis poured more wine and said, "So you trust him."

"He could have let the storm have us."

"Maybe we're being led to a more interesting slaughter."

Laric regarded him thoughtfully. "What don't you like about him?"

"I don't know. It's nothing I can grasp. Just an odd feeling—" He glanced around as cold air blasted through the opened door. "Ah, Rohannon! Come thaw out. This is no place for a Desert lord's son."

"Or a Sunrunner, my lord. Everyone's settled," the squire reported as Idalian helped him off with his cloak and outer tunics. Rohannon's fingers were practically frozen to his gloves. "The horses are a bit crowded, though—that barn's not built for so many."

"Warmer with more bodies packed in. Have some wine." He poured and slid the cup across the trestle table. Rohannon picked it up, thanked him, and took it over to the fire.

"Tell us more about Aldiar," Laric said to Idalian, who sat opposite him and frowned. "Everything he ever said to you."

"Well," the young man began.

"What are you doing?" a sharp voice called from the direction of the ladder. They all turned, including Rohannon, so startled that he dropped the small pouch in his hand. "Is that what I think it is, Sunrunner?" Aldiar demanded.

Rohannon was on his knees by the hearth, scraping together scattered dry leaves. There was something desperate, almost frantic, about the movement that brought Arlis to his feet. Aldiar was at Rohannon's side, shaking his arm.

"No—let me—stop it, get away—"

The sorcerer grabbed the Sunrunner's head in both dark hands. Turning Rohannon's face toward the light, Aldiar sucked in a breath as pale eyes flinched from the brightness of the fire.

"By the Nameless One," he breathed. "How long have you been taking it? How much each time?"

"What in all Hells—?" Arlis asked.

Rohannon jerked away. He scrabbled at the wooden floor again, trying to get all the little leaves up from between the cracks. "Damn you, look what you've done!"

"You idiot—look at *yourself!* See what *you're* doing! Do you want to be like this the rest of your life?"

"Rohannon!" Arlis snapped. "Explain this!"

"He can't," Aldiar said over his shoulder. Rising, he rubbed his face with both hands, then faced the princes. "It's *dranath.* You must know what it does when it's taken too often. He's been taking it for quite some time, I'd say. You only have to look at him to know it—the light hurts his eyes, and see how he's—oh, for the Goddess' sake, leave it!" he cried.

Arlis went to them, knelt beside Rohannon, gently drew him up. "Is this true?" he asked quietly.

"It was necessary." His gaze strayed to the floor where the little pouch lay spilled. "I had to. I didn't know enough—I wasn't strong enough."

"So you—" Arlis swallowed hard. "Even I heard the story of what it did to your mother."

"It didn't take that long to cure her of it—"

"Aldiar?" Arlis looked at the boy.

"I can try. Segev kept her short, you see—so that when he came with wine or taze and the *dranath* in it, she'd associate feeling better with his presence. So all in all, she didn't have that much. As for him—" He shrugged. "I don't know how much he's been taking."

"How do you know so much about my mother?" Rohannon exclaimed.

"We didn't, until after. It didn't take much wit to figure it out—especially as Lady Hollis survived."

Arlis didn't dare ask whether or not Lady Hollis' son would.

"Do what you can. Do all you know to do," he said, more

numb with inner cold than he'd been when the snow had numbed his body.

"You're not going to *trust* him!" Idalian strode forward, appalled.

Sick with guilt, Arlis couldn't speak. Rohannon was his squire and his responsibility, sworn by oaths as solemn and binding on him as they were on the boy. Maarken and Hollis had given their only son into his keeping. Arlis had failed the three of them, Rohannon most of all.

He had not questioned an untutored Sunrunner's performance of tasks he shouldn't have known how to do. He had taken advantage of the prodigy, assuming that thanks to Rohannon's inherited gifts such strength came easily, naturally. He hadn't even questioned how a Sunrunner could sail the open sea without being violently ill. How was he to know it was *dranath* that had done it, *dranath* that had lent power and spared Rohannon the *faradhi* weakness? *Dranath*, the precious herb that cured Plague, the terrible drug that augmented gifts and became an addiction. The sorcerer's herb, forbidden to Sunrunners.

He was about to give a Sunrunner's life into a sorcerer's hands.

Laric answered softly, "What choice is there? None. Aldiar, help him."

"Yes, my lord. I'll try."

"You'd better do more than 'try,' " Idalian threatened.

"Then you'd better be prepared to help me," came the grim reply. "This isn't going to be easy on anybody."

Rohannon glared at them all. "I don't need anybody's help!"

"Shut up!" Arlis commanded. "You'll do as you're told. Aldiar, he's in your hands." And he thanked the Goddess for the snowstorm, praying that it would last a long time; it would prevent Maarken and Hollis from looking for their son.

✳

Maarken and Chay had finished presenting four different battle plans on four different maps spread out on the Attic table. It had been a long afternoon, and stomachs were beginning to rumble. When Pol's gave a particularly loud growl, Chay laughed, rolled up the maps, and told him it was time to feed the inner dragon.

Sioned and Meath came in with Alasen, the latter smiling as she said, "There's a rumor of a spectacular meal—somebody came back with three deer this morning and the cook locked the kitchen door at noon."

"Not three does, I hope," said Hollis, who had been taking notes during the strategy session.

"Of course not," Maarken told her. "That law goes back to—well, I've forgotten his name, but he was an ancestor and forbade killing a fallow doe even if you were starving."

"Yes," Sioned agreed, "but doing so doesn't get your tongue cut out anymore—making sure that fresh venison was the last meal you truly enjoyed."

"I thought it was the left ear that got lopped," Chay said. "Or maybe the right."

"If it was the left hand, I'd be safe," Maarken said, and grinned widely as the others reacted.

"Don't be morbid," Sioned scolded. "From what I know about your delightful ancestors, they'd only take the other one, and then how would you make love to your wife?"

"Creatively."

"As ever," Hollis added, her eyes dancing.

"Might have been the nose," Chay mused. "I forget."

Alasen gave an elaborate shudder. "Can we forget this conversation, please?"

"Don't worry," Maarken smiled. "All we do nowadays is fine the culprit the price of a doe and twin fawns."

"Speaking of twins," Alasen said firmly. "I think someone ought to go down to Skybowl and bring Rislyn here. For her sake and for Jihan's."

Pol glanced up from Hollis' notes. "Oh, no. Nobody but the hunting parties sets foot out of Feruche *or* Skybowl until we've got our plans worked out."

"Rislyn needs her sister—and her father," Alasen argued. "It's not that far, only two days' ride. We could send a good-sized troop for protection. If she's well enough in the next few days—"

"I'll go," Meath offered. "I've really been of no use here, except for teaching—Andry's work, now."

"What's my work?" Andry asked as he came in the open door. "Besides being so hopeless at battle strategy that the rest of you seem even smarter?"

"Teaching Sunrunning to the children," Maarken said.

"In between watching Meig yawn in my face," Andry replied with a grin. "I think I'm boring him."

Alasen tapped Pol's shoulder to get his attention. "Meath could show Rislyn a few things on the way back from Skybowl, you know."

Slow wonderment spread across their faces. Alasen shook her head.

"Sunrunners! You see what happens from the Sunrise Water to Kierst-Isel, but you never see the obvious!"

"Good Goddess—you're right," Andry murmured at last.

"I didn't realize," said Maarken. "Any more than I did about Mother."

Sioned was nodding. "The world doesn't have to be completely dark for Rislyn. She has another way of seeing, just as Tobin has another way of speaking."

"We're all idiots," Pol exclaimed. "Except you, Alasen. You're brilliant!"

"Thank you, your grace," she replied demurely. "Then you'll send Meath down to Skybowl?"

"I'll go myself."

"I don't think so," said Ruala from the doorway. She was leaning against the carved frame, arms folded, evidently having been there listening for some time. "It's an excellent idea, bringing Rislyn here and so forth, but you're going to have other things to do."

Pol groaned. "Not more Merida! By all the Hells that ever—"

"No. You have guests, Pol." She wore an odd expression, compounded of bemusement and apprehension. "You specifically. They're asking for the *Azhrei*. But I'll let their escort tell it."

To general astonishment, Betheyn and Isriam walked in. Chay and Maarken and Andry greeted Sorin's Chosen while Sioned and Pol welcomed Rohan's former squire, now knighted. But the exchanges were brief; everyone had questions.

Riyan got his in first. "What about those pestilential merchants?"

Beth dismissed them with a wave of her hand. "I made Tormichin and Nemthe jointly responsible at Chaldona. If they murder each other, then they murder each other."

"But they won't," Isriam added. "They'd have to share a

pyre. Don't think we haven't been tempted, my lady and I, to arrange it!"

Beth smiled at him. "Don't remind me!" She found Pol with her gaze, sobering. "I don't care what they do to each other. This is more important."

"And 'this' might be—?" Pol asked.

"It's kind of hard to explain." Isriam scratched at his lank, dusty hair, caught himself at it, and grimaced. "Your pardon, ladies. Everyone thinks Chaldona is a lovely manor. Unfortunately, all sorts of tiny livestock agree."

"Talk to Master Evarin," Andry said. "He'll give you something to put in your bath—later. Beth, I'm glad to see you, but why are you here?"

"I could ask the same thing of you," she replied. "Later. For now—well, several days ago we had visitors."

"Exactly ninety-nine," Isriam added. "They made sure I told you that, your grace," he directed at Pol. "Nine of them came with us. They're *diarmadhi*."

Everyone looked at Andry. Andry arched both brows and looked at Pol. Pol said, "What do they want?"

"Nothing." Betheyne shrugged. "They're offering their support in this war. I know, I know—I didn't believe them, either. They scared me half to death, if you want the truth. But there were two things about them that made us hear them out. First, they were unarmed."

"Would a sorcerer need a sword?" Chay pointed out.

"Yes, but—the other thing was what convinced me. Each wears steel—an earring newly placed, so the wound isn't closed up yet. And they can't do their spells if there's iron in contact with their blood, isn't that right?"

Meath, who had experienced what happened when steel pierced a Sunrunner's flesh during a working, nodded emphatically. "Exactly right. So we're safe enough from them."

"Are we?" Andry asked softly. "It would cause terrible pain, but they'd be capable of doing whatever they wanted."

"It was a sign of good faith," Beth told them.

"From a sorcerer?"

"There's more than one kind," she said. "Isriam and I have spoken at length with these nine, and what they've said makes sense."

"It's probably pretty much what we've been hearing from Princess Naydra," Hollis commented. "Those of Mireva's faction are opposed by others who've kept them in check over schemes we never even heard about."

"Because they never existed," Andry said. "It's laughably easy to talk of saving us from plots no one can prove one way or the other."

Beth looked up into his eyes. "I believe they're telling the truth, Andry."

"So do I," Pol said. "Ruala, are they waiting outside? Good. Isriam, escort them in."

"Wait a moment—" Andry began.

"If you don't wish to be present, then leave," Pol said, but—mindful of Maarken—without quite the edge it might have had. "I know what all of you are thinking. Hells, I'm thinking it myself. This could be what the Vellant'im have been waiting for. These people may be here on their behalf. But I fought and beat one *diarmadhi* at his own spells, and I'm willing to bet that a group of them with iron in their skins won't be willing to challenge the Sunrunners here." He picked out each in turn with his gaze—Meath, Hollis, Maarken, Andry, Sioned—then, looking at Riyan and Ruala, added, "Don't forget we also have two of their own kind among us."

Andry said nothing for a moment, then gave a shrug. "If the Lord of Goddess Keep can be any help, then I'll stay."

"Thank you," Pol said, and Maarken relaxed.

Isriam returned, leading nine people ranging in age from old to ancient. As Beth had indicated, each wore a twist of steel wire in one ear, often next to an earring already in place, and the slightly reddened puffiness around the wires showed that they were indeed fresh punctures.

Pol barely had time to glance at each face—three women, six men, only a few with the dark Fironese coloring associated with *diarmadh'im*—when one of the old men let out a gasp. He was looking beyond Pol to Andry. The others followed his gaze and a couple of them clung together, eyes widened.

Isriam cleared his throat and, acting as a squire again, began the introductions. "His Grace the High Prince, Ruler of Princemarch and of the Desert. Her Grace the High Princess Sioned. Lord Chaynal of Radzyn Keep." Isriam paused, uncertain for a moment whether Maarken should come next as eldest son, or if Andry took precedence. Pol solved his problem for him.

"And the Lord of Goddess Keep I believe you know," he said easily. "In fact, I rather think you're familiar with all our faces and titles. If there's anyone you don't know, tell us, and—"

But they weren't listening to him. By drawing their eyes away from Andry, he had focused them not on himself but on what was behind him.

Camigwen's mirror.

The oldest of the old women, with a face lined like a map of the Catha River delta, stuck out a withered finger. "What is that?" she breathed. "Where did you—?"

"Beautiful, isn't it?" Sioned remarked calmly. "It belonged to my dear friend Camigwen—mother of Lord Riyan, whose castle this is." She nodded at Riyan, and he took his cue.

"We think it might be very old, maybe dating back to the time of Lady Merisel. Isn't that what you thought, Meath?"

He responded at once, "The design of the frame, anyhow."

One of the other *diarmadh'im* spoke up, making their game of verbal catch four-sided. "Apologies, my lord, but I believe it may only be a copy."

"Do you?" Riyan asked.

"Sorcerers," said Andry in silken tones, "know a great deal about mirrors."

The old woman had collected herself by now. "In times long past, Lord of Goddess Keep."

He inclined his head slightly, not in acknowledgment but in quiet mockery. "As such, I'm feeling a little superfluous. If you'll excuse me. . . ." He bowed—to Sioned, not Pol—and finished, "Beth, you look exhausted. Let me lend you my chamber to rest in until Lady Ruala finds you one of your own."

Only when the door closed behind the two did Pol allow himself to look at his mother. There was no time for a message to pass between them; the old woman cleared her throat, snagging his attention.

"I am sorry for my clumsiness, *Azhrei*. But your mother called it Camigwen's mirror. Her family is honored among us."

"You reacted to the mirror before you knew whose it was," Pol said.

"Again, I apologize. I am an old woman, and should be more careful."

"May I ask why?" Hollis said, before Pol could be even more blunt about it.

Faded blue eyes counted her rings swiftly, searched her face. "You are *faradhi*. Many of you are."

"And you don't talk about mirrors around *faradh'im*," Sioned interpreted.

"It is a rule," Pol said pleasantly, "that you are about to break. For I, too, am a Sunrunner. And if you're here to help me and mine, then the first thing you can do is tell us about that mirror."

She glanced at her companions, none of whom met her gaze. At last she looked at Pol once more. "We cannot. Not until we have spoken together."

Sioned stepped forward and offered her hands to the woman. "I understand. If you'll permit, I'll take you to a chamber where you may be alone and private."

The old woman accepted the touch and bent her head low. "The *Azhreia* Sioned is gracious."

Sioned gathered Hollis and Alasen with her gaze, and beckoned to Isriam—who was looking vastly confused. They filed out with the *diarmadh'im,* and Pol muttered under his breath, "The *Azhrei* Pol is getting impatient."

"Well, don't," Chay advised. "Remember how proud these people are. And what a shock seeing Andry must've been."

Pol faced the mirror. "I know. I was stupid about it. But they know something about this mirror. This one specifically. It wasn't just that it's old. They *recognized* it. And putting Camigwen's name to it sealed it for them."

"They'll tell you in their own good time," Meath said. "I think that—"

What he thought was interrupted by the arrival of Dannar, captaining a small army of servants.

"Oh, Goddess," Pol said. "Dinner."

"Yes, dinner." Riyan sat at the head of the table. "And things won't be any the better or any the worse if we starve. Ruala, sit down. Chay, where's Tobin? And what happened to the children?"

Nothing, not even a sorcerer's appalled reaction to the sight of a Shadowcatcher, was allowed to interrupt the routine of Riyan's household. In this, as in other things, he was the true son of his mother—whose mirror the Shadowcatcher had been.

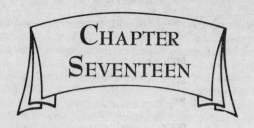

CHAPTER SEVENTEEN

Rohannon fought his way out of a vivid and explicit dream. Hoping it had been acted out only in his mind, his stealthy fingers explored. No luck. The sticky dampness on his belly mortified him. Such dreams were normal, and not what brought the flush of hot color into his face. It was that he knew he wasn't alone. He could sense people around him, feel them—just the way seeing a swarm of crawling insects made his skin itch.

But it wasn't just his skin. His whole body itched from the inside out. As he got his breath back, each inhalation seemed to intensify the jumpiness, freshened blood teasing and tickling every nerve. It was maddening.

He slit his eyelids open. Large, worm-eaten beams supported a sloping low ceiling, fitfully illuminated by a hearth somewhere to his right. He could smell smoke; the chimney didn't draw properly, and to judge by the smoky stains on the ceiling, never had. Turning his head, he squinted into the semi-darkness and was momentarily startled to see that beyond a waist-high wooden railing the room simply ended. Oh—of course. A loft. But he'd never heard that Arlis owned a holding like this—and he knew he wasn't in the Desert, where high ceilings let warm air rise above living level.

The intent here was to warm the sleeping loft, but the result was a tingle of wood smoke in his nose that made him want to sneeze. Hells, his whole *body* wanted to sneeze. The squirmy feeling got worse. He scratched at his chest, then wriggled on the rough woolen blanket beneath his back. This couldn't be one of his lord's holdings—a prince and his squire would have been given silk sheets in private rooms. But he had no idea where he was. His memory had blanked like a parchment scraped clean of mistakes. He twitched again, this time involuntarily, and again, and it was bad enough to scare him into a muffled exclamation.

Someone's hand rested on his forehead for an instant, then brushed his cheeks and lingered at the pulse in his throat. "Stay still. You're coming out of it. Just relax."

Not a particularly pleasant voice, or reassuring—a sound almost as scratchy as he felt. He forced his eyes open and saw a shadow bending over him, no light from the hearth below touching the featureless face at all.

"Who—?" he tried to say, and coughed.

"My name is Aldiar, and you're going through the first *dranath* hunger. It's only going to get worse, so you can make up your mind right now. You can yell your throat raw early on, and have no voice left later when it *really* hurts, or you can keep silent as long as you can."

"Hurts? It doesn't hurt." And it didn't. If only these stupid nonexistent crawly things would get out and leave his skin to its rightful owner.

"Not yet," Aldiar told him. "Personally, I think there are advantages to the first choice. If you shout yourself hoarse to begin with, Prince Arlis might be fooled later that you're not as bad as you will be. And the other way, you use up a lot of strength keeping it all in. But it's up to you."

Aldiar made no sense, and Rohannon was about to say so when it *did* begin to hurt. Just a little, just twinges. But he recognized them.

And finally understood. *Dranath*. He wanted it. Needed it. Was addicted to it, just as his mother had been. Only she had been tricked and used. He had taken it by choice.

It had happened just as his father had warned him.

"I suppose you thought you were smart enough or strong enough," Aldiar was saying. A damp cloth landed across his brow and stuck there. "Can't happen to you. Not so young, and so immortal. And surely not to a son of your parents, grandson of a princess, kinsman of the High Prince and the Lord of Goddess Keep. *And* a Sunrunner besides. Yes, I know who you are—and that you think nothing bad ever happens to people like you. You're thinking otherwise now, aren't you? And it doesn't make sweet fodder for your pride to chew."

The cloth was removed, moistened, replaced. He loathed Aldiar for reading his thoughts and his humiliation.

"Never fear, you'll get more than your share of punishment for being so stupid. You're going to scream like all Hells were promised you, and puke your guts up as if you were back on board ship with no *dranath* to protect you, and you'll wish me dead—and yourself, too. But neither of us is going to die. Understand?"

He glared feebly at the shadow looming over him. "Shut up."

"Not just yet. This is the part where you have to stay awake. There's not much difference between sleep and unconsciousness right now. So you're going to listen to me, and keep your eyes open—and start hating the sound of my voice."

"I already h–hate *you*." The catch in his voice had come from a spasm of pain through his legs. He gritted his teeth.

"Not a screamer yet, eh? Well, never mind. Let's see— where shall I start? What do you remember about getting here? Do you even know where 'here' is?"

He didn't, and that galled him even more.

"Well, it's a start. You sailed with Prince Arlis to Einar, where Prince Camanto fell over a balcony rail—and by no accident, believe me. I know all about it." The cloth was taken away yet again, and this time the blanket was pulled down to his waist as hands began to wash him. He pushed them away. "Don't be so silly. I know what the dream was. I watched for it all afternoon. It's how I knew what stage of this you're in."

All afternoon? He'd lost a whole day in sleep. "Leave me alone!"

"To die? Not likely. Hold still. You stink up the whole loft, and if I'm to spend the next three days with you, I don't want to faint from the stench."

Three days of this? And it would get worse? He bit his lip and a shudder wracked him.

"Don't fight it so much now. You'll use up your energy." The hands made short work of his chest and stomach, and he was expertly flipped over. Aldiar talked all the while. "So after you left Einar, you sailed around Kierst-Isel and on up to Snowcoves. Anything sound familiar?"

"Yes!" he said through gritted teeth.

"Good. The *dranath* may have eaten a temporary hole in your judgment, but at least it hasn't made a sieve of your brains. Snowcove surrendered without a fight. Prince Laric was very clever about that, by the way. You set off for Balarat, and on the way found Prince Tirel and that blithering fool Idalian. Then the storm blew up, and I sent the good folk of Pimanost to bring you in, and here you are. Turn over."

He did so, washed clean from nape to heels, loathing this awful young man with all his soul. The cloth swiped between his thighs.

"Stop that!" He grabbed for Aldiar's hand.

"Modest, or just shy? Whichever—get over it." The soiled cloth was replaced with a fresh one, dripping wet and laid across his forehead. "Tell me what you want right now."

"You gone!"

"What else?"

"My sword in your guts!"

"What else?"

Rohannon gasped as a cramp twisted his vitals and let go. *"Dranath,"* he muttered, knowing it was what Aldiar was waiting to hear.

"Wait a while—and when that's your first answer, wait a while longer than that, and *maybe* I'll oblige. You can't give it over all at once, you see. It has to be done gradually. But we don't have the days your father did with your mother. So it'll be harder on you by the way of time as well as the strength of its hold. But you're not going to die, Rohannon. I won't allow it."

He could feel another wrenching pain begin in his belly, and before it robbed him of air he managed, "Arlis—would kill you—"

"Quite right," Aldiar admitted readily. "And I'm much too young to die. Almost sixteen, like you. But a lot smarter. Did you know I'm royalty, too? Also like you. Let me tell you the story."

"Not—interested—"

"I know, but you're going to hear it anyway." There was a shifting of clothes, as if Aldiar resettled himself for a long telling. Rohannon had still not seen his face. He had a vague impression from the night before of a lot of unkempt black hair and two big black eyes set in a scrawny face. But the rest of it eluded him. Just as the *dranath* had eluded his scrabbling fingers—oh, Goddess, the memory of the picture he'd made was itself enough to make him want to die now, and not wait for the hunger to kill him.

"Fifteen or sixteen generations ago, the *diarmadh'im* ruled this whole continent, and Kierst-Isel besides. The only place they didn't hold was Dorval, where the *faradh'im* had their ancient keep. Everybody kept out of everybody else's way. Mainly because there were many thousands of us, and much fewer of the Sunrunners."

"Us?"

"Didn't I mention that? I'm a sorcerer."

Rohannon turned his head away. Now he *knew* he was going to die.

"You really are the dumbest—" Aldiar sighed in exasperation. "If I'd wanted to kill you, I would have. It's not that difficult, especially killing a Sunrunner who doesn't really know what he's doing."

How did this strange person always know what he was thinking? It was uncanny, and it unnerved him.

But Aldiar hadn't expected what Rohannon did next. He didn't let himself think about it past the first wild impulse. He called a fingerflame, and it lit the thin, intense face—and flared dangerously as he cried out.

For the face was familiar. He'd seen it raised to the stars on an icy night not long ago, after these very hands had placed a twisted cord around Yarin of Snowcoves' shoulders.

"You!" he cried, trying to scramble off the bed. Aldiar lunged for him, but not in time. He tumbled onto the wooden floor. "Get away from me, you're in it with him, I saw you—oh, *Goddess!*"

Agony took him from his throat to his groin, and tied his insides around themselves, around his skeleton, around the little Fire that jumped and quivered and died as he lost consciousness.

When he came to, it was with the taste of wine in his mouth. He was back on the bed—Aldiar was stronger than he looked—with the blanket tucked firmly around him. He felt too weak to move.

"Where did you see me?" The question was calm, and the eyes lit by a candleflame were only mildly curious.

He stared at the sixteen-year-old face, high-boned and

proud, remembering it in that circle of Fire and stone. "On
... the stars," he managed, too exhausted to resist. "That
night."

"What night? Oh. You mean the Circle of Ninety-and-
Nine. You saw that?" Aldiar chewed his lip for a moment,
then shrugged. "I remember now. I felt something. You, it
seems. Well, that's just one more thing to explain. Do you
feel better?"

"Some."

"I gave you a little *dranath* to take the edge off. But
you'll get less and less, and the pain will get worse and
worse."

He glared feebly. "You're ... enjoying this."

Thick lashes shaded the boy's eyes. "No," he said softly.
"I watched my older brother die of it. But you're not going
to die, Rohannon."

"You ... won't ... allow it. ..."

"No. I won't allow it."

Rohannon sighed. He was helpless, and he knew it, and
there was nothing for it but to submit. His own imbecilic
pride had gotten him into this; if Aldiar could get him out,
then—

"Tell me ... the rest," he murmured.

✳

"We sent out ships, for we do not share the Sunrunner weakness, and explored the nearer parts of the world," said
Thassalante, chosen as spokesman for the nine *diarmadh'im*
at Feruche. Being the youngest—at only seventy-three—he
had the vocal stamina for the telling of a long, long tale. He
had described himself as great-grandson of the *Diarmadh'reia*
Lallante's grandfather's sister. This interested Pol only because if necessary, he could claim kinship and thus loyalty.
Until such time, he wasn't about to mention it.

They were again in the Attic, with the mirror empty and
cold above the hearth. Thassalante had come alone. It had
taken all of the last evening and most of today for the
diarmadh'im to argue themselves into sharing their information with Pol. The wait hadn't been easy on anyone, least of
all him. Seventy-two days of Winter gone now; he recalled
the portents Kazander had mentioned, that the war would
last either three seasons or three years. *Not,* please the God-

dess in her mercy, the latter. Almost forty days—only a third of the number that had passed since this began. Pol counted each day his enemy now. His and Meiglan's. And the man trapped in that mirror? How many days had been his enemies? Thousands? Tens of thousands?

The *diarmadh'im* were polite and respectful to him, even though they thought him *faradhi* only. They knew about Riyan and Ruala—knew more about their ancestry than they did themselves, in fact—and were willing to speak to them. But Pol was another matter. They honored him for ending Andry's incursions into Princemarch against their kind, but from respect to trust was a long step. This afternoon they had finally taken it, or at the very least decided they had no choice. In recognition of this, Pol told them to remove the iron from their flesh. He also asked them to wait for the conference until the sun was down and the moons not yet up. That way, he did not say, no one could watch who was not physically present.

They understood that the unspoken reason was Andry. And in Thassalante's pale brown eyes was gratitude that Pol had chosen to sit at the long table rather than by the windows, where someone might watch on starlight and read the words as they left his lips.

There was no Fire but what Pol himself had kindled, in Thassalante's presence, to the candle branch on the table. The sconces beside the mirror were unlit. Pol intended to save that until he'd heard the whole story.

And it had better be the *whole* story, he told himself. He was tired of guessing games and speculations. He needed knowledge, and he wanted it *now*.

Riyan and Ruala sat at either end of the table. Sioned and Meath flanked Pol on the side with a view of the mirror. Thassalante paused every so often for a sip of the Syrene gold Riyan kept for special occasions—and if learning why his mother had owned a Shadowcatcher wasn't special, nothing was.

"You Sunrunners do not explore," the old man went on, idly brushing a strand of longish gray hair back behind an ear. His fingers brushed the ruby earring hanging there, and he winced as the movement hurt the unhealed wound left by steel wire. "It's said that once, one of you attempted to follow the sunlight all the way around the world. He died, shadow-lost."

"Not exactly," Meath said. "The way I heard it, when he lost sight of land he got disoriented, and kept going because he couldn't do anything else. There's a lot of open sea out there in all directions. Somebody went to find him and couldn't. Sun-lost would be more accurate."

Sioned nodded. "You're the same as we are, you know—you need references of land in order to find your way home."

"But we can sail without weakness. So we did. And of all the lands we found, only the Vellanti Islands were peopled. There are more than forty islands, perhaps as many as a hundred, although most are too small for more than a few families to live on. The Vellant'im were without gifts. They herded their animals, grew their crops, felled their trees for houses and ships, and knew nothing of how to call Fire or use the light."

"In other words," Pol murmured, "perfect victims."

"They were weak," Thassalante said. "That was how my ancestors saw them. For many generations we ruled over them. But eventually they learned how to be warriors instead of slaves. And they rose up, island after island, to fight against us."

"How long did it take them to get rid of you?"

"I'm not certain. But during the last and most vicious of their wars against us, we made the mistake of bleeding the princedoms with taxes and levies of soldiers and food—clanmarches, they were called then. That was when the clanlords went in secret to Lady Merisel and Lord Gerik and Lord Rosseyn. And they defeated us."

"You'd reached too far," Pol said.

"Yes, your grace." Thassalante sipped wine. "We took Vellanti goods and the produce of their lands, which included much iron. We made them build ships for us, vastly superior to those we made ourselves. We even showed them how to treat the wood against fire—of all kinds."

"So *that's* why—" Meath interrupted himself. "Do your people still know how to do that?"

"No. It was lost, as much of our knowledge was lost, when Merisel and her kind destroyed us."

"And yet here you are." Sioned met his gaze across the table. "Tell me, is this an offer to help my son, or to help yourself to his armies in order to gain vengeance?"

"Both, your grace," Thassalante replied frankly. "He is

faradhi, and though my people and I do not believe as those who followed Mireva believe, we have no love for the Sunrunners who all but obliterated us. Our time is past, our seasons of power and influence. And this is a good thing, for we were thoughtless, sometimes cruel, and, worst of all, careless in our pride. We never thought that a pack of weakling Sunrunners would sail as far as Radzyn, let alone to the place where Goddess Keep now stands."

"But we did," Meath said. "And I think we've done a little better than you."

Bony shoulders lifted in a shrug. "Perhaps. History since has been filled with wars, all the princedoms Merisel created fighting with each other, usually over trifles. Until the High Prince Rohan." He nodded respectfully at Pol, then Sioned. "A wise and noble prince. We honored him, and helped when and as we could."

"One day you'll have to tell me all about it." Sioned poured herself a half-cup from the pitcher, then passed it to Meath. "Right now I'm more interested in the Vellant'im. You know them. We have our own ideas, but we'd like to hear yours."

"Especially regarding that mirror," Pol added.

*

"Some of them decided there was profit in working with the *diarmadh'im,* and were sent back here. And those became the Merida."

"Assassins," Rohannon said. He knew now why Aldiar was talking. Not just to keep him awake, but to give him something to think about that would distract him from the spasms of pain and the occasional nausea. He couldn't contribute much to the conversation himself, but had learned that if he didn't say something every once in a while, he was asked that horrible question: *"What do you want?"* And he was damned if he'd make the even more horrible reply.

"Go on," he said.

"The Merida bred among themselves but never with us. That's why there were always so many of them. Women here usually have four or five pregnancies—nobody understands why, because we can tell when a woman is fertile and there's nothing about our bodies that's different from theirs. *Diarmadhi* women had more children by Vellanti men than they otherwise would have. But maybe it's the men, too—because their women didn't have as many children by *diarmadhi* men as they did by their own. Anyway, the point is that mixing the breeds makes for more children. So if you want a big family, Rohannon, find yourself a Vellanti or Merida girl."

"No thanks, I'll—" Rohannon closed his jaw tight around a moan.

"Well, Merida bred Merida, while at the same time getting more and more used to our land and our ways. Lady Merisel offered them a ship to go home, but they refused. They stayed and fought. And they're still fighting, the stubborn fools. It's your bad luck that it's the Desert they want. I could never understand why, myself. It always sounded like a place somebody thought up as an especially nasty Hell for one of his enemies."

Rohannon remembered the vast golden expanse of the Long Sand, the trees and pastures of his home at Whitecliff, the eight proud towers of Radzyn that would be his someday in the far future. He remembered the warm sun on his face and the breezes off the sea, and all the colors of the rainbow blooming on the coastal hills in spring. Hell? Quite the opposite. But he didn't have the breath to say so.

"Let's see, where was I?" Aldiar paused for a long swallow of wine. His voice had grown even rougher during the night, and every so often it broke upward as if he were thirteen instead of nearly sixteen. "Lady Merisel won the war, built Goddess Keep, and settled down to raise Sunrunners while the princedoms were established. She decided who got what according to who'd supported her. Your ancestor was one of them—so he got what he wanted, which was the whole Desert. He could have asked for Syr, or Meadowlord, but he wanted the Desert." He snorted. "Insanity seems to run in your family."

Rohannon said something incredibly filthy that he'd heard Arlis direct at a balky horse (a Kadari stud; no Radzyn horse was so ill-mannered). Aldiar only laughed.

"Physically impossible, but I take your meaning. I'll have to remember that—Idalian will be irritating until I convince him I'm not here to incinerate the lot of you. In fact, my family sent me to keep an eye on Yarin. But Tirel was more important. They would've killed him either way, you know."

"Too kind . . . of you."

"I know. I'm very softhearted. You'll learn that, in the next few days." He paused. "What do you want?"

"The rest of—the story," he hissed between his teeth.

"There's not much else. You know about Mireva, and Ianthe's sons. What Segev did to your mother, what Marron did to your uncle Sorin, and what Ruval tried to do to Pol. So now we're up to the present time, and Yarin thinks that his little group of *diarmadhi* kinfolk are about to make him Prince of Firon. I'm here to stop them, and him."

"How?"

"By helping Prince Laric, of course."

"How?" Rohannon managed again.

"I'm not sure yet. Something will occur to me. This is my trial, you know—getting you through this. Which is another reason you can't die."

"K–kind," he stammered again.

"Aren't I?" He mopped Rohannon's forehead. "That's the thing about *dranath*—it makes you sweat like a horse and smell worse."

"Not the thing—to s–say—to *me*."

"Oh, yes, I forgot. Radzyn-bred, born in the saddle, and you'd bed down with the horses for preference? I rode one of your grandfather's mares once. It was better than walking, but not by much."

Rohannon squinted up at him. "You're—scared . . . of horses!"

"No, I'm not!"

But the reply was too quick to be the truth. Rohannon felt a smug little glow inside, knowing this rotten boy had at least one real fear. When this was over, he'd use that knowledge without mercy.

When this was over.

Three days, Aldiar said. If Rohannon had to listen to that scratchy, cracking voice for even one, he'd go utterly mad.

If the *dranath* didn't get him first.

✳

"Then they don't shout *'Diarmadhi'* as a battle cry—not the way we would 'Radzyn' or 'Feruche' or whatever," Riyan was saying. "They use it as a curse."

"But why kill Sunrunners? In a way, we solved their problem for them by defeating the sorcerers here, so they were too busy to fight for the islands." Pol looked at Thassalante for an explanation.

The old man spread his hands wide. "This I do not know. It's possible they have the two confused. It's been a very long time—fifteen, sixteen generations."

"Maybe they think we should've finished the job by coming to help them," Meath put in.

"Or maybe they just hate anybody with our kind of power." Pol raked his hair back with both hands. It pulled free of the thin black ribbon at his nape. He swore and set about retying it out of his way.

"I know only this," Thassalante went on. "They will stay and kill until one of two things happens: either *we* are all dead or *they* are all dead. They will not stop. They cannot. Their warrior code does not permit it." He hesitated. "It is something they learned from our rule," he ended bitterly. "To fight and never give up."

"Delightful," Riyan said acidly. "What else did you teach them?"

"My ancestors—and yours, my lord—taught them to hate us. It is hate that drives them."

"Why are they afraid of dragons?" Sioned asked suddenly.

"There we delve into legend. It is said, variously, that one was captured and taken across the sea to terrify them."

"If so, it worked," Ruala said.

"Well, it's *un*worked now," Pol reminded her. "They killed Morwenna's Elidi."

"Please, I don't understand," Thassalante said. "A dragon?"

Pol explained it briefly. The old sorcerer pursed his lips, finally shook his head.

"I don't know why this happened. Another of the legends says that certain of the Vellanti were brought here and shown dragons as proof of *diarmadhi* power. Yet another has it that a whole flight of them were persuaded to cross the sea along with *diarmadhi* ships, and their descendants linger in the islands to this day."

"Is it cool or warm there? What about caves?" Sioned asked.

"Nothing I have ever heard tells me those things. I am sorry, your grace."

"Whatever," Pol said impatiently. "They're not scared of dragons anymore. They kill them. If you're thinking of risking them in battle, Mother, then forget it. Thassalante, I want to know about this mirror."

Bracing himself against the table, the old man rose and turned, and walked to the hearth. Staring up at the mirror, he said nothing for a long time. Then: "Has he spoken to you?"

"Has he—?" Sioned swallowed the rest, and a long gulp of wine to help it down. "I can't see anything in that mirror. Riyan and Ruala can. Tell us what *you* see."

The sorcerer called Fire to the sconces on either side of the mirror. His body stiffened almost at once. The tiny flames died, and Thassalante turned, tears seeping down his face.

"It's true," he whispered. "May he forgive me for being of the blood that put him there." Wiping his eyes, he moved slowly back to the table and sank into his chair. "That mirror, that *daltaya,* is the greatest shame of my family. For it was one of us who betrayed him, trapped him. Legends would have it that the mirror was buried in a secret place in the Veresch, or on Dorval, or under the deepest packed ice on the northernmost coast of Firon. It doesn't matter now. He is here, within the *daltaya* my kinswoman of many generations ago fashioned for him alone. She bore him a son and then she betrayed him—because he had betrayed us." He covered his face with one hand. "Why didn't she just kill him?" he muttered brokenly.

Pol refilled the old man's winecup and pushed it toward him. "Drink."

Thassalante did, both hands wrapped around the silver, trembling.

"You knew the mirror."

"From drawings. Legends describing—"

"You know the man," Pol said quietly. "Who is he?" *Who is this Shadow-caught sorcerer? Who is this man who might be* my *ancestor, too?*

The *diarmadhi* drew in a breath that shook in his throat.

"Lord Rosseyn."

✳

"The circle," Rohannon whispered. "That night."

Aldiar stretched his shoulders before wringing out the cloth and returning it to Rohannon's brow. "Did I forget that part? Sorry. It fell to me as the son of my mother—you'd only get confused by the bloodlines, so I won't go into that now—anyway, the one who qualified. There's a rope woven of gold, silver, and bronze, and when a *diarmadhi* claims leadership, and that claim is validated, then the rope is placed around the claimant's shoulders. Yarin doesn't understand all that it means, of course. He thinks it's strictly a token of authority. But it also binds the person to the service of our people, and if something is done our elderfolk don't like, then we have the right to strangle him with it. I'm looking forward to that part of it," he added grimly. "If Prince Laric lets us have him, that is."

"Not . . . likely—" He coughed again. "Damn it!"

"Have some water. You've sweated buckets tonight."

He sipped, and felt a little better. "You—the ceremony. Why?"

"Because it made Yarin feel important. Not to mention invincible. Everyone in the *Ku'al*—that means 'mind circle,' by the way—they were all Yarin's loyal kin. Except me."

"Why trust you, then?"

Aldiar laughed. "Because I'm the one who brought the rope!"

"No—I mean—*us*."

"The reason you *should* trust me is that everything I've done was to benefit Laric. He should get around to that conclusion pretty soon, if he's not there already. But the reason you *have* to trust me is that there's no one else."

They were both silent for a time, Aldiar presumably brooding on this truth, Rohannon concentrating on breathing as painlessly as possible. It was no good. He called up the sickening image of himself as he scraped frantically for the spilled *dranath,* but it didn't work as well as it had. He gripped the blankets, trying not to shift with the restless demand of his muscles.

Aldiar pried his hands loose from the wool. "Here. Hold on to me, instead."

"Break—your fingers—" Rohannon gasped.

"Tomorrow, maybe. Not just yet. I'll knot a blanket for you to yank on. We'll have to rip one up anyway, to tie you down with."

There would be no limit to his humiliation, it seemed. But he had not yet cried out. That was something, wasn't it?

He lost even that morsel of pride when cramps knotted his guts and the first of the real pain began.

✳

"You know," Sioned mused as she watched the moonlight dip into her winecup, "of all the things I've had to believe in my life, this is one of the easiest." She tossed back the remainder of the Syrene wine. "And *I* can't even see the poor man's face."

Meath took the goblet and set it aside with his own. The shelf carved into the crenellation was meant for arrows in time of war; Ruala had refused to clear it and the others like it of herb boxes placed there for color and scent. Leaning his elbows on the low wall between ramparts, Meath stared out at the silvery dunes and sighed.

"Lady Merisel," he said mildly, "wasn't entirely forthcoming in her histories, was she?"

Sioned gave a dry chuckle. "I'd love to have met her. She sounds like she was made up of best and worst, with nothing in between. No compromise to either her virtues or her faults. On second thought, I'm glad she's long gone—she would've scared me to death."

"Frightening people seems to be the only constant about her. Everyone either hated her or adored her—with nothing in between!" He smiled.

"I wonder how Gerik lived with her so long. If she scared him, too."

"Probably. And just because she loved him, I don't think she went easy on him. Or Rosseyn. People like that only demand more of those they love."

She glanced sidelong at him. "Do I hear a rebuke in that?"

Meath shrugged. "A respectful note of caution, maybe. I wouldn't dare chasten you, my lady. I'm too scared of you."

Sioned gave a snort of derision. "Oh, of course."

"It's better than being scared *for* you," he added softly.

After a few silent moments, she shook her head. "That's over. It won't happen again, not any of it. And don't say that you're afraid of me, old friend. It hurts, even in jest."

"It wasn't meant to be funny." Meath straightened and faced her. "You're holding something back. Something you know and Pol doesn't. No, you don't have to tell me, because I'm not asking. But I think you might consider telling him. It's his war to fight."

"Not mine anymore, you mean?"

"He's High Prince, not you. He's the Sunrunner and the sorcerer."

"And his useless, antiquated old mother should stay out of it. You're the second person who's told me that the last few days. Only that time, I was accused of too much meddling, not the reverse."

"I won't ask about that, either. But it sounds like you." He smiled again. "Nothing in between."

"Thanks *so* much," she said, wrinkling her face up as if tasting soured wine. "I'll tell you who else knows something and isn't talking about it yet, and that's Thassalante. He said the frame around that mirror had been described, and there were drawings of it. I'd like to know why, if they thought the thing was buried somewhere nobody could find it, they went to so much trouble to remind all good little *diarmadh'im* what it looked like."

"Interesting point. Here's another. The pattern I found at the old Sunrunner keep was set with jewels. If you've looked carefully at the frame, there are spaces left in it at the same intervals."

Sioned clenched her left hand. Meath noted the movement but said nothing. "It seems the gemstone symbology goes back at least that far, then. But as for its meaning or function—"

"You *do* know something."

She hesitated. "Put the torch out."

He had lit it with a gesture and a thought when they'd come out of the stairwell. Now he extinguished it. The fire-thrown shadows vanished, and there was only starlight and the brighter glow of the moons.

Sioned held up her hand. The emerald Rohan had given her shone dimly. "Watch," she said, and shielded the stone from all light with her other hand.

The secret green heart of it began to pulse with a soft, regular glow.

Sioned let the moons and stars touch the emerald again. "I'm tired, or I wouldn't have slipped and said 'function.'"

"Good thing it was only I who heard it." Meath managed to sound casual, even though he wished the winecups still had something in them. He could use a good long gulp about now. "How long has it been doing that?"

"A while. I seem to have blooded it. I'd bitten my lip, I think, and—well, it's not important how. But ever since, when it's completely dark, it does that." She laughed unsteadily. "So it's not just every mirror that's suspect, it's every pretty rock whose history we don't know."

"Why did Merisel conceal all this? Is it *that* dangerous?"

"I know why *I* would have," she replied softly. "If the frame and the mirror and the gems are all connected in some way—if there are other stones like this one that have a heartbeat after they're blooded—then knowing might get Rosseyn out of that mirror."

"But she and Gerik *loved* him. He was their friend! Surely she'd want to set him free!"

"As what? A shadow without a body? Spirit without substance? We've both seen Sunrunners shadow-lost, Meath. The merciful thing to do is kill their bodies. Their souls are already gone. Lord Rosseyn's body is dust and ashes, and has been for hundreds of years. What would we be setting free?"

"The ritual of Burning," he said slowly, feeling his way through it, "releases the spirit. But that's not really true, because at death the spirit is already gone. It's just the body that's left behind."

"The ritual is for the living," she agreed. "To give time for grief."

"Yes. But with someone who's shadow-lost, there's only—I don't know, a thread left, too fragile to weave the mind back into the body. It's being half-dead—or mostly dead, except the body doesn't know it yet."

"So they are dispatched as painlessly as possible—not that anyone in that state could really feel pain, I think." She wrapped her arms around herself. "But what about Rosseyn, Meath? His body is dead. But his spirit is inside that mirror. Shadowcaught, not shadow-lost."

"Goddess," he murmured, not really comprehending the horror of it until now. "Thassalante was right—why *didn't* the woman just kill him?"

"Whatever he did, or whatever she believed he had done to betray the *diarmadh'im,* she must have thought he deserved it."

"No one could deserve that. No one."

There was another small silence before Sioned spoke again. "Lord Rosseyn, dearly loved of Lady Merisel and Lord Gerik, a sorcerer. Won't Andry have a fit over *that*."

"Speaking of whom—he's bound to ask about the mirror. We didn't fool him, you know."

"I know. But if we'd said nothing, someone would've blurted out the whole thing. Andry needs to be kept ignorant a little while longer. We have to know exactly what it is and what can be done with it—if anything—before we let him in on it."

"You think it's going to be useful?"

"Oh, Meath!" She laughed again, with no more humor than before. "Didn't you ever listen to Rohan? Things happen because they're supposed to happen."

"That doesn't leave anybody any choices, does it?"

"But it does, you know," she said more seriously. "We are what our lives make us. Because we are what we are, we can only act in certain ways. I *could* choose to tell Pol what I think I know now, instead of waiting until I'm sure—and until I think he can use it instead of being crushed by it. Do I obey what is ruthless in me, or what is compassionate—and which choice is weighted more on the side of each?"

"*Crushed?* Sioned, what is it you're not telling him?"

She ignored the question. "I'm ruthless and compassionate because of natural inclination and the life I've lived. So you see I *do* have a choice."

"Sioned—"

"You said you wouldn't ask."

"So I lied!" he snarled. "Wait—is it Meiglan? What do you know? Are they going to kill her?"

"They'll try to kill her. We already knew that, more or less. It's not the why of it, but the how. And that's all I'm going to say." Suddenly fierce: "And if you breathe a word of this to Pol—"

"You'll what?" he challenged.

"Don't push me," she warned. "You're the oldest and dearest friend I have, but do not push me."

"Meiglan is his wife!"

"And his princess. His *Azhreia*."

"As you were Rohan's? She's not like you, she's not a—"

"—ruthless bitch? You think not? Underneath all that softness, there's a woman—a High Princess—who ordered her own half brothers executed. I underestimated her, Meath. When she comes back to us, I intend to apologize."

He breathed a little more easily. "Then you're certain

she'll be coming back. You'll tell Pol what you know in time for—"

Sioned stared up at him in shock, her eyes huge and colorless by moonlight. "What kind of monster do you think I am?"

"I don't," he said curtly. "But I told you before—at times, you scare me."

As she turned wordlessly and went down the stairs, he thought, *And I'll bet Rohan felt the same way.*

CHAPTER EIGHTEEN

It was Prince Tilal's personal good fortune that he cared about his soldiers enough to organize roving medical help during battle. At Goddess Keep and again at Swalekeep, casualties were kept down by the swift treatment of the wounded. In fours—one person with a field kit, three to guard and carry—they darted in and out of the fighting on agile Radzyn horses, killing the enemy only to get to wounded friends.

When Tilal's army combined with Amiel's, physicians from the latter replaced rough bandaging with surer skills. Faolain River had been their first test, but it was nothing like the Firelit chaos of the Second Battle of Radzyn Keep.

One of these twelve patrols—lacking a member who was wounded literally keeping a Vellanti off the physician's back—saw Tilal go down, his horse collapsing under him as a sword plunged into its heart. They didn't know the prince was wounded until they got to him, galloping up just as the Vellanti freed himself from the dying stallion. The sword had caught in the Kadari's massive rib cage. Had he been a lighter Radzyn breed, sheer weight wouldn't have brought the Vellanti down with him—and sheer bad temper wouldn't have kept him there. As the man scrambled up, leaping to one side to avoid bared teeth hungering for his flesh, the physician arrived and skewered him through one terrified eye.

Three days later, fever gone and wound healing and body aching with every heartbeat, Tilal heard how his life had been saved. That physician would be welcomed at Athmyr with all honors whenever he chose to visit. As for Kadari horses, Tilal vowed to ride none other and to defend their superiority against all Chay's boasting about his Radzyn breed.

A rather inhospitable thought, for it was in Radzyn that Tilal was recuperating, and in Chay's own bed. There were worse places to be confined, he supposed. But something was not quite right about Radzyn, and eventually he realized this was because its lord and lady were not here to rule it. He kept waiting to hear Chay's deep laugh and Tobin's light, not-quite limping step.

Princess Nyr and Master Chegry attended Tilal, giving him the details of the battle and the three days he'd wafted in and out of consciousness. The first thing he wanted to do, of course, was get up, get dressed, and get busy. Chegry told him fine, he could do whatever he liked.

Tilal got one knee free of the quilt before stabbing ribs and lack of air felled him onto the pillows. The Vellanti swordthrust had punctured him between the bottom of his chest armor and the thick leather of his belt, angling upward to nick his lung. The fall from his horse had cracked two ribs, wrenched his shoulder, and bruised almost everything else.

"It's much more effective," Chegry observed as the prince gasped in pain, "to let you find out for yourself that you won't be going anywhere for a while."

Nyr clucked her tongue and resettled the quilt. "You're as bad as Amiel—*he* thought he could climb down all these stairs on a broken ankle."

Tilal looked a question at her; he didn't have the breath to ask aloud.

"He tripped jumping into shallow water," she explained. "Just as well he did, too, and was out of the fighting—when their priests found out they wouldn't get much welcome on board ship, they got very nasty."

"If you'll excuse the language," Chegry commented, "they fought as if their balls were made of iron—even though they have none at all."

"What?" Tilal's breath exploded out of him.

"The ones in white are priests, something to do with their rituals and so on. And all of them are castrated."

"Good Goddess," he whispered.

"Utterly barbaric," Nyr agreed. "I'm trying to figure out how they still manage to grow beards."

"I've read about it, at the school," Chegry said. "If it's done after a boy becomes a man, and if enough is left of—" he stopped and grinned, seeing the involuntary shift of his patient's thighs. "Yes, it does give one a certain vulnerable feeling, doesn't it, my lord?"

Nyr giggled, a deliciously wicked sound. "Amiel says it makes him long for a steel codpiece!"

"It's not funny," Tilal said, finding that if he inhaled with exquisite care, he could manage to speak without too much trouble. "Women can't possibly understand. Let's talk about something else. Has Pol been told?"

"Andrev has been working hard, my lord. And so have the rest of us." Nyr lost her smile. "I'm glad Princess Tobin and Lord Chaynal weren't the first back into Radzyn. It would break their hearts."

"Why? What's wrong?"

"Nothing that a lot of money won't cure," Chegry reported dourly. "They used furniture as firewood. The tapestries are mostly in shreds. They made the silk sheets into new robes for themselves—and I don't want to describe what state the great hall is in."

"Tell me."

Chegry paused. "Blood, my lord. Everywhere. And the— the entrails of a mare and twin foals. Ritually slaughtered, it looks like, and left to rot. Either that, or we interrupted them before they cleaned it up."

Tilal swallowed hard. "Don't ever tell Chay."

"No. Anyway, we've begun to put things to rights. It gave the soldiers something to do after they finished burning all the Vellanti dead. And there were a lot of them," he said with satisfaction.

"How many of our own?"

"Over a hundred," Nyr murmured. "Thank the Goddess you weren't among them."

Tilal forced a smile. "I'm too ornery to kill. Now, if I'm stuck to this bed, and it seems I am," he paused for breath, "send Andrev to me and—"

"Andrev is otherwise occupied," Nyr told him, serenely disregarding his scowl. "Everyone else is, too, so don't bother to ask. It's time you got some more sleep. Chegry?"

"I've two sorts of wine here for you, my lord—and you

could weep at the shambles they made of the cellars." He held up two dented silver cups. "The first is an excellent Giladan red—724 was a fine year on their coast. Unfortunately, I've had to spoil the taste with a sleeping draught. The second is pure Ossetian white, from your very own vineyards around the Kadar River valley." He smiled; Tilal glowered. "Which will it be?"

✳

Meiglan's fingers were cramping more and more often. Each stitch was like the dripping of a water-clock—and time was filling up. She had three days left to finish the cloak. The garment itself was done, though not to her usual standards. It was difficult for her to abandon care and pride in her work, but she had no time to make the stitches nearly invisible or to fit the lining so precisely to the outer material that it seemed all one piece of cloth.

The cloak was dull, nubby violet silk lined with slick and shiny blue that folded over to make front plackets and a handspan trim around the hem. She busied herself embroidering the blue in gold-and-white wreaths that would border words not yet stitched. She would leave those for last. But time was running out, and she was no closer to learning the Vellanti purpose at Skybowl than when she started the cloak.

The High Warlord had not been back. He had not come to see the material delivered—probably still too angry. But she understood enough about him now to be certain that when his temper cooled, he would return to watch her sew what he intended to be her husband's shroud.

The silk had come from Radzyn, but not because of her request. It had pleased the priests—of which she had yet to encounter even one—to bring the finest, costliest silks with them for future use in whatever would be done at Skybowl. It seemed that they, too, were sewing these days, in their little enclave set apart from the rest of the army—but the High Warlord, though he had commanded material enough in Pol's colors for the cloak, had not explained exactly what the ritual entailed.

She would find out. She was beginning to understand him. She must play on that combination of the pride he seemed to expect of a High Princess, the meekness he demanded of a woman, and his own need for her to know the "truth" of what had been done all those generations ago. She would find out about the ritual. And then she would find a way to warn Pol.

But as the fourth day of her work wore on, and she had to pause more frequently to flex her aching hands, she began to think the High Warlord would not come back until the cloak was finished. And if that proved true, all her work would be for nothing.

At least she now had something to occupy herself during the long, empty days. But as her fingers moved with expert skill through the silk, she found her mind wandering down worrisome paths. She did not think beyond finishing the cloak. She dared not. But she could not finish until she knew what the High Warlord intended.

She had so little information. Sitting outside her tent in the mornings and afternoons, she had been careful to move her chair with the light and thus view most of the encampment. Yesterday she'd had a bit of luck. Their horses—no, not theirs, Chay's—had been led in groups of ten up to Stronghold for a good, long drink. Evidently someone had grown tired of lugging buckets, or decided no dragons would rise out of the ashes. Meiglan counted, and counted, and went on counting—and knew they'd drink the grotto spring dry. Almost six hundred horses—and Pol with barely six hundred troops total. She considered the masses of foot soldiers she could never number accurately from where she was placed, and couldn't pretend that the tears in her eyes were from a pricked finger.

After that, she concentrated on working out exactly how she would send her message. Never mind that she had practically nothing to tell yet; she would. She must.

The High Warlord was clever. He thought *she* was clever. But she was also a mere woman, fit only for bearing sons, minding her needle, and keeping her mouth shut. Still, she was the High Princess. And that, she reasoned, put him in something of a quandry. She must play both parts to perfection, keeping him off-balance enough to let information slip. Because he considered women inferior, he would not suspect her capable of making use of it. But because he considered her clever, he would expect her to try.

Thus she was faced with a problem to drive anyone mad: give him something to satisfy both attitudes. Her effort to communicate with Pol could not be too obvious, but it must be there for him to see. He must admire her ingenuity while at the same time laughing at her pathetic attempt to outwit him.

And she must accomplish all this while distracting him from what she wanted Pol alone to see—which she also must make sure Pol saw and understood.

Meiglan thought she knew how it might be done. Valeda had sewn gold coins into her cloak. Meiglan would sew a letter made of silk. She had already finished it, stitching in the privacy of her tent by candlelight until her eyes swam with weariness. It was a brief and rather remarkable missive, proud and pleading, a pathetic entreaty to be rescued couched in complaints and demands. It was the way the High Warlord would expect her to write—as the *Kir'reia* and as a woman.

Meiglan would give him something to find, and beseech the Goddess that he would stop looking.

As for what she would tell Pol, and how—those problems must wait until she knew more. And she must know soon.

During the afternoon she finished the last of the wreaths and had no excuse not to begin the words that would tell of Pol's great deeds as High Prince. She started at the right corner of the hem, and for pleasure's sake made the initial capital of her husband's name a beautiful scrollwork of vines and leaves all in gold.

She'd stitched the silken letter in an irregular style—few capitals, no punctuation except where absolutely necessary. She didn't have time. A frown had occasionally crossed her face while sewing, for she took as much pride in the elegance of her writing as she did in her needlework, and labored mightily to instill the same in her daughters.

The High Warlord could read her language as well as speak it—though with odd lapses in fluency. It hadn't surprised him that the *Kir'reia* could read and write, though he considered such skills in a female rather akin to legs on a fish. He probably wouldn't even notice the mistakes in her letter. But if it somehow escaped his inspection and Pol actually found and read it, the raving illiteracy alone would convince him that her wits were scattered to the winds.

Her thumb, raw from plying the needle, stroked the first letter of her husband's name. The threads blurred and she blinked, knowing she ought to rest her eyes before she went blind. She could not rest. She had so little time.

But when would she learn what she must know, what *Pol* must know? And how could she convey the information?

Surely the High Warlord would inspect the completed cloak to learn—and ridicule—the *Azhrei*'s deeds. If she finished a day early, then after he found the silk hidden in the lining she would have a night to repair it and write a second letter. He would not think her so brainless as to try the same trick twice.

Or perhaps he would think her so clever that she *would* try it twice.

Worse, he might sit with her while she resewed the cloak.

It was hopeless. Give him something to find so his opinions of both her cleverness and her stupidity were reinforced. Give him something to find so he would not see what she meant for Pol alone to see—which must remain hidden yet not so obscure as to be missed.

Not even Sioned could have done it.

The High Warlord appeared very suddenly, blotting out the afternoon sunlight. He was nearly of a height with Pol and Chay and Maarken, but none of those men came to her mind as he loomed above her. Though he was bulkier in the shoulders with warrior's muscle, he was exactly as tall as her father. She knew that this association would defeat her before she even began. She banished it to a corner of her mind. But when he stood over her like this, the way her father used to, it was all she could do to remember she was the High Princess.

"Is this all your women are good for?" he demanded, and his usually melodious voice grated on her ears.

She lowered her gaze to her work and said nothing.

"What is your want? All you have asked is this of me—silk for a cloak! No books, no walking, no bath, nothing but this!"

"You seem eager to be thought generous." Meiglan startled herself with that. "What I want, you can't possibly give me. Because you don't have him and never will."

He snorted and began to pace, his shadow passing over her again and again. At last he caught up the trailing length of silk from the sand.

"No words. No lies of his great deeds."

She indicated the hem with its elaborate initial capital. "I've only just started. And I don't have to lie about my lord's power." She placidly began to sew again, sliding bright needle and luminous thread through dark silk.

"*He* is your want. In fifteen days, you may have him— one piece at a time."

She'd been wrong about the date.

"You think he will win? Fool of a woman! Stupid as a priest! I should give you to them now and not wait for the day!"

The eighty-ninth day of Winter.

"You will be theirs, but he is mine! They will have their ritual—and I *will* have mine!"

Two ritual murders, of the *Azhrei* and the *Kir'reia*.

"He will die," the High Warlord said. "I will kill him—my own hand, my own sword!"

She met his gaze for the first time. Amazingly, her heart kept a calm rhythm and her face was serene. His was anything but. Something had happened to annoy him mightily. She gave him a pleasant smile. "You can try."

His fists clenched. Meiglan held herself immobile, knowing that if she flinched he would know the suddenness of her terror.

"You are only a woman. You know nothing. You are without worth. You have no sons. Your husband is a fool to keep you. You are no use to him!"

Something really wonderful must have happened. It was much easier now to smile.

"Clever!" he snarled. "Be clever, *Kir'reia!* It is all you know! At dawn that day he will die, and clever will not save him!"

He strode off, calling for attendants. She listened carefully and heard him say *Radzyn* several times. Had someone besieged it? Or even retaken it? The former, she decided; had the keep been lost, he would be roaring with fury instead of merely taking out his irritation on her.

When the light failed, she returned inside and lit candles. There were enough left for three or four nights of sewing. If Radzyn was no longer a source of supply—well, Pol's need for information was more important than her need for light.

She had finished Pol's name and title on the cloak when a commotion outside distracted her. Voices shouted questions and orders. Gliding to the tent flap, she twitched it open enough to see. Torchlight and cookfires glowed. And her guards were gone!

For an instant she pictured it—a swift horse galloping into the hills—she could lose herself in gulleys and canyons where they would never find her—

From which she might never emerge alive.

Sioned would have risked it, and Tobin before her illness. Meiglan wondered dully if comparisons to them would ever find her anything but lacking.

A straggle of horses limped past, broken-winded, heads hanging. On their backs, riding without saddles or bridles, were exhausted men in white tunics, some of them stained with blood. They left her limited field of vision, but she could hear very well as the High Warlord bellowed a demand in their language—with the word *Radzyn* falling like a boulder into a well.

Meiglan had to know. If she waited to tease information out of him, there would be nothing to tell Pol but guesses and speculations. Smoothing back her hair, she strode straight out of the tent toward his angry voice.

But by the time she reached the knot of warriors around him, he had recovered his temper. "Tilal," he was saying, almost softly. *"Rei* Ossetia Tilal. *Rei* Ludhil. *Rei* Amiel."

Meiglan stepped deliberately into his view. "You've lost Radzyn," she said on a bold guess. "Stop this now, before you lose your lives."

One of the white-clad men slid to the ground, staggered for a moment against the horse, then approached her with a hand uplifted. "Dare your lips open, woman?"

"Kir'reia," the High Warlord snapped.

The man's arm fell. *"Kir'reia!"* he jeered.

"Yes," Meiglan answered, never for a moment believing she was in any danger. Not with the High Warlord there. "The *Azhrei* will destroy you. Leave us in peace, and he will leave you with your lives."

"Peace he will have, *Kir'reia*—in death!" He laughed raucously. Everyone else joined in. The High Warlord deigned only to smile. At first Meiglan felt thoroughly the fool. But after a few moments she realized the laughter was forced and false. They were stung by defeat, these proud barbarians. Gathering herself, she gave them all a superior smile, turned, and went back to her tent.

He came to her shortly thereafter, tautly controlled in speech and gesture. "Speak again in hearing of warriors and priests, the words will be your last."

She glanced up briefly from her needlework. "You need me alive."

"Alive," he agreed. "A tongue is not needed."

"Alive and unmarked," she challenged, remembering the warriors' reluctance to hurt her and Valeda. "No bruises and no wounds." Taking an even greater chance, she went on, "Do you think I don't know what those priests plan for me? You don't dare harm me."

His dark eyes flared and he swore under his breath. Then, grasping her arm, he dragged her upright. "You are truly the *Kir'reia*—unlike any woman I know!"

If she hadn't been so frightened she would have sobbed aloud with laughter. The women of his experience must be fools indeed, if she shone so brightly by contrast.

He let her go, and her knees would not hold her. She landed in the chair, the cloak spilling onto the carpet.

When he spoke again, he was as calm as if his outburst had never occurred. "You will write to *Rei* Ossetia Tilal. You will say he will die for what is done. You will say the Fire will not touch warriors as priests. You will write this now."

Meiglan clenched her fists and folded her arms.

"You will do this," he murmured, "or I will kill you—and find another virgin of clean blood for the priests."

"Virgin?" The word made her laugh with incredulity. "I've been a wife for nine years! I have two children!"

He shook his head. "Daughters."

"But I—"

"Daughters," he repeated, and this time he smiled, his clean-shaven face oddly shadowed by candlelight. "No sons."

✳

The rooms Sionell shared with her children were only a little way down the corridor from Pol's. He could hear laughter, and her fondly exasperated voice as she tried to scold them into bed. He wanted to go in to them, to forget the pain of remembering similar scenes of his own family in the warmth of Sionell's. He had just kissed Jihan good night, where she slept now on a cot in his mother's room, and the echoes of the past had been almost too much to bear.

Something strange had begun to happen to him over the last

several days. He supposed he had learned how to wait. His mind functioned just as usual—observing, considering, reasoning, thinking, planning—but the impatience was gone. And that was curious, for with Meiglan in Vellanti hands he ought to have been frantic to do battle, to win her back.

But because the Vellant'im had taken her, he was compelled to admit they were real.

Killing an Enemy was not the same as killing a man. The Enemy he faced on the field had no reality beyond their swords. They were faceless, without name or personality or family or history. He was just as unreal to them: not Pol, but the *Azhrei*. Not a man, but a thing: Enemy.

Now, in taking Meiglan, these unknowns had ripped a portion of him away. She was part of what made him Pol. The High Prince and the *Azhrei* were not what she loved; it was him. Pol. Husband, lover, father of her children.

They were husbands. Fathers. Brothers. Sons. They had names and faces, the love of their families, lives that had brought them here to seize a part of his life. They would look on Meiglan and think of their own wives, their own children. Through her, they would know a part of the man Pol was.

For they were the same as he.

It was not required to mourn the deaths of those he had killed in battle. They were Enemy: alien and other, unreal, inhuman. But those who held his wife captive—he and they were real to each other now. No differences, no alienness, no otherness. Real; human.

He must believe that they were human. He must believe that they would see their wives in her, and know him as more than the *Azhrei*. Imagining his gentle Meiglan in the power of monsters could not be borne.

But if they were men, just like him, then—

"All right, you've made me curious enough to ask. Why is that door so fascinating?"

He started violently. Sionell stood nearby, mildly amused, no trace of mockery in her smile. Her eyes were sparkling, her dark red hair disordered with the rambunctious bedtime antics of her offspring. And even with Meiglan called to his mind and his heart, he felt his insides knot at the sight of this woman. *I love you both. Goddess help me, what can I do?*

"I was just thinking," he said curtly.

"Don't snarl at me," Sionell warned in a soft voice, all humor dying in her eyes. "I'm almost cured of disliking you. Don't give me new reasons."

And loving me? Are you cured of that, too?

Despair helped him master himself. "Sorry. But there are plenty of reasons without my having to say a word."

"Oh, I don't know. You've changed recently—or at least you're less obnoxious." She leaned a shoulder against the wall, folding her arms. "What were you thinking about just now?"

He hesitated, then opened the door of his chambers. "Come talk to me for a little while. I never see you except in glimpses down the halls or across the courtyard. Even at dinner we never really get to talk."

Sionell hung back, wary. "There are lots of other people to discuss things with."

"Too many other people. They all hear bits and pieces of it and put it together when they talk among themselves—well, except Andry, of course. There are things nobody tells him."

"Rightly so. He makes me uneasy, Pol."

"You? Why?"

She preceded him into the anteroom. "Close the door." When he had done so, she said, "Even with all he doesn't know, I think he feels power gathering around you. And that's not something he relishes."

Pol sat down, sprawling his legs, frowning absently at the scuffs on his once immaculate boots. Strange how that bothered him, where before he wouldn't have given it a thought.

"I sat with the *diarmadh'im* for a while today in the gardens," he said with seeming irrelevance. "Asking questions and getting very few answers. But one thing Thassalante said stuck in my head like a thistle barb. 'Every good sorcerer knows how to steal power.' "

She nodded. "That's exactly what I sense in Andry. What you've got, what you're going to have, he's on the alert to steal."

"It'll be the other way around," Pol replied grimly. "And he won't like it. I just hope the fight he puts up doesn't rip Maarken to shreds."

Sionell perched on a chair opposite him. "You're not worried for yourself?"

"He doesn't know about me."

She was quiet for a time. "He'll have to, sooner or later. That's what all this is about. Sorcerers. I had a talk with your mother," she added when he arched a brow.

"Good. I won't have to explain it to you." Restless, he stood and began to pace. "Goddess, isn't that the Hell of it? The Vellant'im have come to take their revenge on people who haven't held any real power in hundreds of years."

"Life's full of ironies," she said with a shrug. "Do you think telling them would make any difference?"

"Of course not. They hate Sunrunners, too."

"But once Andry learns of the distinction. . . ."

"It'll give him one more excuse to purge the prince-doms?" Pol's turn to shrug. Sinking into the chair again, he eyed her quizzically. "I can't talk to anybody else like this. Oh, they've all got good brains, but they've also got their own goals. Andry's concerned with his own power. Chay thinks only in military terms—and that's good, I need him for that and there's none better. Maarken is waiting for Andry and me to have at each other again, while Hollis holds her breath and begs with her eyes. And then, of course, there's my darling, devious mother."

"But all their goals combine into yours—don't they?"

"In a way. Only Mother's hiding hers. She knows some-thing, I can feel it."

"I'm surprised you haven't wrung it out of her."

"It's funny, isn't it? But I find I can wait. I trust her—the way I should have trusted her and Father to begin with over this war." Pol sighed. "You're the only one who doesn't have an aim larger than going home. I don't mean you don't care about the rest of it—but you don't let what you want get in the way of listening." He paused, then risked it. "I need that, Ell. I need to know you're here."

She gestured with one hand. "Do you see me packing to leave?"

"You know what I mean."

Her shoulders stiffened fractionally. "Not really—and not interested."

"Ell—"

"Stop it, Pol! Why do you have to ruin it? Why can't we just sit here and talk as friends? Damn it, stop *needing* me so much!"

"I can't!" he cried. "And even if I didn't, we have to talk

about this. Don't pretend you didn't feel anything, I know you did—I *know* it!"

"If you were so almighty certain of it, you wouldn't be yelling at me."

For an instant his temper came near to igniting. Then he gave a tired smile. "Do you know how much I hate you when you're right?"

"Hold that thought." She got to her feet and started for the door.

"If you didn't feel anything, you wouldn't always be walking away from me," he called softly to her back.

She stopped with her hand on the knob. After a moment she turned, her face expressionless. "You," she said, "are a son of a bitch."

"And a bastard as well." He spread his hands wide. "Both of them, in fact as well as action. But whatever I am, we've got to clear things up, not pretend they don't exist."

Sionell resumed her chair. "You wanted to talk. So talk."

He couldn't think of a single word to say.

Her lips twisted in disgust. "All right. It happened. It shouldn't have, but it did. We can do one of two things: forget it and be friends, or remember it and be unable to speak a civil word to each other for the rest of our lives. I've been trying to show you which I want, Pol. Evidently you don't agree."

"Isn't there another choice?"

"I won't be your mistress. Even if I wanted to be, which I don't, we both have children and you have a wife. I won't hurt any of them—and I certainly won't repeat the mistake of dishonoring Tallain's memory."

"Are those your reasons?" he asked softly. "Or your excuses?"

"What do you want from me?" she exclaimed. "All right, let's talk about it, shall we? Until there aren't any more words left, and then maybe you'll leave it dead where it lies!"

"Stop it, Sionell."

"You wanted it to start," she shot back. Her voice took on an ugly sneer that made him wince. "Need me, do you? What you really *need* is an imagination, Pol. Let's see— shall I have my own chambers at Dragon's Rest, where you'll come to my bed when you feel the *need?* Will Meiglan and I sit on either side of you at the law courts when you *need* our advice? Just think of our happy family evenings! Her children and my children playing oh-so-sweetly around us—and perhaps *our* children, Pol? Yours and mine? Do you *need* a son, High Prince?"

"I'm not my grandfather!" he cried. "Damn it, Ell—do you think I'd do that to you and Meiglan? Or to myself?"

"Don't like that version?" She rose, pacing as he had just done. "How about this one? You give me some quiet little manor convenient to Dragon's Rest, and I'll wait *breathlessly* for your visits—in secret, of course, so Meiglan doesn't know. My parents can raise Talya and Jahnev and Meig, so not even the children will know! Would that suit your *need,* High Prince?"

Springing to his feet, Pol took her by the shoulders and shook her. "Shut up! You know that's not what I want, not any of it!"

"What in the Name of the Goddess *do* you want, then? I won't be kept, Pol! I won't do anything that makes me hide my face from my own mirror!" She paused, then with lethal softness inquired, "Or were you thinking of putting Meiglan aside to marry me?"

He gasped as if she had driven her fist into his stomach.

"No, I suppose not," Sionell said. "Murder isn't your line of work—and we both know it would kill her." She pried herself from his grip. "All right, we've talked. It's settled. We'll forget our mistake and try to—"

"Ell." He put a hand very gently on her arm. "I love you."

She shook him off. "You're beginning to bore me, Pol."

"I love you," he murmured again.

"That's your problem," she said with a shrug. "Get over it."

"You wouldn't fight me so much if there was nothing inside *you* to fight."

"What I'm fighting is the urge to kick you into the middle of next Summer."

"Perhaps." He let her go. "Do you know why I'm certain that I love you? Every time I'm with you, it's like when I stood in the sand with Azhdeen at my back and watched the Vellant'im advance on me. I'm convinced I'm going to die—and at the same time I feel invincible, and safer than I've ever felt in my life."

Blue-gray eyes flinched. "I don't mean—that's not what I want, Pol. You know it isn't." She stuck her hands into her trouser pockets. "It's just that you make me so damned *mad.* Always demanding things of me. Always knowing where to put the knife, then twisting it just because you *can.* You hurt me—not like when I was young, but you can still hurt me. If that's your definition of love, then maybe I should go home to Tiglath before we *do* end up hating each other."

He took a careful step nearer. "You've never let me show you what I mean by love."

"And if I did? What about Meiglan? Do you think I'd take what's hers?"

"You don't understand. It's not the same sort of love."

"Oh, and that makes it all right? What in all Hells is wrong with you?"

"I don't know!" he burst out. "Do you think I *asked* to feel this? Now, when it's too late? I'm ashamed—because I'm *not* ashamed! What kind of man does that make me?"

"The usual kind," she answered, with a wry gentleness that was the very last thing he'd expected to hear. "Did you think you were special?"

All he could do was give a weary laugh and a shake of his head. "I've tried very hard not to be—while being convinced all the time that I am."

"It's why you love Meiglan, you know," she said seriously. "She's your refuge from all the other things you have to be."

"And it's why I love you," he replied. "You force me to be—'usual'—but at the same time you never let me forget that I'm not."

"She's better for you than I ever would have been, Pol."

"We'll never have the chance to find out, will we?" he asked. "You're right, we've talked—and this is the end to it."

"Yes. With our customary knack for slicing each other up with the truth." She opened the door, glancing over her shoulder. "Friends?"

"Friends," he acknowledged.

She nodded. "Get some sleep."

To his surprise, he did—falling into bed and a deep well of velvety rest.

But toward dawn he dreamed. He walked through the charred gardens of Stronghold, tears stinging his eyes. At the grotto, he knelt to wash the ache away with cool water. Floating on the pond were two royal circlets. One was woven of living flowers, brilliant purple and gold and blue; the other was of silver studded with a rainbow of living jewels. The sun blazed down, igniting both in Fire. He reached out, not knowing which he would take—but he wasn't swift enough. The fragile crown of flowers withered and vanished.

He woke sheened with icy sweat and calling Meiglan's name.

CHAPTER
NINETEEN

The next morning—only two more until the cloak must be finished—Meiglan decided the Father of Winds might be a sympathetic character after all. A brisk breeze blew sand in all directions, giving her an excuse to stay inside. Last night had shown her how precarious was her hold on composure; she didn't want to risk seeing anyone, least of all the High Warlord. She never thought that Pol might be using the sunlight, frantic to see *her.*

About midmorning, a Vellanti entered without asking permission. White-clad against the white walls of the tent, his hair and beard and eyes were all the blacker by contrast. A stark man, all angles and anger, he extended a thin roll of parchment by his fingertips, too fastidious to touch a woman.

Meiglan accepted it, untied the broad ribbon—Radzyn red and white, with Desert blue edgings—and made a show of inspecting the quality. The ribbon already indicated that the page was from Tobin's own desk, and she used only the finest.

"I see you remembered to stuff a few rolls in your pocket as you ran out of Radzyn," Meiglan said. "This belongs to Princess Tobin."

White teeth gritted behind the black beard. "Women not write. It is law."

The sight of a mere woman wielding pen and ink would not be one of the more fulfilling moments of his life. Meiglan smiled, genuinely amused, oddly relaxed. Only the

High Warlord, it seemed, could unsettle her. The thought was both comforting and worrisome.

"No women," he emphasized. "Only priests."

Oh—so *this* was a priest. All the others in white must be, too. She wondered what it was they did besides write and steal Tobin's bedsheets for clothing. Rerolling the page, she heard the soft, dry crackle that meant it had been improperly stored. Good parchment ought to be nearly as silent as fine silk.

Silk. . . .

The priest deposited a pen and inkpot on the empty second chair.

"I need a knife, in case I make a mistake," Meiglan said. When he frowned, she sighed patiently and explained as if to a child, "To scrape the ink clean."

"No knife."

"This is a very important letter. A *precise* letter. Mistakes will cause your High Warlord to be thought of as an illiterate fool." The word was too big for him; she added irritably, "As if he has no written words!"

"No knife."

Well, it didn't really matter. The parchment would tear. The edge would be ragged, but she could probably nip it clean enough with her teeth.

Meiglan shrugged. "Very well. Leave me, I have to concentrate." Another word he didn't own. "To *think*. Isn't that something you do very often, priest?"

The priest took a pace nearer, caught himself, and hissed, "On the day, I will silence your tongue myself!" He turned on his heel, and strode away.

No question about it, twitching these people was exciting—but it left her shaking at her own temerity. By rights she ought to be cowering in terror. These people had killed thousands; she had watched Valeda and Thanys die with her own eyes; they were planning to kill her and Pol and everyone else they could lay hands on.

But that was the kernel of it: she didn't believe in their power. She believed in Pol's. She had no delusions of immortality. She knew she *could* die. She simply didn't believe that she *would*.

When her hands no longer shook, she knelt on the rug before the second chair, using it as a desk. Smoothing the parchment out onto the seat, she nodded at its size—quite adequate for her purposes. She turned a third of it back, then changed her mind and made the fold smaller. After all, he thought she was terribly clever.

She took a long time about tearing it, until she realized she could say that she had spoiled the first part and, lacking a knife, had to get rid of it in the only way available. But she would only say that if he asked. Tucking the piece away in the folds of the cloak, she uncapped the inkpot, dipped the pen, and began to write.

Two mornings later, the parchment would be flung by a Vellanti warrior at a Dorvali on scouting patrol near Radzyn. By noon it would reach Tilal, where he lay fuming and helpless in bed. His blank bewilderment at the letter's colossal arrogance soon gave way to fury that a High Princess should be forced to write such things. Then he inspected the words themselves—wavery, badly spelled, nothing at all like the beautifully written missives that sometimes came to Gemma at Athmyr. Poor Meiglan—she must be half out of her mind with terror, sick with the humiliation of writing this incredible document. He debated about telling Pol, finally deciding it would be kinder not to. So Pol never knew about the letter at all.

✳

"I still don't understand why they don't know about Pol," Riyan said to his wife across their double desk. "I mean, shouldn't they?"

Ruala gave a shrug. "They know all the bloodlines, it seems. But how could they know about Ianthe?"

"Hmm. You'd think they'd be able to sense what Pol is, though, and be mad with curiosity over how it's possible."

She set aside the kitchen inventory and sighed. "I can't think about any of this. All I can think about is that mirror. *Lord Rosseyn!* All those years it hung in the entry at Skybowl, and we never knew anything!"

"And all the years before that, when it belonged to my mother's family and they never knew what they had." He paused and grimaced. "Or maybe they did at one time, and sort of forgot to mention it after a while."

"But you'd think *someone* of sorcerer's blood would have called Fire around it, and seen him."

He spread his arms wide, let them fall to his thighs with

twin slaps. "You would've thought someone would bump into a dragon on sunlight long before this, too. But nobody did. Speaking of which, what are we going to do with the dragons when it comes time for the battle at Skybowl?"

"Do with them?" Ruala chuckled low in her throat. "What makes you think any of us could persuade any of them to *do* anything?"

"I meant we'll have to get them out of the way. Once the fighting starts, they might all do what Azhdeen did and the Vellant'im would kill every one of them."

"Fine," she agreed readily. "You go right ahead and tell that big brute Sadalian to fly away somewhere. Let me know how it turns out."

"He's not a 'brute,' " Riyan protested.

"He's absolutely huge and every time you talk with him your head aches for a whole day."

"Your Azhly isn't exactly pocket-sized. And I've seen you wince often enough after a chat with him." Rising, he went to the window and watched the wind swirl sand around the outer walls—a southerly wind that couldn't find its way into the keep to strip new buds off the trees. He hadn't even noticed that all the dead leaves were long gone and shoots were poking through the garden beds. "It's almost Spring," he mused. "Last year at this time—"

"Don't," Ruala said softly.

He nodded. "It's just that it sneaked up on me. Feels like all this has been going on forever."

"Yes. But it won't. We'll be free of them and able to live in peace."

"But nothing will ever be the same." Someone entered the gardens down below; he reminded himself to have the gate hinges oiled. A dark, lanky young man Riyan barely recognized as Isriam of Einar wandered the paths so sightlessly that several times he nearly collided with a bush or tree. Ruala joined Riyan, seeing his interest, and leaned against his shoulder.

"Pol must've told him," she said. "I hope he was kind about it."

"Who better to tell Isriam that he isn't who he always thought he was?"

"Personally, I'd be glad to find out I wasn't Sabriam's son. I never did like that man."

"Neither, it seems, did Isaura."

"It might be a good idea for Isriam to go down to Skybowl with Maarken this afternoon," Ruala said thoughtfully.

"Give him something to do to take his mind off it? I'll mention it."

Word had come several days ago that Sabriam had divorced his wife and disowned his son for being no true son of his at all. The Sunrunner at Einar had been unable to say what reaction had been at Fessada; Pol had wanted to wait to tell Isriam until Prince Pirro decided whether he would accept the youth as his grandson, fathered by Camanto. But Pirro's Sunrunner was silent, and Pol had chosen to talk with Isriam now, before anyone could let word slip.

"If he's made a Prince of Fessenden, Arnisaya's not going to be happy," Riyan commented. "I'm sure she counts on her little boy's being Pirro's heir."

"With herself as regent, of course. Well, I suppose it all depends on how threatened Pirro feels. Pol isn't happy about his denying Laric passage through Fessenden. If Isriam becomes the heir, maybe Pol won't be so quick to carve up parts of the princedom as a lesson."

"His hands are pretty much tied about Grib and Gilad, too. Amiel's helping Tilal, and Elsen is at Goddess Keep doing the best he can, so Pol can't punish their fathers too harshly for being cowards." Riyan turned from gazing down at the aimless, disconsolate figure far below. "I'm glad I won't have to make that decision."

"Look at it this way—he won't have any trouble at all over Meadowlord. In fact, he'll enjoy himself tremendously. That should make up for any frustration over Grib and Gilad and Fessenden."

"You know, I don't think he *will* enjoy it," Riyan said, brushing back a stray lock of her night-black hair. "Taking isn't half as much fun as giving. I just hope he doesn't decide to give *me* anything. I've got my hands full with three keeps as it is. Although I'm not sure how much of Skybowl is going to be left when this is over."

"Don't worry," Ruala soothed with a wicked little grin. "It's his battle—we'll make him pay for the damages!"

✳

"I still don't like it," Hollis said.

Maarken repressed a sigh. They'd been through this a

dozen times. Two dozen. She would never like it and they both knew it. But they both also knew it had to be done.

"I'll be with her every step of the way," he reminded her again. "With a troop of fifty for military protection and Meath for other kinds if I get busy, we'll be just fine."

"I know, I know—stop repeating yourself," she snapped irritably. Settling his cloak on his shoulders, she went on, "And it's only two days there, and Chayla has to go because she's the best physician we can spare—and in order to get over her fears. Or so Sioned keeps trying to convince me. Everybody will be perfectly safe the whole time—or so *you've* been trying to convince me." She picked up his swordbelt, but when he reached for it held it back. "I'm a little unclear on why *you* have to go," she finished pointedly.

"Because she's my daughter."

"Besides that. There's something else, Maarken, I know there is." She grasped his left arm. "And it has to do with this, doesn't it?"

"Do I have to say it?" he burst out. "Do I have to use words of one syllable to make you understand? It must be seen that I can still lead."

"Nobody doubts it but you!"

"I'm the Battle Commander. My place is with the army." He snatched the swordbelt from her hand. "There's a battle coming, Hollis. They have to know *before* it that I'm still capable—"

"—of arming yourself with one hand? Oh, give that here before you drop it." She slid the belt around his waist and buckled it, then turned for the sword that lay on a table. All at once she gripped the polished wood with both hands, bright head bending, body quivering.

Maarken went to her, touched her shoulder. "Hollis . . . please, my darling, you mustn't. It'll be all right. Just tell me you understand."

"I have to, don't I?" she mumbled.

"Sioned is right about Chayla—I don't like admitting it any more than you do, but she is. Have you noticed how she flinches back from every man who isn't family? She keeps seeing the Vellant'im who stole her from us. I can't do anything about that. But I *can* help her do her work—it's important to her, Hollis. Being a physician is what she *is,* and

Rislyn needs her help—so she can't let herself be afraid. Evarin can't go anywhere, his leg is still healing. Rislyn doesn't know him, anyway."

"You can stop now—I've heard all this." She still wouldn't look at him.

"Besides," he went on, "there's Kazander."

That brought her head up. "What do you mean?"

"She'll want to see him," Maarken replied steadily.

"It's cruel, Maarken. There's no hope in it. He has to know that."

"Of course he does. They both do."

"Then why—?"

"Because this will all be over soon. He'll return to his wives and his children, she'll become a Sunrunner and a physician, and that will be the end of it. Let them have what they can. It's little enough. They both know this is all there can ever be."

She swallowed hard. "It's so damned sad," she whispered.

Picking up the sword, he held it out to her. "I'm late. I have to go."

She slid the sheath into the heavy loop on the belt, made certain it was secure, and reached up to fasten the clasps of his cloak. "All right, I understand," she said grudgingly. "Does that make you feel better?"

"No more than it does you." He leaned down to kiss her lips. "We'll be back in four days."

Arm-in-arm they started for the antechamber. Hollis suddenly pulled up short, a shiver touching her. Maarken opened his mouth to ask, then didn't have to: their reflection looked back at them from the full-length mirror mounted to one side of the door.

"I can't see Lord Rosseyn's face," Hollis whispered. "We're Sunrunners, we're safe from mirrors. But I can hardly swallow a meal in that room these days—and I never see a mirror now without being scared."

"I hope it scares Pol, too," Maarken said grimly. "Have you heard? He's taking lessons in sorcery."

✳

Six hundred horse, two hundred foot, one hundred priests in white to conduct ritual at Skybowl eighty-ninth day of Winter.

Meiglan frowned at the scrap of parchment. Precious little of this would help Pol. She must know more. What did the ritual involve? Why Skybowl? (Well, that hardly mattered. Pol wanted them there anyhow; it was convenient that they wanted the same location.) But the ritual itself—Sioned was powerful and imaginative. She might be able to foul their ceremony in some manner, or use it to mean the opposite of whatever the Vellant'im intended.

His voice outside made her thrust the parchment beneath the chair cushion. She rose smoothly to her feet, capping the inkpot and sliding it and the pen into her pocket. When he took his first step within the tent, making the candles flicker, she was seated as usual, the cloak in her lap, her needle busy and precise.

"Done?"

"Not quite."

He bent to snatch up the bulk of it from the rug. As he read the words he snorted. "Lies. Sword and Fire will not help him live." Sliding the silk through his hands, he came to the place she was working on. "Write that his last breath will taste of fear and knowledge and *my* sword."

"There isn't room."

"*Make* room!"

She shrugged and took the silk back into her lap.

He paced to the bed, then the washing stand to rinse his fingers. His back to her, he said, "In two days you belong to the priests."

"After I finish the cloak, you mean?"

"Yes. After. You will be—eh, what is your word?— cleansed. Washed of sin. Seen to be unmarked and perfect. No thing not perfect may be offered." Turning, he watched her fingers move mindlessly, automatically. "I will not see you again until the day."

"What will they do to me?" she whispered.

"You know." He paused. "You, mother of no sons, mother of dragons reborn."

Meiglan's hands stilled. Dragons? What did they have to do with—

Forcing herself to speak took everything she had—and the strong memory of Pol's face. "Are you sure they'll get it right?"

"It is written. The princess of highest blood who has given no man life will cleanse the dragons of all taint.

Diarmadh'im will have no more power than puling girl-children. Dragons will tear their flesh, and feast on their bones, answer no more to the *Azhrei*'s call."

Information. This was information. She seized on it, clung to it. Even though he was informing her of how she would die.

"You carry no son," he went on. "You bled four days ago. You will be cleansed of that, and all else, by priests." He hesitated. "I will not see you again before the day."

"It sounds as if you've thought of everything," she managed. "Will I be killed with glass, silver, gold, or steel?"

For the first time in her experience of him he looked unsure. It had been an arrow shot with eyes closed, but it had worked.

"The priests decide."

"It makes a difference, you know."

"Then you will say what difference."

She tucked the corners of her mouth into what felt like a ghastly smile.

"You will say!" he snapped. "If not to me, then to priests!" He leaned over her, his breath hot on her cheeks. "They need not harm to learn. They will know, and you will be unmarked still. You will say, *Kir'reia*."

Her arrow dwindled to an insignificant dart, a pinprick. Glass, silver, gold, steel? Which? Glass was the Merida weapon—but this was a ritual murder, not an assassination. Silver? Gold? The Vellant'im already knew that steel killed Sunrunners. But if she was to be rescued, and if Pol was there, steel would kill *him* if he was using his power, and he would have to in order to get close enough, any of the Sunrunners would—

"Gold," she blurted. "It must be gold."

He straightened up and nodded. "Gold. It is honorable. And—" One fingertip brushed over her hair. "—fitting." He kicked the cloak out of his way as he went to the tent flap. "Two days," he flung over his shoulder, and left.

Meiglan felt herself begin to shake again. But she didn't cry. Tears would leave marks on the silk.

✳

Honorable, fitting—and a waste.

The High Warlord walked without seeing the mass of his

army, or the Desert beyond the camp, or the endless blue sky. He saw Stronghold. The Flametower rose as proud as ever, but with its fire quenched. No one feared to enter the castle now. The dragons were all dead.

As if they had ever been alive, he thought acidly. Stupid priests. Stupid, self-righteous, superstitious fools.

And yet he was just as much the fool. He should have left more warriors at Radzyn. They would have been some use there, instead of lolling about the camp waiting for the march on Skybowl. But he'd wanted all available clans here to terrify the enemy. To swell his own pride.

Unable in fairness to blame the priests for the loss of the keep, unable to accuse them of cowardice in the hearing of the warriors, who believed in the priests' words, he could only blame himself. How could soft white priests be expected to fight? They had not dared to blame *him,* of course—but it had been his mistake, and knowledge of it had gleamed furtively in their eyes.

And so he must give up the *Kir'reia* to them, many days before he'd planned. They had lost Radzyn, yet he must give them her. They had abandoned their duty to keep the harbor safe, yet he must allow them charge of her.

By the Father of Wind and Rain, how he hated priests.

She would be safe enough. They would be even more careful of her than he had been. After the initial inspection to assure themselves that she was without flaw, none of them would touch her on pain of death. He had only touched her rarely. The priests would not even be tempted.

But he had been. He had been.

There would be no more sitting near her. No more speaking to her in hope of hearing her speak. No more scenting her skin—ah, she kept herself so clean, even in this filthy land. He had denied her a real bath because the thought of her pale nakedness all polished with water would have maddened every soldier in the camp. He could not have protected her—not even the priests could have protected her then.

She was exquisite, and so exquisitely different from Vellanti women, with her fragile bones and her cloud of golden hair, and her skin the color of milky dawn tinged with gold and roses. She sat serene amid the silken clutter of that accursed cloak, slender, clever fingers always moving, supple, clever mind always working. He never knew what she was thinking. Her huge dark eyes were guileless as a child's one instant and cunning as a wolf's the next. Her voice was always soft, even when she was angry. Her body, tucked small and neat into her chair, was a body to dance in. She was more beautiful than any woman had ever been— and despite his taunts he knew very well why the *Azhrei* did not put her aside, or add more wives to his bed.

Damn the *Azhrei* for making *her* his wife. She was a woman worth the honoring, a prize fit for the offering. But what a hideous, senseless waste her death would be.

Glancing around as a breeze nipped at his hair like a playful stallion, he discovered it was full night and he was nearly at Stronghold. If he turned back now, they would wonder why he had walked so far to no purpose. He had no purpose, of course. Only distance between himself and her, between himself and the priests who would take her as their reward for fleeing Radzyn.

He strode forward, through the tunnel and into the first courtyard. He had given the duty of standing guard in case of stray dragons—what idiocy—to ten youthful warriors with courage to prove, who would not shy in fright from a stray shadow. Two of them came to meet him, bowing.

"That trough," he said, pointing. "Take it to the priests."

They knew better than to react. The stone trough was hip-high and as long as a man was tall, and must weigh more than four horses could drag. But he had ordered it, and it would be done.

A petty use of his power, he told himself in disgust, completely unworthy of him. Had the priests made him as impotent as they?

No. He would prove otherwise. He was the High Warlord of the Vellant'im, he would destroy the enemy who had destroyed the Islands. He was mighty. He had killed so many that he needn't bother displaying his kills in his beard. His slightest word was obeyed instantly.

And, surrounded by priests who would not be tempted— who did not know how to be tempted—the *Kir'reia* would have her bath.

*

The snowstorm jeered at the village of Pimanost, clearing for half a morning before renewing its fury, brooding for half the night before striking out in blasts of wind that felled a score of unprotected pines. Five days of this had scraped tempers raw and turned Laric into a pacing, muttering madman. But no one dared raise his voice in the lodge. They were all painfully aware of Rohannon's voice up in the loft, and that in the last two days his cries had grown feeble.

Aldiar came down the ladder every so often to stretch his legs while Rohannon slept. He said little beyond "No change, my lords." Once or twice Arlis attempted to go up and help. Aldiar discouraged him with a few words, and finally forbade him with a single look. Amazing, the power in those black *diarmadhi* eyes set in that thin Fironese face.

Arlis had never felt so trapped in his life. His world had contracted to the lodge and fifty paces around it. Everything else was a white Hell. What the locals called breaks in the storm were to him nearly indistinguishable from its worst furies. He battled his way outside several times a day to check on his troops and horses, returning exhausted but still restless.

His companions were no help. Tirel could be amused by playing chess only so long, and grew fretful. Idalian reviewed events and Yarin's probable troop strengths until the others could recite the information in their sleep. Laric paced endlessly, the bare floorboards creaking with every step, and asked military questions Arlis couldn't possibly answer. Balarat wasn't *his* castle.

The elderfolk attended their prince at dinner. Conversation was awkward, occasionally interrupted by Rohannon's weakening groans. At such times Idalian would glare up at the loft, and Tirel would be stricken silent, and Laric would make a visible effort to resume talking. Arlis drank.

Four young villagers came every night after dinner to grace the noble group with lutes and singing. Arlis, who had never heard Fironese hill music before and hoped he never would again, applauded dutifully even when the noise stung his ears. By the fourth afternoon he was actually looking forward to the evening concert. It gave him an excellent excuse to stay silent while he got drunk. Their favorite song was about a crystaller who made his lifework the imitation of all the different forms of snow and ice, and finally gave up in despair at trying to out-create the glassy or frosted beauty around him. There really *were* forty-six distinct kinds of frozen water, and a verse for each. And if he had to listen to them one more time, he would slit the singers' throats so they never inflicted it on anyone else again.

But at least it drowned out the terrible sounds from the loft.

On the morning of the seventy-sixth day of Winter, as the storm gathered breath for what the elderfolk promised would be its last assault, there was no music to cover the scream that shook the rafters. Arlis scrambled up the ladder, Aldiar's permission or not. What he saw in the sullen shadows of the hearthfire below made his heart stop in his chest.

Rohannon looked a full silkweight thinner. His cheeks were sunken and gray, his eyes hollowed in dark bruises of pain. He was tied to the bed—wrists and ankles and hips—by thick ropes of wool blanket. Rank sweat poured off him, soaking bedclothes he'd ripped in his agonies. He shook so hard that the cot and even the planks beneath Arlis's feet shook with him.

"Gentle Goddess," the prince breathed. "Aldiar—help him!"

The young man glanced around, nearly as hollow-eyed as Rohannon. "I've done all I know."

Arlis went to the bed, seizing Rohannon's shoulders as he arched up from the bed, pressing the boy back down before he tore the restraints loose—or tore his arms from their sockets. "Help him, damn you!"

"His body is almost drained now, and the hunger is at its worst. He has to get through this on his own."

Arlis struggled to keep Rohannon down. All at once the bucking body went limp and a pitiful whimper parted his lips. Blood trickled from a corner of his mouth. "He's bleeding!"

Aldiar slipped a piece of wood between Rohannon's jaws—polished free of splinters, already imprinted with the marks of his teeth. "He's only bitten his tongue or his cheek." Sitting back on his heels, he drooped as if strength was nothing more than a memory. "He'll live or he'll die. There's nothing more to be done for him."

He glared at the sorcerer across Rohannon's shivering body. "His mother didn't die!"

"His mother was used to less. His mother was older. His mother took twenty or thirty days to cleanse herself of it." Aldiar's head lifted slowly, and the shifting light showed Arlis the swollen bruise on his chin. "If I give him something to make him sleep, his heart will fail and he'll die. If I give him *dranath,* we'll have to start all over. He won't survive this a second time. Now or not at all, my lord."

Arlis smoothed Rohannon's sweat-dark hair. "It's my fault," he whispered. "I needed a Sunrunner. I did this to him. I'm the one who should be in danger of my life right now. Not him. It was my fault."

"No. His. He knew about *dranath.* He's not the first to believe himself stronger than it is. Not the first to find out otherwise."

"He's barely breathing."

Aldiar leaned forward, placing a hand on the thin bare chest to feel the blood-pulse at its source.

"Do you think. . . ." Arlis swallowed hard. "Will he die?"

"I don't know."

Crouching beside the cot, Arlis took one of the boy's hands. Not even a ring to mark him as *faradhi.* Yet no *faradhi* had ever done so much, risked so much, in serving any Lady or Lord of Goddess Keep.

Rohannon breathed. Slowly. Arlis listened, watched, as if every breath might be the last. Aldiar's head had bent once more, hand resting lightly over Rohannon's heart. They stayed like that, as if carved of stone, for a very long time.

Suddenly Aldiar's hand lifted, fisted, slammed down on Rohannon's chest. Arlis cried out and grabbed the sorcerer's wrist.

"Let me go! His heart stopped!"

"What are you—"

"Let me go or he *will* die!"

Arlis flinched back. Aldiar pounded a second time, a third, hard enough to crack ribs.

"Blow air into his mouth!" he ordered, voice breaking, hoarse and frantic. "Fill his lungs!"

Rohannon's lips were blue. Arlis took the stick away, pinched his jaws open, and blew a long breath down his throat. He understood now; it was like helping someone half-drowned. But he had never seen anyone do what this *diarmadhi* did, never heard of keeping up a rhythmic thud over the heart.

"Don't you dare die! *Breathe!*"

Rohannon spasmed and gasped in air. Aldiar slapped Arlis away and pushed with both hands just below the ribs.

"Come on! You've been doing it all your life! You stupid Sunrunner, did you forget how?"

"You can stop." Arlis reached for the boy's shoulder. "He's breathing."

Aldiar's own breath came in a sudden sob. He hovered over Rohannon for a moment, staring at the rise and fall of his chest. Then he slumped against the cot with his hand on folded arms. Arlis nearly did the same. He was sodden with sweat and his hands trembled as he unknotted the blankets.

"He'll be all right now?"

Aldiar glanced up, bewilderment twitching at his brows. An instant later his eyes closed and he slid to the floor. Arlis levered himself up onto his knees and peered over Rohannon at him. Sprawled on the wooden planks, eyes closed, he looked more like a ten-year-old child than a sorcerer who had just saved a Sunrunner's life.

✳

Thassalante closed the Attic door behind him. Pol barely heard the sorcerer leave.

"What is it you know and he doesn't?" he asked the face in the mirror. "I can see it in your eyes."

So late that the moons had long since nestled down to sleep; so late that the whole castle was silent; so late that the candles on either side of the mirror had burned nearly to the sockets.

"Would you tell me if you could? How this happened, why, when? What I can do now to free you? To free myself and all my people? Would you speak if you could?"

Lord Rosseyn gazed down at him. Wild waves of black hair swept back from thin, intense features and eyes as black as pitch.

"What did you do that she trapped you there? Did you understand what was happening to you? Could you have stopped it—any more than I can stop what's happening now?"

Pol took a step closer, bracing his hands against the mantlepiece. His head tilted back and he stared straight up into those eyes.

"I need what you know. I need the power you knew how to use."

For all its remote sorrow, it was a beautiful face: the face of a prince, a bard, or a madman. Perhaps all three.

"You owe it to me, damn it! The Vellant'im came here for vengeance on you and your kind!"

The face remained as it was: proud, severe, beautiful. Silent.

Pol bent his head to one outstretched arm. "No," he said more softly. "*Our* kind. Yours and mine, my could-be ancestor. Is that who Lallante's family came from? The child of the woman who did this to you? If that's so, her viciousness bred true. She'd approve of my blood-mother."

The hearthflames were too hot. He pushed himself upright and backed away from the mirror.

"What can I do?" he whispered. "Wait? Learn what I can? They'll come to Skybowl, I know that. I'll be there, with everything I have. The killing will start again and won't stop until the sand is soaked in blood. Meiglan's blood. They'll kill her if I don't yield. And if I yield, they'll kill everyone else. All the Sunrunners. All the sorcerers. Everyone."

Rosseyn went on watching him. He knew it was a trick of the mirror; the eyes never followed him around the room, and only seemed to meet his when he stood directly before the hearth. But the sensation of being watched was so strong.

"Did you buy lives with your freedom? Is that what's waiting for me? No, if I give in I'll only be the first. It won't end with me. Did it end with you? The most powerful of all sorcerers—Thassalante says all the legends agreed on that. Could you have stopped her, and chose not to? Did you sacrifice yourself to stop the killing? Or was it all for nothing? Is that what's in your face?"

He would never know. The mirror would never speak. He could stare up into that face for the rest of his life and nothing would happen. Nothing would change. Rosseyn would gaze out with sad, resigned eyes, and give no answers.

"Useless, isn't it? You can't help me. I've got to do it. Well, it's not as if I'm alone. There's Maarken and Chay and the armies here and at Radzyn. Andry, if I'm tactful enough to convince him or strong enough to take his power anyway. And that's not to forget my mother. . . ."

A deep, demanding bellow high above the castle turned his head to the shuttered windows. Azhdeen, Pol thought, with a rush of gratitude. He flung open the windows and

conjured Fire in midair so the dragon could see him.
Azhdeen circled, choosing his spot, and came to rest on a
wall with his talons dug into the stone. He folded his wings
tidily against his back and rumbled low in his throat, peering
up at Pol.

"Coming, your magnificence!"

*

Late as it was, not everyone was startled out of sleep by
Azhdeen's roar. In Tobin and Chay's bedchamber, candles il-
lumined a large parchment drawing spread atop the quilt,
upon which he made notes while she mused aloud. They
both looked up at the dragon's call.

"I thought it was time for a sentry to come by," Chay remarked. "Jeni says the dragons hold a conference at
Skybowl afterward, to share the news." He shifted the parchment on the bed. "What were you saying about the kitchens?"

"Inconvenient," she replied succinctly.

"So when we repair the first floor, you want to move
them?"

"No. Make a new great hall."

He moaned. "Forty-eight years you're mistress of Radzyn,
and only now you tell me you don't like it?"

Sionell heard Azhdeen, too. She even recognized his
voice. It seemed she had recently grown an extra set of
nerves that responded to anything having to do with Pol. In
fact, at times she felt physically sick being near him.

Hitching her chair closer to her bedchamber fire, she concentrated on mending yet another of Meig's shirts. How *did*
the child manage to tear at least one seam each day? Simple,
she told herself. He was growing out of his clothes. But
coaxing him into hand-downs was impossible. She'd tried;
he'd flatly refused. A real stickler for his appearance, was
Meig—at least until he ran outside to play dragons.

Azhdeen and all the others absolutely enchanted him.
He'd long since made the connection between being a
Sunrunner and having a dragon to talk to, but he had none
of Jihan's impatience. Sionell had asked him about it yesterday.

"I suppose you want a dragon right now, too?"

Meig answered, "I can wait. Besides, my dragon's not even born yet."

It was hardly the first precocious thing he'd ever said, but it had taken her aback more than usual. Practically from birth, Meig had looked on the world with complete equanimity—never angry, rarely crying, always composed—and with a self-awareness that was positively uncanny sometimes.

Well, she wouldn't have to worry about a dragon taking up residence at Tiglath for years yet. The next hatching would come in 740. No immature dragons had so far expressed interest in any humans, so she could tack on another three years. Still—a ten-year-old Sunrunner with a dragon? Meig would no doubt find it as normal and unremarkable as he did everything else. Something told Sionell that a dragon would be the least of her concerns with him.

She grinned, imagining her mother's face when Meig finally got his dragon. Feylin was as fascinated by the great beasts as she was terrified of them. The sight of her grandson casually scratching a draconic jaw—Sionell chuckled in undaughterly glee. Feylin had written the dragon book partially in an attempt to overcome her fears with intellectual reasoning. But it had never been the legends that frightened her. Dragons were just too damned *big,* and never mind all that nonsense about teeth and talons and—

The shirt slid from Sionell's suddenly loosened grasp. She stared sightlessly at the fire for some moments.

"Dragons," she murmured. "Dragons. Oh, of course!"

CHAPTER TWENTY

Done.

Meiglan had finished the last stitches just before dawn, just before the last of the candles guttered out. Her eyes would barely focus, and her back was one great knot of pain. But the cloak was done.

She lifted both hands from the neatly folded silk in her lap, watching with a remote sort of interest as her fingers curled in a slow spasm that warped the bones. Eventually it hurt so much that she tried the usual remedy—flattening her palms against each other, then bending the fingers back to stretch muscles. After a time the cramp passed, and her hands dropped to her lap again.

She stared down at them, lax and helpless atop silk so sleek that it rippled like water. She could no longer feel the texture. The constant rub of material and thread and needle had chafed her palms raw and swollen her fingertips.

She supposed she ought to lie down and rest until he came for the cloak, or wash and dress in fresh clothes, or inspect her work one last time. But she was too exhausted to do any of those things. Besides, she simply didn't care.

The High Warlord might or might not find what she meant him to find. If Pol saw what was meant for him, he might not understand. There was nothing she could do about any of that now. The cloak was finished.

If the High Warlord did discover what was sewn inside, she must seem frightened. She couldn't seem to summon up much real fear anymore. She remembered feeling it, like the mercifully vague recollections of childbirth. But fear took so much energy.

Not that she felt especially brave. Courage was doing what you were afraid to do. Thus if she didn't feel afraid, she couldn't be courageous. All she felt was tired.

But she knew how to pretend. She had acted everything from a daughter's affection to a highborn's political cunning to a High Princess' power. Fear was something she'd always pretended *not* to feel. Still, she ought to be good at it. She ought to be absolutely brilliant.

Her right forefinger, practically imprinted with the shape of the needle, traced the initial capital of Pol's name without feeling it. She wondered without curiosity if he would understand what she had written. Perhaps; he was clever. Perhaps not; he didn't expect *her* to be clever. Perhaps it didn't matter. There was little of importance that she'd been able to work into the cloak. No really vital information. Nothing that would change anything. Sewing the cloak had given her something to do. All her efforts of mind and body, all her tenacious thinking and cramped muscles, all of it was well-nigh meaningless. Not that she could bring herself to care.

Not even that she knew she was going to die.

Two priests had come by last night. In disjointed sentences and nearly incomprehensible accents, they had told her that she would be moved to their holy precincts. She would be purified in body, if not spirit. She had finished her bleeding and would be given water to wash and white clothes to wear. She would drink no wine and eat no meat. Only white things would pass her lips: milk, certain vegetables and roots, and flowers brought from the Vellanti Islands and carefully nurtured for this purpose. She had a moment of inner hilarity at that—how they must have struggled to keep the plants alive in the Desert!—but nothing showed on her face. They went on to tell her that if she willfully became impure, the ritual purification would not be to her liking. Then they described what would make her impure: any bruise, cut, scrape, or other damage to her skin; any food that was not white; touching or being touched by any man; seeing or being seen by any man who was not a priest; witnessing the rising or setting of the sun, or the moons and stars at any time; touching anything that a priest had not purified; reading; writing; wearing trousers instead of the robes they would provide; uncovering in the presence of any man her hair, her arms, her face. . . .

They droned on in their harsh, guttural voices. Meiglan decided that if even a quarter of this was regularly inflicted on Vellanti women, they would be better off dead. She stopped listening and kept stitching.

Then they described the ritual purification.

Last night it had produced a twinge of fear. This morning it moved her not at all, except in wonder of their logic. A woman who had borne no sons was presumably defective in some way, and "purifying" her might make some sense. But a woman who had borne no sons was still virgin to their way of thinking, a worthy sacrifice to their god—*after* she had been purified for having borne no sons, which was the reason she was pure enough to sacrifice in the first place.

Doubtless they found it logical. Or perhaps not—there was no logic in a belief that dragons died and rebirthed themselves in Fire. Everyone knew they didn't. But "know" and "believe" were sometimes as different as day and night.

Meiglan *knew* she was going to die. She simply didn't *believe* it.

She must have dozed a little in her chair, for the next thing she knew was his voice outside, giving some command to the guards. Righting herself with an effort, she settled more firmly on the cushion—under which were the pen and inkpot the priest had forgotten to retrieve.

His shadow filled the doorway, morning sunlight glancing off the jewels hanging from his earlobe and the golden cuffs that covered each forearm. He was splendid and powerful, and the sight of him hurt her eyes.

"Is it finished? The cloak?"

She lifted it from her lap with both hands. He came to her, boot heels digging into the carpet, and unfurled the mass of silk. Just as she'd known he would, just as she'd hoped. First the whole of it, inspected front and back; then the plackets of embroidered blue; at last the hem, where she had stitched her tribute to Pol. He let the rest of it pool at his feet as he slid the words through his hands, reading silently, lips moving.

" 'Shining eyes,' " he sneered. " 'Ritual fire'—'Dragon seeking prey'—'cloaked in rightness'—'dead at his feet'—bah! What list of his great deeds? What battles, what killings, what enemies?" He shook the cloak at her. "And what of his death? Where is his death in these words?"

So tired. "You didn't honestly expect me to put that in, did you?"

"I ordered." He frowned down at her, crushing the silk in both hands.

"I'm his wife," she said simply.

"Kir'reia!" he accused, and walked to the open tent flap to get a closer look at the stitching. " 'Beloved of Meiglan,' " he jeered over his shoulder. "A woman who gave him no sons!"

She waited, absently massaging her sore right hand with her left. Perhaps the words would occupy his mind to the exclusion of the material they were written on. Perhaps they would make him so angry that he would rip the cloak to shreds and thereby discover everything. Distantly curious, not really involved, Meiglan rubbed her weary fingers and waited.

But he only folded the cloak again, neatly, with the front plackets meeting down the center. Returning to her side, he sat down and smoothed the silk with long, battle-scarred fingers.

"The priests take you at sunset. This tent will move to their place, and the bed, but no chairs. No washing. No other clothes."

"Yes—nothing that isn't white. I've been informed."

Taking the cloak by its neck, he flung it out again so it spread across his knees and spilled onto the rug. "This," he said, pointing to the embroidery on the back. "What is it?"

"You must have seen it before, on my husband's banner."

"But what *meaning?*"

"The dragon is obvious. The scroll in its talons stands for the law."

"And this?" He stroked the outline at the dragon's feet.

"My own addition. It's this cloak."

Black eyes searched hers. "Clever Meiglan," he muttered, and slowly gathered the silk onto his lap. He never looked away from her face as he felt it along the blue plackets, rubbed them between his fingers, and finally smiled.

When he drew his knife, she remembered fear.

He slit a dozen stitches. Slid his fingers within. Slipped out a piece of parchment, closely written on both sides.

"Clever Meiglan," he said once more, and began to read.

She closed her eyes.

"Six hundred horses—yes, that is so," he commented. A moment later: "The number is wrong in warriors not mounted." Another pause. "Yes, all of warrior age are here—no more will come if he kills us now."

Suddenly he grabbed her wrist. She stared at him, at the knife he held before her eyes, and terror was no pretense.

"If I mark you," he said softly, lowering the knife to the back of her palm, "the priests would not take you. I keep you. As mine. To take you home and put sons into you, clever Meiglan. Strong sons." Cold steel rested feather-light on her skin. "Do I mark you, *Kir'reia?*"

Someone gasped; someone frightened. Someone brave marked *him* instead, with a palm cracking across his cheek.

The High Warlord laughed and let her go. Rising, he heaped the cloak at her feet and crumpled the parchment in his fist. "Make it whole, for *him* to die in," he said, and strode from the tent.

A guard replaced him immediately, to watch as she repaired the broken stitches. She did so numbly, not daring to think or feel. When she finished, the guard took the cloak away and tied the tent flap closed.

Meiglan stumbled to the cot and buried her face in the pillow. He had found it. He had done as she'd begged the Goddess to make him do. She ought to feel triumphant at the trick she'd played on him, she ought to be laughing into the silken pillow. Not weeping.

✳

Maarken was not especially concerned about day-to-day commands on the ride down to Skybowl. That was the sort of thing he could do in his sleep; he didn't have to prove his competence to anybody. So he told young Isriam of Einar—or, rather, no longer of Einar but not yet of Fessenden—to see to making camp and getting everyone started again in the morning. To Draza of Grand Veresch went the duties of organizing scouts, sentries, and the general order of the journey, and leading the hundred soldiers. This left Maarken free to enjoy the ride, his daughter's company, and a little project of his own.

With Laroshin—abandoning his usual self-effacing silence, he'd flatly informed Pol he would be Princess

Rislyn's personal escort—Maarken spent the whole of the first day happily plotting maneuvers. The troop was made up of veterans from Radzyn and Stronghold, some of the surviving students from Walvis' training school at Remagev, and thirty soldiers from Tiglath offered by Sionell—though it was Jahnev who made the formal offering. His mother was scrupulous about showing their people that, although only seven winters old, he had taken his father's place legally, if not militarily. Jahnev's chagrin at being too young to lead them had nearly been the demise of his dignity and Maarken's carefully straight face.

He and Laroshin had spent plenty of time with Chay recently, proposing and refining various tactics for Pol's consideration. This trip would give them the opportunity to practice one or two of these maneuvers, most notably something he called Dragon Wings. On the second afternoon out from Feruche, after telling Chayla and Meath to get out of the way (with ten soldiers to whisk them to safety if things got out of hand or the Vellant'im appeared), Maarken gave the signal for practice to begin.

Laroshin, at the head of the Remagev contingent, swept around the main force at the same time Maarken led the Tiglathis in the opposite direction. Then they swung around and charged. The "wings" of twenty riders each folded in, pushing the remaining fifty against themselves. Draza, warned that something would be tried but not knowing what, responded by dividing his troop in half, giving one to Isriam and leading the other himself—the first section riding ahead, the other wheeling smartly to retreat and regroup. Maarken found himself galloping through empty Desert, right past Laroshin and fortunately not into him. The four contingents paused, turned, and sat their horses staring at each other. Maarken burst out laughing.

"Why is it so funny?" Chayla complained to Meath as they watched from atop a sand dune. "It didn't work."

"Lord Draza's a smart boy," the Sunrunner replied. "And Swalekeep taught him how to think fast and give orders even faster. So much for 'Dragon Wings.' I think we'd better rename it 'Torn Cloak.' "

"Father will have to think up something else."

"No, he just can't use it against their mounted troops. I have an idea it'd work rather nicely against those on foot. The Vellant'im aren't as quick as Draza, when it comes to it.

And just imagine all that horseflesh and all those swords thundering down your throat." He unstoppered his water skin and drank, then offered it to her. "While your father amuses himself playing soldiers, would you care to learn a little Sunrunning?"

Chayla nearly dropped the skin. "Me? Now?"

"I see no one else around here who has either the capability—your pardon, ladies and gentlemen," he added to the ten guards, who only shrugged or grinned. "Or the need," he finished more seriously.

Chayla drank, returned the water, and stared at her gloved hands on the reins. "I should have learned a long time ago."

"Not really. You're about the right age to begin," he said, deliberately misunderstanding her.

"I mean that I could have—"

"—been the vexation of your parents, like Jihan?" Meath smiled. "I doubt it. I'm told you can call Fire. Let's see you do it for me now. A fingerflame will do."

She obliged, letting it hover in the air between them. "More?"

"That'll do. Interesting colors."

Peering at the flame—gold with tinges of red and orange, like any other—Chayla asked, "Is it? Does that mean something?"

"Not that. You. I can read *your* colors as you work. Here, let me show you." And around the tiny Fire he conjured the pattern that was Chayla, two sorts of green with blue and red woven through it. "Jihan can do this without even thinking about it. I'm not that talented. But that's you all the same. Emerald is a good color for a healer."

"The other green doesn't shine as much," she said critically. "It's almost opaque."

"We classify it as jade. You should see Sioned's colors sometime, with black onyx so thick you'd swear you could touch it."

"Can I?" Her fingers ventured toward the pattern.

Meath watched her trace the curves and angles in the air. The guards were uninterested, scanning the dunes for possible threats as Maarken sorted out his army. But one of them, a young man wearing Radzyn's silver sword badge, stared intently at what to him should have been empty air.

Meath noted his face and reminded himself to find out his

name. But he had no time to spare for other potential Sunrunners right now. This one needed all his attention.

Maarken rode up, still grinning. "Did you see that? Pitiful! Absolutely pitiful!" He paused as he caught sight of the colors. "Are you doing that, Meath, or is she?"

"I am." He let them vanish, and Chayla extinguished the fingerflame. "But she knows them now, well enough to answer another Sunrunner." He smiled as the girl's blue eyes rounded. "This afternoon I'll show you one or two other little tricks."

"Tricks!" Maarken snorted. "Andrade would have your rings for that!"

"So would Uncle Andry," Chayla said shrewdly. "Father, can't you stop him from trying to get me to Goddess Keep? It's flattering, of course, but I'm tired of telling him I'm a physician first and a Sunrunner second."

"Positive of it since the day you were born," Maarken said.

"If you'll both excuse me for a while, I should justify the rings Andrade gave me," Meath said. "I'll let Jeni know where we are, then look in on Andrev at Radzyn."

"He's never seen it before, has he?" Chayla asked. "And he won't be seeing it at its best, either."

"If I know Princess Iliena—and I do—she'll have it scrubbed from cellars to battlements to get rid of the Vellanti stink." He withdrew to work.

"Has Andry been pestering you?" Maarken asked his daughter.

"A little. Things about my being family as well as *faradhi*." She shrugged. "I think he's using Master Evarin to tempt me to Goddess Keep." When Maarken's eyes widened, she laughed. "Not like *that!* We talk medicine, not moonlight!"

Embarrassed, he growled, "Well, all right, then. Keep it that way."

Chayla made a face at him, then said seriously, "I think I'd like to go to Gilad and study—after Whitecliff and Radzyn are put to rights, I mean. Or do you think I should stay with Sioned wherever she decides to live, and learn Sunrunning first?"

"I hadn't considered it," he admitted. "I've never thought of her anywhere but at Stronghold."

She frowned. "Can it be rebuilt?"

"Yes. But I don't know if Pol will want to." He chewed his lip for a moment. "Rohan always meant things to shift to Dragon's Rest as the High Prince's residence. I suppose he thought Stronghold would go to whichever of Pol's daughters wanted it—or maybe even you."

"I don't think Jihan would give up one stone of it— burned to a crisp or not. And anyway, I don't have any claim on Stronghold."

"You're Zehava's great-granddaughter, just as Jihan and Rislyn are. If you Choose a man without a holding of his own—and you can Choose anyone, I'm rich enough to pro- vide ten dowries—then if Jihan or Rislyn don't want it, you might consider living there."

Her face went very still. "I'm not going to get married. I don't want a husband or ch–children." To cover the slight stammer, she hurried on, "Really, Father, I've got too much to do. And it's not as if there's nobody but me to continue the bloodline. There's Rohannon, and Jihan and Rislyn, and all of Andry's children—"

"Let's see how you feel when you're twenty, or twenty- five," he said, aware that he, too, was talking quickly to cover a nervousness he didn't really understand. "At *Riall'im* or the school in Gilad you'll have your pick of fine young men. And if it comes to it, I'll build you a castle somewhere myself. Nothing so grand as Feruche, mind you. But I promise it won't overlook the sea!"

When she smiled—as he had hoped she would—Maarken had the sensation of stepping back from a cliff. He wished Hollis was here; she would know what to say, how to com- fort.

He found another change of subject as he squinted down at the troops, who had rearranged themselves into formation and waited for his word to ride on. With a glance at Meath, he said, "He'd better get back soon. I'd like to make another fifty measures before dark."

"We could get to Skybowl by dark if we pushed a little." She eyed him. "Or do you have something else you want to try along the way?"

"Caught," Maarken acknowledged cheerfully, and Chayla laughed—her old self again. Thank the Goddess.

Meath blinked and cleared his throat. "I took too long, didn't I—sorry."

Maarken shook his head and lifted a hand to signal resumption of the journey. "How's Tilal?"

"Healing nicely—and with all the gracious good humor of a wolf with a sore paw. They've made a good start in getting Radzyn put back together. Andrev says Ludhil and Amiel are all for marching up to Stronghold. I told them if they left Tilal behind, he'd make them pay for it at *Riall'im* until they're all in their dotage."

They started down to catch up with the troops. "And at Skybowl?" Chayla asked. "How's Rislyn?"

Meath sobered. "Jeni says she still sleeps quite a lot—recovering from the illness. Feylin's with her almost constantly. When she wakes up . . . well, she's not as frightened as she was. Jeni thinks she doesn't realize yet what's happened to her. She thinks it's only temporary." He sighed. "In a way, it is. Sioned's right, the world doesn't have to be completely dark for her."

"Very comforting—for us," Maarken observed quietly. "About as much as telling myself that because I've still got one arm, I shouldn't regret the loss of the other too much."

Meath looked stricken. "I didn't—forgive me, I forgot—"

"But that's what I *want* you to do: forget about this," Maarken replied, gesturing with the stump of his left arm. "In time, I'll bet most people forget Rislyn's blind, too. Sioned *was* right. She has other eyes. She's a Sunrunner."

✳

Meath had found Jeni walking the upper walls of Skybowl, obedient to Sioned's order not to set foot outside the keep. At her side was Sethric, hobbling along with one arm across her shoulders, determined to exercise. After the brief pause for her conversation with Meath, they started off again, and Sethric mentioned something about going riding tomorrow.

"Don't be an idiot, Sethric!"

"Lady Feylin says—"

"I don't care what she says! Look at you—if I let go, you'll fall over."

"Then don't let go," he said with a smile, leaning down for a kiss.

She avoided his lips. "Don't."

He gave a one-shoulder shrug. Her concern was gratifying proof of her feelings for him, but she didn't understand his reasons for pushing himself. A battle was coming, everyone knew it, and he was determined to be fit.

"I'll be careful," he said placatingly. "Just a couple of turns around the courtyard. If anything starts to hurt, I'll stop."

Her shoulders tensed. "Are you patronizing me?"

"It's not as if I'll be heading out at a gallop to meet Lord Maarken!"

"You would if you thought you could get away with it."

He had to admit she was right. "You don't see why, though, do you? I failed, Jeni. I have to make up for that."

"You were wounded and couldn't even stand on your own, but you brought Rislyn here safe—I don't see how that's a failure."

"They still have the High Princess."

Jeni slid out from under his arm and faced him. He balanced precariously with one hand on her shoulder, looking down into clear and angry gray eyes.

"That's not your fault, and you're a fool if you think it is! You're lucky you escaped with your life—that you came away with Rislyn is more than anyone could have hoped! But *you* feel sorry for yourself because you didn't complete the perfect portrait of Hero!"

"That's not true!" he replied hotly. "It was my duty to try and—"

"—and you succeeded! Has Pol blamed you? Has anyone? Anyone but yourself, that is! Goddess, men are impossible!" She strode away from him and he had to brace himself against a nearby wall. "You're *not* going to fight in whatever battle they're planning! It's *not* your duty to get yourself killed!"

This had ceased to be gratifying. Young as he was, Sethric understood that this meant more than her fear or his guilt.

"Camigwen." Use of her full name made her whole body stiffen. "Do I begrudge you your dragon?"

She whirled, sun-streaked brown braids flying. "What does Lainian have to do with this?"

Young as he was, Jeni was younger. Carefully, he said, "Do I get angry that you're a Sunrunner, and others like you will know your thoughts in ways I never can?"

"You're not making any sense at all, Sethric, you—"

"A Sunrunner with a dragon is what you *are*. What you are is what I love." He paused to gather words, propping himself more firmly against the stone, wishing he could go to her and touch her. "After this war is finished, you'll want to earn your rings. When we're both ready, if you haven't found anybody you'd rather Choose, I want us to be married."

She caught her breath; it was the first time that word had been used between them. He couldn't tell whether it pleased her or not, and didn't dare stop to find out.

"But during that time," he continued as steadily as he could, "I'll be in Grib. I'll help my cousin Elsen keep the laws by riding the princedom, the way High Prince Rohan set up the *Medr'im*. I've thought about it quite a bit, and I think it's something I'd be good at. It's what I want to do, Jeni—what I intend to *be*. Will you begrudge me that?"

"But that's *different!*" she cried. "I don't have a choice about being a Sunrunner—"

"Your mother did."

"She was afraid," Jeni snapped. "I'm not. And we'll leave my mother out of this, if you please!"

"What in Hells do you expect?" he exclaimed. "That I'll sit on my ass at Summer River, waiting for you to learn how to be something I can't? What happens if you decide you don't want a man who can never share that with you? If you're scared of losing me to this war—Goddess, Jeni, don't you think I'm scared of losing you to the Sunrunners?"

"It's not the same! You could *die!*"

"Either way," he told her bitterly. "Just to a different degree."

Tears sheened her eyes, but she was too proud to cry. "I hate being afraid for you," she whispered. "I don't know what to do with this, how I'm supposed to behave, what I should say—oh, why did you have to tell me you love me? Why couldn't you have waited?"

"Because I thought I *was* going to die," he answered simply. "And I couldn't leave you without letting you know."

Jeni wrapped her arms around herself, shivering. *If she turns away from me,* he thought, *then I really have lost her.*

"Sethric—"

A sudden shadow swept away the sunlight. He glanced up, seeing the dragon pass overhead. Lainian settled on the rocky ground below and keened a demand that sent Jeni to the walls. Sethric waited, biting his tongue. But she was leaning over the battlements, entirely absorbed in the dragon. Sethric might not have existed. She stood not two arm lengths from him, but she might as well have been atop the highest peak in the Veresch—or at Goddess Keep.

He judged the distance to the stairs, fairly certain he could make it that far. Climbing down them, however, was problematical. Maybe he could call for someone to help. All he lacked at this point was a three-flight fall to reopen his wound and bust a few ribs—and his stupid, stubborn skull.

Her arm slid around his waist. He looked down, startled. She was still looking over the walls at her dragon, not at him—but she was laughing softly. And suddenly he laughed, too, for Lainian was humming and crooning and rocking his head back and forth with what Sethric could swear was a ridiculously blissful expression in his eyes.

"You see?" Jeni said. "He likes you!"

"Looks that way."

"He considers *you* to be his now, too, you know." She slanted a glance up at him, the westerly sun glossing her face in gold. "Dragons are possessive. So it seems I'll *have* to marry you to keep him happy."

Sethric gulped, rallied, and said, "I owe him, then."

Jeni laughed. "I promise I won't mind having to share you with a dragon."

No man in his right mind could have resisted that face or those eyes. Sethric leaned down to kiss her, and the dragon sang loudly enough to rattle the stones of Skybowl.

✳

When Chay went upstairs, he found Tobin seated beside Pol in the moonlight, the dragon book in the young man's lap. Neither spoke a word; they weren't even moving except to breathe and blink. He stood staring at them for a few moments, then shrugged and went into the bathroom to get ready for bed.

Some time later he emerged, wearing a thigh-length nightshirt, his face freshly shaved (a habit formed early in their marriage to spare her delicate skin the abrasion of a day's growth of beard), and his temper ready to ignite. The two sat exactly as before, silent and motionless, discussing Goddess knew what by the bright white light of the moons.

He was tempted. He knew better than to interrupt a Sunrunner at work, but oh, he was tempted. It was late, nearly midnight, and Pol ought to know better than to keep Tobin up when she needed rest. She was doing much better—walked with only one cane to aid her, spoke more clearly, and the damaged side of her face was even showing a little responsiveness. Tobren attended her except when at lessons, and had said only yesterday that Granda was getting stronger. Chay knew what *that* meant. Tobin would try to do more, and exhaust herself, and lose what ground she'd gained. Look at her over there, black eyes wide open—both of them, the way they hadn't been since her illness—oblivious to everything around her. Even him.

From the day they'd first set eyes on each other, she had never *not* noticed him. Good Goddess, nearly fifty years. He remembered every day of them. They'd quarreled, laughed, struggled, made love, fought wars, ruled their vast holding, raised three boys to manhood, wept over a fourth who'd died too young, then wept over another son murdered in his prime. Looking at her now, he knew that they were both old—she coming up on sixty-seven winters, he on seventy. They were grandparents seven times over. Yet through all those fifty years they had never worn away the rough spots, never settled into a comfortable routine.

And never, ever been bored.

Chay wondered occasionally what it might be like to have a placid, agreeable wife—like Meiglan, for instance, or Alasen, or the way Betheyn would have been with Sorin, or even Sioned in her more peaceful moments. He couldn't imagine it. Life without Tobin? Life without *living*.

He heard her laugh. Her eyes caught his and lit with excitement, and it was just the same as always. He forgot everything he'd been thinking, except that she was the most impossible woman who ever drew breath, and—Goddess help him—he adored her.

Pol was laughing, too. "Congratulate us, Chay! Tobin and Sionell and I are brilliant!"

"Congratulations," he growled. "Now get out of my bedchamber so I can get some sleep."

"Don't you want to hear it?"

"Tell me tomorrow. I'm tired and I'm going to bed."

Tobin's smile actually lifted both corners of her mouth—still lopsided, true, but more the smile he remembered. "Cross old d–dragon," she accused.

Pol slapped the book closed, stood, bent to kiss Tobin's

brow, and said, "Be sure to kick him tonight when he least expects it. Sleep well."

When he was gone, Chay narrowed his eyes at his wife. "Do you walk or do I carry you?"

She snorted. "As if you *could,* feeble old fool—"

She finished with a yelp as he swept her up into his arms.

When he had her settled in bed, he climbed in beside her and muttered, "Do something about the lights."

Sunrunner's Fire winked out on a pair of candle branches. A little while later, he whispered, "Tobin?"

"Mmm?"

"What have you and that insane whelp of Rohan's come up with?"

She snuggled up against his back and twined an arm around his chest. "Broken crockery," she said succinctly.

He turned his head, and her face was a pale smiling oval in the moonlight. "What?"

"Thought you were t–tired."

"Tobin—"

"Go to sleep."

"Tobin!"

She laughed and kissed his neck, and would not explain. *Typical,* he told himself, tucking her hand against his heart, and didn't for a moment wish her any different than she had always been.

*

The next morning—the seventy-eighth of a seemingly endless Winter, as everyone would have agreed if asked—brought, among other things, a departure from a village in Firon and an arrival at a castle in the Desert.

Rohannon, weak but recovering, made it into the saddle by himself to prove he'd been right in declining Arlis' offer to wait another day at Pimanost. The storm had blown itself out, and they must start for Balarat again—and they couldn't leave him behind. Aldiar could function as lookout, but only Rohannon could be their Sunrunner. Only he could communicate with other *faradh'im.*

Rislyn, weak but recovering, responded to Meath's voice with a shy smile that stung tears into his eyes.

Kazander, who admitted no weakness and insisted he had recovered completely, greeted Chayla with a delighted smile that didn't hide the pain-weariness in his eyes. His pleasure turned to outrage when she ordered him to undo his nightshirt so she could have a look at his wound. He pulled the sheets up to his chin; she told him not to be a bigger fool than the Goddess had made him and stop this silliness at once. To Visian's amazement, Kazander meekly submitted.

In other places—at Goddess Keep, at Radzyn, at Feruche, and at the Vellanti encampment outside Stronghold—people stayed put and fretted as their differing circumstances dictated.

Elsen, also bedridden, breakfasted with his sister and her husband, and talked of anything but when and if the Vellant'im would attack. The Sunrunners, led by Torien and Jolan, stood on the ramparts and sang in the dawn, shivering in a fog that tucked around Goddess Keep like a blanket, smothering all *faradhi* communication for yet another day.

Tilal, defying the advice of a dozen knowledgeable physicians, got out of bed, took several turns around Chay's and Tobin's rooms, and promptly collapsed back onto the pillows in infuriated exhaustion. Princess Iliena gave him a look to wither grass and told him to behave or she'd tell Gemma on him.

Everyone at Feruche woke to yet another day of questions with no answers and problems with no solutions. Only Pol, Tobin, and Sionell met the morning with enthusiasm, and once Ruala understood why they asked what they asked, she laughed, too, and set herself and Maara and Jihan the task of gathering up every suitable piece of white pottery in the keep.

Meiglan, waking in the white tent to the sight of a white-robed priest setting white clothing on a stool, turned to her other side in bed and shut her eyes and refused to leave the cocoon of Tobin's white silk sheets.

The High Warlord, awake since dawn, spent half the morning watching the northern Desert sky and the other half watching the priests' white enclave.

Elsewhere, three groups of varying sizes moved at varying speeds to their planned destinations.

The first, made up of a priest who had deigned to act as courier and two clanmasters and their ninety warriors, headed due north at a quick canter, skirting the edge of the foothills, toward Feruche.

The second traveled slowly and amid constant complaints,

due west through Princemarch's mountain passes where snow had turned to slush in thin but stubborn sunshine.

The third journeyed due north on the Faolain River, blessing the strength of a wind that quickened their sails and made catching the second group a real possibility instead of just a hope.

None of the three would end their ventures in quite the manner they'd planned.

None of those who waited, worried, or worked; none of those who left safe haven, or reached it, or sought it, or sought to keep others from it—none of them would end the seemingly endless Winter in quite the manner they'd planned.

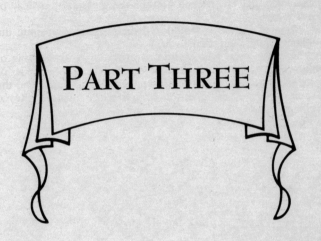

PART THREE

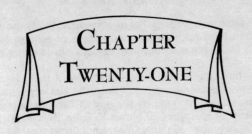

CHAPTER
TWENTY-ONE

Ostvel stood on deck, gloved fists on the rails, and hunched his shoulders beneath a heavy cloak. Ten days of drizzling, miserable rain were behind him. For all he knew, ten more were waiting for him farther into Princemarch. He cursed the rain while blessing the wind that bellied the sails and drove his ships north on the Faolain.

But it was a long river, and his little boats could not compare to the sleek dragon ships of the Vellant'im. What he couldn't have done with one or two of those....

At least he wasn't a Sunrunner, to be cursing the rain *and* the ship in between bouts with a bucket. Still, as a former Second Steward of Goddess Keep who had married two Sunrunners, he was *faradhi* at heart. And as different as his first wife had been from his second, Cami and Alasen would both laugh themselves silly at the irony of his being surrounded by ninety-nine *diarmadh'im* without a Sunrunner in sight.

Before the next ten days passed, he would be laughing, too: at Chiana. Through Naydra's conversations with Pol, Ostvel had offered to sail down the Faolain and join Tilal, march across the mountains to Skybowl, or go anywhere else his prince desired. Pol replied that if Chiana and Rinhoel set a single toe within fifty measures of Castle Crag, Ostvel's reward for dereliction of duty would be rule of all Princemarch when this was over.

He wished the damned boats would go faster. He wished he didn't feel so guilty about going to the defense of his own castle rather than helping Pol at Feruche. Mostly, he wished Pol didn't have such an atrocious sense of humor.

Cami and Alasen would both collapse in laughter at that, too.

Pol's little joke—and the welcome word that Ostvel was to be a grandfather again—had been the last opportunity for communication. At noon on the day of their departure from Swalekeep, this storm had blown in from Brochwell Bay. It was gasping now, slanting the rain in snorting gusts, but there was life in it yet. Ostvel didn't relish the notion of slogging through the muddy hills, chasing down Her Grace of Meadowlord. Still less did he look forward to fighting in the inevitable muck. But he was damned if that bitch and her murderous whelp would get within a hundred measures of Castle Crag. Though it was the ancient seat of Princemarch, repository of archives, built it was said by sorcerers after dragons abandoned the caves, Ostvel didn't care about any of that. His daughter Milar was at Castle Crag. So was Arlis' sister Alathiel, Rialt's daughter Mistrin, his old friend and court Sunrunner Donato, all his servants and retainers, and the work of over seventeen years in making a home and a life with Alasen.

Make that *two* hundred measures.

"I think there's enough thunder, my lord, without your adding to it," said an amused voice at his shoulder.

He turned, getting a faceful of rain, to see Princess Naydra's smile. "I beg your pardon?"

"You were positively growling. Don't worry, the storm will end soon. Look." She pointed southwest, where a ragged swatch of blue had stitched itself below the clouds like a banner tagging along for a wild ride on the gale. "By this afternoon, I think."

"I hope the wind doesn't end with it. We won't have much of an army if all the men are too worn with rowing to lift a sword."

"My kinfolk have said something about calling on the Father of Storms for a decent breeze, if needed."

Her voice was perfectly even. Ostvel struggled to keep his expression neutral—not so much at the absurdity of praying for a wind, but at her acknowledging the *diarmadh'im* as family.

"They say the Sunrunners foolishly limit themselves to Fire," Naydra went on, misunderstanding his lack of reaction. "Some stricture of Lady Merisel's—although if she was truly responsible for half of what they credit her with. . . ." She laughed and shook her head. "Anyway, even with all that's been lost over the years, they still know how to summon up a respectable wind. Their main problem seems to have been getting enough people together who agreed on the necessity and wouldn't take the chance to blast a rival."

Ostvel lost his fight and let astonishment scrawl itself across his face. "What exactly are you telling me?"

Naydra tilted her head slightly in the way of someone who has spoken perfectly clear words that somehow haven't registered. "It's said that when a new Lord or Lady of Goddess Keep is confirmed, they call on the four Elements. But it's only for show, isn't it?"

He nodded.

"Well, the *diarmadh'im* say that if enough of them work together, they really *can* summon a wind."

Insanity. "How many do they need?" he heard himself ask.

"They seem to have a fixation with ninety-nine—threes are important to them, for reasons they don't really know anymore. The ninety-nine with us now are willing to give it a try if you say so."

Too much rain. It had soaked into his skull and rotted his mind. Still—if Sunrunners could mesh their gifts to produce the *ros'salath,* then why not this?

"I don't know if I have the courage to ask what they might be able to do with Earth or Water," Naydra admitted, raking back her wet hair and resettling the hood of her cloak. "I rather hope that's something else they've forgotten."

"Oh," he said. "Um—yes."

"I can understand three regarding the moons," she continued musingly. "That's obvious. And we know they have a third deity, this Nameless One. They're not terribly clear about that, either. Someone hinted that they divided the continent into Desert, Mountain, and Meadow, and a group of three ruled each. I'm not sure how they classified Kierst-Isel, though—and they evidently didn't worry about Dorval, because it belonged to the Sunrunners. It's quite interesting talking with them, but it can be terribly frustrating as well.

I have a talent for asking questions they haven't heard since Lady Merisel's time. And *she* is usually their answer."

One way or another, he was going to get Merisel's history scrolls for the Castle Crag archives. Which brought him back to what had made him growly.

"When the sky clears—if it ever does—I'd like you to forage out a little, if you don't mind."

Naydra held one palm out flat, smiling. "Gracious, no man has ever found my conversation so fascinating that he didn't notice the rain has stopped!"

He looked at her glove. Damp, but no new drops on it. He took the hand and bent to kiss it.

"My very dear *Diarmadh'reia*," he smiled, "when I cease to be fascinated by a lovely and intelligent woman, I will beg someone to put me out of my misery. The sunlight is yours."

It took her longer than most, for she was newer to it. Ostvel wondered what it would be to live a whole life in ignorance, then have this break over one's mind—sudden storm or sudden dawn, either would be a shock. Naydra had accepted it by now, and come to enjoy it; she was smiling faintly as she worked, looking very much younger. He remembered his first sight of her—forty years ago next Autumn, when she and her sisters had vied for Rohan's favor at a tumultuous *Rialla*. He would never have believed that one day he would be the friend and ally of Roelstra's eldest daughter.

Or chasing across Meadowlord after Roelstra's youngest. Not that he'd minded leaving Swalekeep. Not at all. The thirty days of his residence there had been enough to put things in reasonable order and root out the officials who had aided Chiana in her rule. Young Gerwen of Mevricca would be a careful steward. Enough troops had been left behind to impress any would-be malefactors. Work would continue in field, orchard, and pasture. However, leaving Polev and Palila—*that* he minded. So did Naydra, though she said little. Camina, a favorite of his from his own guard at Castle Crag, had volunteered to look after the two children while her broken leg mended. But they both needed the gentleness and understanding Naydra had given—Polev while he came to realize his parents were not coming back, Palila while she recovered from what she'd witnessed the day of the battle. *If* she ever recovered fully.

To Ostvel's mind, there was nothing in life more important than children. But when it came to a choice between these two and his own daughter at Castle Crag, there was no choice at all.

Naydra's smile changed subtly, from the sweetness of youth to an expression that made her Roelstra's daughter. Ostvel held his breath, waiting for her to unthread the sunlight, knowing she must be methodical and not quickfire the way experienced Sunrunners were. When her dark brown eyes met his, however, there was fire enough in them, and more.

"Land here, my lord. In a day, perhaps two, she'll come through Wine-stem Pass."

He nearly yelped with delight. They both knew Princemarch, and the narrow defile that opened abruptly onto a grassy plain. Ankle-deep in mud this time of year, of course, but a day or two of sunshine would make the footing tolerable.

"We've got her," Naydra said, suddenly fierce. "My lord, do what you like with Rinhoel, but I beg you to leave Chiana to *me*."

"My pleasure, *Diarmadh'reia*."

＊

Maarken hadn't thought his dragon would react so enthusiastically to his arrival at Skybowl. But the instant Pavisel recognized him, riding up the north face of the crater, she launched herself into the sky—all black and silver and joyous cries of greeting.

She latched onto him so swiftly that he nearly fell off his horse.

That evening, once his headache had gone away, he made sure Pavisel was contentedly asleep on the heights before taking a stroll with Chadric and Walvis on the lakeshore.

"You know," he mused, "I thought I might shy away from coming here again—after what happened the last time, I mean. Remembering the exact spot, that sort of thing. But not a twinge."

"There was a sandstorm blowing, how could you remember?" Chadric asked, smiling.

"Well, yes—but the rest of my arm is out there somewhere, and my rings."

"Goddess, what an idea!" Walvis said. "Don't be morbid!"

"It's like prodding a sore tooth with your tongue," Maarken explained. "You keep at it to find out exactly where it hurts. I can't do this, that, or the other thing—or I think about part of me buried out there in the Desert—" He grinned as Walvis made a disgusted face. "No, really, I'm serious."

"So am I—in a definite need to change the subject."

"I think I understand," Chadric said. "Rislyn will do the same."

Maarken nodded, kicking at a stone. "I've been trying to anticipate things. Reading, for instance. Watching people's faces to learn what they're thinking and feeling."

"Except for reading, there's not all that much she won't be able to do if there's light to work with." The old prince lifted his face to the moons. "It's clouds that will blind her, and the time between day and night."

"She hears things more acutely," Walvis remarked. "I suppose the other senses compensate, don't they?"

"I hope so." Maarken paused. "Feylin says there's no hope at all?"

"None. She thinks the fever was so high for so long that it damaged the part of her brain that takes in what the eyes gather up." He sighed, then bent and picked up a rock and flung it into the water. "What she means, of course, is that she doesn't have a clue why it happened."

Nodding again, Maarken gave his friend his wish by changing the subject. "Kazander seems to be recovering nicely."

"From a wound that would've killed anyone else," Walvis agreed. "Feylin *says* she's not surprised. Let's see, how did she put it? The constitution of a horse, the hide of a dragon, and brains of solid rock."

"Speaking of which," Chadric put in casually, "my lady wife and I have a little idea that might intrigue you. Why don't we go back in and let her astound you?"

"Am I going to like this?" Maarken asked Walvis.

"Damned if I know. First I've heard of it."

Chadric only smiled.

As the rough soil crunched under their boots on the way back to the keep, Maarken said, "By the way, Pol wants to know who won the bet."

The other two exchanged glances. "What bet?" Walvis asked.

"Daniv, Jeni, and Sethric."

"Oh. *That* bet."

"Well?"

"There were several ... variables," Chadric replied thoughtfully.

"Who, when, and how being the primary considerations," Walvis added.

"Taking into account that some of us were right about who but not when, and some about how but not who," Chadric reminded him rather pointedly.

"—with the prizes pretty much evenly distributed among us, we agreed that the only real winners were Jeni and Sethric," Walvis finished.

Maarken rolled his eyes skyward. "Nobody's willing to own up, eh? How's Daniv taking it?"

Walvis laughed. "He says that since he was the one who gave them the appropriate shove, they'd better Name their firstborn after him!"

Audrite was waiting for them upstairs with hot taze to steal the chill from the evening. Daniv, she said, was in fascinated military conversation with Draza, Isriam, and Laroshin; Meath and Feylin were with Rislyn; Alleyn and Audran were pestering Jeni and Sethric; and Chayla, she added with a smile, was tending Kazander.

"With Visian in attendance, I trust," Maarken replied blandly, refusing the bait. "Her Isulki thistle. Half the time you don't notice him much—he's like Laroshin that way— but if she makes a move he thinks might so much as break a fingernail, he makes his presence known."

"Kazander made him account for every instant since he charged him to protect her," Walvis said, accepting a cup from Audrite with a nod of thanks and seating himself beside the hearth. "It took most of the afternoon."

"So," Maarken said, sprawling comfortably in a chair. "What's this scathingly brilliant idea you've come up with?"

When Audrite completed her five concise sentences of explanation, Maarken didn't know whether to laugh or call Feylin to give the princess something to cure her wits. A quick glance at Walvis showed him to be of the same mind.

"We have to get them to Skybowl," she said when the paralyzed silence stretched out too long. "This will do it nicely, we think."

"Simple, practical, and effective," Chadric added. "My father would've loved it."

This was too much for Maarken. With sure knowledge of Prince Lleyn's sense of humor to prompt him, he snorted, then chuckled, and finally burst out laughing.

"We thought you'd appreciate it," Audrite said demurely.

Walvis divided a bewildered look among them. "You're not really serious, are you? I mean, what's Riyan going to say when you propose to hand over his castle to the Vellant'im?"

Chadric eyed Maarken. "When he gets his breath back, we can ask."

※

"Ouch," said Pol, wincing.

Riyan grinned broadly. "It's only a *little* lie."

"That's just the point," Sioned told him. "It's uncomfortably close to the truth. We *haven't* been protecting our vassals' lands and people."

"Hardly your fault," Ruala soothed.

Sioned nudged her son with fingers in his ribs. "Stings, though, doesn't it?"

"I'll live." He leaned back on the couch beside her. "But I'm going to practice looking terribly, terribly hurt for when I see Audrite and Chadric again!" He looked up as Andry entered the Attic in response to Sioned's summons. "Ah, excellent. My Lord of Goddess Keep, you're just in time to witness foul treachery, high treason, and the breaking of sworn oaths."

"I beg your pardon?" he asked blankly.

"Riyan and Ruala are about to cancel their bargain with the High Prince," Sioned explained.

Riyan nodded, enjoying Andry's bafflement. "We hold our lands the way your father holds his—free and clear, down to the last stick of furniture and the last drop of water in Skybowl's lake. We're sick and tired of bending the knee to the High Prince. So we're canceling him."

"And," Ruala finished sleekly, "inviting the Vellant'im to a peace conference at Skybowl."

Andry greeted this cheerful destruction of centuries of tradition with a whoop of laughter.

"You're not treating this with the gravity it deserves," Pol complained.

"Indeed, your grace," Andry responded, instantly assuming an air of spurious solemnity, "I am shocked and grieved at the—what did you call it?—the foul treachery of this ungrateful pair." He turned to Riyan and Ruala. "Do you kick him out of Feruche as well as Skybowl?"

"On his backside, and his dragon with him," Ruala confirmed.

"And are all his relatives included?"

"Oh, we'll make an exception or two," Riyan said breezily.

"Dare I hope—?" Andry gave them a pleading look, hands folded at his heart.

"Oh, stop it, all of you," Sioned laughed. "I'll admit it has its amusing aspects, but this really is serious. We have to make it look good—and you're right about our being here at Feruche, Andry. How do we get around that?"

Pol answered, "We'll send the Tiglathis back home, carrying my banner with them. That ought to work."

"All right, then," she said briskly. "That's one. The next is how to convince the Vellant'im of Riyan's good will and honest intentions."

Andry joined Ruala on a second couch. "If Skybowl is left open to them, they can't help but suspect a trap. What can be said or done to impress the High Warlord that it isn't?" Barely seated, he sprang to his feet again. "Of course! We give them what they want! No, not you, Pol! What have they been trying to get back since this started? The pearls!"

"Tilal has them—and Karanaya would have a seizure," Pol reminded him.

"Karanaya is the least of your problems. For maximum effect, it should all happen at once. A letter from Riyan and Ruala, along with the pearls as token of good faith."

"Which means whoever delivers them has to come from the north." Pol tapped a finger on his teeth. "Andrev can explain it to Tilal, and he can send a courier. Ours will meet him out in the Long Sand somewhere, make the transfer, and circle back around to approach Stronghold from the north. How's that?"

"We'll have to use people who know the Desert intimately," said Andry. "The Long Sand is a big place to get lost in."

"I'll make a list. I—" He happened to look at his mother, who was smiling in a way that interrupted his thoughts. "What?"

She shook her head. "Nothing."

"No, I want to hear it. Is there something wrong?"

"Quite the opposite."

"I'm glad you approve," he said impatiently, "but what are you thinking?"

Her gaze darted from him to Andry and back again. "Not thinking, exactly. Listening."

Pol met his cousin's eyes. Sheepish smiles spread over both faces.

" 'When dragons sail the sea,' " Andry quoted softly.

Pol nodded. "So they have. And here we are." He rubbed his hands together and went on, "We'll need a letter, and a chat with Andrev—speaking of seizures, Tilal's apt to have one over this—and to choose a courier. Mother, will you talk to Sionell about taking her people back home? Thanks. I'll find Maarken and tell him we're agreed."

"Ummm . . . just one little thing, Pol," Riyan ventured. "Almost insignificant, really."

"Yes?"

"Please tell me that my castle will still be standing when you're finished with it."

"If not, he'll buy you a new one," Sioned soothed.

"Mother!" To Riyan, he said, "My word on it—that Skybowl will be intact, I mean, not that I'll pay to rebuild—" Sioned elbowed him ungently. "All right, all right! But you don't have to worry about it, Riyan. It may get slightly torn around the edges, but that's all. I promise."

Andry lingered after the others had left. Pol delayed going to the windows to weave moonlight, wanting to hear what was on his cousin's mind.

"I knew it must be Skybowl," Andry said abruptly. "I dreamed it."

Pol arched a brow.

"It was after they took Meiglan," he went on, his voice low and soft, blue eyes clouded with memory. "I'd been wounded. The Goddess appeared before me, juggling crystal spheres with castles inside. Some she let fall. They shat-

tered. Stronghold, Tuath, Remagev. Feruche as it was before
Sorin rebuilt it. The old Sunrunner keep on Dorval. Of those
that were left, she said one more must fall. And I knew it
would be Skybowl."

"Why?"

Andry's gaze focused on him. "Because it's expendable. I
bought Radzyn's safety with my belief in the dreams she
sent me, dreams of the war. Swalekeep has already been attacked and spared. Tiglath, the same—and too remote in any
case. None of the others made any sense."

"Was Goddess Keep among them?"

Patience obviously strained, Andry said, "She showed me
that another castle would fall and that would end the war!
Why can't you believe me? I dreamed the dragon ships. And
this justifies your own decision that the battle must take
place at Skybowl."

"But it doesn't have to shatter. You weren't paying attention to your own dream. Stronghold, Tuath, the old Feruche,
and the Sunrunner keep are all gone. Destroyed. But the fifth
was Remagev—*and it still stands.*"

Andry paced a few steps, swung around. "If it comes to
a choice between Skybowl and lives—"

"It won't. You say you bought Radzyn with belief. That's
how I'll buy Skybowl."

Andry's lips twisted. "Whose belief? Yours?"

"No." He smiled. "Theirs."

"With a letter and a few pearls?" he exclaimed.

"With their superstitions." It trembled on his tongue to remind Andry that he was no stranger to that sort of thing,
with his sunburst sign and his songs and his "sins," but managed to keep his mouth shut.

"You can't run a war on trickery. Damn it, Pol, if we're
forced to work together, then let me do what I came here to
do."

"Weave all of us together in a *ros'salath*, you mean? Let
you use our gifts as well as your own to kill? Don't you see
that's what I'm trying to avoid?"

"Have you suddenly turned squeamish? Or—no, it's that
you can't bear the thought of subordinating your power to
mine. How it must gall you to know you *need* me."

"You're dreaming again—this time with your eyes wide
open." As swiftly and easily as their minds had sparked
ideas earlier, now did they spark anger. It would be like that

until one of them was dead. He'd been a fool to think he could work with this arrogant, ambitious, bloodthirsty, self-righteous—

"I don't give a damn what you think of me," Andry hissed. "I don't need or want your approval—but, by the Goddess, I *will* have your respect!"

Pol grabbed for his temper and missed. "You sicken me," he breathed, the fury so abrupt and so great that it took all his strength.

"No, I frighten you," Andry shot back.

"I'm afraid of those who might be stronger than I. *You* are merely an annoyance." He took a step closer to Andry, his voice and his hands shaking. "I tolerate you because of your parents and Maarken, and a promise I made to Sorin years ago. But I'm sick of wasting my time." He turned on his heel before his clenched fists could satisfy their need to connect with Andry's face. "You have my permission to leave."

A strong hand clamped onto his arm, dragged him around. "Your *permission?* You insolent son of a whore!"

"Let's leave Ianthe out of this."

Andry's face blanked. Pol tore himself free.

"You knew. Don't pretend you didn't. That mirror of yours—you must have used it to see what I am. I've been waiting for you to say something for years now. Well, surprise, my Lord—your secret knife is dull and you'll get no blood from me. I know what I am and I know that you know it, and I couldn't care less. Now get out before I forget whose brother you are."

"Why remember?" Andry invited, stepping back, body relaxed and ready. "Come on, cousin, let's have at it. Right now."

"Don't," Pol whispered, rigid with tension. "If I started, I'd kill you."

"No, you won't. You need me," Andry taunted. "Admit it, Pol—or let's settle it now. What's it to be—swords or the Star Scroll? It'll come to it eventually, we both know that. Why not now? Are you that afraid of losing?"

He did with his fist what he ached to do with his mind. Andry was flat on his back on the carpet, blood smearing his nose and upper lip. But he was smiling. As if he'd won.

Pol fled. He trembled as if bones would come loose from muscles and flesh and skin. He climbed stairs, not knowing where he went in this castle that stood in place of the one where he'd been born. It wasn't until the chill night air slapped him in the face that he heard his own ragged breaths and felt the quicksilver sweat on his body.

Father was right. I am a barbarian. A savage. But I can't be. I'm a prince. High Prince. I don't have the luxury. I have to be vigilant against what I am—for if I'm not, who else will make peace out of this horror?

But there could be no peace, not until the violence was played out and the enemy who had brought it with them was dead.

I can't let them make of me what they *are,* he told himself, truths blistering his mind, the night wind having no power to cool him. *But it's there inside me. Waiting for rage, for battle. If it hadn't been this war, it would have been Andry, sooner or later. Right now, it* is *Andry. He made of me less than I am—no, he only showed me what lurks inside me.*

I ought to thank him for it. He did me a service. I've seen. I've succumbed. I know what it feels like now. I won't let it happen again.

But he knew that it would. Any kind of power—political, physical, magical, emotional—was addictive. He could use the power of his position to lead men and women into battle, command them to die for his sake. He could use the power of his strong sword arm to kill and kill and kill. He could use the power of his mind to do the same. He could use the power of his feelings to gain him Sionell—wear her down, make it impossible for her to refuse him again. He could have whatever he wanted, because he was a uniquely powerful man.

And with each use, using would become a little easier. A little sweeter. Until its poison addicted him as surely as *dranath.*

I understand now, Father, he said to the starlight. *I know why you were afraid of this war. It wasn't that you'd lose everything you'd built, you and Mother—it was that I'd enjoy being a savage so much that I'd never—*

Forgive me! I didn't understand! I've had an army around me and a sword—your sword—*in my hand, and I could justify the rage and the killing because killing is necessary in war.*

But it was Andry he'd wanted to kill just now. His kinsman. Sorin and Maarken's brother, Chay and Tobin's son.

Lord of Goddess Keep. A man he *did* need. All of it forgotten in his need to kill.

That frightens me the way you were frightened for me. I understand now. Goddess help me, I understand what I really am.

"You're Rohan's son, all right," Chay's voice said behind him, and Pol turned awkwardly to face him. "Whenever he was troubled, he flew to the highest perch he could find. Is it the sight of the Desert you love, or simply being away from everyone else?"

"It's the quiet," Pol heard himself say. "I can hear myself. Listen to myself."

"And tonight's conversation doesn't seem pleasant." He sighed gently. "Andry again."

Pol nodded wordlessly, ashamed.

"For what it's worth to you—" Chay hesitated, then approached and stood beside him at the walls. "Do what you must. Tobin and Maarken and I stand with you, whatever happens. Whatever you decide."

He felt a portion of his heart break. "He's your son."

"You are my prince."

"That's not reason enough! I don't deserve this from you, Chay! I'm not worth what you're offering!"

A short, stunned laugh. "Do I hear correctly? Unworthy? *You?*"

Pol flushed and glanced away from gray eyes luminous in the torchlight.

"And there's a reason for you, my prince. It wasn't Rohan's, you know. He believed in all of us so powerfully that he took us right along with him, whatever his doubts of himself. How can you resist a man who makes you feel you can be so much more than you are?" Standing shoulder-to-shoulder with Pol, he gazed out at the Desert night. "But you—no, your belief is in yourself. Your challenge is different. You expect us to be everything you need us to be, so that you can become what we expect of a prince."

"But—Andry—"

"—expects the worst. He believed sorcerers to be a danger, so he killed as many as he could before you stopped him. He saw an enemy. You didn't. This idea of 'sin'—he expects people to offend against the Goddess or the Sunrunners, and so anticipates it by providing a punishment in advance."

"He doesn't believe that he's right and everyone else is just misguided," Pol blurted. "It's that he's right and everyone else is wrong—*deliberately* wrong. I'm no better. We both believe in ourselves instead of other people."

Chay held his arm exactly where Andry had—and Pol felt the difference between them in that simple touch. "You're learning. Granted, you have to be bludgeoned into it most of the time." He smiled, too briefly. "My prince, there used to be three people Andry felt he could learn from: me, Maarken, and Lady Merisel. Now there's only one."

"And she's been dead for hundreds of years." He bit his lip, then muttered, "I need him, Chay. It curdles my stomach to admit it, but I do need him."

"As I said—you're learning." He rested both elbows on the wall and stared at his clasped hands. "I wish *I* could," he continued softly. "I'm too old for it. I'm glad I've come to the end of my life. When a man can't understand the world anymore. . . ." He shrugged. "When I was young, there were Sunrunners, and there were the rest of us. They had their duties and we had ours. No sorcery, no sorcerers—not where we could see them in our lives, anyway. No Star Scroll spells. No magic. No conversations with dragons. . . ." Another quiet sigh. "Life was simpler, I suppose I'm trying to say. Less civilized, Rohan might call it. Both are correct. But I can't help feeling I've outlived my time. And my prince," he finished in sorrow.

It took several moments for Pol to find words, several more before he could speak them. "I need you, too. More than I need Andry—more than even my father needed you. I think that's what I was hearing in myself tonight. I have to believe in myself—but not because there's nothing else to believe in."

Chay turned his head, his gaze pale and curious. "There's more than your power, your position?"

He accepted the gentle rebuke stolidly, knowing he deserved worse. "All of you—the Desert itself—all the princedoms, the people in them—"

"Hmm. You really *are* learning."

"Chay—I don't want anyone else to die. But if there's another battle—even if it kills all the Vellant'im, our own people will die, too. I have to be able to use what I am to keep it from happening. Goddess, I'm so sick of killing!"

Chay returned his gaze to the Desert and was silent for a

long time. Finally: "Whatever happens, whatever you decide, I am your man as I was your father's. But by the sound of it, this isn't something I'm qualified to advise you on."

"Just—be here," Pol said helplessly. "For me, the way you were for Father. And—for Andry, too."

✳

Sioned held out her cup for more taze.

"Sorry it's cool," Sionell said as she poured. "It's a long way up from the kitchen, and my hearth doesn't have a rack for keeping the pitcher hot."

"It's fine."

"So do you think it will work? Will they have scouts this far north still?"

"We have to assume they do," Sioned replied. "Even if they don't, we have to put up a show just in case they're watching. So take your people back home, my dear, where they belong."

"I'll *send* them," was the immediate correction. "I'm staying."

It didn't even occur to Sioned to argue. She knew her Namesake forwards, backwards, and sideways. "Then perhaps you'll consider coming with me to Skybowl."

Sionell's eyebrows scrambled up her forehead. "What? You? Why?"

"I have always admired the succinct quality of your speech," she chuckled. "In order: *what* I propose is sneaking into Skybowl as a servant to mingle with those few who will be left behind. *Me,* because I'm a Sunrunner witch with a few good spells left in me. And *why*—" Her humor vanished. "To get Meiglan out."

Sionell nodded. "Yes. I'll come."

"No doubts, no misgivings, no questions about what I'm going to do or how?"

A tight, almost feral smile curved Sionell's lips. "Succinctly? No."

They relaxed a little, sipping hot taze, each keeping silent company with her own thoughts. At length Sioned put her cup aside and stretched.

"I'm too old for this. I don't see the future as clearly as I once could."

"You never said you could—"

"Oh, not like that. Except in Fire and Water—but frankly I'm not eager to look." Sinking back in her chair, she mused, "I always felt sorry for poor little Brenlis. She saw whether she wanted to or not."

"Brenlis? Oh—Andry's . . ." She trailed off tactfully.

"Yes," Sioned agreed. "Andry's. But no one's, actually. Not even her own, I think. There was something about her that seemed—brushed by the Goddess' fingertip. Not enough to let her see everything and know exactly what it meant, but a more definite touch than that and she would have gone mad. I knew it the first time I ever saw her, when we visited Faolain Riverport—oh, years ago. She was brought to me as a sort of local curiosity. In some ways, she reminded me of myself, and the way my brother's wife used to look at me from the corner of her eye."

"Brenlis saw the future?"

"Bits and pieces. Nothing to connect with anything else until after it had happened. Which doesn't make much sense, I know. Andry and I were talking about her recently. He told me that in Autumn she saw herself at her parents' farm near Riverport. Word came shortly thereafter that her family needed her, so she left. And she was the first Sunrunner to be killed by Vellant'im."

"But she didn't know it would happen?"

"No. What she saw had significance, but could only be understood later." She gave a shrug. "Just before the *Rialla* this year she caught a glimpse of Arnisaya of Fessenden wearing a white fur cloak, riding through the snow. She told Andry—she told him all her seeings, but of course neither knew what to make of it. Now we know."

"I wonder she *didn't* go mad."

"I suppose she merely accepted what the Goddess chose to show her the way a pitcher accepts wine. Nothing she could do about it, after all." Sioned paused a moment. "I'll tell you something else because it concerns you, but you must never repeat it. Andry says she knew about Meig several days before he was born—that the child was a boy, and what you'd Name him. So keep an eye on him. Someday he'll do something important."

"Or something will be done to *him*." Her shoulders shifted as if to rid herself of the knowledge. "I wish you hadn't told me."

"You're his mother. You deserve to know." After a few

moments' silence, she said, "I won't look in Fire and Water again. I don't want to know what's waiting for us. What *I* see always comes to pass."

"Didn't Lady Andrade always say that nothing was written in stone?"

"And even if it was, the stone could be broken." She paused to sip lukewarm taze. "I saw Pol, you know, long before he was born. I was holding a baby, and there was a scar on my shoulder. But that's not where the scar turned out to be." She touched the crescent-shaped mark on her cheek. "Ruval gave Pol one to match it. What it all means, I've no idea. Because my scar is in a different place, I suppose I could change what I saw—if I looked. But I won't. If Pol wants to know, let him try it himself."

Sionell set her cup down. "What do you plan to do about Meiglan?"

"I have an idea or two. I'm hoping to take Alasen with us. Ruala will come, of course, but as herself, to welcome the Vellant'im."

She noted the names, as Sioned had known she would. "Two *faradh'im* and one *diarmadhi*—I don't fit, Sioned."

"No."

Green eyes locked with blue. Neither woman had to say what both knew: that risking her own life to ensure Meiglan's would be atonement for the wrong Sionell had done her. No words would ever be spoken between them; Meiglan need never know. Sioned had been told to stay out of it, and she would. But she wondered sadly if anything could ever cure the wrong Pol and Sionell had done to themselves and each other.

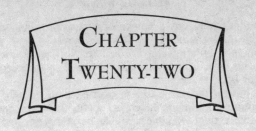

CHAPTER
TWENTY-TWO

"I want to go back to Feruche, Meath. Please, can we go today?" Rislyn walked across the bedchamber with surprising confidence, hands held out to touch. "I'm much better. I can ride with you—"

"I hope you mean with me on my horse!" Meath cradled her fingers in his palms. She couldn't see his expression, so he put the smile into his voice. "Or did you want me to be your dragon, and fly you up to Feruche on my back?"

She laughed, and he rejoiced in the renewed strength of it. Her eyes were as clear and bright a green as Sioned's: no cloudiness, no dull stare, no aimless tracing of things that did not exist. Her pupils reacted to light, contracting as he led her toward the window. It was her brain that was damaged, not her eyes. If one didn't notice telltale reactions to sudden sounds—a voice, a door opening, a footstep, a dragon's cry—one would never know she was blind.

Meath lowered himself into the window seat and settled her on his knee. Turning her face to the morning sun, Rislyn smiled as warmth brushed her thin cheeks with color. Color—how he wished he had Jihan's talent for seeing a Sunrunner's colors without effort. More, he wished he'd had the wits to ask Jihan to share Rislyn's colors with him. Rings didn't make a Sunrunner—and neither, it seemed, did age. He'd made the same mistake with Jihan that he'd made with Pol as a little boy at Graypearl; he of all people should never underestimate the talents and perceptions of a child.

To see Rislyn's colors, he must first teach her to call Fire. But she couldn't see to place it where it would do no harm.

He couldn't hold out the hope of Sunrunner sight until he was able to show her how. Stroking her silky hair, freshly washed this morning and brushed to glorious gold, Meath cursed his own inadequacy. All he could do for her was to take her back to Feruche.

But not today. Her frailness worried him, though Feylin was optimistic. Having taken her sight, the fever had vanished like a thief. Recovery would be complete, and fairly quick, for all her delicate looks. Or so Feylin said—even as she cautioned against taking the long ride to Feruche too soon.

"Meath," Rislyn said again, "can't we leave today? Please?"

"Not even your father says 'yes' when Lady Feylin says 'no.' Such is the power of physicians." He paused, seeing movement in the courtyard below. "Laroshin is waving to you, my lady."

Rislyn waved back. He shifted her subtly in his lap so her greeting went in the right direction.

"Now he's giving you a bow as elegant as Lord Maarken's, and a great deal more elegant than your father's."

"Papa doesn't get much practice bowing," Rislyn observed slyly. "Except to Granda Sioned! If we can't leave today, can I take a walk to the lake instead?"

He knew no reason why not. Mild exercise was allowed. Holding her hand, he escorted her out of the room and into the hallway. She didn't reach to feel for doorways or walls—trusting him to guide her. It half broke his heart.

"Jihan swims all the time at Dragon's Rest," she said. "I can't. Does that mean I'm more of a Sunrunner than she is, or less?"

"Maybe a different *kind* of Sunrunner," he equivocated.

They had reached the stairs. She tugged her hand free. "I can do this myself, Meath. I practiced."

Finding the banister, she laid her hand firmly atop its polished smoothness. The first three steps were hesitant. But once she sensed the rhythm of the risers, she went down them with perfect ease.

Visian, in the entry hall applying charm and flashing dark eyes on a lissome young soldier from Graypearl, called up the stairs, "The Goddess has sent a second sunrise this morning, and her name is Princess Rislyn!"

The child giggled, and the guard winked at Meath. "With a handsome escort, too," she said. "You Desert ladies have all the luck!"

"Your wits have curdled, my girl," Meath growled.

"Meath!" Rislyn exclaimed. "You *are* handsome! And besides, Samlia's with Lord Visian, and that shows she knows handsome when she sees it. Jihan says he talks almost as pretty as Lord Kazander, and only half as crazy!"

Meath and Samlia burst out laughing. Visian bowed low. "Your grace honors my unworthy self. My poor words have failed with the Warrior-Lady Samlia."

"Keep talking," Meath advised. "Sooner or later you're sure to find a few she likes."

On their way out of the keep, many people greeted Rislyn. She answered some of them by name, separating familiar voices from those she wasn't yet sure of. Meath wished she could see the delight in their eyes that had replaced worry— but he was just as glad she couldn't see their pain and their pity. She'd react as Maarken had.

"My princess," said Laroshin, hurrying to her side. "Should you be up and about?"

"Oh, please, Laroshin?" She groped for his hand. He clasped her fingers gently in his huge, battle-scarred paws. "Meath is going to take me out to the lake. If I get tired, I promise I'll tell him and we'll come back."

"I'll come with you, if I may." He glanced at Meath, who nodded and mouthed *Thank you.*

They left through a postern gate, walking at an easy pace down the road to the lakeshore. Both men kept close watch on the child, alert for any signs of fatigue or fever. But Rislyn seemed to soak up strength along with the sunlight. Not yet strong enough to run riot, as she had done with her sister and the other children at Feruche, still she looked bright and lively. Meath began to think that leaving tomorrow might be possible after all.

"I can smell the water," she said. "And the dragons. How many are there today, Meath?"

He squinted at the far shore. "Maarken's Pavisel is curled up with her tail in the lake, taking a nap. I don't see Abisel—it must be his turn to go up to Feruche and see Hollis. That big bronze monster of Riyan's—"

"Sadalian," she supplied. "And he's not a monster. And more greenish than bronze."

"As you say, my lady. Anyhow, he's circling around as if he can't make up his mind—ah, there he goes. Off hunting, I guess."

"What about Granda Sioned's Elisel and Papa's Azhdeen?"

"You know them all, don't you?"

"Of course she does," Laroshin said. "They're here, dozing in the sand. And one of the strays, as Lord Maarken calls them, he's—"

"—taking a bath!" Rislyn exclaimed. "I just heard the splash! Where's the other one? And is Azhly up at Feruche, too, visiting Lady Ruala?"

"Maybe he's out hunting with Sadalian," Meath said.

"They must miss Dragon's Rest as much as we do," Rislyn sighed. "All they have to do there is pounce on the sheep. I love watching them—"

She broke off, and Meath traded an agonized glance with Laroshin. The latter said quickly, "Ah, here's the other stray now. She's a pretty thing—black as soot, blue underwings. Her talons look almost silver. Good growth, too, for a youngling. She just flew in from the southeast—looks like she's had her breakfast and now she wants a nap."

"A bath, from the way she's circling the lake," Meath observed. "Actually, Laroshin, I think she's colored more like the cliffs around Goddess Keep on a rainy day."

And she was flying right toward him, he noted, frowning. The wild thought occurred to him that she might have fixed on him, a Sunrunner, to become hers. He didn't want a dragon—he didn't have the time or the iron head that seemed to be required. The females were gentler with their humans than the sires, but he'd seen Sioned wince often enough after a conversation with her dragon, and Maarken had been fairly staggering yesterday after Pavisel's attentions.

The black dragon landed with delicate precision a little way from them. Meath felt Rislyn's fingers clench around his.

"Oh, Meath," she whispered. "I can hear her—wouldn't it be wonderful if she wants to talk to *you*? Then you'd have a dragon just like Papa and—"

She broke off with a soft cry. Laroshin drew his sword; Meath gestured frantically at him to put it away. The dragon was making low, gravelly noises, her wings folded, her neck stretching out toward Rislyn.

The little girl's eyes were closed. She let go of Meath's hand. Slowly, surely, she walked toward the dragon as if she could see every stone, every glint of lakewater, every wisp of distant clouds in the vast blue sky.

✶

Pol barely felt Meath's colors fade back toward Skybowl. He stumbled a little, then crumpled hard onto the steps behind him, put his head in his hands, and wept.

The people in the courtyard respected his privacy, though speculation sent darting glances among them. A disaster would see him shouting orders, wouldn't it? Or was the calamity so terrible it had crushed him? Someone had the presence of mind to run into the keep by a side door, looking for anyone who could approach him, help him—find out for everyone what new horror had befallen them.

It was a long time before a hand fell lightly on his shoulder and a voice murmured his name. He looked up, and through tear-blurred eyes saw the dark red hair and pale triangular face that meant Sionell. As if he'd needed sight of her to confirm what his senses had already told him.

"Lir'reia," he said. Confusion knit her brows. Pol cleared thickness from his throat. "Rislyn's dragon. She's Named her Lir'reia."

Sionell gave a start like a hawk unhooded in too-bright sun. "Goddess," she breathed. "Pol, are you sure?"

"This morning, at Skybowl. Just now." He scrubbed the moisture from his eyes and tried to stand, making it on the second try with her help. "I can't quite believe—I didn't mean to make a fool of myself, but—"

She shook her head. " 'The Princess' Eyes'—isn't that what it means?"

"Yes." Drawing in a shaky breath, he managed a smile. "Meath can see and pattern her colors now. The dragon did it for him, in a way. He says not to be surprised if by tomorrow I can speak with Rislyn on sunlight."

Sionell's answering smile was wry, still a bit bemused. "Jihan will be wild to have a dragon of her own, you know!"

"She'll just have to wait until a dragon picks her out the way Lir'reia did Rislyn. We don't choose them, they choose us. And Lir'reia has chosen Rislyn!" Laughing, he seized her around the waist and swung her in the air.

The servant who had fetched Sionell—and lingered in a shadow to listen—breathed a sigh of relief and hurried to spread word of the dragon who had become Princess Rislyn's eyes.

"Put me down, you idiot!" Sionell demanded breathlessly.

He did so, flushed and grinning, filled with joy as he had not been in longer than he could remember. His father had been right: Sunrunners, dragons, and the Desert, none would ever fail him.

"I hate to spoil your mood," Sionell said as she tucked her shirt back into her belt, "but your mother commands—her exact word—your presence upstairs. She and the *diarmadh'im* are waiting for you in the Attic."

"Nothing could spoil my mood, and my mother was the second person on my list this morning. Riyan was first, but he'll have to wait." He beckoned a groom over. "You'll find Lord Riyan in the back garden. Please give him my apologies and tell him we'll talk later." To Sionell, ushering her back up the steps, "Have you thought about taking your people back to Tiglath in aid of our little deception?"

"They'll leave whenever you give the word."

He paused at the foot of the main stairs, one hand on the banister. "They?"

"I'm staying," she said blithely. "Don't even try, Pol. I have a direct order from your mother, whom I've been obeying a lot longer than I have you."

"When did you ever?" he asked sourly.

She smiled. "Exactly."

"What does that impossible woman have in mind *now?*"

"I'll let her tell you." She started up the stairs. "Did Meath say anything about Lord Kazander?"

"Doing just fine." Pol caught up with her in two long strides. "You're fond of him, aren't you? All the ladies are. He's a maniac, but eminently lovable!"

"His father offered to marry me." She chuckled at the memory. "I was about ten years old at the time. He was so tall I had to tilt my head all the way back to look in his face, and he had the most wonderful laugh and brought me such lovely presents." She flicked a finger against the pendant white jade earring that swung near the corner of her jaw.

"There's a necklace that goes with these, all the beads carved like fringepod flowers."

"After so skilled a courtship, I wonder that you refused him," Pol teased.

"No wonder at all. I would've been his seventh wife—or was it the eighth? Whichever, I was rude enough to inform Lord Velianpashevisel that I was honored but intended to be an *only* wife."

She was smiling as she said it, but he winced inwardly anyhow. To cover it, he blinked his eyes wide and said, "Lord Velian-what?"

"Velianpashevisel. Roughly translated, it means 'My sword is like the wind, and the air turns to fire beneath my wings.' " She laughed at his expression. "That's nothing, oh you of a single syllable! *His* father's name was—let's see if I remember—" She frowned in exaggerated concentration. "Barcataliznartiel."

"You're joking."

"Certainly not." She slanted him a laughing look.

"But Kazander has a short name."

"His mother's reasoning was that by the time you finish yelling the *korrus'* name in battle, the battle shouldn't be over."

Pol heaved a great sigh. "I can see it coming, but go on—tell me what Bar-and-so-on means."

"It's fairly straightforward. 'Many bows feast on red victory'—otherwise known as blood."

"I'm beginning to feel decidedly inferior with my paltry single syllable!"

"Why do you think Kazander calls you all those outrageous things? He has to make up for the neglect somehow. It would be insulting not to address a great highborn with enough sounds to impress the common folk."

"I'm glad my mother believed in simplicity. My hand would fall off if I had to sign everything with a name like Barcatal-whatever."

"Mama! Mama, come make Uncle Lord Andry Goddess Keep teach us Sunrunner lessons!"

Sionell gave a martyred sigh as her youngest's piercing demand rang down from the next landing. Pol laughed at her.

"Meig likes plenty of impressive sounds, too—the louder the better. But when did Andry become his uncle?"

"Jihan claims the relationship to irritate Tobren, and Meig calls you Uncle Pol, so in logic—" She shrugged. As her son's mouth opened wide to yell again, she called up the stairs, "Meig! Hush up! I'm coming, I'm coming! And if you've been plaguing Lord Andry, I'll tack your hide to a wall and paint you purple!"

Meig chortled at the threat. Although at not quite five years old he was not quite as tall as the banister, lack of height didn't prevent him from scrambling up as if it were a saddle.

"Meig!" Sionell cried. "No!"

Too late. The child skimmed down polished wood, crowing with laughter, feet and hands waving wildly. Pol's stomach lurched as he glanced down the stairwell at the three stories of thin air between Meig and the floor. He and Sionell ran to catch the hurtling little boy. Meig saw them coming. He flung his arms wide and launched himself for all the world like a dragon taking off. Slamming into his mother, he clamped his arms around her neck, nearly throttling her.

"I want to go *all* the way down like that!"

"Not a chance!" Sionell dealt him a resounding thwack on the backside. "And there'll be ten more just like that one if you ever do that again!"

Meig didn't cry; he looked absolutely stunned, thoroughly insulted, and so betrayed that Pol had to look away to hide a grin.

Sionell set her son on his feet, latching onto one hand. "You come with me, bandit, and we'll go find Lord Andry. If his grace will excuse us—?"

"Uh—yes," Pol managed in a slightly strangled voice that earned him a disgusted look from Sionell.

Meig didn't have to recover his dignity; he'd never really lost it. He gave Pol a serene smile and a nod, and decorously descended the stairs with his parent. Pol had to bite both lips between his teeth to keep from laughing when he heard Sionell mutter, "And *this* is to be a great lord someday! Goddess help us!"

A few moments later Pol sauntered into the Attic with a grin on his face that even his own mother's acid glance couldn't dim.

"What was all that racket?" Sioned asked. "Have you been inciting children to mayhem again?"

"Me?" Pol greeted Thassalante and the four elderly *diarmadh'im* present graciously enough, hiding his surprise—and his curiosity at the configuration of chairs. Seven had been taken from around the table and the other furniture moved aside so they could form a half-circle facing the *daltaya*. Even more interesting was the fact that the curtains had been drawn against the sunlight and the room was lit only by a candle branch on the table. He looked briefly at the mirror; nothing. The angle of its mounting kept the Fire from its reach.

"Sit down, Pol," Sioned told him, indicating the chair in the middle. The others did likewise, while Sioned stood behind the chair nearest the window. Her hair, clean and curling, shone red-gold-silver by candlelight, her eyes oddly dark with a kind of repressed urgency.

"When Meath found the old Sunrunner keep on Dorval, he saw a pattern repeated several times in the ruins. The same pattern of leaves and apples that frames this mirror. Now, Master Thassalante says that this pattern is familiar to *diarmadh'im* of education. All of you recognized it. I saw this mirror for years in Camigwen's room at Goddess Keep, and years more at Stronghold. When Ostvel was given Skybowl, it was taken there. In all those years—and countless more before Cami owned it—thousands of people passed by and never saw anything but their own reflections. Even though Cami was *diarmadhi,* and her son Riyan is as well, and we must assume others called Fire near this mirror, it wasn't until Princess Alleyn and Prince Audran of Dorval looked into it that this was revealed as a *daltaya*. A Shadowcatcher.

"I won't speculate on the whys of all this. Lord Riyan and Lady Ruala have looked into this mirror—and she says that the face within it is uncannily like her father's. We know now that Riyan and Ruala are distant cousins. All of you people seem to be. How Alleyn and Audran fit into this, I haven't a clue. But whether only Lord Rosseyn's descendents can see him in the mirror or whether all *diarmadh'im* can is of but passing interest to me. I'm concerned with the frame."

Sioned moved around the chair and stood before the mirror, her back to it. "Meath saw this pattern in tile set with colored crystals." She paused as if waiting for a reaction. Pol sensed nothing—and was instantly suspicious. There should

have been *some* sort of response at finding out the
Sunrunners had used the same decoration as a sorcerer's
mirror.

"Meath made a drawing for me, with the crystals colored
in. Very pretty, very elegant. Very puzzling. For there are
spaces on this frame that correspond to the places where
crystal was set. But I don't think mere colored glass was
meant to be put there at all." She clasped her hands at her
waist, then brought them to her lips, watching her audience
with brilliant green eyes over the equally brilliant emerald
on her finger. "I think the frame was meant to be set with
jewels."

Pol glanced involuntarily down at the amethyst of
Princemarch, then the great topaz of the Desert. He thought
of Lady Andrade's rings and wrist cuffs, glittering with the
whole rainbow of gemstones. Her moonstone was also on
his hand. But his gaze returned at once to Sioned's emerald
ring.

"Special jewels," she went on, very softly. "Jewels that
for one reason or another have more meaning than the usual
symbolism—garnet for constancy, pearl for purity, sapphire
for truth, and so forth. Jewels that possess power."

At Pol's side, Thassalante trembled. "Lady," he begged in
a hoarse voice, "please—you don't know what you speak
of—"

"Don't I? Not all of it, perhaps. But—watch."

Her fingers unlaced in a supple, graceful movement, and
the candleflames vanished. Pol flinched, knowing how much
she feared absolute darkness, and why.

But the darkness was not absolute.

The emerald ring glowed. Pulsed. *Lived.*

Thassalante moaned as if a sword had pierced his heart.
The other *diarmadh'im* gasped or shifted in their chairs; one
of them muttered something too low for Pol to hear.

Fire danced once more atop the candles. Sioned finally sat
down in her chair, hands folded in her lap.

"The stone has been blooded," she said quietly. "And now
I ask you to tell me why."

Thassalante was stricken mute, head bowed, Another of
the sorcerers quavered, "Lady, it is not a thing *faradh'im*
may know."

"I assumed that, Master Pandradi," she replied. "But consider this. I am *faradhi,* you are *diarmadh'im.* Aside from some small differences, the gift of power is the same."

"No," Pandradi whispered, but Pol was unsure if the woman protested the equation or the sharing of knowledge. He gathered himself to tell them who and what he truly was, but before he could speak, Sioned addressed them again.

"Why does a blooded jewel beat with the heart of its wearer? Why do such jewels fit into the frame around a *daltaya* with Lord Rosseyn trapped inside? I am not asking for myself. The mirror is empty to me, its power beyond my reach."

Thassalante looked up. "How did you know—?" Then he compressed his lips and shook his head. "It doesn't matter," he said dully. "Your cunning is well-known. You cannot see Lord Rosseyn, but you saw everything else that is there to be seen. It is true that you cannot use the mirror. But we will not. We *cannot.*"

"Is it forbidden?"

"It is death to *diarmadh'im!* Worse—it is no death at all!" He leaned forward, bracing his hands on his knees, ignoring Pol as his gaze fixed almost desperately on Sioned. "Of all the things that were lost or stolen from us, I wish this evil had been among them!"

Pandradi shook her silvery head. "With respect, Thassalante, I disagree. If we did not know, we could still be caught. Because we know, we are safe. I regret, your grace, my lord, but we fear for our lives. The mirror will remain silent. We *will* not use it—and neither of you *can.*"

"You're wrong," said Pol.

✳

"Well," Sioned murmured. "*That* was interesting."

Pol looked at her with shock-dulled eyes. After a moment he said, "I will never understand how Father managed to keep his sanity around you."

Smiling tiredly, she rose to open the curtains. Sunlight flooded in at an angle that surprised her. "Is it really that late? We must've been in here all day."

"Are you sure it's the *same* day?"

Turning, she laughed at him. "*That,* my son, is how your father kept his sanity. He never lost his sense of humor."

Pol stood and stretched, joints cracking. "I'm serious. It's been at least a hundred years since I walked into this room. I feel as old as Pandradi."

The sorcerers had left them a short while ago, exhausted by revelations and by telling Pol everything they knew about the mirror. Sioned had been an intrigued observer, and occasionally an appalled one. For the mirror was not what she had expected.

"We'll need some time to assemble the appropriate jewels," she said. "So you'll be able to rest up." One of the dozen display cabinets had recently been redecorated with rolled-up maps and parchment for notes; she selected a few clean pages, a pen and inkpot, and sat at the long table. "My emerald, to begin with. Your amethyst and topaz—"

Pol dragged a chair over and sat beside her. "If we're borrowing power that seeped into the gems from previous owners, then neither of those will do, will they? Roelstra wasn't gifted. Father was a halfling."

Sioned merely shrugged. "You'll have to ask Naydra who gave her father that ring. The way things are going, it probably belonged to Lord Rosseyn himself."

"Or his betraying lady."

She watched him eye the ring slightly askance, and smiled. "Power is power. We can't be choosy."

"If the cap fits, wear it or get out of the rain?" He smiled back, but his voice had an edge to it.

"Mmm. Not a Desert expression, but I can think of one that applies to that mirror. If one undertakes to ride a dragon, one had better not try to get off."

"You're comforting tonight."

"These are comforting times." She started a list of the needed gems in order of their placement in the frame. "By the way, I wouldn't disparage that topaz if I were you. Rohan had more gifts as a so-called halfling than most trained Sunrunners. Let's see—amethyst, sapphire, emerald, topaz, garnet, ruby, and a diamond in the center. The only one we have for certain is my emerald. But I'm betting your two will work as well, after they're blooded." Giving him a sidelong glance, she added, "I think that can wait. It's been a long day."

"Tell me," he muttered.

She put down the pen and folded her hands. "No, *you* tell *me*."

He lost ten winters in a single smile. "I was going to,

earlier. But you didn't give me a chance. Rislyn has a dragon. Or, more properly, the dragon has Rislyn."

Sioned felt her lips move. No sound came out.

Pol held both her hands between his own. "She's called her Lir'reia."

Her brain gave her the translation effortlessly, and he saw it in her eyes and nodded.

"Meath has Rislyn's colors now. She's sleeping off the initial contact—and don't we both remember how *that* feels!—but when she wakes he's going to teach her how to use the sunlight to see what her eyes no longer can. You were right, Mama—about Tobin, about Rislyn—you're worse than Lady Andrade," he teased. "Don't you ever get *tired* of being right?"

She laughed and flung her arms around him. "Not in my whole life!"

He hugged her and let her go. "Back to work, High Princess—I'm feeling much better and would feel better still for a little wine."

"On an empty stomach?" She poked him playfully, then frowned and felt at his ribs. He squirmed away, ticklish. "You're too thin, Pol."

"So are we all. War has that effect on the figure." Then he smiled and lifted a dismissive shoulder. "I was getting fat, anyway."

Sioned returned her attention to the list of gems to disguise her worry. Three new holes had been cut into his belt to keep it snug around his waist; the seams of shirt and tunic had been resewn to accommodate warrior's muscle. But there was no flesh left to support that muscle. His face was leaner, its lines taut with day after day of strain: width of jaw more pronounced, nose sharper, blue-green eyes dominating his features more than ever. War had taken things from him, demanded its price in flesh and youth. But it had not diminished him, or tarnished the brightness that was so like his father's. And yet—the shining of him was fiercer, harsher than Rohan's had ever been.

"We can't test every ring and necklet at Feruche for latent power," she said briskly. "No matter how old the gems are or who once owned them. We have to think first about which would respond."

"Or people will start asking some very awkward questions," Pol agreed.

"People, meaning Andry," she interpreted. "My emerald, your amethyst and topaz—you know, if we had all the princes assembled, we'd have a pretty good collection of very old jewels. All of them go back so far as symbols of princely power that people have forgotten who originally owned them. Velden's ruby, for instance—it's a sixteen-facet table-cut that doesn't let half enough light in, and no one has worked gemstones like that in hundreds of years."

"Can you imagine prying our dear cousin away from it? And anyway, we don't have the princes within reach. All we've got is—" His eyes lost focus, almost as if he was Sunrunning, but the light from the window was nowhere near him.

"Pol? What is it?"

"—Andry," he said as if there had been no pause. "Lord of Goddess Keep."

Sioned looked at her hands, picturing the ten rings, some set with rubies or diamonds, and the wrist cuffs with their great chunks of sapphire and moonstone.

"There's power for you," Pol went on, leaning back in his chair. "Power and to spare. We can only get three out of him—ruby, diamond, and sapphire—but I don't know of any other stones we can be as sure of." He gave a bitter laugh. "Andry kept insisting that I need him, and so I do. For a sorcerer's spell!"

Sioned felt something dart teasingly past the edge of her mind, too quick to catch, too elusive to recognize. She let it go, knowing it would come back to demand her attention if she ignored it. She said, "So it was you who split his lip. I thought so."

"He's lucky it was only that. I wanted to split his skull." He contemplated the hands that had done the damage. "Mother, I wanted to *kill* him."

"You remind me of two little boys squabbling over who gets the last slice of pie—and neither of you sees that someone's sneaking up to steal it behind your backs."

He looked up angrily. "Go on, tell me to grow up. But you'd better give Andry the same lecture."

"He's not my son," she replied. "The question is, does he care more about trying to beat you than he does about the thief?"

"He wants both. He's positive he'll *get* both. He's wrong. Believe me, Mother, the mighty Lord of Goddess Keep is wrong!" Pol brought a fist down on the table. "But why do I have to go to *him* for what I need?"

The idea settled smugly right in front of her, and spoke with her voice. "It doesn't have to be the Lord of Goddess Keep."

"I hate the idea, too, but where else can we be sure of finding stones of sufficient power?"

Sioned stared at the list of gems. Emerald they had; amethyst and topaz, probably. That left sapphire, garnet, ruby, and diamond, And the hands she pictured as she stared at her own were not the strong, capable hands of a man in his prime. They were very like her own hands, long-fingered, confident, beautiful still but showing the marks of age. They were as familiar to her as her own.

Tiny chains crossed the back of each palm, joining the glittering rings to heavy wrist cuffs. And crowning each circle of gold or silver was the complacent sparkle of an old, old jewel.

"Not the Lord," she said. "The *Lady*."

Pol caught his breath. Then, slowly and reverently: "Mother of Dragons."

"No," Sioned told him, grimly amused. "Only Andrade."

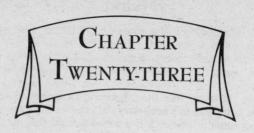

CHAPTER TWENTY-THREE

When Ostvel woke, Camigwen was kneeling beside him, smiling as she held out a clay mug of steaming taze.

How lovely she was—the laughing tilt of her black eyes, the soft dark sheen of her skin, the warm length of her hair knotted carelessly at her nape. And so young . . . and he so old now, the hand that reached for her knot-veined and shaking. He had lived more than half his life without her, and grown old.

Then he remembered. "Camig–gina."

He didn't know how much his face had revealed, but the stammer brought instant understanding and regret to the woman's eyes. "Forgive me. I didn't think. I should have realized—"

"It's all right." He gulped taze around the lump in his throat.

"We let you sleep late," Camigina said after a moment. "They're barely stirring in Chiana's camp."

He nodded. She made another little gesture of apology and left him alone.

The morning was spectacularly bright, as if the sun had confused the eightieth dawn of Winter with the same day in Summer. All around Wine-stem Pass light fairly blazed. Flowers, poking their heads up from the soggy soil, decided it would be churlish not to bloom in response. Animals left shelters to forage, insects buzzed happily by, and birds sang their hearts out.

All that energy pained Ostvel's eyes.

By midmorning Chiana still hadn't emerged from the

damned ravine. Ostvel's little army had been in hiding on either side of the meadow since the previous afternoon. For all the new sunshine, it was still chilly and damp. They'd dared no cookfires, brewing taze one cup at a time over well-shielded fingerflames. The *diarmadh'im* would risk no more than this, knowing what their kind were capable of seeing, and how. Ostvel didn't need magical reasons for prohibiting fires. A column of smoke was a column of smoke, no matter how one chose to look at it. But their words of caution set him to wondering how they had lasted so long if the only senses they relied on were their weirding ones.

It was those senses, however, that would fight this battle. Camigina had been most specific. The sorcerers with Chiana and Rinhoel were their ancient enemies, with blood-claims going back a hundred years before Ostvel was born. He agreed to leave the fight to the *diarmadh'im*—not wanting to risk a single one of his three hundred soldiers on the worthless Chiana and Rinhoel—but the gleam in their eyes worried him. Hungry wolves tracking coveted deer for fifty measures would have softer eyes.

The sorcerers were grouped to one side of the meadow, as close as they could get to the mouth of the pass without leaving effective cover. The budding trees never even rustled. If, among the thick stand of thin trunks, there were a few more shadows than usual, they seemed only bushes in early leaf.

The regular troops were farther back, just as hidden, but not as silent. They didn't have to be. Chiana, Rinhoel, their guards, the *diarmadh'im*—somebody was supposed to see them. There was an invisible line stretching all the way across the dewy grass, half a measure to the trees opposite Ostvel's own hiding place. That line would not be crossed by anyone who came out of Wine-stem Pass. The half-full mark on the cup, he would have called it, had the place been set upright with the hollow stem widening upward into the goblet of meadow. But the glass lay on its side, with half its bowl made only of sky.

Which thought brought him naturally to the Desert, where it seemed his elder daughter had acquired a dragon, and thence to Feruche, where almost all the rest of his family were. Alasen and Dannar, Riyan and Ruala and Maara and a new baby coming—and him hundreds of measures away, unable to do a thing in their defense. Thank the Goddess that

Milar at least was safe and snug at Castle Crag. He wondered when and if he could say the same for the rest.

Safe he himself could not be, not with half an army of *diarmadh'im* coming through that bottleneck sooner or later. Snug was only a wistful memory. He'd take out every instant of worry and discomfort on Chiana's pride. He was too damned old for this.

He could hear Alasen's voice: *"Yes, my lord. Old, decrepit, indolent, selfish, set in your ways, and all the rest. I know the whole list by heart. Now, come to bed and let me make a liar of you."*

Andry was at Feruche.

The thought sidled into his mind, smirking. He kicked it out. Just in time, too, for a trickle was draining now from the stem of the glass: riders wearing the proud green of Meadowlord that Chiana and Rinhoel had defiled.

Twenty, thirty—*Where did they get so many horses?*— moved forward into the brilliant chill morning. There was no attack by the defending sorcerers. Ostvel's stomach churned with the suspicion and then the near-certainty of betrayal. *Camigwen's eyes in a stranger's face—Goddess, what a fool I am!* More riders came, wearing brown or dark blue cloaks. Forty of them, fifty—and still the sorcerers did nothing.

The order to charge had come up from his lungs to the back of his throat when a rider tumbled to the grass. And another. And a dozen more, cloaks spreading like broken wings.

Then someone began screaming, and did not stop.

It was like his first sight of dragons: knowing they were real, not believing in the *fact* of them until he saw them in all their fierce power, soaring across Desert sky. He'd known Sunrunners most of his life; he'd seen what they could do. But he'd never seen anything like this. Never heard of it, never imagined it—and, like the first sight of dragons, barely believed it.

Many fell. Many others screamed. Whatever the *diarmadh'im* were doing, it was selective. Of the hundred or so in the meadow, only about half now lay in moist grass. But they were silent as death, and as still. The rest howled their terror, cloaks flying as they dug heels into equally terrified horses.

Ostvel had drawn perhaps ten breaths since the first rider went down. Now he climbed into the saddle to show himself to his troops, bellowing with all the air in his lungs, *"Azhrei!"*

His soldiers didn't need him. They chased down those who tried to escape—or those who had lost control of their horses; they killed every man and woman they caught. Though this was war, Ostvel decided grimly, it was not a battle. The slaughter of fifty soldiers by three hundred could not be called "battle."

He watched as every single rider who had come through the pass died. The sorcerers he assumed, were taking care of the rest. He had no part in it. He was waiting for his prizes to appear.

He heard them before he saw them. Rather, he heard Chiana. She was trying to control a pretty Kadari mare who was of a mind to escape the appalling noise of her rider's shrieks. If Chiana would only shut up, Ostvel thought, and stop heaving up and down like that as she sucked in air, the horse would quiet.

Rinhoel caught up to her and grabbed the reins. They were now well away from everyone else—beautifully, perfectly alone. And no one came after them. So much for their loyal allies. Rinhoel stood in his stirrups, a fine target if that had been Ostvel's intent, sword raised to protect his darling mama.

Ostvel signaled to the twenty he'd chosen as a personal guard—not for himself, but for their graces of Meadowlord—and galloped forward.

"Good morning!" he shouted cheerfully. "Lovely day, isn't it? I bring you the High Prince's invitation to attend him at Feruche!"

Chiana saw him and let out her shrillest cry yet. Ostvel slowed his horse to a walk, gesturing to one of the guards.

"Do something about Rinhoel's sword before he hurts himself with it." To the furious princeling, he continued, "Well? Shall you accept the invitation? I strongly suggest that you do, by the way. Who knows, after his grace annihilates the Vellant'im, he may be in a forgiving mood." He grinned.

Chiana spat at him. Travel did not agree with her. She wore tattered clothes, her boots were caked in mud, her auburn hair tangled its way out of its pins, and she looked nearer sixty than forty.

"Then again," Ostvel added, "maybe not."

By the time he had escorted them back to his own camp—such as it was, but made cheerier by the fires they could now light—it was all over. Ostvel gave orders for a huge pyre and kept Chiana and Rinhoel close enough to watch the construction. He was delighted to discover that although there were wounded, not one of his own people would lie on that pyre tonight. All of Chiana's would—and the ninety-nine men and women who had been caught with their spells unwoven.

More sobering was the word sent by Camigina through one of the *diarmadh'im* that nearly fifty of their own had died. Ostvel ordered a second pyre, unwilling to soil the ashes of friends by mingling them with those of traitors. For he did count them as friends now. They had proven their loyalty—or at least their hatred for those they considered outlaws among their own kind. Trust would have to wait a bit longer, but it was with genuine pleasure that Ostvel welcomed Camigina to his campfire and the kettle of wine warming on it.

"Drink—it's the best from Chiana's cellars." He ladled it out himself into a clay cup, smiling. "It's hot, mind. Don't burn your tongue."

When Camigina had sipped and given a long, satisfied sigh, Ostvel indicated the blanket spread near him and sat down. She did, too, folding herself into a brown-and-blue huddle beside the fire's warmth.

After a moment she looked up. "They were smart. They mixed their own in with the regular guards—the ones wearing Meadowlord's green. I apologize for not anticipating it. We hadn't meant for any of your people to fight at all."

"Little harm to them. Cuts and bruises." He drank from his own cup. "You went after the *diarmadh'im* only, then."

"It was judged the best plan. Some of them rallied against us for a time."

"I heard. I'm sorry you lost so many."

"It was good to fight in the open," she mused. "We don't, you know, and haven't since Merisel's day. Tell me, what will you do with Roelstra's get?"

"That's for the High Prince to decide. May I ask you to come with me to Feruche? He'll want to thank you personally."

"Most gracious. We will consider it." She drank deep, the wine cool enough now for a long draught. "Oh, that *is* good!

Teachers never mention how much such a thing takes out of you, do they?"

Ostvel set his cup down and stripped off his gloves to warm his hands over the fire. "Would it be tactless of me to ask exactly what it was?"

She arched a brow. "You are Camigwen's Chosen. You may ask anything. It was not the *ros'salath,* if that's what you mean. It doesn't even have a name. Sunrunners needn't fear it. *Diarmadhi* to *diarmadhi* only, and dangerous at the best of times. Unless the surprise is total, as it was today." She hunched her shoulders a little, adding, "It felt very good indeed, and I think that's the greatest danger of all."

"High Prince Rohan would have understood perfectly."

"And his son?"

"With all that's happened in this war, I'm sure he's beginning to. I'm very sure he'll want to do something about your situation."

She frowned. "My—?"

"You don't have to hide what you are anymore. Not in Princemarch, not in Meadowlord, not anywhere." It wasn't his secret to tell, so he didn't, but he said the next best thing. "Camigwen's son is one of his dearest friends. He knows what Riyan is. It's time to bring all of you out of the shadows."

"I don't know. It's been so long ... perhaps we wouldn't. ..." She shook herself and smiled. "Old habits. We'll consider that, too. Thank you."

"—*demand* to see Ostvel at once! Do you hear me, you stupid lout? Obey me! I am the ruling Prince of Meadowlord!"

Camigina glanced over her shoulder, murmuring, "Think again, boy."

Ostvel sighed and stood. "Excuse me. I have a small matter to deal with."

"Very small," she agreed, and helped herself to more wine.

As he approached the circle of guards hemming Rinhoel and his mother, Chiana's voice rose loud enough to address the whole princedom. "How dare you hold us prisoner as if we were common thieves!"

Two soldiers stood aside so Ostvel could see and be seen. Wrists loosely bound, otherwise untouched, mother and son were spitting venom. Ostvel wondered how, by the sweet green eyes of the Goddess, this woman could be Naydra's sister—and how either of these prizes could be related to Pol.

"How about uncommon murderers?" he asked.

Chiana gasped in outrage. "Peasant! Liar!"

"Butcher," Rinhoel added.

Ostvel remembered the dead who were dead because of these vipers. Rialt, with his blithe good humor; Mevita of the sharp and witty tongue; gentle Cluthine; the stalwart strength of Kerluthan. He even remembered Halian, the Parchment Prince, inoffensive and ineffectual. Aurar, also killed by one or the other of this pair, Ostvel could very well do without. But they were murderers many times over—not even counting the battle fought because of their treachery, in which so many more had died.

"Be glad I'm too tired to get angry," Ostvel said. "If I had the energy, I'd slit your throats myself."

"You don't dare lay a finger on us!" Chiana raised her mirror-scarred fists. "Remove these ropes at once! I want horses and a guard to take us home!"

"Whose home?" Ostvel asked. "Yours—or mine?"

Chiana spluttered.

"If the latter," he went on, "I don't recall having invited you. If the former—I take leave to inform you that Swalekeep and all Meadowlord now belong to the High Prince. So you see, you have no home to go to. I'd take Pol up on a room and a roof at Feruche. You're not likely to get any other offers."

The soldiers were openly laughing now. Rinhoel seemed to have misplaced his powers of speech entirely, but Chiana sucked in a breath, eyes flashing. Odd, Ostvel mused, how they were mottled like a lizard's scales.

"You fool! Don't you understand? We were used! These foul, scheming sorcerers—we were innocent pawns, used by them to—"

"Oh, do shut up," Ostvel sighed. "You sang that song nine years ago, and it was out of tune then."

Rinhoel lunged for him, and was shoved back by a Castle Crag regular who looked as if he wanted to do a lot more than shove.

"The High Prince and I are both musically inclined," Ostvel continued, liking the turn of phrase, "and we know a dead string when we hear it."

Unhappily, Rinhoel had found breath and words. "You've become their creature! They're using *you!* Sorcery was done here today!"

"When Lord Andry finds out he'll have you executed!" Chiana flung at him. "He's wanted an excuse to get rid of you for eighteen years! He'll take his revenge at last—and he'll take Alasen, too!"

Ostvel went very still. He had stopped being jealous the night his wife had agreed to become his wife. He knew he shouldn't react, unless with laughter. But this bitch had dared speak Alasen's name. All other crimes were not his to punish; that was the High Prince's privilege. But this was too much.

He slapped Chiana across the face, so hard that she spun halfway around before she fell. Rinhoel gave a roar of fury and struggled toward him again, and this time it took three men to hold him back.

Ostvel couldn't remember ever having raised a hand to a woman in his life—except this woman's sister. And Ianthe, he had killed.

Chiana gasped with pain and helpless rage. Blood ran from her nose; he hoped he'd broken it.

"That's a good place for you," he said. "In the mud, where you belong."

Back at his own fire, he sat and drank a full cup even though the wine nearly blistered his mouth. Camigina stayed silent while he drank, but as he poured another cup she said, "Now you know how it was for us."

His palm still stung a little; a satisfying pain. "Yes. I think so. It felt very good—and no regrets."

After a time, she said, "Light makes shadows. We all cast them. We'd be foolish to believe otherwise. But that one—" She tilted her chin over her shoulder. "She darkens those near her. She was a shadow before the sun ever touched her."

"I don't know that it ever did," he replied thoughtfully. "From the moment she was born. . . . Her father Named her appropriately, it turns out."

" 'Treason.' Yes." Setting her cup on one of the rocks that made the fire pit, she pushed herself to her feet. "I must see to my people, your grace."

He looked up with a weary smile. "My dear lady! Kin or not to my Camigwen, if you call me that just once more—!"

"Get used to it," she advised.

✻

While Ostvel waited for Chiana and Rinhoel, Maarken waited for Chadric and Audrite, muttering his mental list as he donned clothes, cloak, and sword. He knew he'd forgotten something. Before any journey, his mother invariably stopped at Radzyn's gates to send a servant back upstairs for whatever had slipped her mind. But his concerns were more important than a gown, a gift, or a book, and he'd look a proper shattershell riding back up the slope of Skybowl to mention arms or tactics.

The selection of the courier to Stronghold had been made last night—a delicate matter of some contention. Daniv attempted to assert his rank as ruling Prince of Syr. This of course disqualified him.

"Yes, you're Prince of Syr—the only one we've got!" Audrite scolded. "I know you're still young, but try not to be so silly!"

Draza of Grand Veresch considered himself perfect for the task. Maarken told him to consider his wife and two children.

"Besides, it has to be someone who knows the Desert," Maarken added.

"Someone highborn," Walvis said, "with an impressive title to spout at them—and whom Meiglan recognizes so identity can be confirmed."

Feylin snapped, "I do hope you're not suggesting yourself!"

"They wouldn't believe me," he sighed glumly. "I'm Lord of Remagev, and they already came calling to my place."

Neither Kazander nor Sethric could sit a saddle yet, let alone ride across half the Desert twice. Though the former could have made the Vellant'im believe the moons were made of goat cheese, and the latter swore he could lie six ways to Snowcoves in a good cause, they were thanked and told to go heal.

Laroshin volunteered out of duty. He was not highborn, however, and his real duty was to protect a lady who needed him. Visian offered and was refused for the same reasons. Maarken, Battle Commander of the Desert, was obviously impossible. Jeni opened her mouth and closed it again without saying anything when Sethric glowered at her.

All at once Isriam got to his feet.

"Send me," he said simply.

Maarken nodded at once. Audrite handed over the master-work of treason she had concocted the night before, along with the text of his speech to the High Warlord and a map.

Isriam and Daniv, friends since the start of their fostering at Stronghold, drew to one side of the hall with Visian and Walvis to discuss horses, routes, water holes, and provisions. Maarken reminded himself to do something really nasty to Pirro in payment for Isriam's emotional torment.

Any of the others could have performed the task of courier just as well, but none had better reasons. Isriam's diffidence was not characteristic of him. He'd been very quiet since Pol's news that Sabriam had disinherited him and Pirro had not acknowledged him. Highborn he was—higher than anyone had thought, as the grandson of a Prince of Fessenden as well as old Prince Clutha of Meadowlord—but the revelation had mortified him. He saw himself as unwanted, unneeded, next to nothing, with no right to assert himself. But he also knew he was the perfect, expendable choice.

Maarken had seen Isriam's dark eyes burn with the need to prove himself *to* himself. He understood that very well; it had undoubtedly been in his own eyes the day Rohan had given him the garnet ring on the middle finger of his right hand. His first Sunrunner ring—though unofficial, with a gold one from Andrade added later; his first confirmation that he would not go the neutral way of most Sunrunners. His gifts would be used in the service of his prince.

So the courier had been chosen and that part of the plan set. In a little while Maarken would lead his people back to Feruche. The castle would be empty in two days' time, at which point Ruala would take possession. The High Warlord would come, welcomed with a wary smile and vehement castigation of Pol's rule.

And poor Meiglan would have a decent roof over her head again.

She would be incredulous at Riyan and Ruala's treachery, deny it to the skies, not believe it for an instant—but doubts would gnaw at her and until this was resolved she'd feel herself utterly abandoned. Maarken regretted her anguish, but that was war.

And he had forgotten something about the war. Damn it, what?

Chadric and Audrite entered his rooms, and he was grateful for the interruption of futile worries that wouldn't settle into specific thoughts. "Everything's ready?" he asked.

"Not quite yet," Audrite said.

Chadric frowned at her. "I thought you said packing began before dawn."

"It did. But what we can't take with us has to be hidden in the cellars. Or do you want all the best furniture splintered for firewood and knives dug into the rest? Not to mention what they'll do to the rugs and tapestries."

Maarken bit his lip. They had all heard by now what state Radzyn was in; he didn't dare think about his own Whitecliff. However— "Don't strip the place bare," he had to say. "Skybowl is a lived-in castle, not a derelict cottage."

Audrite sighed tolerantly. "Are there any other obvious facts you'd care to point out as if they were vital military secrets?"

He grinned. "Sorry. What I need to ask you isn't obvious—in fact, it's perfectly obscure. Pol rousted me out of bed with the first sunlight to ask about it. I know you left Graypearl in one Hell of a hurry. But did you happen to bring along a certain sapphire earring?"

Chadric arched both brows. "I was *wearing* it. I always do. I always have, since my father gave it to me shortly before he died." He lifted the fringe of graying hair from his ear. An unfaceted sapphire the size of a dried bean, and just as dented, pierced the lobe.

"Pol would like to borrow it, if you don't mind."

"Not at all," Chadric agreed readily, removing it. "How offended would you be if I asked why?"

"As offended as I am that he didn't tell me."

"Hmph," he grunted. "I thought we taught that boy better manners."

Maarken unhooked the pendant gray agate from his own ear—a present from Hollis—and slid it in a trouser pocket. "Audrite, can you help me put this on? I hope it's all right that I wear it," he added as she rose to comply. "I know only you and Prince Lleyn ever have, but—"

Chadric shook his head. "And Lady Andrade. It was a gift from Urival after she died, one of the stones from her rings." Blue eyes brightened with sudden speculation. "Oho!"

Audrite's reaction nearly made her drop the earring. Maarken steadied her and told Chadric, "It doesn't really explain why, but it's a hint. I promise I'll let you know through Jeni when I find out all of it."

"Only if Pol thinks we ought to know," Audrite cautioned. "There—that's got it." She stepped back. "Maarken—"

"Yes?"

"There are other gems from her rings still around."

"The amber is in my wedding necklet," he agreed. "I don't suppose I'll ever see it again—we left it behind at Whitecliff."

"But there are others," she insisted. "Your mother has the ruby, doesn't she? And your father got the diamond."

Searching her eyes, he asked, "What is it you're trying to say?"

But all at once he knew, and felt sick. This was what had been nagging him—not some *thing* he was forgetting, but this particular thing he didn't want to acknowledge. Andrade's jewels, in Andrade's rings—but not really hers. They had been sized over and over again to fit each successive Lady or Lord of Goddess Keep. Who knew but that they dated back to Lady Merisel's day?

Andry had chosen to wear all new rings, the first indication of the changes he would make in Sunrunner tradition.

Was Pol gathering the ancient gems to make new rings— *for himself?*

High Prince, Sorcerer, Sunrunner—

"I'm probably wrong." Audrite's eyes said something else. "Pol isn't that foolish, or that ambitious."

Chadric had not yet made the connection. "Would you please tell me what you're talking about? Or will I have to read it in the history books, or hear it sung by a bard?"

"Books." Maarken seized on the word as a bulwark against intolerable ideas. Instantly he knew that this was what he'd forgotten. "Audrite, of everything you take out of here, make sure Feylin's dragon book is in your own hands."

"I'm not a fool, either," Audrite reminded him. "Time you left, my dear. It's a long ride back to Feruche."

Chayla had told Kazander the same thing last evening. "And it's a ride you won't be taking until the New Year. Your Isulk'im can hide you perfectly well in the hills when the Vellant'im get here. Oh, stop looking furious, it only wastes energy you need to heal."

Like Feylin, she marveled that Kazander wasn't dead. As she mounted up in the bright morning sunshine and made sure her traveling kit of medicines was lashed securely behind her saddle, she wondered if there might be time for her to slip upstairs for one more look at his wound, just to make sure he was—

No. She'd said her farewells last night, crisp and clean.

Laroshin rode on one side of her, Meath with Rislyn in his lap on the other, the Sunrunner and the soldier's sword ready to protect her. Chayla smiled at her little cousin, happy for this one thing to be purely and simply glad about. Lir'reia waited near the lake, and no one doubted that the dragon would follow them all the way to Feruche to take care of her new possession.

Chayla's own watchful swordsman rode his black Radzyn mare through the gates just ahead of her. Visian's new title of "lord" had been confirmed with relish by Kazander, even as he charged his brother-by-marriage yet again to become a hundred swords if anything or anyone dared threaten her. She sighed to herself. If she had been tall, sturdily built, and vividly colored, like Sionell or Feylin or Audrite, they wouldn't hover around her, anxious lest she blink too forcefully and lose an eyelash.

As on the ride down, Lord Draza led the way. Chayla saw her father's sun-streaked brown head several rows of riders up from her; he was in close conversation with Isriam. The young man would leave them at the bottom of the road and gallop for some featureless speck of sand to meet Tilal's courier. The pearls would be handed over, Isriam would gallop north again, and appear to come down to Stronghold from Skybowl to deliver them and the letter.

Perhaps she had lost her sense of humor, but the trick that amused the others so much that amusement seemed their whole reason for it didn't strike her as funny at all. On the one side was practicality: getting everyone out and getting the Vellant'im in. As a physician, she appreciated the tidiness of reverse surgery that would excise healthy flesh to let disease flourish. But on the other side were the shameful words in that letter, and the shocking notion behind it. Whatever a prince's failings, no one *ever* summarily negated the established order and kicked him out. History was replete with wars to oust the corrupt, the rapacious, or the simply foolish—and assassinations aplenty, too. But an *athri*'s uni-

lateral decision to cancel all oaths of fealty as a legal remedy
for redress of grievances—unthinkable.

The Prince and Princess of Dorval had highly original
minds. Scant comfort to hear Chadric laugh that his father
would have clapped him on the back for his cleverness with
one hand while slapping him senseless for his temerity with
the other.

Just outside the gates, the road curved on its way toward
the crater's summit, and it wasn't that much of a turn of her
head to look back at the keep. Sure enough, Kazander was
there at his windows. His face, paled by sickness, was divided in thirds by thick black brows and the sweeping black
mustache. She'd see him again at Feruche, and then at the
celebrations after the victory, and then he'd be gone.

Better so. She wasn't the girl he'd seized onto his knee at
Remagev; she didn't think he was that man anymore, laughing and wild and brimming over with song. There'd been so
many things between then and now. Too many.

She was older now. She knew more about herself. So she
understood why it hurt to see Jeni and Sethric on the wall
above the gatehouse, she tucked under his arm as they
waved good-bye.

The pair on the walls watched until the last riders vanished. Then Jeni leaned her head on Sethric's shoulder and
sighed.

"I'll be glad to leave—to see my mother and Dannar
again," she said. "But I'll be sorry, too. I'm not sure
Skybowl will survive this."

"If Lord Chaynal at his age can rebuild Radzyn, your
brother can rebuild Skybowl."

"Yes. Of course. But it won't be the same."

"Nothing is, not from one moment to the next." He held
her closer. "Not even love, when you think about it. If
you're lucky, the way we are, it gets better each day." He
paused. "Do you think your mother will like me?"

"Are you worried?" She smiled up at him.

"Some. And about what your father will say." He shifted
uncomfortably on his sore leg. "But it's not as if I'm stealing you away from them immediately, so maybe they'll get
used to the idea in time."

"You won't be stealing anything. We don't marry *out* of
our family. Other people marry *into* it. You'll see—Pol will

give you a holding in Princemarch or the Desert, and when we're ready to be married, that's where we'll live."

She sounded very complacent about it. He undertook not to resent the power of her powerful relations. But pride compelled him to say, "It may be that my uncle or my cousin will find something for me in Gilad, you know."

"Then we'll have two homes." Smiling, unworried, she slid both arms around him, tilting her head back. "Two, a hundred, none at all—what does it matter?"

"We have each other?" He grinned.

"That was the general idea," she purred.

He kissed her, wondering if her mouth would ever be anything less than irresistible. Goddess, he hoped not. No other girl had ever tasted the way Jeni tasted. Fit in his arms the way she fit. Dug her fingers into his back with innocent passion—that had better ease off now or her father would come after him with a naked sword and finish what the Vellant'im had begun.

Sethric had only just drawn reluctantly back when a great shout went up from the courtyard behind them. With Jeni's help, he hobbled through the gatehouse door and out to the balcony. Every horse left in the stables was being saddled, every man or woman who could hold a sword was arming for battle.

"What in all Hells—?" Sethric's gaze skimmed over the chaos and widened as he caught sight of a familiar figure tottering against a wall. "Kazander! What are you doing out of bed?"

The *korrus* pointed southeast. "Vellant'im!"

✳

Draza, in the lead as the company rode north, didn't see the cloud of sand. Neither did Maarken, or Meath, or Chayla, or even the watchful Laroshin. It was Visian, Isulki-alert to every nuance of the Desert, who sensed them first along his nerves. He peered into the distance, saw a telltale smudge just poking up over the horizon, and bellowed the alarm.

Laroshin snatched Rislyn from Meath's arms and kicked his horse to an all-out gallop. Maarken and Draza shouted orders and the company split in thirds: one to protect, two to fight. Isriam, already past a rise of dunes to the east, halted for only a few breaths. He was one man, one sword. He

might make a difference in a battle—but the task he had
been assigned might make all the difference in the world. He
clamped long legs around the ribs of the fastest stallion at
Skybowl, leaned over the glossy russet neck, and rode as if
all Hells were after him.

Sethric swung up into the saddle, unable to hide a wince
but keeping the groan of pain imprisoned between his teeth.
He had to fumble to fit his foot into the stirrup, the injured
leg balking. He'd get no strength out of it, no help for balance. But he'd manage.

When he could speak again without his voice shaking, he
shouted to a passing groom. "Here, girl! Get me a sword!"

"Sethric—no!" Jeni clung to his knee. "If you do this—"

"Don't say it," he warned. "Just—don't." The sword was
in his hand. No belt, no scabbard, just plain sheened steel.
"Let go, Jeni."

He pried her hands loose, dared to kiss one of them, and
rode through the gates to join Walvis and Daniv and everyone at Feruche who could sit a saddle and hold a sword.

Maarken called Meath forward on sunlight, explaining
what he wanted to know that he didn't have time to check
for himself. Then, while his old friend worked, he struggled
to knot his reins one-handed. They must be loose enough to
keep the stallion's head free but not drag on the ground and
trip him. He swore luridly, wanting his other hand back, but
eventually succeeded and stuffed the loose ends under the
saddle blanket. He drew his sword and was ready for battle
by the time Meath rode up beside him.

"Two of their divisions of forty-five each, both under the
High Warlord's flag," Meath reported. "We outnumber them,
but just barely. They're riding in rows five abreast at a fast
canter. I don't think they've spotted us yet—no swords out."

He thought for a moment. "Sand Dance, I think. Yes. How
far?"

"Just over five measures. The one out in front wears
white, by the way. No sword, and flops about in the saddle
like a sack of sand."

"Sounds like some kind of ceremonial leader. Excellent!
Off you go, Meath. This is no place for a *faradhi*."

A broad grin was the reply. "And what are you, then?"

"You know what I mean, damn it! Get out of here! And
take Chayla with you!"

"Visian's seen to it, so that excuse is gone. I've got a sword, Maarken. I may be old, but I can still use it."

"Meath—"

"Are you going to argue or kill Vellant'im? I'll go tell Draza where and what and how many." He galloped off.

"Stubborn Sunrunner!" Maarken signaled his horse with his heels and his troops with his sword. They'd played at this only two days ago, on the way here; now they would not be playing.

As two thirds of his army moved out to meet the enemy, Maarken admitted deep inside himself that he was afraid. Better to acknowledge it head-on than have it sneak up behind his back. So he gripped his fear tight in his missing hand, gripped his sword in the one he still had, and rode into battle.

Ninety of them, Draza learned from the Sunrunner with relief and regret. Lovely to have it an even match; lovelier to kill as many as he could of these accursed savages now so there'd be that many fewer to fight later on. He wouldn't have minded another fifty or sixty at all. He knew what an adamant line of cavalry could do. He brought his group up alongside Maarken's—twenty across now, a deep and solid swath of galloping hooves and unsheathed swords—and rose dangerously in his stirrups to wave his readiness. For Swalekeep, he thought as he settled back down, for all the good men and women he'd lost there, and for Kerluthan and his widow, and for his own wife and son and daughter at Grand Veresch, so he could go home to them soon.

They slammed into the astonished Vellant'im, who barely had time to draw their swords. As a dragonsire sidled across the sand, talons raking the sky and mighty wings displayed, so was the enemy forced to dance out of the way of the onslaught, but with no elegance and less power. The first charge killed many and unhorsed more. Maarken and Draza rode through, wheeled their army around, paused for proper order that was worth the time, and hit the disorganized foe again from the rear.

Or would have, if half the remaining Vellant'im hadn't simply scattered in all directions. The collapse of enemy ranks made the skirmish take longer than it should have. Pity, Draza thought as he chased down a fleeing warrior, that they didn't have sense to recognize the inevitable, and hold still and die.

In the torrent of sand and swords and horses, Maarken lost

sight of the white-garbed rider. Ah, well—someone would find him. But as he broke free of the mess and scanned the area, he scowled. Surely more of their own were here than there should be. If those guarding Rislyn and Chayla had left their posts, he'd—

Good Goddess, was that Daniv, hacking away at a bearded head? And Sethric, tall and lopsided in his saddle, but killing as efficiently as anyone could wish? And that imbecile Walvis, riding down an escaping Vellanti with two of his Remagev guard at his side—

"Damn it all—we'll end up getting confused and killing each other!" He urged his stallion to the top of a dune and roared dragon-loud for a regroup. He might as well have whispered; no one heard over the din. Fire would get their attention, but he'd learned back at Stronghold that conjuring anywhere near a battle was foolhardy.

Yet fool he was, or madman, to ride at a full gallop with an unsheathed sword in one hand—the only hand he still possessed. Others saw him thunder past, and later they would admire his horsemanship and marvel at his trust in his mount. Their immediate concern was to abandon or dispatch current opponents and hurry to join their Battle Commander as he raced to protect his daughter.

Laroshin was already measures away, Rislyn tucked safely to his chest. The soldiers assigned to guard Chayla would not leave even when she ordered them to. So she had deliberately held back from top speed. Her father might need these troops—and her skills as a physician as well.

But now thirty Vellant'im were riding straight for her, and she turned to stone.

"Go on!" Visian cried. "We'll hold them here!" He leaned over and grabbed reins, yanking her mare forward. "My Lady, please!"

She stared at the dark Isulki face. Stone broke and walled-up terror gushed from her lips in a terrible shriek. *Him*—black eyes black hair he wasn't dead he had returned to take her again shut her away in the dark again suffocate her claw at her rape her again—

Maarken slowed his horse, seeing the banner of his daughter's golden hair whipping behind her with the wind of a wild gallop. Visian followed her. So did the Vellant'im.

And so did a cluster of Isulki warriors, summoned by some silent and arcane understanding, angling to intercept the enemy.

The clash of it was enough to rend the rock below the sand. Howling, screaming, shattering, hideous noise—over within ten heartbeats.

Maarken slowed to a canter, then a trot. He sheathed his sword. He reined in, flung a leg over the saddle, and slipped to the ground beside a pile of bodies.

Fifteen, twenty—twenty-seven bearded faces. Fifteen just as dark, but clean-shaven. The horses had escaped. Thrifty, canny Isulk'im, to spare horses rather than themselves.

Kazander had been spared nothing. Maarken knelt beside him, touched his face. Not spared the violent rupture of his previous wound—blood bubbled at his lips with every breath, bright red blood, the brightest in the body. Not spared the sword that had ripped open half his shoulder. Not spared death. Not this time.

Black eyes opened, saw him. A smile lifted the corners of the passionate mouth. "Mighty Battle Commander . . . unworthy servant . . . begs pardon f–for—" He coughed, very lightly. Without strength.

"It's all right," Maarken said. "She's safe."

"Ah." Softly, on a sigh.

Not long now. He glanced up, hoping for Kazander's sake that Chayla would be here, hoping for her sake that she wouldn't.

"She's coming," he lied, for there was no sign of the girl. "Just a little while, my friend. You can wait that long."

"Regret . . . I cannot. . . ." The undamaged shoulder lifted in a little shrug. "Not even for . . . my *Zabreneva*. . . ."

"Your—oh. I see." The secret Name, the one whispered to a new wife when she graced her husband's sleeping silks for the first time. Golden dawnfire.

". . . pardon," Kazander was saying, so low that Maarken must lean down to hear. "Yours . . . hers. . . ."

Maarken shook his head. "No. Not needed. I understand."

Another small, surprisingly sweet smile. "Great Lord . . . thank you. . . ." Then he drew in as much air as his blood-filled lungs would hold—and used it to sing. Only a few words, something about a white crown, and with more breath than voice, and with the light dying in his eyes.

*

Most curious. He no longer seemed to have a body. For a time he'd been able to feel his arms still, but his legs had vanished in a flash of pain the instant he'd fallen from his horse and now the rest of him was disappearing. There was a heart beating somewhere, and he supposed it was his own. The neck, too—it ached from the cramped position he was in, and from which he could not move. But he discovered that with monumental effort he could shift his head and dislodge the flies that swarmed indiscriminately around dead and dying alike.

The sun rose high and hot, very hot for late Winter. The flies returned, concentrating on a spot over his right eye, soft-crawly on his skin when they wandered from the gash in his skull. He moved again and they went away.

He could see the bulk of Skybowl's crater now, dark rust and gold beneath a darkening sky and clouds that would never bring rain. Not to the Desert. He would enjoy a little rain. He was so very thirsty.

Rain seemed a very long time ago. Years and years, when he'd been young at Goddess Keep ... ah, how they'd all chafed at the sight of clouds, and rejoiced in the sunlight, using their strong young gifts to weave its skeins the length and breadth of the continent. . . .

He squinted as a shadow passed over him. Oh, of course. The clouds weren't clouds. Dragons. They swept the sky clean with their vast wings, racing down the wind as *faradh'im* raced down the sunlight.

He remembered learning how, and the sweet freedom of it. Like being a dragon, she'd said once ... she who had come into his life a scared and scrawny girl with a river of firegold hair. He remembered a million things, wondering suddenly if Rohan had done the same in the moments before he died.

But Rohan had never seen her as she had been at Goddess Keep—hunched over books in the library, slogging through muddy spring fields, scribbling frantically in classrooms, laughing as he and she and Cami and Ostvel raided the kitchens for taze and cakes late at night. He sank deep into memories: watching as she called Fire for the first time; trying to guess which of the Sunrunner men would go to her that night; swearing to himself that he would not be jealous. Knowing by the strange intensity in her eyes the next day that she had seen things in Fire and Water that meant she would never see him.

His memories of her with Rohan began on a sweltering spring day in the Desert. She, pallid and taut with tension; he, shirtless, bloodied, fresh from killing the dragon that had killed his father; them together, wary and helpless in the grip of sudden Fire.

He remembered that he'd kissed her. Once. How odd that he'd almost forgotten that. He'd startled her—almost as much as himself—after Andrade joined her to Rohan in marriage, playfully bending her backward in his arms.

"I had to!" Laughing, teasing. "I've never kissed a princess before!"

And never had again. She had slept in his arms that horrible night of Rohan's death, but he had not mistaken it for something it was not. Rohan had been everything to her. It was enough simply to hold her in her need.

One thing Rohan had never known was the vibrant touch of her colors. That was a shame. Through the years when he had seen her only on sunlight, there had been the warmth of her and the brightness when they spoke in *faradhi* ways. He was sorry that Rohan had never known that.

Her colors were all around him now, and he smiled. Deep greens and blues of the rich land she had been born in; shades of golden amber for the Desert that she had made her life; and black, shining like the night sky ablaze with stars. He forgot the heat and his thirst, and lost himself in the glow of her and the memory she made for him.

He was a youth again, strong and vital, and she was a young girl trembling in his arms, and it was a time before Rohan was even a face in the flames. He touched his lips to hers and her slim body melted against him.

"Oh, my dear," she whispered, tears in her green eyes. "My very dear—"

"Shh. Don't cry." He stroked her long firegold hair. "It's all right. He won't know."

"*I* should have known. I should have seen—"

"I never meant you to." He smiled. "It really is all right, Sioned."

"Forgive me. I do love you. And if things had been diff—"

He placed his fingers over her mouth. "Hush. It happened

as it was meant to happen. You mustn't regret anything, my love. I don't. I am content."

Her arms twined around his neck. "Kiss me again," she pleaded. "Kiss me—"

He did, and again, and again.

✳

Alasen said she'd gone back up to her rooms. Pol found her there, slumped in the window embrasure sunlight shining on her bent head. He hesitated before touching her shoulder, sick with the news he had to bring her.

"Mother."

She looked up, tears sliding down her cheeks. "Meath is dead."

No. Not Meath. Worse than hearing about Kazander, if it was true.

"He called to me on sunlight. I felt him die." She paused, her throat working. "Gently. Very gently, Pol. I made sure of it."

It wasn't true. Not Meath, first teacher, cherished friend. Maarken had said nothing—

"I should have known," Sioned whispered, rocking slowly back and forth. "I should have seen—Rohan would never have begrudged—"

"Mother—I don't understand."

"I do. That's bad enough." She straightened up. "Leave me, Pol. Please."

He did, blindly. He didn't seek the heights of Feruche this time, but the maze garden, full of living things. Too much death. How much more? When would these latest deaths begin to hurt through the first drugged shock of grief?

"Pol."

He turned from staring at the pond. Sionell. Of course. Always Sionell—his greatest grief, for it went back a lifetime. *Sioned* should have known? *Sioned* should have seen?

"I can't lose you, too," he said in a strangled voice.

He saw in her eyes that she knew about Kazander. Not yet about Meath.

"I can't," he said again. "Not you." Taking her hands, he held them to his lips. "Please."

"Hush." Her arms went around him, warm comfort. "Hush, Pol."

He wanted to hold her so tightly that she became part of him, to wear her like armor against pain. She was strong enough to be his strength when his own ran out. Goddess, how he needed this woman, even more than he loved her.

With Meiglan he had remained himself, owning his heart and his breath and his eyes. He gave because he wished to give. But not with Sionell. She drew him without his volition. And what had he given her but guilt and a single night?

But she had come to him here, hadn't she? Sensing his grief? Wanting to be with him, needing him—didn't she? His strength, his breath, the end of all his paths. Caring for him, loving him in whatever way through all these years, even though he had given her nothing. And he had never known, never seen—

He understood his mother then. And Meath.

Drawing a breath that trembled in his throat, he pulled away from Sionell's arms. "Forgive me."

"Are you all right now?"

He nodded. Lying.

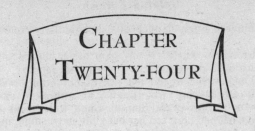

CHAPTER TWENTY-FOUR

That night, Pol blooded the amethyst and the topaz.

They were what Sioned had thought them to be: alive in pitch darkness to the pulse of their wearer's heart. She watched them throb, strong and quick with Pol's astonishment, and wished Meath could know that he'd been right.

"I rather think you'll have to do the same for my ring," she told her son once candles had been lit again in his chambers and she could see his face. "But not just yet."

"No," he murmured, staring at his clenched fists. "This is enough for one day." Then, pouring strong wine, he continued, "Had you thought about the others yet?"

"Tobin brought her jewel coffer with her when we left Radzyn."

"And . . . ?" he prompted.

"The diamond was made into an earring for Chay—thank you, only half a cup—and Tobin had the ruby set into her coronet."

He nodded. "Amethyst, sapphire—what can we use if Chadric doesn't have it with him?"

"I have a feeling he will. It was precious to Lleyn, after all—a remembrance of an old friend. If Chadric wasn't wearing it, then somebody among the servants probably snatched up the valuables when they fled Graypearl. Tibalia did the same with my boxes at Stronghold."

"If you say so. Anyway, there's your emerald, Father's topaz, Tobin's ruby, and Chay's diamond. We're missing a garnet."

"Between my rock collection and Tobin's, there must be

something—though neither of us particularly favors gar-
nets."

"What about Ruala? If any gem has a chance of being
useful, it'd be one that came down in her family."

"I'll ask." She traced the rim of her goblet with one
finger—around and around, like an unbroken circle of
thought or tragedy or Sunrunner's ring. "Rohan had the one
Andrade wore."

Pol gave a start. "I thought the agate—"

"It was supposed to go to Andry," she went on as if he
hadn't spoken. "But by the time Urival could bear to part
with the stones, he was so furious with Andry that he found
another garnet. Identical—but dead, as we now know. I
don't know what Andry did with it."

"Father's was set into an earring, wasn't it?" Pol asked.

"Yes. He may even have been wearing it, you know." She
shrugged. "Who knows but that the High Warlord himself
has it now?"

"If he does," Pol said slowly, "and if there's a—a
resonance—when the other ones come alive—"

"I hope it catches Fire and burns him to ashes."

Pol studied his own rings again. "I'm still not sure I quite
believe this. By tradition, we assign certain qualities to jewels. Emerald for renewal, moonstone for wisdom, pearl for
purity, and so on. But to think there may be some truth in
it—"

"There usually is, somewhere back behind the legends.
Look at dragons. The songs have it that they hoard gold.
And in a way, they do." She finished her wine and rose. "It's
late."

"Yes."

"Go to bed, Pol."

"In a while."

She watched his eyes search hers, and saw *Meath* in them.
They had not spoken of him, the hurt too new. She sighed
impatiently. "No, I'm not going to my rooms and drink myself into oblivion again. For one thing, it doesn't work."

"And for another, you need all your wits about you to plot
something. Sionell hinted at it earlier, but she's not clear on
what it might be."

"Oh, so you two are actually speaking to each other?"

"Don't evade the issue, Mother. What do you have in
mind?"

"There are times, my own, when I could wish you resembled your father a little less."

"Stop it. I'm not in the mood."

"Neither am I." She paused. "You were a rather boring little boy, you know. Always so proper. So mannerly. Chay told me once that it worried him—you never got into any serious trouble, and what small scrapes you did get caught in you always talked yourself out of. It looks like you saved all your childhood shortcomings to live out in adulthood."

Pol appeared unperturbed. "You'll have to tell me eventually."

"Will I?"

"I want the truth, Mother." He held her gaze with ice in his own. "All of it."

"It's better to be frugal with the truth—there's so little of it." Sioned brushed the overlong hair from his eyes. "When you've lived as long as I have, and remember as much as I remember, you'll know that."

"I've enough bad memories. I wouldn't want yours."

"No, darling," she said softly. "Nor my dreams." Bending to kiss his forehead: "Good night."

She was at the bedchamber door when he spoke again. "Don't fight me, Mother. I won't risk you or Sionell or anyone else. You'll tell me what you plan to do or, by the Goddess, I'll have you locked up under guard."

Sioned glanced over her shoulder. "Do you think this castle—*any* castle—could hold me if I wanted to leave?"

Pol sipped wine before asking, "Is what you have in mind that dangerous, or that insane?"

"It seems to me that sometimes what people call 'insane' are usually things they neither know nor understand—nor could possibly guess at. Such is the fate of those cursed by a total lack of imagination. If you use yours, you might know why I want to go to Skybowl before it fills with Vellant'im."

"Tell me or I *will* lock this castle—"

With a little shrug, she replied, "You're becoming predictable—not a healthy quality in a prince. Good night."

✳

There was only one person at Radzyn who knew the Long Sand well enough to ride it successfully without the aid of even a map. Unfortunately, that person was Tilal—no longer confined to bed but in no shape for a solitary four-day gallop. It was a tribute to his good sense that he didn't even try to convince his companions otherwise. But sense had little influence over his temper, already strained by enforced idleness.

He was not so far gone in irritation, however, that he failed to seize instantly on the next best choice. If not someone who didn't need a map, then someone who would never need a map. A Sunrunner. To the point, Prince Saumer of Kierst-Isel.

With the pearls tucked into a pouch around his neck, he rode out of Radzyn at midday on the eightieth of Winter. He was armed with a powerful bow and a quiverful of arrows for discouragement of Vellant'im at a distance; his sword and several knives in case it came to close quarters; food and water; and the firmly memorized colors of the High Prince, the Battle Commander, Lady Hollis, and the elder son of the Lord of Goddess Keep. It was hoped that the only armament he'd require would be his own gifts in spying out Lord Isriam's progress and adjusting his own accordingly if he got off track.

Trouble was, there *was* no track.

Saumer did take a map—for all the good it did him once out of sight of Radzyn's eight towers. One sand dune looked exactly like the next, and the next, and on into infinity. By evening he swore to himself that whatever direction his life might take in the future, if it showed him a road leading to the Desert he'd turn and gallop the other way.

Well before the moons set near midnight, he had found the half-buried way station used that Autumn as shelter on the way to Remagev. He regretted having to stop, but once total darkness swept over the Desert it would be too dangerous to ride farther. He didn't know the land, and he couldn't use the stars. Nor the moons, either, come to it. So he tethered his horse securely outside, dug the sand out of the shelter's doorway, rolled himself in his cloak, and slept with his sword in his hand.

And woke just before dawn to find Andrev seated in the doorway. No mistaking the slight form curled for a nap with his spine against the stone lintel, or the bright blond hair shining even in the dimness.

"What in all Hells are *you* doing here?"

Andrev's head jerked up from his knees. "Wha—? Oh. Don't be angry, my lord," he began.

"Too late for that." Saumer got to his feet, sheathing his sword. A goodly portion of his annoyance was because he had heard nothing of the boy's arrival. He tried to soothe himself with the idea that his senses had registered *friend* and allowed him to sleep on. If Andrev had been a Vellanti warrior, Saumer would never have woken up. "How long have you been here?"

"I was only thirty measures behind you, give or take."

"And Prince Tilal doesn't know you're here."

"I left him a note." Andrev pushed himself to his feet. "If one Sunrunner is good, then two are better for this. Somebody has to keep an eye out for possible danger to Lord Isriam, and—"

"And you've left Radzyn without a Sunrunner at all! Did you think of that, eh?" He dribbled some water from a skin onto a scrap of cloth and used it to scrub his face. "Making a habit of disobedience, I'd say. First sneaking away from your father at Goddess Keep, and now away from your sworn lord. You'll be lucky if Prince Tilal doesn't send you back to your father in disgrace." He flung the cloth against Andrev's chest with a soggy slap. "Wash, have something to eat, and get back on your horse. *I'm* sending you back to Radzyn."

"You can't!"

"No? Watch me." He rummaged in a satchel for bread and cheese. "And by the way, never tell a prince that he *can't* unless you've got either the law or an army behind you."

"I'm sorry, my lord—but you *really* can't. Before I got here last night your horse gnawed through the reins and ran off."

Saumer used several of his mother Hevatia's favorite phrases, making Andrev's eyes pop. Shouldering past the boy, he looked outside. Sure enough, dangling from one of the iron rings set into the stone for the purpose were two strips of leather, ending in chewed ruin. Andrev's gelding was tied to another ring—and hobbled.

"He was gone before I got here," Andrev repeated. "I didn't see any sign of him. My grandsir's horses are trained not to spook during a night in the open, but it's a good idea to tie their front legs anyway, and—"

Saumer shut him up with a single look. He couldn't send

Andrev back—not on foot. The gelding was big and strong,
the boy was small, and there was no choice to be made.

"Get my saddlebags," he ordered, and started cinching the
saddle girth.

Neither said much for the first ten measures. Then Saumer
glanced halfway over his shoulder at the boy perched lightly
behind him.

"Why did you follow me?"

"Because you're not as good at Sunrunning as I am,"
Andrev replied forthrightly, with no hint of conceit. "And
yesterday I saw some scouting parties heading out from their
camp at Stronghold."

Saumer hadn't. "Why didn't you tell me that before?"

"You wouldn't let me."

Saumer relented with a rather sour smile. "Second lesson
in dealing with princes: tell them the facts even if they don't
want to listen."

"Yes, my lord."

✳

It lacked a line before midnight on marked candles when
Maarken rode back into Feruche by the Desert-side gates.
Hollis had seen him coming on the moonlight, and warned
selected persons of the arrival.

Pol took his sleeping daughter from Laroshin's arms,
spared the man a glance of thanks that would be augmented
later, and took her upstairs.

Hollis received her own daughter into her arms, frightened by Chayla's white and rigid silence. Visian shook his
head helplessly when Hollis looked a question at him. His
eyes were swollen and red with weeping.

Sioned accompanied Maarken upstairs after he gave the
proper—and unnecessary—orders for the comfort of soldiers
and horses. None of the grooms bristled with insult that he
told them their jobs; thoroughness was expected of the Battle Commander, and all knew that Maarken—like his father
before him—would delay his own ease until everyone else's
had been seen to.

His steps were heavy and slow as he trudged up the stairs
beside Sioned. On his face was a doubled grief: for Meath
as well as for Kazander.

"Draza stayed behind with the wounded—we sent them

back to Skybowl," he told Sioned as they climbed slowly up
to his chambers. "Goddess, Sioned, I'm tired. We've been
riding without a break since yesterday noon—the poor
horses are near foundering."

"I saw," she told him briefly.

"I had to get Chayla back home as soon as I could.
There's been nothing, Sioned. Not a single tear. Nothing."

"Crying is vastly overrated. I've learned that, if nothing
else." She paused. "Rislyn?"

"Exhausted. The dragon followed us, and several times
spoke with her, so—" He shrugged. "Children are adaptable,
but this—"

"Perhaps she doesn't believe yet that it's forever." She put
an arm around his waist to support him. "Lir'reia got here
just after sunset. I persuaded Elisel to share part of the maze
garden as a nesting place. They flew off to hunt a little while
ago."

Nodding, he said again, "I'm just so damned tired. . . ."

"I don't know why that surprises you." They reached his
door and Dannar appeared to help him disarm. Sioned
poured wine, which Maarken downed in two gulps, beginning to totter on his feet.

"I'm not hungry," he said when she offered soup and
bread.

"Eat it anyway. Dannar went to a lot of trouble—" She
sent the boy a warning glance when he would have protested
that it had been no work at all. "—and he's not even *your*
squire." She set the bowl and half-loaf on a table beside the
bed.

"It would choke me!" Maarken snarled, then rubbed his
hand over his face and sighed. "I'm sorry. It's just—I'm
sorry." Freed now of his armor and the filthy, stinking shirt
and tunic beneath it, he sank onto the bed. Dannar knelt to
remove his boots. "Sioned—Chayla talks to you, doesn't
she?"

She heard the plea in his voice and nodded. "Yes. I'll go
to her tomorrow."

They were silent until Dannar had finished his duties—
laying out a nightshirt, gathering armor and clothes and
boots to be cleaned and repaired, making sure there was
wine enough for their thirst. He bowed his way out, having
said not a single word the whole time. Tactful silence was a
gift he must have inherited from Ostvel, Sioned decided;

Goddess knew, Alasen's branch of the family was loquacious enough, and possessed all the subtlety of an angry dragon. She ought to know—she and Alasen were cousins.

Slowly, dully, Maarken began to spoon soup into his mouth. As Sioned had anticipated, eating a little revived him enough to eat it all. And with the strength of food and wine in his belly, he was brought back from the bone-weariness that made sleep impossible. It was strange, but frequently demonstrated, that after terrible physical and emotional effort, one had to be roused from a stupor in order to collapse into sleep.

She took the empty bowl from his hand, set it aside, and held up the nightshirt. He slid his arms into it like a good little boy.

"She doesn't talk to me," he said. "She won't talk to anyone. Just Rislyn, to see if she is all right."

His head poked through the neck opening and she tied the laces loosely at his throat. "Off with the belt now, my lad. There we go. Stand up. Lean on my shoulder—Goddess, not so hard, I'm old and brittle these days."

"I can get undressed by myself," he complained.

"Of course you can." She tugged his trousers down to his knees, then pushed him with a single finger back down onto the bed. "I'll speak with Chayla in the morning. Don't worry so much, you're getting wrinkles."

"She won't eat." Maarken lay back and Sioned yanked his pants off by the hems. "This morning it was cold—we only slept a little while—Visian brewed some taze and I thought she'd throw up. She didn't see Kazander die, the Goddess spared her that—or maybe it wasn't a mercy after all . . . I don't know anymore." All at once he opened his gray eyes wide. "Oh, Sioned—I'm sorry—Rohan—"

"Hush. I think it *is* better that she didn't see it." She dragged his legs onto the mattress and pulled up the covers. "She's a physician. She would have blamed herself for not being able to help him—even when there was no hope. This way, she wasn't there and it happened without her, so there's no guilt."

"Not over that, anyway." He worked his shoulder into the pillows, sighing again. "He loved her, Sioned."

"I know. And she him—at least as far as she'll allow herself to admit it. I'll talk with her. Perhaps Sionell ought to, as well. We know how it feels."

"Yesss. . . ." Eyelids heavy with curling brown lashes drooped shut. Almost at once they lifted again. "Oh—forgot." He pushed his hair back and she saw the sapphire sparkling from his earlobe. "Chadric's . . . compliments." The last came in the midst of a huge yawn.

After removing the earring, she ruffled his hair. "Thank you. Go to sleep."

"Sioned—" Urgency fought with fatigue. "Why does Pol want Andrade's—"

"So you realized that, did you?" She talked to be talking, using her voice to lull him. "Yes, the sapphire was Andrade's. Isn't it funny, how we didn't have to lure them with the dragon gold after all? Instead—a letter full of lies and a handful of black pearls. I'll tell you a secret, Maarken. I didn't think the gold would work. The feel was wrong, somehow. That's it, close your eyes, that's the way."

"No—wait for Hollis. . . ."

"I don't think so, dearest," she murmured. And she was right. A breath later he was asleep.

✳

When he woke the next morning, he couldn't move. Hollis was wound delicately around him—legs, arms, her head on his chest, her hair a sweet and silken tawny cloud against his face. But he couldn't *move*. Not to shift position or stroke her back or even turn his head to judge the time by the shadows.

"Hollis—"

She stirred drowsily, lifted her head, and smiled—but only for an instant. "Maarken? What's wrong, love?"

He gulped back panic. Had what happened to his mother happened to him? No, he could still speak. He just couldn't get muscles to respond in arms and legs. His heart was pounding and it felt as if a stack of glass ingots pressed down on his chest. He thought of Rohan, and Feylin's guess as to how he'd died, and battled new fear.

"Hollis—I can't move!"

"Well, of course you can't—I'm practically pinning you to the bed. You were having awful dreams last night." She unthreaded her limbs from his. He felt the gentle slide of skin against skin, the caress her foot gave his ankle. But he couldn't move.

"Get Evarin," he said.

Hollis sat up, twisting her hair over one shoulder. "Maarken, what are you talking about? Were you hurt in the fighting? Sioned didn't say—"

"Damn it, I'm telling my legs and arms to move and they won't! Hollis, look at my face. Is it anything like Mother's?"

"You're serious." She shook herself and touched his cheek. "There's no difference. Can you take my hand?"

"No! Didn't you hear me? I *can't!*"

A little while later—Maarken still immobile and flat on his back in bed—Evarin completed an examination and stood back from the bed.

"If it was the same thing that afflicts Princess Tobin, it'd be the damnedest case of it I've ever heard of. But that's not what's wrong with you." He eased himself into the chair Hollis had pulled over, nodded thanks, and went on, "My lord, you are a strong man of forty-four winters who is simply, completely, and utterly exhausted. You've been in one battle after another since the middle of Autumn. You've ridden Goddess alone can count how many measures. You've had scrapes and cuts and minor wounds. You've lost friends and your uncle the High Prince. You've carried more responsibility than any other five men I could name—saving the current High Prince, of course, but he escapes the duties of Battle Commander. You're worried about your son, your daughter, your wife, all your other family, and whole princedoms besides. And as if any three of those troubles weren't enough, you lost half your lower left arm to a sword." He paused for breath. "Now, *you* tell *me* why your body has taken this long to decide it needs to rest."

"I don't have time!"

"That's what your mind will argue—and with perfect futility, I might add. You're going to lie there while your body recovers from what you and the Vellant'im and everybody else have put it through, and there's no way around it. That's why you can't move. Your muscles hear the orders, all right—they just refuse to obey, and with good reason. They're worn out."

"When will he be all right again?" Hollis asked, trying to sound calm.

"By this evening? No. Tomorrow? I wouldn't take bets on it. In a few days, probably. My lady, what he needs is rest.

No visitors, no distractions, not even his parents—nor Lady Chayla, either. And certainly not his brother or the High Prince. I want him to sleep the rest of today—you know how to do that for him? Good. And don't fight her, either," he warned Maarken, pointing a stern finger. "When you wake, eat. Good Goddess, man, you ought to be at least a silkweight heavier than you are right now. And as for you," he added, turning finger and glare on Hollis as he got to his feet, "you join him in eating, my lady, or you'll be joining him in that bed, in the same condition."

Maarken glowered up at him. "If my daughter wasn't one, I'd be tempted to hate physicians."

"But you'll make an exception in my case." Evarin smiled at him. "When you've had enough rest, your body will let your mind take the reins again. You'll be better for it, believe me." His smile faded. "But I'll tell you something else, my lord. When all this is finished and done, none of this going back home and starting in on another sort of backbreaking work. Twenty or thirty days of doing absolutely blissful nothing, or one of these days you *will* go through what your mother did—and probably get a taste of the heart seizure that killed your uncle as well."

And with that parting shot, he limped from the bedchamber.

Hollis sat at the foot of the bed. "Well? *Are* you going to fight me?"

He tried to raise his head so he could see her more clearly. He couldn't. "Hollis, I feel old."

"You look it."

"This couldn't have happened at a worse time," he fretted.

"No? It could have been four or five days from now, when Pol is ready to march on Skybowl. You just think about *that.*"

"If all you're going to do is give me the sharp side of your tongue, then send me to sleep and leave me alone."

Hollis sprang to her feet, shaking. "Damn you!" she cried. "Don't you understand? Didn't you hear him? You're lucky you aren't dead!"

"That's not what he—"

"You weren't listening! Not to him, not to me, not to—oh, I'm sick of talking to you!"

And sleep spun around him so fast and thick that he blacked out like a snuffed candle.

✳

"Lord Isriam!" Saumer halted the gelding a few paces from the dry well and let the reins drop, holding both hands out to his sides to show they were empty. "Put up your sword!" he shouted. "I'm Prince Saumer of Kierst-Isel, and this is Lord Andry's son!"

The lanky young man rode a little closer to the tattered pile of stones between them, naked steel glimmering yet in his hand. "I'll need more identification than that!"

Saumer's hands fell to his thighs. "What do you want me to do, tell you who won the third race at this year's *Rialla?* I can't—I wasn't there!"

"What color are Prince Tilal's eyes?"

"Oh, for—they're green!" he yelled across the sand. "Like my brother Arlis, my aunt Alasen, my cousin Sioned, and my cousin Dannar! Satisfied?"

Isriam sheathed his sword and approached. "You didn't have to run through your whole family, you know. I beg your grace's pardon, but I had to be sure."

"I realize that. What I don't understand is how you could suspect my friend here, with his hair and eyes." He hooked a thumb over his shoulder at Andrev, perched behind him on the gelding. "*You* look more Vellanti than he does."

"That's all right," the boy said. "Lord Isriam was right to question. You would've done the same thing, my lord, if you hadn't seen him on sunlight this morning to know his face."

"Well, yes," Saumer admitted. He delved into his shirt front and produced the leather bag of pearls. "Here's what you came for. Do you have time to rest and share a meal with us? I know we were a little late getting here."

"So was I," Isriam said with a shrug. "They sent me because I've lived in the Desert, but there's a dry well just like this one about ten measures back. I only knew to keep going because I saw your dust." He swung down from the saddle and got out a wrapped package. "Venison—the hunters up at Feruche have had some luck lately."

Andrev dug around for cheese and bread—a little stale—and they sat on the sand with their reins wound around their ankles to make a meal washed down with water. Hard riding had made all of them hungry, so for the first while no one said much. Then, passing the waterskin over, Isriam asked why there were two of them and only one horse.

Saumer let Andrev explain—including the circumstances of his presence. Isriam arched both brows but made no comment, and, indeed, treated Lord Andry's son with respect.

"You'll be glad to know your father has completely recovered from the bump he took on the head. Your sister Tobren is busy these days, learning to be a Sunrunner and taking care of your grandmother. She's better, too, my lord."

"Is there any news of my brother in Firon?" Saumer asked.

"They landed without a fight at Snowcoves, as you probably know. There's been a storm, so nobody's been able to see anything for quite some time. The High Prince assumes they're on the way to Balarat."

"I wouldn't like to be in Lord Yarin's boots when Arlis catches him," Saumer chuckled. "*That's* going to be a battle and a half."

"What about Goddess Keep?" Andrev wanted to know. He tugged at the gelding's reins when the horse strayed a little. "Have the Vellant'im landed yet? Has there been any fighting?"

"No, and it's got your father and everybody else wondering what they're waiting for." Isriam tore off a hunk of dry bread. "It begins to look as if it might be the same reason the Vellant'im are just sitting outside Stronghold. That's why the High Prince wants them to move when *he* wants them to—get them to Skybowl with the pearls and the letter and all that."

"Work to *our* time schedule, not theirs," Saumer approved. "What does he want us to do down at Radzyn?"

Isriam shrugged, chewed, swallowed, and replied, "Wait. Like everybody else."

"Prince Tilal won't like that," Andrev commented. "Even though all he's allowed to do is wait anyhow."

"Is his wound healing well?"

Saumer grinned. "With an army of physicians to hand, he'd really have to work at it *not* to get better!"

The waterskin was passed around once more. Isriam capped it and slung it around his neck. Saumer asked if he wanted one of theirs; he shook his head.

"No, thanks, your grace. Lady Feylin ran up just as I was

leaving and gave me an extra, so I'm fine." He hesitated. "Do either of you know what happened up at Skybowl?"

"When?" Saumer frowned.

Isriam sighed. "I was hoping you'd taken a look. Just as I left Lord Maarken's army to ride here, Vellant'im showed up."

"And you left anyway?"

His spine and shoulders stiffened. "These were more important." He gestured to the pearls in their sack around his neck.

"Sorry, of course you're right," Saumer apologized. "Andrev, you're better at Sunrunning than I am—as you've often told me," he added pointedly. "Take a look, why don't you?"

"It was two days ago," Isriam said. "There's probably nothing to see."

"I'll let you know," the boy said, and closed his eyes.

Saumer spoke softly so as not to distract him. "I understand you're a Prince of Fessenden, so you can stop 'gracing' me, you know. It makes us cousins of the courtesy sort."

Isriam shook his head, so vehemently that the black cord tying back his overlong hair loosened and strands fell in his eyes. "No. Pirro won't acknowledge me—and I don't blame him. There's no proof but my mother's word."

Looking him over, Saumer had to admit there was no resemblance to any of the Fessenden royal line that he'd ever met. Then again, Isriam didn't look at all like Sabriam of Einar, who'd guested at Zaldivar right before Saumer left for Kostas' service at High Kirat.

"I look like my mother," Isriam told him, correctly interpreting the scrutiny. "Prince Camanto was blond."

"Well, Hell—*I* don't look much like anybody else in my family, either," Saumer lied. "I think you'd make a good prince. As Rohan's squire, and now with Pol, you certainly have the training for it."

"Perhaps." Isriam shrugged again. "I'm still trying to get used to the idea. But if Pirro has his way, I won't have to. I won't have anything—not Einar, not any portion of Fessenden. Nothing to offer—"

Saumer, never particularly subtle, couldn't miss how Isriam swallowed the rest of it. "You mean in *marriage?*"

Tanned cheeks flamed with color. "No. I didn't say anything. Understand?"

"Uh—yes." At seventeen, Saumer was barely a year Isriam's senior—and he couldn't imagine marrying anybody, no matter how compelling, for at least five years. Maybe ten. There were too many pretty girls in the world to narrow his view to a single one just yet. But it appeared that Isriam had, and he wondered who she might be. Whoever, she could end up Princess of Fessenden. Or wife of a man landless, disinherited, and illegitimate, no matter how highborn.

But Pol would fix that. Or Sioned would. Through his brother Arlis' influence, Saumer had infinite faith in the power that emanated from their cousins.

He reached over to unwind the reins from Andrev's ankle; the gelding had wandered again. At his touch, the boy blinked and started.

"What—? Oh."

"He was about to borrow your leg. Did you see anything?"

"The remains of a very large pyre out in the Desert. I think that's where they burned the Vellant'im. There's a smaller one beside the lake for our people—not that many, looks like. But there were two more that I don't understand. Individual ones. And that means somebody important died."

"Who's inside the keep? Wait—check on Feruche as well," Saumer ordered.

"That's what took me so long," Andrev replied with a touch of impatience. "Nobody's gone from Skybowl that I know to look for. Lord Walvis and Prince Daniv were crossing the courtyard. The curly-haired one—Sethric of Grib?—he was limping after Jeni, but she was ignoring him. Uncle Maarken is nowhere to be seen at Feruche, but I saw Aunt Hollis and she looks worried but not like a widow, if you know what I mean. I don't know who we lost."

"Lord Draza?" Isriam asked. "He came down from Feruche with us. Tall, about thirty winters old, dark hair, a moonstone thumb-ring on his right hand—"

"I didn't see him."

"Goddess, I hope it wasn't him. Anybody there to ask?"

Andrev shook his head. "I don't know Jeni's colors, and Aunt Hollis went back inside before I could touch her. No other Sunrunners were in reach."

"Not Walvis, Daniv, Sethric, or Maarken," Saumer mused.

"Well, I'm sure we'll hear the worst of it soon enough. That's the one thing you can count on in a war."

"Not even *faradhi* communication works all the time," Andrev said. "We're at the mercy of the sunlight and who's in it."

"If we were infallible, where would the challenge be?" Saumer asked wryly. "Speaking of sun, cousin, you'd better start back before it starts back down the sky."

Isriam's brows quirked in surprise. Then he gave Saumer a shy smile, grateful to be acknowledged as a prince. They mounted up, wished each other farewell and a safe journey, and turned their horses in opposite directions—Saumer and Andrev back to the safety of Radzyn, Isriam to the unknown perils of Stronghold.

CHAPTER
TWENTY-FIVE

Pol sat down that evening to a dinner he didn't want to eat in the company of people he didn't want to see. There were six around the Attic table: Ruala and Riyan, Alasen and Andry, Sionell and Pol himself. One couple who were married, one couple who might have been, and one who perhaps should have been. No one remarked on the pairings or on the careful distance between occupied chairs. In fact, no one said much of anything beyond a few murmured requests to Dannar and Kierun, who served the meal in wary silence. What was there to talk about? Meath? Kazander? Rislyn? Maarken's strange illness, the lack of news from Firon, the departure from Skybowl, whatever might or might not be happening at Goddess Keep?

None of the others present had any appetite, either. But for all their vagaries and variants in character they were practical people. None of them had ever been so foolish as to neglect the physical needs of bodies they relied on. Too many other people and too much of importance depended on their continued health and strength. So they ate, but they tasted nothing.

With the taze came Visian, tense and apologetic. Though it was amazing enough that he had abandoned his post outside Chayla's closed door, the expression on his face alerted all six highborns to something extraordinary.

"Your grace," he said to Pol, "a courier is here. He—" After considerable difficulty, Visian finally blurted, "From Stronghold! A Vellanti priest!"

So it proved to be. Laroshin escorted the man upstairs—

bound in steel cuffs linked by a heavy chain, with Laroshin's sword at his spine. Riyan had quickly changed places with Pol to give him the master's chair; Pol gestured to Andry to sit at his right hand. A glint of bitter amusement had acknowledged the tactic in blue eyes and blue-green.

Before the captive arrived, Ruala mentioned something about leaving. "No, stay," Pol said. "Isriam won't deliver your message until tomorrow sometime—this priest doesn't know about that. You're still only plotting against me, not in open rebellion yet."

"All right. Riyan and I will glower at appropriate moments."

Laroshin and Visian between them prodded the Vellanti through the doorway. The priest was all plain dark beard and black eyes starting from his head at beholding the enemy. The tremors in his knees were due to simple exhaustion, but the intermittent quiver of his hands was an expression of the superstitious terror in his eyes.

He was filthy dirty, his thigh-length tunic and loose trousers more dirt and sweat than white cloth. Tongue flicking nervously over thin lips, his gaze darted around to note everything from the food on the sideboard to the rugs on the floor. He ignored the women. Pol wondered how these ladies would react to being considered of less importance than the furniture.

"Bend your head to his mightiness the High Prince and the dread Lord of Goddess Keep!" Visian commanded.

The priest got control of himself. His chin jutted upward in defiance. Pol, whose lounging posture in Riyan's chair was entirely deliberate, watched from a corner of his eye while, just as deliberately, Andry leaned forward with beringed hands clasped on the table. They were each other's instinctive mirror tonight, amused disdain contrasting with tense interest.

Andry's good, Pol thought with reluctant admiration. *Almost as good as he thinks he is.*

"Speak your name and your message." Laroshin emphasized the order with a jerk of the sword.

"Perhaps," said Andry in the softest of voices, "a little water might serve to ease his dry throat."

"Will it cure his stiff neck?" Pol asked.

Andry was all oil and honey, balm to the priest's weariness and fear. "He's ridden a long way, your grace."

Pol nodded permission. *You be charming and I'll be nasty. Come on, cousin—let's shake him and see what rattles.*

"Tell me, Laroshin," he said as Dannar poured water into a cup and Visian poured some of it down the priest's throat, "why is this man still alive?"

"I beg your grace's forgiveness. I stayed Lord Visian's hand."

Pol made a dismissive gesture. "He's here, we might as well listen to him."

"We brought his saddlebags, your grace," Visian said. He placed the leather satchels on the table. Pol opened one side, Andry the other.

"Let's see. Food, an empty waterskin—oh, here's another dragon for my collection." Pol held up an exquisite little token made of solid gold, outstretched wings glinting by candlelight.

"Sapphire eyes," Sionell contributed sweetly. "It resembles your grace."

The Vellanti, who had gone rigid as the accursed *Azhrei* dared touch the dragon, gave a start when a woman spoke. The outraged look he turned on Sionell fairly screamed that she had no right to be here, let alone open her mouth. She returned the scorn with a serene smile.

Pol appreciated the interplay, but there could be only two players on his side of the game. Delving in the saddlebag for other items, he found only a silver comb. "Lord Andry?"

"Just this, your grace." He extracted a bulky package wrapped in white silk and tied with silver cord.

The priest—well watered by now, under Visian's ungentle ministrations—cleared his throat. "Cloak for *Azhrei,* from Kir'reia."

You piece of filth, what have you done with my wife!

He made himself toy idly with the knotted cord. "My lady is ever thoughtful of my needs. I trust you left her well?" He showed the man his teeth. "If you did not, I will add one day to your death for every discomfort she suffered."

"Killing priest is sin. But I am ready to die."

Pol kept his mouth from curling in disgust. *Andry seems to have something in common with him other than a liking for white clothes.*

"That's good," he said aloud. "I admire a man who's prepared for anything. My Lord, let's see what this cloak looks like."

Andry beckoned to Kierun. After unwrapping the package, he gave the neck of the cloak to the boy to hold. Unfurled, it was a magnificent garment of violet silk lined in blue, lavishly embroidered.

Sionell filled the puzzled silence with an exclamation. "Oh! It's beautiful!" She hurried over, taking the cloak from Kierun, shaking it out so the silk seemed alive with reflected light. "Such fascinating patterns! Look at all the work that went into it!" She sounded as if she'd found it in a booth at the *Rialla* Fair.

But *patterns* was her delicately emphasized clue, and as Ruala joined her in praising the work Pol traced the stitchery with his gaze. Words ran together in one long sentence along the hem. The only punctuation was a series of dashes; the words were badly spelled, the capitalization any which way. Not Meiglan's doing. This had been commanded by the High Warlord. He didn't dare ask why.

The priest, having found his pride and his footing, conveniently told him. "For burning. Your death cloak, *Azhrei*."

His *what?*

He ran the hem through his fingers to read the whole message. As he spoke the words aloud—stumbling over several; the spelling really was atrocious—he kept hearing Sionell say *patterns*. What had she seen that he did not yet see?

Pol—high prince—lord of eigtie manors Nine palaces—Dawn defeating darkness—shining eyes like Sky—Ritual fire clensing—mighty Dragon seeking prey—punissing evil by Ancient law—cloaked in rightness—all Wrongs dead at his feet—he will Keep all sons and daugters by his strength Safe—Pol—high prince—Beloved of Meiglan

The incredible nonsense of it paralyzed his brain. His face turned away from the priest, he looked up at Sionell in complete befuddlement. She used the cover of the heavy silk to dig her fingers into his shoulder by way of warning.

" 'Beloved of Meiglan,' " Andry echoed softly, almost tenderly, as aware as Pol that it was too quiet. "How devoted she is to your grace, to have made you this wonderful cloak to wear at your victory." He bestowed a smile on the priest, kind and pitying. "You know, of course, that we're going to win."

The Vellanti smirked.

"But perhaps Meiglan knows something," Ruala said tentatively. "Why would she have made this cloak for a Burning ritual unless—"

Pol swung around to snarl at her. "Do you dare doubt me?"

Her cheeks flared with angry color. "I didn't say I did!"

"If you do," he went on in a voice of cold menace, "if you think for an instant that we won't slaughter every last one of these vermin, get out of my sight! And take your husband with you!"

"Cousin, cousin!" Andry pleaded. "Lady Ruala and Lord Riyan are your loyal friends and vassals!"

Alasen interposed then, rising to take her stepson's arm, looking desperate to mend the breach. "Of course they are. You know that, Pol. It's only that these are uneasy times, and we know the Vellanti force to be large. Four hundred horse, at least—"

The priest's face was wiped clean of all expression. *More than that, or less?* Pol wondered. *Or is Alasen's guess too accurate for his comfort?*

"—and a thousand warriors," she was saying, and this time the tiniest of smiles twitched a corner of his mouth. The estimates must be low, then. "But we have almost as many, and something more besides," she finished with the most unsubtle flattery Pol had ever heard from anyone in his life. "We have the mighty *Azhrei* and the dread Lord of Goddess Keep!"

Andry inclined his head graciously, not a hint of ironic sparkle in his blue eyes. "Indeed, and I thank you, Princess Alasen."

"Of no matter," the priest announced. "Your sin power will die. You will die. So is it truly written."

"Oh, it is, is it?" Pol deepened his frown. "Beg me nicely enough, and I may leave one or two of you alive to write down what will *truly* happen. Laroshin, take this thing away. He fouls the air every time he breathes."

But the priest had one last smugness, and this one came close to igniting Pol's temper for real. "The High Warlord, may he sire a thousand sons, permits letter written for the *Kir'reia.*"

Oh, Meggie—dear heart, don't be afraid, everything will be all right—

It took everything he had to relax back into the chair and hook one leg casually over its arm. "Now, why should I bother to write her a letter when I'll be seeing her so soon? Get him out of here, Laroshin."

Visian spoke up eagerly. "May I kill him now, mighty *Azhrei?*" He had understood nothing of the game just played and cared even less. Here was a Vellant'im, one of the barbarians who had murdered Kazander.

"I don't think that would be wise," Andry cautioned.

Pol had no difficulty with a sharp glance upward as his cousin rose. Andry returned it innocently.

"Your grace, the man is unarmed and helpless. It's no part of honor to kill someone who—"

"Then I will give him a sword first, to fight with!" Visian said through gritted teeth. "It is *he* we fought at Skybowl, *he* who escaped my sword then!"

"Is it?" Andry blinked, caught off-guard.

The priest looked pained. "A mistake. No battle meant then. You killed and killed—all but me," he added fiercely. "The Father of Winds gave dragon wings to my horse—"

"My *father's* horse," Andry couldn't help saying.

Pol hid a grin. "He knows too much about us," he said darkly. "He's seen too much."

Laroshin, struggling to comprehend which Pol wanted— free the priest or kill him?—summed up the arguments for both. "He's seen the garrison below, your grace—the scouts found him first, then sent for me—and the back stairs. No more than this. But—as your grace has said, too much. He has seen *you,* and the Lord of Goddess Keep."

Pol spoke musingly. "So they took you by surprise at Skybowl, did they? And you're the only one left to tell of it?" He let a smile spread across his face. Not the charming one; the one that made him look like a wolf scenting easy prey. He glanced up at Andry again. "Cousin, honor aside, I think you're right. While the ninety who died will be missed eventually, if this priest doesn't go back and tell them what happened, the High Warlord might think they're wandering around lost in the Desert."

Andry bent his head, with such meekness that Pol nearly snorted. "Your grace is wise. If I may, I will escort him back to his *stolen* horse. Also, his food is scanty and his water-skin empty—"

"Water. No food. He might feast along the way, and grow drowsy, and then one of my dragons might decide to feast off *him.*"

The priest's initial fear returned. Pol was so intrigued by the strike of his little arrow that he almost didn't follow up on the advantage until Alasen gave him the perfect opening.

"Oh, your grace," she said breathlessly, "before you let this man go, you must tell the dragons not to harm him."

"Yes, I'll have to do that, won't I?" He let his smile turn terribly sweet. "Goodness, I *do* hope I don't forget."

Laroshin and Visian led the priest away—the former certain now of his prince's desires, the latter glum at being forbidden his kill. The Isulki's black eyes hinted that although the priest would leave Feruche safely enough, he'd leave with bruises to remember it by.

Leaning down, Andry whispered rapidly to Pol that he would accompany them and find out what he could. Pol told him to do that—and bring Sioned back with him when he returned. The door closed behind Andry, and for a long moment everyone simply stared at everyone else.

"Well!" Alasen said brightly. "It turned out to be an interesting evening after all."

"My compliments," Pol agreed. "Every word sung in tune and right on cue."

"*You* weren't much help," Ruala chided her husband. "I know it offends you even to pretend disloyalty to your prince, but you could have at least looked angry when he yelled at us."

Riyan drew himself up with great dignity. "I was calmly and thoughtfully plotting out my treachery in the face of his irrational complaints."

Sionell ignored all of them. After piling the cloak into Pol's lap without a by-your-leave, she used one arm to sweep all the dishes and crockery from one side of the table. Dannar and Kierun leapt to remove the meal's debris from the other side. With Alasen's help, she draped the cloak over the table, lining down, so it was spread to its fullest and they could see all of it at once. Ruala ran a finger over the hem, shaking her head.

"The work of a whole season, crammed into—how long have they had her?"

"At Stronghold, seventeen days," Pol said quietly.

"You can see how tired she is. Look here—and here," she said, pointing. "The weave is clearly defined. This heavy stuff always is, the separate threads are so big. They form neat intersections that on finer silk you can barely see. But look how she's missed stitching a straight line guided by the fabric. As if she was so exhausted she couldn't work the needle in properly."

Oh, he'd really needed to hear that.

"She must be frightened half out of her wits," Alasen added pityingly.

That, too.

"These words along the hem," Alasen went on. " 'Eighty manors and nine palaces'? There's no sense in it."

"You think not?" Sionell gave her a curious glance. She crossed to the other side of the table, saying as she went, "Kierun, pen and parchment, please." She picked up the hem Alasen was holding and followed the words halfway around the cloak.

"Ell, what are you looking for?" Pol sat forward, flattening his hands on the violet silk laid out in front of him. "What's here to be seen?"

"She was tired when she wrote this, yes—but she wasn't frightened. She was thinking more clearly than any of us could ever hope to!" She met his gaze, blue eyes blazing, and walked back to the beginning of the sentence. "See how she abuses the language to her own purposes. Words spelled wrong, the oddest placement of capitals since my elder son learned to write his name—"

"I saw that while I was reading it."

"But you didn't see what she was doing. Take just those strange words, and forget the others. Kierun, write down what I say."

"Yes, my lady."

"Pol, eighty, nine, dawn, sky, ritual, cleansing—" She paused to pull more of the hem through her hands. "—dragon, punishing, ancient, wrongs, keep—" Impatiently she yanked the silk from under Pol's elbow. "—daughters, safe, Pol, beloved, Meiglan!" she concluded triumphantly. "Wrong capitals and misspellings, those are the words she wanted us to know!"

"Gentle Goddess," Riyan murmured. "She's told us where, when, and why."

Pol nodded, his fingers clenched now around emptiness. "But not how."

*

The priest was singularly uncommunicative. Andry soon gave up trying to trick him into revelations through a careful show of sympathy, and let Laroshin and Visian take him back down to the garrison. Then he went to find Sioned.

The gift of the cloak was beyond an oddity. Sionell had seen something, he had discerned that much. What? And would Pol reveal the information to him?

Once again they'd worked together like hand and hammer, nailing that fool of a priest. Andry liked best of all Pol's casual claim that the dragons were *his*—and Alasen, bless her, had picked it up instantly. As he climbed to Sioned's rooms, he reflected that even at nineteen, he'd had very good sense to love her. None compared—not even fey and gentle Brenlis.

Ah, well, he thought. First love—one never really lost all of it, even when its object was lost for all time.

Sioned was not in her chambers. He knocked on her door, opened it, poked his head in, went through the anteroom calling her name, found nothing. Back in the hallway, he tried to guess where she might be. With Jihan and Rislyn, most likely. He turned for their rooms, then hesitated. Evarin had forbidden Maarken's bedside to everyone except Hollis. But perhaps—

Pivoting smartly on one heel, Andry made his way to his brother's chambers. His knuckles were just about to connect with the door when it opened to reveal the Master Physician's surprised and then accusing face.

"Aha! I knew it!"

Andry felt absurdly like a child caught filching sweets. "Knew what?" he parried, lowering his hand quickly.

"You know very well what." Evarin stepped out and shut the door firmly behind him. "He's just nodded off without either my help or his wife's, and I won't have you disturbing him. Your lady mother was here this morning, and the High Prince this afternoon. I sent them packing and I'll do the same for you, my Lord. I've been waiting for you to show up."

Andry sighed. All physicians were tyrants. "How is he?"

"Better." Taking Andry's arm, he walked firmly away from the door. His limp had almost vanished. "He ate like a horse tonight, and that's an excellent sign. He'll be fine in a day or two, I'm sure. No, you can't go visit him tomorrow. Perhaps the day after."

Sketching an elaborate, mocking bow, he replied, "I hear and obey, oh mighty lord high physician!"

Evarin snorted.

"What about your other patients?"

"Lady Feylin was correct about Princess Rislyn. The fever burned away her sight. Thank the Goddess for that dragon—who's currently skulking around the garden, trampling the flowerbeds. Although," Evarin mused, "I think Princess Jihan is a little jealous."

"That's to be expected. She takes the lead in everything. Rislyn's having a dragon first would—"

"No, that's not what I meant. Jihan wants to be her sister's eyes herself."

Knowing Jihan, that surprised him—but only until he thought of his own twin. "Ah. Of course. Well, between Jihan and the dragon, Rislyn will be all right."

"Tell your brother he'll hardly miss his arm," Evarin retorted. Pausing on the landing to lean against the banister, he said, "It's not my affair, of course, but are you and the High Prince in conflict over something? More than usual, I mean." His gaze descended from Andry's eyes to his healing lip.

"Nothing special."

"Good. Keep it that way."

"You're right, it's none of your concern," Andry observed smoothly. "But I'd like to know why you ask."

"Your niece has the makings of a brilliant physician." Evarin paused a moment while Andry wondered what Chayla had to do with any of this. "But while she knows how the body works—and how to make it work again after a battle wound—she treats *only* the body."

"So?" he asked, impatient.

"So there's no physical cause for your brother's malady."

Andry nearly slugged him. "Are you saying it's something to do with his mind? Maarken's the sanest man I know!"

"Did I *say* he'd lost his wits?" Evarin growled. "He's exhausted in body, naturally, and that's part of it. But there's a tired mind to go with it. Yes, I know, everyone's feeling that way. Not everyone is lying in his bed, unable to move more than his arms."

Andry tried to picture his vigorous brother helplessly paralyzed. Impossible. He opened his mouth to say so, but Evarin spoke first.

"Yesterday he couldn't move at all."

"He—" Andry clutched the physician's arm. "Why?"

For a moment Evarin searched his face. "No, I didn't think you'd see it. Andry, it's coming down to it now—all the fighting, all the worry. Whatever happens at Skybowl—he can do what needs doing. He proved to himself that he's nearly the warrior he always was. No, it's the battle between you and Pol he fears." He sighed, shaking his head. "It took most of this afternoon while he was sleeping to coax even half of that out of Lady Hollis. I'd guessed some of it from his relief—he tried to hide it, but he's not much of a liar, is he?—when I told him neither you nor Pol would be allowed in to see him."

"Oh, dear Goddess," Andry breathed, understanding too much. "He's afraid of having to choose between us."

"His duty as a Sunrunner and his duty as Battle Commander and *athri* stare back at him whenever he looks at the two of you. His mind can't turn to one side or the other, so it decided his body wouldn't be able to, either." Evarin shrugged again. "He doesn't realize it, of course. His wife does—she's one smart woman, your sister-by-marriage. And she'll skin you both without a second thought if she feels you're threatening his peace."

"Well, then, we won't."

After a slight hesitation, Evarin ventured, "You'll submit to Pol?"

"I'll create circumstances wherein submission won't be necessary. And even if I fail, and have to slap Pol down—Sunrunnerly speaking—Maarken won't know about it. I'd sooner cut off my *own* hand than do that to him."

"Persuade Pol of the same, and perhaps tomorrow I'll let you both see him. No false smiles and sweetness-and-light, mind you—there's nothing wrong with his eyes and he knows you both." More briskly, he continued "Now, what did you come to ask about?"

"What? Oh—do you know where I can find Sioned?"

"With Chayla. Where else?"

✻

While Pol was reading the hem of the cloak aloud in the presence of the Vellanti priest, Sioned sat with Chayla in the girl's bedchamber, waiting as she had waited throughout their shared dinner. Not for tears of grief over what had never been—Sioned didn't think she could stand that, it was too close to her own guilt and sorrow. No, there was something else in the lightless blue eyes, something more than Kazander's death. Something worse.

At length Sioned poured out the remainder of the taze into her own cup; Chayla had earlier refused with a sharp shake of her head and a sudden unexplained pallor.

"Chayla. Tell me what's wrong."

She stared straight at Sioned without seeing her. Slender, clever fingers twisted around each other like tangled skeins of sunshine. With a startling burst of nervous energy, she rose, paced to the hearth, then drew a deep breath and faced Sioned.

"I'm pregnant."

When Sioned utterly failed to react, Chayla went on feverishly, "I can't tell my mother. Do you understand? I didn't tell her about—how could I talk to her now about this? I haven't told anyone but you. You're the only one who knows what happened to me. I know you do—everything you said that day, about forgetting—" Her hands clenched in the hem of her tunic. "I thought I *could* forget, in time. That it would go away. So I didn't tell anyone." She paced a few steps, arms hugging herself tight. "How could I? If my father found out what happened—I was afraid of what he'd do."

Rightly so. Maarken would rage out of Feruche to slaughter Vellant'im until he dropped dead of exhaustion. Chay would be only a half-step behind.

Sioned rose and locked the door. Leading Chayla to the window seat, she coaxed the girl to sit down and pulled a chair over so they were knee-to-knee. With the cold hands folded between her own, she said, "I understand. And you're right, I knew what happened to you from the start. But first things first, my dear. Are you quite certain?"

"Yes. I think I knew several days ago, but I didn't want to." She tried for a physician's calm voice, but succeeded only in a colorless monotone. "My cycle is regular. It always has been. When I didn't bleed, I thought it was from shock. That happens. It's not uncommon. I'm not giddy or sick to my stomach—just at the smell of taze. It's only been twenty-three days since—since it happened. But I feel . . . different, somehow."

She thought of Ianthe, who had *known* scant days after conceiving Rohan's son. "I've felt it several times. I know what it's like—the difference."

"Then you think I'm right."

"I believe so." She hesitated. "You're very young, dearest, and the women of your family don't bear easily. What I'm trying to say is that there's a good chance that your next bleeding—"

"No! I want it *gone!* Now!"

Sioned had never known this unique horror. Long before that time at Feruche, the Plague had damaged her so that she would never conceive again. But she knew only too well how rape could violate the mind and spirit long after the body had healed. She had denied it, walled it up for half a lifetime, and nearly gone mad when the memory finally broke through. Chayla did not have the luxury of years of denial. She must face it *now.*

"What do you want to do?" Sioned asked softly.

"I told you. I want it gone!"

She hated herself for the images her next words would bring to Chayla's mind, but she had to ask. "You are certain you could not carry it, give birth, and raise your baby?"

Chayla yanked her hands away. "Goddess, Sioned—how *can* you? It's not mine! It's not a baby, it's not a life—it's a *thing* inside me and I don't want it!"

"Then you're asking me to help you rid yourself of it."

"Yes!"

For years all Sioned had wanted in the world was a child. Every hope she'd ever had was taken from her in sudden blood. How cruel life could be to some women. How brutal to others.

Chayla spoke stiffly. "Will you help me?"

Sioned nodded. "I only wanted to be sure you couldn't—"

"Never!" She rose, quick and adamant, pacing again. "I could never look at it and not be reminded. I won't give birth to something that would look at me with *his* eyes!" She wrapped her arms around herself again, shuddering. "It's not just that. No child should be hated by its own mother. That's as evil as what he did to me. I won't do it!"

Sioned got slowly to her feet, feeling a thousand winters settle in her bones. "It doesn't happen often, and I wouldn't expect you to know anything about it. But sometimes at Goddess Keep the count of days is wrong and a girl is made pregnant on that first night. A friend of mine long ago—well, I know what must be done."

She was unlocking the door when Chayla whispered, "Sioned? If this were Kazander's baby—I would have loved it. I should have loved *him*. And now it's too late."

"He knew. I promise he knew that you loved him." Turning again, she saw tears slide down pallid cheeks. "Oh, my darling, no. You mustn't." Swiftly she went to embrace the girl.

"It's inside me," Chayla stammered, trembling. "It's his leavings inside me—I can't stand it, Sioned, I hate even the thought of it—"

"Hush, love." She smoothed the bright hair. "Hush now. It will be all right. I promise."

✳

Pol spread the cloak wide on the table, too stunned by Meiglan's achievement to hear the others decide on the exact meaning of the words sewn along the hem. The dragon on the back reared up in golden splendor on violet silk—beautiful work, even though so quickly done.

Alasen set the pen down with a snap that snagged his attention. "Here's what we have. At dawn at Skybowl, on the eighty-ninth of Winter, the Vellant'im will perform a ritual to cleanse the dragons and punish an ancient wrong."

"A ritual cleansing," Riyan mused. "To free them of the *Azhrei*'s taint and influence?"

"That's how I read it," Sionell agreed. "As for the ancient wrong—that was the *diarmadhi* invasion of their lands."

"The eighty-ninth—six days from tomorrow." Ruala shook her head, glossy black braids sinuous around her shoulders. "That's not very much time, is it?"

"Compared to the last hundred and thirty or so days?" Sinking into a chair with the parchment copy of the message before her, Sionell tried a smile. "I was beginning to feel this would last forever."

"It won't," Pol said abruptly. "Ell, look at this."

She sat forward to inspect the dragon. "The same as on the battle flag, and the tapestry."

"Look again."

After a moment she met his gaze with wonder in her own.

"He's holding a parchment scroll, not the emerald ring. And look what he's standing on."

She traced a finger over the threads. The others crowded up to see. Pol and Sionell both ran their hands flat over the silk, neck to hem.

"Nothing."

"The seams?" she asked.

"Yes."

Alasen gasped as each took up a table knife and ripped at the stitching. "What are you doing? You'll ruin it!"

She was ignored. The center seam yielded, and those that curved the cloak at the shoulders. Sionell tore at the fabric and spread it wide.

And there, thin and soundless and aglitter with golden thread, was a letter written on violet silk.

" 'Cloaked in rightness,' " Alasen murmured. "I've never felt so stupid in my life."

Pol lifted the scrap of cloth and smoothed it on the table. Long, swift stitches spelled out terse words and numerals, punctuated only where absolutely necessary. He read them aloud.

600 horse 2000 foot 100 priest. All men here. No threat for generation. High Warlord revenge only—others believe dragon legends. Skybowl ritual gold knife cancels power over dragons, immediate battle victory assured. Priests dangerous.

"So they think their little ceremony will cancel your power, do they?" Ruala asked. "They're in for a shock."

Pol had once more locked gazes with Sionell.

"The priests are dangerous," she murmured. "They believe the legends."

*

Sioned returned to Chayla's room carrying a small pouch of powdered *belmayce*. Feruche's entire stock of the herb was in Sioned's possession, taken from Ruala's medicinal stores several days ago for another purpose entirely. A pinch in a glass of wine acted as a mild purgative; a handful in a cauldron of soup would kill. But mixed with a few things from

Chayla's own medicines, a carefully measured amount of *belmayce* would induce a miscarriage.

Like sensations Maarken sometimes felt in a hand no longer there, Sioned remembered how it felt to miscarry. She also remembered rape. Chayla, at not even sixteen, had known one already and would soon know both.

Opening the door, she called softly through to the bed-chamber, "It's all right, dearest. It's just me. By tomorrow it will be over and no one will ever know—"

She stopped cold in the anteroom archway. Chayla stood by the hearth, rigid with nerves. Between her and Sioned was Andry.

"What is there to be known, Sioned?"

✻

"So *that's* why you've been shattering crockery!" Riyan exclaimed. "Dragon's teeth!"

"Yes," Sionell said. "And if all of you work together on a conjuring, we just might be able to pull it off."

Alasen sat down hard in a chair. "A whole army?" she asked faintly. "You're asking them to conjure a whole army?"

"I don't think we'll have to," Pol mused. "My father was fond of saying that very often it's the *impression* one gives that counts. If they believe that thousands of warriors will spring up from the Desert, that will work more in our favor than if it actually happened. If they think broken dishes are dragon teeth, they'll believe anything. I'm more worried about the priests."

"Leave that to your mother and me," Sionell told him.

"She's been avoiding me on that topic. I await enlightenment."

"You'll wait a little longer. It's not my idea to share."

"Ell—"

"What else can we use?" Ruala asked quickly. "Sionell's idea about the pottery was inspired, but why stop there?"

Kierun stepped forward shyly. "Could we put red dye onto our arrowheads? Like dragon blood?"

Riyan shook his head. "It's supposed to be poisonous, and they'd know it wasn't the moment they touched—no, wait! That paste you smeared on everything at Remagev—why not mix up some and color *that* red to dip our arrows in? I'm told it burns like the Long Sand in midsummer."

Sionell scribbled it down. "That's one to me, and one each to Kierun and Riyan. Ruala? Your turn!"

She thought for a moment, then smiled. "I could show them the dragon gold at Skybowl. If they start arguing over it—"

"They might not, though," Riyan said. "They took nothing but horses everyplace else. And Meiglan says the High Warlord is here only for vengeance."

Ruala shrugged. "There aren't many who don't covet gold, so anything he says to forbid looting may not work this time."

"Whichever," Sionell said impatiently. "The idea is to give them things to see that will make a better foundation for their superstitions. One to Ruala. Alasen, you're next."

"Oh, thanks," the princess said with a grimace. "All the good ones are taken! We want to take the fight out of them before the battle begins, right? They're not frightened of dragons anymore—not enough not to kill them—so turning them to stone with a dragon's glance is out. The hatchlings are all gone south and they're too old now to breathe fire anyway. What's left?"

Sionell caught Pol's gaze again, and what had been formless a little while ago became crystal-sharp for them both. He saw it in her eyes before he knew it in his mind.

Not *what* was left. *Who.*

Meiglan.

*

"I was raped," Chayla said bluntly. "I'm pregnant. By tomorrow I won't be."

Sioned didn't breathe. She knew Andry would not rest until he had learned the truth; Chayla had been brave enough to tell him. But now the girl wilted into a chair by the fire, arms wreathed around her drawn-up knees.

"And *that's* what there is to know," she mumbled, bending her head.

Andry turned to Sioned, asking with an arched brow.

"Yes," she answered.

He said nothing for a long while. His eyes had gone

opaque, his face immobile. Then, slowly, he said, "This is a Goddess-given life. You have no right to destroy it, Sioned."

Chayla's head snapped up, her eyes huge with disbelief. Sioned marched forward, grabbed Andry's arm, and hauled him by main force through to the antechamber. She slammed the connecting door and set her back against it.

"Explain yourself."

His shoulders set into hard lines. "No matter what the reason, it's wrong to kill the gift of the Goddess."

"A 'gift' left inside her after she was raped—as you damned well know!"

"But the child doesn't know that."

"A child? Andry, I've seen what emerges at fifty days from a womb—*my own!*" she flung at him bitterly. "For her, it's not even thirty!"

"I believe that it *is* a child, a life," he said stubbornly. "You were about to kill it. And that is a sin."

"What about the sin committed against Chayla? Violence was done to one of your sacred holy Sunrunners, Lord of Goddess Keep! And that sin is still inside her—"

"A *life* is inside her."

"It has no mind, no breath, no existence apart from hers—I can't believe I'm hearing this!" she exclaimed. "You *know* what happened to Chayla! She's not even sixteen! How can you condemn a child to bear the child of rape?"

"How the baby was conceived doesn't matter!" His voice rose, as passionate as hers. "What you're doing is wrong. It's *always* wrong, no matter what the circumstances."

"Is that what rape is to you? A 'circumstance'?" She took a step toward him, her voice a low and menacing hiss. "Shall I help you see what it's like, Andry? Can you imagine it? Can you? Violence and pain shoving into you over and over again—the blood, the fear—think about having that done to *you!*"

"I know what rape is," he snapped.

"Do you? Has it ever happened to you? It did to me—I don't even remember how many times. You can't breathe, you can't fight, you're less than an animal, less than the dirt!"

"That has nothing to do with—"

"It's still inside her, Andry. The memory of it is growing inside her. Can you imagine feeling it in your body, day after day—and then giving birth to it in more pain, more blood?"

She turned away from him, sick with disgust. "Be glad you're not a woman."

Coldly, he replied, "Taking a life given by the Goddess is a sin."

"Given by the Goddess?" She spun around. "Was *she* the one who raped Chayla?"

Ruby and diamond fire trailed from Andry's rings by candlelight as he gestured his frustration. "Don't you understand?" he cried. "Either *all* life is sacred or *none* is!"

"Oh, very noble! What about Marron's life? Was that sacred? I don't recall you had much trouble killing him! And with your gifts, too—now, there's 'sin' for you, my Lord! Against the vows you swore as a Sunrunner!"

"He deserved to die!" Andry shouted. "For what he did to Sorin—he was guilty and he deserved—"

"His death I'll grant you willingly—him and that walking pestilence Miyon. But what about the others, Andry? The sorcerers you murdered? You had no qualms about executing *them!* Their only guilt was the blood in their veins!" She paused, narrowing her eyes. "What if it had been a sorcerer who raped Chayla and fathered a child on her? Would you still be prating of sin?"

He flushed. "There's a difference between—"

"Either all life is sacred or it isn't! Make up your damned mind!"

Andry paced off a threatening step of his own. "What I do as Lord of Goddess Keep is no concern of yours. You threw away your rings long ago, and with them your right even to discuss such matters with me. Definition and punishment of sin are not on your list of duties, High Princess. You have no rights here. And Chayla isn't even your blood-kin."

"Don't you wave the Radzyn family banner at me, you hypocrite! If you cared about Chayla at all—"

"I'm tired of arguing with you," he said flatly. "Chayla is a Sunrunner. The child she carries has the potential to become one as well. That makes them my responsibility. As a Sunrunner, one of the Goddess' own chosen—" He shook his head impatiently. "Who's to say that this was not the Goddess' will?"

"Oh, no," she whispered. "No, not even you could be that cold, to see that girl as nothing but a—a brood mare!"

"Stop it, Sioned! Stop twisting what I say!" Andry bit his

lip, regaining control. "I don't give a damn what you think. The fact remains—"

"—that *you* will say what is a sin and what is not?"

"I am the Lord of Goddess Keep," he said, as if that justified all.

Trembling, her fists clenched, Sioned understood at last Pol's instinctive loathing of this man—deeper than any act of will to work with him, to coax him into sharing his power freely, to tolerate him for Sorin's or Maarken's or Chay's or Tobin's sake.

"Get out." Her voice shook with the thunder of her heartbeats. "Get out of my sight before I forget whose son you are."

Andry didn't even flinch. "I forbid you to kill that child."

Sioned searched his eyes for a long moment. Slowly, very softly, she said, "If you go to Maarken and Hollis with this . . . I swear by Rohan's ashes, I swear to you that I *will* break you."

Scorn glittered in his half-smile.

"You have never tested me, Andry," she continued. "Never found my limits. Never pushed me far enough."

All he did was shrug. "Can you be so certain you know *my* limits, Sioned?"

She allowed an answering smile, as chill and ruthless as his, to lift one corner of her mouth. "I'm certain that you don't want to discover mine."

They faced each other across the narrow flowered carpet, white and rigid with rage, ready to test all limits right there and then. Ready to tear each other's minds apart, to send color and power and Fire howling across the whole Desert, to bring Feruche down stone by blazing stone.

"No. Stop this."

Chayla stood in the bedchamber doorway, one pallid hand clutching the frame for support.

With a gentleness that made Sioned want to claw his tongue out, Andry said, "I'm sorry you had to hear this, Chayla. I didn't mean to upset you. But surely you must see that killing your child is wrong."

"It's not *mine*," she replied quietly. "It's not a child."

"I understand why you might feel that way." He came toward her, hands open and outstretched. "But I would hope that you'd be strong enough to give this baby life no matter how it was conceived or who its father was."

"And what would you know about it?" Chayla's voice was calm. "I hate what he did to me and I hate what he left inside me. If it was born, I would hate it as long as I live. And *that,* my Lord, would be a sin."

"Chayla—don't do this," he pleaded. "We'll talk, you'll come to see how wrong it would be—"

She met his entreaty with quiet self-possession. "You said nothing to her that I hadn't already considered on my own. But what she said to you doesn't even begin to describe—" She paused. "If I could conjure it for you, or somehow make you feel what I felt, I would. Maybe you'd understand. But please understand *this.* As my kinsman or as Lord of Goddess Keep, you have no say in this. My life is mine."

"Please wait. Once the child moves within you and you feel its life—"

"*My* life!" she cried. "And I will not give any of my life to this thing!" She drew in a long breath, composing herself again. "I've tried to respect your position and our shared blood, but I will hear no more of this."

Andry's gently persuasive tone did not change; neither did Sioned's desire to flay him alive for it. "The Goddess gave women the privilege of creating new life. It *is* a gift, Chayla, no matter how it happened. Abortion is wrong."

Though her blue eyes blazed, her voice was cool as she said, "My Lord, when *you* can get pregnant, *then* you may have an opinion."

Sioned opened the hallway door in silent invitation to get out. But she winced back, startled—Pol stood just outside, hand raised to knock. His eyes sparked with surprise at being anticipated. Then his brows knotted and Sioned had the frightening impression that his fist was about to descend on her.

"You *knew*—Goddess damn you, you *knew!*"

Taken completely off-balance, she could only echo stupidly, "Knew—?"

He dragged her out into the hallway and slammed the door shut. "It was all there to be seen—but you made damned sure I never looked in the right direction, didn't you?"

"Pol—I don't know what you're—"

"When were you going to tell me?" He shook her by the shoulders, his face contorted with rage. "When they had the knife at her throat?"

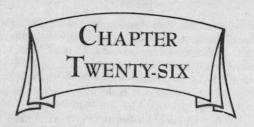

CHAPTER TWENTY-SIX

In a castle crammed with people, Pol spent the entire day alone. Not that it had been difficult to arrange. Not for the High Prince. All he'd done was give orders to Kierun and Dannar, and they had done their duty as his squires. If anyone attempted to see him, he never knew about it. Neither did he care.

Enduring his own company was trial enough. Besides, he wasn't really alone. For he spent the day in the clutter and quiet of the Attic, sometimes pacing, sometimes working, sometimes sprawled in a chair, but always in view of the Shadowcatcher.

Now it was night. Curtains shut out the light of moons and stars. A candle burned with steel-and-flint fire in his hand, flametip flickering with his shallow breaths. Feruche all around him had been locked out, forgotten. His own face stared at him: sun-gilt hair raked back from lean bones and sunken eyes and a pulse throbbing too quickly at his temple. He'd taken the mirror down this afternoon, propping it in a cushioned chair so that his face was even with the mirror face. Meeting as equals? No. If this man was what Pol knew he must be, he had no equal now living.

Other candles rested in silver holders on tables flanking the chair, waiting for other Fire. Fitted into the mirror's frame were seven jewels, also waiting for light, still dark with his blood.

Each gem had been freed of its setting and secured in its proper position in the frame. The prongs, half-hidden in the stems of six silver apples, had mostly been fashioned for larger stones, but he bent them gently into place, three for each. The diamond, raised above the center of the arc, nestled within a sprig of silver leaves.

His own amethyst of Princemarch was first in the spectrum, to his left. Then the sapphire that had been Andrade's, provided in all innocence by Chadric. Sioned's emerald was next. Not an innocent stone, that one—nor the amethyst, nor the garnet. They fit their prongs perfectly. He gazed at the emerald that had left Sioned's finger only once before since Rohan put it there. Beside it was Rohan's own deep golden topaz.

Without the two rings of his two princedoms, his hands felt naked.

The garnet, colored the dark orange of angry fire, was Ruala's. She'd searched her jewel box this morning, and though the design of the rarely worn necklet argued for great age, she could not say who had owned it before her. He wasn't sure of this gem, but he had no alternatives.

The ruby completing the spectrum was from another of Andrade's rings, given to Tobin and set into her formal coronet to honor her aunt and her husband's colors. The diamond that surmounted the whole—Andrade's as well—now was Chay's, taken from its silver earring found in the same coffer as the coronet.

If Pol was right—if Meath had been right—then within these inert rocks was power stored and augmented down generations.

His, now. If he was right. If Meath had been right. If Sioned's emerald was not some freak of long-lost sorcery.

She had sent the ring to him early this morning. Dannar had delivered it, wrapped in a piece of green velvet that concealed what it was, along with a one-sentence note: *Andry will be with Maarken tonight while you work.*

Of all the people he didn't want to see, his mother topped the list.

Andry still didn't know the truth about the mirror, much less that Pol planned to use it. The sorcerers at Feruche did—all of them. And most of the Sunrunners as well. His presence alone in this room all day was signal enough, but there was something else to indicate it, like a faint wind he couldn't quite feel or a tentative scent he couldn't quite smell. In the same vague way, he could sense their power within the keep, and with them the hundreds upon hundreds of other lives for which he was responsible.

High Prince. Sunrunner. Sorcerer.

I understand, Father. When it's necessary, I must become the battlefield.

He searched his own eyes in the mirror. All the striving all the uncertainty, all the rebellion and rage—gone.

It's not just my duty, my responsibility. It is my right.

No light but a single candle—and when he blew it out, even that was gone.

Replaced by a muted pulsing rainbow.

The blood in his body and the blood on the stones beat in sharp, identical rhythm. Faint sparks flashed from each gem, never quite touching, growing fiercer with every failure. He could almost feel them yearn for completion, his own body throbbing in time to the heartbeat of the stones.

He called Fire and the candles on either side of the mirror flared to life. Gemlights leapt for each other, embraced like lovers in a blur of purple-blue-green-yellow-orange-red. A fragmented rainbow spun into a brilliant arch of multicolored Fire that burned all his blood from the jewels—and the diamond ignited. Power subsumed and blanched all the colors of the other jewels into a pure, stark, shining white.

Suddenly his right hand jerked involuntarily toward the mirror. For all that it was unblooded, the moonstone ring—his first, only, and unofficial Sunrunner's ring—burned deep in its milky center with a tiny white Fire. He stripped it from his finger, both hands shaking, and set it before one of the candles. Andrade's moonstone glowed nearly as bright as the flame.

"Fire wakens me."

A soft voice. Quiet, resonant.

Alive.

Black eyes looked at him from a sad, proud face. A changed face. Not frozen anymore. Alive.

Behind the man was a room. Ordinary: a parchment-strewn desk, a chair pushed back from it on the large flowered rug, scrolls piled on a small table. Tapestry curtains were drawn shut. Candles were lit on either side of the man, picking out fine silver embroidery on a black tunic, the sparkle of a plain gold ring on a lean dark hand. That had moved, rising to brush raven-wing hair back from one ear, where a small silver circle pierced the lobe.

"Who has called Fire, and set the *selej* around my head?"

"My Name is Pol," he replied, not quite of his own will.

Silence; a thoughtful frown. "I do not know this Name. Your father was—?"

He swallowed, remembering how Thassalante had formally identified himself. "I am the son of High Prince Rohan, son of Zehava, son of Zagroy, son of—"

"I know none of these. Who was your mother?"

Sioned.

"Ianthe," he replied. "Daughter of Roelstra, son of Rinhoel, son of Roelstan." But that was not where the *diarmadhi* blood flowed. "Ianthe," Pol said again. "Lallante's daughter."

Dark eyes closed tight, in pain. And something else, something deeper than pain. Pol waited, watching the struggle with unknown emotions visible in the tensing of the thin face.

"So," came the whispering voice. "She who trapped me now has freed me."

Questions tumbled in Pol's mind. But black eyes opened again and he forgot them all.

"This is a Name I know. Now I will give you mine: Rosseyn. Son of no one," he added, the faintest of smiles curling one corner of his mouth. "My line began with me. I am glad to see it did not end with me, my son."

Pol felt the shock flinch through the muscles of his face. Rosseyn's smile lit his eyes now, singularly sweet, still sad.

"You are of my blood. Perhaps you'll forgive me for it one day. I will tell you how I know. This was all very cleverly done. Only someone of my blood, and Gerik's, and Merisel's, all three—and both *faradhi* and *diarmadhi*—can use this mirror. No one ever dreamed it would happen, so they thought themselves safe—and me safely here—for all time." Rosseyn paused. "But I sense a difference in the *selej*. Some of the gems are not ours."

"Y—yours?"

Heavy lashes half-hooded his eyes, as if he listened to the colors of the jewels. "Ah—the emerald, the amethyst, and the garnet. Those I know. The others are powerful in varying degrees, but those three belonged to us."

Pol cleared his throat. "To you and Lord Gerik—and Lady Merisel?"

"The amethyst was his," Rosseyn murmured, his gaze softening. "I gave it to him myself, for the color of his eyes in sunlight. The garnet, they gave to me—for the color of *my* eyes in rage, they said!" He smiled wider, remembering.

"Then—the emerald was hers."

"For the color of her eyes in firelight." He paused. "They never dreamed that someone of our blood, all three, would ever blood jewels we had blooded, all three. So you see I know what you are, even if I did not know your Name. It seems," he added almost whimsically, "that it has been a *very* long time."

Pol didn't answer the implied question by telling him how long.

"But now you are here, son of my blood and hers and his. Tell me why."

"I—I need your help. The Vellant'im—"

Rosseyn's black eyes flashed. "They dared come here?"

"They attacked in Autumn. Thousands have died—burned in their cottages and castles, slain in battle. My father—" He stopped, steadied himself. "My father died. I am High Prince. Five days from now my wife will stand as their victim in a ritual they believe will free the dragons from my influence—"

It sounded insane. But this man understood. *"Azhrei?"* he asked suddenly.

Pol nodded. "Yes."

"Gerik would be pleased," Rosseyn said, eyeing Pol thoughtfully. Before the obvious question could be asked, he went on, "I know the rest. She has no sons—they count as virgin any woman who has borne no male child. She will be their white sacrifice. And when they have destroyed you and all your people, they will claim the white crown from the Isulk'im."

"The Isulk'im? I don't underst—"

"This you see above me now, created by Earth and Fire, is the true *selej*. There is another, a symbol, to wear. It was given to the Isulk'im in trust, to hide in the Long Sand." Rosseyn frowned. "Tell me, have they the Tears?"

Sickness rose in his throat. "By now, yes."

"Unfortunate. No white sacrifice may be offered without the black pearls."

Meggie—oh, Goddess, I've done all this, it's my fault! Sent you back to Dragon's Rest, away from me and right into their hands—gave them the Tears—

"None of it will matter, of course," Rosseyn went on. "Not even Gerik could command dragons as the Vellant'im believed. This ritual murder is meaningless. Her death will be for nothing but their ignorance and superstitions."

"Then tell me what to do!" he begged. "Tell me—show me—"

"How to kill them?" Rosseyn shook his head, black hair shining in the light of the *selej* that reached into the mirror and surrounded him like a silken veil. "If so much has been lost, as Merisel hoped, then it is not for me to help you find it again."

Pol took a step forward, as if he could touch this man, shake him into sharing the urgency. "They're going to kill her! I need what you know! I can feel the power in this mirror—Goddess, it's *seething!* Show me how to use it!"

"No."

Pol cried out his frustration. The Fire on either side of the mirror jumped and shimmered in response.

With gentleness and with compassion, Rosseyn said, "That isn't what you want. To kill again, to kill with your gifts—no, that's not what you want."

The face of his ancestor was nothing like his own face. Rosseyn's eyes were black, his bones thinner, like delicate knives beneath dark skin. But Pol saw in that face a weariness of killing that found answer in his own heart as surely as the jewels of the *selej* had answered each other with light.

"I'm sick of killing," Pol whispered in a kind of defeat. "I'm good at it. Too good. I've enjoyed it. But it makes me the same as *they* are—"

"—and you have realized that despite everything, *they* are the same as *you*. It's not an easy thing to admit. Or to describe, even to yourself. But I *do* understand, my son."

He'd never thought to hear another masculine voice call him that, now that his father was dead. But hearing it from Rosseyn was a little like hearing it from Rohan. There was comfort in the claiming; tenderness, and pride.

Pol gestured helplessly. "I don't want any more deaths. But they're forcing me into it . . ." —*into doing the only thing I* can *do: use what I really am. Sunrunner* and *Sorcerer.*

He bit his lips between his teeth. How much more of his father's wisdom would crystallize for him too late?

"This mirror was originally of my making," Rosseyn said abruptly. "I will tell you how you may use it." The resonant voice assumed a lecturing tone. "The Vellanti mind is essentially simple and direct. The more subtle among them—but you need not concern yourself with those, I think. Your goal must be to show them they cannot hope to win."

Gathering himself, Pol replied, "We're already using legends against them—"

Brows arched. "Indeed? How?"

"Broken white pottery as dragon teeth—we might have to do a massive conjuring, but just sowing the sand should frighten them enough."

Rosseyn laughed low in this throat. "Lovely! What else?"

"We'll dip our arrows in a red paste that burns skin from bones."

"Dragon blood? I like this more and more."

Pol was unable to keep an answering grin from his face. "I thought about trying to convince my dragon to breathe fire, but only hatchlings do that. He'd be mortally insulted!"

Black eyes widened. "You have a dragon?"

"Well, Azhdeen has me, to be more precise."

He shook his head in wonderment. "Gerik always said—ah, but he'd be proud to claim you, *Azhrei!*"

"Did he have—?" Pol ventured.

"In his youth." Rosseyn hesitated. "Should I ask how long it has been since *my* youth?"

Pol was astonished by the vulnerability. Before he could think what to say, Rosseyn sighed.

"No, I don't think so. Your face says it's been longer than I care to know. Very well, then—if you're ready, I will tell you how this mirror works."

Pol's eyes flickered to the glowing, pulsing white light of the gemstones. The power of them *did* seethe, hungry and barely controlled.

Rosseyn understood that, too. "Take as long as you like to decide. I'm good at waiting—I've had plenty of practice."

He flushed. "I'm sorry. It's just—the mirror—"

"I am trapped. You will not be. I promise you, my son. Do you have that much trust left in you, to believe in me?"

As a child trusts a father; as a young man trusts an older, wiser one; as a prince trusts a valued counselor—as a sorcerer trusts one of his own blood, his own kind.

"Yes," Pol said quietly. "Show me what to do, my lord."

✳

Although Pol thought him safely out of the way in Maarken's chambers, Andry did not spend the evening there. He spent it with Alasen.

He presented himself at her door with her five fellow students of the *faradhi* arts, none of them over the age of twelve. Alasen recovered instantly from surprise and invited them in. She sent a page downstairs for apple cider while her guests made themselves comfortable on the carpet before the hearth.

With Tobren snuggled in the crook of his arm, and Jihan, Maara, Antalya, and Meig completing the circle, Andry began talking of noteworthy Sunrunners and their deeds. Alasen settled herself close to the fire, stirring cider in a copper pot, and listened to the tale of Ardanala of Fessenden, riding through a four-day snowstorm to warn a castle of impending attack. He had a gift, did Andry, and one she had never suspected; though she'd heard the story many times, Ardanala's peril took on an immediacy not entirely the result of Alasen's identifying it with her own recent journey.

He spoke next about Talath of Sandeia, who'd set beacon Fires on water for two days and nights, guiding home a Dorvali fishing fleet blown hopelessly out to sea by a gale. While the hearthflames burned low, Andry told of a Sunrunner whose name no one knew, braving the sea itself to take the newborn heir of Einar safely away from treacherous kinfolk who would have murdered him.

Alasen knew why he spoke of such people. He was helping the children to think of Meath as one of those *faradh'im,* noble of heart, resolute of purpose, willing to risk mind and life for others. They had lost their kindest friend and teacher. These stories might help them understand why.

She appreciated his tact in not mentioning anything to do with sorcerers; Maara was *diarmadhi,* after all. She and Tobren and Antalya listened in rapt fascination to the authoritative version of stories they knew only as bardsong. Meig perked up at the exciting parts (wild rides, sword fights) and fidgeted at any description of political wrangling, however simplified for children's minds. Only Jihan kept herself distant, staring into her clay cup of cider, her golden hair falling forward to hide her face.

"One last story," Andry said, setting down his empty cup. "Time was when a Sunrunner was commanded to a certain place by the Lady of Goddess Keep."

"Which one?" Meig asked.

"Doesn't matter," Tobren replied. "When the Lord or Lady commands, *faradh'im* obey."

"Mostly," said Andry with a smile. "Anyhow, this Sunrunner and some of her friends traveled for many long days through the beautiful spring countryside. Then they came to the Faolain River. There was no bridge, just a raft that ran on thick ropes to the other side. Now, because it was Spring, the Faolain ran high with meltwater from the Veresch. The raft couldn't carry everyone at once, so they sent some of the group over with the horses and pulled the raft back to the western shore to fetch the rest. Well, you can imagine how the Sunrunners felt at being on a flimsy little raft in the middle of a great big river."

"*I* can," muttered Talya, and Alasen recalled something about a boat ride on Skybowl's lake, and how befuddled Tallain and Sionell had been to discover they'd hatched a Sunrunner.

"Me, too," Alasen admitted, hiding a smile; the tale sounded very familiar.

"It's no fun," Andry agreed. "The ones who crossed first collapsed on the riverbank, sick and dizzy, not even knowing where they were. But as the raft started across a second time, the river grabbed it and wouldn't let go." His voice lowered to a swift whisper. "The raft shook and lurched in a powerful current, for Water had sensed the presence of Sunrunners and wanted to claim them for its own. The ropes began to fray—and all at once one of them snapped!

"The Sunrunner on the opposite shore, the one the Lady had commanded to come to the faraway castle, saw the danger to her friends. She knew she was their only hope of reaching safety, but she hadn't yet recovered from being on Water. Still, somehow she crawled over to her other friends and shook them awake. One of them was a tall, strong young Sunrunner—the kind who has to bend his head when he goes through doors, and go through sideways as well, because his shoulders are so wide. He struggled to stand up, and when he had his footing—more or less—he waded out into the river to grab the only remaining rope. That rope was all that kept the raft from whirling downriver in the torrent."

Andry paused. "Well, together the two Sunrunners got hold of the slippery rope and hauled with all their might. They tied the end to a horse, so they could use its strength to pull the raft safely across the wild river. They were still water-sick, remember, and for a while they didn't know if up was down or backward was forward. If they made the slightest mistake, the rope might snap or even drag them into the river. But after a long, long time, they succeeded."

Gentle-hearted Antalya gave a relieved sigh.

"That's the way they all felt, too," Andry agreed. "Of course, after everyone was safe, everyone simply fell over! When they could think again without the very thoughts in their heads making them dizzy, they turned to their two Sunrunner friends and thanked them for their lives."

Not *quite* how it happened, Alasen thought, aware that another young man had been there—how she wished she'd known Ostvel in his youth!—but the telling served very well for what Andry said next.

"Do you know what? All of us should give thanks, as well. For among those Sunrunners at the Faolain River were—" He smiled at Maara. "Lord Ostvel and Lady Camigwen—your grandparents." She blinked in surprise, but Andry was already looking down at his daughter. "Andrev's grandmother was there, too."

"She was?" Tobren was as startled as Maara.

"She was. So I'm very grateful that she survived and had Andrev's mother—and you should be glad, too, even if you and your brother *do* have the occasional disagreement," he teased. "And because Maara's grandfather is now Princess Alasen's husband, she's grateful to those Sunrunners as well."

"Indeed I am," Alasen chuckled.

"What about us?" Meig wanted to know. "What about Talya and me?"

"Well," Andry said, "think about this, Meig. If things had happened differently at the Faolain, all that followed would have changed. Maybe *your* grandparents might never even have met!"

Alasen bit back another grin, thinking Meig's snort an expression of his understandable inability to imagine circumstances that negated his own existence. But she had underestimated him.

"That's silly. People do what they're s'posed to, so things happen right."

It was as succinct a summary of Rohan's philosophy as she had ever heard.

Andry didn't know quite what to make of the boy, either. His brows quirked in reply to her look, and he cleared his throat. "Ummm . . . anyway, by now all of you should know who those two brave Sunrunners were."

Jihan roused at last. "My granda and—and Meath."

"Yes. Sioned and Meath," Andry said softly. "To borrow Meig's words, they did what they were supposed to do. Just as everyone else tries to do what's right, so things can happen the way they're supposed to."

Rohan's philosophy from Andry's lips was even more startling. Alasen fairly itched to ask him how he would have ended the lesson if Meig hadn't spoken.

"But why did Meath have to die?" Jihan exclaimed suddenly. She sprang to her feet, knocking over the empty cider jug. "It's not fair! He wasn't supposed to die! And what about Grandsir Rohan? And—"

She was about to cry out other names—people she knew, friends and kin—names like Rihani and Kostas, Jahnavi and Rialt and Mevita. And if Tallain was mentioned around his children, Alasen knew that all of Andry's careful, gentle words would be for nothing.

"I know it's not fair, darling," Alasen said. "It hurts to lose people we love. But do you think Meath would have run away from helping those *he* loved?"

"There are wicked people in the world, Jihan," Andry continued. "People who do terrible things. It's not fair when good people are hurt trying to stop them—but if good people *didn't* fight, then the wicked ones would be able to do as they pleased." He hesitated. "I don't understand it either. Nobody does, I think. All I know is that we have to do what we can. What we feel is right."

Jihan trembled. Tears she was too proud to shed glistened in her blue eyes: dark-circled beneath, and too big in a face that was too thin. Alasen reached out, ready to soothe her as she did her own children. But Jihan shied back.

"You could've stopped it," she accused Andry. "You *knew* about the war before it started. I heard your own father say that you knew! Why didn't you stop it? *You're* the one who should be dead! I wish you were!"

"Jihan!" Alasen started to her feet.

"I hate all of you!" she cried, and fled.

Maara rose at once, giving Andry a glance of apology, and followed without a word. The two adults looked at each other helplessly.

Meig leaned over to pat Andry's arm. "Don't mind Jihan. She says bad things all the time."

Antalya nodded. "She didn't mean it, my Lord. She's worried about her mother and Rislyn."

But Tobren was staring up at her father with wide eyes. "Papa—is it true? Did you know?"

"Some of it." He bit his lip. "I saw ships, and battles—but I didn't know that Rohan or Meath or—"

Alasen's heart went very still. She had seen Andry's face like this only once before—haunted, desperate, loathing his gift as a curse. He'd stood on the banks of the Faolain and raised a tempest atop the water, hating what he was because she was afraid of what he was.

She had run from him then, terrified, rejecting him and her own unwanted power. She was older now. Experience had taught her compassion; Ostvel had taught her how to give. She had never seen anyone more in need than Andry was right now.

Meig astonished her again, this time with ruthless logic. "Jihan's stupid. You're just one person, even if you are Lord of Goddess Keep. There's lots more of them than there are of you."

Andry drew in a steadying breath and nodded. "That's true, Meig. But it doesn't make it any easier."

A little while later, after they put the three children to bed, they stood together in the quiet hallway. Alasen touched Andry's arm. He still wore that haunted look, and it ached inside her as if the pain was her own.

"Even if you *did* know, Meig is right."

"Yes, but it's humbling to be reminded of my deficiencies by someone who's still reading *Nibbles the Mouse and Thimble the Cat,*" he replied sardonically.

"Andry, that boy would make short work of Hoeloth's *Fourth Treatise* and point out the inaccuracies besides."

She succeeded in making him smile. As they started for the stairs, Andry asked, "Does Sionell know what she's raising? I mean, Talya's a sweet little thing and quite gifted, and from what I've seen of Jahnev, he's a copy of his father. But Meig—!"

"At least tonight you didn't bore him. I didn't see him yawn once, in spite of its being so late."

"Very reassuring." They descended to a landing before he said, "Someone should go check on Jihan. *I* can't."

"No. But Maara's probably calmed her down by now. They're good friends. Jihan really didn't mean it, Andry. Too much has happened for a seven-year-old to understand."

"Oh, she understands, all right. She knows exactly what's going on. She just doesn't know why." He stopped on the step below her and turned to look up into her face. "Alasen—do you?"

"I'm not sure," she temporized. "Tell me."

"The dreams—I'd wake up suffocating. All the death and fire and destruction—" His eyes glazed over in the torchlight. "I couldn't stop it, no. But I tried to do something—yet how do I know that by changing certain things, I didn't cause worse to happen?"

"Andry—"

"Not even Brenlis saw it," he went on, not hearing her. "She—she *knew* things, saw them before they happened. She saw herself near her parents' home, then word came that her brother was ill, and she left Goddess Keep—" He choked suddenly. "She was the first Sunrunner they killed."

Whoever Brenlis had been, Andry had loved her very deeply. Alasen heard it in his broken voice, and grieved for him.

"I saw Radzyn in flames, and that didn't happen. I bought its safety—perhaps with her life, though the Goddess told me not. She said the price was my belief. I don't know. I can't be sure of anything, no matter what the dreams and visions show me—"

Eighteen years ago Alasen had run from his pain and his power. Everything he was saying now frightened her just as it had then. But this time she cradled his face between her hands and spoke softly, as if to a hurt child. "Hush. It wasn't your fault, Andry."

His eyes sharpened to shards of blue ice. "How do you know? How does anyone know? There's truth in what Jihan said—I *did* know what would happen, I might have been able to stop it if I'd done something else, something different—"

"Andry, didn't you hear what you told the children? We all do what we feel we must. We are what we are, no more and no less. We try to do what we believe to be right—"

"*You* did," he whispered, and she flinched. He held her wrists gently, keeping her hands at his face. "And it *was* right. I know that now. It was a long time before I understood—" His lashes lowered, making silken shadows over his cheekbones. "Just tell me you don't hate me, Alasen."

"Hate you?" she echoed incredulously.

"I've been wanting to say that for so long. I could never seem to find—"

"Andry, how could you ever think that?"

His shoulders lifted in a tiny shrug. "Forgive me, then. For being wrong all those years ago. Forgive me, Alasen."

"Don't you dare use those words to me ever again!"

His head lifted. He caught and held her gaze. The boy she had hurt long ago had vanished; the man who looked up at her now was—a man. Below the spill of brown hair, threaded with gray now, was a strong and compelling face. The blue eyes were almost the color of his uncle Rohan's, and the passionate mouth reminded her of Chay, and the fine high forehead was like Tobin's. But the wild, warm softening of his face as he looked up at her was all Andry's own.

A man's look, a man's face—a man's hard, lean body pressing closer to her. The boy she had loved and feared was half a lifetime gone.

Alasen froze. Andry turned his head slightly, never relinquishing her eyes, and brushed his lips against her palm. The kiss burned. She winced a little, her icy skin reacting to the touch of his Fire. Torchlight behind and below struck gemfire from his rings and the jeweled cuffs circling his wrists.

Sunrunner. Lord of Goddess Keep. Not the Andry she had known, cared for, run from. Half a lifetime gone—a life spent using the power she'd fled.

He leaned up, drawing her gently down with his fingers circling her wrists. She felt heat wash over her: his need. His mouth was a breath away from hers, and she could not look away from his eyes.

"Is this something else you *must* do, my Lord?"

The spell of his eyes shattered around them, and she stumbled slightly. Freeing her wrists, she groped at the banister for support.

"Alasen—" Her name was a low moan of anguish. It moved her not at all. *"Alasen,"* he said again, and even when she saw the shadow of a heart-wounded boy return to his face, she simply looked at him, silent and angry.

A moment later he was gone, his boot heels a rapid clatter down the stairs.

✳

"My lord, it was exactly as I will tell you. He is a tall man, even when seated. His hair is pale and his skin gold with the sun. His hands are the hands of a scribe, not a warrior—not a scar on his fingers, not a nail broken. He was dressed as a prince in gold and silver, brighter than torches, without color but for his eyes and rings. His eyes change from green to blue and back again, showing the two separate and distinct demons within him—not one, as is customary with his kind. These demons take turns looking out from his eyes."

And how, thought the High Warlord, *would* you *know what is "customary" for a prince, a warrior, or even a man—let alone the* Azhrei?

"His rings are of gold. One is a golden stone circled by emeralds, cut and faceted so that the light is captured and made dizzy before it is allowed to escape in flashes of fire. One is a purple stone so dark that light cannot escape, with another golden stone at its side. The third is as if he stole a fragment of the moons and captured it to wear on his hand."

Very pretty. Very poetic, thought the High Warlord, forbidding himself to shift impatiently from one foot to the other. The spring dawn was warm, the sun strong; he would be sweating by noon. All praise to the Father of Winds that he would not have to linger in this miserable land until summer—a season certain to kill man and beast with suffocating regularity.

The priest went on after moistening his dry throat with a sip of water. "He rose from his chair then, and became taller still. He has the shoulders of a quarry slave, the thighs of a horsemaster, the chest of—"

I know the man is strong in battle, thought the High War-

lord. *If this fool goes on stating the obvious much longer. . . .*
"And his face?" he interrupted.

Jolted summarily out of the eloquent rhythm planned on the long ride, the priest took a moment to advance his speech to the appropriate place. "Carved of rock. Though its color is gold, it is not a malleable face, in the way gold is soft and pliant. His nose is straight and sharp as a sword blade. His lips are as a slash of blood across a sacrificial throat."

And I suppose he has excellent teeth, as well, thought the High Warlord. *Is this idiot frightened of him or in love with him?*

He listened with half his attention to the rest of it. The encounter had proceeded much along the lines he'd anticipated—taking into account the priest's self-aggrandizing eloquence and slicing away a good two-thirds of the reported speechmaking. All priests were liars, anyhow.

The cloak had been delivered, the *Azhrei* had mouthed defiance, the priest had replied with smug superiority, and all was as it should be.

Yet there were aspects of the tale that intrigued him. The Lord of Goddess Keep, for instance. What was *he* doing at Feruche? The cousins shared no tender regard for each other, that much had been known to him for years. If they had overcome their differences and worked together, their combined strengths might be a problem. But that sword had two edges—for if Lord Andry was not at Goddess Keep, then Goddess Keep's defenses would be easier to breach. If, during the precisely timed battles, Lord Andry abandoned the *Azhrei* to bolster Sunrunner efforts far away, then the *Azhrei* would be the weaker. And it was far from certain that the two men would indeed set aside their mutual distrust and function as a single power.

The other item that caught his attention was, oddly enough, one of the priest's fanciful interpretations. Two demons looking out from the *Azhrei*'s blue-green eyes, eh? His desire to have his wife back unharmed, and his desire to see the High Warlord dead and all his armies with him—those were the demons, and they were at war within him. And that was a very good thing. The first would urge him to caution; the second, to recklessness.

A very good thing. Fighting Lord Andry, fighting

himself—and about to fight the vassal who owned Feruche, by the sound of it. The *Azhrei* would be so worn out by all his other battles that he would have little left for the real one. That had been the plan all along: to isolate, to batter, to back him into a corner until he had no choices left. He must come out and fight now, with everything he had—against everything the Vellant'im had.

Which did not include magic, but which did include something the High Warlord put more faith in: the faith of his warriors in their sacred war, and their faith in him.

Yes, all was as it should be—but for one thing.

"Why is it," the High Warlord asked all at once, interrupting an assessment of Lord Riyan's disaffection, "that you return alone?"

The priest had been waiting for this one, all the while hoping he could flood the morning air with so many words that this uncomfortable matter might be overlooked. He should have known better. But he did have an answer, plain and ungilded, and the truth.

"My lord, you know of the rivalry between the Clan of the Silver Oar and the Clan of the Stone Sail. Until now, this has been put aside. But on the journey, two young warriors, barely blooded, disagreed—"

—*as those two Clans are accustomed to do over how to lace up a boot,* thought the High Warlord, frowning.

"—and although I was able to settle it in peace, as is your order and the wish of all righteous men, the settling stopped our progress for half a day. Thus we did not pass Skybowl at the anticipated time." The priest shrugged and spread his hands, filthy white tunic sprinkling a little sand with the movement. "I do not know how they knew, but they knew."

"And so Silver Oar and Stone Sail are all dead."

"Regrettably, my lord, this is true. But I endured, and triumphed."

And, of course, your life is worth more than all those warriors put together, thought the High Warlord. *The first thing I do when I get home is execute every priest—no, why wait that long? I'll put them all on the same ship and make sure it sinks. And that, you cut-crotched coward, is my definition of triumph.*

"It pleases me that you survived," he said smoothly. "And performed your task so well. Now go. You have my thanks."

The rare accolade made the priest blush like a girl. The

High Warlord stood alone for a time watching the white tents at the other side of the camp.

She was there. Comporting herself as a true princess, impressing even the priests with her dignity and pride. He had discovered the letter, and she must know she had no hope. Her courage in the face of despair was remarkable.

What a waste of a magnificent woman.

Will he value your life more than my death? thought the High Warlord. An interesting question. The answer should provide much entertainment.

✳

She knew it was a dream because she could feel the weight of her hair spilling down her back, see it blowing firegold across her face as she laughed in the wind. Rohan was laughing, too, as young as she, playing "dragon" for Pol. The boy chased his father around and around the fountain at Stronghold, slipping on new spring grass and unsteady three-year-old legs, giggling as he waved a wooden spoon as a sword. Rohan wore the sleeveless gold silk cloak his mother had made for him, the one he wore when he rode off to Remagev before Pol was even born. He flung his arms out, his face bright with laughter, the gold silk billowing— becoming wings as he became a golden dragon with clear blue eyes. With a single perfect leap he took flight into the sky.

She called out to him, neither astonished nor frightened, only anxious that he wait for her, that he not leave her behind. But Pol was tugging her hand now, and in his fist was not the toy weapon but Rohan's own princely sword.

That frightened her.

"Mama!"

She cried out her husband's name as her son pulled her toward the grotto, toward the rent in the rocks where they could escape—for Stronghold was burning. The golden dragon spiraled high above for a moment, then vanished on the Desert wind.

"Mama—"

Sioned sat up straight, both hands clutching Pol's arm. He gripped her shoulder with his free hand—*No sword,* she thought, *thank the Goddess, no sword*—

"Mama?" Pol said again. "Are you all right?"

She nodded and dug her fingers deep into her hair. No weight to it, no length, just a mass of ragged curls. Graying, she knew; she'd seen it, those few times she'd been able to look into a mirror.

"Just a dream," she said, and cleared her throat.

Pol searched her eyes, then drew in a deep breath. "Mama—it worked."

Worked? Oh—that mirror. "Did it?"

"Yes. I'm sorry about what I—"

Her mind had reordered itself; she knew what he was talking about. "No, you were right. I should have told you."

"You know what I would've done." He shrugged awkwardly and rose from his perch on the side of her bed. "Chayla left a message for when you woke up. She says everything is all right now. Maybe you know what that means. I don't."

"Nothing that need concern you. We talked night before last. She's still upset about what happened to her." How glad she was that he couldn't read a lie in her face. Not that she'd told any; just not all of the truth. Rohan would have seen it. Pol would not. "Is Maarken better?"

"Much. Andry spent the evening with him and Hollis." He paused, fingering the lacy cloth half-covering the bedside table. "It *is* Lord Rosseyn. The jewels form a kind of crown over his head—he called it the *selej*. Like in Kaz—the Isulki song. The white crown."

Sioned tucked her knees under her chin, sheets and quilt and all. "He spoke to you?" She didn't know why she wasn't especially surprised.

"Half the night. The garnet Ruala gave me—it was his. The amethyst was Lord Gerik's." He met her eyes. "Your emerald belonged to Lady Merisel."

And Tobin had said to her once, winking, that it had a magic all its own.

"I'm descended from all three of them. That's why the *selej* worked for me."

"What did he teach you, Pol?"

His shoulders shifted, settled uneasily. "As much as he thought I needed. He's ... a lot like Father, in many ways. There's no blood connection, but the wisdom is the same. Even though his is so much sadder than Father's ever was."

She hugged her legs to her chest and repeated softly, "What did he teach you, Pol?"

"Sorcery," he replied, staring at nothingness. "Not the Star Scroll kind—that's a child's toy compared to the mirrors."

"And what do you plan to do with it?"

"Keep my wife alive. Keep everyone alive. Don't ask me how yet. I haven't worked it out that far. But I can do it, Mother. With the mirror—and without Andry or any of the rest of you." He looked at her again, a tiny smile hovering around his lips. "Will it help any to know how much that scares me?"

"You don't have to do it all alone," she murmured.

"How many times did you say that to Father?"

"Quite a few," she admitted.

"I promise I won't do anything without talking it over with you first."

Once more she nodded, not telling him that she trusted his decisions—now—as much as she had trusted Rohan's. Not telling him that she would not be here for him to talk to.

"You look as if you've been up all night, not just half of it," she said.

"I got a little sleep around dawn."

"Go get some more."

His mouth quirked in a real smile. "Yes, Mother."

"That's what I like to hear—meek and obedient."

Bending over to kiss her cheek, he avowed, "I inherited it from you."

✳

Isriam knew he had a good chance of getting killed before he could deliver his message and the Tears of the Dragon. Even if he succeeded in his task as emissary, there was an equally good chance that he'd be killed after.

That would solve a couple of problems, he told himself sourly. His grandfather, Prince Pirro, needn't acknowledge their relationship and his rights in Fessenden; the High Prince needn't apply pressure to gain him those rights. It would even solve his own dilemma of the heart.

But Isriam, fast coming up on seventeen, squire to one High Prince and knighted by another, trained in statecraft by the first and in war by the second, had no intention of being butchered by a bunch of gold-decorated barbarians. He would fight for what was his and for what he wanted to be his.

So he extracted from his tunic a little golden dragon given by Prince Pol, and as Vellanti scouts thundered up to slaughter him, held the token dangling by its short chain.

It worked. They stopped dead, swords wavering and then sheathed. Isriam marveled at the power of discipline enforced by superstition, wished briefly that he was a Sunrunner with a real dragon flying guard duty overhead, and haughtily accepted escort toward the enemy camp.

Someone in white came to meet him on its outskirts. Isriam looked down at him from astride his tall Radzyn mount. Imitating Chiana at her worst as noted at the last *Rialla,* he said, "I am the Prince Isriam of Fessenden. I am sent by his noble highness the Lord Riyan of Skybowl and Elktrap and Feruche, to speak with the one you call High Warlord."

The dark face below him darkened further. "You speak to holy priest. Now."

"I will speak with the High Warlord and none other."

There ensued a boring and fruitless debate, solved by the arrival of the only other unbearded man in a hundred square measures. He, too, rode a Radzyn horse. He was tall and even more impressive than Isriam would have guessed, his body built for battle, his face built for tyranny. He gestured the priest to silence and spent several moments taking Isriam's measure.

"Good," he said at last. "Left in the *Azhrei*'s army are only little boys."

Isriam's arrogant posture could not stiffen more, so his reaction showed only in the twitch of his jaw muscles.

"I am the High Warlord."

"I am the Prince Isriam of Fessenden." The young man pulled the rolled parchment from his tunic. The priest reached up a hand for it; Isriam let it drop to the sand.

This time a corner of the High Warlord's mouth twitched. Isriam swore the sight of the priest bending to retrieve the letter amused him.

"I assume," Isriam said silkily, "that you can read."

The High Warlord didn't even look at him. As he scanned the masterpiece of treason concocted over Riyan's name, a brow quivered once or twice. But that was all.

At length his black eyes met Isriam's. "Lies."

"I will do you the favor of not reporting your insult," was the cold reply. "As stated by the Lord of Skybowl, Elktrap, and Feruche, you are invited to make a treaty to end this war. The castle of Skybowl will be made available to you and your army while talks proceed."

"Skybowl—" exclaimed the priest.

As if he had not spoken, the High Warlord said, "There will be no talk. No treaty. Skybowl will surrender."

Isriam had known this was coming. He shrugged. "If you refuse Lord Riyan's offer to make peace, he will shut Skybowl tight. He has no wish to see his property ruined and burned."

"By anyone?" Black eyes sparkled in the eerily shaven face. "You were a servant of the old *Azhrei*. Why do you betray his son?"

"I am a prince! I was his squire, not his servant." Isriam composed himself and told his love for Rohan and Pol, his conscience, and especially his honor to shut up. "I am the grandson of the ruling Prince of Fessenden—and I'm sure you know that he has neither love nor help to give the new High Prince in this hopeless war. And it happens that I agree with Lord Riyan. The war must stop." He paused, judging his moment, sternly keeping his glance from the priest. "As a sign of his sincerity he presents you with these. They are of some small value to you, I believe."

The pearls he did not toss onto the sand. He opened the pouch and drew out the chain Karanaya had hung them on, so they appeared one by one in all their black-rainbowed beauty.

The priest reached up both trembling hands. Isriam saw this from a corner of his eye as he watched the High Warlord for reaction.

There was none. Only a few casual words: "Some small value, yes."

He let the pearls drop back into the pouch. He tossed it over and the High Warlord caught it easily. The priest's head turned with the arc of its flight, greed and awe scrawled in equal measure on his face.

"Very well," said the High Warlord, the pearls enclosed in his fist. "You will say what trick took them from Prince Tilal—but later. I now write to Lord Riyan, accept his treaty. Come to my tent."

"I would prefer to wait here."

"We are now friends, Prince Isriam of Fessenden," the man reminded him, his eyes laughing.

"We are no longer enemies," he corrected.

"So. I ride to Skybowl, but no welcome."

"That would be a wise assumption."

The noon sun descended only a little before Isriam was galloping once more through the Desert. He urged his horse to put quick measures between the two of them and Stronghold, then finally slowed to a walk and mopped the sweat of heat and nerves from his face.

He'd done it. He'd told all the right lies and mixed them with enough truth to make them plausible. He'd succeeded and was alive to tell of it.

Taking a pull at his waterskin, he settled himself for the rest of the long ride to Skybowl. For just a moment he put his hand to his breastbone, where the Tears had been. In their place was a brief letter from the High Warlord and the golden dragon on its chain around his neck. Both felt as dangerous against his skin as those pearls.

Shaking himself free of all thoughts but those of his freedom, he touched his heels to his horse's ribs and galloped on, while the Vellanti army broke camp twenty measures behind him.

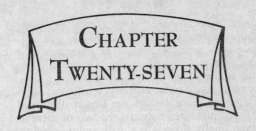

CHAPTER TWENTY-SEVEN

Never, never, never again, Arlis swore, *will I spend a single day in the snow. I hate the snow. I hate the cold. I hate the wind. No, I'm a sailor at heart, I don't hate the wind. But I hate everything else about this misbegotten, Goddess-forsaken place!*

Laric's recommended remedy was a drink called Fironese Frostbite: grain liquor (damned near raw alcohol) heated just to boiling and poured into a cupful of snow. Of course, Laric was out of his mind. Eighteen winters of this gigantic icicle he called a princedom had warped his wits. How else to explain the smile teasing his lips, the bright excitement in his eyes, the despicably supple way he swung up into his saddle?

All day sun had competed with wind to a maddening standstill, alternating relative comfort with numb insensibility. Arlis shivered, then sweated, then shivered some more. The only constant was the single needle of burning ice that pierced each joint at random. *Wonder if Pol has a spare castle in the Desert he'll lend me while I thaw out. Shouldn't take more than a couple of years. . . . Hells, I'd settle for a tent outside Rivenrock. Demalia, darling wife, pack up the children and let Saumer run Kierst-Isel for a while!*

"Only another thirty-five measures," Laric said cheerfully.

Only. Wonderful. They'd stopped to rest the horses, gnaw off something to eat, and attend the demands of nature. Arlis stayed on his horse. Once he got out of the saddle, he'd never get into it again. Besides, he'd let his bladder explode before he exposed a certain very valuable portion of his anatomy to the cold. Like as not, it'd freeze and fall off.

"We'll stop at Ramblewalk. It's a village about ten measures from Balarat. Yarin knows we're coming, so surprise is out of the question. We'll rest and get warm—"

Arlis made astonished eyes. "Don't tell me you're feeling *cold* on this sweet and balmy morning?"

Laric grinned. Arlis hoped his teeth froze.

"Want some wine?" the older prince asked maliciously, knowing very well why Arlis remained in the saddle during these rest stops.

Any liquid he put into his body would eventually want out long before that nice, sheltered, *warm* village. "No, thank you."

"I didn't mean for drinking. Alcohol doesn't freeze, you know."

Arlis stared at him.

"You could pour some over your—"

"No—*thank* you!"

The blue eyes were all innocence—why was it people with blue eyes could do innocence so much easier than those with dark? "It was just a suggestion."

"You can take your suggestion and—"

"My lord? Everyone's ready to ride again." Idalian reined in beside them and shrugged his cloak back from his shoulders. "Getting warmer, anyway."

"Warmer," Arlis growled. He kicked his unwilling horse out into the snowy road again, leaving his princely cousin chuckling behind him.

Laric had no business being so damned cheerful. Even given his intimate knowledge of his castle and Aldiar's inside knowledge of what was going on within it, Balarat presented a formidable problem. It was full of traitorous ministers, disloyal vassals—and sorcerers.

Arlis had been considering methods of taking the place. Laric shook his head to all of them. "I haven't fought a battle thus far, and I don't intend to if I can help it. And certainly not a battle that will wreck my own keep. No, we'll think of something else."

A siege was out of the question. Shelter against vicious winters of always uncertain duration, Balarat was stuffed to the seams with provisions. It might begin to feel a slight pinch in its stores of food by next Summer. Maybe. As for fresh water—Arlis squinted into the dazzling white landscape and snorted. While they had fuel to burn—or a *diarmadhi* to call Fire—they could drink until they sloshed, take six baths a day each, and still have water enough to sluice the middens and wash the castle from spires to foundation stones.

No battle. No siege. There remained two alternatives, neither of which Arlis particularly relished. The first was to infiltrate, kill Yarin and all the sorcerers, open the gates, and take their chances with the regular troops. This was assuming that everyone with the power to kill could be killed quickly.

Unlike his kinswoman Sioned, Arlis wasn't that much of a gambler.

The second choice was the one he suspected Laric would put forth as the only feasible one: Sunrunner help. Arlis wondered sourly where he thought it would come from. Pol's duty as High Prince was to do everything he could to help everyone else—but he was hard-pressed himself and besides, only the Sunrunners at Goddess Keep had any real experience in working together for defensive purposes. They had their own problems, in the form of Vellanti ships waiting for nobody seemed to know what. And *this* was assuming that Andry would even allow his *devr'im* to come to Laric's aid.

Arlis considered that for a time, deciding eventually that if helping Laric was possible without serious danger to Goddess Keep, Andry would not just allow it, he would order it. What a chance to increase his influence and standing—and make Pol furious.

A pretty state they were in when people did what was right only for what it would gain them. Arlis was honest enough to include himself in the indictment. No prince worthy of the trust his people placed in him did anything that didn't sooner or later provide an advantage to those people. This little adventure hadn't cost *him* much so far but frozen toes. But he would have suffered much more for the prospect of favorable future trade with a grateful Firon. It had been in his mind from the moment Laric asked his help back in Einar. He wasn't ashamed of it. Why should he be?

Why should he damn Andry for thinking much the same things?

Because Sunrunners are supposed to help everyone, *no matter what. Because Andry wants power over the way peo-*

*ple think and believe. Because his instincts aren't the same
as mine. Because I don't trust him.*

Aware that his familial connections had a lot to do with
his reactions, he ended the mental meanderings and turned
to Idalian, who rode at his side.

"So. What do *you* think we should do when we get to
Balarat?"

The young man's answer was prompt and emphatic. "Not
trust Aldiar with our plans, my lord, whatever they may be."

"You don't much like him."

Idalian flexed gloved fingers, as if readying them to connect with Aldiar's jaw. "I know what he did for Rohannon.
I know he was right about getting Tirel to safety. I ought to
feel grateful—but I don't trust him!" he burst out. "I spent
too long locked up in Balarat, I couldn't *do* anything—"

"Personally, I'd say you accomplished the damned-near
impossible. You kept Tirel alive."

"And Yarin still sits in Prince Laric's chair, and his sorcerers with him."

"Are they his? Or is he theirs?" Arlis shook his head. "I
don't especially trust the boy, either, But he's done all right
for us so far—" Reminded of his recent musings about why
people did what they did, he wondered suddenly what Aldiar
thought to gain. Changing the subject, he asked, "How's
Rohannon?"

"Avoiding everybody," Idalian said.

The prince grunted and wrapped himself more tightly in
his cloak. Warmer, his ass.

✳

Pol slept until midmorning, waking only when Azhdeen's
howls outside his window became too loud to ignore. At
least sorcery didn't leave one with an aching head, unlike
encounters with a dragon who demanded to know what was
going on. Unable to tell him in words, Pol braced himself in
the spill of late winter sunshine and tried to communicate reassuring confidence.

Azhdeen countered with a swirl of colors that resolved
into impressions of the Vellanti army on the march from
Stronghold.

They fell for it? They fell for it! He broke contact himself,
earning an outraged yelp from his dragon and a stab of pain

from one side of his skull right through to the other. When his vision cleared, he grabbed up a robe and pelted down the hall to his mother's rooms.

"Mother! It's going to work! They've started for Skybowl and—"

He stopped and stared at the neatly made bed.

"Mother?"

But Sioned's rooms were empty.

So were Sionell's.

And Alasen's.

By noon he had the truth from Tobin—though she refused to speak to him on sunlight, thus drawing out the interview with what he was positive was an exaggeration of her difficulties in speaking. She was perfectly unrepentant about the part she'd played in the escape from Feruche. Her only regret was that she wasn't strong enough to go with them.

"How *could* you?" Pol raged, while her husband and younger son glared their own accusations. "Of all the stupid—why did you help them?"

Andry was the one who answered. "Because none of their rooms has the right kind of hidden exit—isn't that so, Mother? I know the plan of Feruche, too."

Pol rounded on him. "Well, I don't! What's so special about this one?"

"Sionell's fireplace stairs lead to the kitchen. The passage from Alasen's room goes down only one floor to a closet beside the main stairs. Neither is practical for getting out in secret. There's a steep spiral down from Sioned's antechamber—" He paused to think, then nodded and continued, "—to a passage though the Desert-side wall. Which doesn't help much, either— not compared to the one in this room. It goes to the stables."

Tobin applauded sardonically, clapping her good hand against the one that lay strengthless in her lap.

"Where's the exit here?" Chay asked, fascinated despite himself.

Andry strode to the wood partition between the bedchamber and small dressing room, found a certain pattern in the carving, and pressed it. A catch snapped; a section of the adjacent stone wall became a door. "And there we have it. Right down to a passage under the main hall, and from there all the way under the courtyard to the fifth stall from the right. I'll bet Sioned's own horse was in it, too, all saddled and ready to go."

"Charming," Pol snarled. "When I find the grooms who did the work and the guards who let them through the gates—"

"You won't," Andry said. "Because they didn't. The guards, I mean—I'm not sure if anyone saw them leave the stables."

"Let me guess," Pol said through his teeth. "A trapdoor under the tenth feed bin from the left, triggered by the third bridle hook in the top row?"

"Actually," Chay remarked, "the whole back wall of the tack room. I know a thing or two about this castle myself. Sorin," he added thoughtfully, "had a rather devious mind. All my sons do." He cast a disgusted look at his wife.

Andry gestured impatiently. "Why blame her? We're half yours."

Pol advanced on Tobin. "How did my mother know she'd need *this* room?"

She gazed up at him serenely. "Didn't. Beth did."

Sorin's Chosen—the daughter of the castle's architect. Pol clenched both fists. "So she went with them, did she?"

Tobin nodded. "Ruala, too."

"Damn it to all Hells! I should've put the woman in chains, even if she is my mother!"

"Begging your grace's pardon," Chay said with elaborate politeness, "but I'd have loved to see you try."

Tobin gave a snort.

Chay cast a quelling look at her and went on briskly, "Well, they're gone, all five of them. What can we do about it? Nothing. So let's get on with what we *can* do. Pol, Andry, I'll meet you in Maarken's rooms in a little while. Go."

When they had obeyed—even a High Prince and a Lord of Goddess Keep obeyed the Lord of Radzyn in that tone of voice—the Lord of Radzyn turned a mildly accusing gaze on his Lady.

"You," he said, "are going to be the cause of my death by reason of raving insanity."

She smiled at him—not with the half-smile of most of the Winter (including a few moments ago), but with all her face. When she spoke, her voice was strong and clear, very unlike the quaver with which she'd answered Pol's questions.

"Liar. You loved it!"

"Well, yes," he admitted, with a grin more suited to a

twelve-year-old boy. "I don't often get the chance to twitch my all-powerful nephew and my high-and-mighty son!"

Hitching herself straighter in her chair, she grinned back. "Most fun I've had in years. But if they ever find out we both helped Sioned, I'll tell them it was your idea."

"They'd never believe you."

"I fooled them with my pitiful act," she challenged.

"You would've done even better if you hadn't kept looking at the water-clock." He knelt before her and framed her delicate face very carefully between his palms. "But watching you pretend to be worse again, to drag out the time—it scared all Hells out of me, Tobin."

"Stop worrying." She put both hands on his forearms, caressing the muscles. "It was just pretend, love. I'm fine."

"Let's hope Sioned can pretend humble serving maid to equal effect. That's something I'd *really* like to see!"

"Me, too. I wish I could've gone with them."

"Ha. I can just imagine you bowing and cowering."

"Me! You'd give the game away in two shakes of a d–dragon's tail."

Chay frowned at the slight stammer. Tobin responded by fitting her hands threateningly around his throat.

"Stop *worrying*," she repeated sternly. Her grip eased and she stroked his cheek. "About me, anyway."

He said nothing for a moment, knowing who she meant. They were well on their way to Skybowl by now. Two Sunrunners—one completely untrained—two exceedingly clever young women, and a *diarmadhi* who'd learned all she knew about using power from her *faradhi*-trained husband. If they succeeded, the enemy threat would be defeated before a single sword was unsheathed.

If they failed, they would die. And Meiglan with them. And countless others in the battle Pol would fight with Chay's own sons beside him.

He turned his head and pressed his lips to her palm. "I'd better go. They're waiting for me."

"Chay—we were right to help."

He gave her a crooked smile and rose. "We just couldn't think up better reasons for staying than they had for going."

It was another way of saying nobody could have stopped them. No: stopped Sioned. She had offered no reasons at all, and had merely told them where she intended to go and what she intended to do.

Chay went to his appointment with his sons and his prince, his head filled with a lifetime of military lore and battle experience. *I may be old, but I've got one more good fight left in me—no matter what anybody else says. If Sioned can pull this off, I can hang up my sword without having to use it ever again. If she doesn't ... well, if my ancient carcass doesn't survive the battle, I'd better think up some way to explain all this to Rohan.*

✳

Rohannon wasn't so much avoiding everyone as he was keeping an eye on Aldiar. And since the *diarmadhi* youth held himself apart from everyone else, watching him meant riding the tag end of the army. Aldiar made no secret of his forays on sunlight, and shared the information easily enough with Rohannon. But it nagged at his mind that perhaps scouting the road ahead wasn't all that was being done. He couldn't forget that scene in the woods, with the stone circle and the Fire and the three braided cords.

His wariness shamed him. Aldiar had saved his life. Miserable as drawing breath still was when *dranath* hunger caught him unprepared, he was alive. The need came less often and faded faster each time, but in a perverse way he welcomed the spasms. They meant he was alive. And this was entirely due to Aldiar.

Rohannon didn't lack gratitude. What was missing was trust. Even after all he'd learned from the boy—yesterday his mother had contacted him on sunlight and confirmed the tale as the same told by sorcerers now at Feruche—and even though it all made a dreadful kind of sense, something about Aldiar wasn't quite right.

He wished he could talk it over with his father. But without the *dranath,* he wasn't sure he had the strength to go Sunrunning so far on his own. Hells, he barely had the strength to ride a horse.

They were taking a break four measures out of Ramblewalk when Rohannon decided to end the morninglong silence between him and Aldiar. Their horses were spared the exhausting plunge through snowdrifts that the lead animals suffered, but back here the dangerous slush required an alert rider once the horse was too tired to care. Rohannon ached from straining to see between his horse's ears to the sloggy footing, his eyes stinging with snow-brightness—though not as bad as some people's. A Desert childhood was good training in the fine art of squinting.

"What do you think the princes will want us to do?" he asked, stretching his shoulders to work the kinks out. "As a Sunrunner and a sorcerer, I mean."

Aldiar shrugged. "Keep out of the way, probably. You're not well, and I'm not trusted."

Salient, unanswerable truths, Rohannon closed his eyes against the glare, resisting the urge to rub, and eventually came up with, "But they'll have to use all the resources they've got."

"Depends on what happens, doesn't it?"

"You don't sound very optimistic. If you don't believe we can win, why are you here?"

"Because my family wants to live in the open, without hiding what we are. That's what the others want, too—the ones supporting Yarin. But they're going about it the wrong way. So I'm here, not there."

"Yarin's side wants things the way they used to be," Rohannon mused. "Surely they know that's not possible."

"If Laric isn't very, very clever, they'll keep Balarat, if not all of Firon, and work outward using the castle as their power base."

"But they're fighting the wrong enemy." He listened to what he'd said, and gulped. "Goddess—we *all* are, here in Firon!"

The dark face frowned at him. "What? How do you mean?"

"It's not just that we should be in the Desert or at Goddess Keep," he went on, words tumbling in his agitation. "The sorcerers here know who the Vellant'im are and what they want. They've known from the first. They figured the war would go badly in the south for us, so they felt safe in taking Firon."

Aldiar shook his head, stringy black hair falling in his eyes from beneath a woolen cap. "This was years in the planning."

"But the Vellant'im made it easier—and absolutely essential to succeed! Any way you look at it, your people will need a safe haven. A castle that can withstand a whole army, not just a bunch of obscure villages."

Aldiar's mouth hung a little open. "If Pol wins—"

"*When* he wins!" Rohannon snapped.

"The Vellant'im came for vengeance against us. The war is our fault."

"That's how people will see it," Rohannon agreed. "And if, Goddess forbid, the Vellant'im win—"

Aldiar shivered. "There's nothing to choose between outcomes. Nothing. Either way is the destruction of my people."

"My cousin Pol would never allow that," Rohannon argued.

"But your uncle Andry would be calling for our blood. And you'd be caught in the middle," Aldiar finished shrewdly.

"It won't come to that," he said firmly, sounding more confident than he felt—and understanding all at once the terrible choice his father might have to make between Pol and Andry. "It can't, if the *diarmadh'im* do the sensible thing and join us against the real enemy! They should have, all along! They are, in the Desert. That'll count for something—"

"Not much. We've watched your uncle for a long time, Rohannon. And he'll have plenty of people on his side—and all the power of the *devr'im,* too."

"But if all the sorcerers can be persuaded to fight the Vellant'im—"

Aldiar bent his head. "I hadn't thought it out this far. But others have, be sure of it. They'll hold Balarat now in terror of their lives. If Pol wins, if the Vellant'im win, it's all the same." Gloved hands gripped the reins tighter. "You're right, we're all fighting the wrong war. Arlis and Laric should be with Pol. We *diarmadh'im* ought to be at his side, too, fighting the real enemy." He glanced up with bitter black eyes. "War is so stupid, Rohannon. Stupid and insane."

"So we're all idiots and fools for being here," he replied impatiently. "Come on, we have to tell Arlis and Laric about the sorcerers and Balarat."

"They're both up front." Aldiar paused, giving him a curious look. "Why did somebody as practical as you ever think he could beat *dranath?*"

"I did, though, didn't I?" Rohannon heard the sharpness of his voice and shook his head. "Sorry, I owe you my life, Aldiar. I know that."

"Makes you uncomfortable, doesn't it? But you're too much the highborn to admit it. Always the noble lordling." His mouth curled in a smile too wide for his thin face. Jamming his cap down over his ears again, he went on, "Well, I'm not going to cancel the debt. One day I'll collect, Rohannon."

"A life for a life?" he challenged warily.

"A life for a life." Aldiar kicked his weary horse out of the road's mire onto a snowbank. "But not necessarily my own."

✳

Pol was singularly and uncharacteristically reticent while the battle was planned. He paid attention, asked a question or two, nodded his understanding—but Andry knew that he wasn't entirely present. Given that his wife was in enemy hands and his mother was even now galloping to join her, his distraction was no surprise.

Andry wasn't all that interested either in what his father and brother were better at than he was. Alasen was with Sioned. Why, she and the Goddess who made all headstrong women only knew.

Betheyn's knowledge of Skybowl's secrets was essential; Ruala had to be there or the Vellant'im would suspect a trap; Sioned did what she did and be damned to anyone else. Andry even understood Sionell's reasons: Meiglan and guilt. He had eyes, he had seen the looks she and Pol didn't give each other. He also had ears, and Sionell's name had never once left Pol's lips since he'd learned she was gone.

But Alasen ... what did she think she was doing? She knew next to nothing about *faradhi* arts. The thought of her fetching and carrying for the Vellant'im nauseated him—and he was certain she could no more pretend to be a common drudge than she could take wing and fly. They'd know her for the highborn she was the moment they saw her.

Women! he thought, in the mental tone of voice used by countless generations of men. He'd chased Alasen across two princedoms in the dead of winter in an attempt to keep her safe. And now where was she bound? To Skybowl. The sacrificial castle, the last place to fall to the Vellant'im. *Why* did the woman have to do these crazy things?

A voice readily indentifiable as his conscience answered the exasperation. No mistaking the sarcasm. *She couldn't possibly—just a wild guess, mind—but I suppose it's perfectly inconceivable that she's escaping* you.

All I did was try to kiss her, he argued. *To show her the past is over and done with, and we can be friends now. It didn't mean anything more than that.*

Dry as wine aged to vinegar came the reply: *Really.*

Oh, shut up.

What nonsense. Alasen was no shatter-shelled young girl, panicking over a friendly kiss. (But how very interesting, he thought suddenly, if he *had* gotten to her, just a little . . . ridiculous.) No, she was simply doing what every willful female did: whatever she pleased, and whatever she could get away with. Every woman in his life was the same, starting with his mother. Even gentle Hollis, friend of his youth at Goddess Keep, stood fierce and resentful guard near Maarken's bed, blue eyes glaring at him and Pol for disturbing her husband's rest. Surely she ought to know that showing him they could work together would speed Maarken's recovery. Evarin must have explained it to her—though not in the stern lecturing tone used on Andry and Pol in the anteroom.

"You can have him until mid-afternoon, but no longer. I'll be listening. At the first words of contention, you're out. And believe me, my Lord, your grace, you'd rather be ejected by me than by Lady Hollis."

Sneaking a glance at her now, Andry judged that their time was just about up. Not that a single sharp word had passed between him and Pol. Maarken was simply growing tired.

The bed looked like a child's imaginary landscape. Pillows lumped under the sheets formed the Veresch Mountains; Skybowl was a silver goblet. Bits of bread from the breakfast tray represented the Vellant'im. Cheese stood in for Tilal's forces coming up from Radzyn, Hollis' hairpins for their own troops. Maarken sat at the head of the bed, knees drawn up under his chin, frowning as he and Chay discussed tactics and possible casualties.

They're good at this, Andry thought with pride, *much better than Pol or I. But Maarken's got Father beat in one thing: he's a Sunrunner. He knows how to use his own kind.*

Yet as he listened, Andry realized Maarken avoided almost all mention of Sunrunners in combat. At the outset he'd rejected using the encirclement maneuver he'd named Sunrunner Rings. The Vellant'im would recognize it and do what they had done at Stronghold: shatter it with iron. And after that, magic had not entered the conversation again.

Andry had a good idea why. Any spells cast would be a source of conflict between himself and Pol. Which was ridiculous, as far as Andry was concerned. He was no warrior; Pol was. The Lord of Goddess Keep belonged with his Sunrunners, directing their attack. The High Prince's place was with his troops in the field. But Pol had to be in control of everything, leading everyone, doing it all himself.

That made Andry furious. *If you ever learned anything from your father, it should have been that you tell people what you want and leave them alone to do what they're best at. But not you. Not the Sunrunner-sorcerer High Prince. Has to be your show, doesn't it? All the credit, all the glory—*

—and all the work, he added honestly. Pol was showing the strain of it, too. He looked worse than Maarken. *Goddess, who wouldn't? How long since all this started? One hundred and thirty days, give or take. Battles lost, castles captured or in ruins, his father dead, his mother nearly losing her mind, his wife and daughter seized, Rislyn blind, that mess up in Firon, so many people dead—dear and gentle Lady, thank you for letting me serve you as Lord of Goddess Keep! I wouldn't be High Prince for anything in the world.*

The Hell of it was that if Andry offered to take some of the burden from him, to lead the Sunrunners' efforts in battle, Pol would think it a scheme to become exactly that. How stupid could one man be? Andry had ridden the width of the continent under uniformly miserable conditions, hiding who he was, at constant risk of discovery. He'd almost been killed in the Vellanti ambush arranged by Meiglan's own father. He had done Pol the favor of depriving Miyon of a life that was a burden to everyone who knew him. He had demanded nothing but to help however he could.

But Pol would never understand that Andry, Desert-born and Desert-bred—more truly than Pol himself, if it came to it—could not sit safely in Goddess Keep while his home and his family were in danger.

That's why he thinks he has to do everything himself, Andry thought suddenly. *Not just because of me, to keep me from gaining power I don't even want. The Desert is his now. Every grain of sand is his home and every person who lives here is his family.*

What did Rohan used to say? *"I'm High Prince, that makes it my fault."* Now it was on Pol's shoulders. But Rohan had had Sioned, Chay, Tobin, and a dozen others he trusted to work with him and for him. People he knew shared his purpose and his dream. Pol had nobody to lean on. Chay was old. Tobin hadn't recovered from her illness. Maarken couldn't face the idea of being torn between his brother and his prince—and Hollis would kill either or both of them if that happened. Sioned had gone off on her own without telling Pol anything. And Meiglan was no Sioned.

To any of a dozen exquisite Hells with Sioned, anyway. Just as well that she *was* gone, after what had happened with Chayla. If he lived another hundred years, Andry would never forgive either of them for killing that baby. They'd never forgive him, either.

Neither would Hollis, if he didn't say or do something to ease Maarken's fears. Well, he and Pol were after the same thing in the end, weren't they? So it shouldn't be too difficult. If he swallowed some of his pride, Pol could certainly choke down a bit of his own.

Besides, he really does need me. He's even more alone than I am.

Pol stirred at the foot of the bed: a quick glance at Maarken, then at Hollis, and finally at Andry, who had the uncanny sensation that Pol had felt his compassion.

And resented it.

"This is all very interesting," Pol began.

"He speaks!" Chay clasped a dramatic hand to his heart. "He might even have been listening. Imagine my amazement."

Pol gave him a weary grin, more because it was expected than because he was honestly amused. "Sheer amazement at your brilliance kept me quiet so long," he replied lightly, then sobered. "But everything I've heard confirms a decision I made last night."

"Which is?" Maarken prompted.

Somehow Andry knew what he would say before he said it.

"There will be no battle."

Andry nodded to himself. *Yes; that follows. No surprise.*

Neither Maarken nor Chay thought so. "What in all Hells do you mean?" demanded the Lord of Radzyn. The Battle Commander abruptly straightened long legs out under the sheets, destroying the makeshift map, and warned, "If we've been wasting our time and breath, why didn't you say so earlier?"

"It wasn't wasted. I needed to hear from those who understand war better than I do. And what I've heard is one undeniable truth: for all their lack of imagination, the Vellant'im are superb fighters. They outnumber us. We can deal with that, but even if we win, we lose. Too many dead, too many wounded and maimed. I won't stand for it. Not again."

Maarken shook his head. "Pol—I know how you feel. But we've set them up to be where we want them and to believe what we show them. Thanks to Ruala, they'll be in Skybowl by tomorrow night. Thanks to your mother, we'll have enough people there to listen in more than one place and tell us everything we need to know. Not to mention spreading a few artful lies where they'll do the most good. We can do this, and with minimal losses." He glanced up at his father.

After a moment's hesitation, Chay said, "Meiglan will be safe, Pol. Sioned told Tobin to give you that promise."

At mention of his wife's name, the High Prince jerked to his feet, taut as a drawn bowstring.

"We all do what we must." Andry nodded again to himself. But Pol needn't battle the Vellant'im single-handed—or single-minded.

"Pol," said the Lord of Goddess Keep, "if it's magic you want to use—and we all know it is—you might as well share it. The gifteds among us can help."

Pol searched his eyes with a ruthless intensity reminiscent of Lady Andrade at her worst. Andry endured it, patient and honest and hoping his cousin would finally understand him.

At last Pol drew in a deep breath. "If you *could* help, I'd accept with thanks. Frankly, it scares Hell out of me. But I have to do this alone."

Stubborn, stupid, stiff-necked fool. Andry should have known he'd never—

Pol was continuing, "There aren't many advantages to being the son of the mother who bore me—but if I was only *faradhi* I wouldn't be able to do this."

That stung Andry where he was most vulnerable, and he knew it. So did Pol. "There's nothing a sorcerer can do that a Sunrunner can't. The Star Scroll proves it."

Pol nodded without rancor. "I know. It's no reflection on

you, Andry. I may accept your offer yet, if what I have in mind doesn't work." He paused, smiling slightly. "And it might not. It's a little like having to sing a complicated ballad for the bard who wrote it, when I've barely learned how to whistle for my horse. And the Vellant'im are going to be a tough audience."

Maarken sat up even straighter, slapping his hand on the quilt. "Say that again!" he ordered.

"Say what again?" he asked, confused.

Andry had heard it, too. So had Chay. The three of them traded glances. A grin spread over Chay's face, canceled almost immediately by a grimace.

"Build the pyre and burn me, quick," he grumbled. "I've gone senile. Why didn't I think of that before?"

"Think of what?" Pol looked from one to the other of them.

Hollis spoke for the first time. "Because anytime we've been close enough, the Vellant'im have been there to haul back on the reins."

"Damn it, Chay, if you don't tell me—"

"Hollis," Maarken interrupted, "we need a list of the studs at Whitecliff."

"Will somebody please—"

"Don't forget the two I lent you last summer," Chay said. "I'll put together my own roster. Andry, start thinking about where else they stole horses from—"

"Hey!" Pol banged a fist on the wooden bedpost. "Care to let me in on it?"

Maarken laughed at him. "You go right ahead and sing your lungs out, Pol. We'll just whistle."

✳

Music of another sort was on the minds—and, regrettably, in the ears—of the highborns at Radzyn Keep. Tilal's captain, Chaltyn, had struck up a friendship with Kostas' man, Havadi, and they were warbling the entire songbook of Athelig the Gribain as they kept the evening watch. Neither man could carry a tune if it was knocked unconscious and tied to his back. So with their every pass on the battlements below, those gathered in the sitting room of Tilal's suite paused in their conversation to wince, or sigh, or threaten to throw a boot at them.

Tilal refused to receive any lady other than his wife while lying in bed. He had hobbled to a large, deep-cushioned chair for the occasion. It was a pretty scene of hearthside serenity, considerably improved by the two princesses in attendance. Iliena and Nyr were ensconced in chairs on either side of the fire; their husbands perched on footstools beside them. Andrev and Saumer, tellers of tales for the evening, sat in straight-backed wooden chairs. Master Chegry was apart from the group over in the window embrasure, keeping an eye on Tilal and Nyr for signs of fatigue.

"So you have your Sunrunners back once more, Tilal," Ludhil said after the story of the pearls was completed. "I must say, it's a relief to have a couple of you around again. We were so isolated on Dorval that sometimes I feared we were fighting the Vellant'im all alone."

"I never thought much about it, myself," Saumer admitted. "I mean, Sunrunners are always there when you want them, aren't they? But now that I know I'm one of them, I feel the responsibility. It must've been rough on you, Prince Ludhil."

"It didn't need to be," said Iliena. "If only I'd known. . . ."

"Well, how could you?" Tilal asked forthrightly. "None of us even suspected."

"My brother knew," she replied, and the firelight shaded her dark Fironese beauty, softening the bitter curve of her lips.

"When *my* brother gets hold of him. . . ." Ludhil's jaw set.

"Oh, no," she said. "Laric can do what he likes with Yarin *after* Lisi and I take a few pieces out of him."

"All of you may have to stand in line behind Pol," Tilal reminded them.

"And my father," Andrev put in. "After all, Lord Yarin had the Balarat Sunrunner killed, didn't he?"

The right of the Lord of Goddess Keep as interpreted by his eldest son and as measured against the right of the High Prince and everyone else was not something Tilal wanted to discuss. "Let's not hatch that egg before it's baked, shall we? Saumer, you didn't say if either of you happened to see Princess Meiglan while you watched Isriam deliver the pearls."

They hadn't seen her. Tilal was spared trying to think up another topic of conversation: the songsters were back. This

time they wailed a deplorable drinking ballad as if their
hearts would break for love of the lady whose charms were
graphically detailed in twenty-nine increasingly obscene
verses.

Chegry opened the window to yell down a cease-and-
desist order. Then he leaned out as far as he could without
tumbling to the cobbled courtyard. "Alert the watch!" he
called back over his shoulder. "By the torches, we're about
to host a small army!"

And so it proved to be: over two hundred men and
women, marching beneath the wheat-sheaf banner of
Ossetia. Tilal limped to the window to watch them enter
Radzyn's main gates. He began a growling catalog of curses
that made Andrev's eyes pop. Even Saumer looked
impressed—he whose mother Hevatia had been quite creative with language when moved to it.

Ludhil shrugged. "Look at it this way, Tilal—at least
Gemma didn't come with them." He cast a speaking look at
his own wife, who had jumped from a boat supposed to take
her to safety and fought at his side across half of Dorval.

Amiel, giving Nyr much the same glare for much the
same reason, said, "*Your* wife appears to have some sense,
cousin."

"You don't have to live with her!" Tilal looked around for
anything to use as a cane. "Leaving Athmyr unprotected,
and the children—! Women are idiots! All of them! And I
should know—I've been plagued with them all my life! Not
one was ever born with a shard of—damn it, Chegry, help
me downstairs!"

It was unnecessary for the physician to forbid the plan.
Chaltyn knocked on the door, entered looking slightly dazed,
bowed to his prince, and said, "My lord—your lady wife!"

Gemma strolled in, all smiles.

After everyone had been greeted—briefly, for the look in
Tilal's green eyes made them all hasten to be elsewhere—
and the pair were alone, Gemma sat with perfect calm at
Tobin's dressing table to unplait and brush out her hair.

"Chaltyn tells me your wound is healing very well, darling."

He said nothing.

"Sioneva and Sorin were wild to come with me, of
course."

He said nothing.

"But somebody had to stay at Athmyr to help Allun run things. He's entirely capable, of course—Lower Pyrme is a very large holding—but every keep has its own little ways of doing things. Sioneva should have a lovely time playing lady of the castle."

He said nothing.

She had finished untangling her braids, and now spread her wealth of autumn-bronze curls across her shoulders. He had almost forgotten how beautiful she was. They'd never been apart more than twelve days in a row during the eighteen years of their marriage—and it had been ten times twelve days since he'd last seen her. She knew that, of course. Her little smile as she faced him told him she was counting on it.

But that wasn't what decided him against anger. It was the gray in her hair. He'd noticed it back at Kadar Water, but then it had been only a few strands, fascinating highlights. Now the silver swirled back from her temples as if moonlight had brushed her hair.

He pushed himself to his feet and went to her—fortunately not too many steps, for he was unsteady for more reasons than his wound. "Why did you come?" he asked quietly. "And don't say it's because I didn't specifically tell you not to."

"Or because I was bored and needed a change of scene?" But her smile didn't reach her liquid brown eyes. "How about I missed you—I need you—when I found out about Rihani, I nearly went mad—oh, Tilal, our beautiful son—"

He bent and buried his face in her shining, silvering hair.

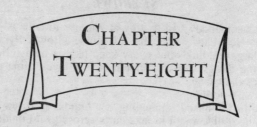

CHAPTER
TWENTY-EIGHT

The departure of the Tiglathis for home some days ago had eased the strain on Feruche's resources. But as people from Skybowl arrived on the afternoon of the eighty-sixth day of Winter, the castle once more threatened to burst at the seams.

Hollis marveled that things were going so smoothly. Then again, they'd all had a lot of practice at this recently. The wounded, both litter-bound and comparatively ambulatory, were seen to first. The garrison below the keep—already housing dozens of injured and a full complement of guards—was stuffed to capacity, the rest were packed into the infirmary. As for the soldiers and servants, Riyan had ordered the great hall cleared of tables and benches.

"So much for civilized dining," he'd said wryly. "People will just have to eat standing up wherever they can."

Sleeping space was definitely at a minimum. So were stalls for the horses, which in Chay's opinion were much more important. The back gardens were therefore sacrificed to threescore additional sets of hooves, and recuperating soldiers paced guard duty to preserve the new vegetables.

The Prince and Princess of Dorval, together with their two grandchildren, were given Sioned's rooms; not a single chamber could stand empty and even the highborns were doubling and tripling up. Maara, very conscious that she was Lady of Feruche in her mother's absence, had taken charge of Alleyn and Audran.

"They're in Maara's schoolroom with the other children," Hollis explained as she accompanied Audrite upstairs for a badly needed rest. "That and the Attic are the only two real sanctuaries at Feruche. Everyplace else is four-deep in bedrolls. But it's only for a little while."

"I understand that the target date is three days from now." Audrite paused on a landing to glance back downstairs. Chadric was still talking with Andry and Maarken—who, thank the Goddess, was now up and about as if he'd never been ill. Hollis didn't know what had been said or not said, but something had ended his terrible inner conflict. *For now,* she told herself with a hidden shiver, and refused to think about it.

"The eighty-ninth," she replied to Audrite. "I only wish I knew why the Vellant'im chose it—not that it matters, but it's puzzling."

"Not really." She leaned over the banister and called down, "Get up here, you old warhorse, before they have to waste their valuable time and energy to carry you!" Before Chadric could answer, she resumed the climb. "It's perfectly understandable. The oratory from the old Sunrunner keep wasn't just a yearly calendar. Some of the references nearly drove me mad until I realized they were calculating events that happen every fifty years, or every few hundred."

"Like eclipses?" Hollis opened the door of Sioned's rooms.

"Those, of course. But those are relatively easy." Audrite eased her tired body into the nearest chair. "Oh, Meath and I did have a time—" She stopped, her eyes closing in pain.

Hollis sat on the couch and stared down at her folded hands.

At length the princess straightened her shoulders. "I spent enough time and parchment scribbling out the mathematics to remember quite well. Starting on the forty-eighth day of Winter two years from now, we'll get a long-tailed star in the night sky for about ten days. It happens every ninety-one years, so nobody's ever seen it twice."

"Lady Merisel did," Hollis said. "It's in the histories. She was born a year before the tailed star appeared, and died a year after it came again, at ninety-three winters old."

"*I* feel ninety-three these days," Audrite remarked. "Anyway, what's going to happen on the eighty-ninth is something that occurs once every two hundred and seventy-four years. It ought to be fascinating, actually. That morning, only two moons will rise."

Hollis blinked. "What? Where does the third one go?"

"Don't worry, it's still there." Audrite smiled. "It'll be hiding behind the biggest one, and come out midmorning. Your ancestral Sunrunners were at great pains to show that in the oratory tiles. It seems there were superstitions about the moon coming down from the sky on that day—all sorts of nonsense about whiteness and purity and so forth, with some special person actually *being* the spirit of that moon."

"Oh, dear!"

"Yes, that's what I said, too, when I heard the date of the battle and made the connection. Which took me long enough," she added in irked tones.

"Do the Vellant'im really believe—" Hollis interrupted herself. "Of course they do."

"I'm told Sionell thought up some delightful things to encourage their silly beliefs. If she's not too busy later, I'd like to congratulate her."

"You mean you didn't—no, I suppose you wouldn't have seen them."

"Seen who? Where?"

"On the way to Skybowl. Sionell, Alasen, Ruala, Betheyn, and—"

"—and Sioned," Audrite finished. "What in the Name of the Goddess has she done *now?*"

Walvis was asking that of Pol at that moment. Pol's answer was Hollis'—but considerably less polite.

"Why ask me? Why ask anybody?" He flung himself into Riyan's desk chair and glowered. "Who *ever* knows what the Sunrunner witch has in mind?"

"Well, yes," Walvis acknowledged, combing his fingers through his beard. "But surely she said something to somebody."

"Tobin. You want to try prying it out of her, be my guest."

The older man sat down opposite him at Ruala's desk. "No, thanks. I've known her longer than you've been alive. What do *you* have in mind? Chadric says you wanted his sapphire earring. He didn't say why."

"He doesn't know." Pol chewed a thumbnail.

"And I'm not to know, either?"

"Everyone will find out—*if* it works. If it doesn't—"

"Then you don't want to be embarrassed, the way you were at Radzyn, trying to burn their ships." Walvis shrugged. "Especially not in front of Andry."

"I couldn't care less about Andry's impression of me. I care about the people here who don't need to see their High Prince fail again."

"We'll leave the 'again' part for another discussion. Tell me what else is going on."

"Nobody talked to Jeni on the way here?"

"How should I know? Jeni's not talking to anybody—including Sethric."

Pol groaned. "Spare me any and all romantic tangles, please!"

"They'll work it out." Walvis propped his elbows on the desk. "What news from Radzyn and Firon?"

"Saumer and Andrev gave Isriam the pearls. He delivered them to the High Warlord. I'm expecting him back here any time now. Gemma brought about two hundred fresh troops from Athmyr—women are all crazy, aren't they? Tilal was fit to be tied, of course. Now he's saying he's fit to sit a saddle. He's not, but they'll start out tomorrow anyway."

Walvis frowned. "Don't you want him to?"

"I hope I won't *need* him to. But that's something else that'll have to wait. Oh, and you'll love this. Laric is camped outside Balarat. He sent a message to Yarin this morning—Maarkin heard all this from Rohannon, since the sky actually had the decency to clear over the Veresch. Anyway, Laric told his precious brother-by-marriage that if he surrendered immediately, he'd be allowed to live, and all his sorcerous allies with him."

"And Yarin laughed in his face."

"More or less. He sent the message back in shreds and the messenger on foot. So there they sit, Yarin snug inside Balarat, Laric and Arlis not so snug outside it."

"With nothing you can do about it."

"Nothing." He hooked a leg over the arm of the chair. "As for Goddess Keep, the Vellant'im still hover offshore. Elsen is bedridden because of his bad leg, Norian is furious, and Edrel is trying to figure out what to do. I learned all this, by the way, late last night, when I *finally* found out who my mother's informant is."

"Antoun." Walvis grinned broadly at Pol's startled exclamation. "Who else could it be? They grew up together at Goddess Keep. He was with the group that came with her to the Desert in 698. All the rest of them worked for her or with her in one way or another—but Antoun hasn't been anywhere near her in twenty years, which should have made everybody suspicious long ago."

Pol snorted. "She does have a way of attaching people, doesn't she? Especially men."

"When I was a lad, I thought the moons rose and set at her command." His lips curved in a reminiscent smile. "Until I found another redhead who made the sun rise."

"What is it about redheaded women?" Pol heard himself ask that question and fought a blush. All he lacked at this point was for Sionell's father to find out about another romantic tangle. Quickly, he added, "They're all insane. My mother, Feylin, Gemma, Sionell, even Chiana—did I tell you what Nyr did, secretly joining Amiel's little army of physicians even though she's pregnant?"

"It's not limited to redheads. Take this lot on their way to Skybowl. Alasen's almost a blond, Ruala's hair is black as a raven's wing, and Betheyn is—well, maybe you're right, there's a reddish tint to her hair in summer, too. And Alasen and Ruala both have green eyes. . . ."

"Like Lady Merisel's," Pol said. "That emerald ring of Mother's—it originally belonged to her."

Walvis scowled. "How do you know that? No, forget I asked. I already know you won't answer."

"Not won't. Can't. I'm sorry." He hesitated, then said, "You've undoubtedly figured this out on your own, but—it has to do with that mirror."

"I thought about asking, then thought better of it. Just tell me if it's dangerous, Pol."

"Not to me." It was the truth; Lord Rosseyn had said so, and Thassalante had told him that Sunrunners were safe from it. But he was half a sorcerer. What if that half was snared by the Shadowcatcher?

No, Rosseyn had assured him he would not be harmed in any way. He trusted the man—who was hundreds of years dead, only a shadow in a mirror.

Had he just accused women of being insane?

"Speaking of Alasen, where's Ostvel?"

Pol was glad of Walvis' training at Rohan's court; he always knew when his prince needed a distracting change of subject. Pol didn't mind being relatively transparent to those who loved him as much as Walvis did. He just hoped Andry couldn't read him even a quarter as well.

Ostvel was an excellent subject, and Pol smiled with genuine pleasure. "He's taking Chiana and Rinhoel to Dragon's Rest. They'll get part of their wish—entry into the palace—but not quite the way they had in mind."

"I suppose he thinks he'll leave them there under guard, then hop over the mountains to Skybowl."

"He won't make it in time—and thank the Goddess for it. But after the festivities with the Vellant'im, there will be another little celebration. That's the one I don't want him to miss—or Chiana and Rinhoel, either."

Walvis arched both brows. "You have something particularly nasty in mind for them, I hope?"

"Nothing definite yet. I thought I'd ask around, get some ideas." He grinned. "My friends and relatives are rather creative people."

Andry was doing some creative thinking based on something Chadric had said to Maarken. An earring was an odd thing to mark the beginning of a path, but Andry followed it as he collected books from the library.

An earring, he thought, pulling volumes down at random to take to the infirmary. Maarken's face had gone momentarily still at Chadric's words and his gaze had stayed very carefully away from Andry's.

"I hope that earring was satisfactory," Chadric had said as they went into the castle.

Andry had been about to ask *What earring?* when he noted Maarken's blank expression. He knew his brother's face as well as he knew his own.

"I've no idea. Sioned took it when I got back here."

At that moment Audrite had called down from the stairs. Andry was certain Maarken had stifled a sigh of sheer relief.

Earring. What sort of jewel would Chadric have that Sioned would want? And for what purpose? He looked down at his own hands, the rubies and diamonds of his rings, the moonstone on one wrist and the sapphire on the other—

Chadric had always worn a sapphire earring. It had been Lleyn's, and before that it had been Andrade's.

But what use would Sioned have for one of Andrade's jewels?

Rubies, diamonds, sapphire, moonstone—

It was only then that he realized that he had not seen what he had been seeing ever since he got to Feruche: an amethyst and a topaz and a moonstone on Pol's hands.

The amethyst of Princemarch, the topaz of the Desert.

Pol's two princedoms. And a moonstone that had belonged to Andrade.

Andry stood as if rooted to the stone floor. Had Sioned been here, he was positive he wouldn't see her emerald, either.

Jewels. Powerful ones, if the traditions were true and gemstones possessed the qualities ascribed to them. Amethyst, sapphire, emerald, topaz, moonstone—lacking only ruby and garnet to make up the spectrum of clear jewels. Moonstone could have no place in it, being opaque like jade and onyx and carnelian.

So. Start again. Amethyst, sapphire, emerald, topaz, garnet, ruby. A rainbow of gems, doubtless stunning to look at, but why?

And why Andrade's sapphire?

Unless—

He stared at his own rings and wrist cuffs again. Perhaps jewels absorbed the power of the person who wore them. Perhaps gifts spilled over or concentrated or were drunk in by pure crystals as Earth soaked up Water during a rainstorm.

If so, Andrade's sapphire would fairly pulsate with power. Her rings had been worn by successive Lords and Ladies of Goddess Keep since Lady Merisel's time.

Until him.

Fool! he raged suddenly. *I should have kept them, I should have had them resized as they've been for hundreds of years!*

But he'd had to be different. He'd had to put everyone on notice that he was breaking with tradition. He'd had to have new rings made, all his, to signal the new beginning he intended to make.

Sioned's emerald—now, there was another potent shard of stone. He'd heard the story a thousand times, how she'd saved Maarken and Jahni from being roasted by a hatchling dragon, and Rohan had presented her with the ring that night in thanks and in private, teasing promise. It had been in the family for Goddess knew how long. And Goddess knew that contact with Sioned for nearly forty years would set the thing blazing.

If his assumptions were true. *If* jewels absorbed some of the power of the person who wore them.

Rohan's topaz had also been in the family for generations,

on the finger of every prince since the very first of their line. The amethyst, however—that one's history he didn't know, other than that it had been Roelstra's.

And *that* scared all Hells out of him.

Amethyst, sapphire, emerald, topaz, garnet, ruby. He'd accounted for four of them. What about the other two?

Who else had been given Andrade's jewels by Urival, after Andry had so thoughtlessly given them up?

The garnet had gone to Andry himself and was back at Goddess Keep. And he knew very well who had received the ruby.

His mother.

He looked at the pile of books on the table, remembering suddenly why he'd come here. He'd take care of that errand—he owed it to himself—and then find some way of finding out why Pol wanted Chadric's sapphire earring.

✱

Isriam had done an incredibly foolish thing the previous morning on his return journey to Feruche. He'd overslept.

He was still kicking himself about it more than a day later. They were waiting for him at Feruche and would be frantic when he didn't show up on schedule. He didn't dare push his weary horse to make up the time. But he was only at Skybowl, visible in the west about thirty measures away, when he should have been well past it.

He reined in, giving the horse a breather while he stared at the mountain. They should all be gone from the castle by now. From the highborns to the servants to the soldiers to even the most precariously healing wounded, Skybowl would be empty. The Vellant'im would ride in to an echoing silence.

Isriam frowned. That shouldn't be. Someone ought to be there as Lord Riyan's representative, to give reassurances that he would be there soon.

The High Warlord knew him now as a traitor to Pol and an adherent of the putative peace plan. There wasn't the slightest shred of trust on either side, but that would turn to active suspicion if nobody was at Skybowl to meet the Vellant'im.

Isriam patted his horse's sweating neck. "What would you

say to a good, long drink and some decent fodder? Yes, I thought so. Me, too."

It occurred to him that Pol might not appreciate his disobedience. But they didn't need him at Feruche to tell them the ploy had worked. There were Sunrunners aplenty to see the Vellanti march for themselves. And if he could assist in furthering the deception of Riyan's treachery, certain persons might look on him as a man instead of a boy.

He was adult enough to recognize a childish wish to prove himself. Still, he felt justified in turning his horse's head to the west, toward Skybowl.

A whole keep all to himself. In a way, Isriam thought with a little smile, it would be a delightful relief after living elbow-to-elbow for so long.

Relief? Not for an instant. Skybowl wasn't just empty. It was spine-prickling, bump-skinned *eerie.*

Isriam rode in through the wide open gates, flinching at every hoof-clop on courtyard stones. It was so quiet he could hear the blood flowing in his own veins. Empty windows shone down on him in the mid-afternoon sunshine like a thousand glaring eyes. There wasn't a hint of movement anywhere. Even the shadows seemed frozen. Had these been normal times, the keep would have been alive with noise and light, patterns shifting constantly as people went about their duties and horses were taken out or brought in from exercise and cats stalked mice.

He walked his horse to cool him down, then stabled him with ample food and water. His own stomach was in knots, but hunger had little to do with it. As he opened the door of the tack room to put away the bridle, a streak of brindled fur shot past his leg with a bloodcurdling yowl.

Isriam jumped half out of his skin.

Hairs rising on his nape, he crossed the courtyard again and entered the keep.

He turned just inside the main door, removing his gloves to wash hands and face in the bowl of water always provided. After a splash or two he felt better and began to think about a nice, long soak in a tub. He raked his hands back through his hair, looking up to the mirror above the basin.

Gone.

A moment later he chided himself for silliness. Of course they would take a valuable object like that down from the walls. Saumer and Andrev had described the mess made of

Radzyn, and Princess Audrite was no fool. Probably all the best furnishings and decorations had been stored in the cellars as well. Isriam just hoped they'd left sheets on at least one of the beds.

First, though, the kitchen. He'd make himself something to eat and take it upstairs, find a bathtub and some clean clothes, and rest for a little while—leaving a candle branch lit. In his present state of nerves, no matter what his brain told him, he was positive that waking to a dark and silent keep would give him a seizure.

He'd never seen a cooking hearth in his life that didn't have at least a small banked fire in it. To find this one cold and swept clean was more disturbing than he would have thought. It was like seeing the Flametower at Stronghold without fire—it was always there, you never thought about it or even really looked at it, but *not* seeing it was a shock of the weirdest kind.

And somehow he couldn't kindle a fire here. He made do with part of a loaf from the hundreds left in a rack taller than he was, dried fruit, some cheese, and a half-bottle of exceedingly ordinary Giladan red wine.

He took a second bottle upstairs, silently toasting his friend Daniv and the bottles of fine Syrene gold promised for happier times. After finding fresh clothing in a servants' storeroom on the second floor, he chose a bedroom on the third that had an attached bathroom. Briefly he wished he was a Sunrunner who could light every candle in the chamber at once—even though it was still only mid-afternoon— and every torch at Skybowl besides. He settled for a branch in the bedroom and a smaller one to keep him company while he bathed.

Water splashed clean and warm into the tub. Laboriously pumped up from the lake into insulated cisterns baked by a Desert sun relentless even in winter, there was enough stored for a thousand baths. To have a really hot soak, he would have had to boil a few buckets over the kitchen hearth and lug them upstairs. But considering the usual reason for a bath in this princedom—to cool off—pleasantly warm water was all that was ever needed or wanted.

Isriam upended the wine bottle into his glass and leaned back in the tub, half-closing his eyes. He estimated that the Vellant'im would arrive by late afternoon tomorrow. There was nothing to do, really—his survey of the kitchen had told him there was food to feed several hundred for a couple of days, and he'd been right about the better tapestries, rugs, and furniture: vanished. All he need do was wait.

Very tired and a little drunk, he listened to the absolute silence and refused to let it get on his nerves. A whole keep all to himself . . . if he'd been a few years younger, he would have had wonderful fun. Fought imaginary battles through the hallways. Sat himself down at the center of the high table to pretend he was lord and master here. Raided wardrobes and jewel boxes to deck himself out as grandly as a prince at the *Rialla*. Done all sorts of things boys dream of when they imagine themselves in the great and glorious future.

Isriam had fought real battles against a ruthless enemy. He had been the master of Chaldona—only over a fractious bunch of merchants, true, but with all the authority of an *athri* nonetheless. He wore in his right earlobe the only jewel he valued, a small tawny topaz given by the High Prince he had worshiped.

His dreams as he lay in the cooling water were a man's dreams. Not of high position, although it was possible this would be his; not of wealth, for which he cared nothing; not even of ruling a castle or a princedom. He dreamed of home and wife and children, and visits from his friends, and peace.

He could almost see Rohan smiling, nodding, as if satisfied with work well done. *Am I what you wanted me to be?* Isriam thought. *Did I learn what you tried to teach me?*

For whoever had sired him, whether the blood in his veins was Camanto of Fessenden's or Sabriam of Einar's, Isriam had known within a few days of arriving at Stronghold that Rohan would always be his real father.

✶

Andry knew Chayla would not welcome him. He sought her out in the infirmary anyway. It wasn't unusual for the Lord of Goddess Keep to visit there; in fact, he'd done so nearly every day since coming to Feruche. He went for the same reason Pol went, and sometimes in Pol's company. Useless at healing broken bodies, yet they could offer words and their presences that conveyed silent assurances of their power, their determination, their confidence.

Evarin had told him that Chayla was different with the

wounded now, even over the last few days. "She talks to them more. They're people to her now, instead of medical problems to solve. Of course, it's worse for her, thinking of them as men and women and not just a head wound or a wrenched shoulder or whatever. But she'll be a better physician because of it."

Andry watched her from the corner of his eye as he moved among the cots and pallets distributing books from the pile in his arms. As he collected those already read to be passed along to someone else, he paused to chat and share what news he felt they should know. Nothing upsetting; only good things like Rislyn's rapport with her dragon or Maarken's recovery or Gemma's arrival at Radzyn with more troops. Whenever he had time, he went Sunrunning before these visits so he could say what the weather was like around their homes, if the vegetables had been planted, if sheep had been moved from one pasture to another. For all their proficiency at arms, most of these people were farmers and herders. It was nearly Spring, the time of year when they felt most keenly their absence from home.

Andry plotted his rounds so he would be near Chayla as she finished hers. She knew he was there. He hadn't caught her glancing at him, but she knew. Now, as he approached directly, hand extended to take the heavy coffer of medicines from her, she met his gaze with a complexity of emotions in her blue eyes—none of them, as he'd anticipated, tender of him. Oddly, there was little of the defiance he might have expected from someone so young who had done something forbidden. It was an adult resistance he saw in her face: one self-aware, self-defining human daring another to condemn her actions.

Taking the case from her, he began, "How are you feeling?"

Low-voiced as they left the infirmary for the courtyard, she said, "The Goddess hasn't struck me down yet, if that's what you mean."

"It wasn't." He searched her face. Tired; but they were all tired. "I just wanted to make sure you're all right."

"I am. Thank you for asking, my Lord."

He wasn't troubled by the stiff formality. "I don't agree with what you and Sioned did," he replied softly. "But I never meant to cause you pain or unhappiness, Chayla."

"My standards of both have considerably altered recently, my Lord."

Meaning that nothing he said or did could cause either.

"I understand," Andry said.

"Is there anything else?" she asked, impatient to be rid of him.

"Only a reminder to take at least as much care of yourself as you do of the wounded. They depend on you, Chayla. I'm glad Feylin is here to take some of the burden from you."

She hesitated, casting a swift glance from beneath silvery-blonde lashes. "It's not, you know. A burden. Or even a duty. It's the only service I can do them—but it's also my own selfishness."

"You may not believe this, but I understand that, too." He held up his left hand. "These rings are just symbols, but in many ways, they're what I am. Just as this—" He hefted the medicine coffer. "—is what *you* are. We can no more stop being what we were meant to be than we can—" He smiled. "I was going to say 'fly,' but 'swim' is probably the better choice for a Sunrunner."

Chayla didn't smile back, but the tension eased in her face. "It's a strange feeling when people thank you for doing things for them. As if it was a favor."

"Or admire you for shouldering responsibility or duty, when you're only being what you are. You're right, it's selfish when you get down to it."

"And embarrassing," she added. "And sometimes it's terrible, when someone's grateful to you for saving his life—after you've had to amputate his leg. It's better when they hate me for it. Sometimes I hate myself."

"For not knowing more," Andry agreed as they walked slowly across the courtyard. "For not doing more."

"You *do* understand." Chayla looked up at him thoughtfully.

"Being me isn't as difficult as being you. But this war has put demands on us both that are unthinkable in peaceful times. And I'll be just as glad to go back to teaching young Sunrunners as you will to brewing snakebite salves."

"Speaking of which, I need another batch of febrifuges," she said, taking back her coffer and angling across the courtyard to the kitchen door. Then she stopped and looked up at him. "If this was your way of making peace between us, Uncle Andry, you didn't have to. You were trying to convince me of what you thought was right. I happen to think you're wrong. But it was my decision to make, only mine—and I'm glad you agree with that if nothing else."

As it happened, he didn't. But he smiled and said, "I'm glad I'm back to being Uncle Andry again. All those 'my Lords' got rather chilly. By the way, do you know where I might find Pol?"

"Try the Attic. He's been spending a lot of time up there lately."

"Probably something to do with the jewels, and whatever Thassalante's been telling him about sorcery."

"I don't know anything about that." She paused. "You don't approve of Sunrunners working sorcery, either."

Andry laughed. "Chayla, *I'm* the one who translated the Star Scroll!"

Because he had, and because this war had given him as intensive a schooling in his particular arts as it had given Chayla in hers, he paused for a time before climbing the one hundred and six stairs to the Attic.

"Who is it?" called a familiar voice from behind the locked door.

"Maarken," said Andry.

✳

It was nothing so gentle as his time-sense or as luxurious as the feel of sufficient sleep that woke Isriam. When the dragon roared, he fell out of bed.

Fighting sheets and quilt, he only tangled himself more securely. He swore and struggled, and flinched as the howl sounded again.

Another, infinitely softer, voice commented, "I hope you had a nice nap."

Isriam blinked up at Ruala, blushed, and hastily unscrambled himself. "I'm sorry, my lady—I—"

"That's all right," she said, her tired eyes dancing with amusement. "There's never been a prince in my bed before."

He became aware of his nakedness, blushed more deeply, and tugged the sheet around him as he climbed to his feet. "I didn't know it was your—I mean, I never would have—"

"Isriam, do stop fussing. It really is all right. Why don't you get dressed and meet us downstairs in the kitchen?"

"Us?"

She was already on her way out the door. "We'll expect you in a little while. Even a prince doesn't keep the High Princess waiting."

He hauled on clothes and caught up with her on the last flight of stairs. "My lady, I'm—"

"Sorry. Yes, I know. The only apology you need to make is for scaring us half out of our wits with that lighted candle branch." Ruala laughed. "Beth turned white as a dragon's tooth."

"Beth—? She's here?"

"And Alasen and Sionell, too. Go on. They're making dinner and you look starved. And speaking of dragons, Sioned and I have some work to do outside, so you go on to the kitchen without me."

The three ladies who labored over hearth and chopping board were unrecognizable. All wore plain, rough clothing: aprons, skirts below their knees, shirts buttoned to the neck. Battered leather shoes replaced the more usual riding boots or fine doeskin slippers. Beth's stockings even had holes in them. Alasen caught him staring and chuckled.

"Yes, we're all proper slatterns, aren't we? Wait till you see Sioned!"

Isriam tried to smile back. The spectacle of three highborn ladies—one of them born a Princess of Kierst—slicing meat and stirring soup was about all he could handle for the moment.

"I'm glad you're here," Sionell told him on her way to the bread rack. "Ruala had planned to deal with the Vellant'im all alone, but now she'll have you to back her up."

"The enemy," Alasen put in, "does not take kindly to women in authority."

"Uh . . . no, I guess not." Isriam jumped to take a heavy cauldron for Betheyn. "I know why you're here—at least, I think I do. To keep everyone at Feruche informed. But what about the dragon?"

"Dragons," Sionell corrected. She sliced into a loaf as if it was a Vellanti arm. "Elisel and Azhly followed us down from Feruche. Quite a bother. Now Sioned and Ruala have to convince them to fly elsewhere before the High Warlord gets here."

"Did Ruala startle you *very* much?" Beth asked as they filled the cauldron from the sink spigot.

"It was the dragon call that woke me," he replied.

"What happened with the pearls?" Alasen contributed an apronful of taze herbs to the pot. "You obviously succeeded, but how?"

The tale took him through the brewing, and by the time he was describing his reasons for coming to Skybowl instead of returning to Feruche, Sioned and Ruala came in.

Like the others, the High Princess wore servants' clothes. Unlike them, her head was covered by wrapped gray cloth in the manner of the Isulk'im. The color was unkind to her face, turning her complexion sallow and her eyes dull. But with her hair scraped back and hidden beneath the cloth, the bones of her face stood out pure and strong.

"Isriam!" She gave him a quick embrace. "I wasn't sure whether to be more angry that you disobeyed or relieved that you're here. Now that I see you, it's definitely the latter. You're all wrung out, my lad. Is dinner ready? Good, let's eat."

They stood around the chopping table, sharing the sketchy meal from the pots and pans it had been cooked in. Both Sioned and Ruala looked the worse for their conversations with their dragons—Ruala perhaps more so, Azhly being a male who sometimes forgot his own strength. The dragons had been stubborn, but eventually were persuaded that all was well, their human possessions were safe, and they ought to return to Feruche.

"I don't like to think what could happen if they're caught here," Ruala said, rubbing her temples against the inevitable headache.

"My lady," Isriam said, "It's stupid of me not to figure it out for myself, but how will you explain that there are only four servants left here?"

"Hardly stupid, Isriam." Sioned speared a chunk of meat with her fork. "In fact, we hadn't discussed it. Ruala?"

"Everyone was too frightened to stay."

Sionell shook her head. "More. That's too simplistic."

"All right, then, when I kicked out your parents and Chadric and Audrite, they took their people with them and most of mine as well."

"Better," Sioned remarked. "But add that many are more terrified of the *Azhrei*'s power than of the punishment for deserting their legal lord and lady."

"You're incorrigible," her Namesake observed.

The High Princess smiled sweetly. "I try."

Later, when everyone but Ruala and Isriam curled into blankets by the kitchen hearth—she went to her own bed, he to a guest chamber—Sioned rose silently from her own pallet. Barefoot, she padded softly from the kitchen to the great hall.

Stronghold had been like this, long ago. She and Tobin and Ostvel and a few servants, waiting out the seasons of Ianthe's pregnancy; Meath's occasional presence like a warm cloak she dared not use for comfort; Rohan far away, fighting Roelstra. Even the emerald ring was once more gone from her hand. All was once more silence, emptiness, just like that helpless wait through an endless Autumn and Winter.

She had thought that time the worst of her life. She had been wrong. At waiting's end had been Pol—what would she find when all *this* was over? Nothing. Her heart was as empty and silent as this keep.

This time she was not helpless. This time she had willingly parted with the ring. This time would be different.

Yes. Very. Rohan would never come home.

Her steps made no sound on the tiled floor. She wandered from the high table to the windows, searching for ghosts. There were none. Only her, alone with a tiny fingerflame following her through the dark.

She tried to remember other times at Skybowl—feasts, dancing, music, hawking, watching dragons. . . .

No ghosts gathered to share her memories. Not even the ones from Stronghold during the desperate year that had ended with Pol cradled in her arms.

Silently, she returned to the kitchen and huddled in a blanket, staring at the Fire until dawn.

✳

"So *that's* why you wanted the jewels," he said, gazing awestruck at the mirror. The stones were in place, glinting by the light of candles and the hearth. He could scarcely believe they could form the white rainbow Pol had described. Still, when he thought of who had worn the jewels. . . .

"Meath was right." Pol rubbed his eyes. "I wish I could tell him."

"He was a Sunrunner, like me. He never would have seen it in the mirror to believe it."

"You think that would've mattered to him?" Blue-green eyes narrowed. "Does it matter that much to you?"

"I take your meaning. And I have to take your word for it that it is what you're really saying. I just wish. . . ."

"You could never talk to Rosseyn, even if you could see him."

"Yes, I know. You explained that."

"If what I have in mind doesn't work, we'll go with the rest of the plan." Pol drained the last swallow of wine from his cup and set it down. "Tonight my new friends and probable kinfolk the *diarmadh'im* will go south. Ruala's crockery will be sown through the sands below Skybowl just before sunset on the eighty-eighth."

"Can they ride that far? Not one of them looks a day under a hundred."

"When Thassalante offered to go, I pointed that out as politely as I could. *He* pointed out that they're the only ones among us who can protect themselves against anything the Vellant'im might try."

"Including iron. I see. It took courage to offer, though."

"Maybe they have something to prove." Pol smiled. "Most of us do."

Gesturing to the mirror, he asked, "Even you?"

Pol sat down at the table, hooking a leg over the chair arm. "I already told you. If it works, you won't have to worry about it. If it doesn't, I may need your expertise after all . . . Andry."

He let Maarken's face and form fade. "How long have you known?"

"Not at first," Pol admitted. "It was only when you kept gesturing with both arms—even the one that wasn't there. Maarken's careful about that."

"Of course. I should have realized."

"What I don't understand is why you thought you had to trick me into telling you. All you had to do was ask."

Andry lowered himself into an overstuffed chair—using both hands. "Can you blame me?"

"I suppose not." Pol studied his fingers, picked at a hangnail. "I loathe what you countenanced at Goddess Keep—both when Tilal was there and what happened to that wretched woman. You don't trust me or any *diarmadhi* as far as you can spit. In fact, I don't like most of what you've done, or your attitude while you've done it. Which is a sentiment you return, I'm sure."

"But?" He arched a brow.

Pol nodded. "But you found Chayla for us. You're here, offering your help. You're the son of your ancestors."

"And so are you."

"I am that." Pol rose, pacing slowly to the mirror. "Andry . . . if this doesn't work—by which I mean if something happens to me—"

"You said Lord Rosseyn promised it wouldn't."

"The *faradhi* part of me is safe. But I'm more sorcerer than Sunrunner. All I can possibly be is a halfling, like my father. Enough to get seasick." He shrugged. "Andry—if the *diarmadhi* part gets caught in the mirror, you'll have to build a *ros'salath*. Don't hear this wrong, but you may be crippled in the working. My mother isn't here to draw on. And you know what she's like."

"I don't deny," he said quietly, "that she'd make it easier. But I've got my brother and Hollis and Evarin. That's a lot of power in just three people."

"If you must—" Pol bit his lip, then shook his head. "If you must, use the children. And your mother. It'll be damned difficult. Raw power like that—and no practice in using it, let alone like this. But you can't let that stop you. Mother says she told you how she sorted everyone out at Stronghold. You may have to do that on your own."

Andry said nothing for a long time. Then, finally: "I thought we'd end up fighting each other over who fights the Vellant'im. Everyone did."

"Maarken," Pol murmured.

"It's not just for his sake, you know. We're neither of us stupid. Not with two thousand Vellant'im ready to sheathe their swords in our guts." Andry smiled wryly. "Besides, if we want anything left to fight over in the future—"

"—we'd better work together *now*." Pol returned the grin.

"Precisely, cousin."

Pol ran his ringless fingers over the mirror frame. "One more thing. Shadow-caught is worse than being shadow-lost. Much worse. Rosseyn isn't really alive—but he's not really dead, either." He glanced up. "If—I want you to kill me, Andry. Or whatever's left of me."

He spasmed half out of the chair. "Pol—!"

"Tomorrow night I'll lock myself in here. You'll have the

only key. Wait until midnight. If I'm not out by then—well, make sure the knife is sharp."

"No! You're Rosseyn's blood, he'd never let anything happen to you—"

"He may not have a say in the matter. But I do. I want you to perform that service for me, cousin. I couldn't trust Maarken or Chay to do it."

"They love you too much, is that it? And your death is my most cherished ambition?" Andry sprang to his feet. "Not a chance, cousin! You're just going to have to make sure you *don't* get shadow-caught!"

He stalked out of the room. Behind him, Pol smiled. Just a little.

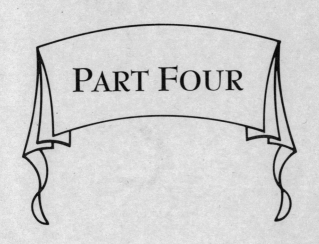

PART FOUR

CHAPTER TWENTY-NINE

In mid-afternoon of the eighty-sixth day of Winter, the Vellant'im were sighted twenty measures from Skybowl. For a few moments five women and one young man stared in bleak dread at the huge dark blot staining the Desert. Then Sionell broke the silence with a single curse, and hurried them all down from the balcony to their stations.

On Sioned's advice and with her help, Ruala dressed in the richest fabrics and gaudiest colors she could find.

"Karanaya did this at Lowland, and it seemed to impress them. They probably don't take much notice of servants, anyway, but I'd like to keep their eyes strictly on you. Hold still while I braid this chain into your hair."

Ruala met the Vellant'im in a bright green brocade skirt and a blazing yellow shirt under a blue velvet tunic to which dozens of earrings had been affixed. Audrite had thoughtfully removed all of Ruala's remaining jewels from Skybowl, but Sioned had brought along a collection of rings, bracelets, and necklets. Ruala was thus arrayed in more gold, silver, and gemstones than she usually wore in the course of a year. As she stood just outside the main gates, she hoped her nerves would hold steady. Every tremor would make her a human wind chime.

"They won't suspect you of spying on them," Sioned told her. "Anybody who makes as much noise as you do just breathing can't sneak around. They'll be paying so much attention to you they won't notice the rest of us at all."

Skybowl seemed to have donned garments of sunlight and shadow for the occasion. The gray stone glowed golden here, purple-brown there, limned with rose-pink as if delicate veils were draped across the towers, floating on the breeze.

Composed and resolute, Isriam waited with Ruala, who joined Sioned in gratitude that he hadn't gone back to Feruche as planned. If she'd had to face the High Warlord and his army alone—well, she would have shimmered in the late afternoon sun with the violence of her trembling.

Mindful of Sioned's comments, when the High Warlord rode within sight Ruala stepped into the light. He lifted one hand, sleeve falling back from a heavy gold wrist cuff that reached nearly to his elbow. All the hundreds of riders behind him stopped. He came forward alone.

"Lady of Skybowl," he said, his voice deep and oddly accented. "You have sense, for a woman."

"High Warlord of the Vellant'im," she replied, relieved that her own voice was steady and cold, "you are near to insulting a woman who can save your whole army from destruction."

He grinned at her. "You of the Desert breed women like horses—for fire. Have you brothers, Lady?"

"No."

"Pity." He looked beyond her to Isriam. "Ah. Prince of Fessenden. My not-friend, not-enemy. What else is there?"

"Allies in good sense, perhaps," Isriam said. "It remains to be seen."

One hand lifting again, he signaled his men to advance. "They will eat, then sleep. You and I will talk, Lady of Skybowl."

"One moment." She took another step forward, tilting her head back to stare up into his eyes. "Where is the High Princess?"

His chin jerked over his shoulder, indicating some spot far back in the march. "With priests."

"I will speak to *her* first." When his brows knotted over his hawk's beak of a nose, she insisted, "I must know that she is safe and well."

He shrugged. "Speak to priests. She is theirs until two dawnings."

"*You* speak to the priests," she countered. "*I* speak with men, not geldings." Before he could reply, she turned on her heel and marched back into the courtyard.

Evidently the High Warlord had given orders that

Skybowl was to be treated with respect. The bulk of the army camped outside around the lake; only the clanmasters and their important warriors were allowed into the castle. And, of course, Meiglan and the priests. Standing in the great hall doorway, Ruala caught a glimpse of her being hurried up the stairs.

"Later," said the High Warlord. "Show me your treaty parchment now."

"There isn't one yet. We haven't discussed terms."

He cast a suspicious glance at Isriam. "You did not say to her no terms?"

The young man gave him a look that said clearly, *Now that you've met her—would you have told her that?*

Glaring down at Ruala, he intoned, "No terms. Skybowl is mine for ritual, fight, feast. Then we go."

"Skybowl is my husband's. There will be no barbaric ritual, no battle, and no celebration. You will take as much dragon gold as you can carry and go home at once."

He snorted. "Do you think me fool, to believe legends?"

"Would you like to see a sample?" She dug into her skirt pocket and came up with a leather pouch. "Open your hand." When he did so, she upended the pouch. Out poured a rivulet of glittering sand.

He stared down at his palm. Ruala caught Isriam's astonishment and sent him a small warning frown. He didn't see it, but his exclamation served her very well just the same.

"Dragon gold!"

A few clanmasters milled about in the entry hall, marveling at its luxury—even denuded as it was of the really valuable items. A few priests were trying not to do the same. They all heard Isriam's words and turned as one man.

The High Warlord closed his fingers around the evidence. "Lies," he said.

"Not at all," Ruala informed him blandly. "I never thought you'd leave us in peace without something to show for your trouble. Here it is. Will you take it in its raw form, like this, or would you rather have ingots?"

"Lies!" He flung the handful away from him; the other men in the hall took an involuntary step toward it, like thirsty cats ready to lap the floor.

"You may inspect the dragon caves at your leisure," she said with a shrug. "And the smelter, if you like."

"If this is true," he said carefully, "why do you offer your wealth?"

"Because gold is worth less than lives. There's plenty more where this comes from, after all. The dragons produce it regularly. Besides, it's not my wealth, or my husband's. It's High Prince Pol's. Why shouldn't I use it?"

He snarled and strode into the great hall. Ruala followed, looking back over her shoulder just once. Sure enough, the clanmasters and the priests were on the floor, scraping up the scattered golden sand. She hid a smile of satisfaction. The High Warlord might be here for vengeance's sake alone, but his people were not averse to profit.

Now, if only the "teeth" and "blood" of dragons worked as well. . . .

"Wine, great lord?"

Ruala nearly gasped aloud. Sioned was humbly bending head and knees to the enemy commander, a silver cup in her hands. He took it, drank, shoved it back at her, and kept walking toward the high table. He didn't look at her once. As Ruala passed, Sioned raised her head slightly and winked.

"Don't take such chances!" Ruala hissed.

"Why not? He doesn't have any idea who I am. Hurry, he's looking for you."

Ruala rattled a bit as she went to join him, and not just with the rhythm of her strides.

He heard her coming and swung around. "Ritual, battle, feast. Then we go."

"Dragon gold to fill your coffers," she countered.

"You are not lord here."

"I am sovereign lady." When she saw that he didn't understand, she said, "I rule here—just as High Princess Meiglan ruled at Dragon's Rest while her husband was away."

This made sense to him, but not on his own culture's terms. "Women are different here," he remarked. And sat down in Riyan's chair.

Ridiculous to feel anger spark at something so unimportant. But she suddenly thanked the Goddess that Sioned had destroyed Stronghold before this murdering savage could sit at Rohan's place.

"Well?" she snapped. "Do you accept the terms?"

He smiled. "Lady," he said with consummate politeness, "it is *my* army outside your walls."

She judged it time for the second part of her task. Putting up a brave show of a proud woman trying to maintain her dignity, she said, "Will you kill me, then, and prove that you have no honor?"

All at once his black eyes sharpened. "Have you sons?"

"N–no." She cursed herself as her right hand went instinctively to her waist. He noted the movement and she realized she might as well admit it. "But I hope to, next year."

"You carry?"

"Yes."

His reaction astounded her. He rose from Riyan's chair and came around the table, taking her arm to escort her to her accustomed seat. "Why did you not say? I would not have frighted you. Rest," he told her, half-scolding and half-solicitous. "Your life belongs to son, to husband."

Given this tally of a Vellanti female's worth, Ruala mentally knelt before the Goddess in gratitude.

"I want to talk to the High Princess."

He looked down at her curiously. "You betray the *Azhrei,* her lord—do you not fear her?"

Meiglan? "Just because I think *he's* wrong doesn't mean I don't care about *her.*" She twisted her fingers together, her many rings clicking and shining. "Take the gold and go. There's more than enough for everyone in your army. You won't be attacked on your way to the sea. Leave us in peace."

He shook his head. "Ritual and battle. Then we go." After a moment's thought, he added, "No feast. And Skybowl left standing."

"You were going to destroy—?" Ruala let her voice quiver. "Please, I beg of you! No more killing! No more death, no more destruction—please!"

"I'm taking Lady Ruala upstairs," Isriam said. "You're upsetting her." He shepherded her from the table. The High Warlord actually bowed. They left him back in Riyan's chair, picking the last of the gold-grained sand from his palm.

*

Between the last of the sun and the first dim glow of the moons through the clouds, one of Edrel's sentries galloped into Goddess Keep. He ignored no fewer than sixteen Sunrunners on his way upstairs. They demanded that he inform them of any problems so they could inform Lord Torien in the proper manner; his response was to snarl.

Lord Torien was seated at dinner in a private chamber, in the company of his wife, two of the *devr'im,* and Lord Edrel and Princess Norian. The guard ignored these Sunrunners, too, heading directly for Edrel.

"My lord—the Vellant'im are coming ashore."

Jolan rose at once. "Then we can fight them—at last!"

"We?" Norian asked sweetly. "I'm so glad you've come to see things our way." She paused a delicate instant before adding, "At last."

Gray eyes below night-black hair ignited. Slightly desperate tact on Edrel's and Torien's parts had recently extricated their wives from this very subject. And now here it was staring them in the face again.

Nialdan cleared his throat with a great rumble. "So whatever they've waited for, this is it."

"You'll notice there's no light for us to use," said Antoun.

Edrel had expected something of the sort from him; after all, he was supposed to be a *devri,* and on Torien's side. Addressing the guard, he said, "Have the sentries pull back. Alert the rest of our people, but don't alarm anyone outside the walls."

"At once, my lord." He saluted and left.

"What?" Jolan exclaimed. "You must attack! They'll be vulnerable coming up the cliffs—"

"As we would be if we were so foolish as to fight in the dark on those same cliffs," he replied. "Unless you'd care to set a few fires in the woods for everyone to see by. No? I didn't think so."

"At least we ought to bring everyone into the keep," Torien said.

Edrel leaned back in his chair with a casualness he didn't feel. "They won't attack until tomorrow, rather late in the morning."

"How do you know?" the Chief Steward asked, frowning.

"Because it'll take that long to get everyone off-loaded and into position. You may sound that horn of yours at dawn." He stood, stretched, and held out a hand to Norian. "And now, if you don't mind, I think I'll go get some sleep. Goddess knows, the enemy won't get any."

On their way to Elsen's room, Norian squeezed his fingers tightly. "Are you really sure about this?"

"Keeping in mind the count of men, longboats, how many can fit into the longboats, and the time it'll take to row back and forth—pretty sure. And if any of these Sunrunners were using the brains they were born with, they'd be sure, too. They're beginning to get on my nerves."

"It's taken this long? Did I tell you what Jolan wanted to do to Jayachin's little boy? Keep him here as if he was apprenticed, with his mother's wealth to pay the fee!"

Edrel smiled down at her. "What did you do about it?"

"I told her that as the city of Waes is under the High Prince's direct protection, so is everyone who calls it home."

"And because I'm Pol's vassal—"

"Exactly. The boy is our responsibility." She hesitated. "Do you mind?"

"Of course not. I feel sorry for the child. And he'll get fairer treatment from us than he would from them." He paused with his fingers on the handle of Elsen's door. "Goddess, what have the Sunrunners come to, that they can think to use a child that way?"

"It's not really all of them," Norian said, trying to be fair. "It's mainly Jolan."

"They're frightened," Edrel mused. "I wonder what of?"

At that moment, Antoun was reminding his fellow *devr'im* why. "You know we can't rely on the *ros'salath*. I don't mean that you can't lead us just as well as Andry, Torien," he added hastily. "It's just that the new ones among us—me included—are still shaky."

"As it happens, I agree with you," Torien said. "And I mean no insult to *you*, either, when I say that if we still had Oclel and Rusina, it would be all right. But four of us are barely trained and, except for Jayachin, we've never worked together in earnest."

"Edrel will simply have to lead his troops and Elsen's in the attack," Jolan stated. "Tomorrow morning, before the Vellant'im can organize themselves for battle."

"How do we persuade him to do it?" Deniker asked. "You know he'll do nothing more than defend Goddess Keep—he won't take the battle outside the walls. He doesn't want to risk any of his people."

"Forgive me for saying it," Jolan said, "but better them than Sunrunners." She grimaced as her husband began a protest. "I know, I know. It's a terrible thing to say. But who has more value in this world, a common soldier or a *faradhi?* And if we attempt the *ros'salath* with half of us inexperienced and their weakness unknown, we'd be more at risk than any soldier with a sword in hand. Given a choice we don't really have, our lives are more important."

Antoun turned a knife over and over in his fingers. "That's a cold assessment, Jolan."

"It's the truth," she shot back. "I've seen that more and more clearly over the course of this war. Why do the Vellant'im linger here instead of going to their High Warlord? Why did he order them to stay at Goddess Keep? Because they hate us. They *fear* us. Whatever Andry told me about their reasons for wanting Pol dead, *we* are the ones they truly fear. If Pol dies, he dies. There'll be another High Prince or High Princess—Maarken as regent for Jihan, perhaps. It hardly matters. *We* are the ones who must survive. Imagine a world without Goddess Keep. Sunrunners would live and die untrained, the *diarmadh'im* would run wild—" She turned to Torien. "Yes, I know you're of their blood. But you're not one of them. You're a Sunrunner."

"What does Andry say?" Nialdan asked.

Jolan leaned her fists on the table and pulled in a deep breath. "Andry . . . says nothing except 'take care of things.' He's abandoned us. Oh, don't look so shocked, it's only what we've all been thinking ever since he left!"

"Doubtless you accused him of it when you spoke the other day." Antoun put down the knife.

"And why not? It's true, isn't it? When he left us behind, he made his choice. It was his dream from childhood to become Lord of Goddess Keep—yet when Goddess Keep needs him most, where is he? Back in his Desert homeland! Don't you see how little we count with him?"

"Perhaps," Antoun offered, "he has more faith in us than we have in ourselves."

"And perhaps," Nialdan said, rising to his full height and towering over Jolan, "we'd better stop this right now. Torien, I'll do whatever you want me to do—be it the *ros'salath* or anything else. As long as nothing you ask of me betrays Andry."

"None of us ever could," Torien replied, not looking at his wife.

Antoun judged it was time for a discreet departure. He

made his excuses and shut the door behind him, hoping he'd said all the right things. If so, then perhaps no one would have to fight in any way, shape, or form. This was why he'd warned of the difficulties of the *ros'salath*. His aim was to get everyone within the walls' protection; then neither bodies nor minds would be at risk.

This afternoon Pol had spoken to him on sunlight. Antoun spared only a wistful sigh for the loss of his secret as Sioned's eyes and ears within Goddess Keep; if Pol needed him, it was time for the secret to be shared. But the others here must not know yet—which meant he could not tell them that Pol was certain the culmination of the war would come on the eighty-ninth day of Winter.

Why and how, Antoun did not know. Neither had he asked. It was enough that there was a time limit now, a day beyond which there was a future that did not include war. He supposed long association with Sioned had infected him with Rohan's ideals of peace and tolerance. But better Rohan's dream than Andry's—of *faradhi* dominance and *diarmadhi* deaths.

✻

Pol handed Kierun the key to the Attic and told him to take it to Lord Andry a little before midnight. The boy's face, scars fading where he'd been cut on the forehead and cheeks, wrinkled up in worry. But he was a dutiful squire, excellently trained. He asked no questions, only nodded and obeyed.

Pol waited until he heard the lock snick into place, then went to close the curtains against all exterior light.

You won't have to kill me, cousin—or so I hope and trust. But I had to make you realize that you don't really want me out of the way. Rather brutally, yes, and the reverse of Father's policy of getting people to do what they would have done anyhow. At least, I think it was the reverse. . . .

He chided himself for being unjust. Andry might want to carve off some of Pol's power, but he could never carve a knife into Pol's heart.

He stood before the mirror. It had been propped at only a slight angle on the floor against a chair, the jewels on a level with Pol's eyes. There was much he might have done with it. Lord Rosseyn had given him spell after spell.

He could spin a killing storm of Air and Water.

He could conjure lightning made of Fire and blast the enemy to nothingness.

He could weave a *ros'salath* so terrifying that they would run screaming into the Desert to die hopelessly insane.

He could fashion a dome of light, the way Sioned had done long ago, enclose them, and then crush them into the sand.

He could project horror into the mirror, from gigantic dragons to monsters from legend to an image of himself a measure high and wreathed in flames.

He could do almost anything he wanted. He had power enough and to spare.

The power belonged to the mirror, and Rosseyn, and the generations of sorcerers who had discovered and sometimes dared to use it.

His to use now. His decision to make. His soul at risk, as Rohan and Sioned would have warned him—as Rosseyn had. If he killed with this gift that augmented his own gifts, he would sin. Not the kind of sin that Andry spoke of and punished, but a wrong done against himself. The irony of course was that *he* had refused to swear the vow that Andry and other Sunrunners had, and had broken.

It didn't make him feel virtuous or superior. He was in a Hell of his own making, inhabited only by him. And only he could get himself out of it.

Pol stared at his own reflection in the mirror, tracing each feature. Except to shave, he hadn't really looked at that face in a long time. He saw a High Prince and a Sunrunner and a sorcerer. He saw a husband frantic for the safety of his wife, a father haunted by the wounds dealt to his children. He saw a son grieving for one parent's death and the other's descent into madness. He saw all that he was, from redoubtable warrior to Azhdeen's personal possession to farmer to horseman to Sionell's lover.

So many of him. Everybody saw him differently, everybody needed him differently. So many of him, crammed into one body, looking out from one face. He was all those things and more, the sum of himself and those who had taught him, and more. The only difference came in the nuances of power.

And power was here before him. Hell was here before him.

Rohan would have understood perfectly.

A thought extinguished the Fire in the hearth. Another thought lit the fresh candles on either side of the mirror. And the *selej* glowed above Rosseyn's living face.

Rosseyn, who had been dead for fifteen and more generations.

"You are determined to do this, my son?"

"I am."

"But afraid?"

"I am," he said again, apologetically.

"Good."

Pol couldn't help a smile. "You sound just like my father."

"Then your father was a very wise man. By the way, don't be alarmed when I seem to vanish. I'll still be here, believe me."

"I'd change that if I could."

"A generous offer. But futile, as I've told you." Rosseyn bent his head and closed his eyes. "When you're ready, then."

Pol laced his fingers together just below his chin, using the pressure to focus concentration. It was easy, really—not unlike a simple conjuring—but he paid attention to every detail. This was no time to grow careless. So instead of damping both candles at once without even looking, he attended to them individually. Instead of a single thought, he ran through the whole sequence as he called new Fire to the already blazing diamond.

Rosseyn faded into a white mist of no more substance than breath on a cold mirror. In his place Pol conjured the great hall at Skybowl. He built the image carefully: windows to his left, the high table in front of him, banners floating from the rafters, fine Kierstian tiles underfoot.

He felt his hands part without his conscious volition, and with the movement something inside him separated, too.

Rosseyn had told him that his mixed heritage would manifest itself in some fashion. The Sunrunner in him could not use the mirror and thus could not be shadow-caught. It would anchor him to this place no matter what happened.

At least, that was the theory.

From the moonlight through Skybowl's windows he twisted a shining plait leading back here, to Feruche. But not across the measures of sand between: through the mirror to where he stood. He seemed to see himself holding it in his left hand where the amethyst of Princemarch had been, invisible in the white crown. His right hand was ringless, too, the Desert topaz set into the frame, Andrade's moonstone discarded when it sparked dangerously in the presence of sorcery. He understood now his mother's words about her long-missing rings still on her fingers like scars.

The twined skeins of moonlight tugged at him. He resisted, using it instead to fill in the details of the great hall as it existed at that moment. When he had seen all there was to see, he consciously transferred the shimmering silver rope to his right hand. Anchored; secure; safe, in the Sunrunner's hand.

He left the Sunrunner in him behind, and entered Skybowl on moonlight.

✳

"I thank you for good food," the High Warlord said to Lady Ruala. "You strengthen the warriors."

"Hardly my intention," she said coldly.

He stifled a sigh. He was trying to be polite, for the *Kir'reia* had taught him that these women valued conversation. It wasn't too great an effort, for he had always enjoyed talking with his favorite wife. He mourned her for more than the additional sons she might have borne him.

How magnificent she would have looked in what Lady Ruala wore: brilliant colors, luxurious fabrics, an entire clanwealth decorating her from hair to fingertips. Especially fine were the matching gold bracelets dotted with dense white stones like dollops of cream. They would set off the scars he'd incised into his wife's hands, emphasizing the proud pallor of his marks as perfectly as they did Lady Ruala's dark skin and the white crescents of her nails.

"Now that you mention it," she said, "I've been wondering how you manage to feed your troops. You haven't taken anything from the keeps and manors you've destroyed. What do you eat?"

He was surprised that so great a lady should interest herself in such matters. Vellanti women did, of course, no matter who their husbands or fathers or brothers were; it was their duty. He would have thought the highborn women of these lands would leave such things to their servants. But a moment's glance at the three who scurried around the tables, pouring water and spooning soup, showed them to be so colorless and cringing that their intelligence was in serious doubt. They sidled and whispered and never looked up at all.

He chose to answer her question with another. "Do you ride the Desert with no water?"

She blinked. Her eyes were very dark green, her hair was very black with a few streaks of silver, and her skin was nearly the color of a Vellanti woman's. "You mean you brought food enough for all these men?"

He nodded, not telling her that Faolain Riverport, Catha Heights, Graypearl, and Sandeia had provided substantial stores before they were burned. And the priests had grown fat enough on the bounty of Radzyn.

His gaze strayed to them now, seated at their own table off to the side. The senior among them were upstairs guarding the *Kir'reia*. They would eat the white food—as if the color of a soup indicated its purity—that was also the *Kir'reia's* lot. He was aware that ever since they had taken her from him, he had less and less patience with their nonsense. He even termed it nonsense now in his mind—though not aloud. He still needed them. They were still useful.

He cast a brief sidelong glance at Lady Ruala. Very beautiful, obviously flawless, highborn even though not a princess, without sons. But she carried a child. If not, he might have . . . no. It must be the *Azhrei's* wife.

But why did the *Azhrei's* wife have to be *her?*

Perhaps Lady Ruala would tell him something of the events that had led to the marriage. He put his winecup down and turned to ask.

Her fists were clenched against her chest, her eyes wide as she stared at the bonfire. Down beyond it, all the raucous jests had ceased. A sword was drawn, and another. A platter of meat crashed to the floor as one of the servingwomen clapped both hands to her mouth.

Through the bonfire unscathed walked a man: tall, fairhaired, plainly dressed but a prince to his fingertips. He paused, half-in and half-out of the flames. His blue-green eyes sought and found the High Warlord's gaze.

"Azhrei!" cried the priest who was the only one among them who had ever spoken to him. "It's him, it's the *Azhrei!"*

A warrior rushed forward, sword flailing. It went right

through the *Azhrei*. Right through him. He took no more notice than if an insect had buzzed past on its way to a dung heap.

The warrior, however, lost his balance and tumbled into the fire. He rolled away from it, the sleeve of his shirt blazing. One of the women, the old and slow one with a gray cloth wrapped around her head, splashed a pitcher of water on him. Some of his clan dragged him back to his place.

"You are the Vellanti High Warlord," said the *Azhrei*.

Rising, he replied, "Yes."

"I have seen you before, on sunlight." He took another few steps forward, and now stood halfway between the high table and the fire. Everything the priest had said about his face was true: pride, strength, power. Twin demons in his eyes.

"I know why you have come here," the *Azhrei* went on. "Why you kill and burn. Why my lady wife was stolen from me. Why you and all your people hate me and mine."

"Then you know why you will die, and she with you."

Beside him, Lady Ruala cried out.

"You know who I am," came the soft answer, eyes calm and fierce. "And because you do, you also know how easily I could slay you where you stand."

"Then do." He made a careless gesture of one hand. The vast majority of his men could not understand a single word spoken here—only the priests knew the *Azhrei's* language, and they not half as well as he—so they must hear the exchange in his tone and his movements. "Your wife will still die. You will still die. It would change nothing."

"I disagree. Who would lead your warriors? The priests?" He tilted his head toward the trembling white-clad ranks, and smiled. "I offer you the chance to live. Lead your warriors back to Radzyn Keep. Board your ships. Leave in peace—or I promise you that you will all die in battle as your ancestors did."

He burst out laughing because they could not be allowed to see that he was almost tempted.

It shocked him, that impulse. He knew how his forefathers had died: horribly. Horribly. They had won in the end, yes; the accursed *diarmadh'im* had been killed, yes. But not before thousands upon thousands died.

To leave in peace. To sail the wide seas where he and his kind belonged. To walk his own fields and shores. To lie beside each wife and cosset each daughter and teach each son to be strong and proud and free.

To let *her* live.

He laughed because he was startled by the bitter revelations of his own heart. Better to laugh than to cry out in pain.

"May the Father of All Storms witness the impudence of this fool!" he called out in his own language. "We sit in his most important keep, we have his wife, and in two dawnings we will destroy all his power—and do you know what he says? He invites us to leave!"

The protest came, but neither as loudly or as quickly as he'd expected. And why should it? There stood the *Azhrei,* clothed in power. The High Warlord knew that if he did not say or do something at once, he would lose them. Oh, not to such fear that they would refuse to fight. The battle would be joined as planned. No, he would lose them to the priests. They would obey the priests. They would die in service of the priests' nonsense.

Just as *she* would.

He could not help her. He was shamed to know he wished to. His duty was to his warriors, to all the clans who had followed him here, who believed in his purpose. His vengeance.

He made his voice a dragon's roar. "Shall we whine and slink away like whipped wolf cubs afraid of our own shadows? Shall we betray our fathers, and their fathers before them back a hundred thousands of days? Shall we be defeated without lifting a single sword?"

The response was much more satisfying this time. He let it wash over him, not daring to cast a look of triumph at the priests. For he had not yet won. He almost had his warriors back in his hands. A few more words, and they would be entirely his once more. But the *Azhrei* was another matter: silent, invulnerable, pitying.

He flung an arm out, finger pointed at the conjuring. "Has he the courage to come before us? He sends his shadow! Has he the courage to come with his whole army at his back? He sends his shadow! Has he summoned the dragons to his aid?" Sweeping his arm around to indicate Lady Ruala, he finished, "Even his own sworn servants betray him! Shall we fear a shadow, obey a shadow?"

Oh, he had them now. They yelled and battered the tiles

with their boots and pounded fists on the tables, ready to tear their enemies apart with bare hands. He basked in their fervor, letting it salve his pride, and then leaned toward the *Azhrei* and spoke in his language.

"Hear their answer, and mine."

"You fool!" the shadow exclaimed. "Don't you understand? I'm offering you your lives! What would your deaths gain me? What would mine gain you? One way or another, you'll leave these lands. You can do it alive and see home again, or you can do it dead with your ships burning to ashes on the sea!"

The High Warlord straightened. "Go, *Azhrei*. Wear the cloak of her making. In it you will die!"

The image wavered, almost as if it trembled in response to the powerful emotions blazing in the blue-green eyes. "How can you condemn your own people to death, when you can so easily—"

The angry bellow of a dragon drowned the rest of his words. Warriors outside shouted in response, warriors within the great hall turning as one man to the High Warlord. Would he kill the *Azhrei*'s dragon, or allow it to live and fly free of the *Azhrei*'s sinful taint?

The *Azhrei* himself swung around and for a moment looked as if he'd run to the windows. Arresting the movement made him stumble slightly. "Azhdeen!" he cried. *"No!"*

The dragon howled with all the strength in his lungs. A piercing shriek from the elderly servingwoman echoed him—but instead of fainting or collapsing into a terrified huddle on the floor, she picked up her skirts and raced out the main doors.

Young Prince Isriam leapt over the high table and hurried to another of the women, who had let out a terrible scream and swayed on her feet as if she would be the one to topple. He carried her from the hall. Lady Ruala half-rose, then staggered against the High Warlord, desperate hands grasping for support.

"He'll kill me!" she wailed. "He's sent his dragon to kill me!"

Picking her off him—carefully, for his instincts around a pregnant woman were blood deep—he placed her in her chair and turned away from her frantic sobs.

The bonfire suddenly spat and flared to the vaulted ceiling, igniting banners, blackening the rafters, blinding him.

When he could see again, the *Azhrei* was gone.

✳

. . . so bright!

(Too bright for such young eyes, infant eyes scarcely open to the world.)

. . . so many colors!

(Red-yellow-green-blue-purple-black-white—)

. . . so many kinds!

(Tobin-Ostvel-Pandsala-Urival-Andrade-Sioned.)

. . . more! Fill empty hurt MORE!

(A child's hunger, but not of the body. A hungry Sunrunner-sorcerer mind. He sees it now, understands it: this, his second memory. The first? Fire.)

Light!

(Starfire woven to enclose Father and Grandfather as they battle to the death—for his life. *That* night: the night of his Naming, the night he has remembered in glimpses of dreams. The hands clasp light between them, like the gemstones in the mirror frame. Other hands are color only—his own hands, Sunrunner and sorcerer—not yet understanding the light.)

—SOUND—

(Steel knife striking the dome, ringing—deadly if not for the sorcerers. Pandsala. Urival. Himself, barely Named.)

So that was how it happened.

He watches colors swirl, catches at some with his right hand, some with his left. But he cannot make the two hands join.

Two hands. He stares at himself from within and without the mirror, right hands—left?—reaching for his own diamond-pearl-emerald-topaz, twinned with him in the mirror. Two men, two reflections, the mirror separating what he is from what he is.

Colors are strewn through the mirror, his own and a million more in shades no human eye has ever seen. He knows he is not really seeing them now, not with his eyes. But he hears them louder than his own trembling heartbeat, smells them stronger than his scorched blood on the jewels, tastes them sharper than his fear.

He cannot touch them. They are trapped in the glass, between his matching hands pressed flat against each other, all four—the mirror that keeps him separate from himself.

There is no feature that does not appear in its exact symmetrical opposite. He stands on both sides of the mirror at once, staring at face and body and shaking hands that claw the glass and leave no scar—

Scar—

Small white crescent on his cheek. The pain of receiving it, like the slash of a Fire dagger across his skin.

No worse than the pain of knowing what he is, who had borne him.

"You are a Sunrunner, Pol. But you are also diarmadhi. . . . Are you anything less than you were before you knew?"

"I'm more."

Said bitterly then, he denies it with serene pride now. The complexity of colors, the shining maze of curves, angles, shadows, depths, bright burning power—he is what he has always been. No more, no less. Himself.

The Sunrunner is the husband is the warrior is the son is the prince is the father is the sorcerer is the Sunrunner. They are not shards pieced together to form an imperfect whole. He is complete; he is all he has ever been. No less, no more.

He presses his fingertips to the glass. Within is all the warmth of light and color gifted to Sunrunner and sorcerer alike. He hungers for it as he hungered that night when Sioned used his raw power and wrapped her own around him, fierce protection and encompassing love as deep and enduring as she'd given Rohan.

For me, he thinks in wonderment. *For me, because of me—and this is what I am. All the light and shadow and color is me.*

From both sides of the mirror, he reaches through it. Hands clasp light, trailing color that sings all around him. Hands clasped tight, he is whole.

✳

Alasen paced the kitchen floor in a fever of nervous energy. Sionell stood at the big sink, scrubbing the glaze off Ruala's soup tureens. She'd missed Pol's performance, having chosen to stay in the kitchens and ready the meal for the others to serve, but Alasen had told her the whole tale. After listening in frowning silence, she'd attacked the dirty pots and pans.

Betheyn moved silently from drying rack to cupboards, putting away utensils that Isriam had finished washing. They neither spoke nor looked at each other; Alasen decided Beth was still irked at the boy for removing her from the great hall.

Ruala had slipped in by a secret staircase a short time ago, and was now stacking logs and kindling for tomorrow morning's breakfast fire. She didn't speak much, either, beyond saying that she still hadn't been allowed to see Meiglan.

Alasen paced, chewed her thumbnail to the quick, and fretted about Sioned.

At last the back door opened, and Sioned trudged in. She looked at no one and nothing, merely sat on a stool by the hearth. Beth went to her instantly with a cup of hot taze. The others stopped whatever they were doing to stare at her. But only Alasen spoke.

"Did Azhdeen leave?"

Sioned nodded, burying her nose in the fragrant steam. She hunched her shoulders, shivering a little.

"You spoke to him?"

"From the gatehouse wall." She drank deeply, eyes closed, then sighed to the bottom of her lungs. "Goddess, that tastes good. Thank you, Beth."

Ruala abandoned the kindling and crouched near Sioned. "Nobody talks to another person's dragon."

Without looking up, Sioned replied, "The dragon didn't much appreciate it, either. My head is splitting, Ruala, please."

"I'm sorry. But are you sure he knows to stay away or they'll kill him?"

She glanced over at last. "Azhdeen—or Pol?"

"Both," Sionell said. Coming into the half-circle of firelight, she went on, "What did he think he was doing? There's nothing he could possibly have said to persuade—"

"He tried," Alasen put in. "At least he had the courage to try."

"So did you," Ruala said. When Sioned looked a question at her, she added. "Somebody sent that bonfire all the way to the ceiling—and since you were gone and it wasn't me, it had to have been Alasen."

Alasen shrugged. "I had to keep them from following you. Beth and Ruala were busy screaming, but that only distracted a few of them."

"So the Sunrunner is no longer afraid of being a Sunrunner." Sioned touched her kinswoman's arm lightly. "Knowing Pol, he chose that moment to make his exit." When Ruala nodded, she continued, "Just as I thought. Rohan always did say that one of the tricks to true style is knowing when to leave."

"He would've been proud of Pol tonight," Alasen mused. "He would've said exactly what Pol did."

Sionell's brow vanished into the untidy tumble of hair over her forehead. "Do you really think so? More likely Rohan would never have said any such thing. From what you told me, what Pol said was mad, idealistic, and total nonsense. Rohan was much too practical."

"No," Sioned murmured. "He simply understood the barbarian mind."

Alasen opened her mouth to argue in Pol's favor, but ended by saying nothing. There were tears in Sioned's green eyes—but whether of sorrow or pride, Alasen neither knew nor dared ask.

✳

Pol opened his eyes.

"About time, too," said Andry.

He levered himself up on one elbow. He was stretched out on a couch—most of him, anyway; his legs were too long. One dangled over the side, the other was propped on the arm of the couch. He glanced around, surprised to find Chay, Walvis, and Maarken also in the room.

"Midnight?" he asked Andry, his tongue thick and fuzzy as if he'd guzzled a whole cask of wine. No headache, though; thank the Goddess for small favors.

"Midnight," Andry confirmed. "Here, have some water."

He sipped, tasted the tingle of some kind of restorative herb, and gulped the whole gobletful. Pushing himself to a sitting position, he returned the cup to Andry and raked both hands back through his hair—glad there were only two hands again—and paused to rub a fingertip against the scar. He was whole. And he had failed.

"I used the mirror," he said to his hands, clasping them together on his knees. "I was at Skybowl—a conjuring, don't ask the details, I'm not sure I understand it myself. I told the High Warlord he couldn't possibly win."

"And he laughed in your face," Chay said. "What did you expect?"

Pol shrugged. "I don't know. Intelligence. Self-preservation. Practicality. They lost against sorcery time and again—"

"But eventually won," Maarken pointed out.

"Did you really think he'd listen to reason?" Walvis asked quietly.

Frustrated and humiliated, Pol shook his head. "It's just—it's so *clear* to me, why couldn't he see it? For just a moment there I thought I had him. He was really listening to me. The look in his eyes—"

"Stop kicking yourself," Maarken said. "That's supposed to be my job. And it's not as if you deserve it."

Pol leaned back against pillows and searched his cousin's gray eyes. "We're six hundred against at least two thousand. That's madness. I don't care how clever you and Chay are—it's madness."

Chay folded his arms across his chest. "If your father was here, he'd slap you across the room for that."

"You forget yourself, Pol," Andry said. "And us. We are six hundred warriors, Isulk'im, Sunrunners, and sorcerers. They are two thousand ignorant barbarians—who just saw the *Azhrei* walk right into their midst."

"Hells," Walvis added, "you probably scared the piss out of them."

Pol knew what they were doing, and resented it. He wasn't a fool, to be coaxed—or bludgeoned—into believing that midnight was noon. But by voicing his despair he'd forced them to this. And it was *his* job to put a proud face on defeat.

So he sat up a little straighter and said, "Azhdeen certainly did. And me as well. Is he back yet?"

"A little while ago." Walvis gestured to the open windows. "We let him have a good look at you, and he settled down."

Andry scowled. "But how did he know—"

"He's a dragon." Maarken shrugged. "Who knows what dragons know? Bet he was confused, though."

"So am I," Walvis said bluntly. "Andry talks about mirrors, you say you were at Skybowl—"

Pol massaged the back of his neck. "I'll tell you everything as we ride."

"Riyan's getting everyone ready now." Chay went to the table and poured wine for all of them. "Mounted troops only, for speed. With the horses Walvis brought, we can field almost seven hundred."

"Tilal will be at Stronghold tomorrow," Andry said. "I've told Andrev to have him send his own cavalry up as fast as they can ride."

So everything was arranged. Pol supposed it was stupid to think he could stop a war with words. Rohan used to say that sometimes you could bury a problem under words until it collapsed from their sheer weight. But not this time.

"To the victory of our seven hundred," Chay said, presenting the five goblets on a silver tray. "Secured through tactical brilliance—" He proffered the tray to Maarken, who selected a cup and bowed. "—sheer bullheadedness—" This for Walvis, with a grin.

"I prefer to think of it as prowess coupled with determination."

"Bullheaded I said, and bullheaded you are," Chay answered serenely. "Where was I? Ah, yes—Sunrunner magic." Andry next; a look of solemn understanding passed between them.

"And sorcery," said the Lord of Goddess Keep to the High Prince.

The toast was drunk. Pol swallowed the wine around the lump in his throat.

Walvis ran a fastidious fingertip along his mustache and put down his cup. "I'm off to organize my students—and to make sure Sethric stays here."

"Good luck," Maarken offered skeptically.

"Would a word or two from a former Battle Commander help?" Chay asked.

"A tear or two from a certain young lady from Castle Crag might be better, but I'll take what I can get."

When they were gone, Maarken cleared his throat. "Pol, I need to apologize. No, don't interrupt. I have to say this. I thought for a time that you might be trying to set yourself up as—I don't know, authority over all Sunrunners. When you had me bring Andrade's sapphire—"

Pol stared. "You must be joking! I don't want Andry's job any more than he wants mine!"

"Want it?" Andry snorted. "I wouldn't take it if the Goddess herself handed it to me."

Maarken nodded, palpably relieved. "Then let's get moving, my lords. It's a long, hard ride to Skybowl—and hard work at the end of it."

CHAPTER THIRTY

"**I've** never seen Stronghold," Andrev murmured.

"You still haven't." Tilal jerked his horse's reins and started back through the outer bailey, much to the animal's relief. He didn't like it here any more than Tilal did.

To be told what Sioned had done; to hear descriptions by Sunrunners who had looked; to know that the splendid castle of his boyhood and youth was nothing but a Fire-scarred ruin . . . to see it with his own eyes. Nothing had prepared him for this. For the sickness that rose to his throat, the tears that stung his eyes. The fury.

He did not say to Andrev, *You should have seen it when Rohan was alive. You should have been here that Spring of 705, when all the princes met under the dragon banner and swore to Rohan as High Prince. You should have heard the music of the fountain and the grotto waterfall on a lazy summer day, played dragons in your great-grandmother's garden, stretched out on your back under the willow tree to watch green and gold shadows. You should have browsed through the library and listened to the servants flirting with each other and climbed the Flametower to see the whole of the Desert spreading out before you beneath the stars.*

Andrev would never know the home of his ancestors as it had been. And Tilal could say none of those things to him. It hurt too much.

He rode through the tunnel, past the long line of riders leading their horses in for a drink at the grotto pool, and back out into the Desert. The signs of Vellanti occupation were everywhere here: the blackened circles of abandoned cookpits, the stench of latrines dug into the sand. But the Desert would take back its own, and cover everything in the next storm.

He wondered bitterly if eventually Stronghold would be buried, too.

Gemma was waiting for him, seated on her cloak in the sand. Cheese, bread, dried meat, a few wrinkled apples, and a bottle of the best in Chay's cellars were spread out before her.

Sympathy gleamed in her eyes as he joined her, but she didn't ask what he'd found within the keep. Instead: "Iliena saw the oddest thing, Tilal. Just the other side of that rise is a stone trough. What could they have meant, dragging it all the way down from the keep?"

"Damned if I know." He sat, careful to keep his boots from the fine blue wool of her cloak. "We'll start for Skybowl just before dusk, I think."

"Are you sure about the timing?" Gemma wielded her belt dagger against the half-round of cheese.

"It's not like it was at Swalekeep. We're not part of the main battle plan. All we really have to do is show up as close to dawn as possible. With luck, we won't even have to draw swords."

"Don't patronize me," she said, but with none of her usual quickfire temper. And she wouldn't look at him, which worried him. Gemma never spared herself or anyone else when she had something to say. "If the Vellant'im turn and run, they'll be heading straight for you. If Maarken's in trouble when you get there, you'll have to take the brunt of the fighting for him."

"But if Pol and Andry manage that *ros'salath* or whatever they call it, there won't be anybody to run or to fight." He bit into an apple, chewed, swallowed, and added, "Too bad, really."

She glanced up and then away, her eyes fierce. But her voice shook. "I lost my firstborn son. I don't want to lose you, too."

Tilal grasped her hand. "It's for Rihani that I want to kill them. It's not civilized of me. Rohan would be appalled to know what I'm thinking right now—that I wish to all Hells I was a Sunrunner, so I could blast every one of those whoresons to ashes for what they did to our boy."

"Don't you think I want the same thing?" Catching his

hand in both her own, she stared out at the late-afternoon shadows pooling between the dunes. "I stopped at High Kirat on the way to Radzyn. Danladi told me—" She choked and tears welled in her dark brown eyes. "She told me everything. What he said at the last. That's what Rohan did to us, Tilal, to all of us. That's why so many died—not just Rihani. We're so accustomed to peace that we can't believe in war even when it's marching across our lands and burning our fields and killing our sons—"

"Gemma," he said carefully, "do you think that Rohan's way has made us weak? Is that it?"

"I don't know!" she cried. "Rihani was *ashamed* that he hated war and death and killing—and Rohan did that to him!"

"What Rihani felt," he replied quietly, "was shame that killing sickened him so. Would you have had him revel in it? Wash his hands in the blood of his slaughters?"

"No! But—"

"As a man and as a prince he wanted only peace. As a man and as a prince, he was forced to become a warrior. He knew he had to fight. He killed more than his share, according to Saumer. But he wasn't meant for such things. He hated what he had to do. But he did it." Drawing a deep breath around the ache in his own heart, he gazed earnestly at the mother of his son. "He understood, at the last, that it *wasn't* a weakness, that he had nothing to be ashamed of. He wasn't meant to kill. He knew he was the man and the prince we always hoped he'd be."

The tears shone in streaks down her face. "Then *I* must be the barbarian. I want them all dead, Tilal—and I'm *not* ashamed of it!"

He put his arms around her, not caring who might see them, knowing that those who did would immediately glance away. "I know," he murmured into her hair, "I know, love."

After a few moments, she pulled away and knuckled her eyes. "I'm not making any sense," she sighed. "First I tell you I don't want you to fight, and then I say I want every last Vellanti dead. You must think I'm insane."

"I have my own kind of madness," he admitted. "I'd love to kill them all with my bare hands—but the thought of another day filled with death and blood nauseates me."

"Rohan did a good job on you, too," she remarked, but with less rancor. As he turned involuntarily to Stronghold, she reached over and coaxed his head back around. "Don't think about it."

"You were right. I should never have gone up there."

"No, you shouldn't." She began picking the bread apart into crumbs.

"I *have* to kill them, Gemma," he said quietly. "For Rihani, for Kostas—and for Rohan. I know what that makes of me. I know I should care about that. I probably will, later. But right now. . . ."

*

Sioned retied the gray scarf around her head, using a polished silver tray to make sure all the ends were hidden. "It's not what it was," she said as Alasen tucked in a few stray curls at her nape. "But still distinctive."

"Not that anyone in his right mind would expect to find *you* here," Alasen replied. "But we have to assume they know certain things about us, and the red-haired, green-eyed High Princess Sioned is famous. There, all done." She was smiling a grim little smile as Sioned faced her. "Well, what shall we feed them tonight for dinner?"

Betheyn answered from the hearth. "Dragon-bane soup with cactus-needle bread."

"Any black-cap mushrooms around?" Alasen asked. "We could make a lovely Nightmare Stew."

"Don't forget the ground glass in the wine," finished Sionell.

"Ladies, ladies!" Sioned chided. "Subtlety in all things, if you please. Beth, do you know anything about cooking a few haunches of elk that have seen better days?"

"You mean how to make it edible?" she snorted. "Do you honestly think these people would know the difference—or even care?"

"Point taken. Do what you can with enough to feed us, then, and warn poor Ruala and Isriam not to have much appetite. Sionell, I'll need your help with the soup. You make the basics, and then I'll play with it a little." Suddenly she laughed. "Oh, how Rohan would've loved it! Me, who can't even brew a decent cup of taze, cooking for hundreds!"

"I'll get started on the bread," Alasen offered. "I've never baked for hundreds, either. I just hope I remember how much beer makes it rise—and how much makes it explode!"

Sioned exchanged a glance with her Namesake, who nodded and cleared her throat to gain the others' attention. "After Sioned finishes with the soup, don't go near it. Don't taste it. Not even a drop. We have a little something planned. We worked it out at Feruche."

"How little?" Beth asked.

"Let's just say," she drawled, with a feline smile on her face, "that the garderobes are going to be very crowded tonight."

"*Belmayce* has that effect," Sioned added.

"*Bel—?*" Alasen gasped, half on laughter and half on surprise. "Forget the garderobes, they'll be using the bathtubs as chamberpots! Riyan and Ruala won't thank you for this, Sioned. They'll have to stay at Feruche or Elktrap until the stink airs out!"

"Sometime next Winter, I'd say," Beth chuckled. "When will it take effect?"

"They should start to feel it around midnight."

It was nearly dusk by the time Sionell pronounced the soup ready. "I've put enough whitespice into it to mask any flavor."

Sioned nodded. Taking the sack of *belmayce* she'd removed from Ruala's stores at Feruche, she began to measure it into the huge cauldron.

"One for health, two for a cure, and three for a purge to last all night long," Sionell said as she watched the powdered herb sift into the soup. "At least, that's what my mother used to say when she dosed anyone stupid enough to complain of an upset stomach. She used pinches, though."

"I should hope so!" Beth said. "Alasen, do you need help with the bread?"

"Done by dinnertime. You know, if I ever get tired of being a princess, I may have a career waiting for me as a master baker."

"You could name your wage and get rich in a year," Sionell agreed. She looked at Sioned then, and caught her staring at the swirls of yellowish powder vanishing into the soup. "Wishing it was poison?" she murmured.

Sioned gave a start. "Actually, I was thinking about when Ostvel lived here. Years and years ago. I've always been a disaster at anything domestic—Cami ran Stronghold for me and Ostvel continued after she died. But when Rohan gave him Skybowl, he found that Lord Farid had two roasting pans and three kettles to his name, and that was all. So he ordered up everything you see here now, and sent us the reckoning—saying that if he absolutely *had* to become our vassal, we could damned well pay for the privilege of eating at his table." She gestured at the array of copper and silver and steel. "I was remembering when all of this was new."

"Sounds just like him," Alasen chuckled. "And speaking of tables, I think it's time we set them."

The plates and cups were already stacked, waiting to be carried in. Sioned stayed behind while the other three went to the great hall. When their footsteps had faded, she again dipped the measuring cup into the sack of *belmayce*.

She had thought, back at Feruche, that she would do this for the living, that they might have their lives back to live in peace. But now she thought only of the dead. What she did was for them.

For Myrdal, who ought to have died peacefully in her own bed at Stronghold.

For Morwenna, killed by iron, and Relnaya, the same—and for Morwenna's Elidi, butchered.

For Meath—oh, Meath, friend and protector. . . .

For those from Faolain Lowland—Miral, Kemeny, Gevnaya, Pelida—who died with Baisath and Michinida at Riverport.

For Tallain. . . .

For Lyela of Waes, who deserved better than to have Kiele for a mother.

For Jahnavi, son of Walvis and Feylin, brother of Sionell—and for his gentle Rabisa, too gentle not to break in this Vellanti storm, and for their little girl, Sioned's Namesake, Siona.

For Segelin and Paveol and Edrelin, dead at Gilad Seahold.

For Latham and Hevatia, and for her kinsman Volog, who died of his grief at their deaths.

For Halian of Meadowlord—Parchment Prince, who deserved better than murder at his own son's hands.

For Rialt and Mevita, executed at Swalekeep, and their Sunrunner whose name she did not even know, slaughtered in secret.

For Cluthine, Lady of Meadowlord, also dead by treachery.

For Kostas, her brother's son, fallen to a Merida knife.

For Rihani—son of her brother's son, who killed the Merida who killed Kostas.

For Kerluthan of River Ussh, dead defending what Chiana and Rinhoel would have given away to the enemy.

For Brenlis, first of the *faradh'im* to die, fey child of seeings and dreams.

For Oclel and Rusina, Sunrunners, Sioned's own kind, and for Valeda, whose courage had not saved her.

And even for Edirne and Camanto of Fessenden, who would be alive if not for this war.

For all whose lives were stolen—and for all the grief and pain these savages had caused.

She hesitated.

But not for Rohan.

Not for you, beloved. You would want no part in what I do here tonight. So this last is not for you.

It is for me.

She threw the empty sack onto the hearthfire. It caught, flared, and burned to ash just as Sionell, Alasen, and Betheyn returned to the kitchen.

Sioned turned to them and smiled. "That was quick work."

*

"Power exists," Aldiar snapped at Idalian. "Like everything else, it can be both good and evil. *Dranath* both kills and cures—but do we eradicate it for being guilty of the one and ignore that it's essential for the other? Evil and goodness in the same substance. It all depends on how you use it."

Idalian hunkered into his cloak as teasing fingers of chill wind stroked into their little tent. "You couldn't possibly have thought up something so trite on your own. Is it standard *diarmadhi* teaching?"

"The way you were taught that all sorcerers are always evil?" he retorted. "Trite, is it? What do you know about power?"

Rohannon judged it time to intervene. "I understand what you're saying, Aldiar. It's the choices we make about using the good and bad parts of ourselves." He shivered, and not entirely because he was the one nearest the open tent flap. "It's hard to admit mistakes, especially when they're based on our own flaws."

"So you learned that, did you?" Black eyes smiled at him, taking the sting from the words. "I guess you're not hopeless after all."

"Thanks," he said sourly. "But what you said about everyone being taught that all sorcerers are evil—that'll be hard to get around after this is over."

Idalian stiffened. "My attitude being evil in and of itself, you mean?"

"No," Rohannon hurried to say. "Not at all. It's how everybody else feels, too, you know."

"And that's what's so stupid," Aldiar burst out. "The ones with Yarin—they think the rest of us couldn't take over an empty barn, let alone a princedom. But look at how they've gone about it. No more subtlety than a rabid wolf."

"Whereas *you*," Idalian purred, "are past masters at—"

"Come on," Rohannon interrupted. "He's on our side, remember?"

Idalian only shrugged.

"Subtle," Aldiar said. "Who do you think worked to get Lisiel married to Laric, and Iliena to Ludhil? The heirs to both Firon and Dorval are *diarmadh'im*. If we'd wanted, we could've put tutors and riding masters and any kind of servant you care to name within their households, and coaxed them in whatever direction we liked!"

"How do I know you didn't?"

"Because we don't want that kind of power! All we want is to live in the open, in peace—"

"So that's why you were so concerned with keeping Tirel alive!"

The younger boy fisted both gloved hands, looking murderous. Idalian's fingers twitched toward his belt-knife.

Both of them got a snowball in the face.

"All right, that's enough!" Rohannon exclaimed as they sputtered furiously. "Idalian, that attitude is going to get perfectly innocent *diarmadh'im* persecuted and maybe even killed! And as for you—" He glared at Aldiar. "If this is your idea of 'subtle,' Goddess help you and all your people!"

"What's the commotion? Any trouble?"

All three looked up as Arlis trudged through the snow toward their shelter.

"None, my lord," Rohannon said, with a quick glance at the others to emphasize it.

"Snowball fights are good exercise for keeping warm, I suppose," Arlis commented, not believing Rohannon for an instant but willing to let it go. "Maybe Laric should challenge Yarin to a duel."

"Is there any response from Balarat, my lord?" Idalian asked.

"Nothing. We assemble for battle tomorrow at dawn. I'd appreciate it if you'd spread the word. Aldiar, Prince Laric would like to see you."

"At once, my lord." He scrambled up and crunched away through the snow.

"No trouble," Arlis murmured, eyeing the two young men. "Good."

Rohannon held himself from a guilty squirm, wondering at the same time what he had to feel guilty about. "Do you want me to tell my father about tomorrow's battle, my lord?"

"Maarken has enough to worry about, I should think." He chafed his fingers together and looked over his shoulder at the castle on the brow of the hill. "Tomorrow will be an interesting day all the way around," he went on. "But I confess I have only one personal objective. I can't *wait* to get warm again."

Getting to his feet, Rohannon flashed an impish grin up at his prince. "Will that make it into the ballads, too?"

✳

Alasen practically skidded to a stop on the kitchen floor tiles. "Ell! Sioned! Hurry—you've *got* to see this!"

"The vegetables—" Sionell began.

"—can wait! They won't start eating for a long time yet. Come on!"

The two women dusted their hands on their aprons and followed Alasen through the torchlit passage to the great hall. She stopped just within the shadow of the door, in view of the high table and the assembled warriors beyond. Ruala, Beth, and Isriam were there, too, staring in silence.

"No bonfire this evening," Sioned murmured.

"After last night's, do you wonder?" asked Beth.

The High Warlord stood on the raised step before the high table. A white-garbed priest who had not been with the others the previous night stood beside him. Both his arms were raised, shortening his robe to expose skinny bare feet and ankles. Sioned bit back a smirk, then lost all urge to merriment as warriors began to separate from their fellows. Scores of them came forward from the disciplined ranks: mute, meek—and on their knees.

Sioned felt her eyes start from her head.

Ruala whispered, "He called down the gaze of the Storm God on them, to judge their worthiness in battle. I'm not clear on some of the words—I only reviewed what I had to in order to understand some of Grandfather's scrolls. Then he described the Hells waiting for those who are unclean."

"Something lingering, I hope." Sionell's voice was half-strangled with astonishment at the display before them.

As more and more Vellant'im crawled into line down the center of the hall, Ruala went on, "All those who are unclean—or maybe 'guilty'—his accent is simply foul—they're to come forward, ask forgiveness, and be cleansed."

"Thus made worthy of killing the Storm God's enemies," Beth interpreted.

"That's not all," Ruala said. "The High Warlord told them that anybody who stays back knowing himself unclean will be executed on the spot. The priest will know."

Alasen, who had slipped away to a window, returned and leaned close to Sioned. "The line of them stretches halfway around the lake!"

With a casual calm she didn't feel, she replied, "Then somebody'd better go back to the kitchen and see that dinner doesn't burn." She had no intention of missing this herself; it was like reading the absurd legends in Feylin's dragon book, only come to life before her eyes.

Isriam vanished down the hallway. A good lad, Sioned thought absently. If Pirro didn't recognize that and recognize *him* as a Prince of Fessenden . . . she'd personally convince him otherwise.

Four other priests stepped forward. One carried a golden fingerbowl—one of Ruala's, Sioned noted, used at the high table—from which drifted a flower-scented column of white smoke. The second held a large pitcher of water. The one beside him grasped a fat white candle between his hands. The last bore a large plate heaped with thick crystals.

"Salt?" Alasen guessed.

"Air, Water, Fire, Earth," Ruala murmured. "But what are they going to do with them?"

The first of the warriors reached the high table. The priest spread his hands, gripped the man's head with his fingertips, and glared down into his eyes. Sioned saw the pallid marks left on the man's dark forehead as the priest let him go. A nice trick, that, she thought; the white prints of the white priest. She was even more impressed—in a detached, intellectual way, she insisted to herself—as the High Warlord extended a hand to help the warrior to his feet.

You have been judged worthy, the gesture said. *And I accept you as my servant in battle.*

Signs and symbols, Sioned mused, even worse than the Isulk'im. As a second warrior took his place before the priest, the first did what she had guessed he would to. He inhaled incense, sipped water, passed his hand through the candleflame, and took grains of salt from a golden spoon onto his tongue. But his mighty grimace at this last set Sioned to wondering.

"Can you *believe* this?" Ruala muttered, shaking her head.

"They do," Sionell replied.

The incense was obvious: Air to cleanse the mind. Water purified the body. The hand-through-the-flame had been the right hand, the sword-hand. That above all must be without taint for battle. But the reaction to salt, repeated by every man who partook of it, that one defeated her.

Why screw up your face like that, with only a few grains on the tongue? It couldn't have tasted that awful. The salt stood for Earth, that much was easy. It was white, and white was the priests' color. But why so emphatic a reaction?

"The salt," Sionell breathed at her side, and Sioned gave her a startled glance. "Of course. Salt is bitter."

"What?" But in the next moment she understood. Bitter, sharp, a powerful jolt to a delicate and evocative sense.

"That's why they're exaggerating the taste. It's a reminder of how terrible it was to sin."

Beth nodded slowly. "What could be more bitter to a superstitious people than being unclean in the sight of their priests and their High Warlord?"

"No—their god," Ruala said.

Barbarians, Sioned thought. *You could lead these people anywhere because they're blinded by their superstitions. They believe in magic and sin and Pol's influence over dragons—and, if we've read them right, in dragon's teeth and blood and all the rest of it. And we* have *read them right. We* can *trick them using their beliefs.*

It occurred to her suddenly that she'd love to hear their songs, their legends, their poetry. She was certain the complexity would dazzle her—as it undoubtedly dazzled them, but for different reasons. The stories she'd heard all her life were probably just as exciting, and just as improbable. But she *knew* them to be stories. All she needed for proof was the way Ostvel—who'd been there and knew perfectly well what really happened—had embroidered the tale of the *Rialla* of 698, justifying his fancywork by saying it was Sinar and Siona he sang about. *"Never let the truth get in the way of a good story,"* he grinned when she and Rohan reacted with embarrassed outrage on first hearing the ballad.

All songs and legends were like that. Moral or political lesson, cautionary tale or heroic saga, love lyric or drinking ballad, hilariously funny or poignantly sad—none was to be taken as literal truth. Everybody knew that.

The Vellant'im evidently believed *everything*. Well, they'd been given plenty to believe—Azhdeen's appearance at Remagev and the use Rohan had made of it and the Sunrunners' Fire; her own conjuring at Faolain Lowland; Pol's visit here last night; the dragon book. They'd swallowed all of it whole.

Contempt dissolved when Sioned glanced at the High Warlord again. His warriors followed him blindly, unthinkingly. Not the way people followed Rohan and Pol, with their eyes wide open and believing with their minds as well as their hearts. But what did it matter *why* a leader was trusted, as long as the trust existed? It might disgust her that fear and superstition united these people, but they'd done damned well so far.

That, she told herself, was about to change. What united them would be their downfall.

She watched hundreds of Vellant'im kneel to their priest, be raised up by their High Warlord. They breathed incense, drank water, touched fire, and tasted salt, positive that by abasing themselves their deity would reward them with victory—just like in all the legends.

Ostvel wouldn't have to embellish this for a ballad. Why bother? Life was usually more improbable than legends, after all.

Legends were just tidier.

*

Just after nightfall, with the stars shimmering across the moonless sky, seven hundred riders stopped for a brief rest and a hasty dinner. Pol and Maarken rode through the loose ranks with a word for every man and woman present, for between them they knew them all.

An odd quiet seemed to tag behind them at a dozen riders' remove. At last, near the back, they heard the reason for the following silence.

Andry was singing. Softly, unobtrusively, but his voice carried in the clear Desert air. As Pol and Maarken returned to the front lines, the words were discernible.

He sang of the beauty of the day just ended and the dawn promised on the morrow. He sang of the Goddess and her many kindnesses, the welcome light of Fire and the sweetness of Water and clean Air and generous Earth. It was an old song and a lovely one, and Pol nearly added his own voice to it.

Andry had changed the ending verses.

Pol froze in his saddle. Maarken wouldn't look at him. When Andry was finished, and a sigh breathed here and there, Pol rode forward to where his cousin stood.

A fingerflame danced gracefully at Andry's shoulder, lighting one side of his face. He looked up at Pol, and all the serenity fled his eyes.

"It wasn't for me, Pol. It was for them."

Pol knew he was perfectly sincere. Andry hadn't wanted to draw attention to his own position or his power. He truly wanted to give their people comfort.

Still, his voice was cold as he replied, "You weren't asking the Goddess for victory. You asked her to help us kill."

Andry arched a sardonic brow. "Considering what we must do tomorrow, is there any difference?"

Yes, damn you—

—no.

Pol jerked the reins around and rode away.

*

After the first hundred or so Vellant'im went by, Sionell returned to the kitchen. She told herself that it was boredom, and the demands of keeping the meal reasonably edible. "Go watch if you like," she told Isriam, "I'll take care of things here."

Once she was alone with the bubbling cauldrons, Alasen's stacked loaves of bread (only a little burned around the edges), and the eight huge wheels of cheese, she could admit that the spectacle in the great hall had made her sick.

It was impossible to imagine any man she knew on his knees like that. Her father, Maarken, Chay, Riyan, Tilal, Andry—they'd rather die.

But Pol would do it, she thought as she started slicing bread. *He'd crawl on his knees all the way from Feruche to Skybowl. He's more arrogant than any three of them put together, and yet he'd do it if it would save lives. They could never humble him, never break him. His pride could withstand anything. He simply wouldn't care. Look what he did last night—of all the damnfool hopeless stunts! And he meant every word of it, too.*

Anybody else would have used the power of the mirror to terrify, even to kill. But not Pol. Oh, no. He must try to reason with the enemy, with their terror a result of Alasen's Fire-calling and not his deliberate design.

Idiot. Hadn't he been able to think up a more effective use of the mirror?

Tallain would've understood perfectly, she thought. *Tallain would've approved what Pol said. He would've done the same thing himself, if he'd been able.* But not because his arrogance was impervious to scorn. Tallain never experienced an instant of arrogance in his life. As unlike as he and Pol were, yet they would still have agreed on what must be done and said.

And this made her admiration for both men either completely logical or utterly insane. They arrived at the same place from opposite directions. Did that make them more alike, or less? Did it justify what she felt for Pol, or make mockery of her love for Tallain?

Bread finished, she started on the cheese, not caring if it crusted over by the time the Vellant'im completed their ceremony. She didn't give a damn what they ate, as long as they ate the soup. It would keep them from any fight more serious than who got to the garderobe first.

She could have told Pol that reasoning with the Vellant'im was futile. Anyone could have told him that. And yet, in a perverse way, she admired him more for what he had tried and failed to do than for anything he had ever succeeded at. Alasen had been right: doomed as the attempt might be, at least he had tried.

She'd give good odds, though, that failure had surprised him. Not closely acquainted with personal defeat, was the sorcerer-Sunrunner High Prince. How it must gall him.

Dangerously close to compassion, Sionell impaled the last round of cheese with her knife and went to stir the soup. She had just dipped the long-handled spoon into the cauldron when once more Alasen raced into the kitchen, breathless and flushed.

"Oh, leave that!" she ordered. "If we climb the main tower, we'll get the best view—"

"Let me guess—they're imitating the dragons' Sand Dance."

"All right, then," Alasen said tartly. "Miss this if you like. But your mother will never forgive you if you can't tell her how it looked to see the legend of the dragon teeth come to life."

A hasty climb later, they joined Sioned and Betheyn on the uppermost floor of the keep. Just visible over the crater's rim, tiny pinpoint Fires were moving outward from a central conflagration as high as a dragon. In stately progression they spread to either side in an ever-widening line, and finally came to a halt when they spanned a quarter measure.

The Vellant'im lined the caldera, holding aloft torches and swords—like a single sinuous, fantastical creature with fluttering gold and silver feathers, Sionell thought, fascinated.

Each sorcerer—and there were well-nigh a hundred of them, all in dark colors—lifted something sharp and white. Sionell knew they were only pottery shards. But from a distance. . . .

The individual Fires fell with the dragon's teeth into the sand. Abrupt darkness ensued, but for the central flames. Then new Fires were kindled, several steps back. New shards were produced, displayed, and dropped with the tiny flames. The sequence repeated seven more times for a total of nine.

By the fifth, Vellanti warriors were screaming with rage that didn't mask their fear.

Sioned was laughing quietly to herself. "Totally unnecessary, of course, with what I've got ready—but it makes a delightful show, doesn't it?"

"Where did they all come from?" Sionell wondered. "You only brought nine or ten to Feruche, didn't you, Beth?"

"Nine. With another ninety left at Chaldona. I suppose they decided to join the fun."

"They're lucky the whole horde of Vellant'im isn't descending on them," Sionell said. "Or was Pol really that convincing as the *Azhrei?*"

Sioned leaned her elbows on the windowsill and cupped her chin in her palms. "Andry's the lucky one, actually. I doubt that even with help he could conjure up—what, nine times ninety-nine warriors? Good thing he won't have to."

The *diarmadh'im* finished their work and the central Fire vanished as if it had never been. So did they, back into the starlit night whence they'd come.

"Dinnertime," Sioned announced sweetly. Then she chuckled low in her throat. Something about the sound grated on Sionell's nerves. "Rohan, my devious darling lord and husband, I do hope you're watching this!"

✴

One more ceremony was performed that night. At Goddess Keep, Torien and Jolan called for silence in the refectory and spent much breath and time honoring the Goddess and beseeching her protection. The chanted responses from hundreds of Sunrunner throats echoed long after the pair sat down again—Torien in Andry's chair.

Edrel, four places down from him, maintained stony silence. Norian's lips stayed closed in a thin line of sheer annoyance. They had been invited to share the meal, but both knew it was really to be impressed with the power and majesty of the invocation.

As, much later, they made their way back upstairs to Elsen's chamber, Norian hissed, "That woman's idea, surely as the sun rises!"

"I was talking with Antoun about her the other day," Edrel murmured. "Jolan bore Torien a stillborn son about ten years ago, after someone caught her up in a working that went awry. She hasn't conceived since."

"And she blames Andry for it? But she's one of his *devr'im,* married to his Chief Steward!"

He shrugged. "For an ambitious Sunrunner, what better place than Andry's inner circle?"

Norian said nothing as they crossed from one wing into another through a long, open hallway. It wasn't until they were outside her brother's room over the library that she whispered, "Edrel—she wants Torien to be Lord of Goddess Keep. And this is her chance."

"She wouldn't dare."

"No?"

He shrugged uncomfortably. "All right, yes. She'd dare. I'll just have to be careful about falling into any traps." He snorted. "Lovely, isn't it? First I have to tiptoe the line between supporting Jayachin's lies and the Sunrunners', and now I'm defending Andry's position against his own people. Nori, my love, when this is all over, would you mind very much if we went home to River Ussh and didn't leave it for, say, twenty years?"

She slipped her arm through his. "Sounds perfect."

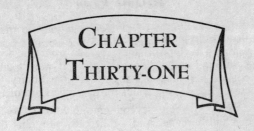

CHAPTER THIRTY-ONE

"Look at us, skulking around the fire," Sioned mused. The six of them sat drinking taze and waiting for the Vellant'im to return—to a dinner none of them would want after the spectacle of the dragons' teeth. "Two Sunrunners, a *diarmadhi,* the daughters of an architect and a dragon-counter, and a Prince of Fessenden, huddling beside a kitchen hearth."

"No, my lady—somebody who might *become* a Prince of Fessenden," Isriam corrected.

"I wouldn't worry too much about it," Sioned advised with a smile. "Your grandsire owes me a favor or three."

Isriam had outgrown his last adolescent gawkiness at Chaldona, and his beard was heavy enough for daily razoring, but she had continued to think of him as a boy until this moment. He met her gaze with quiet dignity and said, "Thank you, your grace, but I'd rather have him acknowledge me because he wants to, not because he has to."

"Of course. I'm sorry," Sioned returned gravely. "However, Pirro isn't stupid. Not only are you the son of his eldest son—and why he passed over Camanto in favor of Edirne always escaped me—but you're eminently worthy."

"Didn't you know?" Alasen asked. "About Camanto, I mean. Pirro intended him to be the next ruling prince all along. But he didn't think it should come easily, the way everything else did for Camanto."

"Death didn't," Sionell murmured. "Not to hear Rohannon's report of it."

Ruala turned to him, her words low and intense. "Isriam,

that's going to have to be part of your job—to make sure Pirro doesn't kill all the *diarmadh'im* he can find because of what one of them did to his son."

"Your father," Sioned added softly, watching the boy's— young man's—clear brown eyes.

He understood the look, and said what she'd hoped he'd say. "I came to know several *diarmadh'im* rather well at Chaldona and Feruche. And we all know now that there are at least three factions."

"Three?"

"Those who killed Prince Camanto, rallied to Chiana and Rinhoel, and took Balarat. Those who work with us now— and seem to have worked for us in the past, even though we didn't know it. And those who either don't care or are too scared to choose either side."

Sioned nodded, but did not praise his reasoning. Rohan always *expected* the people around him to use their brains. "A search must be made through Princemarch, Firon, and Fessenden for just those people—so they'll know it's safe to live in the open."

"But what about the first group?" Beth asked worriedly. "After all they've done, how can they be allowed to go free? One of them killed Sorin, and another very nearly killed Pol. Those who believe with them are still at work—obviously. Look at Firon, as Isriam says."

Isriam got to his feet. "And how do we tell the difference? Excuse me, my ladies, it's time somebody checked to see if the Vellant'im are coming back."

Sioned watched him go, wondering why the notion had hit him so suddenly.

"You're right of course, Beth," Sionell was saying. "But try proving most of it. It's a pretty problem, I grant you. Do we conduct a purge and hope we're right, or simply pardon all of them and hope for the best?"

"Here's another one for you," Ruala put in. "They have power. Shall they be trained in their craft? How? And where? Goddess Keep?" She shook her head. "The Sunrunners will never stand for it."

"By whom you mean Andry," said Alasen. "But Riyan learned there—"

"—before anyone knew what he is. Torien, too, and Urival and Morwenna. Doubtless others are *diarmadhi* as well. But it's never been acknowledged in public. Would Andry do that? I doubt it."

"*He's* not stupid, either," Alasen defended. "Much better to have sorcerers within sight, learning what he wants them to learn, than hidden away. Besides, it's obvious that the Sunrunners can also learn a lot from the sorcerers."

Frowning, Sioned sat forward and leaned her elbows on her knees. "Rival centers of learning would produce exactly what goes on between Goddess Keep and the Physicians School in Gilad. I always thought that was one of our better schemes, Rohan's and mine, until people began thinking there was a difference in Sunrunner medicine. . . ." She sighed. "It seemed a good idea at the time."

"It was, and still is," Betheyn stated firmly. "It was only this—this ritualism and ceremony Andry introduced into all things *faradhi*—"

"Yes," Ruala interrupted, "and now there are *diarmadhi* rituals to be dealt with as well. Can they be incorporated into Goddess Keep? Will the Sunrunners even want to try? And what happens when a Sunrunner student is told there are certain things he can't do because he's not a sorcerer?"

Sioned eyed her. "You're making a very good case for keeping your own people out of the mainstream of our lives."

"Not a bit of it!" She shook back her untidy black braids. "We've seen what *that* brings—Mireva and Ruval, and now this trouble in Firon, and Goddess knows what else besides. I'm only trying to identify the problems to come."

"As if we didn't have enough already," Sionell observed wryly. "But I agree with you, Alasen. Andry's a lot of things, but stupid isn't one of them. He deigned to teach Maara and Jihan and Rislyn, after all."

Alasen and Beth stared blankly at her.

"You didn't know?" Sionell asked. "They're all *diarmadhi*."

"Not—not through Meiglan," Alasen ventured.

"Pol," said Sionell.

Sioned wrapped her hands around her cup. "It seems," she murmured, "that it's a night for secrets. The secret sins for which the Vellant'im are forgiven—but which you'll note they did not confess aloud. The secret of the dragon teeth . . . who we are, and what we're about to do to these people, and what will happen to them tomorrow."

"Pol?" Alasen's green eyes, so like Sioned's, asked to be told how such a thing could possibly be.

"Ruala knows," Sioned told her. "And Sionell—you've known longest, except for me and a few others. I'm afraid you bore the brunt of his anger and hurt. He must've been very cruel."

"To you," she replied. "He told me what he said to you that night."

"Nothing I didn't deserve, in a way." She glanced in turn at Alasen and Betheyn. "Pol is not my son. He is Ianthe's. That is one of the secrets I brought to Skybowl."

Before they could react, Ruala said, "If this is a night for them, then I learned one at Elktrap that perhaps you should know. I suppose it's what prompted my depressing little recital earlier." She sipped from her cup and stared into the flames. "Grandfather's grandmother was a Ruala, too. I was Named for her. She was ten when her great-grandfather Algroy died, and it was from him that she heard the tales she told my grandfather—to which my sister and I rarely listened. Algroy learned them from his grandfather Rossan. And he . . ." She drew a deep breath. "Rossan was the great-grandson of Lady Merisel."

"But—she was a Sunrunner," Sionell said. "So was her husband. When did their descendants marry into a *diarmadhi* line?"

"They didn't. Rossan's grandfather, Merisel's son, was a sorcerer. His name was Rosmer, and he wasn't Gerik's son. He was Rosseyn's."

"Good Goddess," Sioned breathed. The face in the mirror, that Ruala had shied from because he looked so much like her own father—

"I thought about telling Andry," Ruala went on meditatively. "Not that he'd believe me. But do you understand why I said what I did about the *diarmadhi,* and bringing them into the open? All of them? Do you see what Pol is? Not just High Prince, not just a Sunrunner, but *diarmadhi* as well—with every kind of power we know and respect. It makes him High Prince for all of us. And what he does with it tomorrow. . . ."

". . . will determine what kind of High Prince he'll be," Sionell finished.

"Almost by accident," whispered Alasen. "If the Vellant'im had never—"

Sioned poured more taze with a hand that shook only a little. "Rohan would say that there are no accidents." Andrade's rings, for instance—or, more accurately, the stones in them. Everyone had seen them for years, they'd been worn by each successive Lady and Lord of Goddess Keep, until Andry chose to make new rings with new stones and Urival chose to distribute the old ones among Andrade's friends and kin. Thinking of him, she spoke of him. "Urival always told me I was mind-hungry, and so I have been all my life. I've read and studied, educated myself—and been educated by experience—and now I sit here knowing that I know nothing at all." She sighed. "Except that there *are* no accidents, and we all have our own work to do."

"And Pol's," said Ruala, "is to be High Prince for everyone—Sunrunner, sorcerer, and commoner alike."

Sionell broke the small silence. "I think . . . I think he knows that, but he doesn't really believe it. Yet."

"Tomorrow may educate him," Sioned replied. She glanced around as voices and boot heels rang through the great hall. "It's time we educated the Vellant'im. Ladies, our immediate work is at hand."

✳

Careful not to come within touching distance of Meiglan, the priest deposited her dinner tray on the single chair and departed in silence. The door snicked shut behind him. Meiglan decided she didn't much like doors. Walls, either. In her tent she had been able to hear voices and see shadows. And there had been no locks.

They had brought her up here swathed in white veils so none might see her. She'd nearly tripped several times on the stairs, blinded by the silk swirling in front of her nose. She had never been in Skybowl's western tower, identifiable as servants' quarters by its convenience to the kitchen and the large common room on the first floor. She had never been so high in the keep, either—the very top of the tower.

The chamber was comfortable enough, considering the priests' strictures. The bed was sheeted in white silk, the single wooden chair draped in the same material. Hooks high in one wall meant a tapestry had hung there—removed, of course, for being too rich with color. Two iron braziers provided warmth in morning and evening chill, but very little light. The window had been nailed shut, more white silk tacked around the sill. Set into the opposite wall, a white-washed wooden door sealed the small garderobe. This amenity confirmed that the room belonged to a ranking servant.

But all of it was white, floor and walls and doors. Meiglan longed for colors like a Sunrunner gone suddenly blind.

Yes, she was comfortable enough. And trapped. Priests stood guard outside her door. Even if they hadn't, there were over two thousand Vellant'im between her and freedom.

She'd grown used to that over the last eleven days.

Still, she'd had her little vengeances. She smiled slightly, shredding crustless bread in her fingers. Back at Stronghold, she'd once refused to eat the food brought to her until whitespice (naturally) had been supplied. Carefully loading one side of the bowl with the pungent powder, she tasted the other and enthused about how good it was—and wouldn't her attending priest like to sample some? It had been in his black eyes that he hoped he'd finally managed to please her, and that he resented this emotion, as he dipped his own spoon into the colorless mess.

His eyes bulged half out of his head and for a few moments she expected steam to billow from his ears.

She had considered maiming herself in some way, flawing her skin with a cut or bruise, but what would be the point? They'd made it clear they wouldn't waste an otherwise perfectly good sacrifice on a technicality. During the initial inspection—a hideously embarrassing process, worse agony than a physician's examination—they'd found the small brown mark on her left hip. Scrubbing it off hadn't worked; bleaching it with some stinging cream availed nothing. Finally they had given her to understand that they had decided it was the Storm God's fingerprint or some other such nonsense. An indication of her fitness for the ritual.

She had only briefly thought of killing herself. But that would mean she had no faith in her husband's abilities. Pol would come for her. He would make everything all right.

And even if he didn't—treacherous, disloyal thought, but it had sneaked into her mind nonetheless—even if she died in this barbaric Vellanti ceremony, then afterward they would go home and leave her people in peace.

Her people. Not just Pol's, or Rohan's and Sioned's, or the various *athr'im*'s. Her own. It was a strange realization, that instead of just being their High Princess, they were her people. And if she could do this for them, if her death would free them. . . .

How noble I sound, she told herself, *and how defeated. That won't do.*

But it would happen tomorrow. She would live or she would die. And in this, was she so very different from her people?

Or from the Vellant'im, for that matter.

No, there was all the difference in the world. *They* would all have swords. She had nothing.

Except . . . the words she'd stitched *(Oh, Gentle Lady, make Pol understand!)* came back to her. Pol was her sword. He would come for her and kill all the Vellant'im and hold her to his heart and—

The door burst inward, the two priests outside gabbling in outrage. Meiglan jerked back in fear. A woman strode through and stopped dead in the center of the small room. For a moment, Meiglan recognized absolutely nothing about her. Then:

Sionell?

Blue eyes had no glance for her; they fixed instead on the tray set on the chair. Meiglan looked down, wondering in bewilderment what was so fascinating about it. The bread she'd picked apart, a goblet of water, a bowl of soup, a silver spoon—

Sionell fell to her knees on the rugless stone—not entirely of her own volition, Meiglan thought. "My lady," she breathed. "Thank the Goddess—"

The priests were still protesting. One of them almost grabbed Sionell's arm to haul her to her feet, but held back from soiling himself by touching a woman. Meiglan stared down at her friend's pale, strained face, where relief and anguish battled to a standstill.

"Get out," Meiglan told the priests.

None of her guardian priests spoke more than a few words of her language, but they'd heard this phrase often enough in the last eleven days to comprehend perfectly. This time they refused to budge.

"I told you to get out," she said, again softly, remembering how impressed she'd always been that none of the great ladies she knew ever shouted at servants. Tobin, Sioned, and Sionell saved that for their husbands, mainly; Hollis never raised her voice at all. Only women like Chiana had the bad

taste—and the fear of being disobeyed—to yell at underlings.

"Does this look like a man to you?" Meiglan asked the
priests in a quiet tone etched with acid.

They hesitated, then muttered between themselves, then
crossed the threshold to the hallway.

"Close the door," Meiglan ordered.

They did. She decided she liked doors again.

Sionell pushed herself to her feet. Hand shaking, she
picked up the soup bowl and spoon. The first she emptied
into the white ceramic chamberpot; the second she held in
her fist like a talisman.

"I got here in time," she whispered, running a thumb over
the clean, shining spoon.

Meiglan's eyes widened as Sionell struggled with tears.
Quickly she set the tray on the floor and rose, helping her
friend to the chair. "What is it? And whatever are you doing
here?"

"Not just me." She wiped her eyes with her left hand, the
right still gripping the spoon. "Alasen, Beth, Ruala,
Isriam—and Sioned."

It was Meiglan's turn to wilt, weak-kneed. She sat down
hard on the bed. "She shouldn't—none of you should be
here!"

"We had to. And it would've worked—it may still work—
except that the soup was white, and given only to the priests,
and that meant—"

"To me." Meiglan groped for Sionell's icy fingers.

"I thought, we all thought, it would just make them sick.
So they couldn't fight. We were laughing about it—Alasen
and I were laughing as we ladled it into the tureens—" She
shivered. "But then Beth ran in, almost screaming—one of
the priests had made a tray for *you*—" Clinging to Meiglan's
hand now, she squeezed her eyes tightly shut. "Sioned's
face—I thought she'd—it's *belmayce*. She planned it all
along and didn't—"

"Are you saying they're going to die?"

"By dawn. The priests. All of them." Her thumb scraped
against the spoon again, convulsively. "It was almost you,
Meggie—"

"It's all right. You got here in time." Meiglan had never
seen Sionell so jittery. She gently pried the spoon from rigid
fingers. It had bent slightly with the power of her grip.

After a few moments, Sionell managed to compose herself. "I'm sorry. I just—I don't even know how I got up here. Ruala said the priests are all in this tower, so I—but I don't know how I remembered that."

"It's all right," Meiglan said once more. "Oh, Sionell, it can't be real that you're here—for so long I've been—" Tears washed her voice away. She bent her head, ashamed.

Sionell's arms suddenly went around her. Meiglan felt the other woman tremble and knew that she was crying, too.

✱

Ruala had seen Betheyn race headlong from the great hall. Wanting desperately to follow, she forced herself to remain seated between Isriam and the High Warlord, and continued the pattern of deception she had been weaving for two days.

"The source of the dragon gold," she said, "is the innards of butchered dragons. The late *Azhrei* forbade killing them because he wanted to keep all the gold and jewels for himself."

"Jewels?" The High Warlord cocked a skeptical brow. There was amusement in his black eyes, the tolerant half-smile of an adult for a child's harmless flights of imagination.

"From the brain," Ruala said. "Every year at Rivenrock Canyon near Stronghold, a dragon was killed in secret. The gold in its belly and the jewels from its head were gathered for Rohan's coffers." She paused for a sip of wine. "Of course, Zehava—who was *azhrei* before Rohan—was smarter than he. By choosing only the largest and most powerful of sires, he gained even more gold and gems. The bigger the dragon, the more battles he'd survived, and the greater his age, the more treasure."

"Ah," said the High Warlord, spearing another chunk of elk meat with his knife.

"My husband's father, who held this castle for many years, had charge of the caves in Threadsilver Canyon. One has to dig, of course, but the generations of dragons who died in those caves left their bounty of gold and jewels along with their bones."

"And none of us ever saw any of it," Isriam put in resentfully. "No, all the riches went to the *Azhrei,* never to us. And if anyone was ever caught killing a dragon—" He gave an artful shudder.

Though the High Warlord might be unimpressed, the priest sitting next to him was riveted. He said nothing, and Ruala wasn't even sure how much of this little tale he understood, but "gold" and "jewels" and "dragon" registered on his face every time he heard the words.

✱

There was no interruption by infuriated priests. Sionell and Meiglan sat together quietly now, the storm of tears over, their varying stories told.

Except for one or two omissions on Sionell's part.

She steeled herself to speak of the one—for she would never confess the other and bring still more pain to Meiglan's soft, fawn-brown eyes.

"I forgot to tell you that Rislyn has a dragon," she said, keeping her hands easy and relaxed in Meiglan's. "It happened here at Skybowl. A little black female. Rislyn named her Lir'reia."

Meiglan smiled. "I suppose Jihan is jealous!"

She couldn't do it. She couldn't reveal the name's tragic significance.

"Well, yes," she admitted, grateful that her voice was steady, and that weeping had released so much of the tension. *But none of the guilt.* . . . "She thinks that since she knows something about Sunrunning, too, she ought to have a dragon as well."

Meiglan blinked. "Sunrunning?"

"There've been lessons at Feruche. After what happened with Chayla, we all felt that everyone who could be taught, should be. Even Meig!"

"He's—?"

"They tell me so." She sighed. "Goddess help me."

Her smile returned. "Yes, my scamp of a Namesake will make your life even more interesting now!"

"Oh, he can't do more than call a moment's Fire to a candle. He's too young to be concerned with learning to use power. Actually, Andry tends to bore him right to sleep!"

Children; a safe topic, now that Sionell had avoided Rislyn's blindness. It was something better told by Rislyn's father, anyway. Pol would know what to say, how to comfort Meiglan's grief. . . .

Pol was a topic Sionell had mostly avoided. She'd talked about Maarken's injury, the deaths of Meath and Kazander, Chayla's abduction. But briefly, just so Meiglan knew what had happened. She'd concentrated on the better news: the victories of Ostvel in Princemarch, Ludhil at Graypearl, Laric at Snowcoves, Tilal at Radzyn; Gemma's arrival with more troops; the tricks already played on the Vellant'im, and those waiting for them tomorrow. Meiglan had listened in breathless silence.

And then had told her own story.

Sionell had marveled at her composure, her matter-of-fact detailing of all that had happened to her. She faltered only twice: when she described the courage of Valeda and Thanys, and their deaths.

"He gave them honorable burning. I wasn't allowed to watch. And since I finished the cloak, I haven't been allowed to see or be seen by anybody but priests." She gestured to the bed, the chair. "White clothes, white sheets, white furniture, white everything . . . I've been wondering if I'm invisible."

Sionell pressed her hands. "You took a terrible chance with that cloak, Meggie—that we wouldn't be too stupid to understand. We very nearly were."

"No, I *knew* you'd see it. What I didn't know to tell you was the pearls. I only found out about them yesterday from a priest. They were stolen from the Vellant'im long ago. A group was sent to get them, but the sorcerer who had them was dying—so taking them back was easier than they'd planned. That was in 701, you see."

Sionell frowned, not seeing at all.

"They brought the Plague with them," Meiglan said, her voice as colorless as her surroundings. "One of their people had never had it. They didn't know he'd caught it from his children before they left—Ell, they brought it with them!"

"By accident," Sionell heard herself murmur. But— *"Rohan would say there are no accidents."* For they'd all learned about *dranath* then, hadn't they? Not everything, not what had nearly killed Rohannon, but—

"It's only a childhood disease for them," Meiglan went on dully. "A few days of illness. He laughed as he told me. He said maybe they should've saved the warriors the trouble of fighting us, because they could've sent children to do the killing and we'd be just as dead."

But that wouldn't have removed the *Azhrei*'s taint from the dragons. And sitting before Sionell was the means by which the Vellanti priests intended to accomplish this goal.

"What the priests have in mind is much more ambitious." Meiglan had followed—anticipated?—her line of thought. "Tomorrow they plan to use me to free the dragons from Pol's influence. I'll be taken to the highest point overlooking the Desert, and they'll use a golden knife. I told them gold is traditional. That way, if a Sunrunner comes near enough while working and they try to use the knife, it won't have any effect."

"You put us all to shame," Sionell blurted. "Not one of us would have thought of—"

Meiglan tilted her head. "I was trying to think like all of *you*." She hesitated, then lowered her gaze to their clasped hands. "I've . . . learned a lot. I used to play at being like you, Sionell—like Tobin and Hollis and your mother, and especially Sioned. I'm High Princess now, I should—"

"Oh, Meggie—"

"But when I ordered my half brothers killed, I started to learn how to *be* High Princess, not simply behave as if I were. Do you understand?" She glanced up, then away. "Alone like this . . . I found out what *I* can do. And—and I think that now . . . now I can finally be the wife and the High Princess that Pol needs."

✳

Sioned couldn't seem to get warm.

She sat so close to the fire that her cheeks felt scorched. She was sweating under the blanket draped around her shoulders. But she couldn't get warm, not for a long, long time.

We're all going to die for this, she kept thinking. *They're not idiots. They'll make the connection. Only the priests . . . but not Meiglan, please, not Meiglan!*

But they'll kill us for it. Alasen and Beth and Sionell and Ruala and Isriam—I've killed them as surely as I've killed the priests. As surely as I showed the Vellant'im how to kill Meiglan.

The warriors will live. And Pol will have to fight them to-morrow.

Clever High Princess. Clever Sioned.

Someone spoke at her shoulder. She ignored the sound, the words. A hand shook her into accepting them.

"—all right, she didn't touch it. Sioned, listen to me. When I got to her, Meiglan hadn't eaten anything. She's all right."

For now. They'll only kill her tomorrow, just as the dragon book told them. Clever Sioned. . . .

Another voice. Alasen's, perhaps. She didn't care. Meiglan's present safety was cupped between her hands, cherished—and trickling away like sand in the surety of her death tomorrow.

But she heard Sionell's reply as if the words were Fire in her mind.

"No, she's not scared at all. I didn't even think of it until she said it—but with all the priests dead, who's going to perform the ritual?"

With the priests dead. . . .

"And she's right," Sionell went on. "Would Andry allow anyone but *faradh'im* to sing the sun to rising?"

Blood surged to every fingertip, warm and alive. Warm again, and alive.

With the priests dead . . . chaos by midnight . . . Sionell now knew where Meiglan was being kept . . . Beth knew the ins and outs of Skybowl . . . riskier than her original plan but in her mind from the start. . . .

Sioned looked up. "Neither can they perform the ritual if the victim disappears."

✳

Arlis wasn't awake, but neither was he really sleeping. The fantasy he'd concocted to get him there had started out with all the ingredients for relaxation: a big bed, a soft mattress, piled quilts, and a hearthfire nearby in the darkness. Then half-dreams had taken over. A cascade of silky hair drifted over him, followed by a lithe form and a fragrance of starbriar. He sighed in luxurious delight and murmured his wife's name. Only Demalia smelled so good, felt so good—and knew precisely when, where, and how to touch him. And touch him she did . . . oh, yes. . . .

But the hand shaking his shoulder wasn't hers. He snarled into the lamplight and Laric's tense face. His breath steamed in the tent's icy air.

"My steward is here," Laric said. "We'll have to hear what she has to say."

A short time later the woman who had overseen Balarat for Laric and now presumably did the same for Yarin shivered beside the meager warmth of an iron brazier. Laric stood on its other side, next to the folding map table, the fingers of his right hand drumming intermittantly on parchment. The sound grated on Arlis' nerves.

"Well?" Arlis said, stamping his feet inside cold socks and colder boots. "Does Yarin yield?"

"I—I don't know, your grace. I came here on my own." The little fire underlit her face, sinking weird shadows into her eye sockets. "I don't want to die at their hands. That's what they said, my lord." She looked an appeal at Laric. "Anyone who didn't fight until he dropped would be killed where he stood. And by sorcery, not clean with a sword."

"So you decided you couldn't stand to serve them anymore?"

"I never did willingly, my lord, you must believe me. It tore my heart to see him treat the young prince so badly and seize his rights, and with those others to help him now—"

"How many?" Arlis asked.

"Hundreds," she whispered. "Hundreds. . . ."

"All *diarmadh'im?*"

"All." Shuddering, she yanked her cloak across her chest. "Everybody's frightened. That's why they'll fight, even though they don't want to. The death waiting if—"

Arlis exchanged a glance with Laric.

"So you were finally so frightened that you braved the snows and the night to come here," Laric said, fingers beating a rapid rhythm on the parchment. The annoyance was giving Arlis a headache. "You must believe very strongly that I'll win." He paused, his hand still. "Except, you know, I don't think you believe anything of the kind."

She gasped. "I'd rather die out here, clean, than by foul spells!"

"If you'll forgive the term," Arlis drawled, "dragon shit."

Laric nodded. "You're here to tell me I have no hope of winning. You're here to spread lies of *diarmadhi* strength so we'll be defeated before we raise our swords."

She made no reply to the accusations. Her dark eyes glazed over with tears that dripped down her cheeks. Then her gaze slid away and she stared dully at the map table.

"I don't blame you for it," Laric went on more gently, and Arlis repressed an impatient sigh. "Doubtless you're only doing what you were ordered to do, in fear of your life. Go back and tell them I'm not impressed. Tell them—"

Arlis interrupted, "Tell them they have until dawn to surrender or the death they promised will seem merciful compared to what *I'll* do to them."

Still she said nothing, did nothing but stare blankly. Laric cleared his throat, and Arlis just knew he was going to say something imbecilic about giving pardons to those who refused to fight with Yarin's troops. *Still hoping to win without any battles at all,* he thought. *This happens to be war, cousin.*

A small war burst into the tent in the skinny form of Aldiar. Black hair flying, knife in hand, the boy flung himself at the steward and toppled her. He had his knife at her throat before Laric could shout, "No!"

"Let her go!" Aldiar cried with total illogic. "Give her up or I'll cut her, I swear I will!"

"What in all Hells—?" Arlis started for them, bumped into Laric on the same mission.

When they righted themselves, Aldiar was climbing to his feet. He extended a hand to help the steward up. She was shaking violently, sobbing without tears. The *diarmadhi* steadied her, then sheathed his knife and turned to Laric.

"I'm sorry, my lord. I fell asleep when I shouldn't have. And I didn't think they'd try this. I was waiting to sense a shape-change."

Arlis stared at the boy, the steward, and Laric in turn. "I hope you're going to explain that."

"This woman was used by someone in the castle as their eyes and ears. Surely you know that the Sunrunners can do much the same thing?"

"Uh . . . yes. But I don't think it's done anymore. Is it?"

"How should I know?" Aldiar stopped, and added a quick, "—my lord. Sorry."

"Never mind. Go on."

"I'd been expecting a shape-change," Aldiar said again. "I would've felt that the instant she came into camp. But I didn't reckon on this." Raking lank hair from his face, he sighed and continued, "They wanted to see your battle plan. If you hadn't brought her in here, she would've found some way to get in anyway."

Laric glanced over at the map table. "I don't think they saw much," he said doubtfully.

"Even if they did, we can alter our plans," Arlis told him. "Aldiar, why did you say what you did? Why the knife?"

"Because if I'd used steel—iron—on her while they had hold of her, it would've *hurt*." He addressed the steward, who had shrunk back from him in stark terror. "I'm very sorry, but you must believe that it had to be done. You'll be all right now. They won't dare try to use you again."

"Who was it who did this to you?" Laric asked her.

"She won't be able to tell you, my lord," Aldiar said. "Any more than Princess Chiana knew it was Mireva who used *her.*"

The steward had gone pale as death. "You mean—you mean those sorcerers—they—did something to me and—"

"You're free of it now."

That assurance didn't keep her from sliding to the floor in a faint.

A little while later, when everything had been sorted out and a guard put on the steward for her own protection, Arlis stretched out on his bed of blankets and cloak once more. Laric extinguished the lantern. Only the soft glow of the brazier remained.

"Aldiar says that with luck, he won't have to find whoever worked the spell," Laric murmured. "Only that person can break it. . . ."

"With luck," Arlis agreed, "every damned one of them will be dead tomorrow. Had you given any consideration to how we'll manage it?" When the other prince stayed silent, Arlis nodded to himself. "Just as I thought. Me, neither."

"If they're worried enough to make this attempt—"

"Uh-huh."

"Arlis. . . ."

"We've done all right so far, haven't we? Something will occur to us between now and morning. Go to sleep, cousin."

But Arlis lay awake until dawn, courting Demalia back into his dreams without success.

✳

The High Warlord had no time for sleep. At midnight he was still reviewing his own battle plans, sipping from a silver winecup and wishing Varek was with him. He understood his commander's choice to die; after the failure at Swalekeep, even though it didn't matter in the larger scheme, Varek could not in honor have chosen to live.

But he did miss the man. Boyhood friend, kin-by-marriage through his daughter and Varek's son—who would, of course, have to die for his father's shame. All his children would be killed, to remove the taint of failure from Vellanti blood. That was the way of things.

Still . . . perhaps the priests could be persuaded otherwise. Much power would come to the High Warlord when the *Azhrei* was dead. And it hadn't been Varek's fault that Tilal, without honor, had tricked him so foully.

There was no such thing as an honorable defeat.

Pity, he thought as he fought the coming battle again in his mind, staring down at the map. His daughter would weep and plead, being fond of the boy despite his uselessness at the warrior's craft. But someone had to keep the slaves working efficiently, and though Varek's son had never been much good with a sword, he was a marvel with the whip.

This reminded him that Varek's possessions and property would also be forfeit. A goodly portion would come to him through his daughter. The mines, he decided, and whichever of the wives it pleased him to make his own servants. He seemed to recall that one of them was a fine seamstress. . . .

And that made him recall the *Kir'reia*.

Her slim fingers wielding the needle, her golden head bent over her work, her delicate face raised to his as he entered her tent . . . the velvet darkness of her eyes in the pale, milky dawn-glow of her skin.

A waste. Like Varek. A stupid, stupid waste. And all because the priests declared that the sin of defeat was on the commander's shoulders—and the sin of the *Azhrei*'s power over the dragons must be cleansed with the White Sacrifice's blood.

Yes, he told himself, a single ship for them, and an "accident" to sink it. Then all he would have to deal with would be those priests either too old and feeble or too young and unsanctified to have come here with him.

His head snapped up as someone had the temerity to pound on his door. He had barely parted his lips to order the intruder to be gone when a figure in a stained, foul-smelling white robe staggered in and collapsed on Lady Ruala's bed-chamber carpet.

"Dying—" the man wheezed, and a spasm curled him double. The stench grew worse. "Storm Father, h–help us!"

"*Who* is dying? Tell me!"

"All—of us—" The priest writhed in agony, arms clasped around his belly, his eye-whites blood-red.

"The priests? What of the warriors?"

He stared up at the High Warlord for a single lucid moment of shocked betrayal. "Only priests, only—ahhh—!"

Foulness gushed from his body. The High Warlord strode past into the hallway, avoiding the green-black liquid staining the carpet. He didn't run; he would not be seen to run as if he had panicked.

Only the priests. No warriors.

It occurred to him that someone might just have done him a favor.

Long before he reached the western tower he could smell the stink of mortal sickness. Something had rotted the priests' bowels—scant wonder, he thought, resisting the urge to cover his nose and mouth, when they ate only white bread and bloodless meats.

White.

He could see it as if it was before him again: the huge serving bowls carried out by Lady Ruala's women, claimed by the priests. . . .

The rest of the castle was stirring now. Clanmasters honored by rooms within Skybowl were waking, poking their heads from doorways. There were no guards; what need of them in a keep they controlled from towers to cellars?

A mistake much worse than Varek's. A trick reeking of more dishonor than Tilal's. A woman's trick.

He saw several clanmasters drinking and dicing in the feast hall, and bellowed, "Lady Ruala and her people—bring them here!"

"At once, great lord!"

He reached the west tower and stepped over the dead and dying on the stairs. He didn't hear their groans. He no longer even smelled their fetid leavings. *Not the* Kir'reia, *not her,* he thought, unable to bear that she should be convulsing in this same agony, this foulness.

The two priests outside her door were dead. The door itself was wide open. Terrible sounds issued from inside; thin, high-pitched wails like those of a dying animal.

She huddled in the far corner of her bed, as pale as the sheets she clutched in shaking hands. Her horrified eyes were black in the whiteness of her face. A priest lay on the stone floor in his own excrement and vomit. The stench was overpowering.

But *she* was untouched.

The priest opened death-dazed eyes. *"Azhrei,"* he breathed, blood smearing his mouth. "Spells ... evil ... sin to k–kill priest—"

"And she has killed a hundred," said the High Warlord.

"Failed," whimpered the priest. " ... power ... too much. . . ."

"Yes," the *Azhreia* said in a clear, steady voice. She rose from the bed, slender and white and golden, like a pure candleflame. "My husband's power is too great. It has killed them—but protected me."

He prodded the weakly spasming figure with his boot. "Did she eat what you ate tonight? Did she?"

"He can't tell you. He's dead."

He caught her gaze with his own. No defiance shone in her eyes, only a vast serenity that infuriated him.

"Poison, not power! You ate nothing!"

"Prove that to your warriors," she answered. "Tell them that as they burn a hundred priests."

Mindless gratitude that she was alive and unhurt became a raging need to tear her tongue from her throat and her eyes from her head. He had never wanted anyone's death so much in his life as he wanted hers now.

Yet he did not move. Dared not think that perhaps he *could* not move.

They confronted each other for a fragment of eternity that shattered when a woman's voice called Meiglan's name. She spun, white silk robe swirling. Another fair-haired woman, older and green-eyed, slid halfway out of the garderobe, work-reddened hands gripping the wooden door.

"No!" cried the *Azhreia*. "Go back!"

The High Warlord leaped over the priest's body, lunging for the door handle. He grabbed it with one hand and the woman's arm with the other. She gasped, but not with pain.

"Ell, it's him! Close it!"

He hauled her forward and squinted into the darkness behind her, wild speculation distracting him. Sudden light flared from a brazier behind him and he caught a glimpse of a tall, lithe form and masses of dark red hair. *Not her—not the other* Kir'reia, *her hair is—*

She vanished into the stone wall.

As the bonfire had done the night before, now the flames of the brazier surged and spat, filling the room with fire. Startled—and enraged by the emotion—he let go of the woman and flattened himself against the window. Seen through the flames between them, the *Azhreia*'s eyes shone like black glass flung still burning from Dragonfire Mountain.

The green-eyed woman sidestepped the corpse and took the *Azhreia*'s hand, urging her from the room. The High Warlord saw the imminent escape of his prize and roared denial. Magic and fire be cursed, they would not have her. He ripped his sword from its sheath. A careless elbow smashed back through the window. Ignoring the shards that pricked his flesh, he took two steps toward the flames—*no heat, no substance—unreal? Unreal!*—and lunged for the green-eyed sorceress.

She yelped with pain as steel scored her arm. The flames vanished, sucked into the brazier. The high Warlord gained the door in two more long strides and rammed the sword back into the scabbard.

They were trembling, both of them, well and truly frightened. But still proud. He admired that about the women of this land, even as he knew it was unnatural.

"Come," he said in their language.

Frightened, helpless, bleeding—but proud, damn them for it—they followed.

CHAPTER
THIRTY-TWO

She was not what he had thought. She was more.

That it *was* she, he had no doubt. He watched her, standing there with humble shoulders, rough clothes concealing the lines of her body, a gray cloth concealing her hair. It had been wrapped to suggest that the bulk of it was knotted at her nape, but he knew better. He had a strand of it. He had smoothed its silken length between his fingers.

He wondered if she knew that despite the clothing and the posture she gave herself away. He wondered how he had not seen it before, while she was serving his men. Memory envisioned the betraying grace; no common servant would have moved so, every gesture music, every bone and muscle contributing to a harmony that could never be muted, even by graceless clothes.

Ah, but who would have suspected that the *Azhreia* would be here among her enemies? Not just pride in these women, courage.

Such a waste.

She was still beautiful. He had expected that, but not the manner of it. Hers was not the mature beauty of a lovely woman growing older. He could still see her youth in her face, a time when her skin had been perfect and her hair untouched by gray. She was not an older woman who had retained her looks in subtly altered form; she was a young woman on whose face age had imposed itself with reluctance, drawing a line here, changing a contour there, as if the commands of time had been only minimally obeyed.

But he did not notice those things until he recovered from

the shock of her eyes: deep and sharp as a faceted emerald, pure green with no hint of gray or brown. There were lines, and the lids were parchment-thin, but the eyes were young and vivid like the eyes of a hunting cat. Knowledge that he was her intended prey brought a slight smile to his lips and a secret excitement to his heart—and he was honest enough with himself to admit that the latter contained an element of fear.

How he envied her husband. Forty years of this woman—by all the dead and living gods, the *Azhrei* must have been a remarkable man, to have kept such a woman for forty years.

But the old *Azhrei* was dead, and she was living.

Only until tomorrow.

He pierced their palms with needles himself—all but the *Kir'reia*. She must not be flawed. Besides, if she had any sorcery in her, she would have used it long since. The green eyes of the one who had tried to free the *Kir'reia* shone with tears—again, not due to pain. When it came the turn of the harmless-looking little dark one, the boy struggled furiously against his bonds, but didn't even wince when the needle went through his hand.

Lady Ruala, amusingly enough, spit in the High Warlord's face. He slapped her for it. The clanmasters expected it. But he strongly suspected that one could beat these women bloody and not break them.

The great *Azhreia* Sioned had been first, of course. As he held gently to her wire-bound hands and slid the steel needle carefully between finger-joints, he almost asked why she did not ignite him where he stood, or set all his men aflame, or otherwise use her legendary powers.

He already knew why. She had destroyed the necessary walls between herself and her servants. She cared for them. They mattered to her. She could do many things, but any of them would put her servants in danger.

They stood before him now, helpless, shining steel in their flesh. There wasn't much blood. He was as exquisitely careful with their veins as when marking his wives as his property.

A clanmaster came forward, a scrap of parchment fluttering from his fingertips as if he dared not touch more of it or be tainted. "In the search, this was found on her." He indicated the green-eyed almost-blonde.

The High Warlord took it and read it. *Right—right—two floors—left—right—top floor—spring below shelf.*

"Great lord . . . is it . . . sorcery?"

Lady Ruala's fine mouth curled in scorn.

"Yes," he told the clanmaster, sparing a wry crinkle of his eyes for the lady. "These words allowed their entry to the *Kir'reia*'s chamber." He tore the parchment into tiny pieces and threw them on the hearthfire. The clanmasters breathed a collective sigh.

Returning to the captives, the High Warlord said pleasantly, "You will tell me where is the other." He knew the command to be futile—but, again he must give it in the presence of his warriors. Equally absurd was the threat he made next. "You will tell me, or die with the *Kir'reia*."

Silence. Then the small, dark-haired one spoke.

"You'll kill us anyway for what we did to the priests."

He nodded. "But there is killing . . . and killing."

"Tell me," the green-eyed *Azhreia* said calmly, "what sort of killing can you do with all the priests dead? Your actions here in the Desert show that you at least aren't a gelding. But your priests were. Shall you make the sacrifice?" She smiled, knowing he knew which sacrifice she meant.

"I am High Warlord," he said through his teeth. "The *Kir'reia*'s killing is now mine. It is my right."

"Will your warriors think so?"

He no longer envied the old *Azhrei* as much as he once had.

*

Sionell had never in her life regretted so deeply that she had not been born a Sunrunner.

In girlhood, she had cursed her lack of the gift as the only thing standing between her and marriage to Pol. She had long known how ridiculous that notion was. When Pol Chose Meiglan, utterly lacking in Sunrunner blood, she had only shrugged; after she'd gotten over the shock of Antalya's having turned out *faradhi*, the irony had amused her.

But now—now she would have bargained her soul (the parts of it that didn't belong to her children) for one instant's ability to call Fire.

Alasen had lighted their way up the western tower stairs.

Sionell hadn't thought to bring a candle, much less the means to ignite it. Anger at her stupidity was a good thing, however; it kept her from being too scared.

Betheyn had committed the whole maze of stairs and passages to memory at Myrdal's order, with the logic of architecture to aid her. Alasen had consulted the list of turns Beth gave her by the glow of her fingerflame. Sionell had neither memorization nor paternal teachings nor written list to guide her.

In brief, she was lost.

But not hopelessly. She refused, flatly and completely, to admit that she might not find her way out.

She dared not try to get through the garderobe in Meiglan's room again. Goddess only knew what had transpired there. If Alasen had been taken, then probably Sioned, Beth, Ruala, and Isriam would be, as well. One of them must remain free—

—to do what? Attempt a rescue? One woman, not even a Sunrunner, against two thousand Vellanti warriors?

And this was always assuming she could discover where the High Warlord had put them, find a way in, and get them out—when she wasn't even sure how to get anywhere from where she was now.

After a second stumbled flight of pitch-black stairs below Meiglan's room, Sionell sagged against the wall to consider her options. She could try to locate Sioned and the others. Or she could try to find a way out of this maze, somehow get to Pol, and tell him what had happened.

She didn't think much of her chances of success at either. But the first would almost surely see her dead to no purpose at all. The second would at least let Pol know the increased danger—and dump the whole problem on him, she freely admitted. It would put even more responsibility on already overburdened shoulders. But he had an army. She was alone. He was a Sunrunner and a sorcerer. She was only herself, plain and unadorned.

All right, then, she decided. *He has to know what happened here, and I'm the only one who can tell him. If I don't break my neck in the dark first.*

Sparing a few choice imprecations for whoever had last been in these cold stone hallways and not left candles, torches, and the means to light them, she started down. First she had to keep walking—and keep from falling—until she couldn't smell the priests' deaths anymore. When this was accomplished—and surely it must be near dawn by the time the air ceased to reek—she paused to take her bearings. A laughable ambition at best; again she envied *faradh'im* their Fire and their uncanny resistance to getting lost.

I am not *lost,* she repeated firmly—and jumped back against the stone wall as something scurried across her feet.

She very nearly screamed aloud. Inside her, instinct screamed for light as surely as if she *had* been a Sunrunner. Her mind replied coldly that if wishes were dragons, then people would fly.

Feeling her way along the wall, she almost yelped again when her fingers found an opening in the stone. Narrow, more of an access hole than a passage—Sionell put one hand on either side of it and leaned slightly in, breathing the strong scent of taze steeped much too long. She knew where she was now. This was where she and Alasen had started out. Through this slender perforation was a wooden door, guarded by a cupboard, that opened into the kitchen.

In the kitchen were candles.

And the hearth to light them by.

And probably a dozen Vellant'im just waiting for her to poke her head in.

She slid through to the wooden door and held her breath, listening. Sure enough: voices, harsh and angry, and perhaps tinged with a little fear. That was good. That was *very* good. Their terror of the *Azhrei*'s power would increase with this proof of his long and fatal reach. And with the priests dead, Meiglan could not be the centerpiece of their barbaric ritual.

But she and Sioned and the others would die all the same, unless Pol could work a miracle.

Meiglan quite simply expected it. She believed with unquestioning and uncritical trust that Pol could do anything. He couldn't, and Sionell knew it. But if ever she needed to be proven wrong, this was the time.

Well, he has to know about it before he can start scheming. And I can't exactly stroll through the kitchen with a cheery wave, cross the courtyard, steal a horse—reclaim one for Chay, I mean—and ride through the main gates.

Reluctantly, her whole soul begging for the light that was just the other side of that wooden cupboard, she edged back the way she'd come.

They'd used Skybowl's secret entrance in case the High

Warlord had sent someone ahead on a fast horse to investigate before the whole army moved in. This was the location from which the other passages branched. She remembered wondering how Skybowl managed to stay standing with so much of its architecture nothing but air. Beth had answered, "If you think this is impossible, tour Feruche from inside its insides sometime."

One passage led north, back to where they'd entered the keep. But she had no idea how to work the various doors that guarded against unwelcome two- and four-footed guests. After the grueling ride, she'd been too tired to watch. *Stupid!* she accused herself again, and turned to her right.

Although she couldn't see them, she knew stairs to the east spiraled up to the next floor. But she had no intention of threading her way through the whole castle. She really *would* get lost.

The west passage gave immediately onto steps down into the secret repository of dragon gold. When they came through on the way in, Sioned remarked that Rohan had taken her down to see it a long time ago. Perhaps, Sionell thought, perhaps someone had left a candle *there*—

But if she went looking, she might never find her way back up again.

The happy thought occurred to her that once, years ago, when the secrets of Stronghold were being used by Mireva, Rohan had said something about the workers who built the passages and the architects who designed them. *"They became part of the architecture themselves when the place was finished. A ruthless but practical crowd, our ancestors."* Just what she needed: tripping over old bones—or adding her own to them.

As determined as she was not to get lost, she was equally determined not to be afraid. *I'm ambitious these days,* she told herself sourly, and to prove it strode the three steps to the south passage. Beth had pointed out its ending—a cave screened by scrub and a few trees—as they rode to the northern branch. From where Sionell was now, a short walk south to the boundary of the castle would end in a sharp west turn that eventually curved to the north. But beyond the keep's foundations, the passage had been designed by the volcano, not by humans. A river of lava, cooling on top while its molten undercurrent flowed on, had created a natural tunnel. Rough going, Myrdal had warned Beth, a hard climb over boulders fallen from the ceiling, and unused so far as she knew for at least a century.

Sionell gritted her teeth and started walking.

✳

Norian woke with a violent start as steel clanged on stone.

"Sorry," Edrel murmured. He stood near the night-black window, the light of a single candle sheathing his sword like running water. "I didn't mean to wake you, love."

"Edrel, why are you—"

"The Vellant'im are on the move."

As he turned to face her, his scabbard scraped against the wall again. But for helm and gauntlets, he was fully armed. Stiff leather breastplate with brass fittings at the more vulnerable places; thick boots to the knees, reinforced with steel ribs down the sides; greaves from wrist to elbow; the violet belt and golden buckle Pol had given as tokens of his knighthood around his waist. He looked like a highborn warrior out of the ballads, hero of a hundred songs.

Around his neck he tied a length of thin wool, striped in brown and red for his holding of River Ussh. It would protect his nape from being chafed by his steel helm. Adjusting it, he muttered, "I have no choice now. I have to fight."

"So do the Sunrunners," she pointed out. Slipping out of bed, she hauled on a robe, shivering a little in the chill. After a few moments' rummaging in her traveling bag, she found what she wanted.

"I had my sentry—pardon, your brother's sentry—alert Torien. But I have to leave at once. I can't stand around arguing with him."

"I'll take care of him—and his wife," Norian asserted. She unwound the wool from his neck and replaced it with a plain scarf of bright red silk. "This is softer. Wear your own over it and let the ends show. You'll be leading Gribain troops, you should wear Grib's color. And no nonsense from you, either. As my husband and Elsen's brother-by-marriage, you have the right."

"Yes, your grace," he murmured meekly, smiling down at her.

She made sure the cushioning was adequate, then adjusted the folds at his throat to make sure all the colors were clearly visible. She left the short trailing ends free. "There.

That's got it. But that's the *only* red I want to see on you. I hope you take my meaning?"

"Yes, your grace," Edrel repeated.

Before she could succumb to need and fear and throw her arms around him, he turned to pick up gauntlets and helm from the table.

"Tell Elsen what's going on—but *don't* let him any farther than the window. And make certain Torien knows what's expected of him. I'll have the summoning horn blown before I leave. I think that's all—"

"Not quite. But then, we've not been married two full seasons yet." Norian took him by the ears and tugged his head down to give him a kiss on the lips. His helm clattered to the floor as he freed that arm to put around her. The hardest thing she'd ever done was draw away. "Don't exhaust yourself killing Vellant'im. I plan on giving you the rest of that as soon as you're bathed clean of their stink."

He grinned and retrieved his helm, making the movement the sweep of an elegant bow. "Yes, your grace!"

When he was gone, she blinked back tears. Her brother mustn't see them, either. Then she dressed, knotted her hair back with a red lace veil, and went to do battle with Jolan.

✳

The promised rough going didn't bother Sionell, now that she had light. Someone, blessings of the Goddess upon him or her, had left candles and a flintbox on a recessed shelf where the dressed stone passage yielded to natural tunnel. She'd discovered them through the simple expedient of sticking her hand in as she felt her way along the wall. The wax was very old, very dry, and of inferior quality; she'd gone through two candles so far with no end to the journey in sight. She hoped the four left in her skirt pocket would suffice.

But she still wished she was a Sunrunner, able to conjure a little Fire—this time for warmth. Betheyn, or perhaps Myrdal, had forgotten to mention that the lava tunnel was faced not with rock but ice.

It beggared imagination to envision how a river of burning rock twice as high as her head had been transformed into this frozen tube of crystal. As she struggled on, slipping, sometimes falling on her rear, water seeping occasionally onto her head, she worked out how it must have happened. They didn't get much rain this side of the Veresch, but over the centuries since Skybowl had been formed and this tunnel with it, enough had found its way in to form this passage of solid ice. With solid rock overhead keeping out the sun's heat, perpetual winter reigned.

Knowing what had caused it didn't make it any the less remarkable. In other circumstances, she might have found it enchantingly beautiful. Not now. Not with the chill entering her bones so her fingers seemed frozen around the candle; not with the flame casting sickly green-black shadows through ice that seemed to suck in its light and hoard the glow.

And not in this echoing, scentless quiet. The only noises were her own quick breaths and the occasional muffled *plop* of water, resounding weirdly off clear, shining teeth that hung raggedly from the ceiling. The only scents were those of candle wax and her own sweat and the clean, sharp smell of water. Sionell appreciated water as only someone Desert-bred for generations could. But she associated it with the odor of green and growing things, even something as simple as lichen clinging to stone beside a tiny spring. Here, she couldn't even smell the rocks.

"Think of it this way," she muttered, shivering as she picked herself up from yet another clumsy slide on slick footing. "I could be hearing and smelling mountain cats. It's dead certain they'd hear and smell *me*. They might come by for a drink now and again, but even with a fur coat this is no place to snuggle down for a nap." She paused. "And if I don't stop talking to myself, I'm going to start doubting my sanity."

She was an unknown distance from Skybowl and at the end of the third candle when the flame bent to the left. She stopped, watching it. Air drawn out or in? And would the opening be large enough for her to get through? Granted, she'd lost a silkweight since this war began, but she was long-legged and broad-boned—and, as her mother had tactfully observed once, her hips had been built for having babies.

She thought despairingly of her children then, even though she knew them safe at Feruche. Why in all Hells was she here? Not because of anything so primal and pure as a mother's defense of her children. Her reasons were much more complex, much darker.

She didn't much care to delve into them again.

Except—except she'd had no right to risk herself at Skybowl. It was different for the others. Cleaner. They had power or knowledge to contribute. What did she have but a sharp tongue and a reputation for being clever?

That would do her children a lot of good once they were motherless as well as fatherless.

Sionell stared into the candleflame until her eyes stung, as if she could conjure the faces of her children. She should never have come here. She should never have risked her life as if her pain and guilt were all that mattered. Her daughter and sons needed her. Antalya, applying herself to Sunrunner studies that nonetheless frightened her a little; Jahnev, trying so hard to be grown-up about his new responsibilities as Lord of Tiglath, trying to hide how scared he was without Tallain to guide him; and Meig—a wisp of a smile curled her mouth. *Nothing* could ever upset Meig.

Goddess, how she wished she was pregnant right now. Another little girl, a last child for Tallain—

—or a first son for Pol?

No!

The flame swam before her eyes for a moment. Then her brain reminded her that there was no hope for the former—and no danger of the latter. She'd bled five days ago. But in her sudden tempest of confusion, she didn't know if she was more grateful or disappointed.

And standing around being stupefied by her own emotions was no part of her plans—not for the present or anytime in the future.

Shaking herself, she held her free hand to the right side of the flame. Her skin was so numb with cold that she couldn't feel anything but more cold, let alone any stray tease of an air current. But the flame lost its tilt; the breeze was pulling, not pushing.

The ice wall looked impossibly thick. The rock beyond it undoubtedly *was*. She sought into half a dozen shadows before she finally found the opening in the ice.

It was exactly as wide as her fist.

A Sunrunner could use Fire to melt it—and probably bring the whole cavern crashing in when the supporting ice vanished. But a Sunrunner could also have used the moonlight draining through the hole. She could just make out a glimmer of white, winking in mockery. Rising or setting? What time was it? She had no way of knowing.

There *was* a way out. Sionell had seen it. She would just have to keep going until she found it.

Or until her candles ran out.

Or until dawn came, and it would all be for nothing.

*

Chay had advised getting some sleep, or at least pretending for the troops' sake. Pol hoped they would understand that sleep was impossible. He doubted they expected it of him, anyway—not when his wife was due to die with the sunrise.

He sat before a small Fire of his own conjuring, his back resolutely turned on the eastern Desert. He could sense the sun's progress in his guts; no need to keep strained watch for the first pale glimmerings of dawn.

Thassalante had reported personally to Pol about the "dragon teeth." The *diarmadhi* looked older than the Storm God and too weary to stand, but his voice was rich with satisfaction and acidic with contempt for the credulous barbarian Vellant'im.

Pol wasn't so sure. Superstition had driven the enemy to appalling successes thus far. It was a rule of war that people fought five times as hard for their own lands as they would for somebody else's, but it appeared that religious fervor was at least as powerful a motivation.

Against it, he had two weapons in his armory: magic and steel. Andry held a grip on half the former, the Sunrunner arsenal. Maarken was in firm charge of the latter—augmented five or six days ago by a shipment from Cunaxa. Miyon's court functionaries and merchants, currying favor with their new prince, had sent enough swords, armor, arrows, and accoutrements to resupply everyone at Feruche twice over. Pol had eagerly inspected the trove, the finest ever made by smith-crafters acknowledged the best in the princedoms. Eagerly, that is, until he realized it was a peace offering that would enable him to make very efficient war.

You're troubled, my dear.

He gave a violent start as someone's colors touched him on moonlight.

It's only me, Tobin said, her Sunrunner voice as clear as

her speaking voice had once been. *Is there anything I can do to help?*

Can you figure a way for me to get Meiglan back safely without having to fight this battle?

Rohan hoped you'd never have to know anything about war. It's an ugly business.

I know more than I want to—and never enough. How do Maarken and Chay stand it?

It's their function. Battle Commanders are supposed to know such things so their prince doesn't have to. I know it's hard to be strong for yourself when you have to be everyone else's strength as well.

It's not as if they need me—not them or Andry. But that's not what's really bothering me. What I've asked them to do, what I need them for—it goes against everything I know to be right. And I can't say anything to them about it—I shouldn't even be saying this to you.

Yes, you should. Go on.

He hugged his drawn-up knees and rested his chin on them. *This is the last battle we've got in us. We have to win it. But too many people are going to die, Tobin. And the perfect stupid irony of it all is that I'm the one who kept demanding that my father stand and fight.*

Which is what you're about to do, with everything you've got. I see.

He nodded to the Fire. *It's the only thing I can do. And that's right, that's acceptable to me. But there have to be alternatives to what Maarken and Andry want to do. And I'm the only one who can choose.*

You'll know. When the time comes, you'll know.

What if I don't? And what if my choice forces Maarken to choose between me and his brother?

What if it does? she challenged. *Sorin would never forgive you, because of the promise you made him? Sorin is dead, Pol. He was just your excuse for tolerating each other, anyway. For avoiding the issue. Maarken's known all his life that one day he might have to choose between his duty as a Sunrunner and his duty to his prince. His decision isn't your problem. Neither he nor Andry nor anybody else can make your decisions—and if you let them influence you, you're a fool.*

You can say that? Both of them are—

—my sons. Yes. And I've understood every thought in their

heads since I first swaddled them. What I don't understand is why you feel guilty. It's not your fault. It's Andrade's. She was the one who married Sioned to Rohan and began this whole conflict of loyalties. And don't quote your father to me about being High Prince making it your fault. I knew my brother, too, better than you ever could.

Chastened, he hesitated a moment before replying, *All right. I see your point. But that doesn't make it much easier for Maarken.*

Pol, I doubt that anything you did short of threatening Hollis or the children would ever change Maarken's love and loyalty—and even then, he'd assume you had a very good reason. Now, stop all this nonsense and tell me what's going on down there.

He repeated Thassalante's report nearly word-for-word, and was rewarded with the glint of her colors as she laughed. But then he had to tell her that none of the Sunrunners or sorcerers had seen anything of Sioned.

She'll find you when she's good and ready, Tobin answered, not particularly disturbed. *And if she does what she said she'd do, all your emotional wrangling will vanish.*

You're still not going to tell me what they're doing in there, are you?

As you said about the mirror, if it works, then there'll be time enough for explanations.

But the mirror didn't work.

No? Imagine if the Vellanti High Warlord had appeared out of nothingness in the middle of our dinner. It may not have worked the way you intended, but what does in life?

That's about what Maarken and Andry said.

All right, then. I'll keep watch for you on Skybowl—don't any of the rest of you worry about finding Sioned and the others. If I do, I'll let you know.

Don't tire yourself out.

He had the impression of a mental snort of disdain, and then she withdrew. A moment later he almost followed her, for he'd forgotten to tell her about the horses, but then Andry appeared out of the night and crouched down beside Pol's little Fire. The ten rings and two armbands shone almost as brightly as the *selej* over Lord Rosseyn's head. He wore white, already dressed for the battle tomorrow except for his armor. Pol remembered seeing him sort through the Cunaxan goods, settling on a gorgeous but impractical outfit of silver. It was more suitable for a prince presiding over a victory feast than a warrior riding to battle, but Andry wouldn't be among the combatants.

Not physically, anyway.

"I hear your kinfolk had quite an audience for their ceremony. It must've been something to see."

Pol nodded.

"They're like the stars—invisible during the day, working only by night."

"But always there."

Andry shrugged. "Which of us will be the focus of the conjuring?"

"Hollis says it should be you, and I agree."

Andry's brows arched.

"You've got the flair for it." Pol smiled slightly. "And that silver armor of yours will shine like a beacon. They'll be so busy staring at you—and then shielding their eyes from the glare—that they won't notice what's happening with the horses at all."

"I promise I'll give it my best." He grinned wryly. "If it's dazzlement you want, then have somebody call Fire on either side of me while I work. I assume you want this to happen just before sunup. I don't deny I could use Sioned in this, but I can manage with Evarin. You'll be free to conjure up any other appropriate horrors."

"I'll just watch, I think. If you need me, let me know."

"Save your strength for the barrier around Meiglan."

Pol rubbed at a scuff on his boot. "Had you thought how to arrange the conjuring?"

"I won't be able to conjure up a whole army," Andry warned. "I heard the *diarmadh'im* ended with dragon's teeth in some staggering multiple of nine."

"A few dozen ought to do it."

"Good," Andry said with unabashed relief. "There won't be many fine details—just shapes of Fire, waving swords around. You know, I think I'll use Vellanti distance," he mused. "That might get to them on an instinctive level. They tend to stand farther apart from each other than we do, both in battle and out of it."

"Do they?" Pol glanced up curiously.

"Evarin and I noticed it. They even ride more spread-out than we do. Presumably so no one can get close enough on a casual basis to knife them, and so they'll always have room to draw their swords."

Pol shook his head. "I couldn't live like that."

"If this works—and it will—we won't have to. After there are enough Fire shadows to suit, then what?"

"Our people—the real ones!—move up into position, yelling *'Azhrei'* as loud as they can."

Andry grinned again. "At which point the horses stampede."

"That's the theory."

"Some of the most fun I ever had as a child was watching the yearlings gallop madly across a field, thinking they were being summoned to their mamas."

"Only to find Chay, who is *not* equipped to provide dinner! The same thing happens at Dragon's Rest. They nearly trampled Rialt the first time he—" Pol broke off, then resumed with a viciousness that surprised even him, "I can't *wait* for Ostvel to bring Chiana into arm's reach."

"You may have to settle for Rinhoel. Didn't you say Naydra all but issued a summary edict claiming her darling little sister for her own attentions?" He twisted one of his rings, set with a ruby for his birthplace of Radzyn. "I suppose it's too much to hope that the Vellant'im will stampede, too, right into Tilal's waiting arms."

"It'd be nice, but we can't count on it."

Andry was quiet for a time. "I mean no offense, but the *diarmadh'im* should hold back from the conjuring."

"I mean none either," Pol said, stretching his legs, "but do you honestly think they'd consent to be under the command of the Lord of Goddess Keep?"

"I'm willing to work with *them."*

"Not without me. Thassalante made that very clear. When it comes time for it, they won't go anywhere near you unless I'm the one in control."

"You don't know how to work the *ros'salath.*"

"What you mean is that I failed at Stronghold." He said it without shame or bitterness. "I know better now, Andry. Iron can't touch us—*if* we have enough sorcerers in the weave to bear the brunt of it."

At length, Andry said, "Torien."

"Yes. In a small working, one or two suffice. But something this large and this powerful—without me, you'd have

Riyan, maybe Ruala if she's in reach of the sunlight. *With* me—ninety-nine full-blooded *diarmadh'im*."

"So." Andry drew the sibilant out into a hiss. "You've won."

"It's not a competition," Pol said wearily. "Unless with the Vellant'im, to win our lives. That's why you came here, Andry. To beat them—not me."

They regarded each other in silence for a long moment— broken by a bellow of outrage. "Goddess in glory, what did I ever do to earn such women?"

Both men jumped to their feet. Pol intensified the Fire to throw a wider circle of light. Into it came Walvis, eyes blazing like twin blue suns, and—

"Sionell?" Pol gaped at her. She was here, when he'd thought her within Skybowl, and that was enough to stagger him. But the question in his voice was for the apparition she embodied.

Her darkfire hair was knotted at her nape, both to keep it from her eyes and to provide cushion for the bronze helm cradled between one elbow and hip. Bronze as well were the guardplates on stiff leather armor that covered her back and chest. Her shirt was of Tiglathi yellow-and-blue; her tunic, the richer blue of the Desert. Brown trousers thinly piped in orange down each leg—Tuath's colors, her dead brother's holding—ended in matching brown boots to the knees.

She saluted him in the manner of the Isulk'im: brow, lips, heart, signifying that her mind, her breath, and her life were his to use as he would in battle. And fight she was determined to do; her eyes as she looked at him had the sheen of blue-gray steel as deadly as the sheathed sword at her belt.

There was, Pol thought absently, a certain refuge in formality. It kept one from saying other things that would make one out a total fool.

"My Lady of Tiglath," he said, his lips almost numb.

Walvis snarled. "Lady of Rampaging Imbecility, more like it! Would you look at her?"

"We are," Andry said. "How convenient that one of your own Tiglathis had armor that fit you so well."

"Isn't it," Sionell replied flatly. "If you and my father will excuse us, I must talk with the High Prince."

Andry bowed slightly and departed. Walvis took an aggressive step toward his daughter.

"If you think," he warned, "you're going to put that sword to its intended use—"

"But I *do* know how to use it, Papa. You taught me, remember?"

"I'll use the flat of my own across your backside!"

She put a placating hand on his arm. He shook it off. "You can yell at me later. I have to talk to Pol. Alone, Papa. Please."

Pol nodded, assuring Walvis with his eyes that he'd talk Sionell out of whatever she planned to do with that sword. Not that he had any confidence he could do so, of course. After one last fulminating glance for Sionell, Walvis left them, growling under his breath.

Sionell touched Pol's hand briefly. "Make a light for us, and walk with me. I don't want anyone else to hear this."

When they had paced off enough sand to satisfy her, she halted him with another fleeting touch. His fingerflame made fiery sapphires of her eyes.

"The priests are dead. All of them. The ritual can't go forth without them."

Wild hope flashed through his heart. "Then Meggie won't—"

"No. But the High Warlord has taken Sioned and the others."

She told him all of it, as neatly and succinctly as a report from a master of hawks or horses. Her voice was controlled, almost expressionless, as she described what had happened inside Skybowl from the moment of their arrival to Ruala's discovery of Isriam, from Pol's conjuring to their fear for Meiglan's life, from Alasen's Fire to her own flight through a tunnel of ice. Calmly she spoke, yet her eyes revealed emotions—especially her horror at Sioned's deadly alteration of a plan Sionell had helped devise, a scheme meant only to cripple. But moments later fierce pleasure showed that in killing the priests, the ritual was impossible. There was admiration for Meiglan's courage, and for Alasen's; momentary amusement at the Vellanti awe of dragon teeth and the sudden appearance of the *Azhrei;* and, finally, fear.

"I didn't think I'd get to you in time," she confessed, her voice a bit hoarse now, beginning to tremble around the edges. "I only put all this on because the first of our people I found were my own. They insisted I stop and rest, and from somewhere—" She gestured to the armor and the sword. "I had time enough—our horses were outside Skybowl where we left them, so I didn't have to walk the whole way. And I knew I'd never be able to get it all out in any kind of order if I didn't rest a little while."

Pol nodded mutely.

"I couldn't see a way to help them from inside the castle," she went on quickly, guiltily. "There are thousands of them—and I'm not a Sunrunner, either to distract them somehow or be able to tell you on moonlight. I had to decide."

"Rightly," he managed.

"Somebody else might've found a way to—"

He shook his head. "No. Not alone. Not even my mother, alone." He let the flame dwindle out and turned toward Skybowl, a towering blackness against the black hills and star-swept sky. The keep was invisible from here. He could look on the last moonlight, but he knew he'd see nothing. The High Warlord knew about Sunrunners.

"I'm sorry, Pol," Sionell whispered. "I didn't know what else to do."

"You were right to come to me. I had to know this." He faced her again. "I only wish I knew what to do with it."

He could barely see her in the darkness. Only the stray glints of bronze armor and steel sword, and the pale triangle of her face. He could feel her shaking, fine tremors coursing through her muscles. When he put his arms around her, it was as her friend, her prince. She sensed it—thank the Goddess, she wasn't too weary to sense it. He needed her comforting nearness now much more than she needed his. If she'd pulled away from him, he didn't think he could stand it.

But it was so strange to feel the unyielding stiffness of armor, the chill of the breastplate through his shirt. He couldn't even stroke her hair, all scraped back and bound as it was, all the soft warmth of it confined.

"It's all right," she murmured against his shoulder. "It's going to be all right. I know how foolish that sounds. But I'm fool enough to believe it. And I've known you long enough to know that you are, too."

CHAPTER
THIRTY-THREE

The wine, mulled in deference to the freezing cold of the gatehouse chamber, steamed as Torien drained it from a gold pitcher into crystal goblets. Strong Ossetian red would disguise the taste of *dranath* for those still jumpy about its use; Linis in particular dreaded its very name.

She would drink from Rusina's goblet. The stalking cat depicted with consummate Fironese skill had been as appropriate for its original owner as it was laughably inappropriate for Linis. In fact, Torien mused as he watched the green, gray-white, and blue tints darken with the color of the wine, it would be better to give this one to Jolan.

His wife was sifting a precise amount of *dranath* into each cup. He and she were alone, preparing this small ritual for the other *devr'im* who would arrive shortly. She was singing quietly under her breath, some poem she'd written in the old language. He was silent.

The beauty of the goblets never failed to impress him. His own sunset over the sea; Deniker's jade-green waterfall foaming white into a sapphire ocean; the black wolf padding through red flowers beside a brilliant blue river, that had belonged to Oclel. Antoun would use it today, just as Linis would drink from Rusina's, and Valeda's goblet would be Martiel's.

"The last time we did this—" Torien began incautiously.

"You've left Andry's cup unfilled," Jolan interrupted. "You'll be using it, of course. Pour some in."

Everything in him rebelled. He was Chief Steward here, Andry's trusted and valued deputy, center this day of the *ros'salath.* But he was also a sorcerer. He could almost feel the gold rings burning his flesh as if in protest. Or warning.

"No," he said.

"To all intents and purposes, you're Lord of Goddess Keep." Jolan faced him across the small table, eight filled goblets and one empty one between them. "It's a harmless symbol, Torien. Just in here. Just among ourselves."

"No."

For an instant he thought she'd argue. Then she gave an irritated shrug. "Very well. As you wish."

Cold, quiet morning air was pierced by a deafening note from the great horn. Both of them clapped their hands over their ears, then quickly grabbed for the glasses rattling dangerously against each other.

When the incredible noise ceased, Torien had to shout to hear his own words past the ringing in his ears. "Goddess! Is he trying to be heard all the way to Skybowl?"

A few moments later Ulwis and Deniker arrived, the latter complaining that it had taken both of them and Crila besides to rouse Nialdan from sleep.

"And since he's the only one who can lift that damned horn—let alone put enough air into it—he'll be as late getting here as he was in sounding the alarm." Deniker scrubbed his fingers through his pillow-crimped brown hair and grimaced at the wine goblets. "Shouldn't we eat something before we guzzle that? Wine on an empty stomach is bad enough, but with *dranath* mixed in—"

"Always food!" His wife poked him in the ribs. "You just worked off the silkweight you gained gobbling everything in sight at the *Rialla.* I ought to send you out with Lord Edrel's troops to get some exercise."

"Half a silkweight," he grumbled, and picked up his goblet.

How usual *they sound,* Torien thought, *as if this was practice—as if there weren't thousands of Vellant'im ready to tear Goddess Keep apart and weave our rings through their beards. As if Andry were here to lead us....*

Which name reminded him of the decision he'd have to make. He had two choices for the configuration of colors. One put the three *diarmadh'im* in the middle; the other placed Martiel at one end, Crila at the other, with Torien himself taking the center. The first distributed their relative immunity to iron across the whole spectrum. But the second was the more powerful, for it concentrated their strength.

It was rather like castle architecture, he thought, remembering when Sorin of Feruche had visited here and they'd discussed the Castle's design during long evenings around the fire. There were certain ways to construct an arch to stand alone—and other ways to buttress it, if the space to be bridged was very wide. Torien could make a simple, strong arc of power, or use the two other *diarmadh'im* to bolster the Sunrunners.

How much simpler it had been when Andry had taken the center. Then, all Torien had to do was fashion the shield that would keep iron from harming his Lord. Now he must lead as well as protect.

No one else seemed concerned about any danger. Except for Nialdan, they had all assembled now. Antoun looked as if he hadn't slept since Summer, but he calmly lifted Oclel's wolf goblet and went to stand by the balcony windows to await the sunrise. Linis and Martiel had evidently come from the same bed: his shirt was sagging off her shoulders and her cloak was thrown around his. Each had a smile for Torien as they claimed Rusina's and Valeda's cups. But Crila, shivering despite heavy wool clothes and a fur-lined tunic, provided a jolt to Torien's slowly gathering confidence.

She reached for a goblet, then stopped. Nialdan's, shimmering with reds and green, had been filled; so had Torien's own. Andry's was the only one left, and it was empty.

"My lord?" she asked, blinking in confusion. "Which am I to take?"

"Lend her yours," Deniker said to Torien. "I assumed you'd take Andry's."

Jolan sent him a meaningful glance that he chose to ignore. "No," he replied. "We'll find another for Crila."

"Our new *devr'im* don't match the colors of the goblets they inherited, anyway," Ulwis added with a shrug. "A cup is a cup, after all. It's the wine that counts."

By this time the gatehouse was echoing with the noise of those coming into Goddess Keep. Parents called to children, masters to apprentices, and—loudest of all—animals to each other as they were herded inside. As Nialdan finally appeared, disheveled by his struggle through the crowd, Edrel could be heard shouting for passage.

"Let him handle it," Jolan murmured as Torien took a half-step to the door. "That's what he's here for." Raising her voice as well as her crystal cup of *dranath*-laden wine, she said, "Goddess grant us strength to do her work, and success for all we do in her sacred Name."

One by one the goblets—including the plain ceramic one found in a cupboard for Crila—were drained and set back onto the table. The *devr'im* waited for the drug to take effect, eyes beginning to sparkle as the first flush of sensuality slid through their veins. It would be followed by an augmentation of power—and this was what decided Torien on how to construct his arc.

"Martiel," he said quietly. "You're to my left. Then Linis and Antoun." Perhaps it wasn't wise to place the lovers together; Martiel's first instinct would be to protect Linis. But she would work better feeling his presence beside her. If it became necessary for Torien to demand everything Martiel had, Antoun would bolster Linis. "Deniker," he added, "you're on Antoun's left."

Torien looked at each of the others in turn. "Crila, on my right. Nialdan, Jolan, Ulwis." Strongest of the Sunrunners (even including Jolan), Ulwis would be even stronger for the *dranath.*

And if it came to it, which he begged the Goddess it would not, then the five *faradh'im* could be ejected from the weaving for their own safety and the three *diarmadh'im* function alone, with Torien himself as the keystone of the arch.

Such a fine irony: sorcerers doing the work of the Goddess. Torien wondered suddenly if there ever *had* been a sorcerer Lord or Lady of Goddess Keep. That would be the biggest irony of all.

✳

"And wouldn't it be funny," Evarin was saying as he measured out *dranath,* "if they took one look at your conjuring, turned tail, and ran like all Hells were after them? Pol would never get the chance to make us knuckle under."

Andry sipped at the hot taze and made a face. "You could've brewed this a little stronger, you know."

"Don't change the subject. Do you *want* it to be seen that all Sunrunners and even the Lord of Goddess Keep are—"

"You're assuming Pol is powerful enough to take me on. You're also assuming that our aims conflict." Andry glanced at the eastern Desert, where the thinnest swath of deep blue draped the dunes. Morning was coming. Occasionally during this interminable night he'd wondered if it ever would. "He and I want the same thing, Evarin," he went on softly. "A very, very large pyre of very, very dead Vellant'im."

"But it depends on who does the killing, doesn't it?" The Master Physician took a gulp of taze, hands wrapped around the cup for warmth. "I mean, if they really are scared out of their minds by the dragon-teeth trick, then Tilal will get them and most of the credit. But if it's you, working the *ros'salath*. . . ."

"You still don't understand, do you? It doesn't matter who kills them as long as they're dead."

Evarin shrugged. "It'd matter to the Vellant'im. A sword is a lot cleaner. The pile of corpses would be bloody, but at least they'd die sane. And there's this to consider, too—if the *ros'salath* does the work, none of our own people would have to die."

"That's the choice Pol faced. Which lives are more important—ours or theirs? The answer is obvious." Andry paused, swirling the steaming liquid around to catch up the last undissolved particles of *dranath*. "He's had his moments of compassion, of course. Not weakness. He's never that. But at times he's been reluctant to see *any* more deaths, including theirs. It argues well for a prince when he feels that—can you imagine Rinhoel or Chiana regretting the necessity of killing, for instance? But Pol is also practical and ruthless enough to realize that such things have no place when a civilization is threatened." He paused once more, listening to what he'd just said. "Rohan would appreciate the tragedy of that. We must behave like barbarians in order to defend our civilized selves."

"Use a steel knife to excise the putrefying flesh caused by a steel sword," Evarin mused. "I suppose so, my Lord." He glanced into Andry's cup, saw that it was as empty as his own, and poured in fresh, undrugged taze. "I'm not—"

What he was not, Andry never learned. Out of the shadows between campfires came a quartet of flames. The three of Sunrunner's Fire belonged to Hollis, Jeni, and Chayla. Feylin strode along beside them, carrying a more conventional candle in her gloved fist.

"Don't say it," Hollis warned as Andry opened his mouth.

"I've already had enough nonsense from your stone-skulled brother to last me until next Winter."

Andry got as far as drawing breath to speak. This time it was Chayla who forestalled him. "Whoever thought we'd stay behind at Feruche doesn't know us very well."

"I—"

Jeni's turn. "My mother's up there," she said quietly.

"But—"

"But nothing." Feylin eyed him quellingly. "I'm a physician—maybe not in *his* class or Chayla's, but I know my way around the average sword cut."

Evarin began, "I hope we won't need—"

"We hope so, too," Hollis said, dark blue eyes exactly the color of the eastern sky, and flashing with the same quicksilver fire. "But if you do, here we are."

Andry nodded. Then a terrible idea hit him and he glanced around wildly. "*Please* don't tell me my mother came with you!"

Feylin snorted. "Tobin has more sense."

✳

Pol was telling Visian thanks-but-no-thanks regarding a certain piece of armor when Kierun and Dannar showed up, the immense dragon tapestry from Stronghold slung between their saddles.

Sethric rode along behind them, two brass rods taller than most young pine trees propped in one stirrup.

"Forgive me if I don't climb down, my lord," he said. "It was hard enough to get up here. Where would you like your banner displayed?"

✳

"Rohannon? Come on, wake up."

He grumbled and turned a shoulder into his cloak, seeking warmth that wasn't there.

"I know, I know—it's still black as soot outside," Idalian said. "But Prince Laric wants us ready by dawn."

Rohannon's only response was to pull the cloak up over his head.

"There's taze," Idalian added slyly.

He rolled over and cracked an eyelid. "Hot? *Really* hot?"

Idalian grinned and held out a steaming cup.

Rohannon grabbed and gulped. The strong brew scalded his tongue. "Goddess, that's good! All the way to my toes!"

"We've got a little time to enjoy it. I sent Aldiar to saddle our horses."

"That wasn't very nice. Horses scare her, you know."

One instant Idalian was crouching beside him; the next, he was flat on his rear end with astonishment.

"Her?"

Rohannon lowered his face and drank once more, hiding his own sudden shock. He kicked his brain into a rapid mental review of his every encounter with the skinny, black-eyed sorcerer. By the time he looked over at the stunned sprawl that was Idalian, there was a little smile on his lips.

"Well, of course she's a her. What did you think she was? Drink up. I don't know about *your* lord, but mine hates it when I'm late."

✳

"My lady? I have something for you," Pol said, and Sionell turned. "It won't fit as well, but it's more appropriate."

He held up the armor that Tallain had removed from Birioc of the Merida shortly after he'd removed Birioc's head. Though not modern in workmanship and thus unsuited for protection in modern battle, the breastplate was beautifully crafted of thick leather studded with uncut topazes and emeralds. Visian had wanted Pol to wear it, but the moment Sionell appeared Pol had something else in mind.

She was staring at it. So were Maarken, Chay, and Riyan. It pleased Pol that three of his four most powerful vassals—Walvis was off giving Feylin roughly the same lecture he'd tried to give Sionell—would witness this.

"Appropriate?" Sionell asked.

Pol nodded. "After the Merida were defeated at Zagroy's Pillar—" Fifty days ago? Fifty years? "—the Lord of Tiglath was made Regent of Cunaxa. I find the armor a fitting symbol. It would honor me if you'd wear it."

What he didn't say was that when the sun hit those topazes and emeralds and the gold fittings around them, she would be visible at two measures. The Vellant'im might recognize the armor and believe that even the Merida had joined the *Azhrei's* army. More important, if she left the rise he intended her to occupy—right next to Kierun and Dannar with the dragon tapestry unfurled—she would be quickly identifiable and just as quickly whisked away to safety. Battle-canny, Chay, Maarken, and Riyan understood that without his having to mention it.

Sionell wasn't thinking about that at all. For this was the first time Tallain had been mentioned between them except in anger and guilt since the day he died. *Damn you, you clever bastard,* her eyes told him. He acknowledged the accusation with a level look. There was no way she could refuse the armor, the regency, or the "honor"—but she was clearly suspicious of how extensive the trap really was. So he told her.

"Things happen in any battle," he said quietly. "If one of them should happen to me—and to Meiglan—"

"That's enough," Chay snapped.

"If it should," Pol insisted, and glanced at Maarken. "You'll be Regent of the Desert. Riyan, your father will take Princemarch again, as he did for me before. But he'll need your help. He's not as young as he once was. Sionell . . . Cunaxa is yours. Among you, I ask that you raise my children exactly as you've raised your own."

"I fail to see the point of this depressing conversation." Sionell took the leather breastplate from Pol's hands. "Maarken, help me get into this thing, please?"

Well satisfied, Pol bowed slightly to them and walked a few paces away. A brief weaving of the remaining starlight showed him Tilal and his cavalry of Ossetians, Syrenes, Giladans, and physicians from all over the continent. They would not reach Skybowl by dawn, but if everything went as planned, they wouldn't have to.

And if it didn't—which was what he expected, the last thing he would admit to anyone—then Tilal would provide fresh reinforcements for a battle of hideous proportions.

Curiously enough, the certainty that events would turn out much differently than any prior planning could anticipate didn't bother him. By rights he should be a raving madman about now. But his father had been right *(And when had he not been?* Pol asked himself with an inner smile): there was a centered serenity in knowing that whatever happened, there would be only one thing to do about it. He'd know. When the time came, he'd know.

He returned to the others. Visian had joined them. Sionell

was gone. "Giving back the armor she borrowed from one of her Tiglathis," Chay explained.

Pol nodded and told them Tilal's location, finishing with, "Audrite said the moons won't rise until the sun is fully up, but they'll come low and fast. So we have *some* leeway in the timing of all this. If everyone will get into position now, then I think we're ready."

"Not just yet." Chay cleared his throat and divided a look between Maarken and Riyan. Finally his gaze rested on Visian. "It's yours to give."

"Not mine, great Lord of Radzyn," the Isulki said promptly. "My people are only its guardians. It is for Sunrunners and sorcerers both to gift it, as my brother and lord, Kazander, told me to do."

"There's a Sunrunner," Chay said, pointing to Maarken, then to Riyan. "And there's a sorcerer."

"And I'm both," Pol said impatiently. "What are you talking about?"

Visian pulled from his tunic a circlet of beaten gold, set with chunks of white jade. "It is called—"

"—the *selej*," Pol whispered. "The White Crown."

Visian seemed to expect that Pol would know. The other three frowned to varying degrees. At last Riyan's brow cleared and he sighed.

"Yet another tale my wife didn't listen to, I suppose."

Pol couldn't take his eyes from the heavy gold, the dull milky jade. So unlike the fierce bright glow of the real *selej* that had formed around Rosseyn's head: no power, no burning throb of potent stones.

"It's ... a symbol," he said at last. "Given to the Isulk'im for safekeeping a long time ago." He looked hard at Visian then. "You want *me* to wear it?"

"*Azhrei*, Lord Kazander said this to me—'You know who I would have wear it.' And I say to you of my own words—in truth, is there any other who could?"

"If the word of a *faradhi* is required, you have mine," said Maarken.

"And mine, as *diarmadhi*," Riyan added.

After a moment, Chay said, "If all the forms have been observed—even though none of us understands them—then put that thing on and let's get going."

Dear, irreplaceable Chay: a treasure of uncommon sense and bruising practicality. Father of two Sunrunners, including a Lord of Goddess Keep, he considered those gifts just another sort of talent, like music or mathematics.

So Pol accepted the *selej* from Visian and set it around his head without any trepidation whatsoever. It was only a symbol, like the jeweled armor he'd given Sionell. There was no power in it. No magic.

Still, for the moments it took the chill gold to warm against his forehead, he had a sudden image of Rosseyn captured beneath the real one. Beyond his dark, living face in the mirror, Pol imagined Gerik's eyes like amethysts and Merisel's like emeralds, liquid with helpless grief at what had been done to their beloved friend. All these long years of secrecy and imprisonment, sprung from one woman's schemes—and not just Rosseyn's plight, either. The *diarmadh'im* had spent centuries in fear for their lives. The *faradh'im* had never known their true heritage. The population of thirteen princedoms had remained utterly ignorant of those who longed for their destruction because of something that had happened fifteen generations ago.

And all this long while, the Isulk'im had kept the White Crown safe—with only the vaguest idea why.

A symbol, without any power—not the kind of power Pol had come to understand in the past days. For him, the *selej* was a symbol of Gerik and Merisel and Rosseyn, his ancestors. He would wear this crown for them. But for others, as well. Kazander. Chay and Maarken and all the rest of his family. Those who had taught him and loved him. Andry, who had in some ways driven him to understandings he would never have reached without his cousin's constant goading. Rohan. Sioned. Meiglan. Sionell. *All* of them— even the Vellant'im in their fear and superstition. For by using exactly those things, he would spare their lives.

He glanced at the horizon. Not long now. He would know what to do. He was sure of nothing else, but he would know what to do. The serenity of his *wholeness* was absolute.

It only occurred to him at that moment to wonder if, in the knowing, he would have the strength.

If not . . . well, intelligence (Rohan would have been more honest, and called it cunning) would have to make up for it.

Which reminded him. "My Lord Battle Commander," he said to Maarken, "is there any chance of a concert?"

✳

At least he used sterile needles. I'd hate to come so far and fail so spectacularly only to die of blood poisoning.

Sioned and her five companions had spent the rest of the sleepless night locked in a windowless chamber and tied to chairs. Meiglan was with them, plainly glad of the company and not the slightest bit afraid of the dawn. "I've been soiled beyond use. I wasn't supposed to come into contact with anybody but priests."

A massively muscular guard, having planted his boots in the middle of the doorway and his unsheathed sword point between his boots, announced, "I say your words." Presumably this meant he understood their language and would repeat everything he heard to the High Warlord. After this, he neither moved nor spoke again all night.

Foolish, Sioned thought. *If he'd kept his mouth shut, we might have discussed plans he could report later.*

Then: *Plans?* I'm the fool here.

She could do nothing. Not with steel piercing her hand. The High Warlord knew that. So why not make them feel even more helpless by warning them their words would be understood?

So they said nothing as they waited for the morning.

Of them all, Sioned alone knew what Pol intended: to surround Meiglan with the kind of weaving she herself had used so many years ago—and from this very castle—to screen Rohan and Roelstra as they fought. Pol would do it with the help of a few *diarmadh'im* while Andry constructed the *ros'salath*—thus elegantly avoiding any chance of a battle for control.

But now he would have to expand his weaving to include Sioned, Alasen, Ruala, Beth, and Isriam. And with Ruala unavailable to Andry—and Ruala's husband more inclined to help Pol than the Lord of Goddess Keep—where would the sorcerers come from to protect the *ros'salath* from iron?

Sioned had hoped the Vellant'im would all be dead or dying by now—thus even more elegantly avoiding any battles at all. The prospect of disposing of the enemy had brought the others willingly to her aid here. But she hadn't missed their revulsion when they learned she meant not to cripple but to kill.

She gave a mental shrug. Condemn her act as they would, they were glad enough of it. Feeling guilty over it, of course. *There's your precious "civilization" for you, Rohan. I could excuse myself by saying I didn't use my gifts and therefore didn't break my vow—but you'd know that for an expediency the instant I opened my mouth. I was always more of a barbarian than you. Ruthlessness comes easier and quicker to me.*

If not for the needle in her palm, she would have charred the High Warlord and all his minions to a crisp without a second thought.

It was still quite dark when the High Warlord arrived with an escort of twelve. Meiglan arched a delicate brow.

"Two for each of us? How flattering to be considered so dangerous still."

"Terrified of five helpless women and a boy," Alasen added, her biting scorn a perfect foil for Meiglan's sweet sarcasm.

But as she was first to be untied, hauled to her feet, and bound once more, Meiglan said icily, "Hurt her, hurt any of them, and the *Azhrei* will burn you one layer of skin at a time."

The High Warlord's bow was a masterwork of mockery—but their guard and two of the escort cast wary glances at the captives.

As he straightened, Sioned bit her tongue between her teeth to hold back a cry of sheer anguish. The shift of his black hair from one ear had revealed a gold gemstone piercing the lobe, a glowing drop of topaz that she had last seen Rohan wear. The pain was as intense as if someone had made Sorin's Feruche into a whorehouse. *For this alone,* she promised herself, forbidding tears, *for this alone, I'll kill you.*

Outside in the predawn gloom, the courtyard was thick with horses being saddled and warriors coming into formation. The High Warlord led the way through the gates, holding a torch aloft. The clans camped around the lake had assembled to watch the little procession. Silence began to unnerve Sioned. She had been stared at by thousands during every *Rialla* since 698, but never in such profound—and malicious—quiet.

Light flirted with ragged edges of the crater, gilding crags where dragons had perched and preened. Below somewhere, not yet within her sight, was a length of sand strewn with Ruala's dishes; beyond that, Pol's army. Andry should be about ready to play Fire games with the former, while the latter watched and cheered. They would be eager for the battle Sioned had hoped to spare them.

Pol had hoped so, too. But where she had tried to prevent deaths today by killing last night, he didn't want *anyone* to die.

You'd be proud of him, beloved. So am I, when it comes down to it. He understands now what it means to be High Prince. But his way isn't yours, and it isn't mine. He has what you never did, what not even I could give you.

Somewhere among the seven hundred at Pol's command were Thassalante and ninety-eight other sorcerers.

Ianthe's gift. I hope she's watching—and writhing.

✳

"Come on, Alleyn!" Audran hissed. "Don't you want to know what happens?"

His sister frowned. "Princess Tobin—"

"But you don't think she'll let *us* listen, do you? You know how grown-ups are when important things are going on. Nothing but *you shouldn't be here* and *find something to do,* and the battle will be over before we even know it's being fought!"

Alleyn glanced at the bathroom door, behind which their grandparents were dressing by candlelight. A servant had tiptoed in a little while ago to tell them Princess Tobin would receive them whenever they were ready. Alleyn and Audran, roused from their nest of blankets near the hearth, knew very well what *that* meant.

But all they'd been told was to go back to sleep. At thirteen, this galled Alleyn for reasons different from nine-year-old Audran's, but she had to admit she was in perfect sympathy with him. And, she reminded herself, she'd better go along to keep an eye on him. As the eldest, it was her responsibility to make sure he and the other children didn't do something dreadful.

She pulled on woolen stockings in tacit agreement with her brother's plan, but cautioned, "We'll get into *awful* trouble."

"So what?"

"You sound like Jihan," she observed disapprovingly, then paused in reaching for her shirt. "This is her idea, isn't it?"

"So what?" Audran repeated. "It's a *good* idea."

Alleyn was more convinced than ever that her presence was necessary. Jihan was capable of just about anything.

"Mama and Papa are there," Audran said in a voice suddenly gone very small. "Don't you want to know what they—"

"Quick, back under the covers!"

They pretended to be asleep. Their grandparents paused for a little while beside their blankets on the floor, whispering too softly for Alleyn to hear. A loving hand brushed her hair. The caress reminded her of the mother she hadn't seen in longer than she could remember; tears stung her eyes under closed lids. A moment later, the outer door snicked shut.

Audran was up at once, grabbing for his shoes. "Besides, Jihan doesn't believe there's anybody in the mirror. Why won't anybody teach us how to call Fire? Then we could *prove* it."

Both these indignities had rankled Alleyn, too—the skepticism more than the Fire. You couldn't tell high-and-mighty Jihan anything. Antalya said she'd been very princessy for a while and it had been sort of annoying. This was as much condemnation as gently-spoken Talya could manage, followed immediately by the explanation that Jihan was very worried about her sister and her mother. Well, Alleyn hadn't seen either of her parents since the terrible night Graypearl and Sandeia had burned, but *she* hadn't turned all nasty and ordered everyone around.

Alleyn was a princess, too, and if it took a princess to stand up to Jihan, she was more than willing. There *was* a man's face in that mirror, and they'd prove it. Even if they would have to rely on somebody else to call Fire.

The two of them sneaked out of the chamber and down the hall to the stairs. Jihan and Rislyn met them there, holding hands.

"We're going up to the Attic," Jihan said. "Nobody will look for us there."

"Won't they be having breakfast?" Alleyn asked, voicing what to her was a logical objection.

Jihan snorted. "This early? Climb all those steps just for a cup of taze and some bread?"

"We thought of that, too," Rislyn said, and it was hard for Alleyn to believe that such shining green eyes saw nothing. "We're pretty sure they're in Aunt Tobin's room. It overlooks the Desert, so it's easier to go Sunrunning."

"Big windows," Jihan added. "And plenty of sunlight."

Audran frowned. "Pretty sure?"

"Maara went to check." Rislyn's blind eyes turned to her twin. "I still say we should tell Tobren about this. Her father's at Skybowl, too, you know."

"Let's leave her out of this," Jihan replied, and for once Alleyn was in agreement with her. She didn't much like Lord Andry's daughter, either.

"Talya and Jahnev should be here by now," Rislyn said. "Will you run down the hall and check, Audran? Thank you."

He obliged. Moments later, Rislyn frowned slightly.

"I hear four people."

Alleyn blinked. She didn't hear anybody at all.

"Oh, Goddess," Jihan moaned. "They brought Meig!"

*

Alasen clenched her fingers and bit back a whimper of pain as the needle shifted in her right hand. Willing herself to relax, as desperately as she willed herself not to be afraid, she watched helplessly while Meiglan was freed of the white cords that bound her. Alasen's own bonds were heavy ropes that cut into her skin despite Meiglan's warning to the High Warlord. Her right arm was bent at the elbow and lashed to her chest, the rope looped around her neck. She could touch her lips with her fingers but couldn't lower her chin far enough to pull the needle out with her teeth—for her left arm was drawn tightly behind her back and secured with the rope that circled her throat. Bending her head would throttle her; working around to gain some slack for her left arm would wrench her shoulder the rest of the way from its socket.

Sioned, Ruala, Beth, and Isriam were similarly bound. Hopelessly bound. Alasen once more sent an apology to Meiglan with her eyes, and once more received a gentle smile and slight shake of the head in reply.

Meiglan believed utterly in Pol's ability to free her. Alasen wished she shared that belief. All around them—

massed below on the slope of the crater and strung in clanmaster ranks on either side—stood more than two thousand Vellant'im thirsting for Meiglan's blood.

And mine. She heard the blood pounding in her ears with the acceleration of her heartbeat, and forced the rhythm back to something approximating normal. If she didn't control her fear, her body would collapse of it.

She cursed her predicament's irony. She had rejected her Sunrunner gift all her life. Now that she ached to use it, doing so would kill her.

She glanced at Ruala, standing to her right. She, too, looked unafraid, but not for Meiglan's reason. Ruala looked as if she felt this simply couldn't be happening to her. Alasen wished she could share that, too. But Ruala was with child, she remembered. During her own pregnancies she'd been so emotionally attuned to the baby beneath her heart that nothing else seemed quite real.

On Alasen's left, Isriam was purely furious. Betheyn was worried for everybody but herself. Sioned stood beyond them, a few paces apart. Her green eyes, fixed on the High Warlord, glinted with bitter hate.

He was a magnificent sight, resplendent in snowy shirt and trousers, a diamond dripping rubies in one earlobe and a topaz in the other. He needed no weapon to imply physical power, and this morning carried none—only a golden knife in his belt. He stood on the tallest of the crags where all his men could see him—and Pol's army, too, well out of arrow-shot beyond the "dragon teeth."

The thought of the trick about to be played made Alasen feel a little better. But burgeoning confidence dissolved into confusion when a series of high-pitched whistles drifted up from the Desert.

Alasen gave a start when horses began to shift restlessly along the slope. The three whistles, each a different four-note sequence, were repeated. Then a second set of three sounded, and every horse in Vellanti possession either whinnied or began to move.

Sioned was grinning.

Radzyn horses were trained to stay put when their reins dangled. Riders grabbed for loose leather as the whistles sounded again. A dozen mounts escaped and galloped down to the Desert—and then Alasen understood.

Sioned laughed openly now as Vellant'im scrambled to restrain six hundred frantic horses. Many warriors were dragged halfway down the hill before they got control of the animals; several were trampled beneath hooves that dug into the ground in response to the summoning whistles.

Another twenty or thirty horses broke free. Alasen nudged Ruala and whispered, "Foals are taught to come to mama with that whistle—a different one for each stud's get. It's taught to whoever buys them so they can call their horses for saddling."

Comprehension sparkled in dark green eyes. "And all these horses are from Radzyn!"

Sioned's laughter earned her a backhand blow from one of her clanmaster guards. She caught her breath and shook her head as if to clear it, but there was no pain in her eyes: only mockery as she laughed again at the High Warlord.

✳

"Only sixty-two, out of six hundred," Chay complained. "Damn."

Andry shrugged. "Well, it was worth a try."

"It made the Vellant'im even more nervous," Maarken reminded them. "And that's all to the good." He paused to straighten the silver belt around Andry's waist and brush a lock of hair from blue eyes. "Your turn, little brother."

"Goddess go with you, my Lord," Chay said gruffly.

Andry glanced at him, surprised. "I think that's the first time you've ever called me that."

"I don't intend to make a habit of it," was the wry answer. "Go on. And have a care to yourself, son."

Andry grasped his father's hands briefly in his own. "I like that title much better." Turning, he said to Evarin, "You go stand with the ladies—and keep back. This is likely to singe anybody who gets too close."

✳

Evarin made sure the ladies were comfortably seated on their cloaks, then settled onto his own. If Andry drew too strongly on them, they wouldn't be hurt if they toppled over. Feylin stood nearby the little circle of Sunrunners, arms folded and gray eyes sharp as steel.

"We'll be all right," Hollis assured her.

"I hope he knows what he's doing," Feylin replied.

Evarin had slowly grown accustomed to the way these Desert people talked about Andry. It must be difficult, he thought, to hold in any kind of awe someone you'd swaddled, swatted, and sworn at.

Still, it stung him to hear so little respect for the Lord of Goddess Keep. "He knows better than anyone, my lady," he told Feylin.

She snorted. "He'd better."

Chayla's mare nudged her shoulder, and she turned to stroke the animal's nose. "It's not Andry we should be worrying about," she said. "It's what the Vellant'im will do when they see his conjuring."

"Run like all Hells would be my choice," Jeni admitted nervously.

Chayla shrugged. "It all depends on what and how they believe. Those who don't believe what they see and won't be afraid—they'll be dangerous. The ones who believe and are frightened will be easy to beat. But those few who believe and yet are unafraid—they're the ones *we* need to fear."

Hollis touched her daughter's arm. "None of them would be here at all if they didn't believe in their superstitions. That's how their High Warlord and their priests compel them to battle."

Jeni glanced around at the sound of hoofbeats, and scowled. "Whereas some of *our* mighty warriors ride into battle through sheer stupidity."

Evarin followed her gaze. Lord Sethric and Prince Daniv had met near the latter's contingent of cavalry. Their words were inaudible, but the gestures were eloquent: Daniv pointing to the unfurled dragon tapestry on a rise of dunes, Sethric jabbing a finger down at the sand his horse stood on.

"The Prince of Syr has no luck ordering a Lord of Grib to take himself and his useless leg somewhere safe," Feylin mused.

Hollis smiled. "I take it the Lady of Remagev failed, too?"

Jeni climbed to her feet, lightning flashing from her cloud-gray eyes. "Well, a Lady of Castle Crag damned well intends to succeed! Idiot!" she spat, and stormed away across the sand.

Evarin opened his mouth to call the girl back where she belonged. But all his thoughts and all his breath were taken away with the first touch of Andry's *dranath*-augmented colors.

He never saw Jeni stumble to her knees, or Daniv and Sethric leave off their argument, or Feylin leap to keep inexperienced Chayla from collapsing.

✳

Eight young faces were reflected in the mirror, crowding close. In coloring, they seemed to come in two pairs and a trio, with one left over. Jihan and Rislyn were the palest, their fair hair coming from both parents and their eyes taking each color of Pol's, blue and green. Alleyn's braids had been lightened by the Desert sun almost to the red-gold of Talya's; both had blue eyes and an infinity of freckles. Meig, standing on tiptoe in the front, and Jahnev and Audran, just beside him, were all brown-haired and pale-eyed. Maara was the different one, the dark one, her black hair and deep brown Fironese eyes making her seem some exotic changeling.

"So what's it do?" Meig asked.

"It doesn't *do* anything," Audran replied. "But there's somebody inside it."

"Sure," Jihan said.

"Call Fire and you'll see," Alleyn challenged.

"We have more important things to do." Jihan guided Rislyn over to the open west windows. The first full dawn's light shone white-gold in their hair. Alleyn noted with grudging honesty that Jihan changed completely when helping her twin. "I can see Lir'reia—she's circling straight ahead of where we're facing, about halfway up the sky."

Meig eyed the mirror, the nearly spent candles to either side of it, and the gemstones set along the top. "Who's in there?"

"We don't know. A man." Audran looked at Talya. "Can you—?"

"I don't know that I should," she began.

"I can," said Meig, and one of the candles flared to life.

Alleyn held her breath. *He* should be there, that strange dark face she and Audran had seen and Jeni had not. She should be looking into his black eyes, tilted at the corners like her mother's and Lord Riyan's and Maara's.

Nothing.

"So?" Meig asked. "When does it happen?"

Alleyn answered reluctantly, "He ... ought to be there...."

"He's not," Jahnev said with a frown. "Why?"

"I don't know, all right?" she exclaimed, turning away. Jihan would never believe them now. She told herself it wasn't important; she knew what she'd seen and Audran could confirm it. So could High Prince Pol, for that matter. But Jihan's scornful glance from the windows pricked her pride all the same.

Meig shrugged and let the flame go out. He wandered around for a few moments, then curled into a chair near the sideboard. "Jahnev," he said to his brother, "tell me when somebody sees Mama."

And with that, he wrapped his arms around an embroidered pillow and went to sleep.

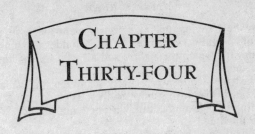

CHAPTER THIRTY-FOUR

And so it begins, Sioned thought. *This thing that was their goal from the first, for which they killed from Graypearl to New Raetia so we would be helpless when this day finally came. One woman, all alone, and a gold knife ready to kill her. They think it's done for the honor—or is it the blood-thirst?—of their God. They think he watches. Does Andry think the Goddess looks on, too? Does Pol? Do any of them understand that it's* people *doing this, and deities have nothing to do with it at all?*

Ruala began her translations in a whisper, but when no command to silence was forthcoming, she spoke in a normal tone. Sioned would rather she'd continued softly. These were things Meiglan didn't need to hear.

Perhaps she can't. Up on that rock with him, he's shouting practically in her ear—Goddess, please don't let her be listening to Ruala as well. How alone she must feel. . . .

". . . don't matter," Ruala was saying. "Not the horses or the deaths of the priests or any of the *Azhrei*'s evil magic. It's what they came here to destroy. The Father of Winds showed them the way, told them how—" She broke off, breath catching in her throat.

How alone she's always been . . . and what did I ever do to help her, love her, make her feel part of us?

"What?" Alasen demanded. "What's he telling them?"

"That the White Sacrifice is set forth in their own—I mean, *our* own—sacred book of dragons."

Left for them by me. Sioned stared straight ahead, stony-faced. *Clever High Princess.*

"Now he's saying that the priests were the *Azhrei's* attempt at a similar sacrifice, to the Goddess—something about sin, for which the *Azhrei* and all who follow him will have to die."

Her last few words were nearly inaudible; the Vellant'im had let out a roar in response to their High Warlord.

"Killing a priest is a sin," Sioned murmured. "And I killed a hundred."

Ruala shifted in her bonds, trying to ease the strain on her shoulder. "He attributes it to Pol."

"Of course. We're only women." *Interesting, this concept of sin. Killing a priest, killing a Sunrunner . . . but you'd never get Andry to understand that.*

The High Warlord waited for the tumult to die down. Reminded of their purpose, the Vellant'im seemed to have forgotten the army waiting down below—or were deliberately ignoring the *Azhrei's* troops to show their contempt.

Ruala continued, a sentence or two behind the powerful bellowing voice above. "Now that the priests are dead, the White Sacrifice cannot take place. That's what the *Azhrei* believes. But he's—" She gasped, all the color draining from her cheeks and the sunlight harsh on the silver in her hair. "Oh, no," she breathed. "No—"

Sioned turned her head as far as the ropes would allow. "Ruala."

"Yes, I–I'm sorry–he says the *Azhrei* is wrong. It's more important now than ever—and *he* will do it. He says they all remember how the High Warlord, with the priests'—permission? Blessing? I don't know—"

A flicker of warm breeze stroked Sioned's skin. The noise of the warriors' approval assaulted her ears. The High Warlord stood with both arms raised, gold knife glinting in one fist.

She moved close to Ruala. "Tell me."

"He killed his own eldest son—oh, Sioned, he used the boy's blood to p–purify the ships, so the Father of Storms would give them fair winds—" She moaned, and if not for the ropes would have doubled over. "I think I'm going to be sick!"

Sioned left it to Alasen and Betheyn to calm and support her as they could. The High Warlord stuck the knife back in his belt and gestured. A young man all in white sprang forward with a rattling necklet of leather thongs and talons and teeth. This, too, was held aloft, to great cheering, before the High Warlord draped it around Meiglan's shoulders.

Morwenna's Elidi, Sioned thought. *Trophies of his kill.*

As if he'd heard her, he turned half around and stared directly into her eyes. A tiny smile curved his lips—neither sneering nor triumphant, nor even ferocious as she might have expected. Rather, he seemed to include her in some private joke that only she would appreciate.

He doesn't believe a word of this, she realized suddenly. *Not a single word or action. He knows what I know: that the God doesn't care what's done here any more than the dragons do. Whoever wins will claim holy favor. But people do what they do for their own reasons, and use Goddess or God or Nameless One to justify it. Nothing he's saying is more than sounds on the wind. He's playing them as skillfully as Meiglan at her* fenath, *every note perfectly chosen—and for him, utterly silent.*

He inclined his head in sardonic acknowledgment of her shocked comprehension, black light dancing in his black eyes.

Yes, I understand, she thought. *You can use their superstitions more effectively than Pol. You've been doing it for years—even to butchering your own son. And all of it because you hate us with the kind of passion most people never understand. Nothing else matters—not even a son. I am impressed by your ruthlessness, my lord. It appalls me, but I'm honest enough to admire it for what it is.*

Actually, we seem to be two of a kind.

No, beloved, said a soft voice, its very gentleness vanquishing her despair. *You and he are nothing alike. How can you think so? What he* does *is in the service of hate. The prize for* him *is death.*

Her eyes shifted wildly, searching rocks and sky. *Rohan?* Only memory—but his voice lived within her more surely than her own heartbeat.

The High Warlord turned back to his warriors. A second youth clad in white climbed up to give him a velvet pouch. From this he extracted a glowing black rainbow split into six tear-shaped shards. Sioned wasn't even looking at them with *faradhi* eyes, and still she could see power shimmering around the pearls, their *aleva* like a Sunrunner's or sorcer-er's.

And it hurt. With the needle stabbing through her palm, the sight of them hurt. She looked away, and the pain faded.

A glance at Alasen told her she couldn't feel it. Ruala didn't, either. An indication of power, perhaps—Johlarian had to concentrate to sense the pearls, but Saumer had no trouble. Neither did Pol and Andry. Merisel had worn them—once. With gifts as strong as hers, their contact with her flesh must have been like black lightning.

The two young men came forward once more, carrying heavy silver poles twice their height surmounted by golden dragons with outstretched wings. Around the poles was wrapped thick white cloth; unrolled, it formed a taut curtain behind Meiglan and the High Warlord, sealing them from Sioned's view. To the left stood yet another youth, supporting a tall staff from which the crowned lightning-bolt banner flared.

More sons? Sioned wondered, noting the set of their bones, their height, the touch of additional arrogance common to offspring of the truly powerful. Then her eyes were drawn to the shadow play on the white cloth. The sun was fully risen now. Meiglan and the High Warlord were outlined against the white cloth like thread-sketchings of a tapestry.

"Sioned—he's going to kill her," Ruala hissed. "What are we going to do?"

"Wait," she said.

"For what?" cried Alasen.

One sketch lifted the long, sharp shadow of a knife. Sioned tensed for the splatter of red blood on white cloth. The Vellant'im bellowed for Meiglan's death—

—and then blurted in surprise and terror.

A subtle, familiar tingle at the edges of her mind announced a Sunrunner's presence nearby. As it strengthened, so did the burning ache in her hand.

Alasen stumbled against her, choking. Sioned almost lost her balance. "Ruala—help us!"

Hard hands held her upright, digging into her arms. The last thing she thought before the pain and the colors swept over her was, *Well, Andry, my lad, you certainly have a sense of timing.*

*

He knew the instant he gathered Evarin, Hollis, Chayla, and Jeni into the conjuring that not even with the *dranath* would he be able to manage it. Not in the spectacular fashion demanded, with dozens of fiery warriors springing from the sand. He disciplined two very practiced and two very raw powers with casual skill, sending Fire across the Desert in a distracting whirlwind. He broke it into separate pieces and began the first few images simultaneously. A few would not be enough. He could establish them and let the others maintain them as he conjured more, but the most he could hope for was ten or twenty. He needed dozens, and to do it, he needed power.

So he reached for the most powerful Sunrunner he knew.

He saw her there, just below the rocks and the white banner stretched behind the High Warlord, sunlight shafting through a break in the crags to strike sparks from her green eyes. Alasen beside her, Ruala, Betheyn and Isriam nearby; each brutally bound. Behind each was a warrior of many, many kills.

Damn them! But he shoved his fury and outrage aside and wove a net of light to fling around Sioned.

Shock ripped through him. *No! It shouldn't hurt!*

Andry—the needles—find Riyan, quick!

He hadn't known he'd sent the words until Sioned answered—a feeble mockery of her usually crisp mental voice. He didn't understand what she meant, but he could feel her colors bleed at the edges, stinking of cruel iron.

Andry, please! Ruala can't shield us alone!

He sought, and found, and wrapped the startled colors through the sunlight. Instinct and familiarity made Riyan weave himself with Ruala, and together they spun protection for the vulnerable *faradh'im*. The pain eased, not entirely gone but bearable.

It was the best Andry could do for them. He began to work.

A dozen columns of flame burst from the sand, growing arms and legs and swords. Dozens more formed behind them, around them. An army sown of dragon teeth rose from the Desert at the Lord of Goddess Keep's bidding, and he laughed within himself as horrified Vellant'im scrambled up Skybowl's hillside, dropping their swords in their frantic haste.

We'll win without even a fight! he exulted. *Sunrunners*

and sorcerers together—under my *direction. Not Pol's. Mine.*

And Sioned made not a murmur of protest, or any attempt to work on her own that would siphon power away from him.

Well, it was time she got into it. With both of them conjuring, they could send the enemy screaming into the Desert for Tilal to pick off at leisure.

Take the west, he told her. When she gave no answer, he called on *dranath* to increase the force of his words. *Sioned! To the west! Another fifty or so, and we'll have them!*

. . . can't. . . . Her colors shivered. *Use me, Andry . . . but I c–can't . . . work. . . .*

He sensed it then: Riyan and Ruala had put their energies into guarding *him.* The Sunrunners would not die, for the conjuring was his alone. But by weaving them into its structure he was causing them unbelievable agony. Sioned, Evarin, Hollis, Chayla, Jeni—*Alasen*—he cursed himself for a careless, thoughtless, overconfident fool.

. . . that's d–*dranath for you. . . .* Sioned's voice was a mere whisper now. *Finish it, please . . . can't stand . . . much more. . . .*

He released them one by one, as quickly as he dared. And heard their moans at the surcease of pain.

The Fire conjurings vanished. Andry barely noticed. He threaded the sunlight and looked at the captive *faradh'im* again. This time, as they sagged into their guards' rough grasp, he saw their right hands trembling in spasms, and the needles through their palms, dark now with the renewed flow of blood.

✳

When Andry strode to the front of the army, newborn sunlight dazzling off white clothes and silver breastplate, Pol exchanged a wry glance with Maarken.

"Nice entrance," he remarked.

"Family talent," Chay growled. "Your family—not mine."

When Fire swept across the Desert and warriors were conjured of two parts flame and two parts Andry's imagination, Pol nodded sincere admiration of his cousin's control.

"That's it, keep 'em coming. . . ."

"They'll have to build a separate tower at Goddess Keep to house his conceit," Chay muttered.

Maarken winked at Pol, each hearing the pride through the gruffness.

When dozens became a hundred, then close to two hundred, Pol's jaw dropped. "How in all Hells is he doing that?"

"Does it matter?" Maarken asked, awe in his voice for his brother's power.

But when Daniv galloped up, leaped from his horse, and whispered urgently to Pol, "My lord, stop him! He's killing them!"—Pol had time only to glance at the young prince before the fiery warriors vanished.

"What the—? What happened?" Chay didn't wait for an answer he knew they couldn't give. Swinging up into the saddle as if he had forty winters instead of seventy, he cantered out to his son. Andry mounted behind him and a few moments later they had returned to Pol, Maarken, and Daniv.

"Damn them!" Andry slid down from behind his father's saddle, shaking with rage. "The whoresons used steel needles—right through their hands! I needed their colors, but the iron—"

"Are they all right?" Maarken asked. "What about Hollis and Chayla?"

"The pain ended with the working." He raked both hands through his sun-gilt brown hair, rings and wristbands bright. *"Damn* them!"

Pol sent Daniv back to the other Sunrunners. Then he walked a few paces away, his movements stiff with fury and helplessness.

Once Andry had conjured the warriors and maintained them for a little while, Pol had planned to set a dome around Meiglan the way Sioned had around Rohan and Roelstra. Once the High Warlord discovered he *couldn't* kill Meiglan, he'd turn his attention to battle. If he convinced his men to fight—doubtful after the priests' deaths, dragons' teeth, and Meiglan's immunity—Pol would use the *ros'salath* to push the Vellant'im into the Desert. Surrounding them with his own cavalry, he would order them to surrender their swords and give them safe passage to their ships at Radzyn. No one would have to die.

He would not—would *not*—use the *ros'salath* to kill.

Andry wouldn't see it that way, of course. Andry, who had entreated the Goddess to help them kill.

Earlier, once what Sionell told him about the priests had sunk in, Pol had blessed his mother even though he was horrified by her actions. He understood why she'd told him nothing: in case it didn't work, he wouldn't be counting on it. There would be no frantic revision of tactics, no scramble to work out an alternative.

But with the priests dead, he'd thought Meiglan safe. Now his thoughts skittered like a thousand frantic, frightened mice. Sight of the High Warlord brandishing a gold knife had stopped Pol's heart. Priests or no priests, Meiglan was going to die.

Pol turned on his boot heel. "Maarken."

"My prince," said his Battle Commander, coming to his side.

"Whatever happens, I forbid you the sunlight. Do you understand? I don't want you even to *think* about Sunrunning."

"Pol—"

"I don't need you," Pol said bluntly. "Not as a *faradhi*. I need you to win this battle for me if I fail." He paced back to where the others stood, singling out Andry with his eyes. "My Lord, I thank you for trying. No one could have done more—or even half as much. I ask you now to yield control of the *ros'salath* to me."

Andry's eyes were startlingly blue, pupils contracted to pinpoints in reaction to brightening sunlight—and *dranath*. "You don't have the experience. Bring Thassalante and his people in, and I'll do whatever you like. But it must be mine, Pol."

"A generous offer that I must refuse. You can't do it without the *diarmadh'im*, and they won't participate unless I'm—"

"You've never done it successfully. I have. Look it in the face, Pol. I can do it. You can't."

"Andry," Pol said quietly. "I beg of you, don't fight me."

Chay grabbed Andry's silver-armored shoulder and Pol's brass-greaved arm. "You think Meiglan has time for this? Look at the sky!"

The first moon was rising, white and full in the pale blue sky.

Maarken had mounted his horse, and was now at the head of the army. His voice rang out in the clear morning air.

"Sorry my father and I couldn't whistle up a victory for you!" he shouted. "But now they'll keep half an eye on their stolen Radzyn and Whitecliff horses—just in case! I'm even sorrier my brother couldn't conjure up two armies instead of only one—these bearded bastards just don't know when they're defeated before they begin! They seem determined to pretend they're brave!"

"Aye," a woman called out derisively. "Brave enough against a whistle and a Fire, m'lord!"

"Exactly," Maarken agreed. "They haven't met up with *you* yet, Hestiba!"

Laughter rippled through the ranks. Pol's gaze still locked with Andry's in a battle of wills that would determine whether these people would fight a battle in blood.

"As for the other eye—after the show my brother put on, you know where *that's* going to be! On every grain of sand in the Desert—just in case! Which by my reckoning leaves them half an eye each. And unless each of them has a *third* eye hidden under his beard, they'll be fighting damned near blind!"

Giving no quarter, receiving none, Pol and Andry called a silent truce and turned to watch Maarken. The Battle Commander resumed speaking, his voice quieter yet still carrying to the four massed groups of cavalry. Walvis led his former students and his own guard from Remagev, with Laroshin as captain. The much-diminished knot of Isulk'im was led by Visian. Daniv was temporarily absent from sharing command with Draza of Rohan's Stronghold troops and the few who had survived Tuath; the last group, the largest, was Maarken's own.

"But we *are* going into this with a third eye—and a fourth, and a hundredth. Remember Stronghold? Remember how they were penned like sheep and you picked them off neat as a dragon's breakfast? We called it Sunrunners' Rings. Well, we've got more Sunrunners here with more rings than sense—as is usual of the breed," he added, and they chuckled again at the self-deprecating humor. "But we also have something else—some*one* else."

His right hand, rings aglitter, pointed to where Thassalante and his ninety-eight sorcerers stood apart from the army.

"Yes, they're *diarmadh'im*. And today it'll be Sunrunners and sorcerers working together, with all the power and Fire they can weave among them."

"Those whoreson Vellant'im don't have a hope!" bellowed an Isulki.

"Hope?" Maarken seized on the word. "Let me tell you something. Going into a fight *hoping* for victory is as futile as if I *hoped* this would be restored to me!" He held up his maimed left arm. "I don't *hope* we'll win—I *know* it!"

"Well, cousin?" Pol murmured under the confirming roar, sensing along every prickle of his skin the Vellanti reorganization up the mountain. "He's made the commitment for us both. He's got us. And we're stuck with each other."

"Just like always? Not quite, Pol."

Before Chay could stop him, he vaulted into the saddle with a born horseman's ease and galloped to where Maarken sat his own horse. Cheers swelled anew as he made his appearance—just as when he'd ridden out to conjure warriors from pottery shards.

Pol watched with a weary bitterness. *To him, anything that's not winning is losing. He'll fight me. With one moon rising and a knife at Meiglan's throat, he'll fight me.*

"My brother the Battle Commander has told you the right of it," he called out. "You don't know me as well as you know Maarken, so I'll tell you my part of it myself. Even if I didn't wear these ten rings, I'd still be here to fight for you and alongside you. I was born here, bred here through all the generations back to the first prince to rule the Desert. I've come back to defend it—and I bring with me all the power of the Goddess' Sunrunners. You've heard how the Vellant'im were beaten back at Goddess Keep. I'm ready to lead the *faradh'im* here in doing the same."

He stopped, looking off to where the sorcerers stood. "You know as well as I what *some* sorcerers have done in the past. I have opposed them with all my strength. But that must be forgotten now. I am willing to do so—to forget even what *some* sorcerers are doing at this very moment in Firon."

Pol's every muscle went rigid. *You self-serving piece of—*

"Yet I'm told they will not work with me because I'm Lord of Goddess Keep. They've put a condition on helping with this task. That condition is *him*."

He pointed at Pol, of course.

"They call him *Diarmadh'rei*—their prince. Why is that? you ask. Why should High Prince Rohan's son, a *faradhi* by gifts if not by formal training, hold authority over sorcerers?"

Maarken's face was carved of stone. His lifelong nightmare was here and real, and it paralyzed him. Pol saw it, and damned both himself and Andry.

But exclusively Andry for something else. *Rohan's son— but not Sioned's. That's what he wants me to admit. What it would do to her—I should've beaten him senseless when I had the chance.*

Daniv, who had returned with Sethric to whisper that the Sunrunners were all right, stiffened as if he'd swallowed a sword. "What is he talking about?"

"How should I know?" Sethric looked down from his saddle at Chay. "My lord, he's *your* son—silence him!"

The old man shook his head gently. "Pol is High Prince now or never at all. For everyone. It's time they knew it."

Hearing him, Pol forced his body to suppleness and walked forward. Some might think it a disadvantage not to be on horseback, but Rohan's instincts ran through Pol strong and sure. He'd never mastered the knack of collecting all attention with a single glance, but this was an acceptable substitute.

As he approached, Maarken dismounted. It forced Andry to do the same or lose the army to resentment of his disrespect for their High Prince.

"They call me *Diarmadh'rei*," Pol said, "because of what I am."

Andry stood quite still, his eyes the eyes of a hunting cat quivering with the scent of a kill. Maarken, just as immobile outwardly, trembled just as hard inside—but as if he was the prey.

"It's true," Pol said, making sure his words carried, "that the *diarmadh'im* will weave sunlight only if I am present within it." He faced the mounted soldiers, rows on rows of them, straining to see him. "It's also true that you follow Lord Maarken because he long since earned your trust. *Trust,*" he repeated. "That's what matters."

And the sorcerers don't *trust Andry, for the reasons Andry himself said. Everybody knows it. Tactical error, cousin.*

He paused, trying to find the words, then shrugged mentally. This was one of those times his father had spoken of, when only one course was possible, and you did or said the only thing you could.

"Their name for me is *Diarmadh'rei*. I suppose I could also be called *Faradh'rei*." Andry's eyes ignited; Pol enjoyed it only for a split instant. The first moon was rising low and fast, just as Audrite had predicted. "Your name for me is High Prince. Whatever words you use, what I am in the end is yours."

They agreed, and left no doubt that they agreed. Pol had heard this roar for his father many times. It was a sound different than what he'd heard for himself since Rohan's death. *You do belong to us,* their shouts told him now, *and we to you.*

He held up a hand for quiet. When he had it, he said, "I will say now what I had thought to wait for until this was finished. I swear to you that I will be High Prince for everyone. Now, with the help of the *diarmadh'im* and the Lord of Goddess Keep, it *will* be finished."

Andry stepped smoothly to his side. "Well done," he murmured for only Pol to hear. "My compliments."

Pol gestured Maarken back up onto his horse, and with Andry beside him paced across the sand toward Skybowl.

"You avoided the issue quite cleverly," Andry continued. "When will you admit to them what and who you truly are?"

"Never." He half-expected the sand to suck at his feet, dragging his steps. He should have known better. Each individual grain was firm under his boots, supporting his every step in dawn-pale gold. He was High Prince. This was *his* Desert. He belonged to this land.

"How will you explain Jihan and Rislyn? You'll have to someday, you know."

Pol shrugged. "Miyon believed what you told him."

"Good Goddess—poor little Meiglan?" Andry forced a laugh. "Another lie for the list. You're that afraid they'd reject you?"

"I'm that concerned for my mother's peace." *And it won't hurt if people believe that Meiglan—but she won't use it, like Alasen—that'll explain—let's see Andry come after the High Princess for being—oh, Goddess, Meggie, Meggie, she must be terrified up there—*

He headed for a tall dune, knowing how exposed and isolated the two of them would be. Out of arrow-shot, but a short ride down Skybowl would remedy that for the Vellant'im.

With an effort, Pol resumed, "While we were talking, so was the High Warlord. Probably about why the warriors vanished, or that the *Azhrei*'s power is waning and they have nothing to fear. But Meiglan is the key. They won't attack until she's—" He paused to clear his throat. "It must be the signal."

"Then you plan to shield just her?" Andry shook his head. "They'll hack their way through—and even with all those sorcerers, eventually it's going to hurt. Besides, what happened to me could happen to you, and you'd catch Sioned and Alasen and Ruala in it. That would redouble the pain. Believe me, I know."

"That's why I'm going to weave the sorcerers into it first, and make a shield. Besides, the knife is gold. If you'll take a quick look, you'll see that none of the Vellant'im up on the rocks carries steel of any kind."

"I'll take your word for it. But that leaves the rest of them to deal with. Which means you don't need the sorcerers, not really. Sunrunners can't be hurt by a gold knife."

"Do you honestly think I'd chance that the High Warlord doesn't have steel somewhere on him?"

Andry grunted. "All right. But give me the weaving, Pol. Give it to me, and I promise they'll all be dead before the second moon rises."

Pol ignored the suggestion. "I'll only need a little while, just until it's seen that the High Warlord *can't* kill her."

"Oh, fine. Then they'll go for your mother and Alasen. Pol, you can't limit this weaving just to Meiglan's protection. You have to let me construct a dome out of the *ros'salath* and tighten it around the enemy."

"To kill them all."

"Yes."

Pol resisted a snarl. "While the High Warlord kills Meiglan!"

"Is one life worth more than the hundreds—"

"If it was Alasen's throat, would you say the same thing?"

Their strides had slowed as they climbed the dune. Halfway up, Andry said, "Why am I here, Pol? You don't need me or the Sunrunners."

"You're right—I don't." Pol gained the top of the rise and swung around sharply. "But think what they'll see—our people *and* the Vellant'im. You and I, working with each other and with sorcerers. You wanted me to admit what I am—and this is it."

"High Prince for everyone?" Andry's lip curled. "How noble. Tell me, do you include in this 'everyone' the kin of those who butchered my brother Sorin?"

I even include you, cousin. Pol glanced southeast, where the first moon was three-quarters risen above the sand. Turning, he squinted up the hillside that seethed with Vellant'im, to the white cloth and the two figures before it.

"Andry, if you meant any of what you said about being born and bred here, about fighting for them and beside them—*don't fight me.*"

Silently, the Lord of Goddess Keep climbed up to stand with the High Prince.

*

Jahnev had dragged over a chair for Rislyn. She sat in the sunlight, blind eyes closed beneath frowning pale brows.

"When can she tell us—?" he whispered.

"Shh." Jihan shook her head. The others—except Meig—gathered anxiously nearby, waiting for word of their parents. *If I knew enough about Sunrunning,* Jihan thought resentfully, *I'd do it myself and we wouldn't have to rely on Lir'reia. I don't know what we'll do if she doesn't understand she's to fly over Skybowl and then come back and show Linnie what she sees. And even if she does, she also has to know she can't get too close or they'll kill her.*

Helplessness was a fluttery feeling near her heart and a sickness in her stomach and she hated it. *She* should be doing this—and not just because she always took the lead no matter the risk. It was her duty as her father's daughter and as a Sunrunner. Duty wasn't a new concept, though this was the first time she'd ever thought it in so many words. *I'm a princess and a Sunrunner, and that means responsibilities. Why didn't anybody ever teach me how to do them?*

Rislyn's fingers pressed her own, and she watched her sister's eyes open. "Lir'reia doesn't understand. I'm sorry, Jihan."

Alleyn pushed in a little closer. "You mean we won't know what's happening at Skybowl until somebody tells us?"

Jihan swung around fiercely, ready with the sharp side of her tongue. The deep rumble of another dragon voice turned her back to the window. Lir'reia crouched on the sand now, wings wrapped submissively along her back. But her neck was extended, her head high with defiance. Azhdeen paced before her like an angry father before a naughty child—

Jihan knew that scene well enough. But Azhdeen's sudden roar outdid any scold her father had ever given *her.*

Rislyn gave a start and caught her breath. Jihan held her hand tighter. "It's all right, Linnie. It's just Azhdeen and he's mad at her."

"He sure is," Audran whispered, and in his eyes was certainty that he never, ever wanted a dragon of his own.

"Shh!" Rislyn commanded. "I'm trying to hear!"

Azhdeen bellowed again as Lir'reia straightened up, her tail lashing up a small, furious sandstorm.

Rislyn was nodding. "He's not mad at Lir'reia. Don't you hear it?"

"No," Jihan admitted reluctantly.

Azhdeen reared and screamed again, and this time other dragons responded. Maarken's Pavisel darted by in a black streak, silver flashing under her wings. Azhly landed near Lir'reia in a froth of sand swept up by red-gold wings, howling a demand that made Azhdeen snarl. Soon all eight dragons had gathered, plus the one who had not yet selected a human for his own.

"What are they doing?" Maara whispered as all the dragons fell silent.

"Sunrunning," Jahnev said. "Talking to each other. Not like people do it, but my Granda says they can. And she knows more about dragons than anybody."

"But why? What are they saying?" Talya asked.

Lir'reia bounded a few steps away from the others, and looked straight up at the window where Rislyn sat. Jihan felt her twin go rigid and tremble in the bright sunshine. The dragon's silvery wings spread wide and the blue shadows of her underwings spread across the sand.

✴

Soldiers on horseback stretched the length of Goddess Keep, with Edrel in the middle—the same keystone position Torien had chosen with the *devr'im.* If he'd looked back over his shoulder, he would have seen them at the gate house balcony, already at work in the thin dawn sunlight. Antoun had mentioned that light wasn't necessary for the *ros'salath,* just made it easier. Edrel couldn't help thinking it was comparable to being a bard: the really good ones could move an audience to tears with nothing but their voices. The lesser kind required a supporting lute.

The gates were shut tight. Between them and the mounted troops were rows of foot soldiers—with a goodly number of castle folk and Jayachin's people mixed in. The Sunrunners, of course, were all safely locked into the keep. Torien—or, more to the point, Jolan—had long since commanded that not one of them risk their precious persons in a fight.

Edrel calmed his restive horse. The Vellent'im marched toward him across the muddy field in total silence but for the squelch of their boots and the occasional clang of armor or sword. Soon enough they'd walk right into that horror of an invisible wall. And even while he prayed it would hold, he was of two minds about it. He'd heard what it had done before; no one should die that way, shrieking in madness. And if it *did* hold, and there was nothing for him to do but gather up the bodies for burning, Torien—or, more to the point, Jolan—could make an effective push for real power at Goddess Keep.

There was a sudden sinister hiss as hundreds of Vellant'im simultaneously drew their swords without breaking stride. Edrel swallowed hard. Even knowing what rose in the morning mist to protect him, he'd never even been close to a battle before. He'd never seen massed ranks of armed men march on him with every intention of gutting him and leaving his corpse for the carrion crows.

If this was what war was, then if he survived it he'd spend the rest of his life gladly tucked away at River Ussh.

A thing he knew to be impossible. He was Pol's man, even more than his dead brother Kerluthan had been. Edrel had been Pol's squire; the belt he wore had been bestowed by Pol's own hands. More immediately, all these people around him knew it, and looked to him for leadership. He'd been trained to it. But no part of him wanted to prove how well he'd learned those lessons. He'd been hoping to experience the fever of battle so often described by those who'd fought. Hoping, fearing . . . but all he felt was a terrible bone-deep chill.

Perhaps it would come to him later. If the *ros'salath* broke, and he had to fight, perhaps it would come to him then.

He begged the Goddess even more fervently that the

devr'im would hold firm, no heart in him to care about the enemy's agony or Jolan's plots for power.

✳

The gold knife was warm in his hand. It shone steady in the growing brightness, token of victory to come as soon as it was slicked dark with her blood. He surveyed his restive warriors, judging the effect of his most recent words. The part of their tension due to the *Azhrei*'s tricks had abated. He had condemned the *Azhrei*'s sin of killing the priests, he had scorned the *Azhrei*'s attempt to summon the horses, he had laughed at the *Azhrei*'s feebleness in creating warriors from sand and Fire who instantly vanished. He had them back, when he had almost lost them. But he knew that only with her death would all the clans believe only in him again.

When the fires died, he mounted the highest rocks to shout his derision. The first moon was fully in the sky now. The second would appear soon. The White Sacrifice would die, and the third moon would begin to slip out from behind the first, and the *Azhrei* and all his minions would be slaughtered.

He saw the man appear on a tall dune, armor shining golden and hair even brighter above it, sword sheathed. The other, the *faradhi* lord, stood beside him all in white, silver breastplate like a mirror. A fine pair they were, magnificently arrayed, knowing as well as he the value of posturing.

The green-eyed *Azhreia* understood, too. He was glad she did; it had been a very long time since anyone had truly understood him. But *she* had, without a word being spoken. Yes, the old *Azhrei* had been a fortunate man.

More fortunate still in not living long enough to watch his son die.

He felt the presence of his own sons, separated for the first time from the clans to which he had given them at journey's beginning. He had not thought of them or spoken their names even in his own mind since the dragon ships sailed. It pleased him that their beards were as full and rich as his own had been, and that many golden kills were woven there. There would be another wife for each of them when they returned home, and more grandsons for him.

He glanced down at his frail white victim, framed by the taut white banner. *How I should like to take* you *home with me, and make you my wife, and watch every man who is a man devour his own liver with envy.*

Such a waste. . . .

The second moon slid into view, small and white and curving as a virgin's breast. His warriors greeted it with a thunder of voices and swords on shields that made their horses cry out in alarm.

He inhaled deeply, savoring the moment. Warm air drifted up from the Desert, bearing scents of horse and leather and sweat and fading fears. The sun was clean on his face, sharp on the graceful arc of the knife. He turned, adjusting his grip. He would be swift. He would be merciful. He owed her that.

He gazed down at her for a long moment. Her beauty was unmatched, her cleverness greater than her beauty—and her courage outshone both as the sun outshone the pale moons.

Such a waste.

CHAPTER
THIRTY-FIVE

Andry knew what Pol was doing, though he could not sense it and had no part in it—yet. Sunlight was alive with power that *dranath* let him feel with heightened intensity. He could practically hear colors seething around Pol, colors previously glimpsed only in a now splintered mirror.

In the end, what matter if Pol didn't draw him into this? He was at Pol's side. It was enough. It was Andrade's vision: Lord of Goddess Keep standing with High Prince. If the actual sharing of authority was an illusion—well, hadn't Rohan always said that it was the impression that counted?

He tried not to let it rankle. Pol needed him for show if not substance. It did him and the Sunrunners no actual harm. And if victory was the result, he would be churlish indeed to quarrel with the manner of it.

And yet . . . and yet it was to *him* the Goddess had shown dreams of what might be, warning him. From his belief—tormented as it had been, unsure of the right of it, his logic protesting despite his faith—had come the *ros'salath*. Because of years of *his* work, it existed for Pol to copy and use.

I won't fight him, Andry told himself, even as the drug burned impatiently in his blood, crying out for the spell all around him, to take it and make it his. *He's keeping my oath for me: no more killing with my gifts.* Sioned had been uncomfortably accurate in pointing out his selectivity. In truth, much as he'd enjoyed immolating Marron, who had murdered his brother, and the treacherous Prince of Cunaxa, he understood the peril. Others might think themselves similarly justified—and that was the reason for the vow, the only reason Sunrunners were trusted. As for Andry himself ... Rohan had been right as well that each use of power made the next use easier, more inevitable.

Andry supposed he ought to thank Pol for sparing him.

But if anyone should take the burden of that shattered vow, it was the Lord of Goddess Keep. Pol might be able to say that because he had never sworn it, he could not break it—but he'd never killed with his gifts. And now he was about to kill more than two thousand.

Andry glanced at his cousin; frowned; looked closer. A trick of the sunshine, it had to be—or else the power whirling in the air around him was potent enough to invade stone. The *selej*'s white jade glowed. Subtle, elusive, seen for an instant and then vanishing—it was like trying to focus on one star's shimmer that flickered teasingly away in the surrounding brilliance. He fixed his gaze just above Pol's blond head—and the whole circle of gold and jade quivered with light.

Fire invading the gems? Or gems remembering Fire, as Pol said those around the mirror had done?

A mirror that contained a face Andry could never see.

This was another issue to be avoided for his own peace of mind. He wove threads of sunlight, careful to keep away from Pol, and sent them up to Skybowl. The High Warlord was watching the second moon. Meiglan was watching Pol. She was beautiful, serene, seemingly oblivious to the barbaric sprawl of teeth and talons draped across her shoulders. The black pearls—Merisel's pearls—glistened at her throat, pure droplets distilled from the midnight sky.

Beyond the white partition, Sioned stared at nothing. Ruala looked ready to collapse. Alasen, he noted proudly, was composed—even with steel piercing one palm and both arms bound halfway to strangulation.

Isriam was anything but calm. He gazed at Betheyn with dark, desperate eyes, as if he knew he was about to die and wanted his last sight to be her face. Andry pitied the boy, whose infatuation was as inappropriate as it was hopeless. Beth was thirty; Isriam not quite seventeen. Well, he'd get over it.

But Andry would never get over the look Beth was giving Isriam.

Sorin's castle belonging to another was bad enough.

Sorin's Chosen Choosing another man—a boy!—was intolerable. Isriam, nameless and landless, bastard of a prince rejected as heir to Fessenden—beloved by Sorin's intended wife?

Andry wished either or both were Sunrunners so he could blister the light between them—

—and half-kill himself with iron poisoning in the process. Never mind. Once this was finished, he'd have plenty to say out loud.

He saw the High Warlord jump lightly to where Meiglan stood, placid as a lamb in the feeding meadow at Dragon's Rest. Her dark eyes shone down on Pol. Andry doubted she even saw the High Warlord approach, knife like a golden snake poised to strike.

Andry's colors danced with laughter as the knife flashed out—and struck a wall of woven sunlight as solid as it was invisible.

*

Torien was not laughing.

Steel bit again and again into the *ros'salath*. Despite his struggle to protect the others while keeping the weave intact, the pain grew worse with each swordthrust.

The spell was working; Vellan'tim flung their bodies forward and had their minds riven by indescribable horrors. Each fell writhing and screaming to the muddy ground. They died by the hundreds soon after, raving.

But Ulwis was screaming, too, silently and steadily. Martiel reacted as Torien had feared he would: protecting Linis at the expense of the others. Antoun tried to shield the young woman so Martiel could return to his task, but Torien could sense the old man's agony. Crila held firm, as did Torien; their *diarmadhi* blood protected them even with Martiel effectively gone from the working. But Jolan and Deniker and Nialdan, Sunrunners only, were hurting. And it would only get worse.

They needed Andry. Torien cried out silent despair, cursing his Lord and his friend for leaving them. *I'm not you! Andry, help us!*

Suddenly he felt a surge of blinding color. *Jolan,* his mind told him dully. Presenting him with Sunrunner after Sunrunner. They were within the sunlight, crammed into the courtyard with merchants and farmers and herders. She had seized them all, and now thrust them into his hands as if skeins of every color in the world were his to weave as he would.

He worked frantically, knowing their cries against iron were terrifying the common folk. The agony was eased by sorcerers scattered among them. None had more than a few rings; none knew what the *devr'im* knew about power. But their power was his to use. Fear strengthened the weaving, spun new horrors into it.

He tried.

He wasn't Andry.

He was shield, not sword arm. Strong foundation, not keystone.

He could almost hear Jolan raving at him for admitting defeat. He ignored her. Selecting a thin thread of sun, he sent it darting toward the Desert.

✳

Sun, sky, and merciless Desert were forgotten. He and she alone existed, inhabiting a world where he bestrode the rocks and she glowed white against white silk, her eyes dark stars, her hair a golden cloud promising dawn. *Forgive me,* he whispered, and was quick with the knife—

—against a wall that wasn't there.

It rang deep and long, like a priest's bronze bell. The shock of impact quivered up his arm. He recovered balance quickly, warrior's muscles responding. He did not make the mistake of trying the knife again—it would only emphasize his helplessness.

She had tricked him—the clever *Kir'reia* had tricked him with beautiful, harmless gold in place of shining deadly iron.

She must die. *Now.*

But he could not kill her.

And a shameful secret voice inside him rejoiced.

She hadn't even flinched.

On your knees! he wanted to shout. *Be a woman, and afraid!* For he had thought of a way to spare her, but only if she submitted. Only if she humbled that enormity of pride and believed that *he* would save her, not her lord.

Yield! Cry out in fear! When the moon comes from hiding I will say that the threat of death was enough, your White

*spirit called the moon forth with the power of your fear. I
will say that you did this not for the Azhrei but for me.*

*For me—and your fear will bind you to me more surely
than your love binds you to him.*

She deigned to glance up at him, with serene dark eyes
and a small, sweet, pitying smile.

She will not. She will never. Somehow, she must die.

He held aloft the golden knife one last time, and to his
warriors called out that the *Azhrei* had so befouled the
woman with his evil that it wrapped her like a shroud. She
would not die until the *Azhrei* died. And he must die *now.*

✳

Andry saw the enemy readying a charge. He and Pol stood
on a lonely sun-baked rise of sand, completely exposed, directly in the path of the coming onslaught. Drawing sunlight
around him, Andry prepared to weave the *ros'salath.*

Pol had beaten him to it. Demanding colors—shining diamond, dark emerald, burning golden topaz, pearl-white
laced with lightning—caught him, used him. He felt others,
Sunrunner and sorcerer, similarly captured. Some struggled.
Andry exerted his strength to calm them as he had calmed
skittish Sunrunners for half his life.

But it won't kill!

It took him a moment to identify the furious cry.
Chayla—? Yes, his brother's daughter: all healing green and
Desert blue and bloody red, and words resounding through
the *ros'salath* that would terrify but not kill.

*They deserve to die! They murdered Kazander—they mur-
dered hundreds,* hundreds—*I watched them die and I
couldn't save them—AND NOW YOU WON'T KILL!*

It was true. Pol had fashioned a weaving powerful enough
to withstand any assault of iron, but there was no killing
strength in it. The images were nebulous, feeble; they would
threaten but not cripple minds that would soon encounter it.

Are you High Prince for them, too? Andry thought bitterly, rage shaking him. *You puling, miserable coward—*

He wrenched himself from the fabric, ready to turn on Pol
and fell him with a fist in the jaw, not caring what it might
do to a mind woven into the light. But another alternative
surged into his thoughts with new colors, long familiar and

tinged with the peculiar sensation of *other* he associated
with a sorcerer.

Torien!

*Andry—help us! They're attacking, it's falling apart, I
can't do it—*

Beyond Torien, tied to him by the thinnest of sunlit
threads, was a true *ros'salath*. One that would kill. Andry
sensed it, and seized it.

✳

Edrel's heart leapt half out of his throat. The Vellant'im
were clambering over their fallen comrades' bodies—and
advancing straight for him. There was nothing between him
and the enemy now.

Nothing but his sword.

✳

*Yes that's it ride to the wall sense it before you touch it
slow down feel the warning you can't get through any
more than* he *could use your swords no more than pin-
pricks fall back now fall back that's it you can't get
through but you won't die you won't—*

—ANDRY!! NO!!

Get out of my way!

Stop this! You're killing them!

How clever of you to notice!

Don't force me to fight you Goddess damn *you STOP!!*
*Take your pathetic whining and huddle around your
wife protect her as you will but leave this to me to
someone with the courage to do what must be done
how* dare *you all you'd do is slap their wrists don't
you understand they've killed hundreds thousands
they'll kill us and everyone else GET OUT OF MY
WAY!!!*

NO! I won't let you do this!

Try to stop me!

✳

From far down the hillside, beyond the taut white wall between her and the rising moons, Sioned heard death. She

knew the sound well. She also knew how and why they were dying.

Steel rang, but not against other steel. Not with battle-clangor. This was hollow music, stones rattling in an empty metal bowl. The Vellant'im cried out, but not because of sword-torn flesh. This was a different agony, one that would leave them whole in body and shattered in mind.

So, she thought, curiously remote from the emotions she knew she ought to feel. *He decided to kill them after all. I wonder what changed his thinking.*

She'd sensed Pol guarding Meiglan, the way Rohan and Tobin and their blood-kin could sense the first hint of dragons in the wind. Pol's touch was careful, delicate after Andry's earlier mistake. Still, she had felt his weaving hover in the morning air. The Tears of the Dragon shimmered in response around Meiglan's neck. And the needle was a sliver of fire in Sioned's hand.

The pain of poisoning iron reminded her of something . . . long ago . . . ah, of course: the poison of crossing Water. The Faolain River—so very long ago, when she'd been so very young, and lives had depended on her overcoming the Sunrunner weakness. She'd used pain then, made it help her regain and hold onto consciousness. The trick was not to fight it or let it rule her—like any kind of power, she thought suddenly. Pain, like power, could be used.

So she did.

✳

How in all Hells was Andry doing it? Scores of Sunrunners, hundreds, mixed with *diarmadh'im*—where had they come from?

Where would *he* find power to regain control of the weaving?

Pol let go, despising himself for allowing Andry supremacy. The Vellant'im broke their minds against the *ros'salath*. Flesh succumbed to fear, and they died. He could hear them screaming, smell their terror on the wind—

Pol.

Weak, stitched with pain, yet it was Sioned. He caught her, wrapped the taint of iron away from her, and felt her sigh.

Pol, why is it that Andry *kills them, not you?*

You, Mother? You can ask that?

Ah. I see. Tenderness seeped through him like sunlight itself, rich and nurturing and strong. *What is it you want, then, Rohan's son?*

*

Alasen stiffened sharply, green eyes blank, blood oozing from her pierced palm as her body jerked once and then froze. Ruala had time for only a startled glance before Sioned took her, too.

And gave them both to Pol.

Thus empowered, his reach expanded.

Near Skybowl, Tilal had called a brief halt to stretch saddle-cramped legs and swallow a little water. He wanted everyone as loose and refreshed as possible for the coming fight. Andrev, Sunrunning to check on events a mere ten measures away, caught his breath and spasmed in every muscle. At the same instant, Saumer and Iliena abruptly turned to stone. After exchanging a worried look with Gemma, Tilal told Ludhil to lift his wife from her horse before she fell. Saumer was more difficult to maneuver; by the time Tilal had him safely down, Andrev had toppled from his saddle, oblivious to the world around him.

Tobin hovered near Skybowl on a cautiously aloof skein of light. When Pol found her and drew her in, he had access to Feruche. Tobren, so close to her grandmother; his own Jihan and Rislyn. Maara. Alleyn and Audran. Antalya was more difficult, for she was pure *faradhi*. But he gathered them all, gently and inexorably. None was afraid.

Now his range doubled.

At Dragon's Rest, Ostvel was trying his best lullaby on small Prince Larien. Suddenly the child stopped crying in mid-breath, dark Fironese eyes fixed and sightless. Ostvel broke off the song with a curse. Neither Lisiel nor Naydra heard him; they sat frozen in their chairs.

In another part of the palace, Camigina and Perchaya stumbled into each other and nearly through a sun-bright window. Hildreth jumped to help them, into the light. She immediately recognized Pol and felt her colors join in a working more extensive than any but those announcing Lady Andrade's death and Lord Andry's accession. *At last!*

Hildreth thought, giddy with the release of long tension. *At last he needs me for more than telling half-truths to Andry.*

This time, with two highly trained, full-blooded sorcerers added to his weaving, Pol's grasp extended across the whole of the continent. And, because they knew their own kind, he felt the shimmer of power at Balarat.

More, he thought, frowning. *I need more.*

It was easy at first. Rohannon knew and trusted him. But he could not guide Pol to the wellspring within the castle walls. These *diarmadh'im* were not like Naydra, untrained but familiar with his colors; they were not like Iliena and Lisiel and her son, untrained but incapable of resistance. Nor were they willing to give him all their strength, like the two unknown women at Dragon's Rest. These were men and women of knowledge and bitter pride who had plotted his destruction, who fought him with all that they knew and all that they were.

The boy, Tirel, was like his mother and little brother: shining raw colors that accepted Pol without fear—without knowing enough to fear. Perhaps Yarin could be reached through him, and with Yarin, the others—

What about me, then?

Blinding white—all shining diamond and glowing moonstone and lustrous pearl—swirled around him. A *diarmadhi* mind, although he wasn't sure how he knew that, and one of rare beauty.

Rohannon says you're the High Prince.

And power. Goddess, the power!

I know them. All of them. Use me.

Pol seized the gleaming whiteness and followed it into the castle. He found them like coins scattered on a rug. He gathered them with one hand, adding to his treasure of power.

They fought him, there in Firon on the morning sunshine, and those who fought him too frantically were discarded. But most yielded. Almost a hundred of them.

No—more than a hundred—twice, three times a hundred. The sudden glut of force staggered him. From outside Balarat, from snowy hills and ice-shrouded mountains of the Veresch, from places not even a pinprick on any map, power came to him. Freely given now, it was a blood-burning rush like the first moments of *dranath* in his veins.

Use us, it called in triumph. *You are* Diarmadh'rei, *you are ours and we are yours.*

From Balarat to Skybowl, the air seethed with color from dazzling white to purest black. All the shades of green and blue and red and yellow ever imagined, some of them tender as dawn and some of them blazing with fire, patterned in impossible complexity and stark simplicity. And as they formed in his mind he touched them all, knew them all. They were his. He was the center of a whirlwind of color tamed to his hand.

His alone.

High Prince for everyone.

✶

Sionell knew she couldn't be seeing this. She wasn't a Sunrunner. She was only a halfling; any gift in her was stunted.

But from the tall dune where she stood with Dannar and Kierun, with the great dragon tapestry spread behind them, she saw colors streaming around Pol. Around his head, the crown of gold and white jade shone like Fire.

"Dannar," she said, her throat dry, "do you see—"

"Yes," he breathed. "It's—shining."

Of course; a son of Alasen and Ostvel, though not a Sunrunner like his sister Camigwen, would see it.

"What's shining?" Kierun asked, puzzled.

"But where's it coming from?" Dannar asked, looking around wildly as if he could see its source, flaming red hair tossing around his head like Sunrunner's Fire.

"I don't know." But she intended to find out. "Stay here," she ordered. "Don't move for anything. If anybody sees that dragon tapestry fall or even waver—"

"It won't," Kierun stated flatly.

No. She didn't suppose it would, not this crowned dragon with the emerald ring in his talons, nor the other one, crowned in light.

Then Dannar cried out, and flung an arm northward. "My lady!"

A storm of dragons darkened the sky.

✶

—come on you whoresons come to me and die as you deserve as you killed Brenlis and Oclel and Rusina

*and Valeda and a thousand others come to me and
die in madness—*

*NO! You can't it's impossible where did you find such
power—*

Come on Andry fight me now *fight the Sunrunners I
hold in one hand and the sorcerers in the other—*

They'll follow me not you give to me not YOU they
want the strength only I can give them the strength to
kill—

*You still don't understand you can fight me and lose and
have all know it or yield and share in the victory you
can't escape me can't win DAMN YOU ANDRY
YIELD!!!*

✳

—and he almost had it almost gathered every skein of the
gigantic tapestry of light into his hands one for the
Sunrunners and one for the sorcerers with Sioned keeping
each mind distinct and whole as only she could and he was
preparing to knot the glowing incandescent silk of the
faradh'im to the tough bright thickness of the *diarmadh'im*
when his senses reeled and the dragons screamed and the
whirlwind became a tempest of sheer primitive fury reeking
color and power and blood.

✳

Jahnev, seven winters old and as blind to Sunrunner light as
Rislyn was to the sun that dazzled him, gave up trying to
pull his sister from the window. Talya was just like the others: as white and frozen and unreachable as the faraway
Veresch. He had to get help—but he couldn't leave them.

"Meig!"

His little brother curled more deeply into the shadows of
the chair, grumbling in his sleep. Jahnev shook him.

"*Meig!* Wake up!"

"Hmm?" Gray eyes blinked drowsily. "What? Did they
find Mama?"

"Not yet. Listen to me and do exactly as I say. Go downstairs and find Princess Audrite, and bring her up here."

Meig nodded, unperturbed. "What should I tell her?"

"That—that we need her help." He gestured to the six

children at the window. "They're all caught up in some kind of Sunrunner work."

Meig peered at them, frowning slightly. He stood, stretched, and took a step toward the window.

"No!" Jahnev grabbed his arm. "Whatever you do, *don't* go into any sunlight or it might catch you, too!"

"Oh." The frown cleared to a smile. "All right, Jahnev. I'll remember."

They wouldn't realize it for many years, but the pattern of their lives formed spontaneously in that instant. It would be that way always: the elder brother compelled to ask the younger to do what he could not, warning meantime of danger; the younger brother obeying without question, while smiling a little at the elder's caution.

"Hurry," Jahnev said. "And be careful."

"I will."

*

The dragons were an infinitely more formidable enemy to Pol's control than Andry. The shock of his first contact with Azhdeen was nothing compared to the assaulting colors of nine utterly enraged dragons who perceived their humans to be in danger.

Images flashed—but through the weaving, not into the air between him and the dragons. Sioned–Hollis–Riyan–Ruala–Jeni—*Andry?* Pol thought, senses battered. The single unnamed dragon had now decided which human to claim. Pavisel alone held back, having found Maarken was not part of the working; a picture of her landing nearby to protect him was instantly followed by Elisel's demand to have Sioned similarly brought beneath her sheltering wings. Azhly shrieked, clawing the *ros'salath* as he looked for Ruala; tangled and insensible as he was, Pol's outer as well as inner hearing rang with the cry.

Silent Lainian was no less fierce in searching for Jeni. Abisel, frantic for Hollis, shot fire-rimmed images through the sunlight that faded only at Sadalian's more vivid—and more painful—conjuring of Riyan. Even Lir'reia, though Rislyn was safe at Feruche, contributed to the drowning madness of color and sight and emotion.

Pol fought them, and with every instant sensed Andry re-

gain another fingerhold on the *ros'salath*. The nameless
dragon flung himself joyously into Andry's grasp, and the
others bellowed triumph as they learned that his influence
meant death to the Vellant'im. The killers of dragons.

All but Azhdeen.

The familiar colors slid past, as if ashamed. Pol snatched
at them, missed, moaned in agony. And fought back, battling
the dragons and their savagery that Andry was using to
strengthen the lethal working.

*Fighting them—no, I can't! They're not the enemy! But if
I don't win them back, if I can't control them—THEY'RE
NOT THE ENEMY!*

Years ago he'd battled his half brother for control of
Azhdeen himself. Ruval had used all the force of a strong
and malignant will. Pol had used his own soul. He had chosen, that night of the Firestorm, to reject the rape and hate
and violence of the night he was conceived. He would not be
such things, nor use them against anyone, human or dragon.

*"What we choose to do comes of what we are. But we are
so many things, Pol—so many!"*

Yes, Father—so many. And together they form the whole.

He found Azhdeen—somehow—and for a moment became the dragon. Primal blood-lust, murderous rage, a mindless *need* to kill—sweet, so sweet, and terrifying. He
trembled, fighting himself now as well, his own fear and his
answering need that shrieked for the kill, and knew he would
lose—for what chance had reason or mercy or his soul
against *this?*

*No. If I die in fighting it, then I die. But I won't allow this.
I won't be* this!

[*KILL!*]

Images slashed at the weaving in response to Azhdeen's
raging emotions. Pol surrounded them, extinguishing each as
he would a Fire conjuring.

No.

[*PREDATORS! KILLED WINGSISTER!*]

No.

[*MAKE PREY! BONES BLOOD FLESH CLAW TEETH
KILL!*]

No! Human. People. Like me.

[*NO COLORS! NOT YOU!*]

Like me. *Legs arms head mouth eyes mind—*

[*PREY! KILL!*]

NO!
[... *no?*]

✳

Andry had been told what happened when a dragon decided on a particular human: crashing, mind-numbing, total possession that stunned for days afterward. It wasn't that way for him. His dragon submitted gleefully to him, adding inestimable force to the *ros'salath* that killed.

The sheer savage beauty of it intoxicated him. *This* was what his gift was for, why the Goddess had chosen to show him the dreams and the castles and the danger—this glory of power in which his faith and his intellect agreed, that was his to do with as he pleased. And it pleased him to kill Vellanti minds. They bled terror as they died; had there been real blood, he would have bathed in it, laughing.

So many Sunrunners! So easy to spin them into a tapestry of fear and death! Insignificant that in the course of his struggle with Pol, so many sorcerers had sided with their *Diarmadh'rei*; those he could grasp through the Sunrunners had mostly negated the sting of iron, and now that he had the dragons there was no pain at all. The *dranath* sang in him, the colors, the gorgeous thing he had woven of terror and vengeance and fury.

When it began to shred, he hardly even noticed.

✳

Sioned had long since dropped to her knees on the broken stones. There was no air, no sound, no light. Pain that was not iron-born burned in her chest and behind her closed eyes. Some remote part of her mind wondered if she was dead.

Where there's pain, there's life. Goddess, what a depressing definition. ...

She couldn't quite understand why she was able to think at all.

She forced her lids open, though they seemed weighted with the foundation stones of Skybowl. White, everything was white, edged in blood-red and black, with tiny darting stars like fish in a pond—but what was she doing underwater? And such strange, pale water, at that? She was a Sunrunner, and she'd drown in no time.

Beloved idiot. BREATHE.

Both hands lifted involuntarily, and the rope circling her neck loosened a fraction that allowed her to breathe. It took several deep inhalations, but soon enough the red and black faded and the odd little fish swam away. The whiteness was revealed as that damned banner between her and where Meiglan and the High Warlord stood above.

Ruala was still on her feet, trembling to the roots of her night-black hair. Isriam and Beth were trying to keep Alasen from falling over and strangling. Their Vellanti guards seemed to have vanished.

Sioned straightened her back. Aching weakness flowed like a river down her spine and in tributary streams to every nerve. She coughed out Isriam's name and his head turned, dark eyes blazing with equal parts anger and effort. He'd half-choked himself in his contortions as his shoulder supported Alasen's back.

"Hold still," Sioned rasped. "I'm going to burn your ropes."

"You can't! The needle—"

"—won't kill me that fast. Just don't move—I'm not very clear yet and I don't want to set Fire to *you*."

Betheyn cried out, "No! Sioned, don't!"

Sioned ignored her. Isriam was her first and only choice. She was too weak to move. Ruala, the same. Alasen was practically unconscious. Beth was too slender to heft a sword, let alone use one.

If there'd been a sword available. She cursed, then told herself Isriam would just have to figure something out.

Goddess, how it hurt! So tiny a Fire, only a thin little knife of it to cut Isriam's bonds, and it was as if the needle pierced every nerve in her body. Long ago, Meath had told her what it felt like; she'd experienced it at Meath's own hand. But this time it went on and on and on, all the colors of sand and rock and crag and clothing brittle, too bright, quivering like glass about to shatter in a thunderstorm.

"Enough!" Isriam shouted. "My lady, stop!"

Sioned had to trust him. She damped the flame and felt herself falling into a blackened pit.

Pol didn't let her.

*

He had all of them now.

With Naydra, the two nameless *diarmadh'im* at Dragon's Rest—and with them, twoscore others called willingly to his service and his need.

With Tobin, Rislyn and Jihan, and the other children's pure young strength.

With Rohannon, that dazzling white mind, shining like snow in sunlight—and close on three hundred more sorcerers, some still feebly struggling, most offering themselves gladly.

And with Andry, Goddess Keep.

He had seen how the *ros'salath* there was connected by merging colors—like yarns dyed in different vats, or gemstones not quite matched in a necklet. For an instant he thought he must examine each pattern individually, shuffle and rearrange them, like to like. The colossal impossibility of it resolved into despair. Then he saw two things: that instinct had guided them to each other, without regard for *faradhi* or *diarmadhi*, and that the whole elaborate structure was supported by nine radiant rainbows.

With Azhdeen, the dragons.

He worked quickly now, curving the long wall into a vast circle, layering power and color upward—just as Sioned had done the length of his life ago. He remembered it now, the fierce beauty and desperate strength of his mother's mind; remembered the tense, sweating faces of his father and grandfather limned in starshine and the thin Fire Sioned raised around them.

Colors and patterns he had never seen before were as familiar and distinct as those he had known since his first forays on sunlight. Yet as he drew each into the larger whole of light and power, identities blurred. He saw all, and he saw none. Concern was dismissed in an instant; Sioned would unravel the weaving as only she could and see them all safe once he was finished here.

One mind, through which so many Sunrunners were brought to him, resisted still. *Don't fight me. I need you. Please, Andry—*

Silence.

✳

Later, they would realize that the dawn had provided a useful tool in determining who had *faradhi* blood.

Feylin and Walvis knew that one of them did—otherwise Sionell could not have made two Sunrunner children with Tallain. They'd never known exactly which until now. What she saw was Pol and Andry standing alone on the rise; what he saw was a bright glimmer of Fire and a glowing white crown.

Chay saw, too—no surprise, with two *faradhi* sons. But there were those who, like Dannar, had never suspected themselves halflings. One was the young man Meath had wondered about while teaching Chayla her colors; another, to his eternal shock, was Sethric. Of the nearly seven hundred men and women who waited to see if they would have to fight and perhaps die that morning, nearly one hundred saw much more.

Maarken saw it all, of course. When the High Warlord struck at Meiglan with the golden knife, his whole body flinched. At his shoulder, his dapple-gray stallion sidled, bumping into Andry's big gelding; he tightened his grip on their reins and planted his own feet more firmly in the sand.

Hoofbeats slurred behind him. "What's going on out there?" Chay demanded, swinging down from the saddle.

"Pol forbade me the sunlight."

"Wise of him, frustrating for you," his father observed. Squinting up the crater's slope, he went on, "Ah. The whoreson just found out he can't kill Meiglan. Wish we could hear what he's shouting to his troops—". He broke off with a blurt of surprise as the Vellant'im began the charge. "Maarken—"

"No. We stay put." He stared at where the *ros'salath* marked the sand and murmured, "Pol took the choice from me. Deliberately. He didn't trust me to—"

"Nonsense!" Chay snapped. "You're his Battle Commander. If this fails he'll need you for the work *I* trained you to do."

Maarken shook his head. "I've known all my life it would come to this. He took the decision away. He either loves me too much to force it on me, or he's scared I wouldn't choose for him."

Chay grabbed the stump of Maarken's left arm. "I don't know how a son of your mother could be so stupid!" he hissed. "You listen to me, boy. You made your choice when you were eleven winters old!"

His remaining hand clenched tight around two horses' reins. Beneath the leather gauntlet was a silver ring set with a garnet, once worn by Prince Jastri of Syr. Rohan had given it to him after he called Fire to Roelstra's makeshift bridge across the Faolain. His first Sunrunner ring—given not by any Lord or Lady of Goddess Keep, but by his prince.

"Yes," he murmured. "I suppose I did." His choice had been made before Pol was born. But it didn't prevent him from feeling he had betrayed his brother.

Vellant'im began to crash into the wall and fall back shrieking. Maarken feared for the horses—Radzyn horses—ridden by the enemy, whose cavalry had held back behind the foot soldiers. Would the *ros'salath* madden them, too? The horses behind him were trembling now, not with fear but with the battle-fervor bred into them. Maarken watched the warriors writhe in the sand and knew there would be no work for Radzyn's finest today—including him. The *ros'salath* would do the killing today.

"Gentle Goddess, Mother of Dragons," Chay whispered, and Maarken wondered if he knew he used Kazander's habitual phrase.

The thought whirled away on an instinctive leap of his heart. He turned, knowing what he would see: dragons, as if summoned by Chay's muttered oath. Joy in their flight was immediately replaced by fear for their lives. They came on powerful wingbeats that pushed the measures behind them at five times the speed of the fastest horse's hooves.

No! he wanted to scream at them on sunlight. *Go back! They'll kill you!*

The Vellant'im surged down from Skybowl, bellowing their defiance of the *Azhrei*'s spells and the *Azhrei*'s minions.

More hoofbeats, at a hard gallop this time, and a moment later Sionell was leaping down from her saddle, shining and sweaty in her Merida armor.

"Don't say it," she warned. "I have just as much right to be here as you do. I want to know what's going on."

Maarken gestured with his left arm. "They're hitting Pol's weave—I assume you can see it?—and they're going mad."

"Yes," she replied tightly. "I can see it. But it's not Pol's doing."

"Sorcery's there, or the swords would collapse it," he said. "Thassalante and his people are there—and they wouldn't be if Pol wasn't in control."

"No!" she insisted. "He never planned to kill! It must be Andry, it has to be. You've got to stop him!"

Chay's quicksilver eyes were dark and lightless. "Andry."

Dragons howled their rage. Maarken staggered against his horse's neck as Pavisel, still in flight, demanded his colors. He was helpless in her frantic grip, incapable of freeing himself. Dimly, he understood that she was trying to protect him, and for an unknown time he felt himself enfolded as surely as if she had wrapped him in her wings.

But when Azhdeen roared an imperious summons, Maarken found that he was woven along with his dragon into the *ros'salath*.

This time, it did not kill.

✳

Isriam's fingers were so numb he could hardly bend them. The rope at his back had only frayed with Sioned's Fire, not burned through, but he'd seen pain in her eyes and knew he must lie to her to save her life. Fumbling at the cords with clumsy fingers, at last he took in a deep breath, tensed the muscles of his neck, and jerked.

The result was freedom—and a burn on his throat that would scar him for life. As quickly as he could, he untied his other hand and yanked the needle from his palm. The trickle of blood was nothing. He spared a moment to rub circulation back into his hands, then worked on Betheyn's ropes.

"Don't bother with me," she said, and he shook his head.

"You have to untie the others." His voice was raspy and every breath hurt his bruised windpipe. "Take the needles out first, so they can work. I'm going after Princess Meiglan."

Her hands were loose. He extracted the needle, cursing the Vellant'im anew. Chafing her fingers as he had his own, he suddenly couldn't look at her. Only a little while ago he'd been unable to look away.

"Isriam." Beth's hands clenched around his. "It was wrong from start to finish—but I do love you, my dear."

Stupefied, he couldn't even breathe. Then he understood: she thought they were going to die. She could tell him, now that she was sure neither of them would live to regret it.

Before he could tell her how wrong she was, she let him go and hurried to Sioned. He would never remember scrambling up the rocks, but he would relive in nightmares the moment he saw High Princess Meiglan.

*

It was the sweetest peace Sioned had ever known, being free of pain. Dulled to a nagging ache by the presence of sorcerers, still it had sieved away her strength. Now she was whole again, the poison was gone, and she was free.

Caught in Pol's gigantic glowing web of Sunrunners and Sorcerers, but strangely free.

This was partly due to Pol himself. He kept her slightly separate, drawing on her but not draining her the way he drained the others. Some of it was Elisel, shielding her in a different way despite Azhdeen's demands, just as the other dragons protected their humans as much as they could. But Sioned realized it was her own doing as well: that, given distance by her son's and her dragon's care, she'd put yet more distance between herself and the *ros'salath*.

When she looked on it as a whole, and saw what Pol had built, and how, and why, she was as stunned by awe and pride as she was by fear.

Elisel, dragon-sensitive to emotion, felt it and slid a little more of herself between Sioned and the weaving. Sioned couldn't spare the time to soothe her; she knew what Pol would want of her when this was over. The slight remove allowed her to inspect the web, to see and identify all those within it. Swiftly, knowing she must sort all the shining, shifting patterns before he finished his work, she called on the memory trained so ruthlessly by Lady Andrade. Many of these people she knew. But the rest—

Merciful Goddess! Over four hundred of them—from Saumer and Iliena near Skybowl to the children and Tobin at Feruche, from the steady glow of Dragon's Rest to the sunburst of power over Firon.

And one solitary mind that seethed amber and amethyst and ruby-red, with a hundred more refracted through him.

He was the glass through which all at Goddess Keep shone, the lens that focused their light.

Andry—

The dragon was helping him, sharing the tremendous burden directed through one formidable mind. Pol was taking more than this from Andry, however. Without the Lord of Goddess Keep and the polished skills of the *devr'im*, Pol could never have done this. They were the foundation, as solid as the stones of Remagev—and on them, as at that castle, the trap was built.

Not elegantly—Sunrunners were crammed together with sorcerers, those in Firon taking the astonished Saumer into their midst, Jeni and her dragon within a group that included sorcerers from Dragon's Rest as well as Antalya and Tobin up at Feruche. No, not at all elegant—but it worked. She wasted a moment appreciating the magnificent chaotic reasonableness of it. *Rohan, you would've loved this!*

Then she saw Thassalante. The old man's colors blazed in a gleeful amethyst-ruby-sapphire dance of pleasure in using his gifts to serve his people and his prince. He didn't care if the *ros'salath* killed or caressed. His was the pure joy of a young dragon's first flight, a colt's first wild gallop, a boy's first kiss from a girl he adored.

But—Thassalante shouldn't be in this at all—

❋

Andry fell to the sand, a smear of white and silver far below her. Pol still stood, golden, shining, his head lifted to the mountain and the dragons wheeling through the sunlit sky at his command. Meiglan smiled. He was tall and strong and beautiful, and more powerful than anyone who had ever lived—even the exalted Lady Andrade, even Andry's precious Lady Merisel, even Sioned.

She saw only him, was aware only of him.

From somewhere very far away, she heard the silvery clang of the poles onto the rocks as those who held the white cloth behind her rushed down to join the fighting. Equally remote, she heard the scramble of boots as the youth carrying the High Warlord's own banner followed them. Someone shouted despairingly behind her.

She did hear the High Warlord say in her own language, "Forgive me, Meiglan. I am sorry."

She did not hear the ringing of the gold knife on invisible
Fire, for there was no Fire left.

She never felt the heartstroke that killed her.

✳

Remembering the mirror, Pol imagined that the dome was
his cupped hands—one *diarmadhi*, one *faradhi*—and
brought them together, fingers lacing, clasping tight.

The Vellant'im toppled like storm-crushed trees.

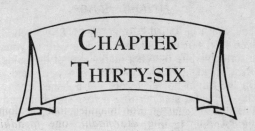

CHAPTER
THIRTY-SIX

The wonder of it was that it all happened so quickly. Chay had spent more time over a single cup of wine than elapsed between the first glow of the *selej* and the moment the Vellant'im began to fall.

And the horses, too. *His* horses. Those moving at a canter or gallop went tails-over-ears; the rest stumbled to their knees or simply toppled over. Scores of riders were trapped, and many crushed, but it wasn't their legs Chay was thinking of when he told himself, *If there's even one bone broken, I'll take it out of those boys' hides.* The oath was hollow, like the feeling in his chest ever since Andry collapsed.

Chay had started forward then, but Sionell's grip on his arm warned him back. Now, with the glow of power gone from the air, Maarken sank to his knees in the sand, slumped, head hanging.

It was incredibly quiet after the din of the Vellanti charge. Chay heard only the muted rattle of harness and a few whispers behind him, and the heavy snorting exhalations of felled horses well beyond Pol and Andry. Chay knelt beside Maarken and cradled the sweat-damp head against his shoulder.

"They're . . . not dead," Maarken whispered. "Tell Walvis . . . disarm them. . . ."

"Yes," Chay said mindlessly.

"Bind . . . but don't kill. . . ." He struggled upright, groping for support with a hand no longer there. "Mustn't kill them—Pol's order—"

"They won't be killed," Sionell said. She touched Chay's shoulder. "I'll tell my father. You take care of your sons."

She scrambled up onto her mare—one of the golden Dragon's Rest breed, given her by Pol years ago—and galloped off. On the bright horse, jewels and polished armor gleaming, she seemed a star hurtling across sun-drenched sand.

Maarken was steadier now, having received Sionell's assurance. "Andry," he murmured. "See to him, Father, I'm all right—"

Chay got him onto his horse, and waved Daniv over. "Take him to Lady Feylin," he said, not knowing what else to do for him. "And send somebody to help me with Andry."

✳

"NO!"

The guttural cry warned the High Warlord an instant too late. He dragged the knife from Meiglan's heart and let her slide from his embrace, but the young man had already launched himself through the air. Turning, he was just in time to take the brunt of the charge in the stomach.

He grunted, breath driven from his lungs. The two of them went sprawling and only swift battle reflexes allowed him to twist in midair so he didn't take the worst of the fall as well.

Still, he felt ribs crack on a ragged stone. Pain momentarily blinded him. The boy lay beside him, stunned but still moving. He brought up his hand—but the gold knife had flown from his fingers, slick with the *Kir'reia*'s blood.

Wriggling free, his vision clearing as he sucked in air beneath stabbing ribs, he pushed himself to his knees. Below him lay his dream and his duty, spreading lifeless down the mountain, across the sand.

Once more his lungs emptied of breath, this time in sickening shock. He could not be seeing this. It was not possible. He rose by sheer force of will, as if by rising he could bring them all to their feet again to attack the *Azhrei* where he stood alone and triumphant in his Desert.

Horses stirred. They gathered long legs, snorted, shook proud heads as if wakening from sleep—or ensorcellment. *But the spell was mine. Now they are free, and I am left with nothing.*

She is dead, and for nothing.

The horses trotted away, fastidiously avoiding fallen bodies. When they were clear of obstacles, they headed for their stablemates at a gallop, manes flying like battle flags.

The banners of fifty clans lay in the dirt. His own wallowed across the rocks down the slope, seeping away from him like water. The lightning bolt struggled feebly in the wind and then subsided, strengthless, as dead as all his warriors.

His sons, easily identifiable in their white clothes—his sons, pride of his loins, his own in feature and form as if they'd had no mothers—his sons lay motionless at his feet.

The *Azhrei* stood alone, victorious, his dragons circling overhead.

The High Warlord stared at the wreckage of his duty and his dream. He could not comprehend what he saw. Had he been wrong? Had he made a mistake?

No. Never. As much as he scorned the priests he had used, the superstitions he had worked to his advantage, it was not a failure of faith that had led to this. He was High Warlord, and *his* faith was in the righteousness of his dream. Not for him a priest's pleas to the Father of Winds for favor.

Neither was it a failure of his belief that such favor was still his. He was still standing. So was the *Azhrei*.

The failure was not his. It belonged to those who had believed too much in superstition and not believed enough in *him*.

He roared challenge, fists raised to the sky. "Fight me, Dragon Prince! I killed your wife—now try to kill me! Take up your sword! Fight *me!*"

✳

Isriam braced himself on one elbow, sickness clenching his belly, storms thundering in his head. There was a warm, wet pain above his right eye; he had to smear blood from his lashes before he could see.

What he'd hoped to find—the High Warlord as limp and helpless as himself, preferably soaked in blood—was instead the bitter sight of the man standing white and defiant above him.

Oh, Goddess, why wasn't I faster? He killed her, the son of a whore killed her—she's dead and it's my fault—

He battled his aching body, his rebellious stomach, and

swayed to his feet. Lightning exploded behind his eyes. If he could just make himself move, he could reach the High Warlord and push. At best, the man would split his skull and spill his brains on the stones below; at worst, Isriam might fall with him.

He lurched forward, stumbling on rocks. The High Warlord had claimed Meiglan's life; Isriam would claim his. *Almost close enough, another few steps—please don't let me fall, please, not until I can take him with me—*

The sudden rush of heat, the sudden scream of animal pain, nearly toppled him. Lightning again—right in front of him, a blinding column of Fire the height and width of a man. This man.

The High Warlord did not scream again.

Isriam reeled back and put one shaking hand in front of his eyes. The stench of charring flesh sickened him even more than the nausea from the wound in his head. He wilted against a jagged stone and retched until there was nothing left in his stomach.

A day dragged by. Perhaps a year. He turned his cheek instinctively into soft cloth. A voice murmured his name; fingers stroked the blood from his face. He opened his eyes. "M—my lady?"

"Hush. You're all right."

His head was cradled in Betheyn's lap. He'd been moved down to the place where Princess Meiglan—he gulped back the memory and looked up at Beth, pleading with his eyes.

"She—" It was all he could say. All that was needed. Her fingers trembled against his skin and she bent her head. Lifting one hand as if to push the knowledge away, he saw that his sleeve was singed, the fine hairs burned from the reddened backs of his palms.

"You were . . . very close to the Fire," Beth said, a small tremor in her voice. "I dragged you back before it could . . . it was an angry Fire," she finished dully.

"You—" *—saved my life,* he wanted to tell her. *But I couldn't save hers.* Once more he could not meet her eyes. He turned his head, biting his lip.

Alasen and Ruala were kneeling nearby on either side of a slender whiteness crowned in golden hair. Ruala's back was to him, and her body hid the wound from him, but he could see Alasen's face—too stunned even to weep. Isriam was passionately glad none of them had seen her die. He had. The knife had found a quick, shining path into her heart, and he knew even before her blood stained the white robe that he was too late.

Sioned alone was on her feet, standing before the massive fountain of Fire. It still burned, though there was nothing now within the flames and the rocks below it had melted to black glass. She glanced over her shoulder. Isriam flinched. Her green eyes were ablaze, her fury as bright and hot as the Fire. When she directed her glare down the mountain, he knew what she was seeing, for he had seen it himself: the piled bodies, the gloss of helpless steel, the tall golden figure of her son.

"It's not you she rages against," Beth said softly. "You mustn't think that, Isriam. It's Pol."

He frowned, regretting the expression as it tugged the gash in his brow. "Pol? Why?"

"The Fire isn't hers. It's his."

✳

Chay cursed the sliding sand as he climbed up the dune, dragging his horse behind him. At the top, he released the reins and the stallion stood quietly, though his nostrils quivered with the scent of newly returning mares.

Crouching beside his son, Chay felt for the pulse in the throat. Wildly erratic beneath chill skin—he swallowed hard and looked up at Rohan's son.

Pol stared at him as if he'd never seen him before. The man who had refused to slaughter his enemies with the deadly madness of the *ros'salath* was perilously near madness himself.

Chay held himself from recoiling from the savagery of those blue-green eyes. It took everything of strength and determination he possessed to meet Pol's gaze. He gathered his son in his arms.

"I killed him," Pol said.

For one hideous moment Chay thought he meant Andry. But Pol had turned that fierce gaze up the mountain to the Fire burning there. Chay hadn't even noticed it. But he knew who it must be.

Had been.

"Pol." He kept his voice low and soft. "Help me."

"I killed him. Too late."

"Pol."

The eyes that looked at him now were stricken by a more human but no less terrible emotion. Tears welled, bitter and luminous.

"She's dead." Madness once more sheened his eyes. "Meggie—she's dead—"

Sensitized now to power, he felt the hairs on his nape rise when the *selej* glowed with light. Very slowly, Pol's eyes closed and he slumped to his knees. As he curled on the sand like a sleeping child, the glimmer faded and the white stones were only stones.

Chay glanced up at the sky. "Whoever did that for him, thank you."

Holding his son more closely in his arms, he called out for help.

✳

Ostvel cradled the baby, careful to stay within sunlight. With half Dragon's Rest, he'd woken at dawn to an incredibly emphatic yowling and was unsurprised when Naydra arrived at his door, begging him to spare them all deafness by singing Larien back to sleep. Goddess, how he wished the noise would return. No child with eyes wide open should be so silent, so still.

Pol was only a day old when it happened to him. Ostvel wondered what it did to a baby's mind, to experience so much power while still so new to the world.

Later, he would judge that Larien's silence lasted no longer than it would take to sip the morning's first cup of taze. Certainly the shadows had not lengthened significantly when he gave a sudden gasp and began to shriek.

Naydra blinked and shook her head to clear it. Lisiel was slower to recover, but the first to ask the obvious.

"What happened?" Then, wincing as she reached for her squalling son: "Gentle Goddess, what an uproar!"

Ostvel handed Larien over, smiling. "Yes, I know. Isn't it wonderful?"

✳

Jahnev was waiting for Audrite at the open door, frantic worry uncannily controlled for a boy his age. He was doing better than she was, she admitted, and once more clenched the trembling hand hidden in her skirt pocket. Meig had hold of the other one, not quite dragging her up the stairs.

"Princess Audrite!"

"I'm here, Jahnev. Meig says you need my help," she began. The sight of the children, washed in sunlight beside the window, took all her voice away. She was frightened, even more than when Tobin whispered, "Pol," and her expression changed from quiet concentration to quivering strain. Tobren had caught her breath and nearly fallen. Audrite was horrified to see that whatever had taken them had also seized her grandchildren.

"Alleyn? Audran?" she breathed, fingers tightening convulsively around Meig's. He gently tugged away. "Dear Goddess, how can Pol do this to them?"

Meig's reply was matter-of-fact. "Don't worry, my lady. If it's Jihan and Rislyn there, it won't hurt."

She looked down at him, not understanding for a moment. The gray eyes were serene as a distant, drifting cloud. Shame made her glance away. Pol would never endanger his daughters—or anyone else, she reminded herself. She of all people should know him; she had helped raise him.

"You're right, Meig. We'll just wait for them to come back."

"Oh, we don't have to wait," he said, looking past her to the window.

Audrite followed his gaze. Maara had put out a hand to brace herself against the wall; Alleyn's knees went weak, too, and Audran held her up. Rislyn reached up a quivering hand as if to touch the sunlight she could not see—not with her eyes. Antalya took a few shaky steps and Jahnev leaped to steady her.

But it was Jihan who drew Audrite's eyes. Her head turned, bright hair aglow in the morning sun, face shining with excitement, blue eyes incandescent with . . . *Power,* Audrite told herself, and shivered.

"Jahnev," Meig asked, "is it all right if I go into the sunlight now?"

✳

At Goddess Keep, the wait was much longer.

Norian and her brother watched from the windswept battlements, unease at the effects of the *ros'salath* giving way to horror when it collapsed. Opposing forces crashed together without hindrance now.

Elsen shouted for horse and sword. Norian clung frantically to his arm, ordering the young page who attended Elsen to stay where he was.

"Don't be a fool!" she cried as her brother shook her off. "You hardly made it up the steps!" Against her better judgment, he'd insisted on being where his troops could at least see him. To ride into battle would certainly undo all the Sunrunners' healing work—assuming he survived Vellanti swords.

"Damn it, Norian, those are *my* people down there!"

"And my husband! I won't risk you, too!"

"If Sethric could ride and fight with one leg useless, so can I!"

Norian did not point out that Sethric had spent time at Remagev honing the skills in which he'd been trained since boyhood. It would only exacerbate Elsen's lifelong sense of inferiority, something hidden so well that she only saw its full bitterness at this instant.

What she did say, just as blunt and even more cruel, was, "I'm sure that will comfort your wife and son when you're dead!"

Selante and Vellanur were the keys to his conscience as a man and as a prince. His death would break their hearts and make a five-year-old boy the immediate heir to Grib.

It was a near thing. Norian watched Elsen hover on the brink, his anguished glance at the battlefield evenly matched by his fingers twisting the ruby ring on his thumb—a gift from Selante to celebrate the birth of their son. She had her husband to thank for what pushed her brother back from the edge: Edrel broke free of Vellant'im and rallied his soldiers with a raucous cry. Those around him echoed it, made it a banner and a weapon against their enemies.

"For Elsen! Prince Elsen and Grib!"

Not Andry, not Pol, not *Azhrei* or Goddess Keep or his own holding of River Ussh. Norian's eyes filled. But it was only when the battle was over, late in the morning, and Edrel lay bleeding and senseless in her arms, that she allowed herself to weep.

*

There was no fighting at Balarat.

The gates opened a few moments after Rohannon, Tirel, and Aldiar were stricken mute. Arlis wasted no time. He shouted for the charge and galloped up to the castle with his army behind him.

The swords, dull gray in the sharp, cold dawn, were unnecessary. Arlis sheathed his, only the chin-strap of his helm keeping his jaw from hanging open. The vast courtyard was packed with castle folk who made not the slightest sound. Not a cough for the wind, not a scraping of boots on cobbles, not even a child's bewildered whimper. At first Arlis thought they imitated statues for fear of how their returning prince would punish them. As his gaze flickered from face to blank face, he realized they were silent because they were simply too stunned to react. Hells, they were barely breathing.

Then he noticed subtle differences between one pair of eyes and the next. Scanning the crowd, he initially rejected what his experience told him must be true. But there was no denying that out of the hundred or so he had glanced at thus far, fully a quarter of them wore the glazed, glassy expression Sunrunners acquired when they worked.

The place was littered with sorcerers.

"Damnedest thing I've ever seen," Arlis muttered.

Suddenly Laric was beside him, saying nothing, staring up at the wide balcony of his great hall. It, too, was packed with people, fifty or more crammed from the stone balustrade to the tall crystal windows. Nobody moved up there, either. Arlis tried to ignore the trickle of ice down his spine that had nothing to do with the morning chill.

Massive bronze doors opened and a little knot of highborns and court functionaries emerged from the great hall.

"Your grace," one began, her voice high-pitched with nervousness. Laric cast one quelling look at her, and she subsided.

A round-faced woman whose apron declared her calling pushed her way from behind the nobles. She descended the six steps and bobbed a curtsey to her prince. "Goddess blessing on you, my lord, and it's more than welcome you are back to your own castle!" She flung a look of fury over her shoulder. "You'll be looking first for that whoreson Yarin. He's likely cowering upstairs with his lickspittles."

Arlis gestured to one of his own Iseli soldiers, who dismounted with twenty of his fellows and went inside to search.

"Nolly?" Laric gave her a faint smile. "Lord Idalian told me how you helped him and my son. I thank you for it with all my heart. Can you tell me what happened here today?"

"Your grace!" said another of the contigent on the stairs, trepidation overcome by outrage that a prince should ask a cook for information. Laric ignored the man utterly; Arlis distributed his best feral smile all around.

Nolly shook her head. "What I heard, my lord, was this. They were all ready to sorcel up their tricks when every misbegotten one of them turned to stone. And so they still are," she added, gesturing to the balcony overhead.

Arlis knew enough about power to believe it. Aldiar would be able to tell them more, he hoped, but Aldiar was still outside with Tirel and Rohannon, all three of them oblivious.

"Secure the castle," Laric ordered suddenly. "I want everyone out here in the courtyard immed—"

One instant, silence; the next, pandemonium. Arlis would later learn that the number of people who collapsed was exactly one hundred—fifty-three of whom were subsequently killed. This was simple mercy; they raved in broken-minded madness, and it was kinder to cut their throats.

But in those first few moments after their release, it seemed the whole courtyard had gone mad. Arlis' soldiers and Laric's quickly moved among the screaming castle folk, separating them from the sorcerers who either dropped to the cobbles in shock or were flailing and moaning in agony. Up on the balcony, feeble shrieks combined with the crash of breaking glass.

Stewards and ministers tumbled down the stairs toward Laric, babbling of sorcery and the foul and wicked spells that forced them to disloyalty. Arlis wondered if they'd taken lessons from Chiana.

Laric's mare suddenly flattened her ears, displayed her large white teeth, and lashed out with one hind hoof. The functionaries beat a hasty retreat. Arlis smiled again. Although he'd missed seeing the twitch of Laric's boot against his gelding's flank, he, too, had been riding Radzyn horses all his life.

Things had just begun to settle down when the erstwhile ruler of Firon was carried out a side door. Yarin flopped like a child's puppet, mouth soundlessly agape, wide-open eyes screaming in silence.

"We'll need help bringing the others down, my lord," said the Iseli to Arlis. "But I thought his grace would want this one first."

"Are they all like—this?" Arlis asked, his throat dry.

"Many are, my lord. Others are just lying there."

Laric's face turned white but for splotches of wind-burned color high on his cheekbones. "Good Goddess—is this happening to my son?"

Arlis wheeled his horse without a word, and everyone between him and the gate scrambled out of his way. *Rohannon—after everything else, now this! Maarken and Hollis will take me apart piece by piece—Hells, I'll sharpen my own sword and knife for them to do it with—*

Three horses were cantering toward him. He reined in, grateful that his own Radzyn mare responded to the faintest of signals, for all the strength seemed to leave his body when he recognized his squire.

Tirel waved from his perch on Idalian's knee, calling out, "Did we miss the fighting, Prince Arlis?"

"Th–there wasn't any to miss," he managed. "Are you all right?"

"Fine!" the child confirmed, then complained, "Except Idalian wouldn't let me ride up here by myself. And I did *not* fall off my horse, either!"

Arlis barely heard him. Rohannon did not look "fine." He looked exhausted. Aldiar seemed near to fainting. But both wore expressions of satisfaction.

"It was Pol," Rohannon said. "He needed us at Skybowl."

"Skybowl?" Arlis echoed weakly.

"It'll take some time to explain, my lord," Aldiar murmured.

"Uh . . . yes."

"It's all right, you know—at Skybowl," Rohannon said as they rode back to the gates. "The Vellant'im were defeated."

"I can't wait to hear how." Arlis paused. ". . . I think."

*

Andrev toppled from his horse before Tilal could catch him. Because Saumer and Iliena were also insensible, neither he nor Gemma thought much of Andrev's state. But when Volog's grandson and Yarin's sister began to mumble their way back to consciousness, Andry's son stayed silent and unmoving.

Gemma called the boy's name. Tilal unstoppered his waterskin and poured a palmful to drizzle over Andrev's forehead.

"Maybe it hit him harder because he was already Sunrunning," he said.

"I don't like this, Tilal." She placed her fingers to the pulse in Andrev's neck, and gave a little gasp.

Tilal pulled the light cloak away from Andrev's body. Soft material stuck and tangled at the shoulder pin: Tilal's spare, given when Andrev lost his. The wheat-sheaf facing dangled free, but the sharp pin itself had hooked into the boy's shirt.

Into the boy's flesh.

"Goddess, no—" He yanked it out. "Andrev!" He tore the shirt from the wound—hardly even that, only a ragged puncture, not even bleeding much—but the pin was stained red. Still attached were a tiny scrap of cloth and a piece of Andrev's skin.

He shook limp shoulders. "No, damn it—Andrev! *Andrev!*"

"Tilal—" Gemma's voice broke.

He sat down hard on the sand. "No," he whispered. "Not you, too—I can't—this isn't—"

But it *was* true. Andrev was dead. He'd been Sunrunning and had fallen and the steel pin had pierced his skin and he was dead. Senselessly. *Meaninglessly.*

A hand grasped his shoulder. He looked up: Chaltyn, tears streaming down weathered cheeks. "My lord," he said thickly, "we're summoned to Skybowl."

"To Hells with Skybowl!" Gemma cried.

The captain nodded agreement, but duty compelled him to speak. "Saumer has been told by High Princess Sioned that we're needed. The Vellant'im must be guarded while they are disarmed, else when they wake—"

"Wake?" Tilal heaved himself to his feet. He stared down at Andrev, and saw another boy dead of a wound that should not have killed him. He knuckled his eyes with one gloved hand, the dry sting worse than tears. "By the Goddess, I'll see to it personally that none of them ever wakes again."

✳

Sioned leaned wearily against the rocks, eyes closed. She could hear them gathering up the white cloth to wrap Meiglan in, hear Beth and Alasen and Ruala weeping softly. *I wonder why it is that I can't seem to cry,* she thought. *Surely I ought to.*

Someone approached, limping slightly: Isriam. She said, "Tilal will be here soon to help down below. But he's not happy. He wants so much to kill them. . . ."

"My lady . . . can you tell me why they're still alive?"

She looked up. He was wiping blood from his forehead, and she told herself they really ought to use some of that pristine white cloth to bandage him.

"It was Pol's doing," she said. "You'd better ask him." *Once he wakes from the sleep that woman spun around him. Whoever she is, Goddess bless her for her kindness.*

"For now," she continued, "if you're up to it, I'd like you to go down and find Lord Chaynal. Tell him to send someone out to meet his infuriated grace of Ossetia. Make it somebody Tilal will listen to. Daniv can go along and take charge of his Syrene troops."

"Yes, my lady." He limped away.

She shut her eyes to the sight of Meiglan's frail body vanishing within the billowing white silk. She was so tired. Never in her life had she felt such deathly emptiness. Perhaps that was why she couldn't weep.

She couldn't even be angry anymore. She had been a little while ago, when Pol had killed the High Warlord. The first time Pol had ever killed with his gifts. *Let it be the first and last. Let it be the only.*

His action had enraged her. Now she couldn't seem to remember why the feeling had been so familiar. A death denied her, claimed by someone else . . . oh, yes. Ostvel. That night at the old Feruche, Ostvel had taken Ianthe's death from her. She'd hated him for thwarting her vengeance. She supposed she'd hated Pol, too. It all seemed very far away now.

Hollow weariness brought with it a remarkable clarity of understanding. She ought to be too exhausted to string three words together in her own mind. But she knew without having to think about it that she was as wrong about wanting the

High Warlord's death for herself as she'd been about wanting Ianthe's. Much more than Sioned, and for more desperate reasons, Pol had needed that kill. He would never have been able to look at his own face in a mirror again—*or anyone else's face.*

But above all, it was imperative that he learn what it was to kill that way. To know that with the power of his mind, with a single thought, he could destroy life and breath and flesh, leaving behind nothing but ash to drift away on the wind.

Well, it was over now. Considering what he'd chosen not to do to the Vellant'im, she supposed that the shock of what he'd done to their High Warlord would be both lesson and warning. He'd needed the death, but he'd also needed to learn.

Sioned couldn't work up much concern over it. *Maybe later. Right now I'm too tired. It's been one Hell of a long day—and not even midmorning yet.*

Alasen and Beth were conferring quietly nearby. She heard her own name, and then Ruala's voice.

"No, leave her be. She's done enough—too much, by the look of her."

Enough? Too much? No. She had done what Pol needed her to do. She had sorted out hundreds of individual minds, separating them back into their distinct colors and patterns. Some had splintered like stained-glass windows, and she doubted their sanity, but couldn't feel any compassion. They had done it to themselves, fighting the awesome strength of Pol's weaving.

Those who yielded survived. She had stitched them back together and left them whole—an impossible task on the face of it, but most had been able to help her. The children had been the most difficult, especially the willful and powerful Jihan. Jihan, though, had been the only one untouched by fear. *Audrite is there, and Tobin, and others who will help the children—and they'll all be here with their parents in a few days anyway. They'll be all right.*

As for the dragons—they'd withdrawn without her assistance, obeying Azhdeen just as they had when he commanded them into the *ros'salath.* Had they held the whole thing together? Possibly. She didn't know, and right now didn't care.

The hardest task had been Andry, for his was the mind

through which all at Goddess Keep had come. She had assumed he would do for them what she had done for the others, but when she finished her work they were all still tightly
woven into the sunlight. The strain was too great; he wasn't
unconscious, down there in his father's arms, but neither
was he capable of the work on his own.

So Sioned did it for him, unthreading each half-trained
faradhi mind first, and then those who had sorcerer blood,
equally inexperienced. Next she found the more knowledgeable, who worked with her as best they could. Finally she
turned to the *devr'im* who had given Pol the technique he
needed. Antoun had helped a little, knowing them as he did.
He had wept, but she had not, at the two lightless deaths at
Goddess Keep.

So it was over now. A few dead, many dying—all of them
of their own resistance. She wondered, without much interest and no real concern, how it must have felt to be Pol during that brief time. To know the power of an entire continent
was his to weave into whatever he liked.

Her light-raw senses told her the third white moon had
emerged from behind her larger sister. Sioned leaned back a
little more, into a shadow. So very little time it had taken;
but it felt like a thousand years.

She wanted never to move again. She sat there in the
morning sun, a breeze rising from the Desert to caress her
face, and thanked the Goddess for her weariness. She had
used up the last shred of her strength in finding Saumer and
making things clear to his groggy, power-drained mind. She
had searched for Andrev, unable to find him, too exhausted
even to grieve when she realized why. She was incapable of
doing anything more. She could not weave the sunlight to
Feruche. So she would not have to be the one to tell Tobin
that her grandson was dead, and her son was dying.

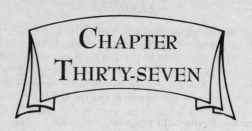

CHAPTER
THIRTY-SEVEN

It took Andry five days to die.

The afternoon of the eighty-ninth, late sunlight crawled across the floor toward the bed. The warm golden touch woke him. It was Feylin who saw his eyes open; it was Evarin who began screaming. All Chay's strength was needed to drag the Sunrunner physician's convulsing body through the antechamber to the hall.

Sioned pierced Evarin back together. Feylin sealed the room to sunlight and forbade *faradh'im* and *diarmadh'im* to enter.

That night Meiglan was Burned on the crags at Skybowl where she had died. Sioned called Fire to her shroud: the silken cloak she had sewn for Pol.

Midmorning on the ninetieth, Andry woke again. Chay heard the rustle of movement and roused from a listless doze. He had barely spoken his son's name when Fire lunged wildly through the room—candles to curtains, rugs to quilt. Chay cried out and tore the burning coverlet from his son's body. Feylin ran in from the next room moments later, yanking the drapes down, stamping them onto the rug to smother the flames. Walvis, just behind her, slammed his fist into Andry's jaw. With loss of consciousness, the Fire vanished.

Shaking, Feylin forbade *all* light in Andry's room.

That night Tilal and Gemma poured sweet oils onto another pyre. Maarken lit the Fire, and at dawn Hollis summoned wind to carry Andrev's ashes into the Desert of his ancestors.

That same dawn, the ninety-first of Winter, Sioned slipped cautiously through an antechamber door, squinting in the gloom. Feylin was alone with Andry. Chay had spent the night watching Fire take his grandson. A sleeping draught ensured Andry would not wake. Sioned conjured the tiniest of fingerflames—all she dared—and tried to touch his dreaming mind.

Afterward, Feylin held her while she wept.

At noon on the ninety-second, thirty people arrived from Feruche. Tobin was forbidden to see her son. When Chay took her into a private chamber to tell her why, she broke as she had not broken in all the long years of her life.

"Nobody gifted can be in the room with him," he said, kneeling before her chair, gray head bowed. "Even I can feel . . . something. I don't know what it is—just at the edges of my mind, as if it can't quite get hold of me."

"Sioned will help him. She can weave his pattern again, the way she did for me the night Father was Burned."

"She tried. Yesterday, this morning—there's been some success. When he wakes now, he doesn't call Fire he can't control. He spoke to Feylin last night. A few words. This morning he woke and he understood when I talked to him." *And asked if he'd dreamed it, or if there really had been a dragon. . . .*

"So it's only a matter of t–time and effort, and—"

He cradled her frail hands in his own. "Tobin . . . too much of him is gone. Not even Sioned can bring back what he's lost."

"No! I don't believe it!"

"Listen to me, my love. At first it was as if he'd been stunned and his brain had just—I don't know, shut down. Sioned says it's something much worse. His mind grabs at light—Tobin, there can't even be a lit candle in the room."

Tobin whimpered. Her child, denied the light that was a Sunrunner's life.

Chay struggled to continue. "I thought Pol could help—but he hasn't opened his eyes since he killed the High Warlord. It's only sleep. But Sioned says that even though he's powerful, he isn't much good at what needs doing. Unthreading Andry from light—I don't understand it, but Sioned says—"

" 'Sioned says'—damn Sioned! *Her* son isn't shut away in the dark!"

He didn't tell her that even with the sandstorm shutters

closed and all the chinks filled, even with the curtains drawn, even with no candles in the room—even then Sioned was in danger. She must fight Andry constantly for control of the fingerflame she used to reach him, to glimpse the mad jumble of color and try to force it back into the orderly elegance that was Andry.

"It's not darkness, Tobin. It's the light. He's not lost in shadows, but in too much light."

"And it's killing him," she whispered.

"Yes."

"Take me to him. I want to see my son."

"You can't." He clung to her hands. "There's nothing you can do for him—and what he'd do to you without even knowing it—"

"I don't care! I want to see him! Andry—!"

She pushed herself to her feet. He caught her in his arms—so slight and delicate, and he so old now, so weak. He sat with her in his lap and rocked her as she cried. He had never seen her cry like this. Never with such hopeless grief, as if her heart had shattered. She had wept for parents and brother and two sons, but never for someone not yet dead.

That afternoon, Tobren sneaked into her father's darkened room while Betheyn was washing her face at the bathroom sink. The child conjured a fragile fingerflame to see by, gasping with joy as Andry's eyelids flickered open.

The gasp became a sob of agony. Beth snatched her up and fled into the hallway, calling for Sioned.

That night, Sioned sat by her chamber hearth, recovering from her work with Tobren's bruised mind and another fruitless attempt to restore Andry's splintering colors. She glanced up as the door opened. Tobin limped into the room and said a simple and terrible thing.

"You helped Meath. Now help Andry. Help my son to die."

✳

Beth counted Andry's breaths—soft and regular with sleep. The chamber around them was blacker than a starless sky. But even in the dark he knew who she was, called her by her name.

"Beth. . . ."

She took his hands. Warm, firm, supple—his body was

strong, unharmed. It didn't seem possible that his mind was dying.

"Beth," he said again, calm and quiet. "Let me die."

"Andry—" Grief choked the rest.

"I want to. Tell Sioned I want to." He sighed. "It's all shining, Beth ... so bright ... always thought death was supposed to be dark...."

"Andry? Andry!"

He was unconscious again, and dangerous to no one. He could conceivably live like this for quite some time. Years, perhaps. If no light reached him, no further harm could come to him or anyone else. But he would never be a Sunrunner again. He would never weave light and power again, never know the colors of another's mind. He was as profoundly blind as Rislyn.

At dawn when Feylin returned to take the watch, Beth heard a dragon call out plaintively, just outside Andry's closed windows. Shivering, she hurried her steps to Sioned's room. Tobin and Alasen sat with her at the empty hearth, keeping each other wordless, sleepless company. Welts circled Sioned's and Alasen's wrists, matching Beth's own; high-collared shirts hid the rope burns at their necks. The marks on their hands were nearly healed. Evarin said there would be no permanent damage, not even scars. The High Warlord had been as precise with the needles as he'd been with the single killing thrust to Meiglan's heart.

Beth could not imagine anyone strong enough to give Andry similar mercy. He needed it desperately—but who would do it?

"Andry says...." She cleared her throat. "He says he doesn't want you to try anymore. He wants it to be over."

Alasen slowly bent her face into her hands. Tobin met Sioned's gaze.

The High Princess nodded. "At sunset, then. If we let the light in, I think it will take him. I've felt it hovering, almost as if it's searching for a way in. If we let it inside ... when it leaves, he'll go with it."

Tobin made a small, strangled sound. Alasen reached both hands to her, covering the thin fingers with her own.

"All he ever wanted was the sunlight. There are worse ways to die than to be claimed by what you love best." Alasen looked up, green eyes liquid with sorrow. "Help him to die, Sioned."

*

On the ninety-third evening of Winter in the Dragon Year 737, Andry died.

Only his father was with him. When Chay opened the shutters wide, Andry seized the last sunlight—or it seized him. No one would ever know.

For a few moments it seemed the light had healed him. He looked into Chay's eyes and smiled. "I've been remembering," he murmured. "All the colors . . . so bright . . . so *good* . . . it's all right, you know. I'm not afraid. Tell Mother that."

"I will." Light danced around him, glimmering even into Chay's mind.

"And how much I love you . . . and my children . . . is Tobren—was she here?"

"Yes. Don't worry, we'll take care of all of them." As shining eyes sought the sun, Chay said, "Maarken and Hollis want them to live at Whitecliff."

"Yes," Andry said slowly, as if from a vast distance. "But let Andrev . . . stay with Tilal. . . ."

Chay replied, "Of course," for Andry didn't know that his firstborn was dead. He groped desperately for something else to say, something that would keep Andry with him just a small, selfish while longer. Stilling the need, he stroked the smooth brow, watching the smile strengthen and the light glow in blue eyes.

"Sleep now. I love you, my son," he whispered as the light and Andry died.

*

That night there was another Burning. Tobren and Chayla poured out the fragrant oils; Maarken and Hollis called Fire. Tobin stood beside Chay until dawn, refusing to leave before Sioned summoned a gentle wind to carry the ashes into the Desert.

At midnight, high above a whisper of breeze and the snap and hiss of flames, one keening cry pealed. It was answered by the other dragons at Skybowl, and then was gone.

At dawn, Sunrunners wove the first light to spread word throughout the princedoms that the Lord of Goddess Keep was dead. No *diarmadh'im* joined them, not even Riyan.

Everyone returned to the castle then. Chay tried to coax Tobin to follow. She shook her head, staring at the empty, blackened stones that had been Meiglan's and then Andrev's and now Andry's pyre.

"He's gone, Tobin. Come inside, love."

"Leave me alone."

"You've been here all night, you're not strong enough—"

"Strength?" She glared at him. "I carried four sons in my body. I gave them life from my life. And now three of them are d–dead. Leave me alone!"

She limped a few paces away. He glanced helplessly at Sioned, who nodded to indicate she would stay and keep watch over Tobin. Chay walked slowly around the lake, back to the castle, wishing it had been him on that pyre. No man should outlive three of his sons.

⁕

All that night, Sionell watched over Pol. Exhaustion and shock made his sleep seem more like a coma, but there was no danger. Sionell's mother came in regularly to reassure herself that it was *only* sleep. Pol's mother looked in once, identified someone named Camigina as Pol's benefactor, and explained that a conversation on sunlight had revealed this sodden sleep to be a normal result of using so much power. Then Sioned had returned to Andry, as Feylin had done.

Sionell was watching at the windows when Andry's pyre was lit. With the first flare of Sunrunner's Fire, she flinched, fingers bunched around a tunic she was sewing for her elder son. Tiglath's colors, blue velvet faced in yellow silk, for Jahnev to wear when the princes assembled to confirm Pol as the new High Prince. It was necessary work, this tunic, for more than reasons of pride. Sewing kept her hands occupied, and sometimes even her mind.

Until tonight, Chayla had shared the task of tending Pol. She was forbidden her uncle's room, and there were no wounded—none that she would treat, for there were plenty of captive Vellant'im still below Skybowl—so she exercised her physician's skills on Pol. Not that she was needed. He only slept. But he must be washed, and food and water must be eased down his throat. Simple, routine, mindless tasks, done in silence.

But not in darkness. Not as it had been with Andry....

And what if we'd had to shut Pol away from the light, too?

Sionell lit a candle on the bedside table, telling herself it was to sew by. The light was shielded from Pol's face by the drape of tapestry hangings. She didn't so much see as sense his eyes open. She let her needlework fall to her lap and folded her hands atop it, waiting for him to speak.

"I already have a cloak to Burn in," he said, his voice thick and raspy.

"What makes you think you'll need one?" Besides, they'd already used Meiglan's work for Meiglan herself. At Sionell's suggestion.

He shifted in bed as if every bone had been bruised. "Why are you here?"

Charming as ever, she thought. "Everyone else is outside and will be until dawn. Andry died today."

"How long?"

"Five days."

"Goddess." He paused. "I couldn't find him. After. I killed him. I took the power and I used it and it killed him."

"No. That's not how it happened. He drew in all the power at Goddess Keep for his own use and died of the strain."

"When did *you* become a Sunrunner?"

Sionell fisted her hands in velvet and silk. "Your mother and Evarin agree about what happened to him."

He was quiet for a long while. She thought he'd gone back to sleep. Then, very softly: "Poor Tobin. . . ."

She allowed more time to pass before saying, "I spoke with Chadric. He and Daniv and Tilal think the princes must meet here as soon as possible. Arlis will sail from Snowcoves. Laric is staying in Firon—Lisiel will come from Dragon's Rest to speak for him. They don't know what you want to do about Cabar and Velden. They assume Isriam will represent Pirro, to force his hand in accepting the boy as his heir."

Listlessly: "Whatever you like."

"What I'd *like*—" she began incautiously, then swallowed the rest. She must control her temper. He had been through enough; she supposed she ought to pity him. She didn't have the option of storming out. There was nobody else in the castle. Everyone was gathered at Andry's pyre, either from love or respect or memories of him as a child or communal need, or simply because it was a singular event in the history of Skybowl. Sionell had no such feelings. She was beginning to wonder if she had any feelings left at all.

"What do you want, Ell?" Pol murmured, and his voice had changed entirely.

I want Tallain back. I want the world the way it was.

The simpler one's desire, the more impossible to obtain. Tilal, for instance, had wanted only one thing: vengeance. When Daniv told him Pol had forbidden any more killing, Tilal had blistered his nephew's ears with his rage before galloping alone to Skybowl, demanding the right to slay every captive Vellanti by his own hand. Sionell had been there when Maarken asked him if killing two thousand would bring back even one.

What I want, you can never give me. No one can.

She shrugged. "It's more a question of what I'll have to settle for, isn't it?" Putting her needlework aside, she rose. "You ought to eat something. There's a tray. Just bread and cheese, but I can brew taze on the hearthfire—"

"I've never had to 'settle' for anything in my life," Pol said suddenly. "I don't know what it feels like. I suppose I'm going to find out."

She heard the shift of silken bedclothes, and a long sigh, and after a moment twitched the bedcurtain aside. Candlelight gilded the tears on his sleeping face. Tenderness hollowed her bones as she smoothed drops from his cheeks and fair hair from his forehead.

He turned his head into the caresses and murmured, "Meggie. . . ."

✳

The day Andry died, three dragon ships sailed from Goddess Keep. Locked in their holds were seven hundred and twelve Vellanti survivors of the assault on the castle. At the helm was Kolya of Kadar Water; in the riggings were fifty of his most experienced sailors. But mastery of the huge vessels did not come easily. Progress along the Ossetian coast was erratic and dangerous.

Next morning a brisk wind blew up from the southwest, and all they needed to do was catch it and skim across the waves. Antoun, ashen and miserable, cursed himself for insisting on joining this voyage. Elsen thrived on it. Edrel, groggy from the fever that accompanied his several battle wounds, kept asking why everything moved. Norian wiped his brow with cool cloths, fed him more medicine, and bade him not to worry about it.

On the ninety-fourth day of Winter, Ostvel arrived with a large group from Dragon's Rest. Lisiel introduced her new son all around, exclaimed on how Alleyn and Audran had grown, and after a tearful private reunion with her sister Iliena went with her to Pol's chamber. They apologized for being related to their despicable brother and urged that Yarin be punished to the fullest extent of the law.

"That's for Laric to decide," he told them.

"But he'll deal more gently with Yarin than he ought," Iliena said.

"Because of us," added Lisiel.

"Why not let him know how you feel about it?" Pol suggested.

They traded glances. Iliena spoke for both. "We ... don't like to bother the Sunrunners...." ... *because of what we are,* hung in the air, unsaid.

"After a few lessons, you'll be able to do it yourselves. Until then, I'm sure someone will oblige you. And I think it's time you got to know the rest of your kin."

He judged it better not to tell them that their brother, though lacking experience with his gifts, had not lacked for panicked stubbornness in fighting Pol. Yarin's mind was more or less still his own. Whether he was sane enough to be tried for his treason was still questionable.

Ostvel came by later, after his own mostly silent reunion with Alasen. Camigina was with him, so Pol finally got to meet the sorcerer who had sent him into merciful sleep. Nothing was said about it, however. They gave a detailed account of Chiana and Rinhoel, who at present occupied a chamber in the western tower—which had been scrubbed from top to bottom. The solvents used were normally kept to clean stables after outbreaks of various equine diseases. It seemed Chiana had a sensitive nose as well as an exalted opinion of where she ought to be lodged; she demanded another room. This one, she said, smelled like a middens.

In Ostvel's opinion, a middens was where she belonged.

"You know," Pol said when Ostvel and Camigina finished, "if life were tidy, we'd be able to prove some treasonable offense and legally execute them. We know they ordered Rialt and Mevita killed. But not only did Naydra not see it done, she killed the guard who did it. We also know that Rinhoel murdered Halian and almost certainly Aurar as well. Palila saw it. But Naydra tells me the child has hardly spoke a word since. Even if she *could* bear witness, how can I force her to condemn her own mother and brother to death?"

"But their alliance with the sorcerers," Ostvel protested.

"I'm coming to that." He sipped wine—a carefully watered cup, for at full strength it sent him right back to sleep. "We know they collaborated with the Vellant'im. But Saumer mentioned that the flag on the shipment from Swalekeep was put there by Kostas' order. Oh, the barge was welcomed right enough, which means the colors were familiar. But that's not proof."

"My lord," said Camigina, "*we* saw them with traitors."

"Yes, you did. And who among those traitors still lives? I'm not complaining, my lady. Your action saved many lives. I'm just sorry it cost so many of your own."

"*Our* own," she corrected softly.

"Yes, of course. That's something we can discuss later. The point is there's no great big thundering crime with a bloodied sword and a hundred witnesses. We suspect, we *know*—but the law requires proof."

Ostvel met Camigina's gaze. "His father's son," he said.

"I hope so," Pol replied seriously. "But it's not just the law. I'd like to kill them. Goddess knows they deserve it. But I'm tired of killing. I wish I could prove any of it—but life doesn't pack itself neatly into a box and tie its own ribbon."

"What will you do with them, if I may ask?" Camigina said.

He shrugged. "Damned if I know."

✳

The next afternoon a strange enclave was established on the sands below Skybowl. Unlike the well-guarded circle that held the Vellant'im, this was a small city of tents. The Isulk'im had arrived.

Visian rode down from the keep at the first sight of them on the horizon, and came back with their request to share water with their kinsman, the High Prince. Pol had talked often enough with Kazander to know that this did not mean they wished to drink from Skybowl's lake. They wanted him to partake of *their* hospitality.

Regrettably, he was in no condition to visit them. Five days of sleep had restored mental alertness, but his body was still exhausted and he could do no more than walk the length of his chamber without growing dizzy.

Visian returned to his people to explain, and extend Pol's invitation—seconded by Riyan and Ruala—to camp wherever they would for as long as they liked. Thus all afternoon tents rose across the sand. By evening, wind chimes of glass and jade and silver were tinkling gently on the breeze.

The next Isulk'im Pol saw were three breathtakingly beautiful young women. They were escorted into his chamber at dusk by Visian—whose strong resemblance to one of them told Pol who these ladies must be.

He saluted them in the Isulki manner, apologized for not being able to rise from his bed, and asked if they would do him the honor of sharing some wine. The eldest—no older than twenty-six, tall, lithe, and approximately halfway through a pregnancy—crossed both slim, dark hands over her heart.

"The *Azhrei* is kind. It is not permitted me, but my sisters thank you."

"Perhaps taze, then, my lady," Pol said.

"The *Azhrei* is very kind."

Chairs were brought by Visian, who also served the wine and taze. In contrast to their husband, who had talked at great and flowery length, these three women seemed content with silence.

Finally, the youngest of them met his gaze directly. She had the blackest eyes and the longest lashes he'd ever seen. *"Azhrei,"* she said, "we have come to see the woman who was worth the *korrus'* life."

Pol froze.

The middle one had a hawk's golden eyes, proclaiming ancestry not wholly Isulki, and the look she shot the younger woman was equivalent to the slice of talons. "You have the grace of a lame and spavined mare!" she hissed.

"But—"

"What she means to say," the eldest said, with a quelling glance in their direction, "is that if the *korrus* thought her worth the dying, she is a woman to be respected and cherished. We would wish to meet her, and speak, and show our people that we agree with him." She paused. "*Azhrei,* will the lady see us?"

"Uh . . . yes, of course," Pol said blankly. There was no bitterness in these women, no rancor, no blame. They had come here because of simple curiosity, and to confirm Chayla's worth to all Isulk'im.

But he was very glad he wouldn't be included in the interview.

They proposed a meeting on the morrow—Pol reminded himself to have someone tell Chayla beforehand exactly why Kazander's wives were here—and then progressed to other business. Namely, that the Isulk'im would guard the Vellant'im on the march south to Radzyn Keep.

Pol smiled. "My lady, that would be perfect. My troops are war-weary, and Isulki sharp-sightedness is precisely what the work requires. Would you consider another task, as a favor?"

"You are kin, *Azhrei.* Ask what you will, and if we can, we will do it."

"First, I will say that I intend to make Lady Sionell of Tiglath my Regent in Cunaxa. I believe you know something of her."

"We do. A woman worthy of respect."

"Yes. Very much so. She and her husband had dealings with the Merida for years. But no one knows them better than you Isulk'im. Would you consider advising Lady Sionell regarding them? While it's true that they won't be much threat after Zagroy's Pillar, their children will eventually grow up and—"

The woman set aside her cup and rose. So did the others. Pol wondered dismally what he'd said wrong.

"*Azhrei,*" she murmured, "you are wise beyond wisdom. They are only children. They do not deserve death for the treachery of their parents. If they become Merida, they will die. If they do not become Merida, they will live."

An interesting way of looking at it, and one he hadn't considered. All he'd wanted was to give Sionell some help in the matter.

"If the Lady Sionell wishes our advice, it is hers."

"I know she'll welcome it," Pol said.

All three folded their hands on their hearts and bowed. Visian came forward from the shadows to guide them out, and Pol saw his eyes go round as taze cups when the eldest spoke once more.

"*Azhrei,*" she said, "my Name is Elizian."

Pol was almost as shocked as Visian. No Isulki wife ever gave her name to anyone but immediate relatives. She had a public name, and a name used by her husband in private, but her real name was for blood-kin. It was doubtful that even Visian, Kazander's brother-by-marriage, had heard it before now.

"You do me great honor, my lady. My Name," he replied in kind, "is Pol."

Elizian's smile was poetry. "The Star that flew into the Sky Dragon."

"I heard about that," he admitted. "And the other prophecies."

"All were true." This from the long-lashed youngest, very eagerly. "The hundred tents felled by the wind, these were castles and manors. The eight of our dead, thus did eight princes die—"

"And the *Azhrei* Rohan?" asked the one with golden eyes.

"*High* Prince," was the tart answer.

Elizian silenced them again with a look. "She is skilled in such things, like all her mother-line. We will leave now, for it is clear you are tired."

"Not at all. I—"

Despite the difference in coloring and age, the look Elizian gave him was so reminiscent of his mother that he couldn't help but smile. She acknowledged it with a brief twinkle of dark eyes, and the three ladies departed.

Pol thought over the conversation, shaking his head in bemusement. He had no doubt that when the list of ruined properties was compiled, the number of castles and manors would total exactly one hundred. Gilad and Syr would be hardest hit, with Ossetia and Grib not far behind. Thanks to Ostvel, Meadowlord could feed almost everyone until spring crops matured. But there was much more work ahead. He would need cooperative princes and *athr'im* in order to do it.

He considered the eight dead princes. He had not a moment's regret for Miyon of Cunaxa, and only scant pity for Halian of Meadowlord and Edirne and Camanto of Fessenden. He would miss, personally as well as at *Riall'im,* Volog of Kierst and his son Latham, and gruff Kostas of Syr.

But his deepest sorrow was for Rihani of Ossetia. Of them all, his was the most tragic death.

Except Andrev. Pol leaned his head back and shut his eyes, grateful that Andry had never known.

And Meiglan. . . .

So many lives wasted. So much lost. Rohan. Andry. Princes, *athr'im*, common folk and their families. Rislyn's sight and Maarken's hand. Meath. Tallain. Jahnavi and Rabisa, Rialt and Mevita. Children dead by sword or fire, dead of disease. Rihani and Andrev and hundreds more like them—young, full of life and promise. Each name was a knife in his guts. The loss of them. The sheer, pointless waste of it.

And Meiglan. . . .

Those who remained would look to him, wanting him to put the world back the way it had been. A dangerous folly. The world that had been was as dead as the man who had created it of his will and his strength and his intelligence and his Sunrunner princess.

Because Pol had wanted to believe that life could resume its former patterns, he'd sent Meiglan back to Dragon's Rest.

It was his task to shape what remained into new patterns. And because of the manner in which Rohan had established the world everyone wanted back, Pol would be able to change things pretty much as he pleased. Though the High Prince's Writ was not all-encompassing, it pervaded the princedoms powerfully enough to be used more extensively than ever.

That structure, enforced by the *Medr'im*, was there to be used, as he had used his gifts, his armies, the Sunrunners, and the sorcerers. With such power, he could do anything. What had taken Rohan forty years of subtlety to accomplish, Pol could do in forty days. And that was if he dawdled over it.

It was his to do, his to fashion as he willed. And he would have to do it alone.

Meggie. . . .

But no one would see the empty place at his side. No one would think to look. He was strong enough to do it all alone, wasn't he? That's what they all thought. High Prince. Sunrunner. *Diarmadh'rei.*

I am what my parents made me, he thought. *All three of them.*

*

The next dawn, the Vellant'im began their long march through the sand to Radzyn. Two hundred of Chay's own cavalry and three hundred Isulk'im prodded them briskly along. Pol was genuinely amused for the first time in a long time when Maarken observed that the whole scene resembled nothing so much as a cattle drive, with the Isulk'im rounding up strays—though they'd be mortally insulted to hear him say so.

Pol was up and about, having decided over Feylin's objections that seven days in bed were enough. The sky was clear over the Veresch and all the way south to the Catha Hills, where the dragons had spent the Winter, but he left the sunlight strictly alone. There was too much else to be done, he told himself, perfectly aware that this was merely a convenient excuse.

So it was Maarken who told him that Arlis' ships were about a day out of Zaldivar, and Idalian and Tirel had stayed behind with Laric at Balarat.

"Aldiara told me Laric sent her along to represent her branch of the *diarmadh'im*. How many branches are there, anyhow?"

"Besides hers, Mireva's, Thassalante's, and Camigina's— who knows?" Pol shrugged, the subject of sorcerers still raw. This morning he'd been told that Thassalante, realizing that abandoning Meiglan had meant her death, had suicided through the *diarmadhi* equivalent of becoming shadow-lost. He left a message for Pol stating that because his was the guilt, his must be the atonement, and he hoped Pol would deal gently with the others.

Pol didn't want to talk about them. Knowing that, Maarken changed subjects.

"Tobren has acquired a dragon."

"What?"

"The one who first chose Andry. Yesterday he made one Hell of a racket and didn't shut up until Tobren looked out a window to see what the fuss was."

Pol nodded. "What has she Named him?"

"Tirita—'my friend.' And she needs one, after—" Maarken broke off. "She stays pretty much to herself. She didn't react at all when Hollis told her that her brother and sisters will be coming to live at Whitecliff, too. But Tirita seems to comfort her."

"Good. I'm glad." Appropriate, that the dragon had chosen Andry's daughter. "Now, about this gathering of princes Chadric seems to feel is necessary. How long before Arlis gets here?"

"Depends on how long he stops at Zaldivar, and the winds down south ... hmm. Landfall at Radzyn maybe the third or fourth of the New Year Holiday."

"All right. Let's plan on the last day of the New Year, then. Banqueting, musicians, the whole silly spectacle."

Maarken smiled. "I'll warn Ruala."

Ruala, dully warned, arrived in Pol's chamber that afternoon bearing a single plate of Kierstian ceramic, glazed in Skybowl's blue and brown. "*This* is what you'd have me use to serve princes?" she demanded. "Or shall I dig up all the 'dragon teeth' and glue them back together to set the tables with?"

Orders were immediately sent to Dragon's Rest and Zaldivar. Pol's *Rialla* service would be dispatched from the former at once; from the latter, unbeknownst to Ruala, would come a complete new service for one hundred to replace what had been shattered in a good cause. Alasen prevailed upon Camigina to ask a *diarmadhi* still at Swalekeep to send Chiana's silver. By dusk, Ruala was satisfied that Skybowl would not be disgraced.

Pol's own cook from Dragon's Rest had insisted on accompanying Ostvel to the Desert. Taking it for granted that there would be a grand gathering of princes, equally convinced that the feast must be prepared by no one but himself, it was said that his battle with the master of Skybowl's kitchen was audible all the way to the stables. Pol was profoundly glad he'd slept through it. Audrite established an uneasy truce, but war was glumly predicted as the great night neared.

Pol resolved to ignore the whole mess. He had decisions to make more vital than which cook would have the honor of seasoning the roasts. This was what he told the two aproned worthies when they accosted him—appropriately enough—in the family dining chamber at Skybowl.

This room was not as large as the Attic at Feruche, and

usually not as cluttered. But when Pol took it over as his temporary office, parchments were quickly strewn across a polished wood table that easily sat ten. At Pol's right elbow was the box containing his seal, brought by Ostvel from Dragon's Rest. A smaller box held Miyon's, from Castle Pine in Cunaxa. Rohan's had been lost at Stronghold. All three were unnecessary now, for one of Riyan's crafters had presented him with a new seal.

The handle was tipped with three small stones—topaz, amethyst, white jade. Otherwise undecorated, comfortable to hold, the seal was as well-balanced as a fine sword. This was a feat in itself, for it was larger and heavier than any ever made, almost as wide as his palm and cast in solid gold.

The impression it left in half a stick of melted wax impressed him. "Lord Maarken's design," the crafter said, adding that he hoped it suited. Pol nodded absently and murmured something about being very pleased.

The Desert's dragon stood within the wreath of Princemarch, wings spread wide, crowned head in profile. A Sunrunner ring was clutched in his right talons, Cunaxa's knife in his left. Written along the wreath's three ribbons knotted at the bottom were three words: *Azhrei, Faradh'rei, Diarmadh'rei.*

Pol's signature, above great irregular circles of wax bearing that seal, was now on five large pieces of parchment. Dorval, Firon, Kierst-Isel, Syr, and Ossetia were taken care of, their princes and heirs confirmed in writing. Cunaxa, the Desert, and Princemarch were his own. Those were the easy ones. As for Fessenden, Grib, Gilad, and Meadowlord. . . .

Pol put an elbow on the table and sank his chin into his palm. Grib and Gilad presented some interesting alternatives. He was actually looking forward to writing out the parchment for Meadowlord. But Fessenden was a problem.

A soft knock at the door brought his head up. "Come in," he said. In walked his own choice for Heir to Fessenden. "Ah. Isriam." He'd forgotten that he'd sent for the boy. Well, now was as good a time as any. "Sit down, won't you."

Isriam remained standing. Tense, haggard with sleeplessness, his face had lost all the not-quite-finished quality of adolescence. War had aged him beyond youth; guilt had made him an old man.

Beth said that Isriam barely spoke to her. He couldn't

even look at Pol. Stiff-shouldered, blank eyes fixed on empty air and generous mouth a hard, tight slash, Isriam obviously expected accusations and punishment for failure.

"Tell me what happened," Pol murmured. "I want to know all you saw."

Stony-faced, Isriam began. "Yes, your grace. High Princess Sioned freed me from the ropes. I untied Lady Betheyn so she could help the others. I climbed up the rocks. He was looking at her, but I don't think she even saw him. She looked down the mountain—at you, your grace, I'm sure of it. She was smiling a little. He put his hand out, as if feeling the air, and—" He stopped and swallowed hard.

"Go on."

"She—she didn't suffer. I know this because I saw her face, after. She was still smiling. It was as if she never felt it, didn't even know. . . ."

Pol forbade himself to react. His feelings didn't matter. "And then?"

"I—I was too late. I knocked him down and fell with him. I hit my head on a rock. I couldn't see very well. But I could see him get up, and I tried to get to him, to push him over the side—"

"And then I called Fire, and burned your arm. I'm sorry for that, Isriam."

"It's nothing, your grace. It's not important."

"Shall we speak of what is?" Pol asked quietly. "Let me tell you why it happened, Isriam. You've heard by now that there was a battle for control over the magic being worked." *Magic*—Andry's word. He schooled his face and thoughts once more. "To fight it, I left Thassalante and many *diarmadh'im* behind, trusting them to protect her. But when they felt the other thing begin, they chose to join. I didn't know that until my mother was freed. She saw their colors where they shouldn't have been, and warned me. Too late."

He paused, wishing Isriam would look at him. Words were fine tools, but anyone could use them; what he wanted Isriam to understand was better said with his eyes.

"I know what you've been telling yourself. If you'd been a little faster it wouldn't have happened."

"Yes, your grace."

"If my mother had freed you just a few moments earlier. If you hadn't taken the time to free Beth."

He flinched, the lean muscles of his jaw tensing.

Pol made his voice even softer. "And . . . if I hadn't abandoned my wife?"

"No! If Lord Andry hadn't fought you—" He stopped, stricken with shame that he could accuse a man who had paid so dearly for his actions.

"Listen to me, Isriam. I've talked with others about this, and reviewed my own memory of it. Andry drew on the Sunrunners working at Goddess Keep. Through him, I saw how the *ros'salath* could be built. But I couldn't control it. So I pulled in Sunrunners and sorcerers from everywhere. I needed their power—and with the *devr'im* showing me how, I could do what I did to the Vellant'im."

"But he—"

"If Andry had not fought me," Pol went on, "the *diarmadh'im* with Thassalante would not have felt my call. Meiglan would have been safe—but I would not have had the knowledge or the power. And if I'd been just a little quicker in using it. . . ." He shrugged. "So you see, I've been thinking just the same as you."

"No! It's not the same! You're the High Prince!"

As if that explained and justified everything.

"Your grace—" The stone walls cracked. All the pent-up emotions were escaping. "I see what you're trying to tell me—but do you? You trusted the sorcerers to protect her. It wasn't your fault they disobeyed—and it probably wasn't their fault they answered to you," he added.

It was something Pol hadn't yet considered. But Isriam wasn't finished.

"Lord Andry was wrong—he shouldn't have killed with his gifts, or forced the other Sunrunners to do it, either! You had to fight him. And all the power you pulled in—I don't understand that, I'm not a Sunrunner, but I *do* know that not one drop of blood was spilled at Balarat! And that was because of you."

It had not been the same at Goddess Keep. Dead and wounded had littered the fields, blood soaking the ground. Was it because Torien had been too afraid of power, or Andry too hungry for it? Or perhaps Pol was much to blame for that, too, for long years of rivalry that had helped shove Andry toward a precipice. He could still hear the echo of his cousin's voice: *"Get out of my way!"* Andry's fall had lasted five hideous days.

"Your mother was part of the working, wasn't she, my lord? So she couldn't have freed me any earlier. And I—"

Pol nodded, for Isriam was now where Pol wanted him to be. The switch from *your grace* to *my lord* confirmed it.

"And because you freed Beth," Pol said, "she pulled the steel from my mother's hand, allowing her a Sunrunner's freedom to warn me."

"Too late!" Isriam cried from amid the rubble of his defenses. "It all happened too late! Oh, my lord, I'm sorry!"

"I know," Pol replied.

It didn't surprise him in the least when the door opened and Beth came in. She gave a fairly natural start on seeing that Pol was not alone, and offered to leave them to their discussion—to which she'd been listening just outside.

"No, my lady, I'll—I have to help Dannar and Kierun with—excuse me," Isriam finished, and strode out.

Beth shut the door behind him and leaned back on it. "All that logic," she murmured, "all that reason."

"And all of it his, with a little help. I think he begins to believe it."

"I wish you did." Without asking permission—rare in her, he realized with sudden wariness—she sat at the table. In Ruala's chair, that would have been her own had Sorin lived.

"He'll be all right, once he understands that it wasn't his fault," he said before she could speak again. "He gave Daniv an earful the other night, you know. About how unworthy he is, and how Pirro would be right to reject him—"

She regarded him thoughtfully. "Do you always babble when you're trying to avoid an issue?"

"No. Usually I walk out." He settled more deeply in his chair. "Well, say what you came to say."

"Thank you for speaking to Isriam as you did."

He couldn't help a smile. "I only followed your suggestions, Beth. *Now* who's avoiding the issue?"

"Not I, my lord. I was about to repeat his question. Did you listen to what you said here today?"

Before now, he would have taken a substantial bet that it was impossible to be annoyed by this woman.

Beth folded her hands atop a sheaf of clean parchments. " 'Being High Prince makes it my fault'—isn't that what your father used to say? Tell me, Pol, is it truly your place to shoulder blame you know doesn't belong to you? Don't you have enough to carry without adding that as well?"

"Shall I surprise you and say I agree with you? I keep asking myself what could have been different, what I could have done—and nothing occurs to me. But it remains that I failed her. She believed I could do anyth—"

"I saw her face," Beth interrupted. "Isriam was right. She never knew. She was smiling, Pol. There was no pain, no fear—"

"What you mean is that she died trusting me. Believing I would save her."

"She died with you in her eyes."

He sat back in shock. "And that's supposed to make me feel—"

Beth spoke much as Isriam had done, to the empty air. "Sorin died in pain. You were there. You saw his face. You were the last to hear his voice—and he spoke of you and Andry, not me. It hurt me deeply, that he loved you and his brother so much that the trouble between you was more important than speaking of me. But gradually I understood. He loved me so much he didn't have to say anything." She looked up, dark eyes serene. "It's nonsense, the idea of a last moment together. Final words. If all the time and all the words that went before haven't proved love. . . ." She shrugged. "What I'm trying to say is that even if she *had* known, even if she'd seen and felt the knife—you may have seen Sorin's face, Pol, but I saw Meiglan's. Yes, she died trusting you, believing in you. She could *never* have believed otherwise."

Even if I'd held the knife that killed her. "That doesn't disguise that I—"

She rose, shoving her chair back so hard it toppled. "Failure, blame—is that all anyone thinks about? Isriam, you—Sioned and Alasen for not killing the High Warlord with Fire that night—what about Laroshin and Sethric and Kazander? Why not blame them? They failed to prevent Meiglan's capture and they failed to free her. And Lady Merisel—after all, she failed to keep the *diarmadh'im* too busy to invade Vellanti lands in the first place!"

"I know what you're trying to do and you can stop right now!" he snarled.

"*It happened,* Pol! There's nothing you can do about it. What you don't seem to understand is that there's nothing you or anyone *could* have done about it."

"If everyone's guilty, then no one is? The coward's excuse!"

"Oh, and the High Prince is so brave and strong and powerful he can take all of it onto himself! Who in all Hells do you think you are? A god?"

For a moment he was so angry he couldn't speak. What came out of his mouth next astonished him.

"This is all wrong, you know. Usually it's Sionell who does this for me—or *to* me, I can never decide which."

A wisp of a smile touched her lips. "Who do you think tutored me?"

He snorted, sprawling back in his chair. "All right, all right. Go on, Beth. Isriam should be ready for reason now. Your work is finished here."

"No, not finished. But I hope I've made a start."

When she was gone, he poured wine and drank it slowly, musing on all the things he'd ever done that merited so many women yelling at him so often.

But not *her*. Not Sionell. She had gone back to Tiglath yesterday. Hollis said she'd promised to return before the princes were assembled. Even with all the people milling around Skybowl, with more to come, he felt the lack of her.

And of Meiglan.

According to the standards of his people, by now he should either be adequately recovered from his wife's death or at least able to consign his sorrow to decent privacy and get on with life. He wondered why. Was it simple practicality, or simply fear? Was it that life was so great a joy, or that death was so profound a horror? Why was it judged enough to spend a single long night in mourning and then immediately resume normality?

He wasn't up to sorting out societal implications.

Perhaps he could not let go because he had not witnessed the Burning. He had not kept the night-long vigil or called Fire to her body or Air to carry her ashes on the morning wind. He had not watched his grief flare, slowly replaced by the softer, comforting glow of memories. That was how Tobin described it to him once, what she had experienced for her parents and two of her sons: an intensity of grief that somehow healed.

The ritual might have soothed his spirit. The mountains of work should have dragged his mind back to the living. He did the work easily enough, even derived honest pleasure from it. But nothing had healed.

Had Meiglan's loss been to him as Rohan's was to Sioned, he would understand the pain better. Half her heart had been torn away; he only bled from a raw wound. That was part of his guilt, of course.

Most of it, perhaps. He could tell himself he could have foreseen none of it—not Miyon's betrayal that led to Meiglan's abduction, not the barbaric ceremony they wanted her for, not the sorcerers' abandonment of her to join in destroying the Vellant'im. How could he have known?

He could tell himself many things. He could even tell himself he believed them.

She had believed in him with a child's unquestioning faith, and he had failed her. That she never knew—that she died with a smile on her lips and him in her eyes—was the Goddess' mercy. He had none for himself.

She had died with her faith intact and perfect. And *that* was supposed to comfort him.

He locked the chamber door, closed all the curtains, shut out the daylight, the sounds, the view of the place where she died alone.

She never felt it. She never knew. One moment alive, and the next. . . .

I can't remember the last words I ever said to her. Beth says it doesn't matter. But I wish I could remember.

Maybe it was "I love you." I hope it was. She knew that. She knew how much I loved her. . . .

She never knew about Sionell.

—a grace I don't deserve.

✳

"I'm quite all right, Chayla," Tobin said to her frowning granddaughter. "I don't need a physician. I need some peace and quiet, away from all this noise!"

Sioned grinned. Nary a murmur of complaint from Remagev to Feruche, but now that Skybowl teemed with highborns and their retinues, Tobin was crotchety.

Chayla, feet firmly planted on the bedchamber rug, stuck her fists on her hips and retorted, "A noise to which you contribute every evening. Granda, you can't regain your strength if you keep using it up. This isn't a *Rialla*. Pol doesn't need you to sound people out for him. He can do it himself."

"I've been serving my princes all my life, and I'll go on doing it until my last breath—or at least until the banquet, day after tomorrow." She waved Chayla away. "Let me be. Go find a fever to cure or a broken b–bone to set."

Sioned put in, "Walvis is holding cross-country races to give everyone something to do, and I'm sure half of them have fallen off their horses."

Chayla divided a disgusted look between them. "Has anyone ever told you that you're impossible?"

Tobin laughed. "And so are you, my darling! You come by it honestly!"

The girl's lips curved in a smile swiftly compressed, blue eyes sparkling. "All right, Granda. I'll come back later. Sioned, make sure she rests, please?"

When Chayla was gone, Sioned observed, "I don't think she sits down except for meals. I wish I had half her energy."

"Is that what you think it is?" Tobin got to her feet and moved to the window—obvious indication that she wished the freedom and privacy of sunlit conversation.

Sioned joined her. Down below, a score of riders crested the crater's rim, thundering toward the finish line Walvis had set up near the castle. Sioned saw the colors of four princedoms and five different holdings—plus the Isulk'im, on mounts descended from "borrowed" Radzyn studs. Spectators cheered and whistled as a young man trailing a battered turquoise pennant won the race: Daniv, earning the honors for Syr.

Chayla's like Pol, Tobin said on sunlight. *Working so hard she doesn't have time to think or feel. But I think she heals herself a little more with everyone she helps heal.*

The hurt of Kazander's death, and what happened with the Vellant'im—

Not so much that. She's a physician who wanted to kill. It'll take time . . . for all of them. The children, the adults . . . especially for Pol.

I don't know how to help him, Tobin. Or even if I ought to try.

You can't. Any more than you could help Andry.

A small silence followed. Tobin unthreaded the sunlight and looked up over her shoulder at Sioned.

"We all say everything except what really n–needs saying. Do you think I blame you? Or Pol?" Tobin shook her head. "I knew my son. And I know Pol. Each d–did as his nature bade him."

An inevitability, beloved, murmured another voice, one Sioned alone could hear. *That they fought so hard and so long against it was the act of noble and generous hearts. Hopeless, of course. We are what we are, and do what we must.*

But they used each other, Rohan. Each believed so strongly in himself that no one else mattered.

"Nothing they did was for themselves," Tobin went on. "For Goddess Keep, for the princedoms, for Sunrunners and sorcerers, for families and children—for total strangers."

Another race had started down below. Young squires and Isulki boys and girls clung to the necks of powerful horses. Jihan was readily identifiable by the banner of golden hair mingling with her horse's thick black mane.

"I feel so useless," Sioned heard herself say, unsure whether she spoke to Tobin or to that remembered voice. "Useless and tired."

Tobin shrugged. "A condition of advancing years. It's not something you get accustomed to, believe me."

Perhaps. Perhaps not.

CHAPTER THIRTY-EIGHT

Sioned stood back from the mirror, shaking her head in wry disbelief.

"What's wrong, Granda?" Jihan asked. "Don't you like it?"

"Oh, very much. It's just that I'd forgotten I could look like a princess!"

It was the tenth and last day of the New Year Holiday, and the banquet would soon begin. Sioned's gown was a gift from Pol, delivered that noon for minor adjustments. She knew he'd plotted something of the kind; none of the maids were seen for days except at meals, and Tibalia vanished completely. But as perfectly as the gown fit, as thoroughly as Sioned understood its purpose, she couldn't quite equate herself with the elegant, glittering woman in the mirror.

Silly woman. There's that look on your face again. You'd think after forty years you'd be used to this sort of thing. Remember that first Rialla *in 698?*

Joy of my heart, people who weren't even there remember *it.*

A gorgeous gown, the work of clever and loving hands. Silk woven forest-green in one direction and dark gold in the other glinted with her every breath. Dozens of tiny topazes decorated the cuffs of long sleeves that hid the rope burns. A high collar, stiffly embroidered, provided the same concealment at her neck. The skirt flowed down to gold velvet slippers and green silk stockings. Her hair had been polished with silk—a ridiculous practice Tibalia insisted on—and arranged in curls from which the emeralds and topazes of her new coronet shimmered. The same stones were repeated in her earrings: green dangled from tawny gold on the left, gold from green on the right.

The whole extravagant display was just a blink shy of outrageous. She knew she was a symbol tonight, not a person; still. . . . *I ought to strangle him.*

Oh, hush. You look magnificent. I couldn't have chosen better myself.

Pol had also given his daughters new clothes. Their dresses mimicked Sioned's in design, but the jewels were missing and the silk shifted from violet to blue. Their circlets were of silver set with a small amethyst, topaz, and piece of white jade each. Like Sioned, each wore a ring given by Rohan.

"But you *always* look like a princess, Granda," Rislyn murmured.

"You're beautiful," Jihan seconded.

Sioned placed a kiss on each crowned golden head. "So are you, darlings. Come, let's go collect Tobin and Chay."

"While there's still sunlight enough for me to see them," Rislyn added.

"When can we learn how to use the moons?" Jihan asked.

"Oh, one of these days," Sioned replied.

"Granda, don't you mean *nights?*" Rislyn laughed up at her, and Sioned growled affectionately.

The Lord of Radzyn and his Lady were a matched set, as usual at great occasions: all red and white, with diamonds and rubies scattered in her hair and down the embroidery of his tunic. They sparkled in the last of the sunlight. Chay gave the twins a low bow—then pretended he couldn't straighten up. While they helped, laughing, Tobin eyed Sioned.

"Pol certainly has been busy spending money, hasn't he?"

"And he does it so well, too." She glanced around. "Where's Hollis?"

"Helping Chayla help Aldiara. I promise you, Sioned, that child has n—never worn anything but riding leathers and wool shirts her entire life. You should've seen her face when the maids came in with her dress."

The two of them proceeded along the hallway to Hollis' chambers, where Aldiara was in pale yellow silk, a white lace shawl, and tears.

"Her hair," Hollis whispered to Sioned.

"Ah." She crossed the room to the dressing table, where Chayla was attempting to twine white ribbons through the girl's lank black hair. "It seems you and I have the same difficulty," she said with a rueful smile, touching a finger to her own hair. "But I'll bet yours wouldn't hold a curl if you used a shape-changing spell on it."

"I'd considered it, your grace," Aldiara sniffled. "It's so stupid—I mean, who cares what my hair looks like?"

You do, little one, Sioned thought with a smile. She glanced at Chayla—lovely in pale coral embroidered in ivory and blue. Trailing down her back were matching ribbons that tied off golden braids coiled around her head. Hollis was effortlessly beautiful in a flame-colored gown that showed off tawny hair, perfect shoulders, and half Whitecliff's worth in diamonds.

I suppose we forget sometimes what we look like, what it does to strangers to see us all in silks and jewels like this.

Light of my life, that was always the point.

"Chayla, hand me that clip, please—no, the silver one. And a brush." The former she held between her teeth; the latter she dipped in the pitcher of clean water on the dressing table. She pulled Aldiara's thick, fine, utterly limp hair back from her face, hoping it was long enough to secure at her nape.

"It'll stay put with a little of this," Chayla said, holding out a jar of clear pinkish stuff. Sioned recognized the faint sweet-spicy fragrance and arched a brow. "There's more to *pemric* cactus than seeds for taze," Chayla explained. "Lady Elizian says Isulki women distill this from the juice. And Feylin says there's a whole new fortune to be made!"

"She and Walvis are going to need one, what with cleaning up Remagev and rebuilding Tuath for Jeren." Sioned applied it sparingly. The sleek result pleased her. "They ought to give you a share of the profits, Aldiara. You'll be its first and best example. Just let me clip this and brush the ends—there!"

The severe style suited her. Her face was all strong bones and tilting black eyes and wide mouth—forceful features that couldn't be disguised by an absurd froth of curls, and shouldn't be.

Hollis approached, smiling. "Perfect! If you'll permit me, I have one more thing to add." She held out a delicate silver chain, from which hung a cluster of three tiny pale gems: pearl, moonstone, diamond.

Aldiara gasped. "My lady!"

"I thought I asked you to call me by my name." She fastened the clasp at the girl's nape, then gently drew her up by the shoulders, turning her around. "Pol told me you look like this on sunlight. I hope you like it, my dear."

"Y–you shouldn't—it's much too—"

"Expensive?" Hollis murmured. "Compared to what? My son's life? Let me and my husband gift you with this, Aldiara. Please."

"Aren't you women ready *yet?*" Chay roared from the antechamber. "If we're not there in two shakes of a dragon's claw, we'll miss Pol's entrance and he'll throw us all in the lake! *I* can swim, but you Sunrunners—!" In the doorway he stopped, stared at Aldiara, and gave a low whistle. "Oh, to be sixty again!"

The girl blushed helplessly. Tobin limped over to him, stood on tiptoe, and whispered in his ear. He gave a shout of laughter that made Aldiara start like a nervous cat.

Hollis made shooing motions and everyone started for the stairs. Sioned slipped to Tobin's side. "What did you tell him?"

"Only that it'll take her a while to get used to his sense of humor—just like it did Hollis."

Sioned began to reply, then stared. "You can't mean—no! At fifteen?"

"She'll have to get over her fear of horses, though. . . ." Tobin mused.

"You can't be serious!" Sioned laughed.

"You just watch t–tonight."

"There'll be plenty to see all around, if I know Pol."

"I'm betting he walks in stark naked. There can't be two coins left to rub together for his own clothes, after what he spent treating us to new finery."

Indeed, no one in Pol's immediate orbit had been neglected. Betheyn was charming in green velvet so delicate it floated; Pol had slyly ordered Isriam a tunic of the same fabric. They, too, wore high collars and long sleeves. Kierun and Dannar wore the violet of Princemarch, which suited black-haired, gray-eyed Kierun admirably but was rather a shock against Dannar's flaming red hair.

Sethric—tall, handsome, and looking miserable—wore a red shirt beneath a vivid blue tunic. The colors of Catha Heights, Sioned noted with surprise and approval, wondering what similar trifles Pol hadn't seen fit to mention during their conference yesterday. He hadn't gone so far as to gift Jeni with the same colors, but the flowers winding all over her silver-gray gown held enough of each shade to complement Sethric's clothes—if they ever got within speaking distance of each other.

Dancing is good for that sort of thing, Sioned mused. *I'll have him partner me, then "grow tired" somewhere near Jeni, and. . . .*

Meddling again.

Well, they're being so silly. They're obviously in love—

As obvious as you and I?

The great hall was awhirl in color from floor to ceiling. The plain blue tiles had been scrubbed until not even a speck of soot remained from the Vellanti bonfire. Princely banners were hung from the rafters, those of the *athr'im* on the walls between windows open to the soft evening breeze. At the main door were the flags of Riyan and Ruala's three holdings: blue and green for Elktrap, blue and black for Feruche, blue and brown for Skybowl. In back of the high table was the dragon tapestry from Stronghold. Between tiles below and banners above, between Riyan's colors at the door and Rohan's at the high table, a living bejeweled rainbow laughed, sipped wine, and tried to keep track of the children.

Nine long tables were set with sparkling crystal from Firon and blindingly bright silver from Swalekeep. Every five places, silk napkins from Dorval sprouted from vases of Kierstian ceramic—flowers being in short supply so early in the year. With the napkins in use there would still be color, for from each vase also bloomed glass roses in shades no spring garden had ever seen.

Jihan scampered off to pluck four from different vases. She kept the blue and gave her sister the violet. The gold on its long green stem went to Sioned. Holding up an orange one, she asked, "Where's Sionell? Do you see her, Granda?"

Sionell's return from Tiglath two days ago had gone almost unnoticed in the tumult of Arlis' arrival. Sioned craned her neck, but she was hampered by not knowing what Sionell wore; in this crush of color, one dark-red head was impossible to find. "Not yet. Maybe we'd better take our places. You can give it to her later."

"It's orange, for her being our Regent in Cunaxa," Jihan explained to her sister as she took Rislyn's hand—by now an automatic gesture. Jihan's care of her twin brought a tightness to Sioned's throat. Pol had decided, rightly so, that soon a servant must be found to attend them—a Sunrunner or sorcerer who could help Rislyn when she needed it. As the girls grew older, duties and lessons as Pol's heir would take Jihan more and more away from her sister.

Sioned saw the children settled, then went to find Alasen. She had an intuition about what her kinswoman might be wearing. She was right.

Alasen was resplendent in a slim, low-cut gown of light green silk slashed in front to reveal a pale yellow underskirt. Lace edged in thin blue and violet ribbons cascaded from wrists to knuckles; looped around her neck from ears to collarbones were six strands of fat white pearls. Sioned awarded her first prize for imaginative concealment—not to mention for working into her gown the colors of no less than four princedoms.

"Did Pol give you that, or just tell you what to wear?" she asked, amused.

Her green eyes guileless as a child's, Alasen said, "He gave me a hint, but this is all mine. Though I had help from Chiana's rather extensive wardrobe."

"Ah. The caravan from Swalekeep," Sioned murmured, the mystery solved.

"I had to have the original dress picked apart, of course," Alasen went on blithely. "She had truly horrid taste in design, but the fabric is quite nice, don't you think?"

"And the color is so . . . appropriate," Sioned murmured.

"Mmm. Yes, wasn't that fortunate?"

Determined to undo such gleeful composure, she asked, "Has Ostvel seen it?"

The reply was a purr. "Not yet. Do you think he'll notice?"

Sioned gave up and laughed. Ostvel always complimented his wife with his eyes while grumbling about the fortune she cost him. But would his deafness of the last nine days over anything to do with Meadowlord extend to color-blindness as well?

Arlis strolled over, his princess at his side, her hand tucked into the crook of his elbow. A brief stop at Zaldivar had allowed poor Rohannon to put food in his stomach that would stay there—while Arlis raided wardrobes for appropriate finery. He had learned more from Rohan than politics and governance. His trousers, shirt, tunic, and a long sleeve-less surcoat layered Kierstian yellow with Iseli scarlet. The diamond dangling from one ear was the size of his infant son's fist. They knew this because Arlis said so.

"Brenoc is going to be even bigger than Roric—and even at five winters old, Roric is wrestling boys of ten! And winning!"

His wife sighed the sigh of all women enduring a husband's paternal raptures. Demalia was small, dark, plump, and neat as a clean kitchen. Knowing she would look ridiculous swathed in styles that suited taller, slimmer women, she had wisely chosen not to emulate the other highborn ladies. The resulting simplicity of plain blue-gray silk and a single diamond on a silver chain was a relief. Sioned told her as much.

Arlis laughed as Demalia blushed all over her round, pretty face. "Yes, we're all as gaudy as those silly sheep of Feylin's, dyed different shades to see if dragons could tell colors." He gazed complacently at his lady. "Thank the Goddess I had the sense to marry my Mouse!"

"You had the *sense*," Alasen pointed out, "to listen to your wise and discerning aunt."

He blinked his bewilderment. "But—you told me Demalia would never make me happy in a thousand years!"

"Exactly. You were always a dreadful child—never paid attention to a word of advice except to do the exact opposite." She smiled serenely. "You may now express your gratitude."

"*He* certainly should," Sioned observed. "But will she?"

Demalia did a good imitation of outrage. "So *you're* the one to blame!"

"I confess it," said Alasen.

Struggling gamely against giggles, Demalia exclaimed, "I—I am speechless with fury!"

Arlis rolled his eyes. "Let it last, merciful Goddess, let it last!"

Rohannon joined them, saying that Riyan's steward was frantic to get people seated. He wore the formal livery of a squire to the Prince of Kierst-Isel—more yellow and scarlet—but Arlis had thoughtfully added Whitecliff's orange and red in the plackets of his shirt.

"You look very handsome tonight, Rohannon," Sioned commented, tempted to ruffle his hair. She restrained herself. He was nearly sixteen; not a little boy. Excited by his first grown-up celebration as anyone his age should be, his smile was bright and his cheeks glowed with healthy color. It was difficult to remember the horror he'd been through. But something haunted lingered deep in his eyes, just as it did in his sister's.

Maarken and Hollis had hardly taken their eyes off him from the moment of his arrival two days ago. Chayla had simply burst into tears at the sight of him, and the twins had been as inseparable as their duties would allow ever since. Sioned wondered what it might be like, having a second self.

You weren't, you know. We were never each other's mirror, Rohan, nor even the other's missing half. What exactly were we?

Sides of the same coin? No, too trite. Seal and matrix, perhaps. . . .

Eventually everyone was seated. The high table boasted more forks, spoons, and knives than Sioned had ever seen in her life. Taking her place between Naydra and Rislyn, she whispered, "What are we supposed to *do* with all these?"

Naydra chuckled and let the black lace shawl drop from her violet-clad shoulders. "I think you start at the outside and work in. Neither of the grand masters in the kitchen wants his creations sullied by contact with a fork that touched his rival's inferior slop."

Glancing left, she saw Rislyn's fingers dance lightly over the silver, pausing at the top of the setting. Sioned smiled. "Oh, bless Ludhil's heart! He sent for lobsters from Dorval! That's to crack the shell with, love. Will you need some help?"

"I . . . I don't know. Maybe."

Naydra beckoned to Kierun and murmured something. The boy looked at Rislyn, comprehension in his gray eyes—but no pity, Sioned noted. She relaxed, sure now that what was served to the girl would be easy for her to eat.

Jihan was on Rislyn's other side. The central chair was vacant, awaiting Pol's entrance. Ruala, Riyan, Maara, Tobin, and Chay completed the high table. Captains, prominent soldiery, and senior physicians were seated near the doors. The other guests, troops, and castle folk would be served outside in the courtyard, ablaze with torches and awash in laughter, flirtation, and wine.

Sioned rather wistfully envied them the informality.

Ruala sank into her chair with a sigh of relief—not at a task successfully completed, but because the whole mess was now out of her hands. She and Riyan were wearing the same shade of blue. He had added a tunic with wide brown and black stripes for Skybowl and Feruche. Her gown proclaimed their holding of Elktrap with two thin green sashes that crossed her chest, gathered at each hip, and draped to her knees. Maara's dress mimicked her mother's, without the collar of opals Ruala wore to hide the marks at her neck.

Sioned decided that by the end of the feast her eyes and Sunrunner senses both would ache with the array of colors and jewels. Whatever Pol wore, how could he compete with such splendor? As delicious aromas announced the opening of kitchen doors and the readiness of the masters to begin the contest, satisfying her hunger became more important than satisfying her curiosity.

If you'll recall, I used to keep everyone waiting, too. A privilege of being High Prince. And part of the game. Remember what I did to Roelstra?

I remember the look on his face when you didn't kneel! Admit, oh light of my eyes, that your action then was a bit in advance of the actual fact.

One ought to begin as one means to go on.

You'd already decided to become High Prince? Even then?

Why not? Better me than him. And with you beside me—

A hand rested lightly on her shoulder and lips brushed her cheek. She gave a violent flinch.

"Sorry, Mother," said Pol. "I didn't mean to startle you."

She caught her breath, trying to still the racing of her heart, and turned to look up at him. He was smiling, all burnished gold hair and dazzling white clothes and shining blue-green eyes.

"You look magnificent," he said, then turned to his daughters. "And *you*—! Last I knew, I was father to a couple of sand rats! But I must say you do wash up very prettily!"

As he took his seat, Chay observed, "That's a new one—making an entrance by not making an entrance."

"I try," Pol replied breezily.

The feast began with a mild culinary skirmish. Riyan's cook opened with cactus soup made from an Isulki recipe. Pol's cook countered with small fish broiled in wine, presented on waves of puff pastry as if they leaped through the ocean. Then came the lobsters, steamed to succulence in silk wrappings, one claw clutching a tiny pearl to be kept as a remembrance of the occasion. These dishes were accompanied by Syrene goldwine in crystal goblets.

As musicians appeared before the next courses, Naydra swirled the last of the wine in her glass. "They even fought about *this*," she told Sioned. "Pol's cook has the roasts and wanted the red wine in crystal. Riyan's cook won—the glasses belong to Ruala!"

The real battle began. Chunks of elk and lamb glazed in mossberry and onion sauce were accompanied by dark Gribain red wine in goblets that were part of Chiana's silver service. Riyan's cook, disdaining the obvious accompaniments, concocted a salad of an astonishing variety of greenery, dressed with vinegar-and-something that set Sioned's tongue deliciously atingle.

"Prince Arlis brought the vegetables," Naydra answered in response to Sioned's question. "I think he raided every garden at Zaldivar."

Plates scraped clean by appreciative diners were taken away. A lone singer stepped forward, silencing the chatter in the hall. A few sad notes from a lute drifted up from near the doors. The young man clasped his hands at his breast in poignant mourning. Sioned held her breath, hoping some ambitious bard had not chosen the occasion to unveil his war epic. The tune was almost a dirge.

> *When there's treachery loose up in Firon,*
> *And fighting around Brochwell Bay,*
> *When the enemy threatens the princedoms,*
> *Who'll shield us all from the fray?*

The singer paused. Lute strings rippled. Suddenly wild chords blared from a dozen instruments, making everybody jump in their seats.

> *Rohannon, Rohannon, the Sunrunner lad!*
> *Just let him get wind of a fight!*
> *He'll weave up the sun in the blink of an eye*
> *And stitch up the stars in the night!*

A rollicking instrumental break followed, during which Rohannon was pushed forward to take his bow, his cheeks as scarlet as his tunic. Sioned gave a resigned sigh. "Ostvel. It has to be Ostvel."

"Do you like it?" Naydra inquired.

"It's absolutely dreadful. But it works!"

> *When rain makes a lake of the Faolain,*
> *And all of the sunshine is hidden,*
> *Who will slog through the mud to the castle*
> *And snatch a black pearl from the middens?*

Arlis joined in the chorus, roaring out his brother's name in an off-key voice that moved everyone else to sing along, too, if only to drown him out. Saumer was practically passed hand-to-hand to take his place beside Rohannon. He swept a laughing bow to the audience, rolling his eyes.

Then it was Jeni's turn, and Sioned nearly choked on laughter when Ostvel indulged in a bit of fatherly chiding.

> *When a dragon is forlorn and lonely,*
> *And his broken heart sighs in his ribs*
> *Who can there be found to console him,*
> *Whom he'd follow from Skybowl to Grib?*

"Papa!" Jeni exclaimed, crimson to her earlobes. Ostvel gave her a *Who, me?* look that radiated injured innocence as everyone sang, "Jeni, Jeni, the Sunrunner lass!" at the top of their lungs. Everyone but Sethric.

Chayla was next, and a more startled subject for a song never existed. The verse extolled her delicate, tender, sympathetic healing touch; those who had endured her forthright ministrations groaned good-naturedly.

Finally, to her stark incredulity, came a verse for Aldiara. Draza of Grand Veresch—who, as it happened, was her kin through a great-uncle—urged her from her seat near Maarken and Hollis. She nearly tripped on her hem as she went to stand with the others while the singers concluded:

> *Where is there a lady courageous*
> *Who can turn diarmadh'im into stone?*

The chorus changed from "Sunrunner" to "sorcerer," but everyone followed it because everyone knew what she was. The singer took his bows to thunderous applause. The five young people, wreathed in blushes, returned to their seats, and dessert was brought out.

Until now, the war had been pretty much a draw. But both cooks knew Pol's weakness. The final weapons were pine-nut pie oozing honey, and a more subtle fruit pastry, countered by small mountains of taze ice festooned with candied flowers. Pol attacked the desserts two-fisted and asked for seconds. Another stalemate.

At last came fruit from Syr and cheese from Gilad. Pol called the cooks out to receive their due tribute. Kierun handed him two identical crystal goblets footed in gold, which Pol himself filled with mossberry wine. Thus did the warring parties end up sharing the honors and a drink. That drink became dozens, and around dawn they staggered arm-in-arm out of the kitchen to greet the sunrise, roaring drunk and the best of friends.

The same wine was distributed at all tables, along with steaming cups of taze. Replete with food and a good, long laugh, at any other occasion everyone would settle back for a time before the dancing began. But there was business to be conducted first.

Sioned sipped taze and prepared to enjoy the show. Great banquets were supposed to feel slightly unreal. Sometimes this came from heightened tension—and the strain of best manners and tight clothing. But the good ones, like this one, always felt a bit like being a child again. Playing dress-up in Mother's best gowns; acting the grand lady with laughter just below the surface for the silliness of it; dancing until breathless; cheerfully disregarding anything beyond the enchantment of crystal and candlelight. . . .

At first, anyway. In Sioned's experience, something rather nasty usually happened to spoil the mood.

But not tonight. Everyone seemed determined to make this night the reality and the war nothing but the memory of a bad dream. And if their laughter was a trifle giddy, it was only because they were so very glad to be awake.

Pol rose, and the hall quieted again. Servants brought out a narrow table, placing it just about where the Vellanti bonfire had been. Kierun and Dannar set a stack of parchment on top, plus pen and inkpot.

Those at the high table left their seats for chairs grouped near Maarken's table. Sioned had insisted on this change of location; she didn't want to miss anything, and had no intention of staring at princely backs.

She had also suggested that each princedom be dealt with in the order of its prince's years of rule—to get the awkward ones out of the way first. Cabar of Gilad and Velden of Grib had inherited when their fathers died of Plague in 701. They had been sent announcements of the gathering, of course— worded so each understood that the invitation to come was really an order to stay home.

So Pol began with, "For Grib, his grace Prince Elsen."

Elsen limped only a little as he walked to the high table to sign his charter. Sioned smiled, thinking how pleased Rohan would be to find his shy, crippled little friend of the long letters turned into this proud young prince—who, moreover, was hailed for his courage. If any good had come out of the mess at Goddess Keep, it was the confidence of Elsen's strides. His sister Norian looked ready to burst with pride, and their cousin Sethric forgot his own troubles and grinned from one side of his face to the other.

Pol didn't mention Velden's name once. Instead, he confirmed Elsen as the next Prince of Grib, and Vellanur as Heir—a distinction lost on no one. He did the same for Amiel of Gilad, adding, "As for *your* heir, cousin, I hear that your delightful princess is even now obliging you!"

Amiel blushed the dusky Giladan pink of his tunic, hiding it by bending to scribble his name. The charters were simply affirmations of each prince's rule. The High Prince's Writ did not strictly extend this far, but Pol had gone Rohan one better.

"If I do this," he'd said yesterday, "and they accept it, then by tacit agreement it *is* law. Implication being that their authority is an extension of the High Prince's, given by him—"

"Or taken away?" Sioned inquired.

He nodded. "Or taken away. This bunch will never stand for that. But eventually, in a generation or two. . . ."

"Very farsighted of you."

"And very unexpected?" He smiled and held up a closely written sheet of parchment in each hand. "This is what I asked for, and this is what they gave me. Don't worry—the first wasn't outrageous, and the second didn't cripple me with compromises. Until the next *Rialla* I have to make sure everything works as well as I can manage, so that I go into it from a position of strength. The *Medr'im* are an unspoken part of the bargain for now, but I'm hoping that will be a very short 'eventually.' The idea is too damned good to waste."

Fessenden was next, Pirro having ruled for nearly twenty-two years. He had not waited to be discouraged from attending; his court Sunrunner termed him the victim of an unspecified indisposition. *Dynastic indigestion,* Sioned mused, and a familiar chuckle teased her mind.

Isriam spoke for his grandfather—looking as if he wanted to sink through the blue tiled floor. Pirro had not yet sent an affirmative answer to Pol's proposed "solution to your inheritance problem," and Isriam keenly felt the lack. Pol had coaxed, cajoled, and at last commanded him to represent Fessenden.

Over Sabriam's wails of outrage, Pirro had already parted with Einar as a fine for inaction and for denying Laric passage through Fessenden. Pol added the port city to Princemarch not only as punishment but because Isriam would feel awkward being the overlord of the man he'd always thought was his father.

Of course, your noble-minded son hasn't the slightest intererst in Einar's highly profitable trade.

My, we are caustic tonight! A prince with dragon gold behind him doesn't need more money. The boy is the real issue and everyone knows it.

Well, if Pirro doesn't see Isriam Pol's way soon, he might find himself deprived not just of a city but a job.

Lisiel represented Firon. Greatly disappointed that her husband and elder son were not here, she perfectly understood why. Aldiara's kin would sort out the *diarmadh'im*, but Laric was on his own when it came to his contrite nobility—who swore they'd been ensorcelled. He'd decided to keep them guessing about whether or not he believed it.

It's a long time since Laric ended up with Firon, Sioned mused. *And Maarken ended up with Hollis, Ostvel with Alasen, poor stupid Halian with Chiana—*

And Andry with Goddess Keep.

Yes. But whose will it be now? Torien died, and Jolan with him, and Antoun says the rest are devastated at losing Andry.

Rather naughty of Pol, wearing white.

Startled, she studied her son's clothes for a moment—a

vide-sleeved silk shirt caught tight at the wrists with thick embroidery that matched the wreath pattern on his velvet tunic. White from neck to heels. . . .

She knew he hadn't intended it to be seen that way. He must mean it to honor Andry. And Meiglan.

She's the only one who could have done it, you know. And she did what none of you others could have done. You're all too tough. You'd break, not bend.

I suppose so . . . and the Sunrunners among us could've become deliberately shadow-lost, depriving them of their sacrifice. Meiglan was condemned to live out the whole senseless horror of it.

Does Pol still feel that way? Condemned to live?

It'll take time. Sionell—

Keep out of it, Sioned.

Oh, everyone's doing just fine without me.

Sionell had returned from Tiglath rested and serene. Chayla had found understanding with her brother, and forgiveness with Kazander's wives. Her crushing guilt over his death and her own ravening need to kill was easing—for who in her circumstances would not want her enemies slaughtered?

As for Sethic and Jeni . . . well, Sioned would take care of that tonight, and be damned to any scolds for meddling. She could do nothing for Tobren. Too much resentment stood between them, along with Tobren's unspoken accusation that Sioned could have helped Andry if only she'd tried harder. Jihan and Rislyn had each other, and Rislyn's dragon. Perhaps Tobren's would help her, too.

Pol didn't need her, either. He was arranging the princedoms according to his own lights. He'd even taken care of the Merida. They would not pose a threat for at least a generation—if at all. Perhaps the same would be true of the Vellant'im. Sioned didn't bother her mind about it. Whatever happened, she'd be long dead and wouldn't know a thing.

Chadric came forward, proudly flanked by the next two generations of Dorvali princes. A few days ago Sioned had spent a quiet afternoon with him, listening to tales of Stronghold long ago. As Zehava's squire during the first six years of Rohan's life, Chadric had been tormented by a child at once scholarly and rambunctious. Tobin's stories were always tinged with older-sister irritation—their childhood relationship had been rather like Pol's with Sionell—but

Chadric had known Rohan from a different perspective. He understood, as few did, that Sioned *wanted* to talk about him now. Tilal and Ostvel could still barely look at her without grieving for the empty place at her side.

The rulers of Ossetia approached the high table together, for Tilal had become its prince by marrying Gemma. His voice was steady as he named as Heir his younger son, Sorin, but everyone remembered the elder son all the same. Saumer, who had been Rihani's friend, bent his head.

"For Kierst-Isel," Pol called out, "his grace Prince Arlis."

Sioned was glad of the chance to smile again. She was as proud of Arlis as if he'd been born hers. In the person of Volog's grandson were finally united the island's two princedoms, just as Rohan had planned. In some ways, Arlis was their finest work. *At least* something *came out right....*

More than one "something," but I agree. This *turned out just as we planned.*

Arlis gave Pol a bow both casual and respectful. "My lord, I am commanded by your cousin his grace the Prince Roric of Kierst-Isel—and belive me, that's exactly how he told me to word it—to confess publicly that I am a rotten father and an even worse prince for not allowing him to come with me and present him to you as my heir."

"He's absolutely right," Pol said, grinning. "And I'll tell him so myself, if he'll consent to come to Dragon's Rest in a few years."

Arlis grimaced. "Damn it, Pol, do you have to guess everything in advance?"

"Go on with your speech. I'm sure I'm going to enjoy it."

"I just bet you will! I am further commanded by your cousin his grace and so on to plead his cause in becoming your squire as soon as you think he's ready for the honor." He paused. "Speaking for myself, and from experience of my son, you'd be crazy to take him. Waking or sleeping, he's a terror."

"Oh, I don't know," Pol replied. "My father seems to have civilized *you.*"

Daniv, splendid in turquoise and black, was called forward then. Sioned saw his gentle mother Danladi in his face—but she saw his father Kostas, too. And there were hints of his grandfather as well—her brother Davvi, not Roelstra. She wondered if Pol would ever tell him the real connection of their kinship.

He had promised to tell his daughters the truth—someday. The conspiracy to explain Jihan and Rislyn was to Sioned both expedient and humiliating. Meiglan, *diarmadhi.* Unaware of it, of course, which accounted for her helplessness in the clutches of the Vellant'im. Whether or not Miyon had known was the subject of intense speculation; everyone knew he'd thrown the girl in Pol's path hoping for a marriage, but his complicity in a presumed *diarmadhi* plot was hotly debated. The sorcerers' allegiance to Pol was because of his marriage to Meiglan, and would be transferred to Jihan when she came of age. They had all sworn that Meiglan had been one of them—and were concocting imaginary bloodlines to prove it.

So I am spared, Meiglan is seen in a new light—never mind what color—and the lie is perpetuated.

It was the only thing he could do. Even after all these years, do you think they're ready for the truth?

She ignored the murmuring voice.

Daniv, of course, had no heir. He produced the first astonishment of the proceedings when he asked Tilal's permission to make Sorin *his* heir as well.

"It's only until I have a wife and children and all that," he said with a shrug that indicated a total lack of personal interest in such things. "But Cousin Pol—the High Prince, I mean—says it's best to get these things settled, so I was wondering if I could dump it on Sorin."

"Uh—yes, of course," his uncle Tilal said blankly.

With an unsubtle wink, Gemma added, "Just so long as you *un*dump it as soon as possible!"

Accurately foreseeing the shape of the next years from family gatherings to *Riall'im,* Daniv protested, "I'm only sixteen! I don't *want* to get married yet!"

Pol circled a fist high in the air like a merchant attracting customers to his booth at the *Rialla* Fair. "Wagering on year and Chosen begins tomorrow noon! Who'll hold the stakes?"

"Cousin Pol—!" Daniv wailed.

Sioned leaned forward. "Pol! Behave yourself!"

Unrepentant, he laughed. "Well, I suppose we can work that out later. For now, Sorin of Ossetia is Heir to Daniv of Syr—on a purely temporary basis, of course."

"Not *that* temporary," Daniv shot back.

Pol had kept his own princedoms for last. Well, *next* to last. The Desert and Princemarch were his directly, with

Jihan his heir. She was somber as she joined the other princes and heirs. Rislyn, holding Sioned's hand now, said wistfully, "I wish I could see her."

"I know, love."

It had been one thing when Rohan held the Desert and Pol ruled Princemarch. But the two combined were a substantial swath of the continent. Pol was entirely capable of governing both, and everyone had always known this day would come. The addition of Cunaxa, however, put him in possession of even more land. *"I don't mind the work, but all those square measures make everybody very nervous. So I'm going to do what Father did, and give people a few years to get used to the idea."*

Cunaxa would be administered by Sionell as Regent. She rose from where she sat with her parents and two oldest children, bronze silk skirts whispering beneath panels of black lace, candlelight glowing from the jewels at her throat. They had been removed from the Merida armor and made into a necklet. The armor itself she had ordered melted down for use however the crafters saw fit. No one would ever wear it again.

She accepted her parchment charter with Pol's new seal appended, and took her place beside Daniv without saying a word.

Pol calmly treated her silence as natural. The next moment his eyes began to dance. Sioned sat forward in anticipation. Now came the fun part.

"For Meadowlord—"

Alasen stood.

Ostvel's jaw dropped in horrified comprehension. Then he snapped, "No! Absolutely not!"

"For Meadowlord. . . ." Pol said again.

Alasen hauled her husband up by an elbow.

"I won't do it!"

"Oh, yes, you will."

"I don't *want* to run a princedom!"

Riyan cleared his throat and in a reasonably controlled voice reminded his father, "You've done it before."

"And I didn't want to then, either!"

Pol, barely repressing laughter—few others were as self-possessed—called out, "You'll take it and there's an end to it!"

"But I *like* Castle Crag!" Ostvel cried plaintively. "I don't *want* Swalekeep, let alone all Meadowlord!"

"You'll get over it," Alasen said firmly.

Dannar took a few hesitant steps forward. "Mama? What's Papa so mad about?"

Sioned quivered with laughter as Ostvel latched onto his son's presence the way he'd grabbed the guide-rope on the Faolain forty years ago. "Dannar—Pol wants to give us Meadowlord. Do you want that? To be a ruling prince someday?"

The boy scrubbed his red hair with one hand as if polishing the thoughts inside his brain. Then he shrugged. "Sure. Why not?"

Ostvel groaned. Alasen turned in triumph to Pol. "There you have it. We accept—on one condition."

He managed a suspicious scowl, direly demanding, "And that might be—?"

"Before I set foot in Swalekeep again, that damned bathroom of Chiana's has *got* to go!"

Arlis raised his voice above the shouts of laughter. "That's it, Aunt Alasen! Make him pay for the privilege of having you run the place!"

Ostvel signed, of course. He glowered at Pol, flung a look of furious accusation at Sioned, and didn't speak to his wife until well past midnight.

He did, however, break into a wide and startled smile when Pol gave Jeni Castle Crag.

The timing's not the best. Sethric looks positively ill.

To quote Alasen—he'll get over it.

Pol then made public what he'd already told Johlarian on sunlight: that Lowland and Riverport would be combined and known as Faolain Hold, with Mirsath as its lord.

"But—what about Lady Karanaya?" Rislyn asked, and Sioned answered, "Wait."

There were no changes at Radzyn, Whitecliff, or Skybowl; each *athri* merely stood to acknowledge possession. For all three men, however, there were loud cheers. Walvis received a double tribute, for he rose when Tuath Castle was called and again for Remagev, naming his grandson Jeren as ruler of one and heir to the other. His other grandson, Jahnev, spoke for Tiglath. Sionell looked torn between tears of sorrow and tears of pride.

On to Princemarch—where Karanaya was announced as

Lady of Rezeld Manor in her own right. When Johlarian had told her that afternoon, she nearly fainted. She never said a single word about the pearls again.

Pol also provided for Idalian. When Laric could part with him, he would come home to the Faolain—but only for a little while. Idalian was to be the new Lord of Waes.

Sabriam was smoothly and briefly confirmed in Einar—Pol's city now Sabriam's nephew Anheld was the new heir. Then Pol turned to Arlis, who had an announcement of his own.

"Your grace, if you'll forgive me," Sionell said, stepping forward unexpectedly. "As Regent of Cunaxa, I have decided to grant the manor of Catchwater to Lord Visian and the Isulk'im."

Sioned's brows shot up. Catchwater had been Birioc's home, right in the middle of lands Miyon had given the Merida, very near the Desert border. That was odd enough—but since when had the Isulk'im ever wanted stone walls?

"Agreed," Pol said, after recovering from this surprise.

"Further," she went on, "I ask your grace's permission to similarly grant Castle Pine to my younger son, Meig."

"Also agreed—with pleasure."

Chay moved to Sioned's side. "What's she up to?"

"Besides using her new position to give her second son land of his own?" She smiled. "Consider how Rohan sneaked Pol into Princemarch's affections."

He scratched absently at his embroidered collar, nodding. "Give them someone to watch grow up. Smart girl, our Sionell."

"Very. But do you understand why she gave Catchwater—" As he shook his head, she finished, "Damn. Neither do I."

It was the responsibility of each prince to affirm *athr'im* in their holdings. Most were as expected. Pol stood back, smiling, his eyes occasionally aglint with amusement at surprises only he had been privy to.

Arlis declared that Port Adni and Adni River were now a single very large holding to be known by the area's ancient name of Reiza—"prince's gold," for the nuggets that sometimes washed downstream. Then he gave it to his brother Prince Saumer.

Prince Saumer almost fell out of his chair.

Naydra, whose childlessness meant Port Adni would revert to Kierst-Isel at her death, smiled as Sioned stole a glance at her. "I gave it back yesterday. I have no interest in it, with my husband Narat dead. And Ostvel has very kindly asked me to administer Castle Crag until Jeni comes of age. So I will again live in the place I was born—much more happily this time."

"I'm glad," Sioned told her, and clasped her hand.

Lisiel named her new son Larien as heir to Snowcoves. Amiel declared Gilad Seahold a crown property to be rebuilt and presented to the physicians as the new home of their school. Daniv, trying to maintain proper dignity and failing utterly, announced with a broad grin that Catha Heights was too vital a holding to be left in the hands of a steward, so would Lord Sethric of Grib do him the immense favor of becoming its *athri?*

Lord Sethic emulated Prince Saumer.

"So much for the landless dependent living off his wife's riches," Tobin said with satisfaction.

"It does make things a bit easier," Sioned observed. "Chay, when you see me partner Sethric, ask Jeni to dance. Leave the rest to me."

He snorted. "You're incorrigible."

"So I've been told."

There was one last castle to be dealt with. Everyone looked to Pol, expecting him to take it for himself and put one of his own people in charge.

Instead, he nodded to someone far down the tables. Sioned's mouth fell open as Antoun—friend of her youth, companion on her journey to the Desert so long ago, and secret source of information for eighteen years—walked slowly up to Pol and bowed before facing the rest of the hall.

"Your graces, lords, ladies," Antoun said, "never in the history of Goddess Keep has the Lord or Lady died without naming a successor. We have been at a loss to choose from among us one who will rule us. The senior *faradh'im* have asked the High Prince to select someone for us. This he has refused to do."

There was a murmuring through the hall. Sioned held her breath.

"Rightly so," Antoun went on. "The stones and lands of Goddess Keep are held of the High Prince, but the Sunrunners belong to no one."

If anyone felt a skeptical brow begin to rise, it was forced back down.

"As you know, Lady Feylin and Lady Betheyn attended the Lord of Goddess Keep in his final days. During times when he was awake and aware of what had happened to him, he spoke to them of several things. And one of them was his choice for his successor."

Feylin's head snapped around and stared at Beth; surprise was scrawled over both faces. Sioned came very close to demanding of each why they hadn't informed her—but instantly understood their reticence when Antoun spoke again.

"After conferring with my fellow Sunrunners at Goddess Keep, I had long consultation with Lord Andry's choice. It pleases me to say that Lady Chayla has consented to—"

The rest of it was drowned out in exclamations—some of shock, many of approval, some of dismay. These last came from her family. Chay marched down the tables to where Maarken gaped at his daughter and Hollis looked ready to weep. Tobin limped along behind him. Sioned caught up to her and put a hand beneath her elbow to steady her.

Rohannon, seated next to his sister, did not look at all surprised. Beth avoided Hollis' anguished look and stared down at her hands. Feylin had come over from her own table, braced for the argument.

Before anyone could say anything, Chayla murmured, "I want to do this. Andry must have had his reasons. I—"

"I'm damned if I know what they are!" Chay snapped. "You're not even sixteen!"

With perfect calm she asked, "How old was my mother when she went to Goddess Keep? Or Father, or Sioned, or any other Sunrunner?"

"You're not just another Sunrunner," Tobin said softly.

The golden head tilted. "Why?" she asked, genuinely curious.

Hollis was as white as her diamonds. "My dearest," she began, her voice trembling, "your grandfather is right. Sixteen is very young to be in a position of such—"

"How old was Andry?"

"Too young!" Chay shook off Tobin's cautioning hand on his arm. "Damn it, Maarken, say something!"

The only son left to him glanced up. "What would you have me say?"

"That it's impossible!"

"Is it?" Maarken met and held his daughter's gaze. "Chayla, answer one question for me, please. Do you truly want this?"

"Yes."

He nodded slowly. "Very well."

Hollis bit her lip and swallowed hard. Chay was less restrained. "What in all Hells do you mean, 'very well'?"

Maarken started to his feet, saying, "Just exactly what you think it means. I remind you that she's *my* daughter."

"That's enough," Sioned ordered. "Feylin, Beth, I want to know what you know about this."

Few things ever ruffled Feylin, but at the moment she was twisting the lace sash of her copper-colored gown in nervous fingers. "I didn't know *Beth* knew, that's for certain. He was conscious, asking if the Sunrunners were all right. Especially Chayla. And then he said—" Her slate-gray eyes closed briefly. " 'A Lady of Goddess Keep must be able to survive storms.' "

Sioned was careful not to look at Chayla. "What did he tell you, Beth?"

Still studying her hands, she said, "It was the third night. He seemed to be asleep, but then he asked if I thought Sorin would approve of treating Goddess Keep as if it belonged to the family. I—I assumed he meant Andrev. But then he said very clearly, 'Chayla's first of all a physician. She'll have to find a very good Chief Steward.' "

She paused, lifting her head at last to search Chayla's eyes. "And then he asked if I thought you'd *want* to be Lady of Goddess Keep. Before I could answer, he slipped away again."

Pol spoke from behind them, having pointedly kept himself at a distance from the discussion. "My lady, will you indeed accept, as Antoun has said?"

Chayla rose. Tobin, Sioned, and Feylin stepped aside; after a few moments, Chay finally did, too. His eyes were quicksilver shot with lightning as his granddaughter said, "I will."

For just a moment various emotions chased each other across Pol's face: compassion and respect, loss and tenderness, speculation and approval. Then he gestured, and Chayla went to take her place with the princes.

Sioned sent her son a single speaking look: *Did you know?* He shook his head slightly to indicate that he had not.

She did not resume her seat. Instead, she, too, joined the princes. Pol stood alone. Kierun brought him a large golden cup, which Pol did not touch. The boy looked up at him in confusion, then followed his gaze to Chayla. She came forward and cradled the wide, plain goblet in her palms.

Pol spoke into an absolute silence.

"I will keep faith with the law, and with all people in all princedoms."

They believed it of him as they had believed it of Rohan—and had not believed it of Roelstra.

"I will defend all persons, no matter their rank, station, craft, or heritage, as promised under the High Prince's Writ."

This was new. So were his next words.

"I will never again use my gifts to kill. Nor shall I use them against those who keep faith with the law, and with me."

At last, the Sunrunner oath Sioned and Rohan had demanded of him last Autumn—with a distinction reiterated by what followed.

"But to those who would destroy peace, flout the law, persecute the innocent, or threaten any law-abiding person living in the princedoms, I remind them that I am High Prince, *Faradh'rei*, and *Diarmadh'rei*, and they shall not escape justice."

She wasn't sure it was the wisest thing to say, but she knew why he felt he had to say it. He would be what no High Prince had been before him, and they all knew it.

"Will you have him as your High Prince?" Chayla called out, and they roared their assent.

Well, what else can they do? But beneath the cynicism was hope, and trust in him, and pride—and, at last, peace.

Kierun poured the wine, and Pol drank. Chayla presented the cup in turn to Chadric, Edrel, Arlis, Lisiel, Tilal and Gemma, Ostvel, Isriam, Amiel, and finally Sionell. It came to Sioned empty but for a few pale golden drops.

We did our work, beloved. Not elegantly, perhaps, and not quite the way we planned, but we did it. And it is our work— not Andrade's, not Roelstra's, not Ianthe's.

His to do now, Rohan. His own work in his own way. It's hurt him, getting here. Nearly killed him. But to be born, every dragon must break its shell.

Speaking of dragons—

Ah, yes. Of course.

She drained the last drops down her throat, then stood near Pol. Turning, she faced the high table and behind it the Stronghold Tapestry. Oh, it had been a *very* long time since she'd first done. this—more than thirty years. But her gifts were more supplely controlled than ever, and a mere thought conjured a dragon made of Fire.

It rose from the cup, expanding in every direction as it reached for the rafters. Sioned's skill gave the dragon wings that trailed the colors of every princedom; whimsy gave the creature vivid blue eyes. With one powerful downsweep of wings, the dragon leaped for the tapestry, and vanished.

Sioned gave a long sigh. *That is absolutely my last dragon conjuring.*

You outdid yourself. My congratulations to the Sunrunner Witch.

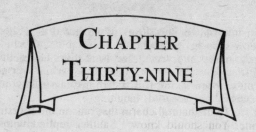

CHAPTER THIRTY-NINE

Tables were pushed against the walls, musicians assembled near the tapestry—giving it one or two apprehensive looks, as if the dragon just might come back—and the dancing began.

"You really ought to have begun with Ruala, you know," Sioned told Pol as they led the first set.

"She'll understand. The conjuring was perfect, by the way. Thank you."

"Glad you liked it. Next time, do your own." They separated, and when the figures brought them face-to-face again, she flicked a finger against the topaz hanging from his ear. "Your hair's gotten so long I didn't see it earlier. I'm surprised it's still in one piece."

"The gold was a trifle scorched," he said. "Alasen retrieved it for me and the crafters here polished it up. But I don't know why you're surprised. No jewel worn by Rohan could be harmed by Fire."

The pattern parted them again. When her hand rested once again on his shoulder, he asked, "Do you mind? About the earring, I mean."

Sioned blinked up at him. "Whyever should I? He always meant you to have it—along with everything else. Take me over to Maarken when this dance is finished, please. He's being silly about his arm."

A curative Ossetian country dance later, Maarken bowed to Sioned and relinquished her to Saumer before claiming Hollis for a wild reel.

"I'm too old for this," Sioned protested as the new Lord of Reiza spun her around.

"You make everyone else look like hobbled horses, cousin."

"You've been taking lessons from Chay in how to sweet-talk ladies," she accused, laughing.

"It's only the natural charm that runs in the Kierstian family line. You should know," Saumer replied with a grin. "How about using a little of it on Sethric?"

"Steer the old plow-elk over there, then, and let's see how well I can do."

The exchange was made. After a decent interval, Sioned suddenly exclaimed, "Oh! There's Chay. I need to talk with him, Sethric." A moment later, and very sternly: "Forgive me for stealing your partner, Jeni, but I have matters to discuss with his lordship of Radzyn Keep."

"Later, Sioned." Chay made as if to whirl Jeni away.

"Now," she commanded, taking his elbow and turning for a window.

Behind them came a glacial, "My lord of Catha Heights," and an actually frosty, "Your grace of Meadowlord."

"You idiot!" Sioned hissed as she marched Chay along. "Don't look over your shoulder! You'll give the whole thing away!" Safely out of range, she spun around, took a half-step to her right, and poked a finger into his chest as if furious with him.

"No fair!" Chay growled. "You get to watch and I don't!"

"Oh, hush." She squinted around the other dancers. "That's it, Jeni, sneak a look at him—excellent! Feylin just bumped into Sethric on purpose!" She chortled, ruining the picture of reprimand. "Good boy! There's more than one way to get your arms around a pretty girl!"

"Are you quite finished?" Chay inquired.

"Kiss my hand and look contrite," she grinned.

He did so, then slid an arm around her waist and tickled her ribs. *"That's"* for making me look the fool."

"All in a good cause."

✳

"It's impossible. I'm too young for you."

Beth laughed softly as she tugged on his hand—as the dance very conveniently demanded. "You'll get older. That's the way life works. Besides, most people are saying that *I'm* too old for *you*."

Isriam missed a step. "Tell me who and they won't say anything else until midsummer!" Realizing his vehemence had attracted stares from the couples around them, he blushed. The music ended, and he escorted Beth over to a handy corner. "I know how much you cared for Lord Sorin. I'm not asking you to feel about me the way you—"

"Good," she said forthrightly, "because I don't. How can anyone feel exactly the same way about two different people? I love Tobin and Sioned equally, but for different reasons. I loved Sorin—but not the way I love you."

He bit his lip. "Even if that's true . . . I don't have anything to offer. If my grandfather doesn't acknowledge me, I'll have nothing. Nothing!"

Beth's fingers dug into his arm, her eyes suddenly fierce. "I don't care if Sabriam took away what could have been yours and Pirro never gives you what ought to be! It's *you* I want, and be damned to what anyone thinks!"

Caught speechless between the uncertainty of his public future and the joy Betheyn promised for his private one, Isriam could only stare down at her.

Another voice, softly feminine, murmured at his shoulder, "It's customary at this point for the man to ask the woman a certain question, you know."

And a male voice added, "Marriage, and all that. Go on, Isriam. Don't make her do *all* the work!"

His head snapped around, but Hollis had already glided by on Tilal's arm to the dance floor.

✳

After regretfully surrendering the lovely and laughing Princess Norian to Lord Draza, Chay ambled over to the refreshments table. Pouring wine, he said, "Ah. Just the boys I want to see."

Arlis and Elsen exchanged glances. "Why don't I like the sound of that?"

"Well? How much will it cost me for wood and so forth to repair my fleet?" He wagged a finger at them. "Bear in mind that if my ships don't sail, Dorval's silk stays put, Kierst-Isel's produce doesn't leave the island, and Grib loses a lucrative market in the Desert."

"Actually," Arlis said with a thoughtful frown that couldn't hide the wicked gleam of green eyes, "after seeing the dragon ships up close, I'm inclined to build a few. With their bigger holds to carry more cargo and our triangular sails for speed, there won't be anything to touch them."

"Now, you just stop right there, boy—" Chay began.

Elsen coughed politely—an equally inadequate cover for glee at Chay's expense. "*Actually* . . . we kept four. They're still at Goddess Keep. If you'd care to examine them, cousin—take them apart, see how they work, that sort of thing. . . ."

Arlis gave a sigh. "How much will it cost me?"

"You make the outsides in Kierst-Isel, we'll make the insides in Grib. One for you, one for me, one for you, one for me, and so on. I'm going to buy into Waes as a home port for my new fleet."

"New fleet?" Chay scowled. "We'll see about that. Pol!"

*

"So then he looked the pair of them right in the eyes and said, 'If I could, I'd send you to a corner of the world so remote that the sun hasn't found it yet.'" Sioned paused for a sip of cool wine; telling Sionell all that had transpired during her absence at Tiglath was thirsty work.

"And then?"

"He told them where he *was* going to send them. Chiana fainted, of course."

"You wanted to rule? Very well. I give you your heart's desire. There's a whole princedom waiting for you—if you survive the trip."

Rinhoel's green eyes narrowed. "What do you mean?"

"Exactly what it sounds like," Sioned answered. "Once you arrive, declare yourself High Prince if it amuses you. None of us will mind."

Pol smiled thinly. "Enjoy yourself, cousin. Be sure to build your darling Mama a replica of Castle Crag."

"I don't underst—" Air left his lungs in a sudden gasp, as if his heart had stopped.

Chiana's gaze shifted from Pol to Sioned to Rinhoel, then fixed on Naydra. "What is he talking about?"

"Mercy," was the icy reply. "Despite my protests.
Take what you can get, Chiana. Your life is more than
you would have received from me."

"My life? You dare imply you'd—"

"Be quiet, Mother!"

"No I will not be quiet! I demand to know where he
thinks he's sending us!"

"Hell!" Rinhoel snarled.

"If you make it that far," Naydra added.

"After all," Sioned murmured with every evidence of
sincerity—which fooled her Namesake not at all, "he had to
send *someone* to the Vellanti Islands to tell them what really
happened."

Sionell winced. "Yes, but it really is a rotten thing to do—
even to a conquered enemy."

"They all deserve each other." She paused a moment.
"Roelstra Named her *Treason*. She spent her whole life de-
serving the name. I'll admit that Rinhoel conducted himself
with a certain dignity, though. It's too bad we won't get any
reports on how he fares." After another swallow of wine, she
went on, "By the way, clear something up for me. I understand why you gave Castle Pine to Meig. An excellent move.
But I don't have a clue about what's behind Catchwater."

"Last night I had a long talk with Visian and Lady
Elizian." With one finger she traced the pattern of black lace
over her knees. "It's a Merida place, of course, very near
Tuath and Tiglath. With my new duties, I can't keep more
than half an eye on them. So I persuaded the Isulk'im to do
it for me."

"But how did you get them to agree to live within stone
walls?"

"You've never seen Catchwater," Sionell smiled. "The
only wall in the whole place is a fence around the kitchen
garden to keep out the sand rats. It's just a wooden manor
house, and some outbuildings and stables. Nearby, a few
small villages. Mostly open space—and you know how they
feel about open space!"

Kierun approached with a chilled pitcher of wine, and
Sioned held out her cup. "Thank you, my lord. But, Sionell,
I just can't see them making it a permanent camp."

"Well, no. Various of them will take turns administering
the place. I left it to them to work out." She laughed. "You

know, they rather like the idea of owning their own water. But not too much of it! Elizian says the lake here makes them nervous—so much water is positively unnatural!"

✳

Arlis bowed his thanks to Ruala for the dance just concluded, and looked around for his wife. He found her talking with Rohannon.

"Well, 'Sunrunner lad,' " he smiled, "didn't I tell you you'd be in all the ballads?"

Rohannon sighed. "Rumor is it was Lord Ostvel's doing—I mean, Prince Ostvel. If I were a few years younger, I'd stuff his pillow full of pudding."

"But of course you're too old for that sort of trick," Demalia added.

"Chayla suggested whitespice," he replied with a straight face.

Arlis felt a sneeze coming on at the very idea. "Don't worry. With so much happening to so many people in so many places, there are stories enough to embarrass everyone equally—and keep the bards fully employed for the next five years! Now, if you don't mind, my lady and I are about to show everybody how the Iseli three-step ought to be done."

Rohannon meandered around the edge of the dancing, looking for his sister. He caught sight of her slipping through a side door with a man in black and gold. Wanting to know what she and Visian had to talk about—hoping it wasn't Kazander, a wound only beginning to heal—he started after them.

Someone blundered into him. He instinctively caught at an elbow. A sleek, dark head turned and an apology stammered from a wide mouth. "It's the skirt," Aldiara finished morosely. "I hate it."

"But it looks nice." Knowing this inadequate response was unworthy of the grandson of a man famous for appreciating pretty ladies, Rohannon smiled and added, "In fact, you look beautiful. Would you like to dance?"

Tobin—over whose cane Aldiara had stumbled—chuckled complacently.

✳

Amiel and Tilal stood on the main steps of the keep, waiting for a couple to be detached from the happy chaos of dancing in the courtyard. At last Audran returned with the pair in tow, awestruck that their young prince had come to fetch them personally.

"Many thanks, your grace," Tilal said to Audran. "Neither of us would ever have made it through that riot!"

Amiel cleared his throat and addressed the young couple. "You gave up something very precious to you in order to aid us against the Vellant'im—"

From Tilal's fingers suddenly trailed two thin rivulets of gold and tiny emeralds. The physician gasped; her Chosen, a soldier who'd fought on Dorval and at Radzyn, opened his eyes even wider than at his first sight of the enemy.

"—and I hope these are adequate replacement for the bracelets you lost at the Faolain," Amiel concluded.

"Your g–grace!"

"It's too much—we can't—"

"Oh, of course you can," Audran scolded.

"Hear that?" Tilal smiled. "Your prince has spoken. So when's the wedding?"

A bit later, as they returned to the great hall, Amiel said to Audran, "And that, cousin, is some of the best fun a prince can have."

"Expensive fun," Tilal added, "but worth it."

✳

In the small back garden, Chayla sat down rather abruptly on a stone bench. "Are you asking me," she said carefully, "for permission?"

"I would be happier," Visian admitted. "But it is a charge placed upon me by the *korrus*. I will obey it with or without your consent."

"My lord—I'm very grateful, and it's very kind of you, but have you thought what it would be like? Goddess Keep is absolutely nothing like the Desert. You'd be terribly homesick."

He smiled. "Will you not be, as well? But there will be me to remind you of the Long Sand and the wide sky. It is not so very far a distance my Lady—only a few rivers away."

A few rivers? Good Goddess, it was twelve days' hard

riding in fine weather, through half the Desert and all of Syr and Ossetia. She opened her mouth to tell him so when a rustle of skirts announced a new arrival.

Three new arrivals, one of them carrying a sleeping infant. Chayla gestured without thinking to a torch that was going out, and the stronger light of her Fire showed her Kazander's wives approaching through the garden. Their feet made no more noise on the loose gravel than if it was sand.

"My friends!" Chayla rose. "I'm glad to see you—for yourselves, and because I need you to help persuade Visian not to—"

"Why, when we approve?" Elizian asked, genuinely puzzled.

Suddenly Chayla was holding the small bundle. She and Feylin had spent much time at the Isulki camp, restocking medical supplies and treating cases that troubled the clan physician. This baby was one of them. Kazander's three sons—aged six, three, and just over two—and twin four-year-old daughters Named for Feylin, were robustly healthy. But this new little girl, expected after the first of Spring, had arrived thirty days early.

Chayla's experience was of battle wounds. Until that first afternoon in the Isulki tent, she'd forgotten there was any other use for a physician. But to help a sick baby, and in time to teach others how to do the same plus a thousand more things that had nothing to do with swords or knives— *that* was what she wanted for her life's work. And at Goddess Keep, where her other gifts would not be neglected.

She had no idea why Andry had fixed on her as his successor—especially after the matter of the abortion. But while she was unsure of her uncle's reasons for the choosing, she was positive of her own for accepting. It was right that she do it: right for the Sunrunners, for the princedoms, for herself. Goddess Keep would welcome someone of Andrade's and Andry's blood. The princedoms would breathe easier knowing that Sunrunners and High Prince would not conflict as they had for so long. (The princes would also appreciate her youth, believing that until she was older and more knowledgeable, she would be relatively powerless. Thinking how little they knew her, Chayla smiled— and wondered abruptly if her stubborn convictions had decided Andry in her favor.) That her family was unhappy grieved her—but she knew she must do this if for no other reason than herself.

She wanted, quite simply, to leave the Desert and its memories. Kazander; rape; abortion; the war, the deaths, the pain and blood. And especially the memory of her demand of Pol's *ros'salath*—deaths that would have betrayed both the physician and the Sunrunner in her. A lifetime of healing the sick and of teaching others the dangers as well as the joys of *faradhi* powers might make the remembering a little easier. But she would never forget. She would not—could not—wall the memories away as Sioned had done.

Chayla smiled down at the baby. Feylin had decided that the trouble was nothing more serious than a delicate stomach. Special herbs were brought from Skybowl. Proof of the cure rested now in Chayla's arms, eyes wide open beneath extravagantly arched black brows. A fist freed itself from the blanket, reaching for the glinting jewels around Chayla's neck.

"Ah, now, little lady," she chuckled. "Wait till you're older!"

Zenaya—the child's mother, youngest of Kazander's wives—said, "When she is of an age, we will send her to you."

"I—I beg your pardon?"

Visian spoke up. "My sister and all Isulk'im claim kin with Zehava's line, my Lady. This fostering, it is better when it is family, not strangers."

"It is common among our people," Zenaya went on, "to share children and provide blood-bond. Do not children of highborns go to other castles? I wish the bond with you and your Sunrunners. It is my choice, and we are agreed."

"She will be your daughter, your sister, your friend," Elizian told her.

"But—I can't just—"

"You do not want her." Zenaya bit her lip, eyes downcast in shame. "She is small, I know this, but the Lady Feylin says she will grow strong and—"

"No, no, that's not it. It's just—" Chayla gazed helplessly into smoke-blue eyes she knew would turn as dark as Kazander's in time. "Why?"

"Why not?" asked Zenaya. "If you do not want her with you, then at least please Name her. It would do her great honor."

"A Name you would give your own daughter," said the middle wife, Karalain.

Chayla finally understood. Softly, she said, "When she's old enough, I would be very proud to have her with me. And—and I think a good Name for her, an honorable Name, would be Andra."

*

Sioned went looking for Pol around midnight. Questioning three different people in three different parts of the hall, she got exactly the same response. When she heard it a fourth time from Dannar, the conspiracy was confirmed.

"I think I saw him on the other side of the room, your grace."

So had Walvis, Chadric, and Hollis. "That's what he told you to say, isn't it?"

"Well. . . ."

"It's all right, Dannar. He probably just wanted some time alone. This is quite a crush, after all."

Another circuitous search pattern told her that Sionell was missing, too.

Perhaps . . . ah, who can say?

You promised to keep your meddling fingers out of it, Sioned.

She let Tilal lure her back to the dancing, and forgot all about Pol and Sionell when she saw a group of children—up much too late, but no matter—form their own set. Alleyn and Jahnev, Maara and Audran, Dannar and Antalya—Jihan snagged Daniv to partner her (naturally; he was a ruling prince). Isriam, abandoning the dignity of his seventeen years and another dance with Beth, coaxed shy Tobren to join in. Jeni and Sethric presided over dancing class amid much giggling confusion.

Best of all, Sioned saw with delight, Kierun led Rislyn into the circle. Soon she was twirling across the floor, laughing.

*

He wedged the single candle against the rocks and stood watching the flame for a time. Remembering. Saying her name to the night, just once.

He closed his fingers around the pearls in his pocket. He'd thought to leave them here, but two days ago his daughters had dissuaded him. Indirectly, of course.

Glancing up from his work, he smiled when he saw that the interruptions were his favorites in all the world. His hand quickly covered the pearls—but Jihan had seen them with her eyes and Rislyn with her senses.

"You're not going to give them back to Lady Karanaya, are you, Papa?" Jihan asked.

"You can't, you know," Rislyn said softly. "They're too important."

"Important? Why is that?"

"Because even when they're hidden, you can still see them as a Sunrunner."

Jihan nodded emphasis. "We can always know where they are."

"And so . . . ?"

"Somebody can always find them," Rislyn explained. "And that means that whoever carries one can't be lost."

An interesting notion, and one he might make use of one day. So he would keep them.

Perhaps he ought to give one to Sionell.

He descended the slope toward the lakeshore, where the dragons were curled in sleep. One or two lifted their heads at his approach. A soft growl from Azhdeen sent them back to dozing—or at least they closed their eyes and lowered their chins to tucked-up forelegs. Pol had the uncanny sensation that they were listening.

"So you've forgiven me for being so rough with you?" he asked his dragon, who blinked at him in the moonlight. "Andry was wrong, you know. He shouldn't have used anyone like that, least of all you." Reaching to stroke Azhdeen's neck, he drew back at the rumbled warning. "Oh. So I'm *not* forgiven. Well, I suppose you don't exactly see it my way."

The dragon glanced from side to side, as if to judge the others' attention. Then he did a remarkable thing. Rolling to one side, he stretched his neck out and presented the length of his throat to Pol—just as a young male dragon did when yielding, in play or in earnest, to an older and more powerful sire.

Pol stepped back, astonished, dismayed—and thinking that this was more or less what everyone else had done tonight. Submission. Acknowledgment of him as their master. Well, that was what he wanted, wasn't it? Even Andry had been unable to oppose him.

"I understand what you mean by it, old son, but it's not necessary," Pol said. He used both hands to scratch Azhdeen's jaws, careful of gleaming white teeth and wickedly sharp spines. The dragon opened an eye. "What I did— well, it won't happen again. And don't you ever do *this* again, either." He ran the flats of both palms over and over the silky hide between the dragon's eyes, smiling when Azhdeen hummed in pleasure. "That's better, isn't it? And probably prophetic as well. Just like you, they yielded, and now I'll be a good High Prince and make them all happy."

"Yes, they *are* like Azhdeen. They never would have yielded if they didn't trust you."

Sionell's words almost made him leap out of his skin. Usually Azhdeen growled at everyone else. But the dragon settled peacefully back onto his belly in the sand, still humming. Pol turned. Sionell's gown and jewels shimmered by moonlight. A warm breeze that teased music from the castle and from Isulki wind chimes down below ruffled tendrils of loosened hair at her cheeks and nape.

Leaving Azhdeen and the other dragons, they started back toward the castle. Light blazed from Skybowl, music and laughter drifting across the water.

"What will you do with the mirror?" Sionell asked.

Thinking himself prepared for anything, this question took him by surprise. "Give it back to Riyan, of course. It's useless without the jewels."

"And those? Returned to their owners?"

"Yes." He'd debated it with himself, wondering if he shouldn't lock them away someplace safe—or do with them what he'd asked Visian to do with the *selej*. But it wasn't these particular stones that keyed the mirror; any gem of sufficient power would do. So hiding them wouldn't do much good.

As if hearing his thought, Sionell said, "But not the *selej*."

"I told Visian to bury it somewhere very very deep—and forget where he put the shovel."

She was quiet for a time, her thin slippers almost soundless against the pebbles underfoot. At length she said, "You spoke with Lord Rosseyn before you gave back the jewels. You couldn't *not* speak with him."

Pol shrugged. "I asked if he could be set free. But there's nothing to be done. Not even smashing the mirror—he'd only shatter with it, a piece of him in each fragment. Goddess, what Lallante did to him—" He stared out at the water. "I can't imagine hating anybody that much."

Sionell replied, "She had the integrity of her passion."

He stopped walking. "What?"

"I don't mean 'integrity' as in 'honor,' but—a sort of purity of purpose. Like Chiana. She wanted Castle Crag. She'd do anything for it."

"I . . . see what you mean," he said slowly. "Absolute single-mindedness. Anything to fulfill that passion. Like Andry with Goddess Keep."

"But never his own power. I think I finally understand that. I wish I could tell him so." She sighed. "Maybe everyone has a world within, part dream and part reality. It doesn't matter how unattainable the dream might be—it's the power of the vision that counts."

"Andrade," he said.

"Yes. And your father. But he had the exterior power to make his interior world a reality."

Pol thought that over, watching moonlight ripple across the water. At the start of the war, he'd feared that his passion would turn out to be for killing. Lately, he'd feared it was for power. No dream-and-reality had ever clarified within him, no single purpose, no vision of himself beyond the serenity of Dragon's Rest.

But suddenly that world-in-small told him everything about his own passion. People came to him for approval or consultation or ideas and then went about the tasks their talents dictated, trusting him to maintain the peace that allowed them to live their lives.

Wasn't that what he'd begun tonight throughout the princedoms? Sunrunners, sorcerers, common folk, princes, *athr'im*—why else had he termed himself *Faradh'rei, Diarmadh'rei*, and High Prince?

Rohan and Sioned had built Dragon's Rest for him. He had ruled it, mainly by following his father's philosophy of turning loose competent people to do what they did best. The princedoms in small. . . .

Meiglan had been so much of his life at Dragon's Rest. He knew suddenly that he would feel her absence there even more than at Skybowl. With him, she had ruled their perfect little world.

But it was to Sionell that he instinctively turned now. *The integrity of passion*. . . . As much as he'd thought he needed her before, he'd been wrong. She was as essential to him as Air to breathe and Fire to light his path.

His expression must have changed in response to his thoughts, for she took a step closer—almost reluctantly, almost as if drawn against her will. "Pol—"

"We'll never stop mourning them," he said. "Meiglan, Tallain, your brother, my father—that's as it should be, Ell. They *should* be remembered, even though it's painful. Maybe *because* it's painful, I don't know."

"Pol," she said again.

He placed a finger lightly on her lips. "I can't stand back from what I feel and stare at it, pick it apart to find out how it works. I can't tell you why or how, I don't have any reasons." He brushed curling strands of hair from her neck. "Maybe if I'd looked in Fire and Water the way my mother did, maybe I would've seen you the way she saw my father. I like to think I would have. All I can tell you is that I love you, Sionell. I love you."

✳

Sioned gradually extricated herself from the crowd, pausing to speak with this prince and that *athri*, moving so subtly that no one noticed when she slipped out a side door. Making her way to the courtyard, she let herself be delayed in talk with some of the soldiers, physicians, and castle folk whose celebration showed no signs of waning. Like the highborns inside the hall, they'd drink until the wine was gone and dance until their shoes wore through, and tell their grandchildren that no night had ever been like this one.

At last she slipped away. There were no guards on duty at the gate. None were needed. Stars reigned unchallenged in the night sky, the third moon having just set. The light showed her a tall, fair-haired man in white and a young woman in a dark gown walking slowly back to the castle.

She stood in a shadow of Skybowl, waiting for them to enter through the gates, wishing she was close enough to see their faces. Not that it mattered all that much; the woman's hand rested on the man's arm, and their easy strides kept the same rhythm.

Well, look at that! And I didn't even have to poke my nose in.

There was no reply, not even the wisp of a presence hovering near her. She'd stopped wondering if it was her imagination, her memories, or her conscience that answered her. She'd decided that it really was him.

But she could not sense him now.

When the couple vanished through the gates, Sioned started around the edge of the lake. She paused now and then to gaze at the ruffling silver water, the breeze dancing across its surface, the stars lacing its deeper darkness with shining light. She walked slowly, in no hurry as she climbed the crater's rim and stood watching the Desert.

The wind smelled of water and Isulki campfires, Skybowl's ancient stones and the clean, golden sand. Nearby a single candle burned in the place where Meiglan had died. But this place where Sioned stood, this was where she had Named Pol, used starfire for the first time, kept Rohan safe. Starlight spilled over the curves and hollows of the dunes below, pooling in the flat plain beyond Isulki tents. Silvery Fire, spreading like Water over the Earth, teased by Air that shifted the gleaming sea. Goddess, how beautiful it was.

"We won, Rohan," she whispered to the night sky. "Not Roelstra, not Andrade. We did. He's not the prince either of them wanted. He's the man *we* taught him to be. You always said that people do what they're meant to, because of who and what they are. But our work is finished. It's his work now."

The light beckoned her, and she spun it on a broad loom. Endless, blazing stars, such incredible light—and voices now, borne on the wind and the fire. They whispered to her: *Daughter* and *Sister* and *Friend* and *Kindred* and even *Mother*, shimmering bright tears in her eyes. Some voices she knew. Others were strangers to her ears, but not to her soul. Not to the Fire.

One voice whispered *Beloved*. She spread her colors on the starshine to embrace this land he had given her, and there were no shadows to darken the Fire soaring across the sand. Only light, only joy.

✳

No one heard Elisel scream. Only the dragons saw her rise into the night sky like an arrow, mute after that one keening wail. It was two days before she returned to Skybowl.

Long before that, they found Sioned.

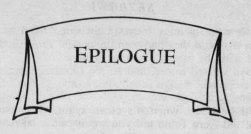

EPILOGUE

So. This *is what I won.*

Did grass spring up beside the fountain? Did roses bud on the garden walls? Did he find here renewal, rebirth, the promise of life resumed?

Stronghold was charred rubble from gatehouse to Flametower.

Sunlight winked and sparkled off bits of glass clinging to the windows, mocking him with rainbow colors. He stood in the garden staring up at the blackened stones. His birthright.

His Feruche?

Sioned had insisted that Rohan raise a new castle on the ashes of their nightmare. Could Pol do less? Could he leave Stronghold to the Desert wind, silent testimony to the failure of a dream?

... for as long as the sands spawn Fire....

He trod the seared ground beside the stream, trying to re-member Chay's words about where they'd found him. Here, perhaps? Or there, where the water curved gracefully be-neath the dead branches of the willow tree? That was as good a place as any. He bent, placing the heavy golden box onto the gravel, and unlatched the lid. Eventually the wind would empty the casket of her ashes in this place where Ro-han and Stronghold itself had died.

"It must have been like Andry," Feylin murmured, *tears streaking her face in the dawn. "Lost, but not on shadows. On light."*

"Papa?"

He turned. Jihan and Rislyn walked hand-in-hand toward

him. He went to meet them, not wishing them to see the golden casket as they had seen the pearls. "You should have stayed with the others," he said gently.

"No, I wanted to see, and so did Linnie," Jihan replied.

"It feels sad," Rislyn added after a time. "I don't like it so sad here."

"It'll be better when it's clean again," her sister said. "Papa, did Aunt Tobin tell you we started a tapestry?"

Pol blinked. "A tapestry?"

"Well, just the drawing. Maarken is going to sketch it for us and I'm going to do some of the stitching."

He smiled. "I thought you hated to sew—and I'm positive Tobin does."

"Well, yes," she admitted. "But it's something we have to do, isn't it? I mean, it'll take a long time to sew, but it'll take a long time to make Stronghold the way it was again, too."

"We're only almost eight," Rislyn reminded him.

"Ah, of course," Pol said. "You have plenty of time, then."

He watched them explore, trying not to remember that he'd said almost the same thing twenty days ago.

> *"Please don't say that, Pol. Not now."*
>
> *"Not ever?"*
>
> *"I care for you. Not the way I did when I was a little girl, but . . . I'm not sure how I feel. I need time."*
>
> *"I'm not asking for a decision right this moment. We have time. I just—I want you to come with me. Just as far as Stronghold—"*
>
> *"No."*
>
> *"Ell—"*
>
> *"Even if I wanted to, I can't. Why are you making me say these things? My parents need my help with Remagev. And Jeren—he's only two years old. He needs me even more. My children need me most of all."*
>
> *Pol watched the stars dance across the water. "Antalya's afraid of me now, isn't she?"*
>
> *"Yes." She didn't lie to him; when had she ever?*
>
> *"I've seen it in her eyes. I wish you'd give me the chance to show her she doesn't have to be."*
>
> *But they weren't really talking about Antalya.*
>
> *"I'm going home to Tiglath, Pol. I need time to think, and put our lives back together—"*

"I understand."

He hadn't even felt it, that she was slipping away from him. He'd never held more than a portion of her heart. In their youth, he could have had everything.

"I love you, Sionell. I need who I am when I'm with you."

"You are what you are, Pol—with me or without me." She paused, then murmured, *"You are my lord and my prince—but more than anything else, I should like us to be friends. Perhaps there can be more . . . but I have to ask you to wait."*

He nodded, and she put her hand on his arm, and they returned to Skybowl: the High Prince and the Regent of Cunaxa. Nothing more.

There was time. He would wait, in patience and however much silence she required. That was all he could do. There were no choices. The future would take shape, and order would return to their lives. In time they would know if what was between them was enough, or if what was between them was too much.

Maarken had said once, when Pol was twenty-two and halfheartedly thinking about finding a wife, that there was a sly paradox to love: in making you whole, it cut you in half. Pol hadn't understood. Not then, not after he married Meiglan, not even after he lost her.

He understood now.

Friends. Something else he'd have to settle for. *Friends*— What a terrible, damning, hopeless word. Hope, along with his youth and his parents and his Meiglan—and Sionell— was gone.

He watched his daughters splash cool water on their faces. They took it for granted that Stronghold would be rebuilt. Well, what they wanted, he would give them. He had been the center of so much for so long; it was a surprising relief to realize he was of only temporary importance. Jihan and Rislyn would live the future he would shape for them.

"Papa?" Jihan called. "Is there enough water?"

He joined them at the fountain. "For what?" he smiled. "Were you thinking of taking a swim?"

"No," Rislyn said seriously. "We have to wash the Flametower."

". . . Tobin and your grandmother scrubbed their hands

raw—I'd only just met your mother, so she didn't help them—it's supposed to be women who are officially *part of the family, although everybody knew why Sioned was there. When it comes your turn, tell Meggie not to worry about the inkstain on the floor. It was Chay's fault and if anybody cleans it up, it should be him!"*

He tilted his head back and stared at the pointed arches of the windows. After Rohan's fire had burned there nearly forty years, and Sioned's Fire had burned for three days, the stones would be—

What would they use for fuel, anyway? And who would he leave behind to make sure the flames didn't go out?

There would be plenty of volunteers: people who understood the significance of the Flametower and why it must be lighted. But they all had other places they must be. Ostvel and Alasen were on their way to Castle Crag to pack. Hollis and Maarken would accompany Chayla to Goddess Keep, where Arlis would leave them and set sail for Kierst-Isel with Rohannon. Tobin and Chay were bound for Radzyn tomorrow morning, along with Chadric and the rest of the Dorvali, none of whom could wait to get home. Walvis and Feylin would stay at Radzyn a few days, then go to Remagev and cautiously spring what deadfalls the Vellant'im had missed. Daniv was needed at High Kirat; Draza at Grand Versch; Tilal and Gemma at Athmyr. The *diarmadh'im* had already returned to their homes.

Who could he ask to maintain the symbol of the past and the future?

Ah, of course. Who else but the Isulk'im, his kin, whose place Stronghold also was?

He held out his hands. Rislyn took one, Jihan the other. "Let's find some buckets and brushes and get to work. We'll have to be quick about it, you know, if it's to be lighted at nightfall."

"But—" Rislyn frowned up at him. "Tradition says it's the women who—"

He smiled, and though she couldn't see it, he knew she sensed it. "I'm starting a new tradition."

✳

They all helped. All his kin, his friends, his people. They scrubbed the stones clean and gathered up pieces of Stronghold itself—blackened wooden doors and floorboards, sticks that had been furniture, the tattered remains of tapestries, anything that would burn. Tomorrow the Isulk'im would bring fresh fuel from the Vere Hills—but not much, for in the cellars, hidden near the cisterns, had been found a dozen mirrors that had escaped destruction. They would be used to amplify the fire.

Pol had called Sunrunner's Fire to none of them. Perhaps one day . . . but not now. He'd had enough of mirrors and Fire and power.

Everyone helped prepare the room. But at dusk, he climbed the stairs alone.

He supposed the Flametower was nothing more than superstition. No, the Vellant'im had shown him otherwise. Superstition did not permit the mind to question; the meaning of its rituals and symbols was deliberately obscured.

Faith, then? He thought of Tilal, and his easygoing relationship with the Goddess. A serene faith, separate from the intellect used to confront his problems. The Goddess was always there when he needed her, like a parent's warm and comforting love. The great passages of life—Naming, Choosing, Burning— had their rituals, bringing faith into the rhythm of existence. But, unlike superstition, faith did not infuse every action.

Pol suddenly knew this fire must be a symbol of *belief*— which required the mind to explain the heart's faith. He wanted people to see the flames, know they burned, and believe in his ideas and his dreams.

Andry had wanted the same thing for Goddess Keep. For the Sunrunners. He had tried to codify faith, to reconcile it with logic. Dangerous and difficult: reason and logic pulling in harness with ritual and faith.

But it was the only way Pol could reconcile himself to the symbol waiting to be reborn in this room. All people— sorcerer, Sunrunner, prince, *athri*, commoner—believing in Pol with their minds and trusting in him with their faith—

—trusting that he could create a world where *their* ideas and *their* dreams could burn as brightly as his own.

He looked out at the Desert for a time, waiting for night. Stronghold was empty again. They were all out at the camp, waiting for the fire. His fire. When the sky was dark and the stars glowed like the jewels of the White Crown, he set the last remains of Stronghold alight.

His fire. For all of them, for however long it would burn.

Melanie Rawn

EXILES

☐ **THE RUINS OF AMBRAI: Book 1**   UE2668—$6.99
                  (hardcover)   UE2619—$20.95
☐ **THE MAGEBORN TRAITOR: Book 2**   UE2730—$6.99
                  (hardcover)   UE2731—$23.95

Three Mageborn sisters bound together by ties of their ancient
Blood Line are forced to take their stands on opposing sides
of a conflict between two powerful schools of magic. Together,
the sisters will fight their own private war, and the victors will
determine whether or not the Wild Magic and the Wraithen-
beasts are once again loosed to wreak havoc upon their world.

THE DRAGON PRINCE NOVELS

☐ **DRAGON PRINCE : Book 1**   UE2450—$6.99
☐ **THE STAR SCROLL: Book 2**   UE2349—$6.99
☐ **SUNRUNNER'S FIRE: Book 3**   UE2403—$6.99

THE DRAGON STAR NOVELS

☐ **STRONGHOLD: Book 1**   UE2482—$6.99
☐ **THE DRAGON TOKEN: Book 2**   UE2542—$6.99
☐ **SKYBOWL: Book 3**   UE2595—$6.99

Prices slightly higher in Canada   **DAW:190**

Payable in U.S. funds only. No cash/COD accepted. Postage & handling: U.S./CAN. $2.75 for one
book, $1.00 for each additional, not to exceed $6.75; Int'l $5.00 for one book, $1.00 each additional.
We accept Visa, Amex, MC ($10.00 min.), checks ($15.00 fee for returned checks) and money
orders. Call 800-788-6262 or 201-933-9292, fax 201-896-8569; refer to ad #120.

Penguin Putnam Inc.   **Bill my:** ☐Visa ☐MasterCard ☐Amex_____(expires)
P.O. Box 12289, Dept. B   Card#_____
Newark, NJ 07101-5289

Please allow 4-6 weeks for delivery.   Signature_____
Foreign and Canadian delivery 6-8 weeks.

Bill to:

Name_____

Address_____ City_____

State/ZIP_____

Daytime Phone #_____

Ship to:

Name_____ Book Total $_____

Address_____ Applicable Sales Tax $_____

City_____ Postage & Handling $_____

State/Zip_____ Total Amount Due $_____

This offer subject to change without notice.

THE GOLDEN KEY
by
Melanie Rawn
Jennifer Roberson
Kate Elliott

In the duchy of Tira Virte fine art is prized above all things. But not even the Grand Duke knows just how powerful the art of the Grijalva family is. For thanks to a genetic fluke certain males of their bloodline are born with a frightening talent—the ability to manipulate time, space, and reality within their paintings, using them to cast magical spells which alter events, people, places, and things in the real world. Their secret magic formula, known as the Golden Key, permits those Gifted sons to vastly improve the fortunes of their family. Still, the Grijalvas are fairly circumspect in their dealings until two young talents come into their powers: Sario, a boy who will learn to use his Gift to make himself virtually immortal; and Saavedra, a female cousin who, unbeknownst to her family, may be the first woman ever to have the Gift. Sario's personal ambitions and thwarted love for his cousin will lead to a generations-spanning plot to seize total control of the duchy and those who rule it.

• Featuring cover art by Michael Whelan